ETHNOMUSICOLOGY

ETHNOMUSICOLOGY

A Contemporary Reader

Edited by Jennifer C. Post

Routledge
Taylor & Francis Group
New York   London

Published in 2006 by
Routledge
Taylor & Francis Group
270 Madison Avenue
New York, NY 10016

Published in Great Britain by
Routledge
Taylor & Francis Group
2 Park Square
Milton Park, Abingdon
Oxon OX14 4RN

Printed in the United States of America on acid-free paper
10 9 8 7 6 5 4 3 2 1

International Standard Book Number-10: 0-415-97203-5 (Hardcover) 0-415-97204-3 (Softcover)
International Standard Book Number-13: 978-0-415-97203-1 (Hardcover) 978-0-415-97204-8 (Softcover)
Library of Congress Card Number 2005013598

Library of Congress Cataloging-in-Publication Data

Ethnomusicology : a contemporary reader / edited by Jennifer C. Post.
    p. cm.
  Includes bibliographical references (p.   ), discography (p.   ), and index.
    ISBN 0-415-97203-5 (hardback : alk. paper) -- ISBN 0-415-97204-3 (pbk. : alk. paper)
    1. Ethnomusicology. I. Post, Jennifer C. II. Title.

ML3799.E79 2005
780'.89--dc22

                      2005013598

Visit the Taylor & Francis Web site at
http://www.taylorandfrancis.com

and the Routledge Web site at
http://www.routledge-ny.com

Contents

Acknowledgments   ix

Contributors   xi

Introduction   1
JENNIFER C. POST

Part I   **Commodification and Consumption**   15

1   Sultans of Spin: Syrian Sacred Music on the World Stage   17
JONATHAN H. SHANNON

2   Sounds Like the Mall of America: Programmed Music   33
and the Architectonics of Commercial Space
JONATHAN STERNE

Part II   **Cultural Tourism and Travel**   53

3   Culture, Tourism, and Cultural Tourism: 55
Boundaries and Frontiers in Performances of Balinese Music and Dance
PETER DUNBAR-HALL

4   Folk Festival as Modern Ritual in the Polish Tatra Mountains   67
TIMOTHY J. COOLEY

Part III   **Gender and Sexuality**   85

5   *Taiko* and the Asian/American Body: 87
Drums, *Rising Sun*, and the Question of Gender
DEBORAH WONG

6   Empowering Self, Making Choices, Creating Spaces: 97
Black Female Identity via Rap Music Performance
CHERYL L. KEYES

7   The Frame Drum in the Middle East: 109
     Women, Musical Instruments, and Power
     VERONICA DOUBLEDAY

Part IV   Globalization and Glocalization   135

8   On Redefining the "Local" through World Music   137
     JOCELYNE GUILBAULT

9   The Canned Sardine Spirit Takes the Mic   147
     MARINA ROSEMAN

10   A Musical Instrument Travels Around the World: 161
     Jenbe Playing in Bamako, West Africa, and Beyond
     RAINER POLAK

Part V   Media, Technology, and Technoculture   187

11   Mozart in Mirrorshades: 189
     Ethnomusicology, Technology, and the Politics of Representation
     RENÉ T. A. LYSLOFF

12   Technology and the Production of Islamic Space: 199
     The Call to Prayer in Singapore
     TONG SOON LEE

13   Acting Up, Talking Tech: 209
     New York Rock Musicians and Their Metaphors of Technology
     LESLIE C. GAY, JR.

Part VI   Nationalism and Transnationalism   223

14   The Sonic Dimensions of Nationalism in Modern China: 225
     Musical Representation and Transformation
     SUE TUOHY

15   Russia's New Anthem and the Negotiation of National Identity   243
     J. MARTIN DAUGHTRY

16   "*Mezanmi, Kouman Nou Ye?* My Friends, How Are You?":   261
     Musical Constructions of the Haitian Transnation
     GAGE AVERILL

17   "Indian" Music in the Diaspora: 275
     Case Studies of Chutney in Trinidad and in London
     TINA K. RAMNARINE

Part VII   Place and Embodiment   293

18   The Embodiment of Salsa: 295
     Musicians, Instruments, and the Performance of a Latin Style and Identity
     PATRIA ROMÁN-VELÁZQUEZ

19   Dueling Landscapes: Singing Places and Identities in Highland Bolivia   311
      THOMAS SOLOMON

Part VIII   Racial and Ethnic Identities   329

20   Native American Rap and Reggae: 331
      Dancing "To the Beat of a Different Drummer"
      NEAL ULLESTAD

21   From "I'm a Lapp" to "I am Saami":   351
      Popular Music and Changing Images of Indigenous
      Ethnicity in Scandinavia
      RICHARD JONES-BAMMAN

Part IX   Social and Political Action   369

22   Cajun Music, Cultural Revival: 371
      Theorizing Political Action in Popular Music
      MARK MATTERN

23   Nitmiluk: Place, Politics, and Empowerment in Australian   383
      Aboriginal Popular Music
      CHRIS GIBSON AND PETER DUNBAR-HALL

24   Culture, Conservation, and Community Reconstruction: 401
      Explorations in Advocacy Ethnomusicology and
      Participatory Action Research in Northern KwaZulu Natal
      ANGELA IMPEY

      Glossary   413

      Research Resources   419

          Books and Articles   419

          Audio Recordings   423

          Video Recordings   427

          Web Sites   431

      Index   437

Acknowledgments

I would first like to thank the contributors to this collection whose research has enriched ethnomusicology and its many related disciplines. I would also like to thank Richard Carlin, Music Editor at Routledge Press, for his encouragement and support, and Shannon McLachlan at Routledge Press, for her editorial assistance. Middlebury College has generously supported my work on this and other projects for many years. I have especially appreciated the support and assistance of administrative and library staff as I completed this project. Many of my students at Middlebury have used their critical and analytical skills—and their creative energies—to provide valuable feedback on the concepts and issues found in the articles collected here. Finally, I want to express my appreciation for my many colleagues in ethnomusicology, anthropology, and folklore—at colleges and universities, at elementary and secondary schools, in libraries, archives, at museums, in arts organization, and in performing groups—whose work has always inspired me.

The author and publishers gratefully acknowledge the following permissions to reproduce copyright material:

Averill, Gage. 1994. "'*Mezanmi, Kouman Nou Ye?*' My Friends, How Are You?': Musical Constructions of the Haitian Transnation." *Diaspora* 3(3): 253–72. Reproduced with permission of the University of Toronto Press.

Cooley, Timothy J. 1999. "Folk Festival as Modern Ritual in the Polish Tatra Mountains." *The World of Music* 41(3): 31–55. Reproduced with permission of Verlag für Wissenschaft und Bildung.

Daughtry, J. Martin. 2003. "Russia's New Anthem and the Negotiation of National Identity." *Ethnomusicology* 47(1): 42–67. Reproduced with permission of The Society for Ethnomusicology.

Doubleday, Veronica. 1999. "The Frame Drum in the Middle East: Women, Musical Instruments and Power." *Ethnomusicology* 43(1): 101–34. Reproduced with permission of The Society for Ethnomusicology.

Dunbar-Hall, Peter. 2001. "Culture, Tourism and Cultural Tourism: Boundaries and Frontiers in Performances of Balinese Music and Dance." *Journal of Intercultural Studies* 22(2): 173–87. Reproduced with permission of Taylor and Francis journals: www.tandf.co.uk/journals.

Gay, Leslie C., Jr. 1998. "Acting Up, Talking Tech: New York Rock Musicians and Their Metaphors of Technology." *Ethnomusicology* 42(1): 81–98. Reproduced with permission of The Society for Ethnomusicology.

Gibson, Chris, and Peter Dunbar-Hall. 2000. "Nitmiluk: Place and Empowerment in Australian Aboriginal Popular Music." *Ethnomusicology* 44(1): 39–64. Reproduced with permission of The Society for Ethnomusicology.

Guilbault, Jocelyne. 1993. "On Redefining the 'Local' through World Music." *The World of Music* 35(2): 33–47. Reproduced with permission of Florian Noetzel Verlag Heinrichshofen-Books

Impey, Angela. 2002. "Culture, Conservation and Community Reconstruction: Explorations in Advocacy Ethnomusicology and Participatory Action Research in Northern KwaZulu Natal." *Yearbook for Traditional Music* 34: 9–24. Reproduced with permission of the International Council for Traditional Music.

Jones-Bamman, Richard. 2001. "From 'I'm a Lapp' to 'I am Saami': Popular Music and Changing Images of Indigenous Ethnicity in Scandinavia." *Journal of Intercultural Studies* 22(2): 189–210. Reproduced with permission of Taylor and Francis journals: www.tandf.co.uk/journals.

Keyes, Cheryl L. 2000. "Empowering Self, Making Choices, Creating Spaces: Black Female Identity via Rap Music Performance." *Journal of American Folklore* 113(449): 255–69. Reproduced with permission of The American Folklore Society.

Lee, Tong Soon. 1999. "Technology and the Production of Islamic Space: The Call to Prayer in Singapore." *Ethnomusicology* 43(1): 86–100. Reproduced with permission of The Society for Ethnomusicology.

Lysloff, René T. A. 1997. "Mozart in Mirrorshades: Ethnomusicology, Technology, and the Politics of Representation." *Ethnomusicology* 41(2): 206–19. Reproduced with permission of The Society for Ethnomusicology.

Mattern, Mark. 1998. "Cajun Music, Cultural Revival: Theorizing Political Action in Popular Music." *Popular Music and Society* 22 (1): 31–48. Reproduced with permission of Taylor and Francis journals: www.tandf.co.uk/journals.

Polak, Rainer. 2000. "A Musical Instrument Travels Around the World: Jenbe Playing in Bamako, West Africa, and Beyond." *The World of Music* 42(3): 7–46. Reproduced with permission of Verlag für Wissenschaft und Bildung.

Ramnarine, Tina K. 1996. "'Indian' Music in the Diaspora: Case Studies of 'Chutney' in Trinidad and in London." *British Journal of Ethnomusicology* 5: 133–53. Reproduced with permission of the *British Journal of Ethnomusicology* (now *Ethnomusicology Forum*).

Roman-Velazquez, Patria. 1999. "The Embodiment of Salsa: Musicians, Instruments and the Performance of a Latin Style and Identity." *Popular Music* 18(1): 115–31. Reproduced with permission of Cambridge University Press.

Roseman, Marina. 2000. "The Canned Sardine Spirit Takes the Mic." *The World of Music* 42(2): 115–36. Reproduced with permission of Verlag für Wissenschaft und Bildung.

Shannon, Jonathan H. 2003. "Sultans of Spin: Syrian Sacred Music on the World Stage." *American Anthropologist* 105(2): 266–77. Reproduced with permission of the University of California Press.

Solomon, Tom. 2000. "Dueling Landscapes: Singing Places and Identities in Highland Bolivia." *Ethnomusicology* 44 (2): 257–280. Reproduced with permission of The Society for Ethnomusicology.

Sterne, Jonathan. 1997. "Sounds Like the Mall of America: Programmed Music and the Architectonics of Commercial Space." *Ethnomusicology* 41(1): 22–50. Reproduced with permission of The Society for Ethnomusicology.

Tuohy, Sue. 2001. "The Sonic Dimensions of Nationalism in Modern China: Musical Representation and Transformation." *Ethnomusicology* 45(1): 107–31. Reproduced with permission of The Society for Ethnomusicology.

Ullestad, Neal. 1999. "American Indian Rap and Reggae: Dancing To the Beat of a Different Drummer." *Popular Music and Society*, 23(2): 63–90. Reproduced with permission of Taylor and Francis journals: www.tandf.co.uk/journals.

Wong, Deborah. 2000. "*Taiko* and the Asian/American Body: Drums, *Rising Sun*, and the Question of Gender." *The World of Music* 42(3): 67–78. Reproduced with permission of Verlag für Wissenschaft und Bildung.

Contributors

Gage Averill, Professor of Music History & Culture and Dean of the Faculty of Music at the University of Toronto, Canada.

Timothy J. Cooley, Associate Professor of Music at the University of California, Santa Barbara.

J. Martin Daughtry, currently completing a doctoral dissertation in ethnomusicology at the University of California, Los Angeles.

Peter Dunbar-Hall, Senior Lecturer in Music Education at the University of Sydney, Australia.

Veronica Doubleday, a musicologist who teaches at Sussex University, United Kingdom.

Leslie C. Gay, Jr., Associate Professor in the School of Music, University of Tennessee.

Chris Gibson, the Geoquest Research Centre, School of Earth and Environmental Studies, University of Wollongong, Australia.

Jocelyne Guilbault, Professor of Music at the University of California, Berkeley.

Angela Impey, Honorary Research Associate, Music Department at University of Natal, Durban, South Africa.

Richard Jones-Bamman, Associate Professor of Music at Eastern Connecticut State University.

Cheryl L. Keyes, Associate Professor in the Department of Ethnomusicology at the University of California, Los Angeles.

Tong Soon Lee, Assistant Professor, Ethnomusicology at Emory University, Atlanta, Georgia.

René T. A. Lysloff, Associate Professor of Music at the University of California, Riverside.

Mark Mattern, Associate Professor of Political Science at Baldwin Wallace College, Berea, Ohio.

Rainer Polak lives and works in Bayreuth, Germany.

Jennifer C. Post, Assistant Professor in the Music Department at Middlebury College, Middlebury, Vermont.

Tina K. Ramnarine, Lecturer in the Department of Music, Royal Holloway, University of London.

Patria Román-Velázquez, Lecturer in Communication and Media Studies, Department of Sociology, School of Social Sciences, City University, London.

Marina Roseman, Lecturer in Ethnomusicology and Anthropology at the School of Anthropoological Studies, Queens University, Belfast, Ireland.

Jonathan H. Shannon, Assistant Professor of Anthropology at Hunter College of the City University of New York.

Tom Solomon, Associate Professor, Ethnomusicology at Grieg Academy, Institute for Music, University of Bergen, Norway.

Jonathan Sterne, Assistant Professor, Art History and Communication Studies at McGill University, Montreal, Canada.

Sue Tuohy, Assistant Professor of Music at Indiana University.

Neal Ullestad has taught at Pima Community College, Tucson.

Deborah Wong, Professor of Music at the University of California, Riverside.

Introduction

Jennifer C. Post

In the fifth annual review of recent world music CD releases published in the *New York Times* in 2003, Jon Pareles wrote:

> The world music category has always been a hodgepodge: field recordings by ethnomusicologists, popular music originally made to please a local audience, traditional music played by traditional musicians or repackaged for tourists, slick international hits in languages other than English. In all of them, Western listeners found the promise of genuine alternatives in both the sounds of the music and its purposes. Visions of otherness could be attached to a nontempered melody, a slinky rhythm or a penetrating voice (1).

The musical category Pareles refers to has taken on a particularly complex identity during the last twenty years. He classifies "world music" as a collection of discrete musical styles subdivided by the social behaviors of some of the participants in its production: ethnomusicologists, music producers, musicians, and consumers. It is *not* a hodgepodge, though; a closer look at all of the players and their roles and responsibilities reveals a contemporary music scene that comprises people and products, social and geographic landscapes, old and new technologies, all carefully interwoven. The interaction and intersection of academic and mainstream media participants and their products creates a confusing terrain, though. Musicians, musicologists, and music producers are all redefining themselves as well as being redefined by others. Ethnomusicologists find the activities that are currently taking place among these various entities fascinating areas for their research. In introductory and advanced level ethnomusicology courses, the changes that are occurring are popular topics for lectures and classroom discussion.

Pareles' statement provides a window into the world of the music industry, but also into the field of ethnomusicology, both historically and in contemporary practice. The vocabulary he chooses and the constructions he uses have been subjects of discussion among scholars seeking to unravel the complex social exchanges that are responsible not only for the musical category now called world music, but also for many other forms of musical expression that are studied today in local, regional, national, and global contexts. The contested meanings of concepts that occur across disciplinary and other professional boundaries are indicative of the transitional period that ethnomusicology is in today.

Before the 1990s, the scholarly focus of ethnomusicology was often referred to as *world music*. Introductory level college and university ethnomusicology courses, offered in music and anthropology departments, typically were called "Introduction to World Music" or simply "World Music."[1] These classes, which remain popular today, concentrate on music as a human activity in a variety of cultural contexts. In early years ethnographic data collected by ethnomusicologists during their fieldwork dominated the content. When the music industry adopted the term "world music" as a marketing category in 1987—especially to classify popular musics from around the world, by and large outside of the mainstream popular and European classical realms—it was applied to many different types of recordings, regardless of the methods used for recording, sampling, and collaborating.[2] The combined ideas and activities of scholars and music industry created a multi-layered social, cultural, economic, and political landscape that contributes to the ever-expanding diversity of styles, genres, and forms of musical expression throughout the world. We see the effects of these developments today both in the music industry and the classroom; mainstream media as well as academic departments in colleges and universities reference world music widely. BBC Radio devotes programming and Web sites to what they call world music. On the Web they provide sound, video, and data bytes on mainly popular performers and their music.[3] NPR (National Public Radio) uses the category to classify selected musics covered in their programs. Their World Music Web site, includes stories and reviews of primarily popular musics and musicians.[4] The "Music Deli" programming on ABC (Australian Broadcasting Corporation) "presents folk, traditional and acoustic music and what is commonly known as world music."[5] Their programming comprises music from local (Australian) artists, singer songwriters, and popular musicians from around the world. In academic music departments today, some courses still retain the title World Music, and many ensembles are referred to as world music ensembles. The courses and ensembles, though, do not focus solely on the popular music genres that have been supported by the music industry, but more typically concentrate on historical and contemporary music-making, including musical systems, as well as issues and topics that impact performance. The departmental ensembles are not often characterized by the fusion that is found in many of the global popular music forms, but instead represent specific musical traditions guided by musicians trained by local artists from countries around the world. There *are* other world music classes, though, sometimes taught in the context of global studies which focus on the popular music forms that have emerged during the last few decades. These classes are especially concerned with the impact of mass media on diverse popular music forms.

Similarly, the term *ethnomusicologist* was once used to identify academically trained professionals who predominantly engaged in ethnographic research and taught college and university classes. Today ethnomusicologists work both inside and outside of the academy; and many are involved in applied work in arts organization, libraries and museums. This has brought information on musics from around the world—and methodologies used to document them–outside of the academy to be shared more widely by the public. In addition, mainstream newspapers and magazines sometimes refer to performers, producers, and journalists who sample, market, and document sounds from around the world, as ethnomusicologists. There is not a clear distinction today in the popular literature between public- and private-sector ethnomusicologists, or between academic and commercial contributors to our bodies of knowledge. It is not surprising then that this blurring of boundaries has produced confusion in the public sector and stimulated discussion about disciplinary identities in the academy: at conferences and in classrooms.

What is understood as ethnographic *fieldwork* was once in a domain claimed largely by anthropologists, ethnomusicologists, and folklorists, but it too has also grown to encompass a broader range of meanings. In the first place, not all individuals engaged in activities that include "in-person witnessing, observing, questioning, tape-recording, photographing, and in some cases performing (Titon, 321)" are involved in order to contribute to ethnographic studies that will enhance the scholarly understanding of performance. They might have aspirations as performers, as filmmakers, or they may be seeking their own individual musical experience or personal growth through extended participation and observation of one or more musical cultures. In fact, there is not always a clear distinction made in the popular literature between the fieldwork data of academically oriented ethnomusicologists and other musics created by musicians and producers for local audiences, tourists, and global-music consumers. Similarly, the *field*, that was identified years ago with remote, rural contexts, typically outside of the researcher's own social and cultural realm, has also been redefined. Today the place for ethnomusicological research ranges from archival collections to live performances; from remote villages to city streets; from local communities to internet discussion groups; from one's own community to sites thousands of miles away.

It is clear then, that during the last twenty years, the definitions associated with ethnomusicology and the fieldwork that often accompanies social and cultural research have changed along with our shifting global landscape. The marketing events of the 1980s will continue to confuse consumers, ethnomusicologists and students, who often use terms such as world music, fieldwork, and ethnomusicology, yet understand their meanings in different ways. The concepts once defined by ethnomusicologists have become sites they must share; once used largely in academic circles—a private social sphere—the concepts and the activities that accompany them are now in the public domain.

For music and musicians around the world, access to information, including our rapidly developing technologies, has often been cited as a primary agent of the recent changes. Yet ethnomusicologists have found that other issues, connected less to production and the products of technology and more to social, economic, political, and environmental effects of change on human behaviors, have played equally significant roles. These events have also brought ethnomusicologists to explore all of the realms that Pareles references in his review: to consider *popular* and *traditional music*, *musicians* and their *audiences*, to focus on the impact of *tourism* and on *local* music production, and to explore the music and socio-economic significance of *international music* and its generators and supporters, both local and global. All the participants in this exchange have also been affected by social, political, and economic events that have taken place in their lifetime and the growing opportunities for wider involvement by local musicians in the production of music in recent years. The current literature demonstrates that ethnomusicologists both observe and experience the effects of the changes on the people and places that they have established their relationships with through their fieldwork and performance experience.

In a way, the term world music may have come full circle. The appropriation of the phrase by the music industry encouraged events that now provide new sites and expanded opportunities for ethnomusicological research. Anthropologist P. G. Toner and musicologist Stephen A. Wild describe the expanded relationship and the issue of agency in a 2004 article in the *Asia Pacific Journal of Anthropology*: "'World music' may indeed be a marketing category developed by the international recording industry to sell the products of musical others, but it is also a set of ideas about music and the world which those others themselves consume, consider, and negotiate" (97). Ethnomusicologists embrace the contemporary musical landscape and are concerned with the broadest range of cultural expression. The dynamic exchange they take part in involves musicians and musical communities, scholars, journalists, politicians, healthcare workers, members of the legal community, religious practitioners, among others, in their own neighborhoods and around the world. Their diverse experiences and points of view offer a wide range of research methods and theoretical approaches. Increasingly their experiences also bring them out of the academy and more actively into communities where they conduct their research, to play multiple roles as researchers and teachers, filmmakers and recordists, performers and activists for social change.

This collection of essays originally published between 1993 and 2003, considers music and musical practices around the world documented by ethnomusicologists, anthropologists, folklorists, sociologists, political scientists, and other scholars. The compilation is a representative collection that concentrates on many of the contemporary concerns that currently engage scholars in their research and in the classroom. The organizational structure for this collection includes nine topical sections, as follows:

1. Commodification and Consumption
2. Cultural Tourism and Travel
3. Gender and Sexuality
4. Globalization and Glocalization
5. Media, Technology, and Technoculture
6. Nationalism and Transnationalism
7. Place and Embodiment
8. Racial and Ethnic Identities
9. Social and Political Action.

The essays offer approaches to research, theoretical frameworks and insights that reach back to earlier ethnomusicological literature of the 1960s, 1970s, and 1980s and connect with current methods and issues in diverse disciplines. We see clear evidence of the influence of the subjects traditionally allied with the multidisciplinary field of ethnomusicology, including musicology, anthropology, dance ethnology, folklore, and sociology. In addition, works from a wider range of disciplines and developing areas of focus have been consulted and—in many cases—fully integrated into the research methodologies, especially cultural studies, gender studies, geography, history, linguistics, political science, psychology, and religion. While the work in this volume reaches across disciplinary boundaries, the studies are also concerned with the points of view and goals of mainstream media and the everyday lives and values of the individuals and communities whose ideas form the basis for research in ethnomusicology. Altogether, they share insights that are propelling the discipline forward. They acknowledge, accept, and sometimes confront our understanding of music in its social, historical, political, religious, and economic contexts—to explore how meanings are variously produced, subverted, mediated, and celebrated in music.

The topics that frame this collection comprise complex issues and ideas that in recent years have played significant roles in literature, especially in the social sciences. Many of the themes are interconnected, and while articles have been assigned to distinct areas, they are sometimes equally aligned with other subjects as well. And because this collection represents contemporary concerns, we frequently find evidence of the ongoing discussions in ethnomusicology: about gendered, racial, ethnic, and national identities; about the effects of globalization and technology on individuals and communities; and about issues connected to intellectual property and human rights that affect so many people across the globe.

Commodification and Consumption: The concept of commodification applied to the study of music encompasses the production, distribution, and consumption of goods and ideas that have been created for the marketplace. Commodities are typically produced for the purpose of exchange, not for use by the producer. Issues surrounding music as commodity and the subject of commodification have been discussed in popular music studies for several decades. Early approaches to the impact of commodification on music expressed the view that the relationship between the market, especially the music industry, and cultural products was oppositional; consumers were identified as passive participants in the process. Research in ethnomusicology and related fields shows that consumers, musicians, critics, ethnomusicologists and other scholars, in addition to members of the music industry, play significant roles in the reception and dissemination process as well. Connell and Gibson in *Sound Tracks: Popular Music, Identity and Place* (2003) discuss the tensions connected to both the "economic and cultural value" of commodified sounds as they circulate (6). They say, "Musical cultures are commodified, but music never leaves the sphere of the 'cultural' or 'social' even when it is being manufactured, bought, or sold" (9). It is not surprising, then, that the flow of culture in the context of the market-driven global landscape finds its way into so many studies of music today, including this collection of articles.

Ethnomusicologist Anthony McCann seeks to expand our view of the concept of commodification by separating the term from its association with objects ("things") and economics to align it with "enclosure," a concept once used to refer to the process of subdividing common lands for individual ownership.[6] He says, "the study of enclosure is the study of attitudes and dispositions, in particular, *commodifying* attitudes and dispositions." He argues that the term commodification needs to be more widely applied. It is "what happens when we engage in strategies of 'closure' and 'separation' in the way that we make sense of our experience. We close 'things' off, ring 'things' round, make distinctions between 'us' and 'them', identify, isolate, eliminate variables, and thereby separate, distance, things from other things, people-as-things from other people-as-things, separate ourselves from acknowledgement of many of the realities of our own experience (McCann)."

Many of the articles in this collection address this broadly defined area. Selected for this section two authors present the commodification in contrasting social and cultural contexts. Issues of global cultural flow and cultural production are at the center of "Sultans of Spin: Syrian Sacred Music on the World Stage" by Jonathan H. Shannon. He examines Islamic music on the "world stage" in a study of the *mawlawiyya* ("Whirling Dervish") performances by a Syrian-based ensemble. He addresses several themes of interest to ethnomusicologists that connect to the transnational processes and practices of mediation and consumption, including classification (of a "sacred music" style with the "world music" genre or category) and revival (of local practice through global performance). In contrast, Jonathan Sterne in "Sounds Like the Mall of America: Programmed Music and the Architectonics of Commercial Space" discusses the commodification of programmed music, which is itself a commodified form. His case study of Muzak in The Mall of America in Minnesota allows him to explore the intersection of music and capitalism and to discuss how music can be viewed as a way of organizing space.

Cultural Tourism and Travel: Cultural tourism and heritage tourism are phrases used widely by the travel industry to describe travel and activities connected to heritage, arts, leisure, and natural resources of a particular locality. The study of the impact of tourism, an integral part of the daily lives of individuals and communities around the world, has been in development in anthropology since the 1970s. In ethnomusicology, tourism studies are relatively new. In the late 1980s the International Council for Traditional Music (ICTM) sponsored a colloquium on Traditional Music and Tourism, and subsequently published an edited volume on the subject in 1988, edited by Adrienne Kaeppler.[7] In 1998 *The Journal of Musicological Research* devoted a volume to the interaction of cultural performances, tourism, and ethnicity[8] and in 1999 *The World of Music* devoted an issue to the topic of "Music, Travel, and Tourism," edited by Mark DeWitt.[9] Martin Stokes referred to "tourism ethnomusicology" in a summary article for *The World of Music* issue and while the specific phrase has not yet caught on, the consideration of cultural tourism as a major force in the contemporary music scene has.

Some issues that interest social scientists, and ethnomusicologists in particular, as they look at tourism in different cultural contexts include the cultural, social, economic, and environmental impacts of tourists and the organizations that support the industry. While some researchers identify cultural tourism as detrimental to the continuation of traditional practices, others have found through their fieldwork that the practice has actually been responsible for renewal and revival of traditional musical forms and styles. Ethnomusicologists look at the social organizations that are constructed in the process of production and ask how music is transformed when packaged for tourists. In this collection, Peter Dunbar-Hall in "Culture, Tourism, and Cultural Tourism: Boundaries and Frontiers in Performances of Balinese Music and Dance" uses case studies of music and dance events designed for tourists by local residents in Ubud, Bali to explore boundaries between culture bearers and tourists and to identify the highly organized nature of cultural tourism in the region. In an example from Europe, Timothy J. Cooley considers the role of tourism in an annual folklore festival held in Zakopane, Poland. In "Folk Festival as Modern Ritual in the Polish Tatra Mountains" he explores how local families use the festivals to create, preserve, and represent their unique identity. Other authors in this collection that comment on the impact of tourism on cultural practices include Jonathan Sterne on music at tourist site in Minnesota and Angela Impey on establishing systems for simultaneously supporting tourism and traditional knowledge systems in KwaZulu Natal, South Africa.

Gender and Sexuality: In the last twenty years gender and sexuality have become fundamental categories of social and cultural analysis in many different disciplines. Both gendered patterns of behavior and sexual identities are explored as social constructs, sometimes along with other systems of power such as race, ethnicity and class. The focus on issues that relate gender, sexuality and music within ethnomusicology is relatively recent. Ethnomusicologists drove it forward with research in diverse locations around the world that was ultimately presented in collections that include *Women and Music in Cross-Cultural Perspective* (1987) edited by Ellen Koskoff and *Music, Gender and Culture* (1990) edited by Marcia Herndon and Suzanne Ziegler. More recently Pirkko Moisala and Beverley Diamond edited a collection of articles entitled *Music and Gender* (2000), and Tullia Magrini edited *Music and Gender: Perspectives from the Mediterranean* (2003). These and other investigations published in major journals are especially concerned with the complex relations between gendered practices, identities, and roles, and increasingly draw on feminist theory, queer theory, cultural studies, and other disciplinary areas for their frameworks.

Contributions to this section illustrate several approaches to the study of gender and sexuality in ethnomusicology. In "*Taiko* and the Asian/American Body: Drums, *Rising Sun*, and the Question of Gender," Deborah Wong identifies *taiko* performance as both racialized and gendered. She explores the cultural dynamics of race and ethnicity that intersect with gender and sexuality in its portrayal in the film *Rising Sun* and in issues of the dominance of the female performer in North American taiko groups. Cheryl L. Keyes in "Empowering Self, Making Choices, Creating Spaces: Black Female Identity via Rap Music Performance," also considers race and gender as she explores African-American women's contribution to and role in shaping rap music. She identifies categories of women rappers and discusses African-American female identity in contemporary urban culture. In "The Frame Drum in the Middle East: Women, Musical Instruments, and Power," Veronica Doubleday examines the widespread association of the frame drum with women in the Muslim world and explores power relationships involving female sexuality with respect to musical instruments in Islamic cultural contexts and beyond. Other articles in this collection that make direct connections to these topics include Leslie C. Gay, Jr. on women in the New York rock scene, Patria Román-Velázquez on gender and the embodiment of salsa in London and Tina K. Ramnarine on Indo-Caribbean chutney, a popular genre drawn from a women's song tradition.

Globalization and Glocalization: The subject of globalization has been central to political and intellectual discourses in many academic disciplines; and certainly it will only grow in importance throughout our lives. Globalization is used in ethnomusicological research as it relates to global interconnectedness and the cultural interactions and exchanges that occur for musicians, their music, and consumers as well as the scholars that study them and work with them. Boundaries and borders around the world are considerably more permeable today than they once were and this has had a direct effect on musical experience. While cultural exchange and the interdependence of cultures and countries across borders has been in place for centuries, the acceleration of the pace and expansion of the possibilities through industrialization, and especially with the rapid growth and development of technology, encourages new musical styles and forms and provides new experiences and areas of study for scholars. The discourse on globalization in ethnomusicology continues to be framed by key works published during the 1990s, especially Mark Slobin's *Subcultural Sounds: Micromusics of the West* (1993) and Veit Erlmann's *Music, Modernity, and the Global Imagination:*

South Africa and the West (1999).[10] These works and others continue to debate issues connected to the circulation of musical practices and the agency of participants in musical production.

Scholars have added the term glocalization to their vocabulary to better represent the dynamic relationship between global and local entities: how the global conforms to local needs through an historical process that bypasses and subverts hierarchies of power. In music, local performers and consumers naturally select and modify different elements from a range of global possibilities providing a wealth of creative opportunities for local actors. In this collection Jocelyne Guilbault explores this issue in "On Redefining the 'Local' through World Music" as she discusses the changing status and redefinition of the concept of "local" that has resulted from the growth of the music industry. She considers the transformation of a local industry in the French Antilles through its connection to production, promotion, and consumption in France and the Caribbean. Marina Roseman also considers these intersections in "The Canned Sardine Spirit Takes the Mic" as she discusses the spirit mediums and song ceremonies that act as mediators for social change among the Temiar, and indigenous group in central Malaysia. She explores the vitality of religious and musical expression, identifying spirit practices as "critical sites for the engagement of local peoples with global processes." Finally, Rainer Polak discusses the local, national, and international uses of the *jembe* (*djembe, jenbe*) drum of West Africa in "A Musical Instrument Travels Around the World: *Jenbe* Playing in Bamako, West Africa, and Beyond." He identifies multiple contexts for performance and the effects of globalization on the construction and production of the instrument.

Media, Technology, and Technoculture: Technologies, the products of human manipulation of materials to make them useful and more efficient, have enabled the rapid expansion of media in the twentieth and twenty-first centuries. This has given rise to radical changes in lifestyle and cultural expression, as well as access to information. Media and technology are both terms that can be used to relate to processes and products during many different periods in human history, although their most common contemporary use relates to their meanings as "mass media" (institutions that create and distribute information electronically and in print) and the technology that is connected to mass culture. Scholars in ethnomusicology recognize that technology is culturally constructed and its uses are culturally defined. As technology becomes more and more dominant in our lives, the term technoculture has been adopted to refer to the cultural reception and interpretation of these new technologies. Technoculture also encompasses the ways the modern world has been transformed by technology and how people negotiate the technological world. While some identify technology as destructive (to local practice, for example) others recognize the possibilities it carries for shared opportunities, including the mobilization of community that it allows.[11]

In current discussions ethnomusicologists acknowledge their "technologically privileged positions" (Lysloff and Gay, 3) through their ready access to audio, video, photographic, and computer equipment for documenting musical practices. This has raised questions that range from issues of privilege and authenticity and concerns about aesthetic value and audio quality.[12] Studies in the discipline have focused especially on the political dimensions and social meanings found in the uses of technologies and on the reshaping of political, social, and cultural boundaries in local and global contexts. Recent articles on the intersection of technology and local culture are in an edited volume bv René T. A. Lysloff and Leslie C. Gay entitled *Music and Technoculture*. These issues can be found in all three of the articles in this volume. In "Mozart in Mirrorshades: Ethnomusicology, Technology, and the Politics of Representation" Lysloff uses a science fiction story to frame a discussion of technoculture, its increasingly sophisticated meanings, and its role in Anglo-European cultural imperialism. In "Technology and the Production of Islamic Space: The Call to Prayer in Singapore," Tong Soon Lee explores the relationship between technology and the spatial organization of social life focusing on the use of the loudspeaker and radio in the Islamic call to prayer in a Singapore community. Similarly, Gay writes about technology as lived experience tied to cultural practices for local New York City rock musicians in "Acting Up, Talking Tech: New York Rock

Musicians and Their Metaphors of Technology." He is especially concerned with how rock musicians establish and reinforce identity, authenticate musicianship and signal social alliances. Other articles in the collection that address the access, use, and manipulation, as well as the social impact of media and technology, include Jonathan Sterne on programmed music and commercial space in Minnesota, Marina Roseman on use of technologies by Temiar peoples in central Malaysia, and Jocelyne Guilbault on local use of new technologies in the West Indies.

Nationalism and Transnationalism: While nationalism is often identified as a political phenomenon it is also connected to cultural identity. Thus the idea of nation refers both to the nation-state, a sovereign nation with borders and government, and to symbolic markers (of nationhood) that include flags, anthems, and geographic boundaries, constructed cultures, and imagined landscapes. Ethnomusicologists have studied aspects of nationalism and artistic expression for decades; the geographic focus of the discipline encouraged scholars often to connect nation (which traditionally was identified with place) and musical expression. Current studies focus on the role of music in constructing notions of national identity, including how music has been used to imagine and legitimize a nation in national and now transnational spheres. Research shows that the growing circulation of people, ideas, commodities and technologies across national boundaries has intensified nationalism rather than subduing it.

In recent years, ethnomusicologists have contributed several significant studies that document the intersection of music and nationalism. In *Performing the Nation: Swahili Music and Cultural Politics in Tanzania* (2003), Kelly Askew explores the ways the new nation of the United Republic of Tanzania used music and dance to imagine and legitimize itself throughout the latter half of the twentieth century. Similarly, in *Nationalists, Cosmopolitans, and Popular Music in Zimbabwe* (2003), Tom Turino shows how music articulated Zimbabwean nationalism during the 1980s and 1990s. Tina Ramnarine uses new folk music in Finland to explore relationships between national and global identities in *Ilmatar's Inspirations: Nationalism, Globalization, and the Changing Soundscapes of Finnish Folk Music* (2003). Finally, in 2004 Philip Bohlman and Michael Bakan edited a handbook entitled *The Music of European Nationalism: Cultural Identity and Modern History* with essays that look at nationalism in both historical and contemporary contexts.

For this volume Sue Touhy traces occurrences of nationalism in China during the twentieth century in "The Sonic Dimensions of Nationalism in Modern China: Musical Representation and Transformation." She presents links between music and nation that are forged both by conscious design and coincidence of circumstance. J. Martin Daughtry discusses the process of adopting a new national anthem in Russia in 2000 in "Russia's New Anthem and the Negotiation of National Identity." He shows how the anthem is used to negotiate a national identity that is not static but is constantly being reconfigured.

Widespread global migration during the twentieth and twenty-first centuries has created complex contexts for diasporic communities who maintain connections with their nations of origin through social relationships and activities. Ethnomusicologists recognize that the forces of globalization contribute to the reconfiguring of economic, social, and geopolitical relations and they see the transformative potential of transnationalism (and thus of globalization). They have witnessed and documented the complex flow of ideologies in transnational spheres—the negotiation of identities and national boundaries, the reproduction of social hierarchies of race and class, the formation of collective memories, and the construction of hybrid forms in music. In this collection, Gage Averill discusses the transnational organization and circulation of Haitian popular music in the reconciliation of homeland and diaspora populations in "'*Mezanmi, Kouman Nou Ye?* My Friends, How Are You?': Musical Constructions of the Haitian Transnation." Tina K. Ramnarine examines the musical genre chutney as an expression of Indian-Caribbean identity in "'Indian' Music in the Diaspora: Case Studies of Chutney in Trinidad and in London." Here she considers the diasporic nature of the tradition and its development in the pluricultural context of the Caribbean.

Place and Embodiment: Place and embodiment are used and applied in various ways in cultural geography, cultural studies, anthropology and other disciplines in the social sciences. In ethnomusicology, research concerned with embodiment, emplacement, and sense of place intersect regularly with scholarship in the above disciplines along with dance ethnology, art history, philosophy, and cognitive psychology. Ethnomusicologists explore the encoding and enacting of identities in historical, social, and geographic contexts as they consider place and space, body and music, and the embodiment of ideas and issues in music and dance, musical instruments, and performance practice. They recognize also that musician's identities over time are built on memories that are continually constructed and reconstructed both cognitively and symbolically. Performance not only mediates and embodies historical memory but also social and political ideas and ideals.

While connections to existing theoretical structures within ethnomusicology and related fields continue to be explored in these developing areas of inquiry, Stokes' 1994 compilation *Ethnicity, Identity, and Music: The Musical Construction of Place* continues to contribute to a re-focusing of research on place and identity as they are connected to issues of gender, race, ethnicity, and nationalism. Ethnomusicologists also increasingly use ideas linked to the composer and musicologist R. Murray Schafer. His concern for education and the acoustic environment began an acoustic ecology movement that called for greater change in the sonic environment as early as the 1960s with "ear cleaning" exercises to improve sensory awareness. Ethnomusicologists have adopted his vocabulary that is concerned with acoustic, geographic, and social elements in sound. Steven Feld became involved in this movement in the early 1990s, noting in his research among the Kaluli in Papua New Guinea "how the ecology of natural sounds is central to a local musical ecology, and how this musical ecology maps onto the rainforest environment (Feld 1994)." His continuing active involvement in exploring and applying musical, geographical, anthropological, and acoustic concepts to ethnomusicological research, including an edited volume with Keith Basso entitled *Senses of Place* (1996), has encouraged others to seek similar geographic, acoustic, and ultimately political connections to landscape issues and to frame work on space and place.

Two articles in this collection introduce concepts connected to these areas of study. In "The Embodiment of Salsa: Musicians, Instruments, and the Performance of a Latin Style and Identity," Patria Román-Velázquez examines the construction of Latin identities as embodied in London-based salsa. She uses music, musical instruments and performance practice to concentrate on how the body and music are informed by ideas of gender, sexuality, and identity. In "Dueling Landscapes: Singing Places and Identities in Highland Bolivia," Tom Solomon discusses how music performance embodies identity and grounds it in a specific place using examples from community performances of indigenous peoples in Bolivia. Other articles in the collection that address issues connected to place and/or embodiment include Tong Soon Lee on the Islamic call to prayer in Malaysia, Chris Gibson and Peter Dunbar-Hall on Aboriginal rock and the land, and Marina Roseman on Temiar spiritual practices in Malaysia.

Racial and Ethnic Identities: Racial and ethnic identities, like gender and national identities, are complex creations that are widely discussed in academic circles. Race, once considered a biological category, is now recognized more appropriately as culturally constructed. The principles and characteristics of race, and the process of reinforcing racial identities, occur through its continuous reproduction in language, ideas, and cultural practices. Ethnicity, often connected to national identity, is generally used to refer to shared characteristics due to a belief in a "common ancestry, memories of a shared historical past, and elements in common, such as kinship patterns, physical continuity, religious affiliation, language, or some combination of these (Shelemay, 249)." Ethnomusicologists, and other scholars in music and related fields, have identified the various ways ethnic and racial identities are played out in music—through interpersonal interaction and global circulation. One of the primary concerns in this area is the construction of boundaries. Research reveals that music variously subverts and reinforces both genre and social boundaries.

As Martin Stokes describes, "how music is used by social actors in specific local situations to erect boundaries, to maintain distinctions between us and them…" (Stokes 1994, 6). These topics are connected also to issues of authenticity, power, and transformation through processes of negotiation of difference.

Articles in this section explore issues connected to race, racial and ethnic identities. In "Native American Rap and Reggae: Dancing 'To the Beat of a Different Drummer'" Neal Ullestad explores identities of Native American performers and musical forms and performances that combine elements of traditional and contemporary popular music. The artists he discusses use hybrid forms to engage their audiences and to undermine and reinforce their sense of place. Similarly, Richard Jones-Bamman examines Saami musicians who construct music drawn from popular and traditional sources to support and confront issues affecting these indigenous peoples of Norway, Finland, and Sweden in "From 'I'm a Lapp' to 'I am Saami': Popular Music and Changing Images of Indigenous Ethnicity in Scandinavia." He argues that their efforts during the latter half of the twentieth century have been focused on creating a new ethnic Saami identity.

Social and Political Action: Music used as a tool to express political sentiments has been connected to scholarly studies on music and politics for years. Political scientists and sociologists who study strategies for control and manipulation through music—by those in power, as well as those seeking social justice—have also framed methods and theories for research. In *Rockin' the Boat: Mass Music and Mass Movements*, edited by Reebee Garofalo in 1992, authors identified issues of social and political action in mass-mediated popular music and political struggles around the world. Two 1998 publications, *Acting in Concert: Music, Community, and Political Action* by political scientist Mark Mattern (a contributor to this volume) and *Music and Social Movements: Mobilizing Traditions in the Twentieth Century's* by sociologists Ron Eyerman and Andrew Jamison, have also impacted research and classroom study of music and social movements. Studies in ethnomusicology explore music and the politics of resistance—how performers use strategies for negotiating social, historical, and political identities and how performers use their music as a form of social action. Scholars explore the complex relationships between local political action and national and international performance, in revolutions, campaigns, and other forms of activism and consider the significance of its transformative power to change perceptions and behaviors at key moments in a community's history. Political action also includes issues arising around globalization and the debates related to protection versus regulation of performance on a local and global scale.

Social action also encompasses activism from within the field of ethnomusicology. While advocacy and music have been linked for years, especially through the music education field, ethnomusicologists have only recently actively embraced the subject to relate it more directly to their own research. An advocacy anthropologist is an activist who facilitates community-based action, providing data and technical aid and sometimes becoming involved in decision-making due to their experience and knowledge in a region. Advocacy ethnomusicologists today are beginning to do the same. The new advocacy ethnomusicology for music, musicians, and their communities—grows out of applied anthropology and applied ethnomusicology where knowledge gained through scholarly research is used to seek solutions for contemporary social problems.

The growth of social and political activism among students and scholars in ethnomusicology is encouraging to see, and will undoubtedly generate even greater advocacy and activism in the future. Between 2003 and 2005 ethnomusicological societies and programs presented numerous calls for research in this broad area. This included graduate program sponsored conferences at Brown University and University of California, Los Angeles that focused not only on music education and community activism, but also on the social responsibility ethnomusicologists have to the communities in which they work.[13] The Society for Ethnomusicology and the International Council for Traditional Music have explored different forms of advocacy in roundtables, conference papers, and calls to action. In the 2004 SEM Newsletter, the president of the Society for

Ethnomusicology, Timothy Rice urged the society to "take positions on public policies, and civic and political issues that impact, or are relevant to our work and missions and on which we possess some expertise;" and to "convey those positions to public figures, to the citizenry at large, to college and university teachers and administrators, and to our membership" (Rice, 3).[14] Using the Internet, ethnomusicologist Dale Olsen at Florida State University has established a series of Web sites he calls "Ethnomusicology as Advocacy." He describes the "Internet information project" as an effort to teach the public about musics and musical cultures that are "in peril or transition" and encourages ethnomusicologists to be advocates for cultural survival.[15]

The papers in this category represent three approaches to studying social and political action. Mark Mattern in "Cajun Music, Cultural Revival: Theorizing Political Action in Popular Music" (1998) identifies distinct forms of social action associated with Louisiana Cajun music. Mattern defines three types of political action (confrontational, deliberative, and pragmatic) and explores and discusses how they might be applied to this popular genre. In "Nitmiluk: Place, Politics, and Empowerment in Australian Aboriginal Popular Music" Chris Gibson and Peter Dunbar-Hall present a case study using the song "Nitmiluk" by the popular group Blekbala Mujik. This piece that combines traditional and contemporary practices, multilingualism and political strategies for improving aboriginal lifestyle in contemporary Australia. Their study explores Aboriginal rock and the (re)construction of postcolonial space in the Katherine region of the Northern Territory in Australia. Finally, in "Culture, Conservation and Community Reconstruction: Explorations in Advocacy Ethnomusicology and Participatory Action Research in Northern KwaZulu Natal," Angela Impey explores the relationship between ethnomusicology, environmental conservation and sustainable development in the Dukuduku forests of northern KwaZulu Natal. She identifies the songs, dances and ritual as agents of local knowledge on the environment and discusses how communities can participate to generate a more effective system to support the environment and regional development. Other authors in this collection that engage directly with some of these issues include Neil Ullestad on identity politics in contemporary Native American music, René T. A. Lysloff on music, the politics of representation and technoculture, Richard Jones-Bamman on political and economic mechanisms employed by Saami musician to support new identities, and Deborah Wong on performance and the politics of ethnicity.

The articles in this compilation sample some of the significant research in ethnomusicology that has been published over the last fifteen years. In addition to offering in-depth topics for learning and discussion, they illustrate how the blurring of boundaries is reshaping the field. The discussions that take place among the academic disciplines, by actors in public and private sectors regarding music in commercial and non-commercial settings, has given ethnomusicologists, scholars in related disciplines, as well as other individuals and communities, new opportunities to document their musical practices and to share procedures, practices, information, and experience.

Notes

1. Today these courses are more commonly called "Music Cultures of the World," or "Musics of the World," or "Music of the World's Peoples."
2. See: Ian Anderson. 2000 "World Music History." *FRoots Magazine*. Available: www.frootsmag.com/content/features/world_music_history/ for a historical view of this event. See: the "Minutes and Press Releases." attached to this article for a collection of documents that document these events: Available: www.frootsmag.com/content/features/world_music_history/minutes/.
3. This site is available at: www.bbc.co.uk/radio3/worldmusic/
4. This site is available at: www.npr.org/templates/topics/topic.php?topicId=1044
5. This site is available at: www.abc.net.au/rn/music/deli/
6. Commons was used especially in Europe to describe public land in a village that was shared by all. A series of enclosure movements that began as early as the twelfth century gradually moved land from public to private status.
7. See Andrienne Kaeppler and Olive Lewin. *Come mek me hol' yu han': The Impact of Tourism on Traditional Music* (Kingston: Jamaica Memory Bank, 1988).

8. The 1998 issue of *The Journal of Musicological Research* 17(2) included articles by Helen Rees, Frederick Lau, Margaret Sarkissian, and Clark Cunningham, and Regula Qureshi;
9. The 1999 issue of *The World of Music* 41(3) included articles by Martin Stokes, Jeff Todd Titon, Mark DeWitt, Timothy J. Cooley (included in this volume), and Vicki Brennan.
10. See Stokes (2004) for a discussion of these and other studies on globalization .
11. See Wong (2004, chapter 5) for a discussion of this in the context of Vietnamese Americans in Orange County, California.
12. For a discussion of the issue of audio quality and aesthetic value, see Feld and Brenneis (2004).
13. In 2003, the Graduate Program in Ethnomusicology at Brown University sponsored a conference entitles: "Invested in Community: Ethnomusicology and Musical Advocacy." They said: "This will be the first conference in the United States to focus on the vital role of the academic in advocating community music. Applied ethnomusicologists work as musical and cultural advocates, using skills and knowledge gained within academia to serve the public at large. They help communities identify, document, preserve, develop, present and celebrate the musical traditions they hold dear. Pioneering scholars will speak about creating useful projects with communities both nationally and internationally." See their archived conference announcement at: listserv.brown.edu/archives/cgi-bin/wa?A2=ind0302d&L=gscomm-l&F=&S=&P=2826. At UCLA the graduate program planned a 2005 conference on applied ethnomusicology, entitled "Ethnomusicology At Work and In Action." For this event they invited participants from a wide range of disciplines, including "ethnomusicology, musicology, music performance, cultural studies, anthropology, media studies, folklore, music journalism," to share insights and explore the place of applied work in ethnomusicology. This includes the issues of "community activism" and "grassroots organizing" among other forms of engagement. See their 2004–2005 newsletter for further information: www.ethnomusic.ucla.edu/newsevents/newsletters/newletter2004-5.pdf
14. In 2003, the president's roundtable, under the direction of then president Ellen Koskoff, focused on "SEM and Political Advocacy" with contributions from members representing diverse issues. This was followed by Timothy Rice's statement on advocacy in the March 2004 *SEM Newsletter*. One of the themes for the 2004 annual meeting for the Society of Ethnomusicology was "Taking a Stand? Ethnomusicology and Advocacy," which generated papers and discussions on this topic throughout the conference. And there has been a call for papers on "advocacy and cultural democracy" for the 2005 annual meeting of the society as well. Similarly, the 2005 call for papers for the annual meeting of the International Council for Traditional Music includes applied ethnomusicology, with a focus on, "issues of advocacy, canonicity, musical literacy, cultural property rights, cultural imperialism, majority–minority relations, and many others." See the society Web sites for further information; for SEM: www.ethnomusicolog.org and for ICTM: www. ethnomusic.ucla.edu/ICTM.
15. He says, "How can ethnomusicologists be advocates for cultural survival? Dissemination of knowledge to the Internet masses is perhaps a step in the right direction. With these music cultural surveys we wish to share our ideas about world cultural diversity, beauty, value, and survival through music" (Olsen, Web). See www.dolsenmusic.com/advocacy/ to access information on this ongoing project.

References

Askew, Kelly. 2002. *Performing the Nation: Swahili Music and Cultural Politics in Tanzania*. Chicago Studies in Ethnomusicology. Chicago: University of Chicago Press.

Bohlman, Philip V., and Michael B. Bakan, eds. 2004. *The Music of European Nationalism: Cultural Identity and Modern History*. Santa Barbara: ABC CLIO

Clayton, Martin, Trevor Herbert, and Richard Middleton, eds. 2003. *The Cultural Study of Music: A Critical Introduction*. New York: Routledge.

Connell, John, and Chris Gibson. 2003. *Sound Tracks: Popular Music, Identity and Place*. London; New York: Routledge,

Erlmann, Veit. 1996. "The Aesthetics of the Global Imagination: Reflections on World Music in the 1990s"*Public Culture* 8(3):467–87.

———. 1999. *Music, Modernity, and the Global Imagination*. New York: Oxford University Press.

Eyerman, Ron, and Andrew Jamison. 1998. *Music and Social Movements: Mobilizing Traditions in the Twentieth Century*. Cambridge: Cambridge University Press.

Feld, Steven. 1994. "From Ethnomusicology to Echo-Muse-Ecology: Reading R. Murray Schafer in the Papua New Guinea Rainforest." *The Soundscape Newsletter* 8. Available: interact.uoregon.edu/MediaLit/WFAE/readings/ecomuse. html.

Feld, Steven, and Keith H. Basso, eds. 1996. *Senses of Place*. Santa Fe: School of American Research Press.

Feld, Steven, and Donald Brenneis. 2004. "Doing Anthropology in Sound." *American Ethnologist* 31(4):461–74.

Garofalo, Reebee. 1993. "Whose World, What Beat: The Transnational Music Industry, Identity, and Cultural Imperialism." *World of Music* 35(2):16–32.

———, ed. 1992. *Rockin' the Boat: Mass Music and Mass Movements*. Boston: South End Press.

Hartley, John. 2002. *Communication, Cultural and Media Studies: The Key Concepts*. London; New York: Routledge.

Herndon, Marcia, and Suzanne Ziegler. 1990. *Music, Gender, and Culture*. Intercultural Music Studies, 1. Wilhelmshaven, West Germany: Florian Noetzel Verlag.

Kaeppler, Adrienne, and Olive Lewin. 1988. *Come mek me hol' yu han': The Impact of Tourism on Traditional Music*. International Council for Traditional Music. Kingston: Jamaica Memory Bank.

Koskoff, Ellen. 1987. "An Introduction to Women, Music, and Culture." In *Women and Music in Cross-Cultural Perspective*, edited by Ellen Koskoff, 1–23. New York: Greenwood Press.

Lysloff, René T. A. and Leslie C. Gay, Jr. eds. 2004. *Music and Technoculture*. Middletown, CT: Wesleyan University Press.

Magrini, Tullia, ed. 2003. *Music and Gender: Perspectives from the Mediterranean*. Chicago: University of Chicago Press.

Mattern, Mark.1998. *Acting in Concert: Music, Community, and Political Action*. New Brunswick; London: Rutgers University Press.

McCann, Anthony. "Understanding Enclosure." Beyond the Commons. Web site. <www.beyondthecommons.com/understandingenclosure.html>

Moisala, Pirkko and Beverly Diamond, eds. 2000. *Music and Gender*. Urbana: University of Illinois Press.

Nettl, Bruno et al., ed. 2004. *Excursion in World Music*. 4th ed. Upper Saddle River, NJ: Pearson/Prentice Hall.

Pareles, Jon. 2003. "Critics Notebook: Oh the Music of Our Sphere." *New York Times,* June 27, 2003, section E, 1.

Ramnarine, Tina K. 2003. *Ilmatar's Inspirations: Nationalism, Globalization, and the Changing Soundscapes of Finnish Folk Music*. Chicago: University of Chicago Press.

Rice, Timothy. 2004. "SEM and Political Advocacy." *SEM Newsletter* 38(2):1, 3–4.

Schafer, R. Murray. 1977. *The Tuning of the World*. New York: Knopf.

Shelemay, Kay. 2001. *Soundscapes: Exploring Music in a Changing World*. New York: Norton.

Slobin, Mark. 1993. *Subcultural Sounds: Micromusics of the West*. Hanover, NH: Wesleyan University.

Stokes, Martin. 1994. *Ethnicity, Identity and Music: The Musical Construction of Place*. Oxford: Berg.

———. 1999. "Music, Travel, and Tourism: An Afterword." *The World of Music* 41(3):141–55.

———. 2004. "Music and the Global Order" *Annual Review of Anthropology* 33:47–72.

Taylor, Timothy D. 1997. *Global Pop: World Music, World Markets*. New York: Routledge.

Titon, Jeff Todd. 2004. *Worlds of Music: An Introduction to the Music of the World's Peoples*. Belmont, CA: Schirmer/Thomson Learning.

Toner, P. G., and Stephen A. Wild. 2004. "Introduction—World Music: Politics, Production and Pedagogy, A Special Thematic Issue of *The Asia Pacific Journal of Anthropology*." *The Asia Pacific Journal of Anthropology* 5(2): 95–112.

Turino, Thomas. 2000. *Nationalists, Cosmopolitans, and Popular Music in Zimbabwe*. Chicago: University of Chicago Press.

Wade, Bonnie C. 2004. *Thinking Musically: Experiencing Music, Expressing Culture*. New York: Oxford University Press.

Part I

Commodification and Consumption

1

Sultans of Spin
Syrian Sacred Music on the World Stage

Jonathan H. Shannon

Understanding the transformations of culture in an age of transnational connections (what in the past decade has been both celebrated and maligned as "globalization") has been at the forefront of critical anthropological scholarship for over a decade (Featherstone 1990, 2002). Transnational musical genres, often collected under the category of world music and world beat, provide the soundtrack to these processes and transformations—from Franco-Maghrebi *raï*, sonically marking and challenging the contradictions of postcolonial North African diasporas in France (Gross et al. 1996; cf. Schade-Poulson 1999), to "Pygmy Pop," bridging the rain forests of New Guinea and the transnational flows of pop music and culture (Feld 1996a), among myriad other examples. Choose pretty much any area of the world, and no doubt artists from there will be performing their "world music" somewhere in the global ecumene. In the seemingly unending quest for new sounds for new times, widely disparate styles and genres of music are increasingly caught up in transnational processes of commodification, distribution, and consumption by much wider audiences than those of their "authentic" homes. What is an "authentic homeland" for genres and styles that increasingly are produced not only in the transnational circuits of migrants and performers, but *for* these circuits? What constitutes "style" in a globalizing aesthetic discourse? How are categorical distinctions produced and marked in the emerging world music market, and how are these distinctions appropriated, reconfigured, and challenged by artists in performance?

These important questions, among others, beg ethnographic investigation. Yet, to date, musical analysis of globalization and the global analysis of music have remained in the quiet margins of anthropological literature despite recent writings by anthropologists and ethnomusicologists that have encouraged a largely tone-deaf anthropology to listen to how global cultural flows are sonically charged and mediated (Erlmann 1999; Feld 1995, 1996b, 2001; Guilbault 1993a). If we are to understand what Veit Erlmann terms "the global imagination" characteristic of cultural production in an era of globalization, we need an ethnography that seeks "why and in what way people's measures of the real, the truthful, and the authentic change and through which discursive and expressive genres and by which technological means they create a sense of certainty about the world in which they live" (Erlmann 1999, 3–4). This article is an ethnographic exploration of the ways the authentic and the real are mediated and constituted in the global imagination through musical performance. Rather than promoting certainty about the world, this example reveals the sites of performance and consumption of world music to be "heterotopic" (Foucault 1986), that is, fraught with disjunctures between the competing authenticities and realities promoted and consumed by artists, audiences, and culture brokers operating within the shadows of the transnational music industry.

I analyze the performance by Syrian ensembles of the musical and kinesthetic elements of the *mawlawiyya* (or "Whirling Dervish") *dhikr*, which draws its spiritual heritage from the teachings and practices of Jalal al-Din Rumi.[1] In Syria, especially in Aleppo, a number of contemporary ensembles perform material adapted from the mawlawiyya dhikr, including its songs and particular dances. The mawlawiyya rite is not commonly practiced in Syrian mosques today and few Syrians listen to this variety of music, either at home or in mosques. However, elements of the mawlawiyya spiritual–musical tradition can today be found performed on stages and in restaurants in Syria, across the Arab world, and now abroad on international stages where it is presented for global consumption as world music. The performance of this variety of music in transnational circuits helps to legitimate the idea of a category of "sacred music" while simultaneously producing the idea of an authentic "local" musical culture. Following Timothy Mitchell's exploration of representational practices that underlie—and undermine—modern subjectivities (Mitchell 1991, 2000), I use the concept of the "world stage" to examine how musical performance practices that are represented as authentic local spiritual traditions obtain their authenticity and locality through their enactment and staging in global performance contexts. The performance of "sacred" music on the world stage requires a conceptual differentiation of "sacred" from "nonsacred" musical genres, and their promotion as distinct "styles" of world music.

If musical aesthetics is based on the naturalized or iconic associations of stylistic patterns, as Steven Feld (1994a) has argued, then the aesthetics of world music styles such as sacred and Sufi must be sought in how such styles are constructed and naturalized in representational practices and processes of commodification and consumption in global political and cultural economies. I analyze how style emerges as a naturalized category in world music discourses, and how artists, agents, concert promoters, and journalists construct such styles as "sacred" and "Sufi" within the wider relations of power and associated representational practices of the world music industry. The result of these processes of differentiation and commodification is the reconfiguration of concepts of both local and global identities, as well as new understandings of style.

Syrian Sacred Music—Al-Kindi in New York City

It was a cool March evening in New York as I stepped out of the subway on my way to the recital hall. I had received a call a few weeks earlier from my Syrian *oud* (lute) teacher—the master performer and teacher Muhammad Qadri Dalal—notifying me that he and the group with whom he tours, the Ensemble al-Kindi, would be performing in New York. The Ensemble al-Kindi (see Figure 1.1), led by the Swiss-born *qânûn* (lap zither) player Julien "Jalaleddine" Weiss, who resides part of the year in his home in Aleppo, is among Syria's most well-known orchestras today. Aleppo is famous in the Arab East for its long tradition of *tarab* music,[2] but it is also known as the second city, after the Turkish city of Konya, for the practice of the mawlawiyya or *mevlevi* Sufi rite, named (like Weiss) after Mawlana Jalal al-Din Rumi. This was to be, however, their first concert in New York.

As the performance hour approached, the trickle of aficionados in the hall became a swarm of people lining up outside the doors for a rare chance to hear the Damascene *munshid* Sheikh Hamza Shakkur perform "Sufi songs" with the accompaniment of the "Whirling Dervishes" (*darâwîsh*) from the Umayyad Mosque in Damascus. The audience included U.S. and Arab fans of Arab and world music, music critics, and their friends. By 8:00 p.m. the hall was packed—some six hundred and fifty souls gathered for an evening of instrumental and vocal pieces that the program said derived from Syria's mawlawiyya repertoires. The lights dimmed and a representative of the World Music

Figure 1.1 Ensemble al-Kindi, New York. March 12, 2001. Photo: Jonathan H. Shannon.

Institute, the evening's primary sponsor, took the stage and introduced the ensemble. In addition to welcoming us, the representative noted that the show would not have any intermissions but would rather consist of a series of interrelated suites of songs from Syria's "Sufi music" repertoire. Finally, this individual added, "Because this is sacred Music, you should refrain from applauding during the performance." The implication was that this music—*sacred* music—demanded a different kind of reception from what usually happens in the performance of tarab-style Arab music—that is, the shouts, sighs, gestures, and applause that constitute the conventional responses of the tarab culture and which index both the quality of the performance and the emotional states of the performers and the audiences (Danielson 1997; Racy 1991, 2003; Shannon 2003a).

I found this remark strange because in my experience Aleppine performers and audiences do not usually distinguish between sacred and nonsacred performance genres in this manner, even in the context of the mosque or Sufi lodge (*zâwiya*), in which audience participation is pretty much mandatory and one finds similar responses to what happens in tarab performances. Furthermore, much of the repertoire, both vocal and instrumental, is shared between sacred and nonsacred domains, undermining any strict distinction between sacred and profane repertoires. At any rate, the performance began with this admonition and after perfunctory introductory applause we settled in for an evening of sacred music.

Unfortunately for the speaker, a number of audience members arrived late and missed the introductory admonition to silence. Because a high percentage of the latecomers were Arabs or Arab-music enthusiasts, and because the music was very engaging, as a consequence they reacted to the performance as any good and skilled Arab listener would: with shouts of *Allâh, aywa!, yâ salâm!*, and *yâ 'anî!* as well as applause after moving vocal phrases and skillful improvisations.[3] In response, some of the more punctual audience members responded with shushes and arched eyebrows: I heard some people behind me whispering to a latecomer to "Be quiet! This is Sufi music—You're not supposed to clap." I was reminded of Syrian connoisseurs of European music who would shush their uninitiated friends when they applauded between the movements of a symphony at concerts in Syria (of course the same thing happens in the United States). I too felt restrained, wanting to react to the playing but wondering if perhaps Sheikh Hamza or Julien Weiss had told the concert organizers that applause was not appropriate in the "Sufi" context, and that they were only passing on the artists' preferences in trying to restrict the audience's responses. And so went the concert: What to my ears were beautiful performances by the artists, met with hesitant reactions from a mostly silent audience.

After the show, I went back stage to congratulate the artists on a good concert. I especially praised the *nây* (reed flute) player, who had played several moving *taqâsîm*, or improvisations. After exchanging pleasantries he asked me if the sound quality had been poor or his playing off, since no one reacted to his solos, which I had interpreted as highly skilled. I assured him that his playing had been great. For his part, Dalal, accustomed to critical acclaim wherever he performs, was unimpressed by the silent New York audience. His response to my congratulations was a laconic "*mâshî al-hâl*—Whatever. It's over and done with." Finally Weiss asked me, "What was the matter with the audience? Why were they so quiet? Didn't they like [the performance]?" I told him that we had been told not to applaud or shout during the concert because it was "sacred music." He and the others to whom I mentioned this fact were surprised; they had given no such indication to the organizers, and for the most part were disappointed that they got what seemed to them to be half-hearted responses: hesitant applause, an isolated *yâ salâm!*—but not the usual effusive responses they were accustomed to getting in the Arab world, Europe, and elsewhere.[4]

Diverging and Converging Representations of the Sacred and the Local

The admonition "Do not applaud: This is sacred music" can be interpreted as the singular vision of the individual who pronounced it. The remarks about not applauding might ostensibly have referred to an indigenous distinction between sacred and nonsacred genres and what, borrowing from linguists, might be called the "co-occurrence" rules for musical performances: that is, what forms of audience coparticipation are deemed appropriate for specific musical performance contexts (see Ervin-Tripp 1973; Stross 1976). The insights of sociolinguistic research shed light on the ways in which, in musical performance, the audience is a key coperformer (see Duranti 1986; Duranti and Brenneis 1986). In musical performances, audiences and performers (often the same individuals; see Schutz 1977) negotiate the meaning of performance by making what Feld has termed "interpretive moves" (1994b, 85–89) that locate performances in time and place and associate them with generic and stylistic conventions. Among these latter conventions are appropriate co-occurrence or coperformance rules. Can audience members applaud during the course of performance, or must they remain quiet? Is dancing an appropriate mode of coperformance, or is stillness? When we speak of a genre or style of music (classical, jazz, world music), we invoke these types of associations. In the performance of the Turkish mevlevi rituals, for example, audience interaction in the form of applause and vocalizations is deemed to be inappropriate, and the World Music Institute representative probably had Turkish mevlevi co-occurrence rules in mind when introducing the Ensemble al-Kindi, which was performing a related music. Moreover, this individual, accustomed to presenting a wide variety of often very unfamiliar musical cultures to U.S. audiences, advanced a reading of the event as sacred through the warning not to applaud during the performance; invoking a principle of nonparticipation was akin to invoking a genre or style of sacred music. Indeed, for most educated Western audiences, however appreciative of Middle Eastern musical genres, a default coperformance rule might just well be what in the context of European classical music is often a principle of nonparticipation out of respect for the performers and other audience members, as opposed to a rule of respectful applause and shouting associated with the Arab tarab culture that many Arab audience members and others familiar with the tarab culture observed (albeit hesitantly, given the admonition) during the New York City performance.[5] Hence the admonition to silence may have been the result of a confusion between Turkish and Syrian coperformance rules, and an unspoken and implicit principle of nonparticipation by a respectful if uninitiated New York audience.

In my research in Syria and in my conversations with the artists after concerts in the United States and abroad, I noted that Syrian musicians generally do not distinguish between sacred and nonsacred categories in this fashion. In practice, the sacred–profane distinction tends to refer more to different *venues* than to different *repertoires*. Of course there are well-known forms of Islamic chant (*inshâd*) performed in Syria that are distinct from songs performed in nonritual contexts by their association with prayer, other forms of ritual, and by their lyrics, which refer to Allah, Muhammad, and the prophets.[6] Yet the lyrics of the "sacred" songs often have both spiritual and profane connotations, as is well known in Sufi poetry and song texts in praise of wine and the beloved, for example (see Kennedy 1997). Moreover, a number of the songs in the "sacred" repertoire are also performed in nonritual venues such as on festival stages and in restaurants. Vice versa, many secular songs and song melodies are performed in sacred contexts such as the dhikr, though the words are often altered or revised to reflect the different context; this is the case with the genre known as *al-qudûd al-halabiyya,* a variety of the *muwashshah* in which sacred lyrics are substituted for profane, and vice versa, while the melody remains essentially the same (see Shannon 2003b). The ambiguity of the distinction between sacred and nonsacred song texts is mirrored in the coperformance conventions in modern Syria; where audiences and performers are expected to interact in similar ways—via shouts, sighs, and bodily movements—in the context of a *sahra* (evening musical soirée) and during dhikr.

The sacred–nonsacred distinction is more fluid in practice than in the discourse of concert organizers and some participating artists. We should think in terms of a continuum of performance practices, musical genres, and styles (see Abrahams 1976) that range between those anchored in specific spiritual practices such as dhikr and those that are more associated with nonspiritual gatherings such as a *hafla* ("party" or "concert") or sahra. Although the performance venue (club, restaurant, festival stage, zâwiya) alone is not sufficient for delimiting the genre or for predicting audience coperformance, it is often a key marker of where on a broad continuum a given performance or genre lies.

The ambiguity of the sacred-profane distinction was illustrated for me at a number of other performances in Syria. For example, in late 1997 I attended a performance by Aleppo's Firqat al-Turath (Heritage Ensemble), featuring the octogenarian vocalist Sabri Moudallal. The concert was held in the amphitheater of Aleppo's medieval citadel, where an audience of approximately five hundred—almost all Syrians—enjoyed some three hours of music, some of which overlapped with what the Ensemble al-Kindi performs (the two groups often share performers as well). Once warmed up, the audience exhibited the typical tarab responses: energetic shouts, sighs, gestures, and (for some young men) burlesquelike dancing that serve to index the emotional appeal of the music as well as the emotional responsiveness of the audience. At the end of the concert the ensemble performed a short sequence of songs from the mawlawiyya repertoire, including the "whirling dervishes." The audience, which up to this point had energetically engaged with the music, did not significantly change its reactions with the onset of the mawlawiyya set but continued to respond to the music with characteristic tarab responses, though obviously when Moudallal chanted the call to prayer (*adhân*) people did not dance—they shouted Allâh! and yâ 'aynî! and other responses typical of the Aleppine tarab culture. I had noted such responses while attending dhikr in Aleppo and Damascus; certainly participants were more subdued than at a hafla or sahra, but they exhibited similar responses in both contexts.

Framing Performance as Sacred

The significant overlap between sacred and profane repertoires and performance practices in these brief examples suggests that where on a continuum of sacred and profane attributes a given performance falls depends on how it is framed as one or another style. Often the performance frame more than musical content determines the classification of musical genre (Feld 1994b, 85–89; see also Bateson 1972; Goffman 1974). Claiming that the music is sacred (e.g., by invoking coperformance conventions appropriate to a ritual context) establishes or keys (Bauman 1977) a frame of reference in which both audiences and artists interpret the flow of events in performance as sacred. For the New York concert, charging admission to the musical event and distributing a program with information on the spiritual background of the performers and the music served to key the performance as sacred. So did the fact that the performers wore "traditional" garb—the musicians in embroidered gowns, the darâwîsh in flowing white robes, and Weiss in a simple black outfit. It, perhaps, goes without saying that Aleppine musicians do not wear these outfits outside of performance contexts; they constitute modern performance costumes rather than "traditional" garb. These and other markers of "authenticity," however constructed and reified by these practices, served to key the overall frame as sacred; they also sought to mask the fact that the performance took place in a New York City hall—and not in a Syrian mosque, where one is *not* likely to hear such music anyway.

Moving beyond the confines of this single performance in New York City, the sacred frame helped to promote not only the idea of Ensemble al-Kindi as exemplars of "sacred" music but also the very idea of a cross-cultural category called "sacred music" characterized by a unified aesthetic with respect to performance practices and appropriate coperformance conventions. The table of CDs in the lobby of the hall attested to the wide array of artists associated with such a frame, or with multiple and overlapping frames: Arab, Middle Eastern, sacred, Sufi, and so on. Indeed, the World Music Institute and such festivals as the Fez Festival of World Sacred Music tend to include in the Sacred Music category seemingly diverse groups; for example, the Gyuto Monks of Tibet are lumped with Sheikh Hamza Shakkur and the Ensemble al-Kindi presumably because each group's music addresses the sacred aspects of life. Interestingly, in these categorizations of sacred and Sufi styles of music, the "spiritual" is marked off from the "religious."

In fact, the promotional material and website for the 2002 Fez Festival states that the annual event celebrates the "sacred music of monotheist religions, including Christianity, Judaism, Islam, and Sufism."[7] Aside from the fact that "Sufism" is distinguished from Islam in this phrase—perhaps reflecting what Ted Swedenburg (1999, 2001) has discussed as the erasure of Islam from musical cultures from the Muslim Middle East as they enter world music performance and consumption circuits—the festival's programming over the last four years has included both representatives of nonmonotheistic faiths (such as Buddhism) and performers of popular and traditional musical styles that in other contexts may not have any relationship to faith-based musical practices. For example, recent festival programs feature performances of Portuguese *fado* music, a genre of lament; Arabian *muwashshahât*, which can be both "sacred" and "profane"; folkloric music of Tunis; and a variety of other musical genres and styles that could equally fit the programming requirements for a folk or traditional music festival. For many of these performances, there is nothing essentially "sacred" about the music; rather, it is their presentation at a sacred music festival that gives them a sacred aura.

Stylizing Sacred Music

Given the indistinction between sacred and nonsacred genres and styles of music within Syria, and the similarities in co-occurrence rules that characterize sacred and nonsacred performances, the admonition not to applaud during the performance of Ensemble al-Kindi in New York seems to be the result of a misunderstanding. Yet I would like to suggest that it can also be seen as an example of how the growing world music industry attempts to delineate categories within the world music classification. Through concerts such as that of al-Kindi or those at the Fez Festival, these categorizations become naturalized as different styles of music: sacred, Sufi, Middle Eastern, and so forth. Framing performances such as those of al-Kindi as "sacred" contributes to the formation of what in many ways is marketed as a more serious and more "authentic" subset of world music—sacred music. World music entrepreneurs and agents market and promote sacred music as a purer style distinct from other (nonsacred) styles of world music, which tend to celebrate hybridity. As Timothy Taylor notes (1997, 23–26), whereas world music and world beat are generally associated with globalization and transnational cultural economies, "sacred music" is the domain of the spiritually authentic and the local. The example of al-Kindi reveals how the authentic local spiritual traditions are in fact produced within the same sets of discourses and representational practices of the world music market.[8]

The differentiation of these categories can be found in the World Music Institute's online book and music catalogue, which interestingly classifies "sacred" as a *style* of music, other "styles" including: bows, compilation, cross cultural, flutes, lutes, percussion, reeds, Sufi, vocals, and zithers. Following the categorizing trend mentioned above, in this catalogue Sufi is distinguished as a separate style from sacred, though there is some overlap between the 28 entries under "Sufi" and the 85 under "sacred."[9] The latter "style" encompasses groups and genres as diverse as the Gyuto Monks of Tibet, Muezzins of Aleppo, African American spirituals, the "Mysterious" voices of Bulgaria, Afro-Brazilian Candomblé, Moroccan Gnawa ritual music, "Uhuru-Rhythms of the World," "Traditional Drum Dance Chants" from Hawaii, and others.

Although the World Music Institute is not responsible for the titles of the recordings it markets, it is worth mentioning that a large percentage of the sacred music titles in their and other catalogues refer to soul, mystery, spirit, essence, masters or master musicians, and, often, tradition, folk, and peoples, whereas much of the music sold as world music by such companies as the Putumayo World Music and Mondo Melodia labels, among others, refers instead to groove, spice, odyssey, journey, eclectic sounds, and flavors, not to mention influences, dynamism, danceability; these labels less often make recourse to a sense of pure tradition and essences and rather celebrate hybridity and idiosyncratic connections such as Putumayo's "Music of the Coffee Lands" and "Tea Lands" compilations. In this manner, sacred and Sufi "styles" of music trade in the currency of cultural authenticity and purity, and their promotion should be read as constructing a domain for consumption considered style to be a characteristic of the frame; it marks the distinction of code or medium from message, in communicative and metacommunicative terms (see Feld 1994a, 110; see also Bauman and Briggs 1990). Thus the result of successful framing of a musical performance is the creation and promotion of a distinct understanding and experience of *style*. In a classic study, Leonard Meyer (1967, 116) defined style as consisting of replicable patterns of formal musical elements such as melody, rhythm, texture, timbre, instrumentation, and voice. Following Feld (1994a) and others (Duranti 1986), we can add extra-musical associations to Meyer's formal musical properties to include venue, costume, audience, audience–performer interactions, and appropriate co-occurrence or coperformance rules, among others. Medieval Arabic texts, for example, correlated the modes *(maqâmât)* with times of the day, bodily humors, and celestial configurations, among other extramusical factors (Farmer 1994; Wright 1978). When these correlations and evaluations are experienced as natural in the course of performance, an iconic relationship between them develops so that each element implies the other; as Meyer asserts, in these cases, style is felt as predictable and natural (Meyer 1967, 116; cf. Keil 1994). Feld (1994a) has likewise argued that in such cases we find the basis of local aesthetics—in the iconicity of styles that themselves develop as networks of associations between formal musical properties and diverse framing strategies.

Constructing Sacred Syrian Music

The distinction of sacred from other styles of music reflects the larger processes of differentiation and homogenization at the heart of the representational practices associated with world music. These processes include journalistic and academic writing that, as Feld has analyzed (2001), alternate between the celebration of transnational "world" grooves and beats, on the one hand, and anxieties about cultural loss, homogenization, and (more importantly) appropriation and com-modification, on the other. I now turn to an analysis of recent journalistic representations of the Ensemble al-Kindi in order to trace the ways in which they promote an understanding of a sacred music style in world music discourses.

To a large extent, performers and their agents willingly go along with the "sacralization" of their musical traditions. For example, links to spiritual ancestors are an important component of al-Kindi's self-presentation. The promotional literature for the Ensemble al-Kindi and its press file stress the link between the ensemble and the "Sufi traditions" that the group claims to have resurrected from obscurity and now perform around the world. As in Sufism itself, spiritual genealogy (*isnâd*) is a key principle in establishing the authenticity of the group in their literature and self-presentation. The evening's program begins with an epigraph from the ninth-century Iraqi Sufi master Junayd on the effects of "sacred music" on the body:

> The great master Junayd was asked why the Sufis felt such powerful emotions in their spirit and the urge to move their bodies when listening to sacred music. He replied: "When God asked the souls in the spirit world, at the moment of the First Covenant: 'Am I not your Lord?,' the gentle sweetness of the divine words penetrated each soul for ever [*sic*], so that whenever one of them hears music now, the memory of this sweetness is stirred within him causing him to move." [The Whirling Dervishes New York, program notes, March 11, 2001]

Yet despite these claims for spiritual ancestry, for the performers, the music's purported "Arab-ness" was more important than its "sacred" character; given the tarab-like responses of some audience members, it seems that the ethnic dimensions of the concert and not only spirituality was a major motivation for attending the concert. The members of the Ensemble al-Kindi, as noted earlier, expressed surprise at the statement about not applauding during the performance, but they did not necessarily contradict the overall presentation of the concert as "sacred"; indeed, their self-presentation as exemplary performers of Syrian "tradition" in many ways confirmed it. In conversations with the performers in Syria and after their concerts in the United States and Morocco, the artists stressed that they performed "authentic Syrian works." Weiss, in remarks to the audience after the New York performance, stressed that the works they performed were "Arab" and not "Turkish," in order to clarify what he and others perceive to be a confusion between the Turkish mevlevi and the Arab mawlawiyya practices (and that quite probably resulted that evening in a confusion with respect to co-occurrence rules in the different types of music).

Similarly, the artists claimed that their show represents an Arab-Syrian "tradition," not a Turkish one. Dalal, the group's unofficial artistic coordinator, claimed that he performs not for the money but to spread Aleppo's heritage (*turâth*) and make it known around the world; he asserted that financial concerns were a secondary motivation for him. Dalal, proud of his efforts on behalf of Aleppo's and Syria's musical heritage, pointed out that the repertoire consisted entirely of "Arab" pieces (instrumental and vocal), not "Turkish." It did not seem to matter much that some of the "traditional" selections were by 20th-century composers, such as Tawfiq al-Sabbagh (a Christian), not known for their participation in the mawlawiyya rite or their interest in it, and others show clear Ottoman influences in terms of structure and treatment of modes.[10]

Even with respect to the spiritual genealogy of the music, the performers emphasized the "Arabness" of the music, more to promote the authenticity of Aleppo's claims to the mawlawiyya rite than to celebrate its sacred character. Both Weiss and Dalal remarked that Rumi lived for a period in Syria, and that Aleppo is considered to be the second home after Konya in Turkey for the mawlawiyya order; because the performance of the related mevlevi rite was until recently strictly limited in Turkey, they suggested that Aleppo's continuous mawlawiyya tradition is in fact "more authentic" than its contemporary Turkish cousin because of its longer uninterrupted history. By associating their musical practices with the founder of the rite, and by localizing the genealogy in a

Syrian-Aleppine spiritual geography, both artists underscored the authenticity of their performance practices, marking them as similar but distinct from those of the "Turkish" mevlevi practices.

The legitimizing function of these spiritual and ethnic genealogies is reflected in the diverse manifestations of the Ensemble al-Kindi itself. Their promotional literature includes information sheets for the six incarnations of the group, each specializing in different repertoires of "sacred" and "profane" music; "The Whirling Dervishes of Damascus" is only one manifestation of Ensemble al-Kindi. Yet all versions feature the same group of musicians performing on the instruments of the traditional Arabian *takht* ensemble: qânûn (lap zither), oud (Arabian short-necked lute); nây (open-ended reed flute); and *riqq* (tambourine); sometimes the Iraqi *joza* (a spike fiddle not unlike a *rabâb*) is added for the performance of their "The Passion of the Thousand and One Nights" program, featuring the Iraqi singer Husayn al-'Azami. According to the style they wish to present, they add either vocalists associated with the mawlawiyya or other types of spiritual music, or those who sing the more tarab-inspired "profane" music.

We might see the multiple incarnations of al-Kindi as an example of niche marketing of music in a post-Fordist era of "flexible accumulation" in the global marketplace (Averill 1996; Harvey 1989). Their diverse programs and incarnations reflect both the musical interests and skills of the performers and the promotional and self-presentational skills of Weiss and his agent, who skillfully navigate the growing world music markets as aptly illustrated by the various music label catalog classifications discussed above. Moreover, as I remark later, the diverse manifestations of Ensemble al-Kindi must also be read as illustrating the representational dynamic at the heart of world music aesthetics—what I term the "world stage." Indeed, with the exception of Hamza Shakkur, who performs only inshâd, and al-'Azami, who performs the Iraqi maqâm repertoire, each of the vocalists performs and records both "sacred" and "profane" repertoires. For example, Sabri Moudallal and his protêgê 'Umar Sarmini perform both "sacred" and "profane" repertoires and often will mix them in a given performance.

Sultans of Spin

Moving from the performers' self-presentation to journalistic impressions of their art, one notes immediately how the international press and especially those writing world music columns have been drawn to the personality of Weiss—his having been charmed by the Orient, his conversion to Islam, his role in "reviving" traditional musics (Hudson 2000, 11; Thomas 2001, 66), and, especially, his attraction to "Elusive Aleppo" and the "Oriental way of life" (Hudson 2000, 11). One of Weiss's interviewers, for his part, was so mesmerized by the music of the "Whirling Dervishes" that, "sitting in the front row, the white cloth of their skirts flapping against me, I wonder, not for the first time since I arrived in Syria, if I'm dreaming the whole thing" (Hudson 2000, 2). Clearly, this writer has succumbed to "Elusive Aleppo" as much as Weiss.

Journalists predictably make much of Weiss's "conversion" to Islam, the former Hippie guitar player leaving the highs of his youth for the purer life and tones of Islam; indeed, Weiss has undergone the *hâjj* (the pilgrimage to Mecca) several times. Moreover, Weiss's conversion tends to be framed in journalistic accounts not in terms of spirituality, but in terms of its service to his musical pursuits: "I realized I couldn't go further in this music without becoming a Muslim," claims Weiss in a published interview excerpt. Weiss continues, "The spirit of Middle Eastern music comes from the mosque and the church" (Hudson 2000, 2). These statements suggest that Weiss had to "go native" in order better to understand and perform the music. While this may be the case, it is interesting that the aesthetic factors in his conversion are highlighted in the same manner that the world music industry marks Sufi music as a style—again, one distinct from "sacred" or Islamic music in this de-Islamicized context, with little if any attention paid to the spiritual dimensions of Muslim prayer, dhikr, inshâd, madîh, and so on. In the context of Ensemble al-Kindi's self-promotion, Islam serves as a legitimating factor, as in the spiritual and Arab genealogies of the repertoires and performers, and as an exoticizing device in the case of Weiss's Muslim identity, one that appeals to a sense of cultural purity and authenticity. Weiss could not master the music without going native, but going native is an exotic, aesthetic adventure and not necessarily a spiritual one.

The liner notes of the Ensemble al-Kindi's recent recordings make much of Weiss's home (described elsewhere by one journalist as "ultra-authentic" [Singh-Bartlett 2000]) and the fact that he "chose [Syria] so as to live in a world teeming with symbols, where he could contemplate the Divine Being through music" (*Les Croisades sous le regard de l'Orient* 2001). Moreover, many writers have been intent on giving Syrian mawlawiyya music the particular "spin" of world music journalism, playing artfully (or less so) on the theme of whirling dervishes, and emphasizing the romance and mystery of the music and its exotic provenance.

Not surprisingly, Orientalist discourses of the passive, erotic, and violent Arab are resurrected to serve the interests of constructing and marketing the music abroad. The images and titles of both the press material and Weiss's own statements pander to the most common Orientalist stereotypes of the Arab world: despotism ("sultans of spin"), sensuality ("seductive rhythms"), mystery ("mysterious," "Elusive Aleppo"), and, of course, the *hijâb*—whose image serves as an iconic representation of *all* of these characteristics combined: despotism, sensuality, *and* mystery. One writer even complained that, instead of gazing on the "kohl-rimmed" eyes of local women during his stay in Aleppo, he only encountered "women . . . sheathed in black; buttoned-up in coats of strangely Edwardian cut, their faces draped in shawls [presenting] an utter ghostlike blankness" (Hudson 2000, 1).[11] Thus the Orientalist metaphors of veiled sensuality become naturalized as a central aspect of the aesthetics of this emerging "style" of world music: sacred *or* Sufi music. In this manner the press and promotional literature draws on a stock of Orientalist images and associations to put a particular spin on this type of music, packaging it for consumption by audiences drawn to things elusive, mysterious, and exotic.[12]

That Weiss and his agent include these selections in Ensemble al-Kindi's press packet indicates their tacit approval of the images, Orientalist and otherwise. It also indicates their media-savvy understanding of the appeal and marketing value of such images in a world awash in Orientalist ideologies. Indeed, many Arabs have internalized Orientalist stereotypes and might find the images and associations of the press package appealing, even accurate. Weiss is a skilled marketer as well as a skilled performer; the press packet represents just one small part of a larger set of images, recordings, films, and concerts that Weiss has organized for al-Kindi in order successfully to navigate as an independent culture broker in the risky commercial waters of world music.

In addition to allure and exoticism, a common theme of this journalistic spin is the claim that Weiss is responsible for reviving Syrian "classical" music; it is the Westerner who, through his enchantment with the Orient, is able to out-do the Orientals and resuscitate what one writer calls the "flagging fortunes of Syrian classical music" (Thomas 2001, 66). Weiss's significant achievements notwithstanding, I think even he would argue that the journalistic conceit is an exaggeration; today there are many groups who perform the "classical" (or, better, "classicized") music of Syria. Yet, while acknowledging Weiss' important role in generating interest in this music (both in Syria and abroad), we must also acknowledge two important points. First, echoing Orientalist understandings of the Arab world, it takes a foreigner (specifically a European) to reform and revive "true" Arabian culture. Second, and more importantly, Weiss is "reviving" this music largely for presentation to foreign audiences. The primary reason such music has fallen into decline in Syria is that fewer and fewer people are interested in listening to it; contemporary Arab pop music is far more "authentic" in terms of how accurately it reflects the tastes and interests of the majority of Syrian listeners today who—with approximately fifty percent of the population urban and under the age of 15—are largely youth. While the dominance of Arabic pop music in the contemporary market may be a shame (and as a lover of the older music I would concur), Weiss's reformation of Arab music would seem to serve the interests of a global market of world music consumers more than it does a local one. Even today, few Syrians have CD players or internet access in their homes, few can afford to attend concerts abroad, and few are able to attend Weiss' celebrated *sahārât* (soirées) in his fancy home. Thus, authentic "Syrian sacred music" is in many senses music that is produced, recorded, and performed primarily for non-Syrian audiences outside of Syria. I return to this point below.

The stewardship of Third World or Fourth World musics by First World personalities is a common feature of the world music and world beat phenomena, illustrated by the collaborations with a variety of indigenous musical cultures of Western artists such as David Byrne, Peter Gabriel, Paul Simon, Sting, and others (Erlmann 1999; Feld 1995, 108–110; cf. Byrne 1999). Yet the power relations between this European interlocutor and the "ethnic" musics he curates and performs are not the same as those of the former artists. Of course, Weiss does not (yet) enjoy the same renown as these international stars (though he is well-known in Syria), but, more importantly, he is perhaps more sincerely interested in the music and technically accomplished in its performance. His is not a one-song, one-album, or one-year adventure but, rather, a more than 25-year engagement with Arab and Middle Eastern musics and musicians. Although purists may critique him for lacking "oriental spirit," his recordings are among the best documented and professional recordings of Arab music produced anywhere to date. It is more accurate to read Weiss's experiences with Arab music as illustrating how cultural brokers operate in the shadows of the music industry to promote their own agenda rather than as an example of how the culture industry appropriates Third World music for First World consumption and profit.

The World Stage: Staging Sacred Music

Festivals and performances such as the one I have described are the main sites for staging the sacred, the local, and the authentic. These individual performances—from New York to Fez, Paris, and Aleppo—can be interpreted as actualizations of potentialities inherent in what I am calling (to drag out a tired metonym) the "world stage." In this formulation, I borrow from Timothy Mitchell's discussion (1991) of the representational and administrative practices in colonial Egypt and England that promoted the conception of what he (borrowing from Heidegger) terms "the world-as-exhibition" (Heidegger 1977). In such representational and exhibitionary complexes as the World's Fair, urban planning and cartography, museums, department stores and arcades, among others, the "real" is constructed as a realm of experience distinct from its representations; for example, urban spaces are understood as conforming to a implicit plan or cartographic order. However, as Mitchell points out, analysis of the supposed reality behind the representation reveals further layers of representations, the entire complex being built on a fundamental deferral of meaning, in Derrida's sense (1978); thus, the referent of the "real" does not exist except as a series of representations.

The world stage, while it incorporates aspects of the panoptic principle inherent to the late-19th-century exhibitionary constellations, is structured by the representational practices inherent to what Erlmann (1999) refers to as the "global imagination" of the (post)modern condition in the late 20th and early 21st centuries. The complexes of signs, texts, and representations of the global imagination are themselves intimately involved in the processes of production, distribution, and consumption of global cultural forms—what, to borrow Appadurai's insightful (if cumbersome) terminology, we should analyze in terms of the disjunctive flows of culture within specific constellations of media, population, finance, technology, and ideology "scapes" (Appadurai 1990, 1996). The world stage, then, is the representational and performative nexus of the global imagination in specific complexes of these "scapes."

I intend the term not to refer to a determined site but as a representational practice, a *staging* through which we can understand the global mediation of "local" musical styles. International festivals such as the Fez Festival represent the actualization of an inherent potentiality for staging spiritual authenticity that resides at the heart of world music; the concert that formed the basis of this article is another such example of a staging of the sacred and the authentic. As I theorize it, the world stage is not a specific site or stage per se within the global cultural and political economy but, rather, a principle of siting and staging at the heart of the global imagination as it operates in specific temporal and spatial limits. We might think of the world stage as the representational performance principle behind the actual physical stage on which a given performance takes place, akin to the map that provides a panoptic understanding of an urban space. In its sonic manifestations (and I would argue that contemporary performances of kinesthetic and other forms of expressive culture are also structured to a large extent by the "world stage" principle), the world stage operates as a mediator of the global musical imagination, an imaginary Third Space—distinct from the "home" of local musical productions and the global stage on which they are performed—where, again to borrow from Erlmann (1999, 189), difference is constructed, enacted, and negotiated. It is a space of mediation and consumption of globalized cultural forms and above all sounds. Moreover, it constitutes a space for desire—both that of the artists seeking broader audiences and larger profits, and of consumers seeking the pleasures of cultural difference. The performance of al-Kindi in New York City thus can be understood in part as an actualization of the world stage principle: a staging of a music-dance complex constructed, rehearsed, and performed for a transnational audience of consumers.

Artists, agents, producers and other culture brokers working in the shadows of the multinational music industry—one dominated by five conglomerates that control over 90 percent of the world's music market[13]—construct their performance repertoires and frame them in such a way that the larger vision of the whole, a sonic "panaural" world music, informs the detailed everyday practices of formulating, rehearsing, and instantiating cultural performances in specific locales and stages. It is significant that the performances prepared and executed for the world stage often do not take place in their presumed sites of their origin. Rather, they more often occur in the context of festivals and cultural programs away from their putative sites of origin, and in an important sense are made for the world stage. Indeed, as many scholars have noted, the "local" and the "authentic" in world music circuits are often those cultural practices which can best be packaged and presented globally (Erlmann 1993; Garofalo 1993; Guilbault 1993b; Swedenburg 1999, 2001; Taylor 1997). Often it is musical cultures that are marginal or forgotten within their sites of local origin that are most easily appropriated for this role in the world music market, as in the case of the "Master Musicians of Jajouka" (Schuyler 2000).

Importantly, these same practices that are performed on the world stage in turn are reimported to their putative sites of origin as "authentic local tradition." As mentioned above, "authentic" Syrian sacred music is, to a large extent, music that is produced, recorded, and performed for primarily non-Syrian audiences outside of Syria. In recent years it has come to be performed within Syria as representative of tradition and authenticity—but in restaurants, at festivals, and other locales that are not in any sense the "traditional" or customary performance venues for these repertoires. In other words, if we travel back to Syria to experience "authentic mawlawiyya music" we will meet the repertoires and performance practices prepared and perfected for the world stage. Indeed, aside from a few holidays and festivals a year, and on an extremely limited basis in mosques, one cannot experience the mawlawiyya music and dance in contemporary Syria: It barely survives as a living tradition.[14]

Conclusion: Sacred Music and the Representational Practices of Modernity

Analysis of the representational practices associated with sacred music reveals that concert promoters and performers themselves have a number of increasingly overlapping concerns. Among these are the promotion of a more serious and cross-culturally valid category of human experience called "sacred music," the revival of a "local tradition" (to some extent its invention), and, finally, the ability to profit from this category, at home but, especially, abroad. These areas of concern overlap considerably so that the promotion of a category and style of sacred music for the world stage contributes to the formulation of a local "tradition," and this in turn allows world music promoters and performers to realize profits.

The concern with promoting "sacred music" as a more serious style of world music arises partly in response to the perceived excessive commercialization of world music and its often hybrid nature. The category of "sacred music" suggests a purer musical culture and reflects a desire among artists such as Weiss and audiences such as the one in New York City for the preservation of this purer musical culture in which the spiritual dimensions and not just commercialism are accessed. In some senses sacred music as a stylistic category can be understood as a response to the anxieties of globalization about which Feld (2001) has written. Sacred music thus comes to define a cross-cultural category—not unlike the musicological category of ritual or liturgical music—that encompasses musical traditions which are considered more authentic than popular varieties of world music and world beat fusion musics (cf. Byrne 1999).

Yet it is unclear what qualities such diverse groups as the Bulgarian Orthodox Church Ensemble, Sabah Fakhri, Meredith Monk, and the Agape International Choir have in common aside from being featured at the same international festivals (in Fez, 2001, for example). To say that they are all examples of "sacred" or "spiritual" music obscures more than it reveals about the different styles, genres, and performance practices associated with these performers. It also obscures the fact that these are largely products of and for the world stage, global in their orientation and aesthetic, and reflecting what Appadurai in another context has termed "production fetishism" (1990, 306)—the masking of the transnational forces of production and consumption that produce commodifiable "local" cultural products such as Syrian sacred music. If anything, the sacred music designation reveals the extent to which universalizing narratives of spiritual essence are behind the marketing strategies of record companies and festival organizers, and also how they self-destruct on closer examination.

With respect to the revival of local tradition, in contemporary Syria mawlawiyya music does not enjoy widespread popularity. However, with the success of this and other Syrian groups abroad at international festivals, that is, as a result of its promotion on the world stage, it has gained increased popularity at home, leading to the elevation in status of previously marginal groups (musicians) and marginal genres and repertoires among local consumers—chiefly Syria's middle class and bourgeoisie who now patronize these performances, although in the safety of a restaurant or festival, or on television, and rarely in a mosque or Sufi zâwiya. This has contributed to the construction and elaboration of the concept of a local "tradition" or heritage (turâth), one that requires patronage and preservation. It is worth repeating that contemporary interest in and indeed the very concept of a "Syrian" mawlawiyya tradition arose in Syria *after* it had been formulated and promoted on the world stage in global performance circuits abroad and was reimported "home." The "tradition" is in fact a highly selective sampling of what were and to some extent remain diverse musical–spiritual performance practices, now standardized as a singular mawlawiyya repertoire.

Finally, the world music industry and performers alike seek to profit from the classification and commodification of what they label as "sacred music." Sacred music festivals and concerts have become increasingly popular in Europe, the United States, and in the Arab World. Foreigners and émigrés are willing to pay a lot to hear "sacred" music at festivals; they may also be motivated by a desire to recapture the spiritual in the face of a sense of loss of this dimension of life—what the organizers of the Fez Festival of World Sacred Music may have had in mind when they came up with the motto "Giving Spirit to Globalization" (Schuyler 2001). Yet, as indicated above, it is often the ethnic associations of the music that draw audiences and compel performances: al-Kindi's New York City performance was produced and consumed as much for its appeal to ideologies of Arab ethnicity as for its supposed spirituality. This marks a disjuncture between the aims of the World

Music Institute, the concert's chief promoter, and the artists and audiences concerning the proper aesthetic response to the music and indeed its appropriate stylistic category—predominantly "sacred" for the former, predominantly "Arab" for the latter.

Many would argue that all music is in a sense "sacred," but this generalization (however valid) must be understood not for its presumed truth value but in terms of how it allows for the commodification of diverse musical cultures as "sacred" in order to serve the interests of the growing world music market and the culture brokers that inhabit this emergent space. In this respect, the construction of Syrian sacred music on the world stage entails the simultaneous production of an idea of musical and spiritual authenticity at the site of the local and its packaging for export abroad as a style of world music. The concept of the world stage as a representational practice and staging principle for the production of authentic local musical cultures helps us to understand the interface between small agents and culture brokers such as world music journalists, concert promoters, and artists, and the transnational circuits in which their diverse musical repertoires and performance practices are stylized and categorized. As I hope I have made clear, such concerts and the representational practices of staging that drive their aesthetics also have the effect of bringing not only spirit to globalization but, as it were, aspects of globalization to the spirit.

Acknowledgments

This article is based on field research in New York City in 2001 and in Syria from 1996–98. Earlier versions were presented at the Annual Meetings of the Middle East Studies Association and Society for Ethnomusicology 2001, and at the Center for Middle East and Middle Eastern American Studies, CUNY Graduate Center, 2002. I thank Deborah Kapchan, Michael Frishkopf, Vincent Crapanzano, and the editors and reviewers of the *American Anthropologist* for their useful comments. I thank Muhammad Qadri Dalal, Julien Weiss, and the members of Ensemble al-Kindi for insights on their performance practices.

Notes

1. Jalâl al-Dîn Rûmî: b. 1207, Balkh, Persia (now Afghanistan), d. 1273, Konya (now Turkey). Rumi is considered to be the spiritual father of the Mawlawiyya Sufi order. He is the best selling poet in America today, largely through the translations of Coleman Barks: *The Glance* (1999), *The Essential Rumi* (1997), and *The Soul of Rumi* (2001), among others. The Sufi dhikr is the ritual invocation of God through prayer, song, and codified bodily motions. It may take place in a *zâwiya* (Sufi lodge), a mosque, or home.
2. *Tarab* refers to a state of musical "rapture" or "enchantment" experienced by listeners in the course of performance. It is generally associated with "classical" styles of Arab music in the Levant (see Racy 1991, 2003; Shannon 2003a).
3. These exclamations, literally meaning God!, Yes!, O Peace!, and O My Eye!, are common expressions of tarab.
4. Their performance a few weeks earlier at UCLA was not introduced with a restriction on applause, and, hence, according to the performers and some who attended the concert, was full of tarab-style audience-performer interactions (Kathleen Hood and Jihad Racy, personal communication, October 2001).
5. Michael Frishkopf suggests that one analogy might be the respectful silence most tourists display when entering a cathedral or similar place of worship (personal communication, October 2001).
6. These include *tajwîd* (Qur'anic recitation), *madîh* (songs in praise of the Prophet), *adhân* (the call to prayer), *ibtihâl* (prayers of supplication), and others. See Frishkopf 2000.
7. http://www.fesfestival.com, accessed May 5, 2002.
8. Although a large percentage of total music titles are categorized as "world music," only about three to four percent of total music sales are within this category (see Swedenburg 2002).
9. http://www.heartheworld.org, accessed March 22, 2002.
10. As many scholars have pointed out, the distinction of "Arab" from "Turkish" music (especially instrumental genres) is largely a product of Arab nationalism and does not refer to clear differences among the musical traditions of Istanbul, Aleppo, and Cairo; prior to the 1930s the music was usually referred to as *al-mûsîqâ al-sharqiyya*, "Oriental music" (Lambert 1997; Racy 1977; Shannon forthcoming).
11. Although some of Aleppo's Muslim women wear such attire in public, even in conservative neighborhoods one finds a variety of sartorial styles.
12. Weiss packages his recordings with extensive notes and biographies of musicians and composers in ways that undermine the stereotypes and offer insights into the everyday life of music making in Aleppo.
13. These are BMG, EMI, Sony, Universal, and Warner/Time. For more on what Charles Keil terms the "Musical-Industrial Complex," at the forefront of which are these transnational conglomerates, see Keil 1994.
14. Other Sufi order (*turuq*, sing. *tafîqa*) remain active in Aleppo, including the Qâdiriyyâ and Rifâ'iyya. For more on everyday Sufi ritual practice in Aleppo, see Pinto 2002.

References

Abrahams, Roger. 1976[1969]. The Complex Relations of Simple Forms. In *Folklore Genres,* edited by D. Ben-Amos, 193–214. Austin: University of Texas Press.

Appadurai, Arjun. 1990. "Disjuncture and Difference in the Global Cultural Economy." *Public Culture* 2(2):1–24.

———. 1996. *Modernity at Large: Cultural Dimensions of Globalization, vol.1: Public Worlds.* Minneapolis: University of Minnesota Press.

Averill, Gage. 1996. "Global Imaginings." In *Making and Selling Culture,* edited by Richard Ohmann, Gage Averill, Michael Curtin, and David Shumway, 203–223. Middletown, CT: Wesleyan University Press.

Bateson, Gregory. 1972. *Steps to an Ecology of Mind.* New York: Ballantine.

Bauman, Richard. 1997. *Verbal Art as Performance.* Prospect Heights, Ill.: Waveland Press.

Bauman, Richard, and Charles L. Briggs. 1990. "Poetics and Performance as Critical Perspectives on Language and Social Life." *Annual Review of Anthropology* 19:59–88.

Byrne, David. 1999. "Crossing Music's Borders in Search of Identity: 'I Hate World Music.'" *The New York Times,* October 3, 1999. Electronic document, http://query.nytimes.com/search/articlepage.html?res=9901EED8163EF930A35753 C1A96F958260, accessed October 31, 2002.

Danielson, Virginia. 1997. *The Voice of Egypt.* Chicago: University of Chicago Press.

Derrida, Jacques. 1978. *Writing and Difference.* Chicago: University of Chicago Press.

Duranti, Alessandro. 1986. "The Audience as Co-Author: An Introduction." *Text* 6:239–247.

Duranti, Alessandro, and Donald Brenneis, eds. 1986. "The Audience as Co-Author." *Text* 6.

Ensemble al-Kindi. 2001 *Les Croisades sous le regard de l'Orient: Musique arabe et poêsie du temps des croisades.* CD Le chant de Monde/Harmonia Mundi—CMT 574 1118.

Erlmann, Veit. 1993. "The Politics and Aesthetics of Transnational Music." *The World of Music* 35(2):3–15.

———. 1999. *Music, Modernity, and the Global Imagination: South Africa and the West.* Oxford: Oxford University Press.

Ervin-Tripp, Susan. 1973. *Language Acquisition and Communicative Choice.* Stanford: Stanford University Press.

Farmer, Henry George. 1994[1929]. *A History of Arabian Music to the 13th Century.* London: Luzac Oriental.

Featherstone, Mike. 1990. *Global Culture: Nationalism, Globalization and Modernity.* London: Sage.

———. 2002. "Islam Encountering Globalization: An Introduction." In *Islam Encountering Globalization,* edited by Ali Mohammadi, 1–13. London: Routledge Curzon.

Feld, Steven. 1994a[1988]. "Aesthetics as Iconicity of Style (Uptown Title); or, (Downtown Title), 'Lift-Up-Over Sounding': Getting into the Kaluli Groove." In *Music Grooves,* edited by Charles Keil and Steven Feld, 109–150. Chicago: University of Chicago Press.

———. 1994b[1984]. "Communication, Music, and Speech about Music." In *Music Grooves,* edited by Charles Keil and Steven Feld, 77–95. Chicago: University of Chicago Press.

———. 1995. "From Schizophonia to Schismogenesis: The Discourses and Practices of World Music and World Beat." In *The Traffic in Culture: Refiguring Art and Anthropology,* edited by George Marcus and Fred Myers, 96–126. Berkeley: University of California Press.

———. 1996a. "Pygmy POP: A Genealogy of Schizophonic Mimesis." *Yearbook for Traditional Music* 28:1–35.

———. 1996b. "Waterfalls of Song: An Acoustemology of Place Resounding in Bosavi, Papua New Guinea." In *Senses of Place,* edited by Steven Feld and Keith H. Basso, 91–135. Santa Fe, NM: School of American Research Press.

———. 2001. "A Sweet Lullaby for World Music." In *Globalization: Millennial Quartet,* edited by Arjun Appadurai, 145–172. Durham, NC: Duke University Press.

Fez Festival. 2002. *Fez Festival of World Sacred Music.* Electronic document, http://www.fesfestival.com, accessed May 5.

Frishkopf, Michael. 2000. "Inshad Dini and Aghani Diniyya in Twentieth Century Egypt: A Review of Styles, Genres, and Available Recordings." *Middle East Studies Association. Bulletin* 34(2):167–183.

Foucault, Michel. 1986 "Of Other Spaces." *Diacritics* 16:22–27.

Garofalo, Reebee. 1993. "Whose World, What Beat: The Transnational Music Industry, Identity, and Cultural Imperialism." *World of Music* 35(2):16–32.

Goffman, Erving. 1974. *Frame Analysis: An Essay on the Organization of Experience.* New York: Harper and Row.

Gross, Joan, David McMurray, and Ted Swedenburg. 1996. "Arab Noise and Ramadan Nights: Raï, Rap, and Franco-Maghrebi Identities." In *Displacement, Diaspora, and Geographies of Identity,* edited by Smadar Lavie and Ted Swedenburg, 119–155. Durham, NC: Duke University Press.

Guilbault, Jocelyne. 1993a. *Zouk: World Music in the West Indies.* Chicago: University of Chicago Press.

———. 1993b. On Redefining the "Local" through World Music. *The World of Music* 35(2):33–47.

Harvey, David. 1989. *The Condition of Postmodernity.* Oxford: Basil Blackwell.

Heidegger, Martin. 1977. *The Question Concerning Technology, and Other Essays.* William Lovitt, trans. New York: Harper Row.

Hudson, Mark. 2000. "Elusive Aleppo." *Sunday Times* (UK), April 23: Travel, 1.

Jakobson, Roman. 1960. "Linguistics and Poetics." In *Style in Language,* edited by T.A. Sebeok, 350–377. Cambridge, MA.: MIT Press.

Keil, Charles. 1994. "On Civilization, Cultural Studies, and Copyright." In *Music Grooves,* edited by Charles Keil and Steven Feld, 227–231. Chicago: University of Chicago Press.

Kennedy, Philip F. 1997. *The Wine Song in Classical Arabic Poetry: Abu Nuwas and the Literary Tradition.* Oxford: Clarendon Press.

Lambert, Jean. 1997. *La médecine de l'âme: le chant de Sanaa dans la sociêtê yêmênite.* Nanterre, France: Sociêtê d'ethnologie.

Meyer, Leonard. 1967. *Music, the Arts, and Ideas: Patterns and Predictions in Twentieth-Century Culture*. Chicago: University of Chicago Press.

Mitchell, Timothy, ed. 1991[1988]. *Colonising Egypt*. Berkeley: University of California Press.

Mitchell, Timothy, ed. 2000. *Questions of Modernity*. Minneapolis: University of Minnesota Press.

Pinto, Paulo. 2002. "Mystical Bodies: Ritual, Experience and the Embodiment of Sufism in Syria." Ph.D. dissertation, Department of Anthropology, Boston University.

Racy, A. Jihad. 1977. "Musical Change and Commercial Recording in Egypt, 1904–1932." Ph.D. dissertation. Department of Music, University of Illinois.

———. 1991. "Creativity and Ambience: An Ecstatic Feedback Model from Arab Music." *The World of Music* 33(3):7–28.

———. 2003. *Making Music in the Arab World: The Culture of Artistry of Tarab*. Cambridge: Cambridge University Press.

Rumi, Jalal al-Din. 1997. *The Essential Rumi*. Coleman Barks, trans., with John Moyne, et al. San Francisco: Harper.

———. 2001. *The Soul of Rumi: A Collection of Ecstatic Poems*. Coleman Barks, trans., with John Mayne et al. San Francisco: Harper.

Rumi, Jalal al-Din, and Nevit Orguz Ergin. 1999. *The Glance: Songs of Soul Meeting*. Coleman Barks, trans. New York: Viking.

Schade-Poulson, Marc. 1999. *Men and Popular Music in Algeria: The Social Significance of Raï*. Austin: University of Texas Press.

Schutz, Alfred. 1977[1951]. "Making Music Together: A Study in Social Relationship." In *Symbolic Anthropology*, edited by J. Dolgin, 106–119. New York: Columbia University Press.

Schuyler, Philip. 2000. "Joujouka/Jajouka/Zahjoukah: Moroccan Music and Euro-American Imagination." In *Mass Mediations: New Approaches to Popular Culture in the Middle East and Beyond*, edited by Walter Armbrust, 146–160. Berkeley: University of California Press.

———. 2001. "Giving Soul to Globalization: The Fez Festival of World Sacred Music, 1995–2001." Paper presented at the Annual Meeting of the Middle East Studies Association, San Francisco, November 20.

Shannon, Jonathan. 2003a. "Emotion, Performance, and Temporality in Arab Music: Reflections on *Tarab*." *Cultural Anthropology* 18(1):72–98.

———. 2003b. "*al-Muwashshahât* and *al-Qudûd al-Halabiyya*: Two Genres in the Aleppine Wasla." *MESA Bulletin* 37(1):82–101.

———. forthcoming. *Among the Jasmine Trees: Music, Modernity, and the Aesthetics of Authenticity in Contemporary Syria.*. Middletown, CT: Wesleyan University Press

Singh-Bartlett, Warren. 2000. "Weiss's Oriental Love Affair with Music: Child of the 60s Who Transformed Himself into a Master of the Qanoun." *The Daily Star* (Lebanon), August 17.

Stross, Brian. 1976. *The Origin and Evolution of Language*. Dubuque, IA: William C. Brown.

Swedenburg, Ted. 1999. "Arab "World Music" in the U.S." Paper presented at the Annual Meeting of the American Anthropological Association, November 19.

———. 2001. "Trance-National Islam, World Music, and the Diaspora." Paper presented at the Annual Meeting of the Middle East Studies Association, San Francisco, November 20.

———. 2002. "The Post-September 11 Arab Wave in World Music." *MERIP* no. 224, 32(3):44–48.

Taylor, Timothy. 1997. *Global Pop: World Music, World Markets*. New York: Routledge.

Thomas, Karen. 2001. "Syria: Sultans of Spin." *Arabies Trends*, February 2001:66.

World Music Institute. 2002. *World Music Institute*. Electronic document, http://www.heartheworld.org, accessed March 22.

Wright, Owen. 1978. *The Modal System of Arab and Persian Music, A.D. 1250–1300*. New York: Oxford University Press.

2

Sounds Like the Mall of America
Programmed Music and the Architectonics of Commercial Space

Jonathan Sterne

Shopping malls have become icons of consumer society. The prophets of advanced capitalism—whether they be post-Marxist academics or developers—have given us the shopping mall as emblem and microcosm of this cultural epoch (see Morse 1990; Shields 1992; Karasov and Martin 1993). Visions of the shopping mall become social visions. Yet the visual bias in cultural critique tends toward the assumption that all that matters presents itself to be seen. What if we were to *listen* to a shopping mall instead? What could be heard?[1]

At the Mall of America (Bloomington, Minnesota), beneath the crash of a roller coaster, the chatter of shoppers and the shuffle of feet, one hears music everywhere. Every space in the Mall is hardwired for sound. The apparatus to disseminate music is built into the Mall's infrastructure, and is managed as one of several major environmental factors. Music flows through channels parallel to those providing air, electricity and information to all areas of the Mall. "Facilities Management," the department responsible for maintaining the Mall's power supplies, temperature, and even grounds-keeping, also keeps the Mall's varied soundtracks running. Throughout the many stores and hallways, one can see the blonde circular speakers which are the programmed music industry standard. The Mall of America has three main sound systems: a set of speakers in the hallways plays background music quietly; a set of speakers hidden beneath the foliage of Camp Snoopy (the amusement park built into the Mall's atrium) broadcasts the steady singing of digital crickets; and each store is wired for sound so that it may play tapes or receive a satellite transmission. The Mall of America both presumes in its very structure and requires as part of its maintenance a continuous, nuanced, and highly orchestrated flow of music to all its parts. It is as if a sonorial circulation system keeps the Mall alive.

In places like the Mall of America, music becomes a form of architecture. Rather than simply filling up an empty space, the music becomes part of the consistency of that space. The sound becomes a presence, and as that presence it becomes an essential part of the building's infrastructure. Music is a central—an architectural—part of malls and other semi-public commercial spaces throughout the country, yet for all the literature on spaces of "consumer culture," little or no mention is made of the systematic dissemination of pre-recorded music that now pervades these places (a notable exception is Frow and Morris 1993). This article can be thought of as an answer to that absence, but it is really part of a larger experiment: What happens when we begin to think about space in industrialized societies *acoustically*? How is sound organized by social and cultural practice? How does it inflect that practice? These are old questions for ethnomusicologists, yet the field has really just begun exploring music and sound in industrialized and recorded forms. Since Charles Keil's call for studying mass mediated music (1984, 91), there has been a growing field of interest in the circulation and culture of recordings (see, for example, Wallis and Malm 1984, Meintjes 1990, Guilbault 1993, Manuel 1993). Much of this work is concerned with the relationships of performers and audiences, with the manner in which music influences or connects constructions of identity, or with music industries themselves. This article takes these problems as a point of departure, but explores them at two different layers: (1) where music and listeners' responses to it are themselves commodities to be bought, sold and circulated; and (2) where this commoditized music becomes a form of architecture—a way of organizing space in commercial settings.[2]

The centrality of music as an environmental factor in commercial spaces should come as no surprise. To the contrary, the idea of music pervading quasi-public commercial spaces is the height of banality. Programmed music, better known by one of its brand names, "Muzak," is one of the most widely disseminated forms of music in the world. Alex Greene notes that "we take Muzak for granted, the word having transcended its status as a product trademark and entered into the realms of everyday language, as a label for all 'easy' listening music" (1986, 286). Americans take for granted that almost every commercial establishment they enter will offer them an endless serenade during their stay. This banality itself is a cause for reflection: in 1982 it was estimated that one out of every three Americans heard programmed music at some point every day; that number has steadily increased since then. Americans on average hear more hours per capita of programmed music than any other kind of music (Jones and Schumacher 1992, 156). As I will shortly discuss, programmed music now encompasses both "easy listening" music *and* original recordings heard elsewhere. In other words, one cannot tell simply by listening to music whether it is "Muzak" or not—*all* recorded music is at least potentially Muzak. (For consistency, I will refer to the service itself—"programmed music"—rather than adopting this common usage of a specific brand name. Currently, the three largest programmed music services are the *MUZAK* Limited Partnership, 3M, and Audio Environments, Inc. Programmed music has been in practical use since the 1930's, and *MUZAK* remains the predominant service in the industry; it is the model on which other services are based.)[3]

The economics and social organization of programmed music presumes and exists on top of a whole culture and economy of recorded music. In other words, programmed music presumes that music has already become a *thing*—a commodity. This reification is represented in the economics of the service, and in the presumptions on which this economy is based. For instance, programmed music requires the absolute separation of performer and audience fostered by many recording industries, thereby circumscribing the experience of music for the majority of the population to that of listening: "Today's Baby Boom generation grew up with music as an integral part of their lives. From the clock radio to the Hi-Fi to the stereo to the CD player, music has always been present. They expect it everywhere they go. In fact, respondents of all ages in survey after survey unanimously agree they prefer to shop, dine and work where music is present. Music moves people" (*MUZAK* 1992b). Here, musical experience is understood entirely as listening and cultural value is attributed to the very *presence* of music as a kind of sound. These are two key cultural assumptions underlying the production and deployment of programmed music.

I want to be absolutely clear here: while the capitalist and consumerist market structure of mass mediated music contributes to a larger divide between performer and audience, with fewer performers and a larger audience, this is not necessarily a quality inherent in the recording and transmission (mediation) of sound itself. In other words, we should be wary of critiques of mediation *qua* alienation. Also, we should be careful to recognize that the treatment of music as purely a kind of sound (as opposed to a whole ensemble of practices such as dancing, playing and so on) is a specific cultural construct, and not universally valid. However, this construct of music as sound is very much alive, and exerts real effects, as the case of programmed music demonstrates.

If—under certain conditions—music exerts effects primarily or solely as sound, then we have to begin asking questions about the very act of listening under those conditions. In a media-saturated environment, listening designates a whole range of heterogeneous activities involving the perception of sound. Everything from aesthetic contemplation in a concert hall to the mere act of turning on a radio or a sound recording in one's everyday environment can be understood as "listening." Here, I will use the term "listener" to denote a person perceiving sound in either the active or the passive sense, or both. This ambiguity is important in thinking about programmed music, since such music certainly isn't meant for contemplative listening; it also isn't always "heard" in an entirely passive fashion—rather, it tends to pass in and out of the foreground of a listener's consciousness. Thus the necessity for understanding "listener" as an ambiguous term that shuttles between activity and passivity. In part, this ambiguous status of listening—especially as it pertains to programmed music—is an effect of the social organization of music in a capitalist mass media environment. Peter Manuel (1993) and others have suggested that recorded music be considered from a "holistic" vantage point that examines its production, circulation, and consumption. The context of programmed music adds a whole second layer of circulation to this economy: *re*production, *re*distribution, and secondary consumption. The "producers" of programmed music are the programmed music services themselves, who assemble already existing songs into soundtracks. The consumers of programmed music are stores and other businesses that purchase the services.[4] Clients generally subscribe to a programmed music service and pay a small monthly fee. The service will provide the subscriber with a tuner and a choice of approximately twelve satellite channels to choose from, or a special tape player and a catalogue of hundreds of different four-hour programs. Clients with tape subscriptions generally receive new tapes every month, or every few months, depending on the type of music. Thus, as Manuel points out, in a thoroughgoing analysis of mass mediated music the analytical tools of ethnomusicology need to be supplemented with those of communications (1993, 7; see also Wallis and Malm 1984). A detour through the political economy of programmed music will clarify my own analytical orientation.

Essentially, the use of programmed music in a shopping mall is about the production and consumption of consumption. Programmed music in a mall produces consumption because the music works as an architectural element of a built space devoted to consumerism. A store deploys programmed music as part of a fabricated environment aimed at getting visitors to stay longer and buy more. Other commercial establishments may use programmed music to other ends, but in all cases its use is primarily concerned with the construction of built and lived commercial environments. Having deployed the music, subscribers such as a store or a mall consume consumption insofar as they are interested in listener response to the music itself. They are purchasing the music so as to consume listeners' responses to it—for instance, if listener responses to music lead to increased average shopping time, increased sales, and increased number of customers (see *MUZAK* 1990, 1992b). In other words, while the people who go to a mall to shop may hear programmed music, the consumers of that music (and listener responses to it) are actually the stores and the mall itself. A thoroughgoing analysis of these relations requires an adjustment in critical orientation. Rather than focusing purely on listener response—that of people we normally think of as "consumers" in a mall setting—I am primarily concerned here with the production, distribution, and consumption of that listener response (or what I called above the second "layer" of circulation). I have focused on the frames of possible experience and the ways in which those frames are constituted, rather than cataloging all possible listener experiences in the Mall of America. I am less interested in an exhaustive survey of possible meanings listeners (or "hearers") may attribute to programmed music than in the uses to which those attributions may be put.

Two other obvious problems obstruct a proper ethnography of listening. As I discuss below, actual hearing and listening practices are not necessarily at the forefront of participants' consciousness—sounds can be quite ephemeral, and therefore my calling attention to the music would not necessarily elicit responses from people that reflected what would happen in my absence. Furthermore, because the music in the Mall comes from a larger field of circulation, it would be an error to isolate music heard in the Mall from other contexts in which the same music is heard. In other words, if I were to do a proper ethnography of listening, given that my subjects would be visitors and not *dwellers* in the Mall, the Mall ceases to be useful as an exclusive site of inquiry. Finally, ascertaining exactly what music means to listeners in the Mall still begs the question of how that experience is put to use by the Mall itself.

A Suburban Ethnomusicology?

Given these concerns, in this article I examine the deployment of programmed music in the Mall of America. While this mall may be more spectacular than other malls, its spectacle is a self-conscious one: a tourist visit to this mall above all others is about the spectacle of consumption itself. The Mall's utter extremity on one hand and everydayness on the other offer a unique perspective on a place where consumerism is conflated with nationalism, and where a private commercial space can be hailed by developers as an "alternative urbanity." The Mall has been promoted by airlines and travel agencies as a tourist destination to rival downtowns; some local architects have echoed this assessment, suggesting that the Mall is a downtown for an outer suburb and that *this* downtown offers what Deborah Karasov and Judith A. Martin call a "facsimile of urban delights with almost no urban responsibilities." (1993, 27) But Karasov and Martin are quick to qualify this assessment: "What this commercial imperative suggests is how poorly we understand our cities, present and future, if we view them as little more than accumulated land uses. There is little expectation that shopping malls will contribute to urban design and social goals, no matter how big these malls become or how many people they attract. In the end, the Mall of America is no more a city than Sea World is an ocean" (ibid.).

In this facsimile of urbanity, speakers in the ceilings and walls cascade travelers with an endless flow of music. Perhaps, then, as a footnote to Bruno Nettl's call for an "urban ethnomusicology" (1978, 13), essay could be understood as a suburban ethnomusicology. Although they are a distinguishing aspect of the space, a mall's acoustical features cannot be understood apart from its other general thematic and structural features. Acoustical space is an integrated and substantial element of cultural practice, not an autonomous sphere.

The Mall of America is the largest mall in the United States; it is second only to Canada's West Edmonton Mall. (For a discussion of the West Edmonton Mall, currently the largest in the world, see Crawford 1992.) Also known as the "megamall," it has become a major tourist and leisure site in the area: It has attracted over 10,000 bus tours (each averaging fifty people) since its opening in August 1992, and the average visit to the Mall for all customers is three hours, close to triple the industry average. In addition, adult shoppers spend approximately $84 per visit, which is almost double the industry average (based on Nordberg 1993, 1). You can find billboards advertising the megamall—"the place for fun in your life"—at least as far away as the middle of South Dakota.

Aside from its size, the Mall's most unique feature is its national theme (Petchler 1993). It was built with a self-consciousness about its cultural purpose: while striving valiantly to be "all things to all people," the Mall cultivates itself to simulate a whole range of generic "American" experiences that will appear nonthreatening to its desired middle class clientele (Karasov and Martin 1993, 19, 25). While most malls serve as regional centers, the megamall attempts to present itself as a center of national culture. Its tenant stores are well-known national chains, and the four department stores—Sears, Macy's, Bloomingdale's, and Nordstrom's—combined, represent the paradigm of national department stores (it is worth noting in this respect that neither Bloomingdale's nor Nordstrom's had any locations in Minnesota prior to the construction of the Mall). Even the Mall's home state is demoted to one region among many, as evidenced by stores with "Minnesota" themes. Considering that the West Edmonton Mall claims to be "the world" in a shopping mall, that the second largest mall in the world should devote itself to an entirely "American" theme illustrates the self-importance of American nationalist ideology.

The Mall's national identity requires a very narrow conception of the nation, centered on the mainstream of retail marketing. There is a great deal of product duplication, and with a few exceptions (like souvenirs), one could find almost all the products available in the megamall at many smaller malls. Similarly, although there are a great number of specialty stores, all specialties are geared toward an assumed mainstream population. Ideologically, the Mall of America adds an explicit national theme to the usual consumerist and white middle-class worldviews represented in mall design.

While the Mall of America derives special significance from its size and theme, it also represents the cumulative wisdom of almost forty years of mall design and management. Architecturally, the Mall embellishes on industry standards, but not much. Any difference in scope between the Mall of America and other malls is a result of scale. In contrast to the traditional suburban shopping mall surrounded by smaller strip malls, movie theaters, bars and fast food joints, the Mall of America has simply enclosed all the surrounding activities under one giant roof. As Karasov and Martin put it, the spaces separating the shopping mall from its surroundings have been transformed from "highway to hallway" in the Mall of America (ibid., 23). The Mall thus foregrounds the connections between consumption and leisure so prevalent in American culture, while keeping each activity in its place: to wit, the Mall has an unusually large entertainment complex—the amusement park is joined by a "Lego Imagination Center" and an indoor mini-golf course. As Rob Shields has remarked, there is a critical interdependence among private subjectivity, media and commodity consumption, and privately owned semi-public spaces like shopping malls (1992, 1). In the Mall of America, they can feed off one another.

Great care was taken to produce an "urban shopping district" sensibility for the interior. Each major corridor of the Mall is called an "avenue" and is painted, carpeted, lit, and named differently from the others. The "entertainment districts" are isolated from the shopping areas—Camp Snoopy is located in the Mall's gigantic atrium, while the movie theaters, bars, and an arcade are located on a separate floor, away from retailing. The Mall compartmentalizes specialized functions like eating and entertainment, and retains a general cohesion of design throughout its interior.

In theory and execution, the Mall's soundscape is entirely consonant with other design goals, in part because programmed music is a phenomenon divided according to the same logic as the other commercial enterprises in the Mall: according to a reduction of identity to consumer taste and a universe of taste that rotates on the axis of a consumer class. The music also works because programmed music has become a design feature integral to *any* mall, and therefore doesn't seem the least bit out of place. The acoustical design of the Mall is a result of similar philosophies to those underlying other design features, but it is structured to somewhat different ends.

Sounding Out the Mall

A social space is as much defined by its constant influx and expenditure of energies, by the movements which maintain it, as it is by any stable or structural construct (Lefebvre 1991, 93). Music can therefore be considered as one of those energy flows (such as electricity or air) which continually produce the Mall of America as a social space. In this way, programmed music is both an environmental and an architectural element of the Mall. The acoustical space of the Mall is structured around a central musical tension: the quiet, nondescript music in the hallways contrasting with louder, more easily recognizable and more boisterous music in the stores.

Background Music

The 3M Corporation provides quiet background music for the Mall's common spaces. According to their programming director Tom Pelisero, 3M "did nothing unusual for the Mall of America" (1993). Pelisero himself suggested that the megamall was a hostile environment for background music, because the common hallways are all filled with the din of Camp Snoopy. So what would the Mall want with a standardized form of background music that is barely audible?

The music for the hallways is known within the industry as "environmental" or "background music." This is the kind of music usually brought to mind by references to "Muzak": symphonic arrangements of well-known tunes, both contemporary and traditional, that make prolific use of stringed instruments but stay away from brass, voice, and percussion. In the last ten years, programmed music providers have begun updating their collections. Instead of hearing "Lucy in the Sky With Diamonds" performed by the Czechoslovakian State Orchestra, one is now likely to hear it adapted for a four- or five-piece jazz group (McDermott 1990, 72). These relatively generic ensembles are chosen in service of background music's ultimate design goal: anonymity. The quest for anonymous or "unobtrusive yet familiar" music animates the entire production process.

All environmental music has certain essential characteristics. All vocals and those instruments considered by programmers to be abrasive are eliminated; both would call attention to themselves and thereby disturb the backgroundness of the music. As several authors have noted, mass-mediated music tends to focus more on the performer than on the song (see Chopyak 1987, 441). In the case of programmed music, this tendency must be countered by stripping the music of any distinctive elements. Background music strives toward anonymity, and can thus be understood as the inverse of most industrially recorded and disseminated music. Arrangements of popular and traditional songs are thus performed in "a style devoid of surprise" (Radano 1989, 450) in an effort to render the music familiar and unthreatening—and nondescript.

Background music programming operates according to a technique called "stimulus progression," where each musical selection is rated on a scale from one to six and arranged with other songs in an ascending or descending order to evoke certain emotional responses in listeners. Although *MUZAK* does not share their criteria for stimulus ratings, it is clear that the differences between low and high stimulus ratings are based primarily on rhythm, tempo, and melody. The more upbeat a song, the higher its stimulus rating. (Of course, all background music already operates within a limited range in these respects given the constraints on musical content and style mentioned above.) Stimulus progression was invented to combat worker fatigue in weapons plants during World War II, functioning on a principle of maintaining a stable stimulus state in listeners at all times. Programming is designed to slow people down after exciting parts of the day and speed them up during sluggish parts of the day. It is an aesthetics of the moderate: not too exciting, not too sedate. While environmental music is no longer used exclusively in factories and production centers, it is still programmed along this line of thinking. In a shopping center setting, stimulus progression could be justified—to pick up visitor movement during the middle of the morning and afternoon, and to slow people down after lunch and at the end of the day.

Thus, background music in the hallways has many possible uses, despite its precarious audibility. To paraphrase a corporate slogan, the music in question is not meant to be listened to, but to be heard. A great deal of market research shows that the presence of quiet, leisurely music increases the duration of shoppers' visits (see Bruner 1990). But even if the din of Camp Snoopy counteracts the kind of psychological effects Gordon Bruner seeks, the simple presence of the music itself—when it can be heard—does carry some significance. For instance, it constructs a continuity among the hallways, bathrooms, and entrances. These spaces are somewhat distinguished by architectural motif, but the background music reinforces their common characteristics through its own non-distinctive and generalized character (Greene 1986, 288). Background music is not devoid of meaning, but its meaning is entirely located in its presence, rather than in the songs in the soundtrack. Even controversial songs that contain a catchy tune may still wind up in an environmental program: for example one may hear quiet jazz arrangements like Madonna's "Like a Virgin" or Nirvana's "All Apologies" with a piano or saxophone playing the vocal melody. This practice is quite common, although it invites a kind of recognition on the part of listeners that may actually be disruptive—the song, if recognized, could still call attention to itself, even in an anesthetized version, thus contradicting the "backgroundness" of the environmental program.

This soundtracking further serves to structure the hallway as a transitional space, a space of movement. Besides the nondescript (or vaguely familiar) environmental music and the echoing amusement park, the hallway has no markers of its own identity other than a vague architectural theme. The mall management does not intend the hallways as destination for Mall visitors. (Despite the management's intentions, these transitional spaces often serve as a place for youth to congregate and socialize—to hang out. As this has become a point of contention, I will consider the issue in further detail below.) Through the contrast of clearly identified architectural, visual, and musical markers, stores construct themselves as the identifiable localities within the Mall.

The tensions within the acoustical space both affect and reflect the contradictory flows of movement throughout the Mall—into and out of stores, through hallways, among levels, and into and out of the parking lots. Musical programs constantly produce the space; their continuous presence is an insistence or reminder to listeners. Programmed music can be said to territorialize the Mall: it builds and encloses the acoustical space, and manages the transitions from one location to another; it not only divides space, but also coordinates the relations among subdivisions. As they divide and demarcate, sonorities create "a wall of sound, or at least a wall with some sonic bricks in it" (Deleuze and Guattari 1987, 311). To get anywhere in the Mall of America, one must pass through music and through changes in musical sound. As it territorializes, music gives the subdivided acoustical space a contour, offering an opportunity for its listeners to experience space in a particular way: "music…calls forth our investments and hence, our affective anchors into reality" (Grossberg 1991, 364).[5] It also constructs the limits of that experience.

Foregound Music

In contrast to the halls' quiet, sometimes inaudible soundtrack, stores may have varying volumes of foreground music. Foreground music is the industry name for music programming that consists of songs in their original form, as recorded by the original artist. The music itself it still meant to serve as a background wherever it plays, but it is "foreground" in that it can draw attention to itself in ways that background music cannot. So while on the environmental channel we might hear a jazz group quietly working out "Faithfully" by the band Journey, on a foreground channel we'd hear Journey playing the song themselves, complete with wailing vocals and soaring guitar solos. This louder and more audacious foreground music emanating from stores works in tension with the background music in the hallways. If the store is open to the mall (rather than being closed off by a front wall with a door), music distinguishes the store's interior from the exterior hallway. If the volume of the store's music is moderate, the placement of the speakers within the store will determine a sonic threshold: on one side the ambiance of the hallway is primary in a listener's auditory field, and on the other side the sounds of the store will be primary in a listener's ear. This sonic threshold, often a discernible physical point, behaves as a store's front wall. Through clear acoustical delineation, the music produces a sense of inside and outside.

If, on the other hand, the volume of the store's music is high enough, the music will spill out into the hallway. In this way programmed music produces a transitional space from outside in the hallway to inside the store, much as stairs up from the street or a canopy and carpet on the sidewalk would do. Its louder relative volume also directly hails people in the hallway in an attempt to get their attention—it more or less invites them inside the store. Thus, from the hallways, stores can become identifiable by how they sound; this sonic quality is the central preoccupation of foreground music programming.

Foreground music sounds like radio: it "broadcasts" already existing recordings, but is itself carefully programmed according to a logic called "quantum modulation." If background music strives toward anonymity and gradual changes in mood, foreground music strives for an absolutely consistent identity and unchanging mood. Quantum modulation produces continuity and maintains flow in the overall soundtrack through assigning each song a composite numerical value based upon a variety of criteria: rhythm, tempo, title, artist, era, genre, instrumentation, and popularity. A flow of music is established through song compatibility and cross-fading so that all transitions from song to song are seamless. This stress on maintaining a flow that does not vary in "intensity" is again based upon the posited listener of the music: it is assumed that the person will hear the music for a shorter duration of time (for instance, while browsing in a store). Therefore, rather than try to gradually alter the listener's mood over time, the music remains at a consistent value (*MUZAK* 1992b; Ritter 1993).

Unlike in environmental music, where services will provide only one program choice (usually just called "the environmental channel" or some such), there are a multitude of foreground programs. Foreground music operates at the levels of taste and distinction, differentiation and association. The standard satellite programs are based on the categories of *Billboard* charts, adjusted for certain demographics like age and gender. Rather than organizing music according to style categories, foreground music organizes it according to marketing categories like "top 40" or "adult contemporary"—which is similar, but not identical, to the way commercial radio stations organize their play lists. Foreground music programs available on tape are more specialized according to genres such as "classic jazz" or even "Hawaiian," or they are programmed for other specialized uses, such as "holiday music" (*MUZAK* 1992a). Two illustrations will clarify the continuities and discontinuities of foreground music programming.

In programmed music, the recording medium is inseparable from its message: music acquires its value as much from the manner in which it is recorded as the supposed "content" of the recording. Figure 2.1 is part of a "Mixed Tempo Classic Pop" tape in a *MUZAK* catalog. The tape appears under the catalog's "Nostalgia" section, with this description under the heading "Classic Pop": "This series features Pop's all-time greats from the top of the charts of the 1960s, '70s and '80s. This series differs from "Classic Rock" by including only the smoother side of Pop music. These programs provide a timeless feel for an audience looking for the best popular music" (*MUZAK* 1992a, 29).

This sequence of songs is notable because of the diversity of artists represented. The songs do, however, have several characteristics that bind them together. They all come from a six-year span: 1972–78. Although the songs were produced in differing styles, they all operate within a narrow range of production values and techniques endemic to 1970s pop, and a limited range of timbres.

Creedence Clearwater Revival, "Have You Ever Seen the Rain?" (1972)
Jim Croce, "I Got A Name" (1973)
O'Jays, "Back Stabbers" (1972)
Hall & Oates, "She's Gone" (1973)
The Steve Miller Band, "Fly Like an Eagle" (1978)
Queen, "Bohemian Rhapsody" (1975)
Dave Loggins, "Please Come To Boston" (1974)
Olivia Newton-John, "Please, Mr. Please" (1977)
George Harrison, "My Sweet Lord" (1976)
Bob Seger, "Night Moves" (1976)
Leo Sayer, "You Make Me Feel Like Dancing" (1976)

Figure 2.1 Tape 4016: Mixed Tempo/Classic Pop (track 4 of 4) (MUZAK 1992a).

Johann Strauss, "Tales from the Vienna Woods, Op. 325" performed by The Vienna Johann Strauss
    Orchestra (1982)
Giuseppi Verdi, "La Donna E Mobile" performed by Andre Kostelanetz and His Orchestra (1989)
Boccerini, "Minuet from String Quartet, Op. 13, No. 5" performed by Academy of St. Martin-In-The-
    Fields (1980)
Edvard Grieg, "Morning from Peer Gynt Suite" performed by the Orchestre Philharmonique De Monte
    Carlo (1989)
Vivaldi, "Spring-Allegro 1" performed by the Vienna Philharmonic (1984)
Beethoven, "Symphony No. 7-3, Presto" performed by Staatskapelle Dresden (1987).
Mozart, "Overture from The Marriage of Figaro" performed by the City of London Sinfonia (1986)

Figure 2.2 Tape 6023: Mixed/Light Symphony Favorites (track 1 of 4) (MUZAK 1992a).

The ordering of the songs represents gradual changes in tempo from song to song, but no radical shifts in speed from one song to the next. To the devoted fans of any particular artist or group on the tape, the program may appear to juxtapose different music inappropriately; to a more casual listener, the differences will likely be overshadowed by the consistency among songs in overall production values (dynamic range, mix, timbre, use of reverb, and so on). Figure 2.2, from a tape of "Mixed light Symphony Favorites," is again organized by sound, tempo, and timbre. The selection appears in the "Classical" section of the catalog; "Light Symphony" is described as follows: "This series contains popular movements from the great symphonies. Favorite melodies recorded by some of the world's best orchestras provide a full sound without being imposing. Suitable for a sophisticated environment" (*MUZAK* 1992a, 59). The program limits itself to orchestral recordings since 1980, so that the timbres, mixes, dynamic ranges and overall production values are consistent on the tape, as in the first example. One could chart similar tendencies throughout the various music programs. Although programming may be totally inconsistent along lines of genre, it is carefully regulated in terms of other musical characteristics that might be lumped together under the headings of "affect" or "mood." However, musical periods and histories can re-enter this framework: in the "Classic Pop" example, the selection's period determines the parameter of a production aesthetic; and as I discuss below, periods such as "the 1950s" can themselves become tropes in the rhetoric of programmed music. Programmed music is organized according to an aesthetics of production, where the recording itself is analyzed and programmed as much as the content or style of the musical selection the recording ostensibly represents. While many theories of recording treat the medium as an instrument to reproduce existing music, programmed music is more concerned with the substance and texture of the medium itself.

Foreground music utilizes these programming techniques to create consistent musical programs with which stores can then associate themselves. Retailers are encouraged to choose music styles to cultivate a business image considered most appealing to whatever demographic group of customers they hope to attract (*MUZAK* 1990). Although *MUZAK* and its main competitors produce mostly generalized programming, the choices of programs, the placement of speakers, the volume and the texture of the music are all determined at each individual site.

That this music resembles radio—but isn't radio—is further advantageous to stores. Playing radio stations in commercial establishments without paying royalties to musicians' unions is illegal. Thus many stores find it cheaper to subscribe to a programmed music service than to play the radio, because all such services pay their royalties in a lump sum. But a resemblance to radio is advantageous to businesses because radio stations are often instrumental in constructing local communities (Berland 1990). Not only is FM radio a part of regional community construction, but it also hails its listeners according to age, race, and class. In short, this resemblance mimics the use of FM radio in other spaces and thereby produces at least the possibility that a store will be able to associate itself with the other spaces in which the music resounds. This enables retailers to construct a "business image" through the music and possibly connect with other places listeners have heard the same music. Although the musical program does not necessarily conform to any rules of genre, it can appeal very strongly to consumer identity. Pierre Bourdieu has demonstrated the continuities between taste and social position (1984).[6] By knowing the tastes of a desired clientele, a store can position itself as within—or as a "logical" extension of—an already existing taste culture.

Generally speaking, stores within a particular chain all use the same or similar music programs to achieve a uniformity of corporate image, just as they use similar design and lighting techniques. However, this corporate image is itself an amalgamation of what the company wants potential consumers to think about it, and what the company wants potential consumers to think about themselves and the products they are browsing. In other words, programmed music can become a key that frames the experience of shopping in a store. Not only can it suggest a particular affective stance for listeners toward the store and their experience of it, foreground music can frame the context to suggest a whole range of possible responses to the commodities and experiences within, and a whole disposition toward those possible responses. This is no different than the use of music to frame other kinds of activities (see Goffman 1974 on framing; see Booth 1990 and Turino 1993, 218–232 on musical framing). Or as Regula Burkhardt Qureshi puts it, "extra-musical meanings in musical sound give music the power to affect its context in turn" (1987, 58). I will illustrate the variations on this process with four examples from the Mall of America.

1. Victoria's Secret, a store specializing in lingerie, not only plays classical music in their stores, but sells tapes of their music programs. "Romantic" selections like Mozart's Piano Concerto in E Flat, the allegro from Schubert's Symphony No. 5 in B Flat, or Beethoven's Romance No. 1 in G cascade over supple decor. While the store's merchandise and visual displays differentiate it in terms of gender, the music program, along with the decor, offers listeners an index of class and a coherent frame within which to experience the store and themselves.[7] The music plays to an American bourgeois identity by suggesting a refined, European, aristocratic taste. As a form of music that is generally associated with refined taste and prestige, it functions to legitimate the store as a respectable place to shop.[8] More generally, it helps to produce the atmosphere within the store. The store itself is decorated in plush style, and the lighting is particularly soft. While the music plays, sale displays encourage the visitor to take advantage of "a special opportunity to indulge yourself" in a lingerie purchase. The music suggests a continuity among the wide array of commodities available in the store (clothing, accessories, and perfume, as well as more general merchandise), some of which are only related to one another in that they are being sold in the same store.

The store is full of references to England and Europe (where displayed, the "Victoria's Secret" name is always pictured with a London street address). The programmed music, European classical music, supplements the rhetoric of the store's appearance. For many Americans, "Europeanness" can itself be an index of high-class status and refinement. To the other design features, however, classical music offers the possible pleasures of recognition: recognizing the music can be as important as enjoying the music, both for the cues it gives toward experiencing the store itself and for suggesting that proper customers of Victoria's Secret are people refined enough to recognize the music. In other words, knowledge of the music is a form of cultural capital: it suggests membership in a certain social stratum.

But Victoria's Secret goes one step further by selling the music it plays. Victoria's Secret can sell tapes of the music in their stores because their music is programmed by an independent contractor, and was arranged especially for them, as opposed to having simply purchased a "light classical" program from one of the major programmed music services. This has been a hugely successful venture for the store: according to a June 1995 *Forbes* article, they had sold over 10 million tapes and CDs since 1989 (Machan 1995, 133). The tapes offer their purchasers a chance of enjoying the music at home, but also of learning the music and thereby being able to recognize it upon return visits to the store (see Bourdieu 1984, 13–14, 272–273). In other words, should one find oneself outside the refined taste culture upon entering Victoria's Secret for the first time, one can undertake an education to culture taste and refine the senses. This has a metonymic effect: insofar as the music works with other aspects of the decor, it suggests that one needs a cultivated, refined sensibility to enjoy all that Victoria's Secret has to offer. The liner notes to their tapes combine these purposes, offering rudimentary knowledge about composers' lives and trivia concerning the music, while extolling the sensibilities of composer and listener, patron and performer:

> This spectacular recording includes some of the world's best loved and most romantic music composed by Wolfgang Amadeus Mozart. You will thrill to the lyrical magic of this romantic collection recorded exclusively for Victoria's Secret by the London Symphony Orchestra. Victoria's Secret is proud to be among the distinguished individuals and corporations, who through their endowments, have been designated Diamond Patrons of The London Symphony. In his short life, Mozart lived amidst kings and courts, brilliance and despair, dying almost penniless at the age of 34. In this collection, you will celebrate Mozart at his most majestic and compelling. Inclusion of several intricate and intimate compositions, lesser known than most, gives this volume its singular quality (Victoria's Secret 1993).

The irony, of course, is that the music in question is the most common and most easily recognized variety of European classical music. Thus the liner notes take time out to assure readers that *this* tape of Mozart is special. Victoria's Secret offers an experience of itself and the tools to sophisticate and heighten that experience. It offers potential consumers an image of themselves, as if that image could be actualized through the consumption of the experiences in the store and the commodities it offers.

2. Compagnîe Internationale Express, a more conventional fashion store, plays only French pop music, and it plays this music at a relatively high volume. Near the cash register, the store proclaims itself to be "a world of French style." But the design within the store is quite common to fashion retailers in the Mall. The entire store is brightly lit, and track lighting allows individual displays to be highlighted. Most of the color comes from either the clothing or the displays in the store. Aisles are wide, but not too wide, so that one moves through the selection slowly. Most of the clothing for sale comes from places other than France. The window display features (at this writing) "grunge" fashions (faded flannel shirts and faded jeans) that are decidedly American. So "Frenchness" refers more to an affect the store would like to convey than to any trait that the store or its patrons actually possess. "Here again, the sign [in this case French pop programmed as foreground music] is ambiguous: it remains on the surface, yet does not for all that give up the attempt to pass itself off as depth" (Barthes 1972, 28). Or to make our French theorist speak to the matter at hand directly: The sound is like another layer of packaging laid over commodities. This packaging contains the real instructions for use—how to *feel* when using the products in the store. The French rock music envelops the commodities in an effort to stand in as their essence. As at Victoria's Secret, programmed music works with other environmental factors to confer certain meanings onto the merchandise and the people in the store—these meanings having no intrinsic connection to the people or products. However, there are crucial differences here: the volume of Express' music makes it more insistent—making conversation more difficult, and making the music much more present. But then, it has to be: while the programmed music in Victoria's Secret works in concert with other environmental factors to simulate an aura of sophistication and indulgence, the music here works all by itself. The music is authentically French, or at least *in* French; little else in the store is. The music suggests a particular experience of shopping or a way to experience a wide range of products. In suggesting these experiences, the music also offers a mode of experiencing the self. The actual nature of that experience depends on what one takes "Frenchness" to mean. Clearly, Express intends its "Frenchness" to connote sophistication of taste, affluence, luxury, and a touch of exoticism—after all, Paris is the capital of international fashion. But this is a particularly American

representation of what it means to be French. Compagnie Internationale Express exemplifies this: they are headquartered in Columbus, Ohio.

3. In addition to framing space and offering affective cues, foreground music can be used to help construct time and movement by its presence rather than its content. A Levi's store uses programmed music and video to these ends. The back of the store contains a giant nine-screen "video wall" and the store actually plays music videos. The store acquires these on laser disc from a parent company, and true to form, the discs only appear coherent in terms of programming concerns (for instance, offering a program that is a combination of popular rap, alternative, and "top 40" musics). The store is itself otherwise unremarkable. The floors are a wood grain, and the store uses the usual bright lighting and track-lit displays. They sell a complete line of Levi's clothing. An eclectic range of musical genres would disallow any simple identification of music with a particular mood as in the above examples. Neither does the store sell itself as an experience; it relies primarily on its products. By essentially saying nothing, the store says everything it has to: as if the choice of basic decor was the result of the products speaking for themselves, and not a deliberate marketing strategy. Relieved of its ostensible content function, the programmed music and video wall can provide a generalized hip atmosphere—one that echoes or displays current fashion trends—while helping to structure the movement of people inside and outside the store through a process of distraction. Since the video wall is visible from the hallway, it is to the store's advantage that passers-by stop and watch the video. In so doing, they will also look at the available merchandise and sale displays. Moreover, for a visitor to stop shopping momentarily and watch the video is not a liability to the store: it is conventional wisdom among retailers that the longer people spend in a store, the more likely they are to make a purchase. In this way, Levi's is able to use the video screen's power to distract to its own advantage: the distraction may or may not gel with the rest of the shopping experience, but it affects that experience by prolonging it. Unlike music programmed according to stimulus progression, this music and video usage does not attempt to speed up or slow down customer movement by tempo, melody, or rhythm; but rather, it functions as an interruption that becomes integrated into the shopping experience. By hailing people into the store, and by distracting them in the store (thereby increasing the duration of their stay) the programmed music and video juxtapose consumption and entertainment without having to fuse them in any meaningful way. Or to play on writers who treat the mall as a postmodern phenomenon: the music video serves to decenter shoppers (its "subjects"), but this decentering is not necessarily endowed with a resistant or subversive political potential. Rather, the discontinuity works in service of the one unifying "signifier of value" for the store: the point of sale. Any other effects of this decentering (as there may be) are incidental.

4. Johnny Rockets, "The Original Hamburger," is located on the edge of The Mall of America's south food court. There it is sandwiched between an Asian fast-food restaurant and a larger sit-down bistro. It is far less enclosed and far less set off from neighboring businesses than are the clothing stores discussed above. Through its volume, programmed music frames the experience of Johnny Rockets by physically differentiating the space from those around it and enveloping other noise within its frame. It spills out of the restaurant and touches every listener in the food court. The restaurant is a representation of a 1950s-style art-deco diner, and includes a long counter and a row of seats in front of it. It is the only restaurant in the food court to provide its own seating, in addition to the tables and chairs in a large common area. The employees are all wearing 1950s-style soda jerk outfits (white shirts and hats) as the programmed music, 1950s pop (mostly love songs), comes blaring out of the restaurant. It is by far the loudest music in the food court. The menu is conventional—hamburgers, fries, sodas, and so on; one can get this food from a variety of sources at the Mall. Thus, rather than differentiating itself by its product, Johnny Rockets is about consuming an experience. On the west wall, a poster pictures a teenage man seated on a couch

with two women seated very close to him and clearly enraptured with him. They are dressed in fifties clothes, and the slogan on the poster reads: "Johnny Rockets—Hospitality." The restaurant invites its customers to experience a nostalgic 1990s representation of a 1950s diner, complete with regressive gender roles and sexual mores. Here programmed music performs a double function: it is at once part of the experience to be consumed (as atmosphere) and simultaneously calls attention to the possibility of consuming that experience. Here the experience becomes crucial, because the product for sale is unremarkable in any other way. Yet it doesn't seem to offer the same cues for self-understanding as the clothing stores. It seems less about constructing an identity (being "1950s-ish") than suggesting that *anyone* can now enjoy the experience of a 1950s diner. Certainly, anyone in the food court can hear the music from the diner. The volume of the music here may be a more blunt and demanding message: it demands a reduction of all context to the nostalgia booming through the diner. Perhaps the music's blistering volume exists in quiet deference to the knowledge that the party never happened this way the first time.

In each of the above examples, programmed music plays a role particular to its context, but it also serves a more generalized function which could best be termed "articulation." Stuart Hall defines articulation as "the form of the connection that *can* make a unity of two different elements, under certain conditions. It is a linkage which is not necessary, determined, absolute and essential for all time" (1986, 53). Articulation is the process through which otherwise independent meanings, ideologies, or people are unified in some sense. In all four of my above descriptions, a musical program articulates specific meanings to the purchase of a commodity or service. Thus, underwear at Victoria's Secret becomes refined; "Frenchness" is conferred on flannel at Express; music and video distract visitors at the Levi's store, making them better and more valuable shoppers; and eating a hamburger becomes part of a "1950s experience" at Johnny Rockets. None of these connections are natural—rather, they have to be produced or performed.

Although the above are all examples of planned and deliberate uses of musical programs, intention on the part of the store is not necessary for this process to take place. Upon informally questioning the employees of an art gallery and a shoe store in the Mall, I found that in both cases, the music playing had been brought in from home by the stores' employees. Rather than specifying a particular kind of music to be played, the management of each outfit had simply defined a range of possible music, and allowed employees to select the music they wanted to hear. On that particular day, Bob Seger resounded in the shoe store, and the Beach Boys could be heard in the art gallery.[9] Both of these musics could easily perform the same kind of articulatory functions I outlined in my previous examples, but any coherence with other environmental factors (such as decor) would be more coincidental. However, this arrangement may prove to have other benefits, since it is the employees, not the customers, who must spend hours in a store; and the employees I spoke with tended to find preselected music programs repetitive. This could benefit the store as well: in giving up control over the sound space to the employees, it allows workers to take control of one aspect of their environment. In so doing, it offers underpaid service workers the comforting illusion of some ownership in the retail process. Even if the workers entertain no such illusions, it still offers a degree of comfort. Who wouldn't want to make a bad job a little bit better? Regardless of intention, the music can still function at the level of articulation, and it still builds acoustical space.

Building a Better Consumerism

Clearly, music's various functions within stores are always socially determined and constantly changing. My intent here has been to provide an illustration of how these processes work, rather than an exhaustive survey of programmed music's uses (or listeners' responses)—possible or realized—in the Mall. The Mall's handling of spatial difference is intimately tied to its handling of social difference. In considering the Mall of America's construction of space, elements are excluded and are juxtaposed together and enclosed. The structure and movement of the Mall's acoustical space—and more generally its social space—congeals around a clear set of priorities: "interior space protects the germinal forces of a task to fulfill or a deed to do" (Deleuze and Guattari 1987, 311). Consumer culture is given priority in the Mall by decree, not by consensus. Yet the Mall is far from a closed or seamless system. An awareness of cultural struggle and cultural difference plays a part in its very constitution. In particular, three issues concerning difference warrant some further exploration:

1. If the Mall's play on a national and consumerist identity requires a narrow mainstream to be represented, the programmed music refines that mainstream ideology in both its spatial and its interpretive functions. The bell curve and "the charts" determine the presence of any song or kind of music on a musical program. The ubiquitous *Billboard* charts depend on a laser scanning system that records sales in 11,000 music stores nationwide. *Billboard*, by its own admission, has to rely on larger retail chains, because smaller independent stores cannot afford the necessary survey technology (Ellis 1993). So the charts are determined by chain sales, but sales figures say little about taste. They don't reflect, for instance, the practice of sharing or "passing along" a recording common in many communities (see Rose 1994, 7–8). Moreover, buying power is not equal among all sectors of the population. Thus, a chain of effects occurs: social stratification is reproduced in the statistical—that is, commercial—distribution of taste; the statistical distribution of taste is foundational in the construction of programmed music; programmed music then becomes part of the Mall's architectonics; and the Mall thereby mobilizes social difference and makes it useful, all the while denying that it's anything but good clean American fun.

2. The forms taken by Mall design and programmed music are connected with larger political concerns. 3M is very careful to assure potential clients that nothing "controversial or offensive" will ever appear on the soundtrack which might upset a customer (Pelisero 1993). In other words, they wish to keep social tensions and the differences which embody them out of listeners' minds. In reducing all traces of real social difference to taste preference, the programmers and the Mall must necessarily draw their lines of exclusion precisely along traditional axes of social difference, lest drawing different lines call attention to the process itself. Although music programmers and the Mall do differentiate by gender, age, and taste (which often stands in for race or class) all of these differentiations exist within a very limited field. In this particular case, difference is circumscribed by a mainstreamed construct of "Americanness," and to a large extent, middle-class whiteness.

The "nation" as it is used by Mall planners and music programmers is a narrow construct, corresponding exactly to empirical data, but not to any living human being. (Of course, the data themselves are influenced by collection procedures that are biased toward a consumer public; again, see Meehan 1990.) By deploying a range of social scientist norms in the service of building a better consumerism, the Mall of America and the programming of music function in the reproduction of a stratified society.[10] Decisions about what will be in the Mall or the soundtrack contain, implicit within them, three kinds of normative prescriptions: those pertaining to normative behaviors (signs in the hallways indicating appropriate behavior, and the repeated encouragement to identify oneself through consumption—sensing, looking, listening, and ultimately buying); those pertaining to normative tastes (the stocking of the stores, the songs that are used for programmed music); and those pertaining to normative differences (what kind of variation is allowed within and among stores and what kind of differences are and aren't allowed to be represented in the Mall—evangelical Christians can set up a kiosk to sell tapes and books, but Greenpeace cannot because mall management considers the latter to be political. Further, Devin Nordberg has noted that although the Mall does have an environmental booth, it is run by Browning Ferris Industries, a notorious corporate polluter [1993, 18].) The result is a perpetuation of taste through programming. One might ask whom the Mall is hailing through their programmed music or more precisely, what kinds of identifications the Mall wants to encourage, and who is most likely to make those identifications.

Music programs correspond to the demography of the Mall's *desired*, rather than *actual*, visitors. While the Mall desires an affluent (and usually white) adult middle-class population, there is strong evidence to suggest that the real enthusiasts of the Mall are teenagers from a diversity of racial backgrounds (Karasov and Martin 1993, 27). But these teens must make use of an environment that is not immediately welcoming to them; or rather, which welcomes them as consumers first, and people second. African-American teens, for instance, have reported being trailed by uniformed guards (ibid.).[11] Indeed, the Mall has displayed a great deal of ambivalence toward the population that seems to have taken to it most strongly: there are now signs outside of Camp Snoopy detailing expected appropriate behavior, and more security staff has been added. Such signs become a clear marker of difference: they prohibit "loud, boisterous behavior" precisely at the entrance to a sometimes deafening amusement park. Considering the loud, drunken revelry on Friday nights in the "bar district" and the joyful screams emanating from the roller coaster, it becomes clear that these prescriptions can be pretexts for enforcement of social boundaries rather than clearly delineated rules. Thus, the management of sound becomes one political strategy in the management (and collapsing) of difference.

3. Listeners have to negotiate programmed music. This negotiation is rarely a conscious or intentional thing—how many people reflect on a store's wallpaper?—yet the contradictions embedded in mall and musical design leave open the possibility for alternative readings (I use this phrase with some caution). As statistical categories and behavioral ideals, the scientist norms animating music programming are neither internally consistent nor do they correspond to living individuals.[12] Such a system is necessarily clumsy, because no person or group of people is fully inside it at any given time. Since potential listeners' affective investments vary widely and are themselves overdetermined, there is always a range of possible engagements with programmed music, whatever the statistical and scientific rhetoric of marketing research might suggest. Thus, mall design can manifest itself in several ways for visitors: the intended result is a process of identification, where the (ideal) consumer identifies with the environment, the music, the spectacle, the mall, or simply (and most importantly) the commodities being offered. But any differentiating process—and here I return to programmed music specifically—can also alienate people. Because the acoustical landscape reflects the mall's desired rather than its actual visitors, the environment could cause some cognitive dissonance. If this alienation does not chase people away, it can, at the very least, foster some kind of ironic distance. (But again, ironic distance alone is not necessarily a resistant or subversive stance, unless it is coupled with some kind of collective and active opposition. Any store will readily accept money from any customer, whatever level of irony the latter may read into the transaction.) By trying to paper over differences that may be entirely visible and audible in the hallways of the Mall (such as race), the environment itself may reveal its own biases more clearly. Ronald Radano views programmed music as an attempt to "domesticate" public spaces by placing familiar music in an unfamiliar space (1989, 452), but this familiarity does not guarantee a positive identification with the music.[13]

Several authors (such as Schaefer 1977; Lanza 1991; Jones and Schumacher 1992) have expanded these possible contradictions and tensions into a political program—they have felt the need to consider the ways a person might "resist" programmed music. Each winds up suggesting that a resistant response to programmed music would simply be to listen to it more closely. Joseph Lanza claims that "we can subvert the corporate canon by actually LISTENING with a fresh, ironic ear" (1991, 48). In a call for devoting more energy to discerning programmed music these authors reproduce it as some kind of autonomous practice, removed from its surroundings. This is the very dichotomy that the *MUZAK* Limited Partnership sets up in their advertising: in the slogan "Music is art, Muzak is science," art and science are both constructed as socially autonomous truths. A call to ironic listening ignores any sense of context. Nobody is escorted from the Mall of America for listening to the music too closely. Jacques Attali claims that programmed music works to silence the listener, or more precisely, to hide the listeners' own silence from themselves (1985, 111). A finely tuned, ironic ear only reinforces this relationship. Or rather, those listeners who choose this political route will always wind up "resisting" all by themselves.

What disrupts the Mall environment is noise, the voicing of differences. The signs prohibiting "loud, boisterous behavior" located at the entrances and exits to the roaring amusement park are reminders that the Mall is attempting to construct a very specific kind of consumerism, and interference with that goal is grounds for ejection. This is a concern not only for visitors to the Mall who might not fit so neatly into its imagination of "America," but for the residents of the Mall itself—the stores.

Mall space is now an eminently familiar environment to many Americans, even to those who find it alienating. In addition to policing their images, stores have to worry about conflicts from outside communities arising in the Mall. In fact, there is a great deal of anxiety among stores in this respect. This is one reason that programmed music services all assure their potential customers that nothing "offensive" will appear in the soundtrack. But the soundtrack itself may be offensive. To illustrate: a popular urban legend has two adjacent stores in a shopping mall quarreling.[14] One plays light classical music, and sells upscale clothing. The other sells the latest fashions, and plays Top 40 music, which includes some rap. The former store fears that the latter's music will chase away its customers and petitions the mall management to have the latter keep their music at a lower level. The latter, of course, pleads that turning down their music would make their store design less effective in luring in potential customers. The moral of this story is simple: programmed musics in malls do not form a seamless and totally coherent system, nor do they always work together or as they're supposed to. Yet this divergence from designer intention should not be taken as cause for celebration. This is not *subversion* but *contradiction*—part of the everyday functioning of capitalist societies. Chance and coincidence play their part in composing the rhythms of acoustical space.

Conclusion: Ethnomusicology and the Problem of Reification

If all music is ethnic music (McAllester 1979, 183), then the ethnicity of programmed music is capitalism. Programmed music presupposes and builds upon an already-constituted commodity status for music and the experience of that music. In order for there to be programmed music, music must already have become a thing—it must be lived through its commodity status. The logic of programmed music follows Georg Lukács' description of reification all too perfectly: "The essence of the commodity-structure has often been pointed out. Its basis is that a relation between people takes on the character of a thing and thus acquires a 'phantom objectivity,' an autonomy that seems so strictly rational and all-embracing as to conceal every trace of its fundamental nature: the relation between people" (Lukács 1971, 83). In the case of programmed music, a relation of listening (itself highly structured by commodity circulation) is reified into a thing that can be bought and sold. That is why I have focused here more on rationalities underlying programming and design than on listener response. The latter is presupposed by the former.

If we follow Steven Feld (1988) and others in understanding sound in fundamentally social terms, then the problem of reification in mass mediated music should become a fundamental question for ethnomusicological inquiry. Ethnomusicologists tend to take mass-mediation as a problem or a point of departure—media are thought of as external to communities, impacting them or existing alongside them. In these accounts, the media begins as Other to the community. How the advent of a music industry affects local musicians, how it impacts on musical pedagogy, how music industries function on a global scale—these are the questions currently preoccupying ethnomusicological thought (see Chopyak 1987; Wallis and Malm 1984; Erlmann 1993; Guilbault

1993; Manuel 1993; Meintjes 1990). While there is certainly much research remaining to be done in these areas, in order to fully understand mass mediation in music, ethnomusicologists will have to move beyond a paradigm primarily concerned with distinguishing between tradition and change. This paradigm tends to understand mass mediated music in terms of its difference from other music; its main concern with the mass media is in distinguishing between music that is mass mediated and music that is not (as is evident in the theoretical models proposed by Seeger 1987, Malm 1993, and Manuel 1993, for example). This approach tends to bracket mass mediation as a problem at the point of its advent, thereby overlooking the kinds of social conditions that emerge as a result of its proliferation. Ethnomusicology will have to consider formations like programmed music, that arise as a result of *the results* of mass mediation. To paraphrase an argument advanced by Ulrich Beck: in places like the Mall of America, mass mediation becomes reflexive; questions of the development and employment of media technologies are eclipsed by questions of the social, cultural, political, and economic "management" of the results of actually and potentially utilized media technologies (1992, 19). If ethnomusicology wishes to recover and critique modes of experience in a society fully saturated with the mass media, it will have to consider the phantom objectivity—the reification—of experience itself as a pervasive social phenomenon. In mass mediated societies, this process is part of an endless chain in which the outside social world of recorded songs, mass mediated images, and programmed spaces and schedules is folded into that which is most inside and private: the substance of affect and experience.

Notes

1. This essay is part of a larger work in progress on the culture and history of programmed music in work and leisure. I am deeply indebted to the following people, all of whom provided essential contributions to this project: John Archer, Greg Dimitriandis, Ariel Ducey, Lawrence Grossberg, Richard Leppert, Alex Lubet, Lauren Marsh, Roger Miller, Radhika Mongia, Negar Mottahedeh, Carrie Rentschler, Carol Stabile, Gary Thomas, Tom Turino and Mike Willard. I'd also like to thank Leslie Ritter of *MUZAK*, Tom Pelisero of 3M, and Michael Ellis of *Billboard* for taking the time to answer my questions. Much of my analysis stems from personal observations during repeated visits to the Mall of America over the Fall of 1992, the Winter and Spring of 1993, and follow-up visits in late Fall of 1994 and late Spring 1995 for the purposes of this study.
2. Although the history of programmed music is important for understanding its significance, a thorough historical account is beyond the scope of this article. There are several varying accounts of Muzak's Industrial and cultural history. Jerri Husch (1984) and Jane Hulting (1988) both provide detailed accounts of the corporation and products evolution. Both of these accounts focus on the history of the *MUZAK* corporation in their account of its development as a cultural form. Joseph Lanza (1994) focuses on Muzak (programmed music) as a kind of easy-listening music. For shorter discussions of Muzak history, see Jones and Schumacher 1992 or McDermott 1990.
3. "Muzak" (which refers to a programmed music product) is a registered trademark and "stimulus progression" and "quantum modulation" are registered service marks belonging to the *MUZAK* Limited Partnership. The degree to which "Muzak" stands as a synecdoche for the industry can be illustrated by my conversations with both 3M and Audio Environments, Inc.: each time I raised more detailed technical questions, I was referred back to the *MUZAK* Limited Partnership. Much of my information on programming logistics thus comes from the *MUZAK* corporation, although the corporation does not provide most of the programmed music considered in this particular case study.
4. There is an important analogy to radio here, where broadcasters sell audiences to advertisers through programming and ratings (see Meehan 1990). However, as I will demonstrate below, programmed music presupposes the circulation of music through radio. It is thus a secondary mode of distribution, whereas radio is a primary mode of distribution. For Instance, another economic function of radio is to advertise the music itself for purchase, thereby serving the needs of the music industry directly. Programmed music, on the other hand, pays royalties to musicians' unions because it then sells the music (and its popularity) as a service to clients. While programmed music could occasionally result in increased sales of recordings, this would be a purely accidental result.
5. I am engaging two important theoretical issues here. The first is territorialization, a term I borrow from Gilles Deleuze to connote the literal "embodiment" of space. Territorialization is enclosure, but it is also the filling up of space, its endowment with a certain kind of meaning (or affect) and the exclusion of others. (For a more extended discussion of territorialization, see Deleuze and Guattari 1987, 310–350). The second issue is music's spatiality—its spatial character and behavior, as well as the ontology of space in which music resounds. While it is one of the questions which got me interested in programmed music to begin with, there is very little written on it (in addition to the above chapter from Deleuze and Guattari, see Attali 1985 and Grossberg 1991).
6. Bourdieu's analysis focuses mainly on class distinctions within France, although his model appears demonstrable along the many lines of affiliation and difference in American culture, such as class, gender, race, sexual preferences, and age. In the American case, it seems less likely that one can correlate taste and class in any meaningful way, in

part because Americans' experience of social class is itself so strongly mediated by other axes of difference (see, for example, Perlman 1993 for a summary of this position). Yet, given the importance of demographics in marketing (and the success of demographic models of marketing), dismissing connections between social difference and taste difference seems premature.

7. While a great deal of feminist scholarship has shown that when gender is not named, it is generally assumed to be male, programmed music is a messy case in this regard. Although *MUZAK* and 3M both offer a few programs pitched specifically to men or to women, the majority of their programs appear not to be intentionally geared toward a specific gender. *MUZAK*'s own research literature verifies that the majority of shoppers are women, which may be one reason for the relative inattention to gender at the level of programming. Another possible reason for *MUZAK*'s approach may have to do with the nature of its service: stores are often already gendered by their merchandise, so music performing that function would be redundant (although redundancy can also be an effective design and marketing tool). Finally, there is the question of what it means to call programmed music gendered. If music is gendered by virtue of its intended audience, then we are left with rather ambiguous clues from the music programs. If we understand the "gender" of a music to be defined by formal characteristics in the music (melody, harmony and chordal structure, as in McClary 1991; or timbre, rhythm and tempo as in Shepherd 1987), then we have to add to this list the formal characteristics of the medium itself (production values, dynamic range, and so on) given that the latter are especially important in programmed music. But here, we have to ask if listeners necessarily understand a characteristic of music as masculine or feminine just because it's described that way in the musicological or technical literature. Even if we turn it into a purely sociological question by instrumentalizing the content of the music ("the text") and consider the genders of performers and audiences, this also becomes a muddled problem as music programs cut across audiences and genres.

8. My argument here is similar to one advanced by Jane Juffer (1996). She argues that Victoria's Secret uses indices of class—both in decor and soundtrack—as a part of an attempt by the store to distinguish itself from pornography and from other lingerie stores.

9. It is worth noting that this practice is strictly illegal, because it qualifies as a "public performance" of the music, and therefore would require the stores to pay royalties on each tape they played. The exception to this rule is the performance of tapes for sale (as in music stores) where the music being played is actually for sale.

10. I am loosely borrowing Michel Foucault's idea of *normalization* from his discussion of the deployment of norms. In some ways, it can be understood as the shadowy inverse of Weberian ideal-type analysis, where a norm is deployed in the service of comparison, differentiation, hierarchization, homogenization, and exclusion: "In a sense, the power of normalization imposes homogeneity; but it individualizes by making it possible to measure gaps, to determine levels, to fix specialties and to render the difference useful by fitting them one to another. It is easy to understand how the power of the norm functions within a system of formal equality, since within a homogeneity that is the rule, the norm introduces, as a useful imperative and as a result of measurement, all the shading of individual differences" (Foucault 1977, 183–4).

11. If one were looking for a population that "resists" this environment, the teens would be as close to that as possible, but we have to keep in mind the context of that resistance. The fact that it is cheaper to ride a bus out to the Mall of America in a distant suburb than to your friend's neighborhood inside the city limits demonstrates the systemic tendencies these teens are up against. A little decentering and a critical attitude may help urban teens survive (and in this sense they are a good thing), but ultimately, these efforts alone will not lead to meaningful social change.

12. A passage by Jean Baudrillard is suggestive of a critique of *MUZAK*'s own appeals to "science" in the name of consumer engineering: "Besides, it will be noted retrospectively that the concepts 'class,' 'social relations,' 'power,' 'status,' 'institution'—and 'social' itself—all those too explicit concepts which are the glory of the legitimate sciences, have also only ever been muddled notions themselves, but notions upon which agreement has nevertheless been reached for mysterious ends: those of preserving a certain code of analysis" (1983, 4–5). Demographic science, for Baudrillard, becomes a trope of legitimation.

13. Radano only discusses background music. Although foreground music uses the same rhetoric of familiarity, I have shown here that it does not work in the same way.

14. I use the term "urban legend" (or perhaps suburban in this case) deliberately. I've heard the same story with a few mutations from several people. It is quite likely this happened somewhere at some time, but as an allegory, it works equally well to illustrate my point. "Anecdotes need not be true stories, but they must be functional in a given exchange" (Morris 1990, 15).

References

Attali, Jacques. 1985. *Noise: The Political Economy of Music,* translated by Brian Massumi. Minneapolis: University of Minnesota Press.

Barthes, Roland. 1972. "The Romans in Films." In *Mythologies,* translated by Annette Lavers. New York: The Noonday Press.

Baudrillard, Jean. 1983. In *The Shadow of the Silent Majorities,* translated by Paul Foss, John Johnston, and Paul Patton. New York: Semiotext(e).

Beck, Ulrich. 1992. *Risk Society: Towards a New Modernity,* translated by Mark Ritter. Newbury Park: Sage.

Booth, Gregory D. 1990. "Brass Bands: Tradition, Change and Mass Media in Indian Wedding Music." *Ethnomusicology* 34(2):245–262.

Borland, Jody. 1990. "Radio Space and Industrial Time: Music Formats, Local Narratives and Technological Mediation." *Popular Music* 9(2):179–192.

Bourdieu, Pierre. 1984. *Distinction: A Social Critique of the Judgement of Taste,* translated by Richard Nice. Cambridge: Harvard University Press.

Bruner II, Gordon C. 1990. "Music, Mood and Marketing." *Journal of Marketing* 54(4):94–104.

Chopyak, James. 1987. "The Role of Music in Mass Media, Public Education and the Formation of a Malaysian National Culture." *Ethnomusicology* 31(3):431–454.

Crawford, Margaret. 1992. "The World in a Shopping Mall." In *Variations on a Theme Park: The New American City and the End of Public Space,* edited by Michael Sorkin, 3-30. New York: The Noonday Press.

Deleuze, Gilles, and Felix Guattari. 1987. *A Thousand Plateaus: Capitalism and Schizophrenia,* translated by Brian Massumi. Minneapolis: University of Minnesota Press.

Ellis, Michael. 1993. Telephone interview by author, 2 September.

Erlmann, Veit. 1993. "The Politics and Aesthetics of Transnational Musics." *World of Music* 35(2):3–15.

Feld, Steven. 1988. "Aesthetics as Iconicity of Style, or 'Lift-up-over-Sounding': Getting into the Kaluli Groove." *Yearbook for Traditional Music* 20:74–113.

Foucault, Michel. 1977. *Discipline and Punish: The Birth of the Prison,* translated by Alan Sheridan. New York: Vintage Books.

Frow, John, and Meaghan Morris. 1993. *Australian Cultural Studies: A Reader.* Urbana: University of Illinois Press.

Goffman, Erving. 1974. *Frame Analysis: An Essay on the Organization of Experience.* Cambridge: Harvard University Press.

Greene, Alex. 1986. "The Tyranny of Melody." *Etc.* 43(3):285–90.

Grossberg, Lawrence. 1991. "Rock, Territorialization and Power." *Cultural Studies* 5(3):358–67.

Guilbault, Jocelyn. 1993. "On Redefining the 'Local' Through World Music." *World of Music* 35(2):33–47.

Hall, Stuart. 1986. "On Postmodernism and Articulation." *Journal of Communication Inquiry* 10(2):45–60.

Hulting, Jane. 1988. "Muzak: A Study in Sonic Ideology." MA thesis, University of Pennsylvania.

Husch, Jerri A. 1984. "Music of the Workplace: A Study of Muzak Culture." Ph.D. diss., University of Massachusetts, Amherst.

Jones, Simon C., and Thomas G. Schumacher. 1992. "Muzak: On Functional Music and Power." *Critical Studies in Mass Communication* 9:156–69.

Juffer, Jane. 1996. "A Pornographic Femininity?: Telling and Selling Victoria's (Dirty) Secrets." *Social Text *48.*

Karasov, Deborah, and Judith A. Martin. 1993. "The Mall of Them All." *Design Quarterly* (Spring):18–27.

Keil, Charles. 1984. "Music Mediated and Live in Japan." *Ethnomusicology* 28(1):91–96.

Lanza, Joseph. 1991. "The Sound of Cottage Cheese: Why Background Music Is the Real World Beat!" *Performing Arts Journal* 13(3):42–53.

———.1994. *Elevator Music: A Surreal History of Muzak, Easy-Listening, and Other Moodsong.* New York: St. Martin's Press.

Lefebvre, Henri. 1991. *The Production of Space,* translated by Donald Nicholson Smith. Cambridge: Basil Blackwell.

Lukács, Georg. 1971. *History and Class Consciousness: Studies in Marxist Dialectics,* translated by Rodney Livingstone. Cambridge: MIT Press.

Machan, Dyer. 1995. "Sharing Victoria's Secret." *Forbes* (June 5):132–33.

Malm, Krister. 1993. "Music on the Move: Traditions and the Mass Media." *Ethnomusicology* 37(3):339–54.

Manuel, Peter. 1993. *Cassette Culture: Popular Music and Technology in North India.* Chicago: University of Chicago Press.

McAllester, David. 1979. "The Astonished Ethno-Muse." *Ethnomusicology* 23(2):179–89.

McClary, Susan. 1991. *Feminine Endings: Music, Gender and Sexuality.* Minneapolis: University of Minnesota Press.

McDermott, Judy. 1990. "If It's to be Heard But Not Listened to. Then It Must Be Muzak." *Smithsonian* 20(10):70–80.

Meehan, Eileen. 1990. "Why We Don't Count: The Commodity Audience." In *Logics of Television,* edited by Patricia Mellencamp, 117-37. Bloomington: Indiana University Press.

Meintjes, Louise. 1990. "Paul Simon's Graceland, South Africa, and the Mediation of Musical Meaning." *Ethnomusicology* 34(1):37–74.

Morris, Mcaghan. 1990. "Banality in Cultural Studies." In *Logics of Television,* edited by Patricia Mellencamp, 14-43. Bloomington: Indiana University Press.

Morse, Margaret. 1990. "An Ontology of Everyday Distraction: The Freeway, the Mall, and Television." In *Logics of Television,* edited by Patricia Mellencamp, 193-221. Bloomington: Indiana University Press.

MUZAK Limited Partnership. 1990. "The Right Music Style Can Successfully Promote the Image You Desire For Your Business." In *Muzak Research Review: Fashion Retail.* Seattle: Muzak Limited Partnership.

———.1992a. *Tones Music Catalog 1992–93.* Seattle: Muzak Limited Partnership.

———. 1992b. "Quantum Modulation—The Story." *MUZAK Special Marketing Supplement 4* (July/August).

Nettl, Bruno. 1978. "Introduction." In *Eight Urban Musical Cultures: Tradition and Change,* edited by Bruno Nettl, 3-18. Urbana: University of Illinois Press.

Nordberg, Devin. 1993. "The Mall of America: A Postmodern Factory of Service and Spectacle." Unpublished paper, University of Minnesota.

Pelisero, Tom. 1993. Telephone interview by author, 31 August.

Perlman, Marc. 1903. "Idioculture: De-Massifying the Popular Music Audience." *Postmodern Culture* 4(1). Available electronically as REVIEW-7.993 from LISTSERV@LISTERV.NCSU. EDU, or on diskette from Oxford University Press.

Petchler, Thea. 1993. "Errands into the Wilderness: The Mall of America and American Exceptionalism." Paper presented at the Ninth Annual Meeting of the Mid-America American Studies Association, 16–18 April, Minneapolis—St. Paul, Minnesota.

Qureshi, Reguta Burkhardt. 1987. "Musical Sound and Contextual Input: A Performance Model for Musical Analysis." *Ethnomusicology* 31(1):56–86.

Radano, Ronald. 1989. "Interpreting Muzak: Speculations on the Musical Experience in Everyday Life." *American Music* 7(4):448–460.

Ritter, Leslie. 1993. Telephone Interview by author, 2 February.

Rose, Tricia. 1994. *Black Noise: Rap Music and Black Culture in Contemporary America.* Hanover: Wesleyan University Press.

Schaefer, R. Murray. 1977. *The Tuning of the World.* New York: A. A. Knopf.

Seeger, Anthony. 1987. "Powering Up the Models: Internal and External Style Change in Music." Paper delivered at the Annual American Anthropological Association Meeting in Chicago, 21 November.

Shepherd, John. 1987. "Music and Male Hegemony." In *Music and Society: The Politics of Composition, Performance and Reception,* edited by Richard Leppert and Susan McClary, 151–72. New York: Cambridge University Press.

Shields, Rob. 1992. *Lifestyle Shopping: The Subject of Consumption.* New York: Routledge.

Turino, Thomas. 1993. *Moving Away from Silence: Music of the Peruvian Antiplano and the Experience of Urban Migration.* Chicago: University of Chicago Press.

Victoria's Secret. 1993. Liner notes to "Two Centuries of Romance: Mozart." *Victoria's Secret Timeless Tributes of Love* #6. Audiocassette.

Wallis, Roger, and Krister Malm. 1984. *Big Sounds from Small Peoples: The Music Industry in Small Countries.* New York: Pendragon.

Part II

Cultural Tourism and Travel

3

Culture, Tourism, and Cultural Tourism
Boundaries and Frontiers in Performances of Balinese Music and Dance

Peter Dunbar-Hall

Introduction

This article debates a number of issues of cultural tourism through analyses of three cases of interaction between culture bearers and tourists on the Indonesian island of Bali. The issues raised touch on and illuminate a range of areas of study. In this way the cases presented are positioned not only as examples of tourism as a "complex set of social discourses and practices" (Rojek and Urry 1997, 1), but also as contributors to the theorising of cultural tourism, and to the investigation of meaning construction and modification in the performing arts at sites where the intentions of performers and audiences can be mapped from their respective perspectives.

Cultural tourism exists somewhere between the anthropological study of culture (e.g., Adams 1995; Macdonald 1997), sociological analysis of the dynamics between groups of people (e.g., Cukier et al. 1996; Lury 1997), human geography's focus on the ways people and places interact (e.g., Connell 1993; McGregor 2000), and the business studies examination of the tourist industry (e.g., Sinclair 1998; Singer 2000). Therefore, a degree of interdisciplinarity is one of its characteristics, one which allows investigation of it to develop from and contribute to a number of directions. In addition, a dependence on music as a regular component of cultural tourism events implies that comprehensive discussion of cultural tourism include levels of ethnomusicological discourse. Whether Merriam's definition of ethnomusicology as "music in culture" (Merriam 1964, 6) or Nettl's as "music as a part of culture" (Nettl 1983, 9) is adopted here is not as important as the realisation that music is a significant cultural tourism product, and that the study of music in relation to culture has something to add to consideration of its role in that context.

In this discussion, investigation of music covers two broad areas. The first of these is the monitoring of conceptualisation and negotiation of musical meaning when pieces of music and the dances they accompany are translated from cultural artefacts in their original contexts to cultural commodities in new (tourist) contexts. The second area concerns reflections of this translation in changes in the roles, form and function of music and dance, and how this translation acts as an agent in ongoing artistic development. As these processes are well documented in Balinese performing arts, often tangentially with reference to tourist presence, study of cultural tourism in Bali which focuses on music and dance is at a substantive advantage (see for example, De Zoete and Spies 1938; Bowers 1956; Becker and Yengoyan 1979; Vickers 1989; Picard 1996; Herbst 1997; Racki 1998; Tenzer 1998, 2000; Bakan 1999; Dibia 2000; Sugriwa 2000).

It is in the translation of music and dance from their original uses to those in Balinese tourist culture that concepts of boundaries and frontiers are useful in this discussion, as tourist access to Balinese performing arts constitutes a map of these notional spaces. Boundaries and frontiers are defined respectively here as sites at which tourists are restricted from or allowed entry to levels of insider experience and potential knowledge. At boundary sites, tourists, although not discouraged from attending, are denied access to parts of events and their meanings. Sometimes this restriction is imposed by culture bearers, at others it results from a lack of knowledge or the means of obtaining it. At sites defined as frontiers, a simultaneity of culture bearer and tourist input to the meaning of events is found. At these sites, there is also a practice on the part of Balinese performers to welcome tourist interest and to respond to it with contextualising information to assist in the comprehension of events and aspects of their significance. Events do not fall exclusively into one or the other of these types, but during performances shift continually between them. Consequently the roles of culture bearers and tourists are in a state of continual flux, one which is mediated through the potential significations of performance of music and dance.

In the cases which follow, the position of culture bearers as the ones who define, delineate and maintain these different types of moderated spaces forms a significant factor in the readings presented. In these readings, various implementations of boundaries and frontiers are identified, and are used to put a case for a cultural tourism which is differentiated both within events, and by event. It follows from this that the cultural tourism debated here is not monolithic, and that a position is adopted in which each case is unique, exhibiting a range of relationships between its participants. Acknowledgement of these relationships has a number of implications. First, that cultural tourism is a discourse of diverse voices. Second, that this discourse cannot be analysed generically as if events for tourist consumption were uniform in their aims, packaging, presentation and outcomes, or that performers do not have a stake in them beyond providing reification through costume, choreography, music and storyline of the exotic, the historical, and the traditional. From this follows a third consideration: deconstruction of the position of the culture bearers in activities of cultural tourism is necessary if the dialogue of cultural tourism is to be recognised and understood. My readings of cultural tourism therefore focus on the "other" (Craik 1997; Wood 1997) or "difference" (Stokes 1999), on whose existence and activities cultural tourism is predicated and defined, as the focus of research and source of information. This is rather than on tourists as the defining factor in meaning construction in performance events, and is used to produce a counter knowledge to canonical readings of cultural tourism, particularly those which propose that cultural maintenance is dependent on cultural tourism (Firat, in Picard and Wood 1997), and that culture and tourism have coalesced to the point where they are indistinguishable (Rojek and Urry 1997).

The cultural tourism presented here is one in which the roles of tourists are set by culture bearers, and are controlled in figurative sites of levels of access to experiences of Balinese performing arts. In most situations, the participation of tourists as the audiences at these events is a superficial interaction, a sampling of music and dance in condensed representations and bounded by momentariness. Often, the sample is presented as a museum exhibit, "frozen" in a traditional past, which is emphasised by contrast with the surrounding day-to-day business of ongoing contemporary culture. In actuality, tourists at these events are unwitting witnesses to a range of cultural agendas and practices, and are present at synchronic moments in the diachrony of a living culture. In this way, they are collaborators in, and at times the instigators of, cultural change and development.

An additional consideration in this discussion is that of location and culture as parameters in theorising about cultural tourism. All three events discussed here are unified in location and culture, occurring in and around the Balinese village of Ubud in a period between May 1999 and August

2000. Literature on cultural tourism demonstrates a concern among researchers for extrapolating a profile of this form of tourism from examples in various cultures and locations, thus emphasising that cultural tourism differs from culture to culture and location to location (for example: Howe 1996; Picard and Wood 1997; Rojek and Urry 1997). In this discussion, I investigate differences in events in one culture at one location, with the intention of removing culture and location as variables from my analytical paradigm, and of highlighting issues other than these contextual differences in relationships between culture bearers and tourists.

Cultural Tourism in Ubud

In research literature, Bali is one of the most discussed cultural tourism destinations (e.g., Bowers 1956; McKean 1979; Vickers 1989, 1994; Schansman 1991; Connell 1993; Hill 1994; McCarthy 1994; Warren 1995; Cukier et al. 1996; Hobart et al. 1996; Picard 1996, 1997; James 1999; Rubinstein and Connor 1999). Developments by which coincidental tourist experience of Balinese performed culture became a highly organised and government-sanctioned enterprise known as 'cultural tourism' is also well documented (Vickers 1989; Schansman 1991; Picard 1996, 1997; James 1999). As Picard notes, cultural tourism in Bali did not simply result from market forces and the presence of tourists on the island. Rather, it was an intervention on the part of Balinese authorities in response to decisions made by the centralist Indonesian government in Jakarta (Java) to exploit Balinese culture as a tourist drawcard:

> faced with a *fait accompli*, (the Balinese authorities) nevertheless attempted to appropriate tourism as a tool for regional development. In response to the (national) masterplan, the Balinese authorities proclaimed in 1971 their own conception of the kind of tourism they deemed the most suitable to their island—namely what they termed "cultural tourism." (Picard 1997, 182)

Among sites frequented by tourists on Bali, the village of Ubud has become the most significant one for cultural tourism; ethnomusicologist Bakan (1999, 23) describes it as "the cultural tourism center of Bali" and Balinese writer Nyoman Pendit labels Ubud as "where the tourists are" (in Vickers 1994, 205). That this constitutes the usual view of Ubud, and that the events described below took place in and around this village is already an indication of official demarcation of physical and conceptual space in tourism in Bali; it is symbolic of the establishment of a "boundaries and frontiers" approach to tourism on the island. This village is at the apex of a triangle (Kuta, Sanur, Ubud) designated officially as areas to which tourism could be confined (Vickers 1989, 196) so the rest of the island would remain relatively untouched by its undesirable traits. Tourists would not only be physically channelled into a tourism precinct in this way, but would also be figuratively manipulated in their experience of Balinese culture there. As Picard notes:

> to save tourists the discomfort and long waits characteristic of (Balinese music and dance) performances—quickly tiresome for non-Balinese spectators—it was recommended that dance performances be organised especially for tourists, freely transposed from the traditional forms and adapted for a diverse foreign audience. (1996, 46)

Cultural tourism in Ubud revolves around nightly music and dance performances organised by Yayasan Bina Wisata (Tourist Management Foundation) and run through the Ubud Tourist Information Office in Jalan Raya, the village's main street. Performances are timetabled to commence between 7 p.m. and 7:30 p.m., and to finish by 9 p.m. In 1999–2000, a weekly roster of 32 performances was in place, from a maximum of six a night to a minimum of three. Not all advertised performances were always presented, and others not listed might also take place as they became available. As some of these performances, such as *Kecak* and *Calonarang*, discussed below, are given in neighbouring villages, free transport to and from them is provided by the Ubud Tourist Information Office. In addition to these performances, which are designed and staged specifically for tourists, observance of local culture, especially that required to fulfil the religious obligations of the Balinese–Hindu calendar, can also be witnessed. It is one of these, a *Karya Piodalan* (Temple Anniversary) of the *Pura Dalem Ubud* (Ubud Temple of Shiva the Destroyer and his wife Durga), which forms a counterpart to the *Kecak* and *Calonarang*. Together, these three events provide a range of interactions between culture bearers and tourists through which the enterprise of cultural tourism can be critiqued and a cartography of boundaries and frontiers in Balinese cultural representation inscribed.

Kecak

A *krama desa adat* (*krama* = collective membership; *desa adat* = village) to the north of Ubud, performs *Kecak* for tourists once a week. *Kecak* is one of the most popular Balinese tourist shows. Its storyline is not uniform in all cases, in this performance presenting the *Ramayana* story of the abduction of Rama's wife, Sita, by King Rahwana and her return at the hands of Sugriwa and his army of monkeys. Rather than the more commonly heard *gamelan* (instrumental ensemble) used with much Balinese dance, *Kecak* is accompanied by a mens' chorus. The preparation and performance of *Kecak* is a comprehensive activity for this village, involving members of all families as performers or as support staff in organising details of the performance, driving tourists to and from it, and selling food and drinks to the audience.

Kecak is such a usual event for tourists in Bali (there are nine advertised in the Ubud area each week and numerous others within driving distance) that motives for its performance beyond those of entertainment for tourists, and its authenticity as a work of Balinese traditional culture, are rarely questioned. This *Kecak* is a commercial manoeuvre, as the members of this village, needing a new *bale banjar* (community meeting pavilion), decided to rehearse and perform *Kecak* for tourist consumption as the means of raising funds (personal communication, May 1999). Performances commenced in August 1998; by May 1999 the cement for the floor and some of the support pillars for the roof of the new *bale banjar* were in place. The building was completed by August 2000. The first aspect of this tourist performance to note, therefore, is that it was not solely intended as an example of performed Balinese cultural representation for tourist elucidation. Rather, it demonstrates a multiple intention of use, one which accommodates tourist wants and expectations, and villagers' financial needs. Commodification of performance to fund communal projects in this way is not an unusual occurrence in Bali, either in performances for Balinese audiences or those for tourists. This was noted by Bowers, for example, in his description of Balinese dance in the 1950s:

> Dance is also of practical service to religion. If a community is poor and in need of specific funds for rebuilding a temple, or if the temple's relics are dilapidated and need to be replaced, then a troupe sets out to collect funds. Wherever they are invited they will perform, and the length of the performance depends on the amount of money given. (1956, 240)

Moreover, this practice can be read as contemporary manifestation of an ethos of commodification of the performing arts in the Ubud area since the 1930s. Two sets of influences can be observed there at that time. The first of these is the work of Western researchers, who utilised an ethic of payment for performance as a means of securing music and dance events for observation. As anthropologist Margaret Mead commented about her months in Ubud in 1936: "every theatrical performance is also an offering to the gods, those who wish to make a thank offering...sheer heaven for the anthropologist" (Mead 1972, 231). Also at that time, according to MacRae (1999,

133), the activities of the local royal family, the Sukawati, mediated Ubud music and dance to non-Balinese audiences and 'insinuated into the local cultural economy the distinctly global idea of cultural products as commodities'.

A second aspect of *Kecak* through which its presentation to tourists can be problematised is its identity as a work of traditional Balinese culture and the processes of signification by which that identity has been and continues to be constructed. The exact details of *Kecak's* development remain obscure. Suryani and Jensen (1993) maintain that it was created especially for tourists, while others such as De Zoete and Spies (1938) and Dibia (2000), are less conclusive. There is agreement, however, that in its present form, *Kecak* is the result of relatively recent collaboration between Balinese and non-Balinese. Taking the rhythmic chanting which accompanies *sanghyang* (trance) dance, building on existing Balinese adaptations of it from the 1920s devised by I Wayan Limbak from the nearby village of Beduluh, and utilising it as the accompaniment to a danced version of a story from the *Ramayana*, Walter Spies, a German artist living in the Ubud area, and dance researcher Katherine Mershon, are credited with the form of *Kecak* seen today for use in a 1938 film by German producer Victor Baron von Plessen (Neka Art Museum, no date). Depiction of it not long after that in travel writing as essentially exotic and "one of the last remaining primitive orgies to be seen on the face of the earth" (Clunes [1944] in Vickers 1994, 250), and its use in films from the 1948 *Wake of the Red Witch* (Vickers 1989, 126) to *Baraka* in 1992 have guaranteed it an aura quintessentially ancient and Balinese. Constructed from source materials of a religious nature still in use, *Kecak* has no ritualistic implications. Through the symbolism it utilises and the sacred ethos it invokes, however, it retains the power to influence the spiritual state of its performers and to play a role in the religious consciousness of a community by whom or for whom it is performed. A level of ambiguity in its meaning for Balinese is evident in the way that, despite its non-ritualistic nature, *Kecak* has assumed ritualistic implications and now sometimes appears as a component of *bebali* (ceremonial dances) in religious settings (Racki 1998, 91). Through its history and derivation, conversion into a tourist spectacle, commodification, representation in writing and film, exemplification of culturally accepted and historically established uses of music and dance, and religious implications, *Kecak* can be viewed as a site with multiplex intentions and meanings, a frontier zone between Balinese and tourist expectations about and uses of music and dance.

The contribution of non-Balinese to its construction and dissemination notwithstanding, the aural and visual components of *Kecak* provide tourists with a clearly identifiable sample of Balinese music and dance materials. In this way a prerequisite of cultural tourism—an experience in observable form of "otherness"—is fulfilled. As with much cultural tourism, high levels of tradition are referenced here, and there is a tendency to present Balinese culture as a museum exhibit in the trappings of the past. What tourists attend, however, encapsulates two major aspects of living Balinese culture which form a third level of interpretation of this event. These are implementation of the ethic of *kreasi baru*, and actualisation of the ideology of *gotong-royong*.

Kreasi baru (new creation) is a term used by Balinese musicians and researchers into Balinese music to refer to a new piece of music, dance or performance event which is created from existing materials. This is distinct from the term *komposisi baru* (new composition), which refers to an original new work. Often in this process, a change of signification from the religious to the secular is involved if the materials used have sacred implications. Where much performed art has been desacralised to allow its use before tourists, this is often the case in tourist culture in Bali. The characteristic manipulation of earlier material in the production of new Balinese music and dance is symbolic of a cultural ethos of change, which Hobart et al. refer to as "the important principle of transformation in (Balinese) culture...that flux is inherent to all things" (Hobart et al. 1996, 135), and is remarked upon by numerous writers in discussion of different types of Balinese musical repertoires. McPhee, writing about his time on the island in the 1930s, noted that in *gamelan gong kebyar* music "while much of the musical material...is newly composed, much is borrowed from traditional repertoires" (McPhee 1966, 342). Speaking of the work of I Wayan Lotring, active in the inter-War years, Tenzer describes how the Balinese practice of reshaping existing music to new purposes was a mainstay of Lotring's output, and how he "made use of melodies and rhythms" in secular pieces from types of ritual music, and "opened the door for other composers to rearrange, invent, alter and discard musical ideas and materials" in *kreasi baru* (Tenzer 1998, 55). Discussing the musical relationship between McPhee and Lotring, Oja comments on the former's fascination with this aspect of the Balinese composer's work: "Lotring enthralled McPhee... because he gave a close up view of how the Balinese imaginatively reworked existing material" (Oja 1990, 86). Bakan quotes a Balinese musician talking about *kreasi baru* in *gamelan beleganjur* in the following terms: "for the *kreasi baru*... we would copy off cassettes, develop our own arrangements..." (Bakan 1999, 199), while Heimarck sums up the idea: "In musical composition, Balinese composers often begin with a traditional model and then add to or alter it in order to develop a "new" piece or a new version of a traditional art form" (Heimarck 1999, 12). In its construction from existing components, and concomitant shift from religious to secular contexts, *Kecak* can be aligned with the arts ethic of *kreasi baru*. What tourists witness therefore in a *Kecak* performance is not only the "otherness" of aural and visual materials from which Balinese performing arts are constructed, but reification of a mainstay of the thinking behind those arts, and one which has strong connections with artistic developments in the creation of works for tourist consumption.

A second cultural factor observable in this *Kecak* is the Balinese communal ideology, *gotong-royong* (community self-help, mutual cooperation), the practice of group endeavour in which there is an expectation that everyone will participate, and in which the whole is more important than an individual's contribution to it. The clue to this aspect of the *Kecak* under discussion appears on the printed programme distributed at performances, which attributes the performance to the *krama desa adat* involved. Here, *krama* clearly indicates the participation of the whole *desa adat*, and 'identifies the individual with the group... (with) a non-individualistic connotation' (Warren 1995, 9–10). The concept of *gotong-royong*, which Hobart et al. define as "mutual-aid activities to the advantage of the village or the *banjar* (village ward) community" (Hobart et al. 1996, 239), is explained by Eiseman (1990b, 72–73) through reference to Balinese society as "tightly knit and highly collectivized... a place that requires collective participation in almost every aspect of political, social, economic, and religious life." Eiseman explains that members of a *desa adat* are "bound together" and that it is normative in Balinese society to engage in "group projects for the welfare of the community" (Eiseman 1990b, 72–73) as the members of this *desa adat* have done to procure the funds needed for a new *bale banjar*. Warren (1995) also discusses the input of *gotong-royong* to *adat*, and cites other examples of communities which financed *bale banjar* through such activity. As much as tourists witness *Kecak* at this performance, they are present at a performance of *gotong-royong*.

Calonarang

Performances of the *Calonarang* story take place in a village to the south of Ubud on a weekly basis. Based on events in Java in the 11th century, *Calonarang* concerns villagers' attempts to counter the powers of a black magic practitioner, the witch Rangda, who causes sickness and destruction. In common with *Kecak*, this event mediates a story symbolising the opposition of beneficent and destructive forces through music and dance. Both events summarise the basis of Balinese Hinduism which:

> embraces the principle that for every good, positive, constructive force, there is a counterbalancing evil, negative, destructive force. The two sides are inseparable. They must necessarily coexist, but preferably in dynamic equilibrium, so that neither gets the upper hand. The principal efforts of the Hindu-Balinese religion are devoted to maintaining a balance between positive and negative forces. Equilibrium and balance are the key goals. (Eiseman 1990a, 128)

As with *Kecak*, tourists attending this performance experience visual and aural materials of Balinese performing arts, in the form of costuming, singing, storyline, dialogue, and the sounds of instruments. Also like *Kecak*, what on the surface appears as an event for tourist entertainment covers a number of other factors through which different readings of it can be formed. The first of these is an element of revivalism.

The opening section of this performance is a purely musical one: in succession three short musical segments occur. First, a group of men play on *okokan* (large wooden "cowbells"). This is followed by a procession of the men of the *banjar* (village ward) which is presenting the performance accompanied by *kulkul* (hand held bamboo slit drum) players. The third segment consists of the musicians who will accompany the performance playing the instruments of a *gamelan tektekan*, that is *kendang* (drums), *ceng-ceng kopiak* (small cymbals), *kulkul* and gongs. In the storyline of *Calonarang*, as in Balinese cultural practice in general, these noisy musical segments are meant to drive away evil forces. In local cultural terms, the incorporation of *okokan* and *kulkul* into this performance constitutes an act of musical revival, as these instruments and the music played on them had been falling into disuse in the area. Their appearance in this performance was considered by villagers as a means of reviving an aspect of local music-making, and had required the finding of instruments and teaching of relevant repertoire (personal communication, January 2000).

This *Calonarang* is unusual among the tourist performances run by Yayasan Bina Wisata in that delineation between tourist spectacle and village religious observance is obscured within it. In other tourist shows, performers perform and tourists watch. Events, whatever the spiritual influence they have on their performers out of tourist sight, are clearly defined as tourist entertainment by the sale of tickets, provision of transport, distribution of printed programmes, staging which addresses the audience, and setting up of performance spaces with lighting and seating. In this *Calonarang*, ambiguity of the identity of personnel in the performance places performers and tourists in unclear and shifting positions.

The performance opens with the *pemangku* (priest) of the temple compound where the performance takes place and two attendants making an offering in the middle of the performance space, the *jaba* (public/outer courtyard) of the compound. As an offering is the usual practice at tourist performances, indeed at all performances touristic or not, this seems to be a pre-performance event, one tourists witness regularly. However, it becomes clear from the outline of the story given to tourists that this and the subsequent entry of the music groups described above, rather than being preludes to the performance are in fact the opening scene of it. This introduces a degree of ambiguity to the presentation: are the priest and the village musicians those of the village presenting the performance, or those of the story's setting in its historical past? Is the story historical, or a working out of its tensions in the present? This ambivalence returns throughout the performance when the two attendants appear as characters in the drama, and in the concluding section of the performance. Here the plot requires that the villagers of the drama hold a temple ceremony to celebrate the results of their efforts against Rangda. At this point, the village of the drama and the village presenting it conflate as the members of the village, the men of the opening procession and the women and children who have been watching the performance from outside the tourist seating area, enter the performance space—the women dressed in temple attire and with *bebangkit* (temple offerings of various kinds of food) on their heads—and proceed to the *jeroan* courtyard of the temple to take part in what has obviously moved from presentation of a tourist spectacle to a village religious observance.

That performance of *Calonarang* inhabits both the secular world of tourists and the religious one of villagers is reflected here by its performance in the *jaba* of the temple. This middle courtyard of the temple compound is bordered on one side by the *jeroan* (most sacred courtyard of a temple) and on the other by the *bale* (pavilion) where the audience has been seated, the worldliest part of the complex. It is thus in the physical space where sacred and secular influences intermingle. That it raises spiritual forces which require acknowledgment with a temple ceremony, and that the performance has entered a new and different phase of its presentation at this point is stressed not only through use of religiously differentiated spaces within the temple grounds, but also by a member of the village addressing the audience and explaining the significance of the drama in terms of Balinese religion, especially the ongoing conflict between beneficent and maleficent forces. Through conflation of a village in a drama with the village of a performance and the shift from performance event to religious observance which coincides with this, the position of the tourist audience also shifts, from momentarily observing an historical drama to witnessing a Balinese Hindu ceremony. The audience's position at this point is doubly confusing; their context as observers has altered, and the explanatory talk by a village member indicates that their interest in the ceremony which has just begun is welcome. But at the same time, despite the fact that the ceremony has commenced in full view of them, they are kept firmly in the *jaba* and are soon politely ushered from it while the ceremony continues.

Odalan

The drawing of boundaries between religious observance and events considered suitable for, or aimed specifically at, tourists evident in the performance of *Calonarang* can also be found in the celebrations of a *Karya Piodalan* at the Pura Dalem Ubud in January, 2000. *Odalan* is a "regularly scheduled festival … to celebrate the anniversary of (a temple's) dedication" (Eiseman 1990a, 249) held every 210 days (six Balinese months of 35 days each). An *odalan* such as this one lasts from five to seven days (see Belo 1953). The one under discussion is referred to as *karya* (special) *piodalan* (*pi* = grand, *odalan* = festival) as it occurs in one of the three main village *pura* through which the religious, and thus cultural, cartography of Ubud is marked out.

Music and dance are important aspects of *odalan*. Their presence indicates that a temple is inhabited for a short time by gods, as for the remainder of the time temples are empty and silent. *Odalan* music and dance includes ceremonial repertoires, performances for entertainment, and music for street processions. Balinese divide music and dance at *odalan* into three types, depending on their use and consequent place of performance. To summarise Racki's (1998) and Sugriwa's (2000) explanations: *wali* are sacred dances performed in the *jeroan* (inner and most sacred courtyard) of a temple and have religious functions; *bebali* are ceremonial dances performed in the *jaba tengah* (second courtyard) of a temple, they tell a story; and *bali-balihan* are secular dances which are not linked to ritual, are performed in the *jaba* (third courtyard) of or outside a temple, and may require payment. (Racki 1998, 23; Sugriwa 2000, 7) Although these classifications vary over time and place, through them aesthetic boundaries which are reified in physical spaces of allowance can be seen to exist in Balinese conceptualisations of the roles and significances of music and dance. How are these cultural protocols applied to tourists intending to watch parts of an *odalan*?

For this *odalan*, leaflets were distributed through hotels and shops informing tourists that parts of the festival would be open to tourists: performances classifiable as *bali-balihan* of *gamelan*, dance-dramas, *topeng* (mask) dances, *wayang kulit* (shadow puppet plays), and *kreasi baru* dances. The times and dates of these were made public. Other parts of the *odalan*, however, those defined as *bebali*, were only open to tourists willing to wear proper Balinese costume, as set down by the rules of *adat* (local custom). This is not a simple matter of adding one or two items of Balinese clothing to Western dress, but a serious undertaking involving clothing with religious implications. For men, this consists of: *baju* (shirt with sleeves), *kain* (sarong), *saput* (over-skirt), *umpal* (sash) and *udeng* (headcloth); for women, *kain*, *kebaya* (blouse), *sabuk* (belt), and *selendang* (oblong sash over *kebaya*). Beyond that, some parts of the festival, including music and dance classifiable as *wali*, could not be seen by tourists:

this short introduction will hopefully serve as a guide to visitors in understanding the essence of Balinese life and customs and to help those who wish to witness and participate in some of our religious ceremonies, large or small. Once in Bali, some visitors seem to forget that, as in their own societies, religious ceremonies are not commercial performances staged for the pleasure of the tourist, but are a very important part of the daily life of the community. As the ceremonies in Bali display spectacular and colorful scenes, they have become great attractions for visitors who, when they do not understand the procedures, may unwittingly become intrusive...at times, outsiders are not permitted to attend ceremonies...the visitor who sees Bali just as a photo opportunity without regard for the sensibilities of the Balinese...will not be welcome. (Desa Adat Ubud 2000)

While boundaries were clearly drawn around parts of the *odalan*, the community was, however: "only too pleased to welcome you to our ceremonies and celebrations and there are always people willing to assist whenever you have doubts, problems or questions" (Desa Adat Ubud 2000).

As "myth, art, ritual and theatre are intimately connected in Bali" (Hobart et al. 1996, 199) the roles of music and dance in *odalan* are extensive. Performances of specific genres of Balinese music and dance at *odalan* have the potential to provide tourists with some idea of their contextualisation in ongoing Balinese Hindu culture, something which is missing from tourist performances of the same or similar works. *Odalan* processions along the main street of Ubud allow tourists another experience of music as a part of lived Balinese Hinduism. These processions, valued camera opportunities and with a high degree of tourist presence, inscribe another level of music use in *odalan*, one which remains relatively unrecognised by tourists although they are present along its routes. These routes connect the temples which constitute the religious geography of Ubud. All Balinese villages require three main *pura*: Pura Puseh (temple of the village's origins and Brahma), Pura Desa (dedicated to Wisnu), and Pura Dalem (dedicated to Siwa and Durga, and associated with death). These are built in accordance with architectural regulations which reflect Balinese Hindu beliefs, both at the level of individual temples and in relation to each other and the overall geography of the village they serve (Eiseman 1990a; Hobart et al. 1996). Through these positional protocols, they lay out Balinese cosmologies in physical space. Movement between them in procession, which is always accompanied by the sounds of mobile *gamelan* and *kidung* (womens' singing), inscribes religious thinking onto the landscape through music. This indicates physical and conceptual relationships between the temples, and in turn emphasises symbols which express the identity of the village and its sphere of influence. Like *Kecak* and *Calonarang*, sound and image are obvious signs of culture which tourists witness; other less apparent aspects of culture are also present in the form of actualised cultural ideologies.

Conclusion: Culture Performed

These cases of interaction between culture bearers and tourists at performances of music and dance indicate the highly organised nature of cultural tourism in the Ubud area. They also indicate ways in which tourist roles at events are controlled by organisers and performers. This is achieved through various means: physical positioning of audiences, timetabling and timing, subtle suggestions of when it is appropriate to leave, in one case the mandation of Balinese costume, and notification of whether or not tourists should be present. At times tourists are excluded from events and boundaries are clearly drawn; at other times they are allowed into areas of interaction with performers. Information is provided—formalised in spoken explanations or printed programmes, often in conversation with performers and organisers, sometimes through printed materials in hotels and shops. Local cultural policies and practices thus become the means of constructing tourist presence in accordance with Balinese agendas.

Through these agendas, Balinese ensure maintenance of cultural integrity. While *Kecak* has a history of tourist performance since at least the 1930s, *sanghyang* dance, the origin of its musical accompaniment, continues to be performed in religious settings away from tourists. Calonarang acts out her conflict with the forces of good for tourist entertainment. At the same time, her actions effect the religious sensibilities of her Balinese audience to a point at which religion in ceremonialised form takes over, and the performance ceases to exist for the tourist gaze. A temple *odalan* delineates allowance or not of tourist access. The strength of cultural tourism in the Ubud area would seem to be a result of the strength of local cultural maintenance. Moreover, to suggest that tourism and culture have coalesced so they are indistinguishable is clearly not tenable in situations where such definable boundaries can be found.

Another factor to which the success of cultural tourism in this area can be attributed is the existence of established practices of payment for arts events, their use as fund-raising activities, and systems of patronage as integral to ways in which the performing arts were already aestheticised in Bali before the rise of cultural tourism. Researchers into Balinese culture emphasise that performances were and continue to be "for the gods," but that they could also include payment in some form. Transference of this to tourist contexts is not difficult. This analogy is also relevant in the reading of tourist events as coinciding with cultural matrices. In cases such as *Calonarang*, where a certain ambivalence in signification follows from the use of a location at which sacred and secular worlds meet, or the translation of religiously significant music into *Kecak*, a tourist show, and the ways in which that translation actualises the arts ethic of *kreasi baru*, this functions in favour of both sets of participants. Tourists are provided with experiences rich in potential significations, while culture bearers obtain new fora for the presentation of ongoing artistic development.

The potential significations of these events arise from three levels of application of the term "culture" in this discussion. The first of these is that at which "culture" refers to the observable materials of performance—musical sounds, costuming, etc.—the exotic "other." A second level, one less visible to tourists, is the use of the term to discuss practices in the arts, such as that of *kreasi baru*. This compositional process can be positioned as an example of the third level of meaning of the term "culture," as a way in which tourist culture presents Balinese culture as a whole. While *kreasi baru* is generally discussed as specific to the performing arts, it is a guiding principle of Balinese culture in that it reifies aspects of Balinese religious doctrine. Namely, that materials re-used symbolise a cyclic ethic, and in this way maintain the cosmic balance which is the basis of Balinese Hinduism. A music and dance performance can thus reflect Balinese cultural ethos on the highest, and broadest, levels. That this applies across a range of cultural practices and in other performances can be extrapolated from the similar situation with *gotong-royong*, when a performance presents actualisation of an ethos of communal cooperation, and aspects of music and dance during an *odalan* which indicates the presence of gods, and maps religious thinking onto the landscape. At this level, music and dance events at which tourists are present assume meanings beyond the merely theatrical experience of "otherness," becoming performances of culture.

References

Adams, Kathleen M. 1995. "Making-up the Toraja? The Appropriation of Tourism, Anthropology, and Museums for Politics in Upland Sulawesi, Indonesia." *Ethnology* 34(2): 143–154.

Bakan, Michael. 1999. *Music of Death and New Creation: Experiences in the World of Balinese Gamelan Beleganjur*. Chicago: University of Chicago Press.

Becker, Alton L., and Yengoyan, Aram, eds. 1979. *The Imagination of Reality: Essays in Southeast Asian Coherence Systems*. Norwood: Ablex.

Belo, Jane. 1953. *Bali: Temple Festival*. Seattle: University of Washington Press.

Bowers, Fabion. 1956. *Theatre in the East: A Survey of Asian Dance and Drama*. New York: Thomas Nelson.

Clunes, Frank. 1944. *To the Isles of Spice with Frank Clune: A Vagabond Voyage by Air from Botany Bay to Darwin, Bathurst Island, Timor, Java, Borneo, Celebes, and French Indo-China*. Sydney: Angus & Robertson.

Connell, John. 1993. Bali Revisited: Death, Rejuvenation, and the Tourist Cycle. *Environment and Planning D: Society and Space* 11: 641–661.

Craik, James. 1997. "The Culture of Tourism." In *Touring Cultures: Transformations of Travel and Theory*, C. Rojek & J. Urry, eds. London: Routledge.

Cukier, Judie, Joanne Norris, and Geoffrey Wall. 1996. "The Involvement of Women in the Tourism Industry of Bali, Indonesia." *Journal of Development Studies* 33(2): 248–271.

Desa Adat Ubud. 2000. *Temple Anniversary—Karya Piodalan, Pura Dalem Ubud, 24–28 January, 2000*. Ubud: Desa Adat Ubud.

De Zoete, Beryl, and Walter Spies. 1938. *Dance and Drama in Bali*. Kuala Lumpur: Oxford University Press.

Dibia, Wayan. 2000. *Kecak: The Vocal Chant of Bali*. Denpasar: Hartanto Art Books Studio.

Eiseman, Fred. 1990a. *Bali—Sekala and Niskala: Volume 1, Essays on Religion, Ritual and Art*. Hong Kong: Periplus.

———. 1990b. *Bali—Sekala and Niskala: Volume 2, Essays on Society, Tradition and Craft*. Hong Kong: Periplus.

Heimarck, Brita. 1999. *Balinese Discourses on Music: Musical Modernization in the Ideas and Practices of Shadow Play Performers from Sukawati, and the Indonesian College*, PhD Dissertation, Cornell University. UMI Dissertation No. 991 4666.

Herbst, Edward. 1997. *Voices in Bali: Energies and Perspectives in Vocal Music and Dance Theater*. Hanover: Wesleyan University Press.

Hill, Hal, ed. 1994. *Indonesia's New Order: The Dynamics of Socio-economic Transformation*. Honolulu: University of Hawai'i Press.

Hobart, Angela., Urs Ramseyer, and Albert Leemann. 1996. *The Peoples of Bali*. Oxford: Blackwell.

Howe, David., ed.. 1996. *Cross-Cultural Consumption: Global Markets—Local Realities*. London: Routledge.

James, Jamie. 1999. "Travel: Ubud, the Heart of Bali." *The Atlantic Monthly* 284(2): 26–32.

Lury, Celia. 1997. "The Objects of Travel." In *Touring Cultures: Transformations of Travel and Theory*, edited by Chris Rojek and John Urry. London: Routledge.

Macdonald, Sharon. 1997. "A People's Story: Heritage, Identity and Authenticity." In *Touring Cultures: Transformations of Travel and Theory*, edited by Chris Rojek and John Urry. London: Routledge.

MacRae, Graeme. 1999. "Acting Global, Thinking Local in a Balinese Tourist Town." In *Staying Local in the Global Village: Bali in the Twentieth Century*, edited by Raechelle Rubinstein and Linda Connor. Honolulu: University of Hawai'i Press.

McCarthy, John. 1994. *Are Sweet Dreams Made of This? Tourism in Bali and Eastern Indonesia*. Northcote: Indonesia Resources and Information Program.

McGregor, A. 2000. "Dynamic Texts and Tourist Gaze: Death, Bones and Buffalo." *Annals of Tourism Research* 27(1):27–50.

McKean, Philip Frick. 1979. "From Purity to Pollution? The Balinese *Ketjak* (Monkey Dance) as Symbolic Form in Transition." In *The Imagination of Reality: Essays in Southeast Asian Coherence Systems*, edited by A. Becker and A. Yengoyan. Norwood: Ablex.

McPhee, Colin. 1966. *Music in Bali: A Study in Form and Instrumental Organization in Balinese Orchestral Music*. New Haven: Yale University Press.

Mead, Margaret. 1972. *Blackberry Winter: My Earlier Years*. London: Angus & Robertson.

Merriam, Alan. 1964. *The Anthropology of Music*. Chicago: Northwestern University Press.

Neka Art Museum. n.d. Curatorial note to exhibition—photographs by Robert Koke. Ubud: Neka Museum.

Nettl, Bruno. 1983. *The Study of Ethnomusicology: Twenty-nine Issues and Concepts*. Chicago: University of Illinois Press.

Oja, Carol. 1990. *Colin McPhee: Composer in Two Worlds*. Washington: Smithsonian Institution Press.

Picard, Michel. 1996. *Bali: Cultural Tourism and Touristic Culture*. Singapore: Archipelago Press.

Picard, Michel. 1997. "Cultural Tourism, Nation-building, and Regional Culture: the Making of a Balinese Identity." In *Tourism, Ethnicity, and the State in Asian and Pacific Societies*, edited by M. Picard and R. Wood. Honolulu: University of Hawai'i Press.

———, and Robert Wood, eds. 1997. *Tourism, Ethnicity, and the State in Asian and Pacific Societies*. Honolulu: University of Hawai'i Press.

Racki, Christian. 1998. *The Sacred Dances of Bali*. Denpasar: Buratwangi.

Rojek, Chris and John Urry, eds. 1997. *Touring Cultures: Transformations of Travel and Theory*. London: Routledge.

Rubinstein, Raechelle, and Linda Connor. 1999. *Staying Local in the Global Village: Bali in the Twentieth Century*. Honolulu: University of Hawai'i Press.

Schansman, R. 1991. "Indonesia 1991: Tourism in the Archipelago." *Cornell Hotel and Restaurant Administration Quarterly* 32(3):84–92.

Sinclair, M. 1998. "Tourism and Economic Development a Survey." *Journal of Development Studies* 34(5):1–51.

Singer, M. 2000. "Culture Works: Cultural Resources as Economic Development tools." *Public Management* 82(8):11–20.

Stokes, Martin. 1999. "Music, Travel and Tourism: An Afterword." *The World of Music* 41(3):141–155.

Sugriwa, Sudhyatmaka, ed. 2000. *Nadi: Trance in the Balinese Arts*. Denpasar: Taksu Foundation.

Suryani, Ketut, and Gordon Jensen. 1993. *Trance and Possession in Bali: A Window on Western Multiple Personality, Possession Disorder and Suicide*. Kuala Lumpur: Oxford University Press.

Tenzer, Michael. 1998. *Balinese Music*. Hong Kong: Periplus.

———. 2000. *Gamelan Gong Kebyar: The Art of Twentieth-century Balinese Music*. Chicago: University of Chicago Press.

Vickers, Adrian. 1989. *Bali—A Paradise Created*. Hong Kong: Periplus.

———, ed. 1994. *Travelling to Bali: Four Hundred Years of Journeys*. Oxford: Oxford University Press.

Warren, Carol. 1995. *Adat and Dinas: Balinese CS state*. Oxford: Oxford University Press.

Wood, Robert. 1997. "Tourism and the State: Ethnic Options and Constructions of Otherness." In *Tourism, Ethnicity, and the State in Asian and Pacific Societies*, edited by M. Picard & R. Wood. Honolulu: University of Hawai'i Press.

4

Folk Festival as Modern Ritual in the Polish Tatra Mountains

Timothy J. Cooley

Every autumn, the International Festival of Mountain Folklore is staged in *Podhale* (lit., piedmont), a well-defined folk region in the Tatra Mountains of Poland on the border with Slovakia.[1] When I first attended the festival in 1992, I misprized the staged presentations of folk culture in favor of what I believed to be more "authentic" in-group music events. Soon, however, I realized that what made tourist festivals interesting was not necessarily the content of the staged presentations—though these are very important—but rather the festival itself. In order to appreciate and interpret the content of a festival, I needed to understand the frame. To this end, I have come to regard tourist festivals as rituals, not unlike other more traditionally recognized calendric rituals that define a people's relationship to their universe and ensure their continued livelihood.

Tourist festivals are "rituals" in two fundamental ways that the term is used in the social sciences. First, they are symbolic representations of objects, beliefs, or truths of special significance to a group (Connerton 1989, 44; Durkheim 1915; Lukes 1975, 291). Second, they are transformative or effective. As in other rituals, participants are transformed, or an entire group's relationship to nature is transformed, as in a ritual marking the changes in seasons or insuring a successful crop (MacAloon 1984, 250; Pertierra 1987, 199–200; Schechner 1983, 131–58; Turner 1984, 21). Interpreting festivals as rituals does not remove and segregate them from other forms of performance. Schechner suggested a continuum that spans the distance between two opposing motivations for performance: efficacy (a quality of ritual) and entertainment (a quality of theater) (1983, 137–38). Most performances move back and forth between the opposing sides of this continuum. This approach is applicable to festival performances in Podhale that contain some of the qualities of ritual, but are intended to be entertainment as well. Festivals in Podhale are indeed entertainment to some, perhaps most, but they function as rituals of singular importance to many, including to the festival performers and organizers.

In this I study, interpret the International Festival of Mountain Folklore as a present-day ritual filled with symbolic objects and acts used by local residents to define a place for themselves in a changing world. The festival is held in the town of Zakopane, the major tourist center of Podhale. The descendants of long-established families from this alpine mountain area call themselves *Górale* (mountaineers), from the root *góra* or "mountain."[2] Górale are a distinct ethnic group within Poland. Those with known roots elsewhere are not considered Górale even when they have lived in Podhale for generations. Festivals are central community events at which Górale represent themselves to the larger Polish and international communities to which they increasingly feel they belong. The conscious development of tourism in Podhale is an important means by which Górale participate in this extended world community. At tourist festivals, this interaction is highly controlled and symbolic. Such festivals are reasonable responses by local people to social, political, demographic, and economic changes experienced in the past century (Baumann 1996; Bendix 1985, 1989, 1997; Grünewald 2002; Hagedorn 2001; Ronström 1996). These highly self-conscious self-representations are "folk culture" inasmuch as they are local responses by individuals in relatively clearly defined culture groups to their own life experiences, including their experiences with tourists and ethnographers. Michael Beckerman, writing about communist folk festivals in the former Czechoslovakia, states that "they were not in any sense 'folk music' but rather a series of performances 'about folk music' or about some concept of folk music that fit the picture of it held by urbanites" (1996, 47). This may have been true, but I find that while folk festival stage performances by Górale in post-communist Poland are "performances 'about folk music,'" they are also folk music themselves. Folk processes must incorporate the "picture of it held by urbanites" because these urbanites have been a part of Górale's realm of human contacts for over a century.

This century of interaction between Górale and others is the first topic I address below in a history of tourism and festivals in Podhale. This is followed by an ethnographic interpretation of the International Festival of Mountain Folklore. As an interpretive device in this ethnography, I employ a series of opposing pairs: isolation versus multiculturalism, preservation versus invention, spurious versus authentic, and tourism versus ethnography. These binary structures are like riddles or questions that function as Hegelian dialectics in which interpretation arises from the mediation of opposites.

A History of Tourism and Festivals in Podhale

Significant numbers of tourists did not visit Podhale until the late nineteenth century. At that time, Poland was partitioned three ways between Prussia, Russia, and Austria. Podhale was part of Galicia and was administered by Austria, the partitioning power that provided Poles with the greatest degree of freedom. The capital of Galicia was Krakow, a university town that, during the late nineteenth and early twentieth centuries, was increasingly connected intellectually with the village of Zakopane in Podhale. Zakopane was little more than a wide spot in a dirt road before it was consciously developed as a tourist destination beginning in the last quarter of the 1800s. A century later Zakopane was compared in *National Geographic Traveler* magazine to Aspen, Colorado, a trendy mountain resort town in the United States (Kostyal 1995, 64). The dramatic views of the Tatras and pure mountain air attracted Polish *inteligencja*, who began to build summer villas and establish sanatoriums in and around Zakopane as it gained a reputation as the informal summer capitol of Galicia (Gellner 1998, 125). In 1873 about 400 guests came to Zakopane; by 1880, 638 guests were recorded in Zakopane; in 1886 the number jumped to 3,123; and to 8,011 in 1900. The arduous journey through mountains to reach Zakopane was greatly eased with the completion of a railroad line to the village in 1899, after which time the number of tourists increased steadily to about 13,000 guests in 1913 (Paryski 1991). A list of the town's frequent visitors and residents reads like a who's who of Polish political, intellectual and artistic history, including the likes of anthropologist Bronislaw Malinowski and composer Karol Szymanowski.

The early tourists to Podhale were also the earliest musical ethnographers, and the period at the end of Poland's partition was when Górale music from Podhale began to be codified as a distinct folk genre. Up to the 1880s, literature on Podhale music presented a diverse repertoire including popular songs and dances of the times, but with little significant resemblance to what is played by Górale today. For example, the most substantial collection of music from this region was made by

Oskar Kolberg between the 1850s and the 1880s (published posthumously in 1968). Of the 161 songs with tunes that he positively identifies as being from Podhale, only about half are in a style consistent with twentieth-century Tatra region music, and only a single tune am I able to identify as still current in the living repertoire. But suddenly in the 1880s, a series of published tune transcriptions by Jan Kleczyński presented a body of tunes still played by Górale over a century later (1883; 1884a; 1884b; 1888). As I explain elsewhere (Cooley 2000; 2005, 102–108), Kleczyński was influenced by one of the region's biggest promoters, physician Tytus Chałubiński who established a sanatorium in Zakopane. Working with prominent Górale musicians, musical ethnographers like Kleczyński and promoters like Chałubiński brokered an image of Górale for visitors, including an image of Górale music. The regional movement in Podhale that they helped create halted during the First World War, but resumed with new vigor after Poland regained independence in 1918 and before the Second World War.

The interwar period was a heady time of nation-building in Poland, and folk music was used as a means of rallying the populace, confirming a sense of region, and by extension, nation. A prominent example is the ballet *Harnasie* by Szynamowski, for which he used folk tunes and folk legends from Podhale. During this period, several influential ethnographic studies of Górale music were also conducted, completing the process that began in the end of the nineteenth century of codifying this music (e.g., Chybiński 1961 [researched in the 1920s] and Mierczyński 1930). Górale music-culture was even actively used beyond the borders of Poland by the *Polskie Towarzystwo Tatrzański* (Polish Tatra Society) and the *Związek Podhalan* (Podhale Association)[3] to encourage the Górale diaspora to return to Poland and to Podhale as tourists, or even to repatriate (see Brozek 1985, 19; Cooley & Spottswood 1997a, 1997b; Wytrwal 1977, 316–17). Podhale and specifically Zakopane did experience dramatic increases in tourism during this period. In 1918 there were 9,373 guests, and the number increased to 60,590 by 1938 (Paryski 1991, 21; Jackowski 1991, 23). Though still a favorite resort area for Polish inteligencja, the region was beginning to see mass tourism and more international guests, usually cultural elites.

Another development during the interwar period especially important for this study is the establishment of the first tourist festivals. These early festivals are directly linked, at least conceptually, to present-day festivals in the southern mountainous region of Poland. The first festival was *Święto Gór* (Mountain Holiday) in Zakopane in 1935, sponsored by local government and regional organizations for the purpose of promoting the region—not just Podhale but the neighboring areas as well. In subsequent years, the festival took place in other villages in and around Podhale before the outbreak of World War II ended the festival. Franciszek Świder-Zbójnik, a senior Górale musician who performed with a song and dance troupe at these first festivals, believes troupes today still use a similar presentation format (interview, 7 August 1995, Bialy Dunjec). Another lasting impact of *Święto Gór* is the idea of a regional festival focusing on mountain folklore.

In 1948 after World War II, the adoption of Marxist-Leninist communism as the official state ideology altered the nature of tourism. To a great extent, tourism was socialized, with the government sometimes determining when and where any individual would vacation. Marek Jenner, a long-time resident of Zakopane, told me with a dry sense of humor forged in the communist era, "The government told each worker when he would vacation, what vacation house he would visit, in what room he would stay, and in which bed he would sleep!" (interview, 11 April 1995, Zakopane). The accuracy of his quip varied with individual situations, but often the vacationing "worker" did stay in one of the many vacation houses in Zakopane built by the *Fundusz Wczasów Pracowniczych* (Fund for Workers' Vacations), established in 1949 by the Sejm (diet or legislature) (Kulczycki 1970, 176). Thus, Podhale was consciously developed by the communist government as a resort area and tourist destination. Though still a popular place for Polish artists and "working intellectuals," the face of tourism in Zakopane changed as laborers and others flocked to the Tatras in increasing numbers. Already in 1948, 150,000 people visited Zakopane, 922,000 in 1960, and over three million annually by the mid-seventies (Warszyńska 1991, 38). More than any other region in Poland, the Tatra and neighboring mountain regions came to depend economically on tourism (Dawson 1991, 198).

Another hallmark of the communist era was the establishment of many folklore festivals throughout Poland. Though these were typically designed to promote the ideology of a unified national "folk," this ideal was not as thoroughly implemented in Poland as it was in other communist states such as Bulgaria (Rice 1994, 26–28). In and around Podhale, the most successful festivals celebrated regional folklore, not national. For example, to the west of Podhale in the Beskid Mountains is held an annual festival called *Tydzień kultury Beskidziej* (Beskid Mountain Culture Week), and to the east, the town of Nowy Sącz hosts a festival called *Święto Dzieci Gór* (Holiday of Mountain Children). The latter is an international festival featuring six Polish children's troupes and six children's troupes from abroad. The director of this festival, Antoni Malczak, cites the pre-war *Święto Gór* festival as his inspiration (1992).

The most successful festival of this sort, and certainly the most influential in Podhale, was Zakopane's *Jesień Tatrzańska* (Tatra Autumn), which began in 1962. This festival was the idea of Krzystyna Słobodzińska, a woman raised in Warsaw who married a man from Zakopane and who spent most of her adult life there. In an interview, she explained to me that neither she nor her husband were Górale, but that she admired Górale and their style (interview, 20 July 1995, Zakopane). In fact, the first festivals were not primarily folklore festivals but events designed to attract more tourists to Zakopane with whatever means possible. Displays of local Górale music-culture were just one among many other attractions. The event was first and foremost a tourist event; concern for promoting and preserving mountain folklore performance was an afterthought that only later gained precedence. By 1968, however, folklore performance was clearly the focus of the event, which was renamed the *Międzynarodowy Festiwal Folkloru Ziem Górskich* (International Festival of Mountain Folklore). It was turned into a contest festival with twenty-four folklore song and dance troupes, six of them from abroad (Reinfuss 1971, 7). This annual festival continues today and serves as a case study in this essay.

Since the end of communist control in 1989, Zakopane and all of Poland have undergone rapid privatization while much of the communist-established tourist infrastructure remains. The state-owned vacation houses of Zakopane still operate, but they compete with private hotels. The state-run travel agency that used to be a monopoly still has its office in the center of town, but competing small private travel agents line the streets. There has also been a change in the clientele. During peak tourist seasons, the main business pedestrian way is crowded with people speaking German, French, Italian, English, Japanese, etc., as well as Polish. Despite the increase in international tourism in Zakopane in post-communist times, informal estimates are that the actual number of annual tourists in Podhale has decreased since the mid-seventies. No longer are Górale and other residents assured a minimum number of tourists each season.

The end of the communist era also resulted in a shift in the symbolic value of Górale music-culture. The desire of the Party to use folk music as a national symbol may have actually had the opposite effect. Some who were resistant to communism shunned folk music when they realized it was being used as propaganda (interview with radio producer Włodzimierz Kleszcz, 22 March 1995, Warsaw). Others worked within the communist system toward goals that were counter to that system. For example, many individuals participated in state-sanctioned song and dance troupes because they provided opportunities to travel outside of Poland. When troupes toured abroad, it was not unusual for many members to defect and not return to Poland. Similarly, some scholars took advantage of the Party's support of folk music research in order to encourage local music traditions instead of the nationalized, centralized interpretations of folk music promoted by the State (see Noll 1986, 668). And some festivals such as the International Festival of Mountain Folklore actively focused beyond the borders of communist Poland. Though festivals and any enactments of folk culture can be understood in diverse ways, generally Górale music lost its significance as a national musical symbol of Poland as promoted by Szymanowski and others before the communist era. By the time communism fell, Górale music had instead become a symbol of regional identity.

After the fall of communism, the International Festival of Mountain Folklore faltered somewhat, but it does continue to the present, emphasizing the international quality initiated in the 1960s. For example, the 1996 festival featured sixteen troupes, including eleven from abroad. The premise of the festival is that all performing troupes should represent music-cultures from mountain regions. Underlying this theme is the widely held belief in Podhale that all indigenous mountain people are similar—a belief that has no doubt been promoted by the Zakopane festival itself. Though claims for the universality of mountain people are dubious, the origins of the festival concept to promote the Tatra regions in the inter-war period were grounded in the very real connections of music-cultures along the Carpathian Mountain chain—music from Podhale is more closely related to music from other Carpathian Mountain regions than to lowland Poland. The Zakopane International Festival of Mountain Folklore draws performers from well beyond the Carpathians, but it still includes a sizable delegation of troupes from the Carpathians.

Krzystyna Słobodzińska, the original director of the festival in 1962 when it was called "Tatra Autumn," recalled clearly her goal for the festival when I spoke with her in 1995: it was an attraction for tourists. A secondary theme of promoting and preserving Górale culture emerged later in our conversation: "I tried to run the festival in a way that Górale would not forget about this, that they are Górale."[4] She believes the festival is responsible for an increased interest in Górale song and dance troupes. The theme of preservation was echoed by Elżbieta Chodurska, the then director of the festival, when I interviewed her in 1995 and in her "welcome" published in the 1996 festival program book (1996, 1). But she interprets the goals of the festival in a dramatically different way. Instead of stressing the increased tourism the festival may generate, she believes the festival is an opportunity to show people how Górale from Podhale live, and for Górale from Podhale to see how mountaineers from other parts of the world live. Though both Słobodzińska and Chodurska see good as well as bad effects of tourism in Zakopane, Chodurska is much more circumspect about the good the tourist industry may bring to the local residents. She says tourists are necessary for *Zakopiańczyków* (residents of Zakopane) to make a living since there is no other industry in the area. Noting that she herself is Górale, she presents much more ambivalent views about the impact of tourism and the festival on Górale culture than does Słobodzińska (interview, 20 July 1995, Zakopane).

In his book *All That is Native & Fine*, David Whisnant offers a comparable case where local peoples and their music-cultures are impacted by outside influences including prominent individuals and broad social and economic forces. In tracing the history of the White Top Festival in Virginia, he shows the influence of elite "cultural workers" on a mountainous region of America from the 1890s, a process of cultural intervention that offers a striking comparison to my study of similar processes in Poland. Around the beginning of the twentieth century, ethnographers such as Cecil Sharp believed the Appalachian mountains contained isolated pockets of racially pure Anglo stock with preserved old folk culture (Karpeles in Sharp 1954, viii). Similar views about mountain isolation and racial purity are part of the Tatra myth (see for example Ćwiżewicz & Ćwiżewicz 1995; Czekanowska 1990, 84; Kotoński 1956, 18; Wrazen 1988, 48). The White Top Festival in Virginia was originally conceived as a means of preserving the festival directors' image of traditional folk music of the region. By contrast, the roughly contemporary (1935) "Mountain Holiday" festival in Podhale and many festivals in the region since were first created to stimulate tourism. The concern for cultural preservation that is now an important justification for folk festivals in Poland does not seem to have been the motivation for the early festivals. However, early Polish writers and "cultural workers" did express a concern for cultural preservation in the Tatras (see for example the introduction in Mierczyński [1930] and the 1920s writings of Zborowski [1972]). The historical context for Whisnant's study is the industrial invasion of the Appalachian regions of southern

America, a process of modernization that ultimately stripped many "indigenous" peoples (meaning "white Anglos" to these early cultural interventionists) of their land and often their means of a decent livelihood. At roughly the same time, similar industrial forces were at work in the Tatras: railroads, logging, mining, and tourism. The impact of railroads and logging is comparable in both locations, but the degree to which mining and tourism changed the Appalachians and the Tatras differs greatly. Whereas coal mining resulted in the forfeiture of land rights and altered traditional lifeways in the Appalachians, mining was never as successful in the Tatras, which are relatively poor in minerals. And though tourism has been a force in both locations since the 1880s, in the Tatra region it became the leading industry. The greater threat to private ownership of land in Poland came later under communism, but even then in Podhale, Górale maintained a high level of land ownership because their small mountainous fields were unsuitable for large collective farms. Finally, the cultural politics so convincingly written about by Whisnant were relatively tame compared to the dramatic political shifts during the same period in this part of Europe as Poland changed from a partitioned kingdom into a new independent nation after the First World War, only to fall under Soviet authority after the Second World War. Extending my interpretation to the present day, folk festivals in Podhale have roots in pre-Communist Poland and continue after the fall of communism, providing a type of symbolic continuity that spans the dramatic changes Poland experienced in the twentieth century.

An Ethnography of a Festival: A Series of Opposing Pairs

I turn now to an ethnographic interpretation of the International Festival of Mountain Folklore using the series of opposing pairs introduced at the beginning of this paper: isolation vs. multiculturalism, preservation vs. invention, spurious vs. authentic, and tourism vs. ethnography. These dialectical oppositions aid me in producing dynamic interpretations of festival and tourist shows that lead to flexible understandings of the constantly moving representations of ethnicity that Górale musicians and dancers create for themselves in music-culture at such festivals. I address these oppositions in reverse order, beginning with tourism vs. ethnography.

By "ethnography" I mean the enterprise of observing and writing about social and cultural activity, often by someone considered outside the group written about. Ethnography also suggests, though it does not necessitate, travel by the writer to a place considered "away" in a process sometimes called today "fieldwork." By virtue of my occasional travel from America to Poland to do fieldwork among and write about Górale, I am an ethnographer, for example. Like ethnography, the term "tourism" suggests travel away from home, though not explicitly for the purpose of writing about what one experiences. Tourism is temporary and voluntary travel away from home primarily for the purpose of leisure but also for business (Smith 1977, 2; Cohen 1984, 374). According to Polish border officials, I enter Poland as a tourist.

The anthropological analysis of tourism began in the 1960s (Nuñez 1963), was recognized as a significant line of ethnographic inquiry in the 1970s (Smith 1977), and in the 1970s and 1980s the uncomfortable similarities between ethnographers and tourists were noted (Errington and Gewertz 1989; Kirshenblatt-Gimblett 1988; MacCannell 1989 [1976], 5, 173–179). In the 1980s and 90s ethnomusicologists began to take stock of their associations with tourists and tourism. This trend can be seen for example in a collection of essays published following the colloquium on tourism and traditional music of the International Council for Traditional Music held in Jamaica in 1986 (Kaeppler & Levin 1988), and in Wolfgang Suppan's 1991 collection of essays, *Musik und Tourismus*. As discussed below, the links between tourism and ethnography were most thoroughly demonstrated by folklorist Regina Bendix in her work with the concept of "authenticity" (1989, 1997). Subsequent publications have continued to develop this theme, including an issue of the journal *The World of Music* devoted to music and tourism (DeWitt 1999), and several recent books by ethnomusicologists (Cooley 2005; Hagedorn 2001; Sarkissian 2000). I have mentioned that the earliest tourists in Podhale were also the earliest ethnographers in the region. The continuing links between tourism and ethnography are annually reaffirmed at the Zakopane festival.

Like many modern-day festivals in Poland, this festival features a contest, and for this reason one particular type of authoritative influence of ethnography is tangibly experienced by Górale musicians and by tourists. Contest folklore festivals in Poland feature a panel of jurors who evaluate stage performances using criteria heavily invested with notions of "authenticity." For example, at the Zakopane festival each troupe is judged in one of four categories arranged in an implied hierarchy: (1) authentic troupes (*zespołów autentycznych*); (2) artistic elaboration (*zespołów artystycznie opracowanych*), (3) stylized troupes (*zespołów stylizowanych*); and (4) reconstructive troupes (*zespołów rekonstruowanych*) (from the 1995 Zakopane Festival booklet). The jurors at this and other festivals are usually academic ethnographers of one sort or another—ethnomusicologists, ethnochoreologists, anthropologists, and folklorists. In the past, members of the communities and ethnic groups represented on stage were not entrusted with the responsibility of evaluating themselves, a value judgment reminiscent of the 1930s White Top Festival fiddle contests in Virginia at which fiddlers themselves were not allowed to judge contests in a top down effort to ensure "standards" (Whisnant 1983, 229). Whether or not active efforts were ever made to exclude Górale themselves from juries, the situation is changing. Since 1994, the Zakopane festival jury has included at least one local Górale member.

The relationship between tourists, ethnographers and performers is ritually established each evening at the Zakopane festival. Before the troupes begin performing on the main festival stage, the emcees turn the attention of all present to a long row of tables in the middle of the spectators' seating area. Seated at these prominent tables is a panel of six or seven jurors who stand as they are introduced and the audience claps. These high priests of the festival ceremony come from Poland and other European nations represented by the festival performers. They are culture-brokers who will judge each troupe performing at the Zakopane festival based on their concepts of "authenticity." The recognition of the jury by the emcees is an important part of the public ceremony, but not symbolic of anything particularly Górale. Instead, I interpret this daily feature as symbolic of a value shared by the organizers and participants—a symbolic acknowledgment of a belief in the authentic. With ritually actualized power and authority, the jurors (together with the festival organizers) evaluate and ultimately control the content of the festival performances.

Ethnographers and tourists alike value what is perceived as authentic versus that which is perceived as spurious, our next opposition. Historically the industries of tourism and ethnography are linked in their quest for authenticity, though the quest itself may take different paths. Musical folklore studies in Europe, folklore studies in Europe and America, and to some extent European ethnomusicology today all bear the mark of Johann Gottfried Herder's imperative to search for national authenticity in folk poetry (see Bendix 1997, 16–17; Suppan 1976, 117–20). The late eighteenth- and nineteenth-century Romanticists' fascination with the "folk" (associated in Europe with the peasant class and in America with the concept of the common man) as the locus of purity and authenticity as contrasted with urban society has been repeated in different locations and times, including in Poland since the late nineteenth century. In academic ethnography, the dichotomous view that cultural practice is either authentic or its opposite, spurious, has been challenged in recent decades, though it still permeates both scholarly and lay people's discussions of Górale music-culture and of folk culture in general (Bendix 1997, 13). The promotional literature for festivals in Poland is laced with evocations of authenticity. For example, a flyer for the 1992 "Beskid Mountain Culture Week" promises to be "an authentic celebration of tradition…" and the stage performances at the Zakopane festival are juried using authenticity as the main criterion.

As I am using it here, "authenticity" is not something out there to be discovered; authenticity is a concept that is made—constructed in a process of "authentication." Like music, it is a cultural construct imbued with meaning. As Barbara Kirshenblatt-Gimblett and Edward Bruner have written, the issue is "who has the power to represent whom and to determine which representation is authoritative?" (1992, 304; see also Little 1991, 160). Similarly, Regina Bendix, who has framed the study of the discipline of folklore in terms of a quest for the authentic, deconstructs the discursive formation of authenticity as an object while retaining the inherent value of the quest for the authentic (1997, 17). She replaces the question "what is authenticity?" with "who needs authenticity and why?" and "how has authenticity been used?" (ibid., 21).

Folk festivals are riots of preservation vs. invention, the next opposing pair. This dynamic is frequently mediated in the realm of "heritage." According to Barbara Kirshenblatt-Gimblett, "heritage" is "the transvaluation of the obsolete, the mistaken, the outmoded, the dead, and the defunct. Heritage is created through a process of exhibition [which] endows heritage [. . .] with a second life" (1995, 369). I believe the circular nature of her argument is intentional: heritage has recourse to the past (preservation) and creates a new cultural production in the present (invention); heritage is created in performance, and performance gives heritage new life. With over a century of heritage exhibits for tourists in Podhale, one can observe the circular nature of heritage. Performed tradition becomes the tradition; the representation becomes the actuality. Heritage begins to reference heritage. I find Kirshenblatt-Gimblett's theorizing of heritage especially attractive because she does not allow for the familiar dichotomies of history or fantasy; old or new; folklore or fakelore. Heritage is all of these things, or rather the negotiation of the false dichotomies they suggest.

The folklore festival is itself a recent invention that brings these dichotomies face-to-face. In Podhale, the first tourist folklore festivals that took place in the 1930s even then referenced the past. Festival directors and performers today often strive to preserve the past. However, by inventing new performance contexts, tourist festivals preserve music-culture while simultaneously transforming it. Musicians re-invent music and make it live in the very act of performance. Kirshenblatt-Gimblett's theorizing of heritage concentrates on physical objects and locations—things that exist outside of individual humans. Perhaps this accounts for her litany of the moribund characteristics of objects of heritage: ". . . the obsolete, the mistaken, the outmoded, the dead, and the defunct . . ." (ibid.). Here I focus instead on objects of heritage that require warm bodies—musical performers—in an effort to understand why individuals who undertake the powerful act of performing heritage on stage do so.

This dynamic between preservation and invention in the form of folklore festivals is, in my view, an appropriate modern ritual. Rituals are always a dynamic balance of preservation and invention—they are re-invented, performative acts with the intention of preserving a memory, a belief system, a way of life, etc. Annually marking autumn, the Zakopane festival augments other more commonly recognized calendric ceremonies such as harvest rituals and festivals of the church calendar. Unlike these ritual ceremonies, though, the Zakopane festival does not pretend to "influence preternatural entities or forces on behalf of the actors' goals and interests" (Turner 1974[1973], 123). Yet, like past calendric rituals performed to insure the success of crops, this newly created public ceremony also works to insure the continued livelihood of the performers. For example, few Górale in the late twentieth century make their living via highway robbery, a legendary Górale profession celebrated in the *zbójnicki* dance that I describe below, but many Górale do earn a living wage in the tourist industry of which this festival is no small part.

One opposition that drives the Zakopane festival is isolation vs. multiculturalism. By "multiculturalism" I mean a state of being multicultural, not a doctrine or principle. The festival hosts an international collection of performers who travel to Podhale bringing distinct music-cultures, yet symbolically the festival celebrates in striking ways the local Górale culture—a culture that is most often described in ethnographic literature as a product of mountain isolation (for example Ćwiżewicz & Ćwiżewicz 1995; Czekanowska 1990, 84; Kotoński 1956, 18; Wrazen 1988, 48).

The festival is a ceremony rife with symbolic objects and enacted symbols of Górale identity. Though an international festival, little attempt is made to include symbols of identity from different cultures in the festival proceedings and ancillary productions. For example, one's first contact

Figure 4.1 1993 Zakopane festival calendar. Owned and copyrighted by the Zakopane and Tatra Bureau of Promotion.

with the festival is likely to be some form of printed advertisement, such as a poster or calendar. The 1993 calendar features a photograph of the Górale music and dance troupe that will represent Zakopane at the festival that year (see Figure 4.1). The troupe is in full regional costume, the musicians are playing, and a couple dances *po góralsku* or "in the Górale manner." Below the photograph is a calendar with months written in Polish and weeks going from Monday to Sunday in the Polish style, though the bold proclamation "XXV International Festival of Mountain Folklore" is spelled out in English. In the lower portion of the calendar appears the festival logo, a stylized dancing Górale male complete with hat on head and *ciupaga* (long-handled, small-headed ax) in hand raised overhead. One who has spent even a short amount of time in Podhale recognizes the logo figure as a male Górale dancing the *zbójnicki* (highway robber's dance).

The 1995 festival calendar is peculiarly local, featuring caricatures of many local personalities, scenes and situations, and, significantly for the topic of this study, it pokes fun at tourists and Górale's dealings with them. Suggesting the ambivalence many Górale hold for tourists, a wooden gate over the road proclaims *Witojce*, or "welcome" in Górale dialect, but it has been violently attacked with a ciupaga and knives (see Figure 4.2). Lurking behind the gate is a modern-day *zbójnicki*, a highway robber, updating his archetypal *zbójnicki* hat with a ski mask and brandishing a modern pistol. To an outsider the poster must appear ludicrous—to the insider, clever. As with the 1993 calendar, in the foreground are Górale (all caricatures of actual musicians) playing music and dancing. Similar

Figure 4.2 Zakopane festival calendar. Owned and copyrighted by the Zakopane and Tatra Bureau of Promotion.

to the festival logo image of a dancing Górale, this calendar is a symbolic representation of Górale identity: Górale are those Poles who play violin, dance their peculiar dance at the drop of a hat, and live off tourists through various schemes from robbery to heritage.

The dynamic oppositions of isolation vs. multiculturalism, preservation vs. invention, spurious vs. authentic, and tourism vs. ethnography are played out in many ways with physical and enacted symbols under the large, round circus-style tent erected each year for the festival. For example, the physical arrangement of ceremonial space articulates the relationships between tourists, presenters and jurors. Nestled within the round festival tent is a square formed by the four massive posts that lift the tent canvas. The large square area is dead center in the round tent. On the top side of the square is the performance stage, the ceremonial altar on which folklore performances are offered. Directly opposite on the bottom side of the square are the jurors seated behind their long table. Roll the circle around and they are on top, reversing positions exactly with the stage. Within this square, in the space between performers and the official evaluators, is prime seating for audience members, and about half of this seating is reserved for festival organizers, press, special guests, and other dignitaries including visiting ethnographers such as myself. Thus, the jurors are separated from performers by a human buffer, half of whom are tourists, and half officially attached to the festival ceremony in some way. The area behind the jurors, and the remaining two sides of the tent around the central square not occupied by the stage are all filled with tiered, curved bleachers adequate to seat several thousand guests—the public. Thus, the jurors and three sides of the performance stage are surrounded by tourists, by the "public" of this public ceremony. The activities of the jury and the performing folklore troupes all take place "in public," though separated from the public through the ceremonial arrangement of space.

Through the use of electronic amplification, the emcees claim the space within the confines of the tent as Górale with the consistent use of a linguistic code. They speak in the strong Góale dialect that is almost incomprehensible to other Poles. Most Górale, and certainly the emcees of the Zakopane festival, are perfectly capable of speaking standard Polish, but deliberately switch to dialect in settings where Górale identity is important. This deliberate code-switching is used in the service of ethnic identity and is an example of heritage "adding value" by using aspects of Górale identity as symbolic code (see Kirshenblatt-Gimblett 1995, 370–72).

Within this contextual frame of Góraleness, each troupe offers a version of heritage (national, regional, local) specific to an ethnic sub-group—authentic heritage on stage. Troupes that compete in the first category, "authentic," frequently present a staged version of a life-cycle ritual or calendric ritual, such as a wedding, a saint's day or a solstice celebration. One year I witnessed a Turkish troupe enact a circumcision rite complete with squirming adolescent boy. This example highlights the assumption that in so-called "traditional" societies, just about any occasion is pretext for song and dance. The audience is obviously aware that these are performances and not "authentic" events; the Turkish youth was not actually circumcised on stage, nor are couples actually married in the numerous wedding rituals that are presented. However, these productions are self-conscious public statements of ideas and beliefs about heritage. The performances are complex creations reflecting complex histories, just as an actual wedding ritual enacts and references history.

Each evening's performance begins with three men in Górale costume walking on stage and playing a fanfare on long wooden alpine horns. The alpine horns are blaring examples of heritage as theorized by Barbara Kirshenblatt-Gimblett; new life is given to objects whose former use is no longer viable (1995, 369–70). The horns' past function as instruments shepherds used to signal their flocks is obsolete, but they now have been given new life signaling flocks of tourists to the start the festival.[5] As the men finish and carry their horns offstage, a man and women also in Górale costume emerge singing "Górale, górale..." The song "Górale, górale" serves as a Podhalan national anthem and, at least since 1992, has always been published in the festival booklets (see Figure 4.3). It translates:

Górole, górole

Górale, Górale
Górale music
I have been around the whole world
and there is nothing like it anywhere.

Górole, górole
góralsko muzyka
cały świat obyjdzies
nima takiej nika.

Figure 4.3 "Górale, górale" as published in the 1993 Zakopane festival booklet. Owned and copyrighted by the Zakopane and Tatra Bureau of Promotion.

This text can be interpreted in several ways. Perhaps those who have traveled from other mountainous regions of the world for this festival of mountain folklore hear the song as an affirmation of some sort of cosmic link between all mountain people and between all mountain music. "Jesteś Górale tesz" ("You are a mountaineer also"), I have heard Górale say when meeting someone who comes from any hilly area. Other listeners may interpret the song as a claim for the superiority of Podhalan Górale's music. Each listener interprets the song their own way, if they understand the text at all, that is: but to many Podhalan Górale who sing this song, it is an enacted symbol of the Tatras and the music from the Tatras (see also Wrazen 1988, 287).

Characteristics of this anthem that make it an unmistakable symbol of Górale from Podhale include the high descending melody, rubato rhythm and, when sung by Górale, polyphony ending in unison, with men and women singing in the same octave register. The anthem reemerges at a party for the international cast of festival participants on the last evening of the week-long event. In a humorous ritual transformation, each group is invited to perform "Górale, Górale" and to dance a Podhalan-style dance in a final mock contest. That is, each group is invited to try its hand at being a Górale from Podhale. Here the anthem is recognized as a specific example of the music-culture of the festival hosts. The alpine trumpets, the costumes of the emcees, the song that opens each concert, even the dialect used by the emcees, all symbolically mark the festival as Górale.

When symbols or representations of other peoples appear, they are often domesticated into the context of Górale heritage (see Figure 4.4). The official pin of the 1995 Zakopane festival is an example. Racist caricatures of guest performers are domesticated within a geometric motif from Górale material arts—within a symbol of Górale heritage. Though this particular design is common throughout Europe, the Zakopane festival pins are generally based on a Górale motif, or a motif thought to symbolize Górale (see Figure 4.5). I believe that within this context, the design is recognized as specifically Górale.

The featured Górale troupe at the 1992 Zakopane festival included in their performance a dance called *zbójnicki*. This dance embodies the opposition of isolation vs. multiculturalism. Zbójniks

Figure 4.4 Official pin for the 1995 Zakopane festival. Owned and copyrighted by the Zakopane and Tatra Bureau of Promotion.

Figure 4.5 Door detail carved by Józef Styrczula-Maśniak, Kościelisko. Photo by the author.

were legendary robbers compared by Górale to Robin Hood. They roamed the mountains especially during the seventeenth and eighteenth centuries, primarily in the Beskid Mountains and in what is now Slovakia (Brzozowska 1965, 464–65). There is some question whether they were ever actually active in Podhale, and most were certainly Slovaks, not Poles. The legend of the zbójniks spans the multiple cultures that populate the regions surrounding the Tatra Mountains, and they embody the spirit of travel, another required activity if multiculturalism is to be achieved. Ironically, the myth of the zbójniks who once gave lowlanders and potential tourists reason to avoid the mountains—thus contributing to the region's isolation—is now transformed into part of a heritage that attracts tourists.

The multicultural quality of the zbójnicki dance is also evident in the music itself. The tunes and accompaniment patterns of the dance show the influence of Slovakian and Hungarian music. This is most clear in the rhythm of the accompanying violins for about half of the tunes for the zbójnicki sequence. In all other genres of instrumental music associated specifically with Podhale, the accompanying violins play only on the beat, bowing invariably on the quarter-note, as this music is conventionally transcribed. The zbójnicki sequence, however, features tunes accompanied with a lilting pattern created by the accompanying violins who add an eighth-note off-beat on the open A-string. The A-string is activated with a quick up-bow on the off-beat, as I have indicated in Figure 4.6, and as can be heard on the CD, recorded at the festival. The result is not a polka, for the zbójnicki is too slow, but a sound more similar to a Carpathian Slovak version of the Hungarian *csárdás*, a version that employs a double-pulse bowing technique for the first slow half. Though produced with different bowing techniques, the result is a similar eighth-note accompaniment. Like the legend of the zbójniks, the music for the zbójnicki dance comes from across the boarder in Slovakia and what was Hungary before 1918. The closest precedent is probably Hungarian military recruiting dances from the time of the Austrian-Hungarian empire.

The dance is a balance of preservation and invention. Early documentation suggests that the zbójnicki was once danced in a circle by a group of men, but that each dancer improvised an individual part within this basic pattern. Today the dance is choreographed or called by a lead dancer, unlike other Górale dances which allow for great improvisation. As danced today, the zbójnicki

Figure 4.6 "Marsz Chałubińskiego" from Mierczyński (1930). Bowings added. The cited audio CD example is a version of "Marsz Chałubińskiego" played by the song and dance troupe Skalni at the 1992 Zakopane festival. Recording by the author.

requires a troupe—a group of dancers who gather with the expressed intention of learning a dance together. Though this type of folk troupe has roots in nineteenth-century Europe (Konaszkiewicz 1987; Noll 1986, 645–95) and a few were established in Podhale between the two world wars, they did not become common in Podhale until after World War II (Cooley 1999, 154–64; 2005, 127–28). Therefore the infrastructure required to perform the type of zbójnicki dance presented at the Zakopane festival is relatively new. The zbójnicki dance does have recourse to the past in that it celebrates a historic legend, but the dance itself is newly invented for exhibition. It is a very modern dance juxtaposing the past idealized for the present day.

The zbójnicki dance also links the histories of tourism, ethnography and Górale music-culture in an interesting way. In 1888, musical ethnographer Jan Kleczyński published the zbójnicki tune described above and represented as Figure 4.6. In his publication, he explained that he encountered the tune on a tour in the Tatras arranged by a medical doctor named Tytus Chałubiński (1820–89). Dr. Chałubiński was the individual most responsible for developing Zakopane as a tourist destination in the late nineteenth century. He built a sanatorium in Zakopane, and in 1873 was one of the founding members of the *Towarzystwo Tatrzański*[6] (Tatra Society), an organization promoting tourism to Podhale. This zbójnicki tune was apparently his favorite. In fact, Kleczyński wrote that Chałubiński was responsible for spreading the popularity of the tune, even suggesting to Górale how to play the accompaniment. Today this tune is known as "Chałubiński's March" and is standard Górale repertoire. I wonder if the tune would still be played today if not for Chałubiński and Kleczyński and their ethnographic and touristic interventions.

The zbójnicki dance is not just good theater, it is highly symbolic of ideas about Górale, especially Górale men. Zbójniks were independent, brave, strong and loyal. When I asked Stanisława Trebunia and Paweł Staszel, two key performers in the Górale troupe that performed at the 1992 festival, why the zbójnicki legend is important today, they explained that zbójniks did not allow the rich landowners to have control of them (personal conversation, 28 April 1995, Nowy Targ). Zbójniks embody an important historical myth about the settlement of the Tatras, the tallest, most inhospitable mountains in eastern Europe. The myth is that people fled there to avoid becoming the servants of others. It is ironic, then, that the tourist industry, which created the modern context for this symbolic dance of independence, may have succeeded in subduing the legendary independence of Górale more thoroughly than any previous attempts.

Conclusion

The Zakopane festival is an international festival about a local people—a multicultural ritual celebrating one culture. This was confirmed when I asked Elżbieta Chodurska, the director of the Zakopane festival in 1995, about the Festival goals. She replied "the first goal is to show how Górale live. [...] The second goal is for tourists and Górale to see how others live" (interview, 20 July 1995, Zakopane). The international quality of the festival provides an ideal platform from which those Górale who so choose can symbolically perform their difference. Under the premise of gathering together people who share mountain living in common, Górale of Podhale then represent what is unique about their own brand of mountain culture. They ritually create for themselves a distinct identity by referencing heritage through an elaborate framework of symbols, enacted and physical, in the face of a changing world.

The Zakopane festival, like other folk festivals, is a ritual for modern times. The survival of Górale as an ethnic group no longer depends first and foremost on successful crops and healthy livestock—frequently the concern of folk rituals in the past and now the topic of many stage presentations at tourist folk festivals. Today tourism is a leading means of livelihood in Podhale, and folk festivals help ensure that this continues. Such festivals also provide a venue where Górale can reaffirm their identity and their distinctive music-culture in the face of increasing contact with the world beyond Podhale. Festivals emerged in Podhale when tourism was becoming a significant social and economic force in the region, a phenomenon that then and now does much to put Górale in face-to-face contact with the rest of the world. The structures of tourism that have transformed Podhale from a relatively isolated mountain region into a tourist destination at the same time provide Górale with a means for effectively preserving their music-culture and ethnic group. Not only does interpreting tourist folk festivals as ritual position them meaningfully in the present, it enables one to better understand the power and meaning of these festivals beyond their value as entertainment.

Notes

1. "Podhale" literally means any piedmont area, but here I use the term to refer specifically to *Skalny Podhale* ("Rocky Piedmont"), the Polish Tatra region. Research in Poland for this essay was funded in part by the American Council of Learned Societies, Brown University, the International Research and Exchanges Board, and the Kosciuszko Foundation. I wish to thank Regina Bendix, Mark DeWitt and Linda Fujie for their helpful comments on earlier versions of this essay.
2. Following Louise Wrazen (1991, 175), when writing in English, I use the plural Polish word *Górale* as both noun and adjective, singular and plural. In Polish *Górale* refers to all from mountainous areas. However, here I use the word specifically for people of the Polish Tatra region.
3. These organizations were founded before World War I during the Podhale regional movement discussed briefly above. They remain important cultural organizations today.
4. "Jak ja prowadziłam ten festiwal, to ja się tak starałm, żeby górale nie zapomnieli o tym, że są góralkami" (interview with Krzystyna Słbodzińska, 20 July 1995, Zakopane).
5. For a description of the alpine horn's structure and use in Podhale. see Chybiński 1961, 333–44.
6. The society was first called *Galicyjskie Towarzystwo Tatrzańskie* (Galicia Tatra Society), was changed to *Towarzystwo Tatrzański* (Tatra Society) in 1874, and was then called *Polskie Towarzystwo Tatrzańskie* (Polish Tatra Society) from 1920 to 1950, when the organization joined with *Polskie Towarzystwo Krajoznawcze* (Polish Sightseeing Society) and changed its name to *Polskie Towarzystwo Turystyczno-Krajoznawcze* (Polish Touring-Sightseeing Society), as it remains today.

References

Baumann, Max Peter. 1996. "Folk Music Revival: Concepts Between Regression and Emancipation." *The World of Music* 38(3):71–86.

Beckerman, Michael. 1996. "Kundera's Musical *Joke* and 'Folk' Music in Czechoslovakia, 1948–?" In *Retuning Culture: Musical Changes in Central and Eastern Europe,* edited by Mark Slobin, 37-53. Durham, NC: Duke University Press.

Bendix, Regina. 1985. *Progress and Nostalgia.* Berkeley: University of California Press.

———. 1989. "Tourism and Cultural Displays: Inventing Traditions for Whom?" *Journal of American Folklore.* 102(404):131–46.

———. 1997. *In Search of Authenticity: The Formation of Folklore Studies.* Madison: The University of Wisconsin Press.

Brozek, Andrzej. 1985. *Polish Americans: 1954–1939.* Warsaw: Interpress.

Brzozowska, Teresa. 1965. "Zbójnictwo." In *Słownik Folkloru Polskiego,* edited by Juliana Krzyżanowskiego, 464–65. Warsaw: Wiedza Powszechna.

Chodurska, Elżbieta. 1996 *Festiwal '96: XXVIII Międzynarodowy Festiwal Folkloru Ziem Górskich* [Festival program book]. Zakopane: Urząd Miasta.

Chybiński, Adolf. 1961 *O polskiej muzyce ludowej: Wybór prac etnograficznych.* Edited by Ludwik Bielawski. Warsaw: Polskie Wydawnictwo Muzyczne.

Cohen, Erik. 1984. "The Sociology of Tourism: Approaches, Issues, and Findings." *Annual Review of Sociology* 10:373–92.

Connerton, Paul. 1989. *How Societies Remember.* Cambridge: Cambridge University Press.

Cooley, Timothy J. 1999. "Ethnography, Tourism, and Music-culture in the Tatra Mountains: Negotiated Representations of Polish Górale Ethnicity." Ph.D. dissertation, Brown University.

———. 2000. "Constructing an 'Authentic' Folk Music of the Polish Tatras." In *After Chopin: Essays in Polish Music,* edited by Maria Trochimczyk, 243–61. Los Angeles: Polish Music History Series, Vol. 6.

———. 2005. *Making Music in the Polish Tatras: Tourists, Ethnographers, and Mountain Musicians.* Bloomington: Indiana University Press.

——— and Dick Spottswood, comps. 1997a. *Fire In The Mountains: Polish Mountain Fiddle Music. Vol. 1. The Karol Stoch Band.* Compact disc recording with notes. Newton, N.J.:Yazoo, a division of Shanachie Entertainment Corp.

———. 1997b. *Fire In The Mountains: Polish Mountain Fiddle Music. Vol. 2. The Great Highland Bands.* Compact disc recording with notes. Newton, NJ: Yazoo, a division of Shanachie Entertainment Corp.

Ćwiżewicz, Krzysztof, and Barbara Ćwiżewicz. 1995. *Music of the Tatra Mountains: The Trebunia Family Band.* Compact disc recording with notes. Monmouth: Nimbus Records.

Czekanowska, Anna. 1990. *Polish Folk Music: Slavonic Heritage, Polish Tradition. Contemporary Trends.* Cambridge: Cambridge University Press.

Dawson, Andrew H. 1991. "Poland." In *Tourism and Economic Development in Eastern Europe and the Soviet Union,* edited by Derek R. Hall, 190–202. London: Belhaven Press.

DeWitt, Mark F., ed. 1999. "Music, Travel, and Tourism." Thematic issue of *The World of Music* 41(3).

Durkheim, Emil. 1915. *The Elementary Forms of the Religious Life.* Translated by J. W. Swain. London: George Allen and Unwin.

Dutkowa, Renata, ed. 1991. *Zakopane: czterysta lat dziejów.* Vol. 2. Kraków: Krajowa Agencja Wydawnicza.

Errington, Frederick, and Deborah Gewertz. 1989. "Tourism and Anthropology in a Post-Modern World" *Oceania* 60(1):37–54.

Gellner, Ernest. 1998. *Language and Solitude: Wittgenstein, Malinowski and the Habsburg Dilemma.* Cambridge: Cambridge University Press.

Grünewald, Rodrigo de Azeredo. 2002. "Tourism and Cultural Revival." *Annals of Tourism Research* 29(4):1004-1021.

Hagedorn, Katherine J. 2001. *Divine Utterances: The Performance of Afro-Cuban Santería.* Washington: Smithsonian Institution Press.

Jackowski, Antoni. 1991. "Rozwój funkcji turystycznej Zakopanego w okresie międzywojennym (1918–1939)." In *Zakopane: czterysta lat dziejów,* edited by R. Dutkowa, 22–36.

Kaeppler, Adrienne, and Olive Lewin, eds. 1988. *Come Mek Me Hol' Yu Han': The Impact of Tourism on Traditional Music.* Papers presented at the Fourth International Colloquium of the International Council for Traditional Music held in Kingston and Newcastle, Jamaica, 10–14 July 1986. Kingston: Jamaica Memory Bank.

Kirshenblatt-Gimblett, Barbara. 1988. "Authenticity and Authority in the Representation of Culture: The Poetics and Politics of Tourist Production." In *Kulturkontakt, Kulturkonflikt: Zur Erfahrung des Fremden,* edited by Ina-Maria Greverus, Konrad Köstlin, Heinz Schilling, 59–69. Frankfurt am Main: Institut für Kulturanthropologie und Europäische Ethnologie. Universität Frankfurt am Main.

———. 1995. "Theorizing Heritage." *Ethnomusicology* 39(3):367–79.

——— and Edward M. Bruner. 1992. "Tourism." In *Folklore, Cultural Performances, and Popular Entertainments: A Communications-centered Handbook,* edited by Richard Bauman, 300–307. New York: Oxford University Press.

Kleczyński, Jan. 1883. "Pieśń zakopańska." *Echo Muzyczne i Teatralne* 1:9–10.

———. 1884a. "Zakopane i jego pieśni." *Echo Muzyczne i Teatralne* 41:419–21, 42:429–30, 44:447–48, 46:468–70.

———. 1884b. "Wycieczka po melodie." *Echo Muzyczne i Teatralne* 56:567–69, 58:588–90, 60:610–11, 62:631–32, 64:653.

———. 1888. "Melodye zakopiańskie i podhalańskie." *Pamiętnik Towarzystwa Tatrzańskiego* 12:39–102.

Kolberg, Oskar. 1968. "Góry i Podgórze," part I. Dzieła Wszystkie. Vol. 44. Wrocław: Polskie Towarzystwo Ludoznawcze.

———. 1968b. "Góry i Podgórze," part II. Dzieła Wszystkie. Vol. 45. Wrocław: Polskie Towarzystwo Ludoznawcze.

Kulczycki, Zbigniew. 1970. *Zarys historii turystyki w Polsce.* Warszawa: Sport i Turystyka.

Konaszkiewicz, Zofia. 1987. *Funkcje wychowawcze dziecięcych i młodzieżowych zespołów muzycznych*. Warsaw: Centralny Ośrodek Metodyki Upowszechniania Kultury.

Kostyal, K.M. 1995. "Eternal Poland: Kraków and the Carpathians." *National Geographic Traveler* 12(2):54–74.

Kotoński, Włodzimierz. 1956. *Góralski i Zbójnicki: Tańce Górali Podhalańskich*. Kraków: Polskie Wydawnictwo Muzyczne.

Little, Kenneth. 1991. "On Safari: The Visual Politics of a Tourist Representation." In *The Varieties of Sensory Experience: A Sourcebook in the Anthropology of the Senses*, edited by David Howes, 148–63. Toronto: University of Toronto Press.

Lukes, Steven. 1975. "Political Ritual and Social Integration." *Sociology* 9:289–308.

MacAloon, John J., ed. 1984. *Rite. Drama, Festival, Spectacle: Rehearsals Toward a Theory of Cultural Performance*. Philadelphia: Institute for the Study of Human Issues.

MacCannell, Dean. 1989[1976]. *The Tourist: A New Theory of the Leisure Class*. New York: Schocken Books.

Malczak, Antoni. 1992. " Święto Dzieci Gór." Interview in newsletter *Latawice* (July–August). Nowy Sącz: Wojewódzki Ośrodek Kultury.

Mierczyński, Stanisław. 1930. *Muzyka Podhala*. Lwów: Książnica - Atlas.

Noll, William Henry. 1986. *Peasant Music Ensembles in Poland: A Culture History*. Ph.D. dissertation, University of Washington.

Nuñez, T. A. 1963. "Tourism, Tradition and Acculturation: Weekendismo in a Mexican Village." *Ethnology* 2(3):347–52.

Paryski, Witold H. 1991. "Powstanie Zakopiańskiego Ośrodka Turystycznego (do 1914)." ("Origins of Zakopane as a tourist center [to 1914].") In *Zakopane: czterysta lat dziejów*, edited by R. Dutkowa, 7–21.

Pertierra, Raul. 1987. "Ritual and the Constitution of Social Structure." *Mankind* 17(3):199–211.

Peterson, Richard A. 1997. *Creating Country Music: Fabricating Authenticity*. Chicago: University of Chicago Press.

Reinfuss, Roman. 1971. *Jesień Tatrzańska: Migawki festiwalowe*. Kraków: Polskie Wydawnictwo Muzyczne.

Rice, Timothy. 1994. *May It Fill Your Soul: Experiencing Bulgarian Music*. Chicago: University of Chicago Press.

Ronström, Owe. 1996. "Revival Reconsidered." *The World of Music* 38(3):5–20.

Sarkissian, Margaret. 2000. *D'Albuquerque's Children: Performing Tradition in Malaysia's Portuguese Settlement*. Chicago: University of Chicago Press.

Schechner, Richard. 1983. *Performative Circumstances: From the Avant Garde to Ramlila*. Calcutta: Seagull Books.

Sharp. Cecil J. 1954. *English Folk Song: Some Conclusions* (third ed., revised by Maud Karpeles with an appreciation by Ralph Vaughan Williams). London: Methuen.

Smith, Valene L., ed. 1977. *Hosts and Guests: The Anthropology of Tourism*. Philadelphia: University of Pennsylvania Press.

Suppan, Wolfgang. 1976. "Research on Folk Music in Austria since 1800." *Yearbook of the International Folk Music Council* 8:117–29.

———, ed. 1991. *Schladminger Gespräche zum Thema Musik und Tourismus*. Tutzing: Hans Schneider. 25–33.

Turner, Victor. 1974[1973]. "Symbols in African Ritual." In *Readings in Anthropology*, 123–28. Annual Editions series. Guilford, CT: Dushkin Publishing Group. First published in *Science* 179(1973):1100–1105.

———. 1984. "Liminality and the Performative Genres." In MacAloon 1984: 19–41.

Warszyńska, Jadwiga. 1991. "Ruch turystyczny w Zakopanem po drugie wojnie światowej." In Dutkowa 1991:37–52.

Whisnant, David E. 1983. *All That is Native & Fine: The Politics of Culture in an American Region*. Chapel Hill: The University of North Carolina Press.

Wrazen, Louise. 1988. *The Góralski of the Polish Highlanders: Old World Musical Traditions from a New World Perspective*. Ph.D. dissertation, University of Toronto.

———. 1991. "Traditional Music Performance Among Górale in Canada." *Ethnomusicology* 35(2):173–93.

Wytrwal, Joseph A. 1977. *Behold: The Polish-Americans*. Detroit: Endurance Press.

Zborowski, Juliusz. 1972. *Pisma Podhalańskie*. Vol. 1. Janusza Berghauzena, ed. Kraków: Wydawnictwo Literackie, 329–46.

Part III

Gender and Sexuality

5

Taiko and the Asian/American Body
Drums, *Rising Sun*, and the Question of Gender

Deborah Wong

Taiko is an ancient tradition of drumming with Buddhist roots; it combines music and the martial arts, and it is both very loud and visually exciting due to the choreography—swinging arms, leaping bodies—that is part and parcel of the music. I focus here on issues of gender and race as explored through the transnational movement of *taiko*.[1] The majority of *taiko* players in the U.S. are Japanese American or Asian American; I got involved with it because it spoke to me as an Asian American, and I am concerned here with the cultural dynamics of race and ethnicity as they intersect with gender as vectors of difference. American audiences do not, however, necessarily see *taiko* in the ways that Asian American performers do. The potential in *taiko* for slippage between the Asian and the Asian American body is staggering. Paul Yoon has written about the ways that American audiences map the Asian (and more specifically the Japanese) onto the bodies that perform *taiko*, documenting White Americans who come up to Japanese American and Asian American *taiko* players assuming that they are Japanese, sometimes even trying to speak to them in classroom Japanese (1999). *Taiko* excites an expectation of the foreign in the White American spectator, and I have played in altogether too many performances where this was precisely what was counted upon.

Let me offer an example: a scene from the film *Rising Sun*, made in 1993, starring Sean Connery and Wesley Snipes, directed and produced by Philip Kaufman, music by Toru Takemitsu, based on the novel by Michael Crichton. San Francisco Taiko Dojo appears in the fourth scene of *Rising Sun* (about six minutes into the film) playing their signature piece, "Tsunami."[2] The physical and sonic presence of the *taiko* players creates a stage for xenophobic anxiety over Japanese corporate conspiracy; their ominous strength completely pervades this key scene. The sound of the drums is a sonic path that draws the viewer into the party and into the entire framework of the film, wherein Japanese businessmen adroitly "manage" their American counterparts with bicultural acumen even as they remain deeply, unknowably foreign, strange, and ruthless.

We have just seen Eddie Sakamura and Cheryl, the high-class White call girl, in her apartment; she's nude, sitting at her make-up table and watching the news on television. He's just stepped out of the shower and wears only a towel. She says, "I don't get you, Eddie," and, deadpan, he says, "So what." With the camera still on his face, faint *taiko* drumming suddenly wells up on the soundtrack for about two seconds and *bam*, we're into the next scene: three members of San Francisco Taiko

Dojo on-stage, filling the screen. They're playing furiously: two young men wearing Japanese workers' aprons (*harakake*) without shirts underneath, and Tanaka-sensei, bare-chested. Cut away to White guests in black tie and evening gowns outside—two couples—climbing the steps outside a skyscraper in Little Tokyo; they're talking amongst themselves, reminding each other to "bow when you're bowed to." The camera pans up the front of the dark skyscraper, which is festooned with a banner reading "Nakamoto Towers Grand Dedication." Inside, the elevator doors open and when we see two geisha bow to us, we realize that we're seeing the scene from the perspective of the White guests. Again, they remind each other, "bow when you're bowed to," and they bow back to the geisha. They move into the crowd, which includes lots of Japanese men and lots of White American women. The camera lingers for a second on a group posing for a snapshot: three small elderly Japanese men in tuxedos with five beautiful White women standing behind them and towering over them. In the soundtrack, we suddenly hear a loud *kakegoe*, "Uhhhhhhh!" One of the new arrivals says to his friend, "*Taiko* drums!" His friend says, "Eh?" He leans over to explain, "*Taiko* drums! Long ago, they were used to drive away evil spirits." His friend says, "Oh," and the camera cuts back to the *taiko* group. Tanaka-sensei is now pounding on a metal bar, creating a fusillade of brilliant sound.[3] The camera cuts to Eddie Sakamura looking at his watch with an *odaiko* player in profile behind him who looks tremendously powerful. Eddie slips up the stairs. The sound of *taiko* continues, but a *shakuhachi* trill is laid on top of it, and the effect is suspenseful and a bit foreboding.

We're now in the boardroom, which is dark except for a few isolated floodlights. Cheryl is there; she says, "Come here," and a man (who we see from behind) grabs her, lifts her, and she wraps her legs around him. The sound of *taiko* continues beneath increasingly foreboding *shakuhachi* and synthesizer sounds. Cheryl says, "No, here," and gestures for the man to carry her over to the huge table that fills the room. From above, we see him plunge his face into her groin, but we still can't see who he is; we assume it's Eddie Sakamura. She's moaning.

The *taiko* is suddenly loud and we're back downstairs at the party: the face of a cocktail waitress fills the screen, staring at us, her geisha-like make-up making her seem all the more impassive. She pivots and the camera pans to the face of one of the White businessmen we followed into the party: he gazes at her and then looks aside in distaste.

The camera cuts full-screen to San Francisco Taiko Dojo on stage. The huge *odaiko* at center stage is now being played by a muscular young man. Cut to the Nakamoto CEO's assistant, who is listening to something coming in on his earphone, hand cupped to ear, looking worried; ominous *shakuhachi* again, and he exchanges a significant look with the White assistant. Back to a full-screen view of the *taiko* group, and Tanaka-sensei is now on the huge *odaiko*: he stands in a frozen *kata* and then strikes, DON! (pause) DON! (pause) DON! Cut to a close-up of Cheryl's crotch, and we see a flash of her pubic hair as the man rips off her underwear. She sinks back onto the table and he tears open her black dress; her breasts spill out and he begins to pump at her with her legs over his shoulders. "Come on," she says. Fullscreen, the *taiko* ensemble, to a close-up of Tanaka-sensei on the *odaiko*. We see him from the back. *Don don don don don don don don, doko doko doko doko.* Back to the Cheryl's face under the spotlight, then a shot of the man from behind and her legs wrapped around him. "Yes," she says, and he folds his hands around her neck. She's moaning. Cut to a close-up of Tanaka-sensei from the back. Cut to the man's hands around Cheryl's neck as she gasps, "Yes, oh yes, oh yes, oh yes." A phone ringing carries us sonically into the next scene as the camera cuts to Wesley Snipes answering the phone, and the sequence is over.

Tanaka-sensei is unstoppable—well, *we* know who he is, though to "the viewer," he is just a generic *taiko* player. We never see the face of the man with Cheryl but the camera and the soundtrack have made it utterly clear that he is Japanese. The huge round face of the *odaiko* is visually analogous to the round spotlight on the boardroom table, and Tanaka-sensei's spectacularly strong work on the drum amplifies (visually and aurally) the man's work on Cheryl. It's not terribly subtle: we see Tanaka-sensei from behind, we see the man from behind. The militarism, volume, and masculine strength of *taiko* = the man's sexual conquest of the beautiful White woman. We get it. Tanaka-sensei's muscled back and arms is the perfect eye candy for the trope of the martial: he is beautiful, invincible, and deeply threatening in his strength and perfection. The entire scene "works" because of its reversal of a coupling more familiar to the American gaze, i.e., the White American man and the Japanese woman, popularized and romanticized in the 1950s through such films and novels as *Sayonara* (1957). As Traise Yamamoto has written, that interracial relationship was constructed as "somewhat acceptable—or at least safely titillating" (1999, 27) because it acted out Japan's defeat in World War II in specifically gendered and ethnicized ways; the Japanese woman had at that point undergone at least a century's worth of Western construction as a "metonymic representation of Japan itself" (23) in need of rescue by Western men. In *Rising Sun,* the gaze figures the sexually aggressive and perverse man as Japanese via *taiko* (both its sound and its visual militarism). The White American woman receives the decidedly unsafe titillation of sexual congress with a Japanese man and more: he overcomes her in ways that could not be more menacing. We know, at some level, that this is an inversion of a relationship we would find satisfying if the ethnicities were reversed. In the film's denouement, we discover that we were mistaken: the White woman's lover was a White American senator. But we are also tricked, as it turns out that he didn't kill her—he was engaging in a consensual act of sexual asphyxiation meant to heighten her pleasure. In a clumsy and confusing scene meant to tie up the loose ends, we learn that a *second* man came in and finished her off—by strangulation—as she lay alone on the table recovering from her pleasure. He was Japanese! No, he was White American! But by then we are so wholly convinced that the Japanese assistant to the CEO has acted out of perverse, knee-jerk loyalty to the company that we hardly care when the White American assistant is thrown out of a skyscraper by *yakuza* into a pool of wet cement. We know who really killed her. Crichton has "proven" that he's not a xenophobe by playing with ethnicity and nationality, but we've still gotten the point.[4]

And it was *taiko* that got us there. My teacher, Rev. Tom Kurai, says that that key scene in *Rising Sun* is a completely inappropriate representation of *taiko* despite San Francisco *Taiko* Dojo's fine performance; how could they know what would happen in the editing room? *Taiko* is visually and sonically constructed as both masculine and sinister: this particular confluence of gender and race presented through *taiko* is built up out of older tropes that 'work' because they are so terribly familiar. The (White) viewer of *Rising Sun* is clearly meant to understand *taiko* as a mimetic standin for Japan, and a masculinist, dangerous Japan at that. I am asking an old and difficult question: how can a single cultural form—*taiko*—be read in such completely different ways by different groups of people?

Taiko players tend to have opinions about that scene in *Rising Sun* and, as far as I can tell, Japanese American and Asian American *taiko* enthusiasts aren't alone in identifying the film's problems: *taiko* players generally (whether of Asian descent or not) focus on the *taiko* scene as a microcosm of the film's xenophobic narrative. As one *taiko* musician, Martha Durham of Austin *Taiko*, wrote to me:[5]

> I saw the *taiko* scenes in the previews 7 or 8 times before the movie was released. So the racy encounter mix wasn't part of my first experience with the *taiko* scenes. When the movie was released and I saw the racy scenes mixed in, I was uncomfortable with those scenes, I thought the storyline was dark and negative.

Durham went on to say that the excitement of seeing San Francisco Taiko Dojo play in the film led her to take a *taiko* class and that she and her husband have been involved in *taiko* ever since:

> Since many people have seen the movie, when I tell someone that I play *taiko*, and they get a blank look on their face, I ask them if they have seen *Rising Sun*. Many have, and they all remember the drumming more than the racy scenes that were mixed in with it. I have to think

we can't be the only ones who were introduced to *taiko* by that movie, and even though the storyline scenes were violent, seeing *taiko* played was worth the viewing, and, in my opinion, a boost to awareness of *taiko* in this country.

Whereas Durham felt that *taiko* basically transcended the film's narrative devices, Tiffany Tamaribuchi, the director of Sacramento Taiko Dan, questioned the juxtapositions created in the editing room:

From what I understand SFTD was not aware that the footage was going to be intercut that way and [Tanaka] Sensei wasn't too happy about it when he found out. Personally, I was disappointed with the movie and disappointed with the way in which the scene was presented. I think the scene with Kodo in "The Hunted" played much better, but in both of the movies Taiko seemed kind of forced in to the story line. Understanding that Taiko is very powerful and primal, I can see why the director might choose to intermix it with a sexually themed "murder" scene, but to me it seemed in poor taste and really kind of disrespectful to intercut the footage the way they did from the drumming to the sex to Tanaka-sensei's face to the sex, etc. I think this is in part due to the fact that I studied under Tanaka-sensei, but even still, just as a fan of Taiko it was just disappointing to see. Taiko has always been a very uplifting and spiritually moving thing for me. The scene didn't match my image of what Taiko is or what its potential as an art form is.

Kenny Endo (Director, Taiko Center of the Pacific) took a pragmatic approach to the matter, suggesting that intervention sometimes involves compromising:[6]

All of us in the music, performing arts, or entertainment business rely on getting gigs to survive. I talked to Tanaka-sensei during the filming of that movie and he was torn between the context that his drumming was used and the exposure that a major motion picture would give to the art of *taiko*. If he didn't do it, they would have asked someone else. I supported his decision and would have probably done the same had I been asked.

Roy Hirabayashi, managing director of San Jose Taiko, asked some very pointed questions:

[The film] was a very controversial issue when it was being filmed. The movie came out at a time when Japan bashing was at its peak. We were asked if we wanted to work on the film, but we turned the project down.
 Did the movie help the "*taiko* movement"? It is hard to say.
 Did the movie project *taiko* in the best light and image? No.
 Did the movie continue to project a negative stereotype? Yes.

In short, *taiko* players' responses to the scene offer a range of indictments ranging from mild complaints that the framing narrative was "dark and negative" to more focused accusations of racist stereotyping. Loyalty to Tanaka-sensei is also quite evident in two of the four responses. All four perspectives suggest that *taiko* players have a strong sense for how representational practices can reframe and redirect meaning in in/appropriate ways, even with a figure as iconic as Seiichi Tanaka. How far they are willing to critique or to assert control is another matter. As bell hooks writes (1992, 128), "While every black woman I talked to was aware of racism, that awareness did not automatically correspond with politicization, the development of an oppositional gaze." hooks suggests that interventionist response can take a wide range of forms, from critical spectatorship to the creation of alternative texts to the maintenance of counter-memories, and that politicization may lie anywhere along the way. For *taiko* players, any politicized discussion of *Rising Sun* is too closely situated near Seiichi Tanaka, entangling matters of authority with questions of representation and thus creating a conundrum.

I now need to carry this matter of heterosexist stereotyping into a broader consideration of *taiko*'s intersection with the construction of Asian/American gender and its reading by audiences. The performance costumes worn by my group, the Taiko Center of Los Angeles, are specifically and authentically Japanese: *hachimaki* (headbands), *tabi* (sock-like shoes), bright Japanese shirts, and the kind of apron worn by Japanese craftspersons (*harakake*). I have moments of confusion, wondering why I have to become so Japanese in order to feel Asian American, and why the identity politics of our performances are so easily and consistently misread by audiences. Paul Yoon has addressed these issues through his experiences as a Korean American member of Soh Daiko in New York City, arguing that Soh Daiko (and any *taiko* group) presents all too many possibilities to audiences every time they perform (1999):

> Within the context of the United States, Soh Daiko, and the music they play, Taiko, can be variously constructed (construed) as Japanese, Japanese American, or just Asian (Oriental), rather than or over and above being Asian American. Without complete control over perception, the members of Soh Daiko must contend with, work with, and/or manipulate numerous identities and assumptions, some favorable, others less desirable. For various audiences the music of Soh Daiko creates spaces that are conceived of as Japanese, Japanese American, Asian American, or Asian (Oriental) and in some of these cases these situations are directly counter to either their intentions or desires.

Yoon suggests that Soh Daiko relies on certain kinds of strategic essentialism (*a la* Spivak) to slip out from under the orientalist gaze, and part of me wishes this were as simple as it sounds. Reception is consistently under-theorized as a space filled with both risk and potential—the risk of misunderstanding, and the potential for activist response (i.e., intervention). Given the susceptibility of American audiences to orientalist pleasure—their willingness to give themselves over to it—I must ask what happens when performers think they are saying one thing and audiences hear something else entirely, and whose responsibility it is to redirect the reading. bell hooks argues for a performative recuperation of the gaze (1992), but I am not only interested in witnessing Asian American empowerment through spectatorship—I am fairly certain that that happens routinely through *taiko*, though I think its specific linkage to "the Japanese" bears scrutiny.

How a single expressive practice can bear the weight of completely different interpretations is the conundrum: Asian American audiences willingly place themselves in the loop of the performative (they see empowered performers, therefore they feel empowered, therefore they *are* empowered), and meanwhile, non-Asian spectators shift easily into the orientalist gaze. Kondo addresses the ways that Michael Crichton used her monograph *Crafting Selves* to create a bounded, racist picture of Japanese culture in his novel and screenplay, and she reflects on how her stint as dramaturge for Anna Deavere Smith's *Twilight: Los Angeles 1992* helped her address the "problem" of reception and its uncontrollability (1997, 250):

> *Twilight* foregrounded for me the salience of the intentional fallacy, for authorial/ dramaturgical intention could never guarantee meaning. In the case of Crichton's reading of my book, the intentional fallacy seems all the more fallacious, for authorial intention not only failed to guarantee meaning, but the text generated meanings antithetical to authorial intent. Once released in language, the subject-positions, histories, and (structurally overdetermined) interpretive schemas of readers and audiences shape reception. We can but do our best to anticipate certain overdetermined readings and preempt them, taking seriously authorial responsibility and attempting to do battle with the misappropriations of our work.

In short, authorial responsibility doesn't stop at the end of the book or the foot of the stage, but the key problem of how, then, to work against the uncontrollable and the overdetermined is the question.

Why are the majority of *taiko* players in North America women? In a cross-cultural context, it is extremely unusual for women to play drums, let alone to specialize in them, and it is even more unusual in the Asian traditional arts (with the notable exception of Korea). A significant number of Japanese American women (and Asian American women generally) are drawn to *taiko* for empowerment, and I don't think they do so in an attempt to map the masculine/menacing onto themselves. Rev. Tom frequently notes that the majority of his students are women—as many as three out of four, and this is true for many *taiko* groups in North America. Two of the leading professional Japanese groups, Kodo and Sukeroku, have a majority of men, but amateur *taiko* groups in Japan also contain large numbers of women, though not as significantly as in the U.S. and Canada. As Mark Tusler notes (1999, 6):

> Since the establishment of *taiko* ensembles in the late 1950s in Japan, women have become increasingly active as *taiko* players. Kijima Taiko of Japan is all women. In North America it appears that more women play *taiko* than men; only 6 out of 25 performing members in the San Jose Taiko are men; approximately two-thirds are women in the Sacramento Taiko Dan, a group founded and led by a woman; the LAMT [Los Angeles Matsuri Taiko] is about even; Soh Daiko in New York City is approximately three-quarters women; the San Francisco Taiko Dojo, a group with around 30 to 40 members, appears almost even; and so on. The involvement of women in North American *taiko* drumming has played an important role in the development of identity for Japanese American women; gender has therefore been an important articulating factor for the continued success of *taiko* groups.

I would venture to guess that the qualities made threatening in *Rising Sun* are particularly attractive to—and transformed by—Asian American women: strength, control, loudness. Certainly these qualities speak to Asian American men in similar ways: given historical tropes that have consistently feminized Asian men (e.g., as addressed in David Henry Hwang's *M. Butterfly*), the strength and power expressed through *taiko* holds a particular performative appeal for Asian American men. Nevertheless, the overwhelming presence of Asian American women in North American *taiko* speaks to a certain reconfiguration of the Asian American woman's body and to a claim made on sonic and social space. As Mary Baba, one of my Japanese American classmates, suggested:[7]

> The *taiko* is a very powerful instrument, it gives a feel of strength and command. In this day and age, even with opportunities for equality, women need outlets to feel power. Playing the *taiko* fulfills a need.

Baba's emphasis on "strength and command" is notable, as the transformation of the Asian/Asian American woman from a delicate, submissive stereotype to a figure capable of moving with power and authority is clearly the appeal. The struggle with silence is also addressed head-on through *taiko*, whether through the sound of the drum itself or through the realization of *ki* as *kakegoe*. Mitsuye Yamada (1983, 36–37) has written at length about the link between Asian American women's silence and invisibility, suggesting that stereotyping and reinscription are deeply entangled:

> [W]e Asian American women have not admitted to ourselves that we *were* oppressed. We, the visible minority that is invisible. [...] I had supposed I was practicing passive resistance while being stereotyped, but it was so passive no one noticed I was resisting; it was so much my expected role that it ultimately rendered me invisible. [...] When the Asian American woman is lulled into believing that people perceive her as being different from other Asian

women (the submissive, subservient, ready-to-please, easy-to-get-along-with Asian woman), she is kept comfortably content with the state of things. She becomes ineffectual in the milieu in which she moves. The seemingly apolitical middle class woman and the apolitical Asian woman constituted a double invisibility.

Similarly, Sonia Shah has written that Asian American women searching for forms of expression were continually brought short by first-wave feminist models that located Asian American feminist responses as "American" (i.e., White) rather than Asian; instead, Shah calls for a "bicultural feminism" or a "pan-Asian feminist agenda" that would work against the Black/White paradigms driving American feminism and engage with "our own form of cultural schizophrenia, from the mixed and often contradictory signals about priorities, values, duty, and meaning our families and greater communities convey" (1994, 154).

I would argue too that part of *taiko*'s appeal lies in its redefinition of the Asian American woman's body and its dialogic relationship to "women's work"—i.e., the nimble fingers behind the clothing and computer industries.[8] The contained movement of women's fingers vs. the woman's body filling space with large gestures; the closed doors of the sweatshop vs. the stage; women taking orders vs. the woman stepping forward, in "leisure," into furious movement. *Taiko* opens up the body: the legs are wide apart and the movement of the arms commands a large personal space. How many of us were taught to keep our knees together and to speak softly? *Taiko* provides alternative ways of moving through physical and sonic space that are passionately appealing to Asian American women for real reasons, but it does so while creating ties of cooperation and collaboration. I am reminded of the only time in a *taiko* class when I found myself intensely irritated, angry beyond reason. Rev. Tom was absent and one of the advanced students in the class, Elaine (a Sansei in her forties), was leading us on *shime*. We were having trouble staying together during a particular phrase in a piece and Antoine, a Swiss man in his twenties, suddenly said, I'll play *kane*. The *kane* is only played by the person in charge, usually Rev. Tom. We tried it again, with Elaine still on *shime* but Antoine now playing *kane*. He slouched against one of the pews, looking down at the *kane* as he played fast and loud, driving all of us. In fact, it was too fast, though he certainly played more "authoritatively" than Elaine, so we were even more ragged. We stopped and people made various cautious comments ("That wasn't much better, was it?"); of course, no one was going to do or say anything confrontational, though I felt that Antoine's decision to seize the *kane* was inexcusably so. After waiting a moment to see if the situation would resolve itself, I said to him, "Maybe it's better with just Elaine." He paused, and just when I thought he was going to argue with me, he shrugged and put down the *kane*. Thinking about it later and trying to sort out my own irritation, I recognized the racialized and gendered shape of the encounter: Asian American woman, White (European) man. He challenged her authority despite her greater experience and in fact her twenty years' seniority; he didn't maintain *kata* or eye contact with her *or* the rest of us when he played; he disregarded—challenged—both the social construction of authority in the class and the group dynamic that we have all grown to depend upon. And it left me completely unsettled.

The women I know who play *taiko* do not necessarily self-identify as feminists, but I do think that *taiko* is a sounded bodily channel for addressing the on-going gendered dialectic of the Asian vs. the Asian American. I don't know how *taiko* speaks to Japanese women or to gendered social practices in Japan; this in itself would make a fascinating study. In a sense, I only have half the picture of *taiko* as a transnational gendered phenomenon, but it is impossible to write about Asian American *taiko* without addressing its elisions and distinctions from the Asian body, and the specific spin that all this has for Asian American women. As the anthropologist Aihwa Ong has written, emancipation-in-diaspora is not a given, nor does feminist ethnography offer a denationalized set of critical practices unless we insist that it do so. Instead, Ong suggests that we develop a "dialectic of disowning and reowning, of critical agency shifting between transnational sites of power" which can result in "a deliberate cultivation of a mobile consciousness" (1995, 367–8). *Taiko* is not a matter of Asian American women "rediscovering" a certain kind of Asian body but is rather an intricate process of exploring a Japanese bodily aesthetic and refashioning/re-embodying its potential for Asian American women. In this sense, I am locating an erotics of *taiko* that reclaims the territory mapped out by *Rising Sun*. How "deliberately" any of us do this isn't really the question: the passionate involvement that *taiko* can instill is simply an example of how belief, understanding, and the body come together in ways that are different from abstracted, objectified thought. In this case, thought and bodily action join in ways that are in fact theorized in the Buddhist martial arts, though few of us explore that route through books. For Asian American women, *taiko* is a true performative act, one so profoundly understood through the body that it is rarely channeled into other media like words.

Which brings me back to experience and its liveness, though this time with a gendered twist. The ephemerality of performance is no less a mode of cultural production than those institutions (i.e., government, religious life, the law, the workplace) often taken more seriously as spheres of determination and influence. *Taiko* is a complex site that highlights the meeting ground of transnational movement, gender, and the insistence on being seen and heard. Lisa Lowe has encouraged a closer examination of "those institutions, spaces, borders, and processes that are the interstitial sites of the social formation in which the national intersects with the international" (1996, 172), and *taiko* is one such location that opens up an Asian American space in conversation with the Asian. Its liveness is fundamentally part of its power for Asian American women. Dorinne Kondo has tried to write about the place of liveness in her own excitement about Asian American theater and her understanding of its link to empowerment; she relates how seeing Hwang's *M. Butterfly* on Broadway made her feel that she *had* to write about it, "as though my life depended on it" (1995, 50). Describing the liveness of theater as "another register," she notes that turning her research toward Asian American theater represented "a kind of paradigm shift away from the purely textual toward the performative, the evanescent, the nondiscursive, the collaborative" (1995, 51). As an anthropologist, Kondo articulates something that I think many Asian American woman *taiko* players know intuitively: that those moments of choreographed sound and movement speak in many different ways at once, channeling power and pleasure through the body and redefining that body through pounding heart and shouted presence. "The Asian" becomes a vexed self, a more authentic shadow self that we didn't know we had, that we're not sure we *want* to have, yet it serves as a vector for how we come together in this vital, comfortable, unspoken way even as it leaves us more unsure than ever about the in/authenticity of the Asian/American.

The politics of ethnicity in *taiko* are thus bottomless, yet I remain sure that I learn something about Asian America when I play. Certainly *taiko* remodulates every category it touches—the Japanese, the Japanese American, the Asian, the Asian American—and the sensual sounded body passes through these noisy historical constructions and emerges asserting yet new presences. The complications and the risks are so fundamentally part of it all that I must end by arguing they are intrinsically part of the pleasure—the pleasure of listening to *taiko*, of learning it, of performing it, of teaching it. Perhaps that is what I take away from it, most of all—that the impossibility of containing the meaning of such a clamorous practice sets up a performative too boisterous to be denied, too loud to be any one thing.

Acknowledgments

I would like to thank Rev. Shuichi Thomas Kurai and Audrey Nakasone for hours of instruction and conversation about *taiko* and the *taiko* community, and my classmates in the Taiko Center of Los Angeles for their camaraderie. Kenny Endo was kind enough to grant me an extended interview after a rather demanding performance. Paul Yoon and Mark Tusler have been constant sources of information, always ready to share their insights as ethnomusicologists and as *taiko* players. Traise Yamamoto, Paul Simon, and René T.A. Lysloff were brave enough to watch the *taiko* scene in *Rising Sun* with me several times, and members of the University of California Performance Studies Group gave me some new ways to think about that scene in the film. Participants in "Audiences, Patrons and Performers in the Performing Arts of Asia," August

23–27, 2000 in Leiden, The Netherlands, also had useful comments. Traise Yamamoto offered detailed suggestions on a late draft that helped me see the forest through the trees.

Notes

1. This essay is drawn from a longer chapter in my book, *Speak It Louder: Asian Americans Making Music* (Routledge, 2004), that addresses the cultural politics of Japanese *taiko* in the U.S. and specifically in the context of Asian American cultural politics.
2. San Francisco Taiko Dojo also played on the soundtracks for *Apocalypse Now, Return of the Jedi,* and *The Right Stuff.*
3. This instrument is called the "cannon" by members of San Francisco Taiko Dojo because of its physical appearance. It consists of three pieces of metal pipe welded together and mounted on a stand so that it stands horizontally at waist height. It takes the place of three *kane* with different pitches (Tusler 1995, 14). Rev. Tom refers to it as a "muffler," again due to its appearance.
4. Dorinne Kondo's indictment of the film along these lines (1997, 240–51) is both thoughtful and sweeping.
5. I posted a query to the Rolling Thunder *taiko* discussion list, asking for responses to the *taiko* scene in *Rising Sun,* and I received several responses from list participants between January 14–30, 2000.
6. E-mail note, 30 January 2000.
7. E-mail note, 16 February 2000.
8. Lisa Lowe has written at length about the historical processes linking Asian and Asian American women's labor in the global economy, and she posits deep connections between capitalism and racialization (1996, 158):

   > [T]he focus on women's work with the global economy as a material site in which several axes of domination intersect provides the means for linking Asian immigrant and Asian American women with other immigrant and racialized women. Asian immigrant and Asian American women are not simply the most recent formation within the genealogy of Asian American racialization; they, along with women working in the "third world," are the "new" workforce with the global reorganization of capitalism. [. . .] They are linked to an emergent political formation, organizing across race, class, and national boundaries, that includes other racialized and immigrant groups as well as women working in, and immigrating from, the neocolonized world.

References

hooks, bell. 1992. "The Oppositional Gaze." In *Black Looks: Race and Representation*, 115–31. Boston: South End Press.

Kondo, Dorinne. 1995. "Bad Girls: Theater, Women of Color, and the Politics of Representation." In *Women Writing Culture*, edited by Ruth Behar and Deborah A. Gordon, 49–64. Berkeley: University of California Press.

———. 1997. *About Face: Performing Race in Fashion and Theater*. New York and London: Routledge.

Lowe, Lisa. 1996. *Immigrant Acts: On Asian American Cultural Politics*. Durham, NC and London: Duke University Press.

Ong, Aihwa. 1995. "Women Out of China: Traveling Tales and Traveling Theories in Postcolonial Feminism." In *Women Writing Culture*, edited by Ruth Behar and Deborah A. Gordon, 350–72. Berkeley: University of California Press.

Shah, Sonia. 1994. "Presenting the Blue Goddess: Toward a National Pan-Asian Feminist Agenda." In *The State of Asian America: Activism and Resistance in the 1990s*, edited by Karin Aguilar-San Juan, 147–58. Boston: South End Press.

Tusler, Mark. 1999. "Taiko Drumming in California: Issues of Articulation and the Construction of Ethnic Identity." Unpublished paper presented at the Society for Ethnomusicology Southern California Chapter meeting. University of California, Riverside, 23–24 February 1999.

Yamada, Mitsuye. 1983. "Invisibility is an Unnatural Disaster: Reflections of an Asian American Woman." In *This Bridge Called My Back: Writings by Radical Women of Color*, edited by Cherríe Moraga and Gloria Anzaldúa, (2nd ed., 35–40) Latham, NY: Kitchen Table, Women of Color Press.

Yamamoto, Traise. 1999. *Masking Selves, Making Subjects: Japanese American Women, Identity, and the Body*. Berkeley: University of California Press.

Yoon, Paul Jong Chul. 1999. "Musical Spaces and Identity Politics: Negotiating an Asian American Existence in New York City, the Case of Soh Daiko." Paper presented at the 44th annual meeting of the Society for Ethnomusicology, Austin, Texas, November 18–21.

6

Empowering Self, Making Choices, Creating Spaces
Black Female Identity via Rap Music Performance

Cheryl L. Keyes

Observers of rap music began to notice the proliferation of successful female rap acts during the 1990s. Though rap has often been presented as a male-dominated form by the media, women have been a part of the rap scene since its early commercial years. In general, "females were always into rap, had their little crews and were known for rocking parties, schoolyards, whatever it was; and females rocked just as hard as males [but] the male was just first to be put on wax [record]" (Pearlman 1988, 26). Rap music journalist Havelock Nelson notes, "While women have always been involved artistically with rap throughout the '80s, artists like [MC] Lyte, [Queen] Latifah, Roxanne Shanté, and [Monie] Love have had to struggle to reach a level of success close to that of male rappers" (1993, 77). Challenging male rappers' predominance, female rap artists have not only proven that they have lyrical skills; in their struggle to survive and thrive within this tradition, they have created spaces from which to deliver powerful messages from Black female and Black feminist perspectives.

Data utilized in this study derive from interviews (1993–96) with "cultural readers" (Bobo 1995)—African American female performers, audience members, and music critics—referred to in this essay as an "interpretive community." In *Black Women as Cultural Readers,* film critic-scholar Jacqueline Bobo explores the concept of "interpretive community" as a movement comprising Black female cultural producers, critics and scholars, and cultural consumers (1995, 22). She writes:

> As a group, the women make up what I have termed an interpretive community, which is strategically placed in relation to cultural works that either are created by black women or feature them in significant ways. Working together the women utilize representations of black women that they deem valuable in productive and politically useful ways. [1995, 22]

Because much of the criticism of Black female independent filmmakers' works stems from male or white perspectives, Bobo finds it necessary to distinguish the interpretive community—Black women involved in making or consuming these films—in order to accurately determine the actual intent and effect of these films. Bobo's thesis of the interpretive community is appropriate to this examination of women in rap because rap music is a form transmitted by recorded and video performances. More importantly, the classifications of women rappers are based on the constructions of an interpretive community, as observed via recorded performance and personal interviews. When rapper MC Lyte was asked, for example, if she felt that there is a distinct female rap category, she separated women rappers into three groups, referred to as "crews," reigning in three periods—the early 1980s, the mid-1980s through the early 1990s, and the late 1990s: "Sha-Rock, Sequence, to me, that's the first crew. Then you got a-second crew which is Salt-N-Pepa, Roxanne Shanté, The Real Roxanne, me, Latifah, Monie [Love], and Yo-Yo....Then after that you got Da Brat, Foxy Brown, Lil' Kim, Heather B" (1996).[1]

Queried about specific categories, both rap music performers and female audience members frequently used the buzz words *fly* and *attitude* (as in "girlfriend got attitude"), leading me to more clearly discern the parameter of categories. My initial category of "Black Diva" in early interviews for the grand posture of these women was later revised to "Queen Mother" after one female observer convincingly said *diva* denotes a posture of arrogance and pretentiousness as opposed to that of a regal and self-assured woman, qualities that she identified with the Queen Latifah types (see Penrice 1995).

In the female rap tradition, four distinct categories of women rappers emerge in rap music performance: "Queen Mother," "Fly Girl," "Sista with Attitude," and "Lesbian." Black female rappers can, however, shift between these categories or belong to more than one simultaneously. More importantly, each category mirrors certain images, voices, and lifestyles of African American women in contemporary urban society. Let us now examine the four categories or images of Black women introduced to rap by specific female rappers or emcees (MCs) and considered by the interpretive community in general as representative of and specific to African American female identity in contemporary urban culture.

Queen Mother

The "Queen Mother" category comprises female rappers who view themselves as African-centered icons, an image often suggested by their dress. In their lyrics, they refer to themselves as "Asiatic Black women," "Nubian queens," "intelligent Black women," or "sistas droppin' science to the people," suggestive of their self-constructed identity and intellectual prowess. The "Queen mother" is, however, associated with African traditional court culture. For instance, in the 16th-century Benin Kingdom of southeastern Nigeria, she was the mother of a reigning king. Because of her maternal connection to the king, she garnered certain rights and privileges, including control over districts and a voice in the national affairs of the state. During his reign, a commemorative head made of brass was sculpted in her honor adorned with a beaded choker, headdress, and crown, along with a facial expression capturing her reposed manner.[2]

It is certainly possible that female rap artists may know of the historical significance of African queens; women in this category adorn their bodies with royal or Kente cloth strips, African headdresses, goddess braid styles, and ankh-stylized jewelry. Their rhymes embrace Black female empowerment and spirituality, making clear their self-identification as African, woman, warrior, priestess, and queen. Queen mothers demand respect not only for their people but for Black women, who are "to be accorded respect by...men," observes Angela Y. Davis (1998, 122). Among those women distinguished by the interpretive community as Queen Mother types are Queen Kenya, Queen Latifah, Sister Souljah, Nefertiti, Queen Mother Rage, Isis, and Yo-Yo.

Queen Kenya, a member of hip-hop's Zulu Nation, was the first female MC to use *Queen* as a stage name.[3] But the woman of rap who became the first solo female MC to commercially record under the name "Queen" is Dana "Queen Latifah" Owens. Queen Latifah's initial singles "Princess of the Posse" and "Wrath of My Madness" (1988), followed by her debut album *All Hail the Queen* (1989), established her regal identity. They include such lyrics as, "You try to be down, you can't take my crown from me," and, "I'm on the scene, I'm the Queen of Royal Badness." Latifah, whose Arabic name means "feminine, delicate, and kind," explains the origin of her stage name:

> My cousin, who's Muslim, gave me that name [Latifah] when I was eight. Well [in rap], I didn't want to be MC Latifah. It didn't sound right. I didn't want to come out like old models. So *queen* just popped into my head one day, and I was like, "Me, Queen Latifah." It felt good saying it, and I felt like a queen. And you know, I am a queen. And every Black woman is a queen. [1993]

Latifah's maternal demeanor, posture, and full figure contribute to the perception of her as a queen mother. Although Queen Latifah acknowledges that others perceived her as motherly even at age 21, she tries to distance herself from the label: "I wish I wasn't seen as a mother, though. I don't really care for that. Just because I take a mature stance on certain things, it gives me a motherly feel...maybe because I am full-figured. I am mature, but I'm twenty-one" (quoted in Green 1991, 33). The ambiguity of Latifah's motherly image follows what feminist scholars Joan Radner and Susan Lanser identify as a form of coding in women's folk culture called *distraction:* a device used to "drown out or draw attention away from the subversive power of a feminist message" (1993, 15). Queen Latifah finds that her stature and grounded perspective cause fans to view her as a maternal figure or as a person to revere or, at times, fear. However, Latifah attempts to mute her motherly image offstage, as evidenced in the above interview, indicating to fans that she remains, nonetheless, a modest, down-to-earth, and ordinary person in spite of her onstage "Queen of Royal Badness" persona.

Despite the ambiguity, Queen Latifah represents a particular type of mother figure to her audience. In *Black Feminist Thought,* sociologist Patricia Hill Collins recognizes that, in the African American community, some women are viewed as "othermothers." Collins explains:

> Black women's involvement in fostering African-American community development forms the basis for community-based power. This is the type of "strong Black woman" they see around them in traditional African-American communities. Community othermothers work on behalf of the Black community by expressing ethics of caring and personal accountability which embrace conceptions of transformative and mutuality ¼ community othermothers become identified as power figures through furthering the community's well-being. [1990, 132]

Queen Latifah's othermother posture is no doubt reflected most vividly through her lyrics, which, at times, address political-economic issues facing Black women and the Black community as a whole. In Latifah's song "The Evil that Men Do" (1989) from *All Hail the Queen,* "she isolates several of the difficulties commonly experienced by young black women [on welfare]" (Forman 1994, 44) and shows how the powers that be are apathetic to Black women who are trying to beat the odds:

> Here is a message from my sisters and brothers, here are some thing I
> wanna cover.
> A woman strives for a better life
> but who the hell cares because she's living on welfare.
> The government can't come up with a decent housing plan
> so she's in no man's land

> it's a sucker who tells you you're equal...
> Someone's livin' the good life tax-free
> 'cause some poor girl can't be livin' crack free
> and that's just part of the message
> I thought I should send you about the evil that men do. [quoted in Forman
> 1994, 44]

Another example of Queen Latifah's role as queen mother of rap resonates in her platinum single "Ladies First" (1989), ranked in the annals of rap music history as the first political commentary rap song by a female artist. The lyrics of "Ladies First" respond primarily to males who believe that females cannot create rhymes:

> Some think that we [women] can't flow
> Stereotypes they got to go,
> I gonna mess around and flip the scene into reverse
> With a little touch of ladies first.

The video version is far more political, containing live footage of South Africa's apartheid riots overlaid with photographic stills of Black heroines—Winnie Mandela, Rosa Parks, Angela Davis, Harriet Tubman, and Madame C. J. Walker.[4] Pan-Africanism is tacitly evoked with these images—South Africa's political struggle against segregation and a salute to Winnie Mandela, the mother of this struggle, who is presented among U.S. Black women—reminders of Black liberation. Additionally, the bond between Black women in the United States and the United Kingdom is alluded to through the appearance of Monie Love of England, whom Queen Latifah refers to as "my European partner." These images locate Latifah as a queen mother and equal partner among those Black queens who struggled for the freedom of Black people.

Perceived by the interpretive community as a queen mother of rap, Queen Latifah opened the doors for other Afrocentric female MCs, such as Sister Souljah. Souljah, a former associate of the Black Nationalist rap group Public Enemy, launched her fist LP in 1992. The LP, *360 Degrees of Power*, features the rap single "The Final Solution: Slavery's Back in Effect," in which "Souljah imagines a police state where blacks fight the reinstitution of slavery" (Leland 1992, 48). With her candid and somewhat quasipreachy style of delivery, she earned the title "raptivist" from her followers. Souljah's fame grew after her speech at the Reverend Jesse Jackson's Rainbow Coalition Leadership Summit in 1992, where she chided African Americans who murder one another for no apparent reason by figuratively suggesting, "Why not take a week and kill white people[?]" (Leland 1992, 48). As a consequence, Souljah was ridiculed as a propagator of hate by presidential candidate Bill Clinton. In the wake of the controversy, her record sales plummeted dramatically while her "raptivist" messages skyrocketed with television appearances on talk shows like *The Phil Donahue Show* and speeches on the university lecture circuit. While Sister Souljah advocates racial, social, and economic parity in her rap messages, she also look within the community to relationship issues between Black men and women in her lyrics and her semiautobiographical book *No Disrespect* (1994, xiv).

Although Nefertiti, Isis, and Queen Mother Rage are categorized as queen mothers via their names, lyrics, or attire, female rapper Yo-Yo is also regarded by the interpretive community as a queen mother.[5] Her lyrics illustrate her political ideology of Black feminism and female respectability, as advanced by her organization, the Intelligent Black Women Coalition (I.B.W.C), which she discusses on her debut LP *Make Way for the Motherlode* (1991). But Yo-Yo's image—long auburn braids and very short tight-fitting *pum-pum* shorts (worn by Jamaican dance hall women performers)—and her gyrating hip dancing also position her in the next category, "Fly Girl"

Fly Girl

Fly describes someone in chic clothing and fashionable hairstyles, jewelry, and cosmetics, a style that grew out of the blaxploitation films of the late 1960s through the mid-1970s. These films include *Shaft* (1971), *Superfly* (1972), *The Mack* (1973), and *Foxy Brown* (1974), a film that inspired one MC to adopt the movie's title as her moniker. The fly persona in these films influenced a wave of Black contemporary youth who, in turn, resurrected flyness and its continuum in hip-hop culture. During the early 1980s, women rappers, including Sha Rock of Funky Four Plus One, the trio Sequence, and soloist Lady B, dressed in what was then considered by their audiences as fly.

They wore short skirts, sequined fabric, high-heeled shoes, and prominent makeup. By 1985, the hip-hop community further embraced the fly image via the commercial recording of "A Fly Girl," by the male rap group Boogie Boys, and an answer rap during the same year, "A Fly Guy," by female rapper Pebblee-Poo. The Boogie Boys describe a fly girl as a woman "who wants you to see her name, her game and her ability"; to do so, "she sports a lot of gold, wears tight jeans, leather mini skirts, a made-up face, has voluptuous curves, but speaks her mind" (1987).

By the mid-1980s, many female MCs began contesting the "fly girl" image because they wanted their audiences to focus more on their rapping skills than on their dress styles. Despite this changing trend, the female rap trio Salt-N-Pepa—Salt, Pepa, and Spinderella—nevertheless canonized the ultimate fly girl posture of rap by donning short, tight-fitting outfits, leather clothing, ripped jeans or punk clothing, glittering gold jewelry (i.e., earrings and necklaces), long sculpted nails, prominent makeup, and hairstyles ranging from braids and wraps to waves, in ever-changing hair coloring.

Rap's fly girl image is, however, far more than a whim, for it highlights aspects of Black women's bodies considered undesirable by American mainstream standards of beauty (Roberts 1998). Through performance, Salt-N-Pepa are "flippin da script" (deconstructing dominant ideology) by wearing clothes that accent their full breasts and rounded buttocks and thighs, considered beauty markers of Black women by Black culture (Roberts 1998). Moreover, they portray via performance the fly girl as a party-goer, an independent woman, but, additionally, an erotic subject rather than an objectified one.

Female rappers' reclamation of the *fly* resonates with the late Audre Lorde's theory of the erotic as power (Davis 1998, 172). In Lorde's influential essay, "Uses of the Erotic," she reveals the transformative power of the erotic in Black women's culture: "Our erotic knowledge empowers us, becomes a lens through which we scrutinize all aspects of our existence, forcing us to evaluate those aspects honestly in terms of their meaning within our lives" (1984, 57). Cultural critic and scholar bell hooks further articulates that Black women's erotic consciousness is textualized around issues of body esteem: "Erotic pleasure requires of us engagement with the realm of the senses... the capacity to be in touch with sensual reality; to accept and love our bodies; [to work] toward self-recovery issues around body esteem; [and] to be empowered by a healing eroticism" (1993, 116,121–122,124).

Black fly girl express a growing awareness of their erotic selves by sculpting their own personas and, as folklorist Elaine Lawless (1998) puts it, "writing their own bodies." For example, Salt-N-Pepa describe themselves as "women [who have] worked hard to keep our bodies in shape; we're proud to show them off": moreover, "we're not ashamed of our sexuality; for we're Salt-N-Pepa—sexier and more in control" (quoted in Rogers 1994, 31).

Another aspect of the fly girl persona is independence. Salt notes that "the image we project reflects the real independent woman of the '90s" (quoted in Chyll 1994, 20). But for many women of rap, achieving a sense of independence from an entrepreneurial perspective has not been easy. For instance, it is common knowledge in the rap community that during Salt-N-Pepa's early years, their lyrics and hit songs ("I'll Take Your Man," "Push It," "Tramp," and "Shake Your Thang") were mainly written by their manager/producer Hurby "Luvbug" Azor, until the *Black's Magic* (1990) LP, on which Salt (Cheryl James) ventured into writing and producing the single "Expression," which went platinum. *Black's Magic* also contains Salt-N-Pepa's "Let's Talk about Sex" (written by Azor), which Salt later rewrote for a public service announcement song and video "Let's Talk about AIDS" in 1992.

On Salt-N-Pepa's fourth LP, *Very Necessary* (1993), the group wrote and produced most of the selections. The songs "Shoop" and "Whatta Man" from that album stand out as celebratory songs that deserve note.[6] In the video versions of both songs, the three women scrutinize desirable men, ranging from business types to "ruffnecks" (a fly guy associated with urban street culture). The "Shoop" video turns the tables on the male rappers; in it "ladies see a bunch of bare-chested, tight-bunned brothers acting like sex *objects,* servicing it up to us in our videos," said Salt (quoted in Rogers 1994, 31, emphasis added). In "Whatta Man," on the other hand, Salt-N-Pepa praise their significant others in the areas of friendship, romance, and parenting as the female rhythm and blues group En Vogue joins them in singing the chorus, "Whatta man, whatta man, whatta man, whatta mighty good man."

Other women whom the interpretive community categorizes as *fly* are Left-Eye and Yo-Yo. Left Eye is the rapper of the hip-hop/rhythm and blues hybrid group TLC (T-Boz, Left Eye, and Chili). When TLC first appeared on the music scene with the debut LP *Ooooooohhh…On the TLC Tip* (1992), their baggy style of dress ran counter to the revealing apparel of hip-hop's typical fly girl and invited their full-figured audience to do the same. TLC's T-Boz said, "We like to wear a lot of baggy stuff because for one, it's comfortable, and two, many of our fans don't have the so-called perfect figure; we don't want them to feel like they can't wear what we're wearing" (quoted in Horner 1993, 16). Throughout the 1990s, TLC remained steadfast with the message to women of all sizes regarding mental and physical wellness and body esteem, as underscored in both music and video performances of the single "Unpretty" (1999).

Like Salt-N-Pepa, TLC has made delivering "safe sex" messages a priority. While both groups do so through lyrics, TLC underscores the messages visually through wearing certain accoutrements. Left Eye of the trio wears a condom in place of an eyeglass lens, while other members of the group attach colored condom packages to their clothes. TLC's warning about unprotected sex, emphasized by the condoms they wear, is conveyed powerfully in their award-winning "Waterfalls" from their second LP, *CrazySexyCool* (1994). The message is amplified in the video: A man decides to follow his partner's wish not to use a condom. Following this encounter, he notices a lesion on his face, which suggests that he has contracted the virus that causes AIDS. TLC's espousal of being fly and sexually independent undoubtedly comes hand in hand with sexual responsibility via their lyrics and image.

Like TLC, Yo-Yo also delivers a serious message, which earns her a place among the queen mothers. But her gyrating hips, stylish auburn braids, short, tight-fitting outfits, and pronounced facial makeup also categorize her as fly. Yo-Yo writes about independent, empowered Black women, championing African American sisterhood in "The I.B.W.C. National Anthem" and "Sisterland" from *Make Way for the Motherlode* (1991). She takes on sexuality in "You Can't Play with My Yo-Yo" and "Put a Lid on It," which, as their titles suggest, explore being sexually in control and being sexually irresponsible.

In 1996, Yo-Yo moved beyond the shadow of her mentor Ice Cube with her fourth LP, *Total Control,* for which she served as executive producer. Following this success, Yo-Yo began a column entitled "Yo, Yo-Yo" in the hip-hop magazine *Vibe*, in which she addresses questions about male-female relationships and interpersonal growth in the name of I.B.W.C.

Since the late 1990s, female MC, songwriter, and producer Missy "Misdemeanor" Elliott has joined the fly girl ranks. Mesmerized by her debut LP *Supa Dupa Fly* (1997) and her single "The Rain," female fans also admire her finger-wave hairstyle, known to some as "Missy [finger] waves," and her ability to carry off the latest hip-hop fashions on her full-figured frame. Elliott has occasionally appeared in television advertisements for the youth fashion store Gap. She no doubt succeeds as a full-figured *fly* woman, breaking new ground in an area too often seen as off-limits to all but the most slender and "correctly" proportioned. In staking her claim to rap music's fly girl category, Elliott further reclaims sexuality and eros as healing power for all Black women, regardless of size. However, with her single "She's a Bitch" from her sophomore LP *Da Real World* (1999), Missy "Misdemeanor" Elliott appends another image to her fly girl posture. Her usage of *bitch* makes a self-statement about being a mover and shaker, on- and offstage, in rap's male-dominated arena, and thus she shares much in common with the next category, "Sista with Attitude."

Sista with Attitude

According to Black English scholar Geneva Smitherman, " 'tude, a diminutive form of attitude, can be defined as an aggressive, arrogant, defiant, I-know-I'm-BAD pose or air about oneself; or an oppositional or negative outlook or disposition" (1994, 228). Prototypes of this category are grouped according to " 'tude": Roxanne Shanté, Bytches with Problems (BWP), and Da Brat are known for their frankness; MC Lyte exudes a hardcore/no-nonsense approach; Boss is recognized for her gangsta bitch posture; and Mia X advances a militaristic stance, all in the name of her predominantly male posse No Limit Soldiers.[7]

In general, "Sista with Attitude" comprises female MCs who value attitude as a means of empowerment and present themselves accordingly. Many of these "sistas" (sisters) have reclaimed the word *bitch,* viewing it as positive rather than negative and using the term to entertain or provide cathartic release. Other sistas in the interpretive community are troubled by that view. These women, such as Lauryn Hill, have "refused to be labeled a 'bitch' because such appellations merely mar the images of young African American females" (1994; see also Harmony, quoted in Donahue 1991). The reclaimers counter this argument with the opinion that "it's not what you're called but what you answer to" (MC Lyte 1993). Some women of rap take a middle road, concurring that *bitch* can be problematic depending on who uses the term, how it is employed, and to whom one refers. As Queen Latifah explains:

> I don't really mind the term...I play around with it. I use it with my home girl like, "Bitch are you crazy?" Bitch is a fierce girl [Or.] "That bitch is so crazy, girl." You know, that's not harmful. [But,] "This stupid bitch just came down here talking...," now that's meant in a harmful way. So it's the meaning behind the word that to me decides whether I should turn it off or listen to it. [1993]

Female MCs revise the standard definition of *bitch,* from an "aggressive woman who challenges male authority" (Penrice 1995) to an aggressive or assertive female who subverts patriarchal rule. Lyndah of the duo BWP explained, "We use 'Bytches' [to mean] a strong, positive, aggressive woman who goes after what she wants. We take that on today...and use it in a positive sense" (quoted in Donahue 1991).[8]

By the mid- to late 1990s, the "Sista with Attitude" category was augmented with rappers Lil' Kim and Foxy Brown, who conflate fly and hardcore attitudes in erotic lyrics and video performances, bordering both "Fly Girl" and "Sista with Attitude" categories. In doing so, they are designated by some as the "mack divas," "Thelma and Louise of rap" (Gonzales 1997, 62), or "bad girls of hip-hop" (Morgan 1997). Foxy Brown, whose name is derived from Pam Grier's 1974 screen character, emulates the powerful, desirable, yet dangerous woman: "I think it's every girl's dream to be fly" (Gonzales 1997, 63). Although Lil' Kim's debut album *Hard Core* (1996) and Foxy Brown's *Ill Na Na* (1997) have garnered platinum status, some members of the interpretive community criticize them for being "highly materialistic, violent, lewd" (Morgan 1997, 77), an impression exacerbated by their affiliation with male gangsta rap-style crews: Lil' Kim is associated with Junior M.A.F.I.A., and Foxy Brown is connected with The Firm.

The bad girl image also parallels the "badman" character (such as John Hardy, Dolemite, and Stackolee) peculiar to the African American oral narrative. African American oral narratives commonly exploit the "badman" or "bad nigguh" types in the toast, a long poetic narrative form that predates rap.[9] In these narratives. Black badmen boast about their sexual exploits with women, wild drinking binges, and narrow brushes with the law, symbolic of "white power" (Roberts 1989, 196). The feminist rendering of "the badman" includes those sistas who brag about partying and smoking "blunts" (marijuana) with their men; seducing, repressing, and sexually emasculating male characters;[10] or "dissin' " (verbally downplaying) their would-be female or male competitors—all through figurative speech.[11]

Some female observers I queried felt that sistas with attitude merely exist on the periphery of rap and are seen as just "shootin' off at the mouth." These artists are not highly respected for their creative skills; rather, they are viewed as misusing sex and feminism and devaluing Black men. In an *Essence* magazine article, hip-hop feminist Joan Morgan states that the new "bad girls of hip-hop" may not have career longevity because "feminism is not simply about being able to do what the boys do—get high, talk endlessly about their wee-wees and what have you. At the end of the day, it's the power women attain by making choices that increase their range of possibilities" (1997, 132). Morgan further argues that Black women's power—on- and offstage—is sustained by "those sisters who selectively ration their erotic power" (1997, 133).

Despite the controversies, sistas with attitude have acquired respect from their peers for their mastery of figurative language and rhyme. They simply refuse to be second best.

Lesbian

While representatives of the "Queen Mother," "Fly Girl," and "Sista with Attitude" categories came into prominence during the mid- to late 1980s, the "Lesbian" category emerged from the closet during the late 1990s. Not only does the female audience term this category "Lesbian," but the artist who has given recognition to this division is among the first to rap about and address the lesbian lifestyle from a Black woman's perspective. Though other Black rap artists rumored to be gay/lesbian have chosen to remain closeted in a scene described as "notoriously homophobic" (Dyson, quoted in Jamison 1998, AR34), Queen Pen's "Girlfriend," from her debut LP *My Melody* (1997), represents a "breakthrough for queer culture" (Walters 1998, 60).[12] "Girlfriend" signifies on or indirectly plays on Black lesbian love interest with a parody of the refrain section of Me'Shell Ndegeocello's "If That's Your Boyfriend (He Wasn't Last Night)." Ndegeocello, who is openly lesbian, appears on "Girlfriend," performing vocals and bass guitar. In "Girlfriend," Queen Pen positions herself as the suitor in a lesbian relationship. While this song may be a "breakthrough for queer culture," other issues still complicate Black female artists' willingness to openly address gay and lesbian culture in their performances.

Black lesbian culture and identity have been concerned with issues of race and role-play, note Lisa M. Walker (1993) and Ekua Omosupe (1991). Drawing on the critical works of Audre Lorde (1982, 1984), Omosupe notes that lesbian identity, similar to feminism, represents white lesbian culture or white women to the exclusion of women of color. In this regard, Black lesbians are at times forced to live and struggle against white male patriarchal culture on the one side and white lesbian culture, racism, and general homophobia on the other (Omosupe 1991, 105). Corroborating issues of race privilege raised by the Black lesbian community, Queen Pen contends that certain licenses are afforded to white openly lesbian performers like Ellen DeGeneres and k. d. lang, who do not have to pay as high a price for their candidness as lesbians of color: "But you know, Ellen [DeGeneres] can talk about any ol' thing and it's all right With everybody, it's all right. With 'Girlfriend,'

I'm getting all kinds of questions" (quoted in Duvernay 1998, 88).[13] She continues, "This song is buggin' everyone out right now. [If] you got Ellen, you got k. d, why shouldn't urban lesbians go to a girl club and hear their own thing?" (quoted in Jamison 1998, AR34).

Queen Pen further stresses in performance her play on image, which suggests "role-play," another crucial issue to Black lesbian culture. Walker asserts, "Role-play among black lesbians involves a resistance to the homophobic stereotype...lesbian as 'bulldagger,' a pejorative term within (and outside) the black community used to signal the lesbian as a woman who wants to be a man" (1993, 886). On her album cover, Queen Pen exudes a "femme" image through wearing lipstick, a chic hairstyle, and stylish dress. However, in performance, as observed in Blackstreet's "No Diggity" (1996), one notices how Queen Pen "drowns out" her femme album cover image by appropriating "B-Boy" gestures (cool pose and bopped gait) commonly associated with male hip-hop culture. Regardless of issues concerning race privilege and role-play, Queen Pen concludes that in "two or three years from now, people will say I was the first female to bring the lesbian life to light [in an open way] on wax. It's reality. What's the problem?" (quoted in Jamison 1998, AR34).

Conclusion

Women are achieving major strides in rap music by continuing to chisel away at stereotypes about females as artists in a male-dominated tradition and by (re)defining women's culture and identity from a Black feminist perspective. Although rap continues to be predominantly male, female MCs move beyond the shadows of male rappers in diverse ways. Some have become exclusively known for their lyrical "skillz," while others have used a unique blend of musical styles or a combination of singer-rapper acts, as is apparent with Grammy awardees Left Eye of TLC and Lauryn Hill.

Women of rap still face, nevertheless, overt sexism regarding their creative capabilities. Female rapper Princesa recalls, "Only when I led them [male producers] to believe that a man had written or produced my stuff did they show interest" (quoted in Cooper 1989, 80). Mass-mediation scholar Lisa Lewis notes that, in the popular music arena, "the ideological division between composition and performance serves to devalue women's role in music making and cast doubt on female creativity in general" (1990, 57). However, female MCs of the 1990s have defied the sexist repression by writing their own songs, producing records, and even starting their own record companies, as with Salt-N-Pepa's *Very Necessary* (1993), Lauryn Hill's 1999 Grammy Award-winning LP *The Miseducation of Lauryn Hill* (1998), and Queen Latifah's record company, Flavor Unit. Additionally, Queen Latifah's Grammy Award-Twinning single "U.N.I.T.Y." (1993) challenges those males who use *bitch/ho* appellations in their lyrics.

While the majority of scholarly studies on female rappers locate Black women's voices in rap, they present only a partial rendering of female representation.[14] These works tend to focus on females' attitudes and responses to sexual objectification, ignoring the many roles and issues of women and female rappers. Rap music scholar Tricia Rose says female MO should be evaluated not only with regard to male rappers and misogynist lyrics "but also in response to a variety of related issues, including dominant notions of femininity, feminism, and black female sexuality. At the very least, black women rappers are in dialogue with one another, black men, black women, and dominant American culture as they struggle to define themselves" (1994, 147–148). In rap music performance, a "black female-self emerges as a variation [on] several unique themes" (Etter-Lewis 1991, 43).

More importantly, female rappers, most of whom are Black, convey their views on a variety of issues concerning identity, sociohistory, and esoteric beliefs shared by young African American women. Female rappers have attained a sense of distinction through revising and reclaiming Black women's history and perceived destiny. They use their performances as platforms to refute, deconstruct, and reconstruct alternative visions of their identity. With this platform, rap music becomes a vehicle by which Black female rappers seek empowerment, make choices, and create spaces for themselves and other sistas.

Notes

Earlier drafts of this article were presented on the panel "Women Performers as Traditionalists and Innovators," at Resounding Women in World Music: A Symposium, sponsored by the World Music Institute and Hunter College/City University of New York Graduate Program in Ethnomusicology, New York, 10–12 November 1995; and as a paper, "'Ain't Nuthin' but a She-Thing': Women, Race and Representation in Rap," at the 42nd Annual Meetings of the Society for Ethnomusicology with the International Association for the Study of Popular Music (USA Chapter), Pittsburgh, 22–26 October 1997. I wish to thank Lou-Ann Crouther. Phyllis May-Machunda, the late Gerald L. Davis, and the anonymous reviewers of the *Journal of American Folklore* for their suggestions on earlier drafts, as well as Corinne Lightweaver, whose invaluable comments contributed to the article's refinement.

1. The following is a list of other artists who make up a roster of female MCs: Antoinette (Next Plateau), Bahamadia (EMI), Conscious Daughters (Priority), Eve (Ruff Ryders), Finesse and Synquis (MCA), Gangsta Boo (Relativity), Heather B (MCA), Lady of Rage (Death Row), Ladybug (Pendulum), MC Smooth (Crash Music), MC Trouble (Motown), Mercedes (No limit), Nikki D (Def Jam), Nonchalant (MCA), Oaktown's 3-5-7 (Capital), Rah Digga (Flipmode), Sol– (DreamWorks), and 350 (Rap-a-Lot).
2. Accordingly, sculpting the queen mother's head was established in Benin by King Oba Esigies during the 16th century. Sieber and Walker (1987, 93) note that, during Esigies's reign, he commissioned a sculpted head made of bronze of his mother, Idia, and placed it in his palace to commemorate her role in the Benin–Idah war, thereby including, for the first time, queen mothers in the cult of royal ancestors. In addition to Sieber and Walker's work, refer to Ben-Amos 1995 and Ben-Amos and Rubin 1983 for photographs and a brief discussion of queen mother heads of Benin.
3. The Zulu Nation is an organization that was founded in the Bronx during the mid-1970s by DJ Afrika Bambaataa. He contends that the Zulu Nation is a youth organization that incorporates a philosophy of nonviolence and in which inner-city youths compete artistically as break-dancers, rhyming emcees (rappers), disc jockeys, and graffiti artists rather dun physically with knives and guns. Bambaataa's Zulu Nation laid the foundation for hip-hop, a youth arts movement comprising the above arts, and an "attitude" rendered in the form of a distinct dress, language, and gesture—all of which is articulated via performance by rap music artists (see Keyes 1996).
4. For a more detailed analysis of this video, see Roberts 1994.
5. Isis once performed with the Black Nationalist group X-Clan. After leaving this group, she also adopted a new stage name, Lin Que.
6. "Whatta Man" is adapted from Linda Lyndell's 1968 hit "What a Man."
7. For a more in-depth discussion of this category, refer to the section on female rappers in my forthcoming book, tentatively titled *Beats, Rhymes and Street Science: Rap Music as a phenomenon of Consciousness* (n.d.).
8. Another aspect of speech play is the manner in which sistas with attitude refer to men in their rap songs affectionately or insultingly as "motherfuckas" or "my niggas."
9. For further information about the toast, see Roger Abrahams (1970) and Daryl Dance (1978).
10. This emasculation can occur when sistas with attitude refer to their male competitors or suitors as "motherfuckas" or "niggas." Because the element of signifying is aesthetically appealing in this style of rap, these terms may have both negative and positive meanings depending on context.
11. Examples of selected rap songs that portray the distinct characteristics of sistas with attitude include the following: Boss, "I Don't Give a Fuck" and "Mai Sista Izza Bitch," *Bom Gangstaz* (1993); Bytches with Problems, "Two Minute Brother" and "Shit Popper," *The Bytches* (1991); Da Brat, "Da Shit Ya Can't Fuc Wit" and "Fire It Up," *Funkdafied* (1994); Foxy Brown, "Ill Na Na" and "Letter to the Firm," *Ill Na Na* (1997); Lil' Kim, "Big Momma Thang" and "Spend a Little Doe," *Hard Core* (1996); MC Lyte, "Paper Thin," *Lyte as a Rock* (1988) and "Steady F…king," *Ain't No Other* (1993); Roxanne Shanté, "Big Mama," *The Bitch Is Back* (1992).
12. While "Queen Pen" is a play on "King Pin," Queen Pen uses this moniker to indicate that she "pens" (or writes) her own lyrics, a skill that some believe female MCs lack in comparison with male rappers. Although "Girlfriend" and other selections on Queen Pen's LP were cowritten and produced by Teddy Riley, inventor of new jack swing style (a rap/rhythm and blues hybrid), Queen Pen's real name (Lynise Walters) appears on all songs. In the music industry, it is not unusual for producers to take cowriting credit on their mentees' debut works. The discussion of Riley's input on "Girlfriend" is discussed by Laura Jamison (1998).
13. When asked about "Girlfriend" in her interview in *Rap Pages* with Duvernay (1998), Queen Pen asserts that there are other nonlesbian songs on her debut album *My Melody,* including "Get Away," which discusses domestic violence.
14. For more on this topic, see Berry 1994, Forman 1994, Goodall 1994, Guevara 1987, and Rose 1994.

References

Abrahams, Roger. 1970. *Deep Down in the Jungle: Negro Narrative Folklore from the Streets of Philadelphia.* Chicago: Aldine Publishing.

Ben-Amos, and Paula Girshick. 1995. *The Art of Bain.* Rev. edition. Washington, D.C.: Smithsonian Institution Press.

———, Paula Girshick, and Arnold Rubin, eds. 1983. *The Art of Power, the Power of Art: Studies in Benin Iconography.* Los Angeles: Museum of Cultural History.

Berry, Venise T. 1994. "Feminine or Masculine: The Conflicting Nature of Female Images in Rap Music." In *Cecilia Reclaimed: Feminist Perspectives on Gender and Music*, edited by Susan C. Cook and Judy S. Tsou, 183–201. Urbana: University of Illinois Press.

Bobo, Jacqueline. 1995. *Black Women as Cultural Readers*. New York: Columbia University Press.

Chyll, Chuck. 1994. "Musical Reactions: Sexy Rap or Credibility Gap?" *Rap Masters* 7(7):19–20.

Collins, Patricia Hill. 1990. *Black Feminist Thought: Knowledge, Consciousness, and the Politics of Empowerment*. London: Harper Collins Academic.

Cooper, Carol. 1989. "Girls Ain't Nothin' but Trouble." *Essence* (April):80, 119.

Dance, Daryl. 1978. *Shudein' and Jivin': Folklore from Contemporary Black Americans*. Bloomington: Indiana University Press.

Davis, Angela Y. 1998. *Blues Legacies and Black Feminism: Gertrude "Ma" Rainey, Bessie Smith, and Billie Holiday*. New York: Pantheon Books.

Donahue, Phil. 1991. Female Rappers Invade the Male Rap Industry. *The Phil Donahue Show* Transcript #3216, 29 May.

Duvemay, Ava. 1998. "Queen Pen: Keep 'EM Guessin." *Rap Pages* (May):86–88.

Etter-Lewis, Gwendolyn. 1991. "Black Women's Life Stories: Reclaiming Self in Narrative Texts." In *Women's Words: The Feminist Practice of Oral History*, edited by Shema Berger Gluck and Daphne Patai, 43–59. New York: Routledge.

Forman, Murray. 1994. "Movin' Closer to an Independent Funk: Black Feminist Theory, Standpoint, and Women in Rap." *Women's Studies* 23:35–55.

Gonzales, A. Michael. 1997. "Mack Divas." *The Source* (February):62–64.

Goodall, Nataki. 1994. "Depend on Myself: T.L.C. and the Evolution of Black Female Rap." *Journal of Negro History* 79(l):85–93.

Green, Kim. 1991. "The Naked Truth." *The Source* (November):32–34, 36.

Guevara, Nancy. 1987. "Women Writin' Rappin' Breakin'." In *The Year Left 2*, edited by Mike Davis, Manning Marable, Fred Pfeil, and Michael Sprinker, 160–175. New York: Verso Press.

Hill, Lauryn. 1994. Panelist. Hip-Hop Summit for New Music, Seminar 15, New York, 20 July.

hooks, bell. 1993. *Sisters of the Yam: Black Women and Self-Recovery*. Boston: South End Press.

Homer, Cynthia. 1993. TLC: The Homegirls with Style! *Right On!* (February): 16–17.

Jamison, Laura. 1998. "A Feisty Female Rapper Breaks a Hip-Hop Taboo." *Sunday New Yak Times*, 18 January: AR34.

Keyes, Cheryl L. 2002. *Rap Music and Street Consciousness*. Urbana: University of Illinois Press.

———. 1996. "At the Crossroads: Rap Music and Its African Nexus." *Ethnomusicology* 40(2):223–248.

Lawless, Elaine J. 1998. "Claiming Inversion: Lesbian Constructions of Female Identity as Claims for Authority." *Journal of American Folklore* 111(439):3–22.

Leland, John. 1992. Souljah on Ice. *Newsweek*, 29 June:46–52.

Lewis, Lisa. 1990. *Gender Politics and MTV: Voicing the Difference*. Philadelphia: Temple University Press.

Lorde, Audre. 1982. *Zami: A New Spelling of My Name*. Trumansburg. New York: Crossing Press.

———. 1984. *Sister Outsider*. Freedom, CA: Crossing Press.

MC Lyte. 1993. Musical guest. *Arsenio Hall Show*, 8 October.

———. 1996. Interview by the author. Irvine, CA., 11 August.

Morgan, Joan. 1997. "The Bad Girl of Hip-Hop." *Essence* (March):76–77,132–134.

Nelson, Havelock. 1993. "New Female Rappers Play for Keeps." *Billboard*, 10 July:1,77.

Omosupe, Ekua. 1991. "Black/Lesbian/Bulldagger." *Differences* 3(2):101–111.

Pearlman, Jill. 1988. "Girls Rappin' Round Table." *The Paper* (Summer):25–27.

Penrice, Ronda. 1995. Interview by the author. Manhattan, 11 November.

Queen Latifah. 1993. Interview by the author. Jersey City, 8 July.

Radner, Joan Newlon, and Susan S. Lanser. 1993. "Strategies of Coding in Women's Culture." In *Feminist Messages: Coding in Women's Folk Culture*, edited by Joan Newlon Radner, 1–29. Urbana: University of Illinois Press.

Roberts, Deborah. 1998. Beautiful Women. *20/20*, ABC Transcript #1796, 30 March.

Roberts, John W. 1989. *From Trickster to Badman: The Back Folk Hero in Slavery and Freedom*. Philadelphia: University of Pennsylvania.

Roberts, Robin. 1994. "'Ladies First': Queen Latifah's Afrocentric Feminist Music Video." *African American Review* 28(2):245–257.

Rogers, E. Charles. 1994. "The Salt-N-Pepa Interview." *Rap Masters* 7(7) July:30–31.

Rose, Tricia. 1994. *Black Noise: Rap Music and Black Culture in Contemporary America*. Hanover, NH: Wesleyan University Press.

Sieber, Roy, and Roslyn Adele Walker. 1987. *African Art in the Cycle of Life*. Washington, D.C.: Smithsonian Institution Press.

Sister Souljah. 1994. No *Disrespect*. New York: Random House.

Smitherman, Geneva. 1994. *Black Talk: Words and Phrases from the Hood to the Amen Comer*. New York: Houghton Mifflin.

Walker, Lisa M. 1993. "How to Recognize a Lesbian: The Cultural Politics of Looking like What You Are." *Signs: Journal of Women in Culture and Society* 18(4):866–889.

Walters, Barry. 1998. *My Melody* (sound recording review). *Advocate* 755 (17 March):59–60.

Discography

Boogie Boys. 1987[1985]. A Fly Girl. *Rap vs. Rap: The Answer Album*. Priority 4XL-9506.

Boss. 1993. *Bom Gangstaz*. Def Jam/Columbia OT 52903.

Bytches with Problems. 1991. *The Bytches.* No Face/RAL CT 47068.

Da Brat 1994. *Funkdafied.* Chaos/Columbia OT 66164.

Foxy Brown. 1997. *Ill Na Na.* Def Jam 547028.

Funky Four Plus One. Rapping and Rocking the House. *Great Rap Hits.* Sugar Hits SH 246.

Lauryn Hill. 1998. *The Miseducation of Lauryn Hill.* Ruffhouse/Columbia CT69035.

Lil' Kim. 1996. *Hard Core.* Big Beat Records/Atlantic 92733–2.

MC Lyte. 1988. *Lyte as a Rock.* First Priority Music/Atlantic 7 90905-1.

———. 1993. *Ain't No Other.* First Priority Music/Atlantic 7 92230-4.

Missy "Misdemeanor" Elliott. 1997. *Supa Dupa Fly.* The Gold Mind, Inc./ EastWest 62062-2.

———. 1999. *Da Real World.* The Gold Mine, Inc./EastWest 62244-4.

Queen Latifah. 1989. *All Hail the Queen.* Tommy Boy TBC 1022.

———. 1991. *Nature of a Sista'.* Tommy Boy TBC 9007.

———. 1993. U.N.I.T.Y. *Black Reign.* Motown 37463-6370-4.

Queen Pen. 1997. *My Melody.* Lil' Man/Interscope INTC-90151.

Roxanne Shanté. 1992. *The Bitch Is Back.* Livin' Large 3001.

———. 1995. Roxanne's Revenge. *Roxanne Shanté's Greatest Hits.* Cold Chillin'/Warner Brothers 5007.

Salt-N-Pepa. 1986. *Hot, Cool and Vicious.* Next Plateau/London 422-828362-2.

———. 1990. *Black's Magic.* Next Plateau/London 422-828362-2.

———. 1993. *Very Neccessary.* Next Plateau/London P2-28392.

Sister Souljah. *1992. 360 Degrees of Power.* Epic EK-48713.

TLC. 1992. *Ooooooooohhh…On the TLC Tip.* LaFace/Arista 26003-2.

———. 1994. *CrazySexyCool.* LaFace/Arista AC 26009-2.

———. 1999. Unpretty. *FanMail.* LaFace/Arista 26055-4.

Yo-Yo. 1991. *Make Way for the Motherlode.* EastWest/Atlantic 791605-2.

———. 1996. *Total Control.* East West/Atlantic 61898.

*piano
maqam: microtones are gone #*

7

The Frame Drum in the Middle East
Women, Musical Instruments, and Power

Veronica Doubleday

Introduction

In many parts of the Middle East frame drums are strongly associated with women.[1] This situation is remarkable because in many other regions—parts of Europe and sub-Saharan Africa for instance—drumming is traditionally performed by men, not women. Given the highly contested status of both music and women in Middle Eastern Muslim cultures, an instrument especially played by women offers a rich field for the investigation of gender and power.

My aim in this article is twofold: (1) to contribute to the ethnography of frame drums, and (2) based on this data, to offer theoretical conclusions on gender and musical instruments. My coverage of the Middle East spans an area stretching from the eastern Mediterranean, Egypt and the Arabian Peninsula, through Turkish, Arab and Persian lands to Afghanistan. As the birthplace of ancient civilisations (e.g., Mesopotamia and Egypt), and of monotheisms (Judaism, Christianity and Islam), the Middle East is a region of great historical importance. In this setting the frame drum has a long and significant history. I draw on sources from a variety of disciplines and also present my first-hand data from Afghanistan.[2]

This is a general survey of women's relation to frame drums in the Middle East. However, I need to point out from the outset that scholarly coverage of Middle Eastern women's music is patchy and relatively superficial, although new material is appearing (for instance, see Campbell 2002, Christensen 2002, Sawa 2002, and Urkevich 2001).

Our lack of knowledge relates partly to androcentric cultural bias in both Western and Middle Eastern conventions. In the early 1980s Nettl expressed concern about an "unbalanced picture of world music, heavily weighted towards male musical practices" (1983, 334, quoted in Koskoff 1989, 1), and feminist scholars have repeatedly drawn attention to this bias. Islamic ideologies about female modesty and seclusion have also contributed to the invisibility of women's traditions and created difficulty of access for research (also see Olsen 2002).

As a generic type, the Middle Eastern frame drum is portable, and played with the bare hands. It is usually single-headed and is most commonly round in shape (but rectangular or multi-sided forms are also found). Its frame is of variable size, and it is sometimes modified with percussive additions (bells, rings, chains, cymbals, metal discs). The drum's skin may be plain or painted.

The most common names for Middle Eastern frame drums are *duff* (principally applied in Arabia and western regions), *daff/def* (Turkey, Iran and further east), *dáireh/dáira/doira* (Middle East and Central Asia), and *tár* (Arabia). These terms have many local variants and the terminology for frame drums is imprecise and sometimes confused, as noted in Iraq (Hassan 1980, 38).[3] Other terms mentioned in this article are *tof* (Hebrew), *mazhár*, *riqq* and *ghirbál* (Arabic), and *bendir* (North African). For further details regarding linguistic, historical and geographical aspects of terminology, see Poché (1984a, 616).

Frame Drums and Women

Middle East scholars have noted close associations between frame drums and women. Shiloah makes a general link between women and frame drums in the Arab world (2001, 830), and refers to the *doira, tár, bendir* and *daff* as "the region's most characteristically feminine instrument" (1995, 159). Touma connects the drum with Arab women's dance traditions, stressing its ancient roots, especially with Egyptian and Israelite women (1996, 135). In Turkish folk music Picken associates the frame drum with women (1975, 142), as do Morris and Rihtman (1984), who say the *def* is "almost exclusively played by women, usually in private." Along the same lines, women's use of frame drums extends beyond the Middle East into Islamic-influenced regions (e.g., North Africa, the Indian subcontinent, Central Asia, the Caucasus, the Balkans, and Iberia).[4]

Some general features emerge regarding gender. In the Middle East women lack exclusive rights over any type of musical instrument, even the frame drum itself, as noted in Iraq (Hassan 1980, 94) and Afghanistan. In some areas the frame drum is one of the few indigenous instruments women play, as in Afghanistan. In Iraq, women traditionally play only idiophones and a limited range of membranophones, including the frame drum (*daff*) (ibid., 94). In Azerbaijan "the only instrument allowed into traditional women's surroundings is the *def* " (Kerimova 1996, 4). No doubt there are other examples. It must, however be stressed that elite women have had access to a wider range of musical instruments. At the same time a considerable number of instruments are traditionally reserved for men. These phenomena point to a multi-faceted gender bias, which is clearly demonstrated in other aspects of Middle Eastern culture (see Ahmed 1992).

The status, rights, privileges and powers of Middle Eastern women vary greatly according to class and region. Women's role in family and social relationships is central (see Beck and Keddie 1978, and Joseph and Slyomovics 2001). Middle Eastern women often enjoy the privilege of all-women space, a setting which facilitates the power of female solidarity and provides the principal context for music-making.

Ideologies about female submissiveness and modesty have caused restrictions in many domains, including music (see below). But, as Tapper observes, inequality of status "does not preclude able women from wielding considerable power within the household" (1991, 104). Koskoff also notes that—across culture—women sometimes "connive" with notions of male superiority (1989, 13). Middle Eastern women may privately condemn aspects of male ascendancy, holding an inner sense of power and worth.

Musical Instruments and Power

Before examining Middle Eastern frame drums, let us consider what powers are invested in musical instruments generally. According to DeVale, such powers may relate to healing, physical strength, farming and hunting, safeguarding villages, or help with family problems, and musical instruments may facilitate spirit possession and exorcism, or serve as vehicles for communication between the worlds of the seen and the unseen (1989, 107).

To this list we may add other quite basic powers. As tools of communication, musical instruments may become sources of authority. The sounds of musical instruments have the power to unite people, coordinating marching or work rhythms, or engendering group emotions. Musical instruments may become icons, they may be revered or reviled, and they may be targets of hatred or fear. Magical powers are ascribed to some instruments, and their sounds may be used to promote the growth of plants or to influence weather conditions (e.g., Stobart 1994).

Cirlot states that of all musical instruments the drum is the most pregnant with mystic ideas (1971, 89). Drums are widely used in rituals and ceremonies, and may be said to possess supernatural powers. Jenkins notes that in the Mataco culture of Argentina one type of drum has multiple spiritual functions and "is a general magical instrument" (1977, 41–2).

1.3. Musical Instruments in Islamic Thought

Ideas expressed by the Muslim religious establishment have had a crucial impact in the Middle East. The legists have generally condemned music. In this, they focussed upon musical instruments, leaving unaccompanied song in a separate and less blameable category. In particular, Qur'anic recitation (*qiráat*) is conceptually distinct from "music." In Muslim cultures, a broad distinction is often made between "musical instruments" and "singing." This is true for Afghanistan, where words for music (Persian *sáz*; Greek *musiqi*) are synonymous with "musical instrument," and singing (*khándan*) is closely related to reading and speech (Baily 1996, 147–8; Sakata 2002, 46–48).

The views of Muslim women regarding musical instruments have rarely been recorded. This is due to androcentric bias and to women's exclusion from the realm of public debate and interpretation of the scriptures. The Prophet Mohammad's wife Aisha is a significant exception, the source of many *hadiths* (Islamic Prophetic traditions) and acknowledged as a prominent authority on the Prophet's legacy after his death (see Islamic Gender Ideologies, p. 115).

Broadly speaking, the male legists ascribed negative powers to musical instruments, saying they cause human beings to lapse into sin. This view has sometimes percolated into the popular consciousness. In Afghanistan, Baily interviewed a range of people (necessarily all men) on this point, and summarised their ideas. In their view, music possessed (1) the power to engross and attract, thus distracting people from prayer, (2) the power to deflect people from work, (3) the power to lead people astray, indulging in illicit activities, especially sex and imbibing "wine," and (4) the power to bring people into contact with Satan (Baily 1988, 146–7).

Conceptual links exist between Satan and musical instruments, especially regarding the shawm. Abu Bakr, the Prophet Mohammad's father-in-law and successor, is reported to have called it *mizmár al-shaitán*, "the pipe of the devil" (Farmer 1929, 26). Satan may also be linked with sexuality: villagers in western Afghanistan sometimes called the *sorná* (shawm) the "devil's penis" (Baghban 1977, quoted in Baily 1988, 146–7). Generally, though, in the Islamic Middle East sexual symbolism is not commonly applied to musical instruments.

Positive ideas of instrumental music are also apparent in popular thought. The notion of music as "spiritual food" finds expression in Persian culture (e.g., western Afghanistan, see Baily 1988, 152–5). Sufis opposed the legists, and some upheld the lawfulness and sacred potentiality of musical instruments (see 3.2, below). Some brotherhoods used musical instruments in their religious rituals, even venerating them as sacred. The reed-flute (*ney*) has always been associated with Mevlevi ritual. Part of its hallowed status derives from the opening lines of its founder Maulana Jalaluddin Rumi's *Mathnawi*, where it symbolises "the soul emptied of self and filled with the Divine Spirit" (Nicholson 1978, 29).

It is important to remember that Islamic legists, thinkers and writers developed a construct of history which labelled the pre-Islamic period as uncivilised; they styled it *Jáhelia* ("Days of Ignorance"). This project suppressed awareness of the pre-Islamic because it was un-Islamic. Accordingly, some early magico-religious attributes of musical instruments have been obliterated from cultural memory. Modern scholars have probably underestimated religious uses of musical instruments in Middle Eastern cultures, as Hassan observes for Iraq: "The uses of musical instruments for religious purposes are incomparably more numerous and diverse than profane uses, and also far less well known" (1980, 11).

The Early History of Frame Drums in the Middle East

The Middle Eastern frame drum dates back at least to the third millennium BCE. For many centuries it seems to have been the principal type of drum in the region, always closely connected with women.[5]

Religious Drumming in Ancient History

Archeological and textual evidence points to the frame drum's particular significance within religious ritual. Earliest sources date from the Sumerian civilisation that flourished in Mesopotamia from c.3000 BCE, and artefacts show both men and women playing frame drums (Jenkins 1977, 40–41). Inanna was an important deity, the goddess of life, death, and fertility, and texts describe her bestowing drums to her people at her cultic centre, the city of Uruk (Warka in modern Iraq). Frame drums and other instruments were used in her temple ceremonies and processions through the city as well as in mourning ceremonies for the dead (see Wolkstein and Kramer 1983; Blades and Anderson 1984; Kilmer 2001). Some type of hand-held drum, very probably a frame drum, was used in laments for the dead (Wolkstein and Kramer 1983, 53, 61, 69). The lamenter "circled the house of the gods" in a circumambulation ritual.

Frame drums were used in an annual "sacred marriage" ceremony that was important to Inanna's cult, later being inherited by the Babylonian goddess Ishtar. Widely documented in poetic and priestly accounts, it became known by the Greek term (*hieros gamos*). This ritual was performed continuously for at least two thousand years to assure prosperity and fertility to the land and its people (Ochsborn 1990, 22). By means of sexual intercourse (in the original drama, at least), a priestess representing the goddess bestowed kingship to the king. Sumerian artefacts show nude female figures holding frame drums, and the art historian Williams Forte links the drums with female seduction and the cults of Inanna and Ishtar (1983, 195–6).

The frame drum was widely used in Ancient Egypt, usually by women. In the Egyptian New Kingdom dynasties (c. 1570–947 BCE) female musical troupes (*khener*) directed by women used rectangular and round frame drums in temple rituals and funerary ceremonies, along with other instruments. Women played frame drums in the important *sed* festival to renew the pharaoh's kingship (see Robins 1993, especially p.105, and Teeter 1995). Frame drums were also connected with birth rituals. Within the temple complex of Dendera, dedicated to Hathor the goddess of music and sexuality, a birthing chapel has bas reliefs depicting a musical procession. Thirty-two priestesses play frame drums as they march down the left wall towards the main shrine area, and twenty-nine priestesses with sceptres and sistrums advance along the opposite wall (Redmond 1997, 102). In another link with women, the frame drum was an attribute of the fierce and grotesque dwarf-like household god, Bes, who scared away evil spirits and protected new babies and women in childbirth (Robins 1993, 85; Teeter 1993, 68; Wosien 1974, plate 25).

Numerous terracotta artefacts and references in the Hebrew Bible attest that Canaanite and Israelite women played the frame drum (*tof/top/toph*) in various ritual contexts, whereas men apparently did not (see Meyers 1993). Psalm 68 is a processional hymn, sung as the ark was carried into the temple (Alexander 1973, 341). Verses 24–27 describe a procession penetrating the inner sanctuary:

> Thy procession, O God, comes into view,
> The procession of my God and King into the sanctuary:

at its head the singers, next come minstrels,
girls among them playing on tambourines [i.e., *tof*, pl. *toppim*].
(Psalm 68, *The New English Bible*)

However, after the exile of the Hebrews the sanctuary was reserved to Levites and priests. In a significant loss of power, women (with their drums) were excluded from the sanctuary (Mays 1968, 464).

Outside the temple, women also sang psalms for victories. In the days of the judges (c. 1220–1050 BCE) women had the task of dividing the spoils of battle and spreading news of victories with psalms accompanied by drumming. One of the oldest writings of the Hebrew Bible, the Song of Deborah, is a victory psalm (Alexander 1973, 221–2). Psalm 68:11–12 refers to victory psalms: "The women that publish the tidings are a great host. Kings of armies flee, they flee." Another famous reference to victory drumming occurs in Exodus 15:20, where women join the prophetess Miriam to sing, drum and dance in triumph after crossing the Red Sea. This event is strongly maintained in the folk memory: Touma states that Jews called the drum, and still call it, "Miriam's drum" (*tof miryam*) (1996, 135).

The frame drum (*duff*) probably has ancient roots in Arabia. As among the Israelites, it was principally played by women in a variety of genres. Farmer argues that the music of Arabian, Assyrian, and Hebrew religious cults was very similar. His evidence is based on the character and etymology of musical genres, and on close connections between musical instruments of all three cultures. For the frame drum, he matches the Arabic term *duff* with the Babylonian-Assyrian term *adapu* and the Aramaic-Hebrew *toph* (Farmer 1929, xiv).

Frame drums were used in devotional singing and dancing (*tahlil*) accompanying the circumambulation of the Ka'aba at Mecca and other cultic centres devoted principally to goddess worship. A Meccan tradition of female ritual performance is consistent with devotion to female deity, and Jargy defines *tahlil* as a "magic incantation" and "religious dance," with accompaniment "especially by women" on frame drums (1971, 14–15). Farmer links *tahlil* with Phoenician-Cypriot terracotta artefacts (Farmer 1929, 8; also see Meyers 1993). The term *tahlil* is close to Hebrew *tahala* (psalm or song of praise) (Fohrer 1973). Circumambulation of the "house of god" is an early practice. As noted above, it occurred in Sumer; it was also part of Israelite religion (Gibb and Kramers 1961, 586), and is still continuously performed by Muslim pilgrims at Mecca (without music).[6]

Ecstatic Cults in the Greek and Roman Empires

As cult instruments, frame drums spread from West Asia into the Greek and then Roman Empires. At first the link with female performance was strong, but then eunuchs began to use frame drums in cult ceremonies.

Greek vase paintings from the fifth century BCE show people (usually women) using them in the worship of Dionysus, the god of fertility and of the vine whose ecstasy cult is well documented. Female devotees, known as maenads, were famed for their wild and frenzied behaviour. Dionysian ceremonies took place at night in woods or on mountain tops: they entailed sexual intercourse, the sacrifice of animals, wine-drinking, and trance dances (Larousse 1959, 178–85, Lawler 1965, 75–77). Rouget stresses the importance of Greek ecstatic cults in understanding later Sufi trance practices (1985, 187–8).

The frame drum was also the cult instrument of the mother goddess Cybele, who originated in Phrygia (Anatolia, in Turkey), and she is often depicted holding it. After the second Punic war in 204 B.C.E., Cybele became an extremely important Roman divinity. Her eunuch priests (*galli*) used the frame drum, double flute and cymbals, and her cult attained great popularity in Rome (Scott 1957, 405; also see McKinnon/Anderson 2001, Anderson/Mathiesen 2001). Under the influence of the frenzied music, men enacted self-castration in order to become her priests, after which they wore jewellery and female attire. These practices caused considerable controversy in Rome, but the cult spread despite attempts to suppress it (Vermaseren 1977).[7]

Family and Tribal Rituals in Arabia and the Eastern Mediterranean

For many centuries frame drums have been used in family and tribal rituals of Arabia and the eastern Mediterranean. All the evidence points to female performance traditions. Early Hebrew biblical texts describe Israelite women using frame drums to welcome home victorious heroes with singing and dancing. In Judges 11:12, the daughter of Jephthah came to greet her father on return from a military mission "with tambourines and dances." This type of performance was probably a sacred duty that extended to any auspicious homecoming. Genesis 31:27 describes rituals of leave-taking accompanied by frame drums and lyres; these were probably also the province of women. Meyers's biblical research supports these points (1993, 58–62).

Evidence from north-western Arabia around the lifetime of the Prophet Mohammad (seventh century CE) suggests a similar situation. Women, girls and slaves used the frame drum (*duff*) when singing improvised blessings to honour an eminent person's arrival. Several instances occur in certain *hadith*s (Islamic Traditions of the Prophet). When the Prophet migrated to Medina in 622, he was greeted in the streets by some girls singing with the *duff*: "We are girls of the tribe of Najjar; what a blessing it is to be a neighbour of the Prophet!"—and he congratulated them on their performance (Roy Choudhury 1957, 66; Urkevich 2001, 328). On another occasion women greeted his arrival, singing and drumming from the rooftops (Farmer 1929, 27). Arabian women played frame drums in battles, singing to encourage their warriors to victory (Farmer 1929, 10). The lament (*marthiya*) and elegy (*nawh*) for heroes were the prerogative of women, also performed to frame drum accompaniment.[8]

Summary

Frame drums have ancient roots in Mesopotamia, the Mediterranean, Egypt, and the Arabian Peninsula, and a considerable degree of continuity emerges across traditions and through time. This drum was used in religious rituals in all early traditions examined; some (e.g., Sumerian and Egyptian) were linked with kingship. In the early period, rituals featuring frame drums occupied primary roles in the cultures concerned—in Inanna's cult, in the Egyptian *sed* kingship ceremony, or the procession into the temple at Jerusalem, for instance. Later examples (e.g., the cult of Dionysus) were more culturally peripheral.

In many traditions frame drums were primarily played by women, often in connection with dancing. The contexts included (1) temple rituals, (2) victory and battle songs, (3) family and tribal rituals, (4) ecstatic trance cults. Women often sang, drummed and danced in the open air—in temple processions, at shrines, on battlefields, in streets, outside homes, and even on mountain-tops and through woods. As well as this, across the Middle East female entertainers used frame drums (and other instruments) from early times and until after the time of the Prophet Mohammad (see Kilmer 2001; Teeter 1993; Farmer 1929).

Some scholars (e.g., Touma 1977, 107; Blades and Anderson 1984, 974) propose that frame drums were exclusive to women. Edwards asserts exclusive use by women and eunuchs in Egypt, and probably also by Israelite women (1991, 19). However, men evidently played the drum in some traditions (e.g., in ancient Mesopotamia). Montagu (1984) more cautiously states that the *duff* and *tof* were "frequently, though not exclusively, played by women," and Meyers concludes that *tof* was occasionally played by Israelite men (1993, 60). The evidence could never be conclusive. Exclusivity, in any case, is prescriptive and exceptions occur.

Music and Women in the Islamic Middle East

The advent and rapid spread of Islam in the Middle East precipitated important social changes. These impacted on women, and on the status of musical performance in different contexts.

Islamic Gender Ideologies

The dominant, prescriptive terms of the core Islamic discourses were founded and elaborated in Arabia at the rise of Islam, and in Iraq in the immediately ensuing period (Ahmed 1992, 3). Despite its message of equality, the Holy Qur'an was open to misogynistic interpretation. One verse states: "Men are in charge of women, because Allah hath made one of them to excel the other" (Sura IV, verse 34). The Qur'an also states that women are unclean when menstruating (Sura II "the Cow"), and thus unfit to perform ritual prayers (al-Bukhari 6.22).

The early caliphs and legists inherited a male bias from the Byzantine and Persian empires that came under Muslim control. During the Abbasid period (eighth to thirteenth centuries) Islamic law was fixed and codified, reaffirming "patriarchal family and female subordination" that were key components of the socio-religious visions of Judaism, Christianity and Zoroastrianism already in place (Ahmed 1992, 4). In a consistent trend towards "closure and diminution" of women's power and freedom—to use Ahmed's phrase—men established ascendancy. They could take up to four wives, and had preferential rights with regard to divorce and patrilineal descent. Through concepts relating to honour, male heads of families exerted control over female sexuality and all aspects of women's behaviour, including musical performance.

Women were not veiled or secluded in early Arabia, but a hundred and fifty years after the Prophet's death the "purdah" system was fully established over a wide area (Levy 1957, 130). Purdah practices took different forms, generally characterised by the seclusion and segregation of women in most echelons of society. Women were gradually excluded or marginalised from communal worship, expected to pray in a special corner or balcony-like gallery of the mosque or at home (Schimmel 1994, 51–53). They were discouraged from gathering communally, which inhibited the possibilities of communal religious music-making (see Ahmed 1992, 115–16).

Lawful Music

Roy Choudhury (1957) and Farmer (1929, 20–38) have examined the sources regarding the lawfulness of music in Islam. Some important facts emerge: (1) there is no pronouncement against music in the Qur'an (Roy Choudhury 1957, 65, Farmer 1929, 22); (2) *hadiths* attest that the Prophet listened to music and enjoyed it, women at that time being the chief music-makers (Roy Choudhury 1957, 66–70); (3) many traditions regarding music derive from Aisha, wife of the Prophet; (4) the *duff* occupied a central place in the debate about lawfulness, "among the instruments most referred to in the sayings of Mohammad" (Poché 1984a, 617).

The frame drum was accepted as lawful and desirable in the context of weddings (Roy Choudhury 1957, 70). In a well-known *hadith*, the Prophet announced "Publish the marriage and beat the *ghirbál* (round tambourine)!" (Farmer 1929, 22).[9] Aisha records that the Prophet personally sent musicians to a wedding she had arranged; he composed some verses for the occasion which would have been sung with the *duff* (Roy Choudhury 1957, 68). At his daughter Fatima's marriage to Ali, a celebrated male performer Amr ibn Umayyu Dhamari played the frame drum, and became "patron saint of tambourine players" (Farmer 1929, 39).[10]

Aisha's *hadiths* provided significant support for the lawfulness of music. She recorded that the Prophet once invited an Abyssinian acrobat and musician to perform for her at home. This performance took place on sacred ground, since the Prophet's home and the mosque shared the same courtyard (Roy Choudhury 1957, 69). Aisha attested that the Prophet listened to music by the professional singing-girls (*qainát*) and upheld it as lawful at festival time (Farmer 1929, 26–27). However, because she led political opposition to Ali ibn Ali Talib, members of the Shia sect revile her as an enemy and reject her scriptural authority, which allowed them to express their disapproval of music more fully (Roy Choudhury 1957, 88).

The Sufi movement evolved largely as a spiritual and political reaction against the corrupt Umayyad and Abbasid caliphates. There were important female Sufis in the early Islamic period, but by the late tenth century Sufism had become organised and consolidated into brotherhoods which strove to exclude women. The influence of the brotherhoods grew in every part of the Muslim Empire (Schimmel 1975, 82), and they began to use frame drums and music in their all-male spiritual rituals.

In a tract about musical audition, Majd al-Din al-Ghazali (d. 1126) argues for the lawful use of music, but solely in the context of Sufi ritual. He condemns musical instruments of "diversion" (such as *jank*, *rabáb*, *'ud*, *barbat* and *mizmár*) but explicitly upholds the frame drum as lawful, basing his argument on two "sound" (properly authenticated) *hadith*s in al-Bukhari and Muslim (Robson 1938, 111). Majd al-Din also expresses concern about possible sexual distractions at Sufi gatherings, requiring that "no beardless youth should be among them, nor should there be a window through which women can look at them; but if pious beardless youths are among them, they sit behind the men" (ibid., 112).

Restrictions on Female Musical Performance

Farmer states that after the death of the Prophet, women's "commanding position" in the realm of music declined. A radical change occurred under the caliph Uthman (644–56). Until then "music, as a profession, was in the hands of the women-folk and slave-girls for the greater part" (Farmer 1929, 44). Prominent Muslims campaigned against music. This period marked the first appearance of the male professional musician (*mukhannath*), "an effeminate class who dyed their hands and affected the habits of women" (ibid., 45). The first of these was the famous singer, Touais, "The Little Peacock" (632–710), brought up in the house of Arwa, the caliph's mother. He accompanied himself on a square *duff* which he carried in a bag or in his robe (ibid., 52–53).[11]

There is evidence of zealotry against women, and against the *duff* as a women's instrument. A polemic tract against music by Ibn abi-l Dunya (823–94) describes how an early convert to Islam, Ibn Masud (d. 652–4), patrolled gateways of enclosed residential quarters through which women needed to pass. He and his companions publicly tore up any frame drums "girls" had. The tract quotes Suwaid ibn Ghafala, the Prophet's contemporary—"The angels do not enter a house in which is a tambourine (*duff*)"—and the famous ascetic, Hasan al-Basri (d.728), who said "The tambourine does not pertain at all to the practice of the Muslims" (Robson 1938, 31–32).

Relatively defenceless, girls were easy targets for Muslims seeking to impose new standards of social behaviour. Asim ibn Hubaira, who lived in the Abbasid "Golden Age" (reputed for its fine court music), never saw a *duff* without breaking it. In old age, trampling one with his feet, he could not break it, and said: "Not one of their devils has overcome me but this" (ibid., 32). He was powerless to attack musical instruments played at court which were protected by the caliphs. The legists' condemnation of music and restriction of women's freedom apparently went—and go—hand in hand.

By the thirteenth century, with the close of the Abbasid rule, the legists had failed to stamp out "unlawful" types of music, but amateur women's music had disappeared from public life. In the Mamluk era (1250–1517) women continued to be professional mourners, accompanying themselves with frame drums (Sawa 2002, 298). In fifteenth-century Cairo funerals were lavish social occasions for women. Professional female mourners (with their drums) were periodically banned by the authorities, but they persisted in performing (Ahmed 1992, 118–9).

Practices relating to women and music (and the frame drum) developed differently in the various particular cultures of the Middle East. Broadly speaking, women continued to make music within their more limited circumstances. The frame drum remained widely available. In wealthy settings women might have access to instruments like the Arabian *qánun* and *'ud*, the Persian *tár* and *kamáncheh* or—for the elite—European imports such as the violin and piano.

The Frame Drum (*dáireh*) in Afghanistan

The frame drum probably arrived into Afghanistan with the advent of Islam. Afghan discourses on gender and musical instruments are founded in Islamic thought, which provides an important link with the Middle East. Although Afghanistan is geographically on the periphery of the Middle East (and should not be taken as "representative"), the following case study examines gender aspects of the instrument in some detail.

Evidence in Persian Miniature Paintings

Persian miniature paintings depict a fictional or mythological poetic world, but they contain naturalistic details of everyday life and provide clues about musical practices of the fifteenth and sixteenth centuries.[12] They show the frame drum played in Sufi religious gatherings, courtly settings, and nuptial celebrations.

The paintings depict ecstatic Sufi religious gatherings as an exclusively male context for music-making. Typically, several Sufis dance inside an assembled circle, with music from two frame drums and one or two flutes (*ney*), a combination frequently mentioned in Persian poetry (During 1993, 561) (for illustrations, see During 1991, 173, 200).

In courtly musical settings, the frame drum is played by both women and men. The memoirs of the Mughal emperor Babur, *Báburnámeh*, provide names of celebrated male musicians of the fifteenth century Timurid courts, whom Baily concludes to have been servants of the court, not people of noble birth (1988, 12–13). We have no information about women musicians; they possibly had a lower status. The paintings show small ensembles—all-female, all-male, or mixed—playing for a prince or king, usually in the company of a consort or guests, indoors or outdoors. Women dance, sing, play frame drums and other instruments: the harp (*chang*), various bowed and plucked lutes, and the hammered dulcimer (*santur*). The frame drum is sometimes shown held against the face, used as a resonator for the voice.[13]

Two miniatures from the Bodleian collection illustrate nuptial rituals in an all-female setting (apart from the male presence of the bridegroom). They both depict the consummation of the marriage of King Khusrau and Shirin. One, painted in 1500–1501, shows Khusrau and Shirin in bed, with three female attendants nearby. One sits at the end of the bed while the others play a frame drum and flute. The other miniature, painted in 1581, shows a large number of women around the nuptial bed (see Figure 7.1). Three female dancers holding handkerchiefs dance in a circle to the accompaniment of two frame drums played by women.[14]

Several hypotheses emerge about Persian music performance practice in the fifteenth and sixteenth centuries: (1) the frame drum was the only rhythmic instrument of courtly and religious music, excluding idiophones used by dancers; (2) in Sufi rituals, the frame drum was played exclusively by men (usually with the flute); (3) women used frame drums in the context of marriage; (4) at court, women musicians played a variety of instruments in prestigious settings.

Figure 7.1 Detail from a Persian miniature painted in Shiraz, 1581, showing two women playing frame drums (bottom right) and others dancing in the marriage chamber of King Khusrau and Shirin. Ms. Elliot 239 folio 243R, Bodleian Library, University of Oxford.

Recent History

It is unclear when frame drums ceased to be used in Sufi rituals in Afghanistan.[15] With regard to courtly music, frame drums fell out of use with the advent of Indian court musicians to Kabul in the 1860s. They established the tabla drums as the principal rhythmic instrument of Afghan classical music (Baily 1988, 25). Nearby, in Iran, the frame drum disappeared from classical music in the nineteenth and twentieth centuries, "doubtless eclipsed by the *darb* or *tonbak*", but in the 1980s the large Kurdish Sufi frame drum with rings (*daff*) began to appear among instrumental groups (During 1993, 561).

In Afghanistan the mid-twentieth century saw a period of secularisation, as the country became more open to Western influences. Frame drums were played solely as instruments of folk and popular music, and the instrument did not carry much prestige. In the extensive instrumentarium of Afghanistan's national radio orchestra, frame drums were not used (Baily 1988, 82).

Before the pro-Soviet coup d'etat of 1978, frame drums were common all over Afghanistan.[16] The drums were made by settled or semi-nomadic groups with outsider status known derogatorily as Jat/Ghorbat, who also made wooden sieves with an identical style of frame.[17] Locally made drums were sometimes sold from door to door, for very small sums of money. Such drums vary in size, and are sometimes fitted with iron rings, pellet bells, or metal jingles to enhance the sound. The skins are sometimes painted, sometimes left plain. Designs painted on the skin include the flowering tree of life common in women's embroidery.

In Afghanistan the frame drum is played principally by girls and women. Slobin summarized the situation stating: "In Afghan life there is a clear distinction of musical roles by sex. In most cases women do not play or even handle musical instruments except for the tambourine and the jew's harp (the latter is also played by children). Men, on the other hand, master a great variety of lutes and fiddles, and generally shun the women's instruments" (1980, 137).[18]

In Afghan life a pronounced ideology of gender separation has been defined and imposed by male authority. This affects musical life in several ways: (1) virtually all musical activity is segregated according to gender, (2) men dominate religious, classical and radio music, leaving only folk music to be shared with women, and (3) men have inhibited women from playing almost all musical instruments.

The frame drum's status is somewhat particular: (1) it is by far the most common instrument, played by the largest body of performers, including women, men and children; (2) it is the only self-sufficient non-melodic instrument; (3) it is the only traditional instrument to be played by women (apart from the jew's harp);[19] (4) through its connection with the Arabian *duff*, it has significance in the religious debate about the lawfulness of music; (5) because of its acceptability to some jurists, its status as a musical instrument is questionable; (6) used within women's quarters, it is the principal instrument for effecting the marriage process; (7) it has certain low-key connections with illicit sexuality (see Evaluation of the Drum, p. 120).[20]

Contexts for Performance

Women use the frame drum for informal musical entertainment (*sá 'attiri*) in the privacy of their all-women domestic space. Inhibited by male authority, they say it is "bad" (*bad*) to play when men are at home and would be disturbed.

Weddings provide the most significant lawful context for women to play frame drums.[21] It is incumbent on the bridegroom's women to drum, sing and dance, unless they hire female professional musicians to fulfill that role for them. Inhibitions and ideas of modesty are temporarily forgotten. In wedding processions fully veiled women may even play the drum in public space (see illustrations in Doubleday 2005).

The drum facilitates the marriage process in many ways: (1) it accompanies songs of blessing whose verses give emotional support to the bride and her close relatives; (2) women's music and dancing promote bonding between the bride and groom's families; (3) the drum announces arrivals, accompanies bridal processions, and advertises the marriage to the neighbourhood; (4) music and dancing provide a "boiling hot" (*por jush*) atmosphere suitable for the eventual consummation of marriage.[22]

Apart from wedding processions, women's legitimate use of public space for drumming is highly restricted. Until recently, New Year festivities at the spring equinox offered a notable opportunity for outdoor music. These celebrations connected with greenery and renewal are of ancient origin, widely celebrated in Persian-influenced regions (Doubleday 2005, 62–67).[23] In 1972 at the mass women's spring gathering in the Gohar Shad Park at Herat, Sakata observed women's open-air music-making, an activity permissible only at that time of year: "Small groups of women sing and dance to the accompaniment of tambourines called *daira* which they bring with them or which they purchase in the park from gypsy-like women who traditionally make and sell them" (2002, 19). By the mid-1970s, in Herat women no longer played outdoor music at the mass spring picnics, inhibited by male guards, although they confirmed that music-making had been their custom.

Even within private female spaces, music-making became difficult during the war years, due to religious pressure on everyone to maintain an atmosphere of mourning for martyrs. During the Taliban period (1995–2001) music-making was prohibited. These factors affected the transmission of drumming skills, and young girls had restricted opportunities for learning the traditional repertoire (see Figure 7.2).

Figure 7.2 Female members of a family making music at home. The grandmother sings and plays the frame drum for her daughters-in-law and grandchildren. In the 1970s it was common for girls to entertain older women, but during the recent decades of conflict and censorship young women have had restricted opportunities for learning to play the drum. Photo Veronica Doubleday, Kabul, 2004.

Evaluations of the Drum

In her fieldwork among Jat/Ghorbat groups who make sieves and frame drums, Rao collected a myth about the origin of the drum. It describes their ancestors making the first frame drum for the Prophet's daughter, Bibi Fatimeh, in Medina, for use at a wedding (Rao 1982, 67). The myth gives the drum positive value, invoking the sanctity and prestige of the Prophet and his daughter, and its use in the lawful context of marriage.

Those who make or use the drum professionally give it value. Zainab Herawi, a female professional musician of Jat origins, was one such person. The drum was the tool of her trade: in the past female entertainers were known as *dáireh-dast* ("drum-in-hand"). As my teacher, Zainab suggested I make a religious vow to "make my fingers flow" on the drum.[24] This vow linked her instrument with a venerable Sufi shrine frequented by the greatest master musicians of Kabul, and she said it would bring me religious merit (*sawáb*) (Doubleday 2005, 181).

Afghan women generally cherish the drum as "a good thing," necessary for celebratory festivities and valuable for entertainment. They say festivities have religious merit, but I never heard them claim merit for the drum itself. They attribute certain apotropaic properties to the drum. Following a birth, they play it in festivities that ward off malevolent spirits (*jinn*) (ibid., 144–5). People believe that music (especially drums) can facilitate the exorcism of spirits (ibid., 200).[25]

Afghan men hold a more negative view of the drum and some deride it as a women's instrument. The drum has no part in prestigious genres like classical or radio music, and male professional musicians scathingly say women do not "know anything" about music theory. Another negative aspect of the drum is its connection with Jat/Ghorbat groups, who have outsider status. Some Jat/Ghorbat groups practised the prostitution of women and boys, with dancing as an erotic lure (Rao 1982, 28–29; Baily 1988, 34, 141–2). Further, professional women musicians collect customary tips and gifts from the bridegroom's family in the drum, behaviour which is also seen as shameful (Doubleday 2005, 189, 201–2).

Baily (1996) discovered that some men resisted classifying the *dáireh* as a musical instrument. In a range of tests of sound perception, he questioned various Herati male informants about a recording of a man singing to his own *dáireh* accompaniment. Two theological students did not consider this to be "music" (*musiqi*). Their judgment was presumably based on a pre-understanding of the drum as lawful and upheld in accepted *hadith*s. Their logic would seem to run as follows: "The drum is not sinful, therefore its sound is not sinful. Music is sinful, therefore this sound is not music and the drum is not a musical instrument."

Another informant, Gada Mohammad, a professional musician, also initially claimed the *dáireh* was not a musical instrument, but for different reasons. Perhaps because it is normally played by unskilled women, he did not see the drum as a "proper" instrument. But when he remembered that a prestigious male singer had played the *dáireh* on Radio Afghanistan, he changed his mind (ibid., 169–70). All three informants sought to categorise the drum according to preconceived ideas about music as defined by male authority.

To summarise, in Afghanistan uses of the frame drum have changed over the centuries. In the past it was intrinsic to Sufi rituals and the principal rhythm instrument of prestigious courtly music. Today it is primarily the instrument of women. Its most important use is in wedding rituals.

Sexuality and Power

Frame Drums, Dance, and Sexuality in the Middle East

Middle Eastern frame drums have important links with dance and sexuality. From a global perspective, Hanna emphasises multiple associations between sex and dance. She identifies "aphrodisiac dancing" as a broad category, outlining several types of which the first two relate to our line of enquiry:

1. Dance in settings with courtship opportunities and at wedding parties (where courtship often occurs)—whether women and men dance together or apart, for the opposite sex or for their own sex—encourages culturally licit procreation. A group's own members may dance, or it may hire professional dancers of high or low status.
2. Dancing may be for the purpose of alluring a pre- or extra-marital affair, including prostitution (1988, 46–47).

This analysis is useful for the modern era, but concepts of "licit " and "illicit" sexual union in or outside marriage did not always apply in Middle Eastern culture.

The region has an ancient history of non-monogamous female sexuality in temple service. Historically remote, it was transmuted and largely erased from cultural memory. In Sumer (Mesopotamia) from the third millennium BCE an important characteristic of Inanna/Ishtar-Astarte's cult was the sacred marriage ritual (*hieros gamos*) in which frame drums were featured (see above). Embodying the goddess, the priestess (hierodule) actively "summoned" the king to her embrace (Long 1992, 133). Buonaventura suggests that the Middle Eastern "Dance of the Seven Veils" was an aphrodisiac "welcome" dance within this ritual (1983, 17–23).[26]

For many centuries the *hieros gamos* fertility drama was an occasion for "love feasts for the whole community" (Long 1992, 132), probably with drumming and dancing. Judaism opposed goddess worship, and biblical writers and commentators reviled temple service and its associated ceremonies, denigrating priestesses of Ishtar-Astarte as "temple harlots" or "prostitutes."[27] Under Judaism, Christianity and Islam, religious laws controlled female sexuality within marriage. However, women's "aphrodisiac" dancing and drumming was sanctioned as an integral feature of Middle Eastern wedding celebrations.

For Middle Eastern women today, weddings are still highly significant rites, usually held over several days at great financial expense. In many areas dancing to the rhythm of frame drums still plays an important role. Frame drums are significant in female ensembles in the Arabian Peninsula (Shiloah 1995, 159; Christensen 2001, 681; Campbell 2001). Hassan (1980) provides information on Iraq; for Turkey, see Ziegler (1990); and for Afghanistan, Doubleday (2000, 2005, and forthcoming). At weddings, girls and women typically perform solo dance improvisations focussing upon female corporeal beauty. Arab dancing, with its emphasis on pelvic movements, is implicitly erotic, and—within its lawful context—has a positive and wholesome ethos.

Erotic dancing to the rhythm of frame drums has a long history as an entertainment in palaces, harems, cabarets, brothels and other places. Outside the context of marriage, legists define it as illicit. Buonaventura's (1983) historical study contains six illustrations of women or transvestite boys dancing with frame drums in Egypt and Turkey.[27] The drum also appears as a "stage prop" in Orientalist erotic constructions of Middle Eastern and North African women, especially photographs (see Figure 7.3; also see Graham-Brown 1988, Alloula 1986).

Figure 7.3 Use of the frame drum (and a plucked lute) as erotic "stage props" in a studio postcard entitled "Chanteuses arabes." Egyptian postcard, ca. 1920, author's collection.

Outsider Status and Gypsies/Rom

Professional female dancers often belonged to Gypsy communities whose traditions set them apart. As outsiders, their subversive power, self-assertion, and independence threatened the status quo and led them to be stigmatised. In eighteenth and nineteenth century Egypt, *ghawazee* dancers were Gypsy women who performed in the open air, social outcasts "seldom admitted to respectable harems and frowned upon by the religious and upper classes" (Buonaventura 1983, 41). During Napoleon's expedition to Egypt in 1798 four hundred *ghawazee* women were captured and decapitated for causing trouble among the soldiers, a barbaric incident which reveals their vulnerable status as outsiders (ibid., 7).

Many related Gypsy/Rom performance traditions survive today. Connections with sieves, frame drums, dancing, prostitution and female impersonation by boys are common. The Afghan Jat/Ghorbat groups have strong occupational links with Gypsies (see Sakata 2002, 79–83). Similar musician groups in north-western India, Pakistan, and Iran have a low or marginalised status and are variously said to be the ancestors of "European Gypsies" (Qureshi 2001, 919).

In south-western Turkey, Gypsy women professionals (*delbekci kalinlar*) play frame drums (*delbek*) at wedding festivities. These Gypsies live outside towns, "never regarded as full members of society." Ziegler comments: "Their role as musicians is closely connected with the flavour of indecency and they are spoken of by Turkish men as the village prostitutes. Whether this is simply an accusation which underlines the ambiguous status of these women, or presents some degree of truth remains to be established" (1990, 89).[29] Similarly, Picken notes that "some stigma" is attached to the frame drum: "Not only is it a women's instrument, it is also an instrument of women of ill-repute [i.e., Gypsies]." Further west, in the Balkans, Gypsy musician groups also use frame drums (1975, 144).[30]

Male Control of Sexuality

Accusations of "harlotry" and "prostitution" reflect male discomfort with active female sexuality. As in all male-dominated cultures, in the Middle East unbridled female sexuality was seen as potentially dangerous (see Beck and Keddie 1978; Ahmed 1992).

Anxieties increase when there is conflict or political instability. In recent Afghan history this was reflected in tight restrictions relating to women and music. During the *jehád* ("holy war"), Afghan resistance leaders controlling the refugee camps of the north-west Frontier Province of Pakistan completely prohibited music. They invoked the customary moratorium on all music-making following death, declaring the Afghan community to be in a state of permanent mourning. With the men away fighting, the camps mainly contained women and children, so the authorities were effectively banning women's use of the frame drum. An underlying concern was the control of women's sexuality.

By contrast, the Afghan communist regime promoted music and recruited schoolgirls in Kabul to dance on television, a move which shocked conservative members of the public as an act of flagrant debauchery. Fatima Gailani states: "[Refugee women] were restricted to their own homes, often no more than tents. Men were of the opinion that the more women were placed in seclusion, the more obvious it would be that this reflected on their own piety. Meanwhile, in another form of exploitation, in Communist-controlled Kabul, attractive young women and girls were picked out of schools and colleges and forced to perform patriotic songs and dances on television" (1996, 60).[31] In 1992, when Islamist leaders took control, music broadcasting on the radio and television was greatly restricted, and women news-readers and announcers were summarily dismissed.

These examples demonstrate how male authorities seek to contain female sexuality, and how the frame drum's close links with sexuality may imbue it with subversive power, especially in the hands of "prostitutes" and outsiders.

Men, Music and Power

Sexuality is not the only domain in which Middle Eastern men wield power. Male dominance in the religious, political, and economic spheres has significantly affected musical life. In part the restrictions placed on female performance relate to the suppression of goddess worship (Inanna, Ishtar, Astarte, Cybele, and Canaanite and Arabian goddesses mentioned above) by incoming male-centred religions. They also relate to economic competition from male professional players.

The Power of the Sacred

Judaism, Christianity, and Islam were all born in the Middle East, and in all these religions male legists reserved the right to interpret sacred texts and codify religious law. The Sufi brotherhoods were systematised as chains of power, with knowledge transmitted from master to pupil. Within them frame drums acquired esoteric significance. Commenting on the *zikr* ritual of the Kurdish Qadiri dervishes of Sanandaj (Iran), During states:

> The masters affirm that there is a secret to the art of *daf*-playing, which summons energies similar to those exploited in martial arts ... only a dervish is able to play the *daf*: in the hands of a profane, even a virtuoso, it doesn't have the same effect. An effect, probably obtained through the spiritual disciplines (moderate but assiduous), the zeal (*himmat*) and the faith of the dervishes, through their taxing moral demands, and also thanks to an unbroken line of initiation passed on from the great charismatic men of the past, mystics, miracle-workers, gnostics and saints (1994, 22).

Among Sufis and heterodox sects, frame drums have been hallowed and rendered exclusive in a number of significant ways: (1) protected and set apart, (2) endowed with sacred symbolism, and (3) physically modified.

Sufi frame drums are usually kept within sacred space. In Iraq, the *daff* is hung from the walls of the *takia* (religious gathering place) when out of use (Hassan 1980, 173). Touma states that in Arab culture the *mazhár* "stays in the mosque and cannot be used outside religious ceremonies." He says each *mazhár* is dedicated to a saint, and that these drums are reserved for religious music: "the zikr of Rifai and Qadiri Sufi brotherhoods, and other festivals such as the Prophet's birthday, burials and healing ceremonies" (Touma 1977, 108). Likewise, in Turkey, the *mazhár* is "reserved for the Mevlevi and other religious orders" and "never used in secular music" (K. and U. Reinhard 1969, quoted in Poché 1984b).

Members of the Iraqi heterodox Yazidi sect hold the *daff* as very sacred. It is used to bestow blessings, and is highly protected. Members of the sect may not touch it except to kiss it in respect. Wrapped in cloth, it is carried by a "religious musician," and everyone seated in the cafés is supposed to rise as he passes carrying it. Granted a brief examination, Hassan inadvertently touched an instrument, and was told it would have to be purified with water (Hassan 1980, 183–4).[32]

Attributions of sacred symbolism may express androcentric ideas. In Persian culture the frame drum's round shape symbolised "the image of both the heavens and the assembled circle of [male] mystics" (During 1993, 561). Majd al-Din's tract on Sufi audition contains an important passage of this kind:

> the tambourine is a reference to the cycle of existing things (*dá'ira al-akwán*); the skin which is fitted on to it is a reference to general existence (*al-wujud al-mutlaq*), the striking which takes place on the tambourine is a reference to the descent of divine visitations (*wáridát*) from the innermost arcana (*bátin al-butun*) upon general existence to bring forth the things pertaining to the essence of the interior to the exterior, the five small bells (*jalájil*) are a refer-

ence to the prophetical ranks, the saintly ranks, the apostolic ranks, the khalifate ranks, and the imamate ranks, and their combined sound is a reference to the appearance of the divine revelations and unrestricted knowledge by means of these realities in the hearts of the saints and the people of perfection (Robson 1938, 98–99).

These ideas, couched in terms of a hierarchy of male prophets and saints, relate to a male communal spirituality.

Physical modifications to instruments may bestow an exclusive sacred identity. In Iraq, chains attached to the Sufi *daff* produce percussive effects which facilitate ecstatic union with God. The four links in each percussive chain symbolise the four poles (*qutb*) of the Sufi orders, or 101 links recall 101 names of God. Sacred names and inscriptions such as "*Yá Alláh*" (Oh Allah) may be painted on the drum skin (Hassan 1980, 173).[33] Gender bias may not be consciously applied, but it is there: Allah's names are in the male gender, and the *qutb* (pole) is the male leader of the Sufi hierarchy.

However, before closing this section, I would point out that outside its area of origin, in the liberal context of the United States, the frame drum is currently being reclaimed as a spiritual instrument for women. American Jewish women are creating new feminist rituals, inspired by their prophetess Miriam (Sered 1994, 38). Awareness of the drum's history as an instrument of goddess worship is also spreading within the Western feminist spirituality movement. In California a women's group called the Mob of Angels performs rituals centered on the Divine Feminine, using early Mediterranean drumming traditions as a source of inspiration (Redmond 1997).[34]

Secular Power and Knowledge

Divisions of labour that deem certain work to be "unsuitable" for women may serve to protect male economic interests. In Middle Eastern cultures professional women musicians were stigmatised, while "respectable" women were excluded from spaces where music was transmitted, such as music conservatories or cafés. In Baghdad, in the first half of the twentieth century, each café had music in the evenings and early mornings before work. Cafés became like "schools" where ideas about *maqám* (the classical modal system) and musical technique were discussed and appreciated (ibid., 110). Women were unwelcome.

Male hereditary professional hierarchies guarded technical and theoretical knowledge. They held exclusive control of many instruments. In the nineteenth century, a small frame drum called the *riqq* became part of the Arabic classical *takht* ensemble, its name distinguishing it from the larger *tár*. The *riqq* was taught in conservatoires, in a virtuoso playing style (Poché 1984c). Its name, context of performance and specially transmitted techniques reserved it for male use, and mother-of-pearl inlay decoration also denoted a special, high status.

Male professional musicians sometimes assert priority of rights when instruments are shared with women. At weddings in Turkey, Ursula Reinhard noted that "professional and semi-professional" women musicians had to concede their instruments to men when required: "The women mostly accompany their songs with the goblet drum *delbek*, or the tambourine, *def*. When the instruments are needed at the moment by the men, they play just as happily on a pot or a serving-tray" (1990, 101).[35] The term "semi-professional" may imply lack of payment or low payment compared with men.

Male professionals sometimes assert their ascendancy by downgrading "women's instruments." In Afghanistan the *dáireh* is partially reduced to a "non-instrument," and the jew's harp is derided as a toy (Sakata 1980b, 144, also see Note 19). Feminist art historians note similar patterns in European culture: male artists denied women access to their profession, and then degraded the products of female creativity.[36]

These examples demonstrate how powerful men have asserted superior rights and status over women with relation to musical instruments, using various techniques of enforcement.

Conclusions

Today frame drums have a wide range of uses, with or without other instruments, played in private or public performance contexts which are variously viewed as lawful, sinful or meritorious. The drums feature in folk, popular, classical and religious traditions. Players are of differing age and status, both male and female, amateur and professional.

Shifts in Gender Usage of Frame Drums

The evidence points to a broad historical shift in relation to gender. The early sources show women playing frame drums in many contexts, whereas men appear to have played them rarely. Some women's traditions have been lost. Middle Eastern women no longer publicly play frame drums in battle songs and victory songs, or their modern equivalents such as military parades. To my knowledge, they do not play frame drums in elegies for the dead, or in public religious ceremonies. Drumming as a ritual of female hospitality has also declined or disappeared; in Arabia male professional drummers now perform this public role.[37]

The situation has changed radically. Frame drums remain important for women, especially in marriage rituals, but connections with female eroticism outside marriage have been curbed. Frame drums now feature in exclusively male or male-dominated traditions (e.g., Sufi rituals and classical ensembles), and men appear to be developing the drum's potential for virtuosity and rhythmic elaboration. In Iran the Kurdish Sufi *daff* is played with impressive masculine bravura.

We note that at certain periods of history frame drums were used by people of indeterminate gender, such as eunuchs and transvestites. The eunuch priests of Cybele may represent a transitional phase from female to male priesthood. Similarly, the *mukhannath* "effeminate" professional entertainers of the early Islamic period entered a performance arena that had previously been dominated by women.

However, several factors have helped maintain women's right to play frame drums in traditional settings. The drums were protected as lawful by the Prophetic traditions. Playing techniques could be transmitted informally. The drums were cheap and easy to produce. Stigmatised professional women musicians (including Gypsies) made and sold them, keeping traditions alive and evading control by male authorities.

Finally—and most significantly—frame drums are linked with rites of passage. Weddings remain as the primary context in which the drum is lawful and desirable. There the drum facilitates transfer of a young woman from the control of her father to her husband. Given the separation of men and women prescribed by Islamic custom—the dominant ethos of the region—men needed women's music to enliven festivities which ensured continuance of the patrilineal social order. Men had a vested interest in the transformative powers of frame drums—in the hands of women.

Powers Invested in Frame Drums

A considerable range of powers have been—and are—invested in frame drums in Middle Eastern cultures. Some are acknowledged, others implicit. My understanding of this is informed by personal experience as a performer, including ritual contexts in Afghanistan (see Doubleday 2005, 187–9, 197–201).

Certain powers may be inherent in the drum's physical essence, its particular sound, and playing techniques. Bodily relationships are notable: close connections with the throat (with singing, or when used as a resonator) and hands and fingers (through playing). The drums are held close to the heart and navel, important spiritual centres. When played in movement (dancing or processions), their rhythms unite people in a communal consciousness.

In common with other musical instruments, frame drums promote emotional bonding. Frequently used in connection with singing, including meritorious ritual blessings, their power to enhance or modify the voice is significant. They possess transformative powers in life-crisis rituals. In connection with dancing, they facilitate physical arousal and trance states.

Supernatural powers are frequently attributed to frame drums. The use of drums—and other loud explosive sounds—at weddings and other life crisis ceremonies may be apotropaic, protecting humans in liminal states (e.g., brides, new-born babies, or women during the forty day post-partum period), when they are particularly vulnerable to attack by the evil eye or *jinn*s.

Some performers believe the sounds of frame drums have the power to ward off or exorcise *jinn*s (Doubleday 2005, 200). Belief in these beings predates Islam, and they have ancient connections with trance and divination. Arab poets were considered to be possessed by them (*majnun*) as a source of inspiration (Rouget 1985, 280; Shiloah 1995, 4), and Shiloah states that the *jinn* "re-emerged" as "an inspirational source among some poets and musicians in Islamic times" (ibid., 4).

There are further beliefs that the sound of frame drums may facilitate contact with other spiritual beings. The Qaderi Sufis of Kurdistan state that, in their rituals, drumming invokes the presence of angels, prophets and saints (During 1994, 21–22). The ritual leader establishes a relationship with the divine throne (*'arsh*), and when angels hear the drum they gather and also dance and sing with the Sufis (During 2002, 180–1). Among the Yazidi of Iraq, the *daff* is used to honour angels (Hassan 1980, 193). In Central Asia, there are links between Sufi zikr and shamanic ritual, in which male and female *baxshi* healers use the drum to call spirits and perform divinations (Levin 1996, 242–58, 306–7; During 2002, 181).

Supernatural uses of drums and sieves appear over a wide area extending beyond the Middle East, sometimes linked with Gypsies and divination (for Egypt and Spain, see Hassan 1980, 38). In Morocco, frame drums and sieves are powerful instruments of sorcery (Philip Schuyler, personal communication). In Macedonia many ritual events are "initiated by a respected woman leading the dance line with a decorated object such as a sieve" (Silverman 1996, 68). Another (apparently rare) supernatural use of the drum, in Iraq, is in prayer for rain (Hassan 1980, 138).[38] Links with the sacred or supernatural may of course be lost, or may not apply to some genres.[39]

Techniques of Exclusivity

The data demonstrate various processes whereby frame drums—and other musical instruments—are assigned to certain classes of performer. These processes may involve restrictions about the performer's gender. We may identify the presence of certain "techniques of exclusivity."

In the Middle East, male musicians have monopolised musical instruments in various ways. These include (1) keeping instruments within all-male performance space, (2) transmission of technical knowledge through an all-male hierarchy, and (3) physical modification of instruments, creating an exclusive identity. In the Middle East, certain powers appropriated by men have been crucial in these processes: the interpretation of sacred texts, enforcement of laws, and the seclusion of many classes of women in domestic space.

These exclusivity techniques are evident outside the Middle East—examples abound in Europe, Africa and the Indian subcontinent, for instance. Other techniques of exclusivity exist that are not evident in the Middle East. For example, in Melanesia, South America and sub-Saharan Africa, powerful taboos on musical instruments pose threats of punishment or death to those who are not supposed to have contact with the given instrument. To cite one example, such taboos protect the so-called "sacred flutes", paired flutes played only by initiated men in Papua New Guinea (Lutkehaus 1998, 245).[40]

It is rare to find exclusivity techniques employed by women: they usually lack the power of enforcement. Our planet is male-dominated. Equality between the sexes is not the norm, and female political, economic, sexual or religious ascendancy is rare. This may explain why—across cultures—women have few musical instruments exclusively of their own.[41]

The Importance of Sexuality

As we have seen, male control of female sexuality underlies gender power struggles and impinges upon musical life. Koskoff outlines three important points about sexuality and musical performance: "Sexuality both self- and other-defined, affects music performance in three important ways: (1) performance environments may provide a context for sexually explicit behavior, such that music becomes a metaphor for sexual relations; (2) the actual or perceived loss of sexuality may change women's roles and/or statuses; and (3) cultural beliefs in women's inherent sexuality may motivate the separation of or restriction upon women's activities" (1989, 6). These points apply equally to musical instruments, as the Middle Eastern material demonstrates.

1. Music as a metaphor for sex. This point recalls the close associations of the frame drum with women, dancing and sexuality. The desire to control female sexuality is intimately linked with restrictions on women's use of musical instruments in the Middle East (and the stigmatisation of those who defy those restrictions). Historical religious opposition by the monotheistic religions towards polytheistic goddess worship and associated sexual rituals is also notable.
2. Loss of sexuality and change of musical role. This point may be expanded to include the whole female life cycle, through puberty, fertility and menopause. In the Middle East the attainment of sexuality and loss of virginity (at marriage) are highlighted. Nubile or newly married girls may experience severe restrictions relating to veiling, education, and musical performance (Doubleday and Baily 1995). Women's access to musical instruments may decline as they age, inhibited by conventions of dignity.
3. Separation and restriction of women's activities. This has been a recurrent theme of this article, evidenced by the segregation of music-making according to the purdah system, and assignment of musical instruments according to gender.

Notes

1. I have taken the opportunity to revise my 1999 article, with some updated information and new references. For reasons of space I have condensed section 2. The inspiration for this work stems from a paper I presented at the 2nd Meeting for the ICTM Study Group on Music of the Arab World, Oxford 1996. I offer thanks to the following people, who in various ways have given valuable advice, encouragement and support for my research on frame drums and on musical instruments and gender: John Baily. Margaret Birley, Abdul-Hamid Hamam, Scheherazade Hassan, Nancy Lindisfarne, Asphodel Long, Bruno Nettl, Martin Stokes, Lou Taylor, Bruce Wannell, Owen Wright, Wim van Zanten, and the anonymous referees for the 1999 article. Translations from French material are mine.
2. I undertook fieldwork in Herat city in 1973–77, in partnership with my husband John Baily. I have subsequently worked on Afghan music in London, New York, Pakistan, and on two trips to Afghanistan (1994 and 2004).
3. Farmer notes the following terms used in the Abbasid period: *duff, ghirbál, bandair, tár, mazhar, tiryál* and *shaqf* (1929, 211).
4. See Cohen's forthcoming article on the Iberian square frame drum.
5. This section has been condensed. For fuller references, see the 1999 article. Please note that the 1999 version contains a misleading statement about Mesopotamia (p. 105): "in the absence of any other type of drum..." I now realise that there were other types of drum in that period (see Kilmer 2001).
6. The Islamic ritual of seven circumambulations (*tawáf*) has its roots in sacred dance (Schimmel 1994, 104; Farmer 1929, 8). Hamam defines pre-Islamic *tahlil* as "the song performed as pilgrims danced around the Ka'aba"(1996, 7–8). However, *tahlil* is complicated because it was apparently performed both around the deities and around sacrificing stones (*nusb*). Hamam's textual research indicates that nubile girls performed *tahlil* in the latter context.
7. Another more peripheral women's cult was known as Adonaism, focussing on Adonis, a dying vegetation god akin to Dionysus and Cybele's lover Attis. In this cult, which was inherited from Greece, women expressed frenzied mourning

for the god, and used drums which were probably frame drums (Henderson 1957, 385). Radice notes that the cult of a mother-goddess and her mortal consort was common throughout the Middle East" (1971, 48).

8. In the Prophet's presence some "little girls" played frame drums and lamented heroes who died at Badr (Robson 1938, 75). In the seventh century, weekly concerts by female ritual mourners (*náihát*) were of a high musical standard (Farmer 1929, 53).

9. The precise meaning of *ghirbál* is "sieve," but in this context the word refers to a drum. Connections between frame drums and sieves are discussed elsewhere in this article (4.2, 7.2, and Note 17).

10. I have been unable to trace details about Amr ibn Umayyu Dhamari (also Baba Amr or Amr Iyar), the "patron saint" of the drum. According to Farmer, he was a male companion of the Prophet (1929, 38). It is possible that he was a eunuch (see Note 11).

11. Touma describes Touais as the first man having access to the frame drum, a "privilege undoubtedly accorded on account of his being a eunuch" (1977, 107). The term "privilege" implies a special or possibly sacred status which reserved the drum for women (or eunuchs as "non-men"), but Touma's evidence for this is unclear.

12. In 1978 I undertook a complete survey and analysis of musical instruments depicted in miniature paintings housed in the Bodleian Library, Oxford (as yet unpublished). I thank the staff who facilitated this work.

13. For the drum as resonator for the voice, see Ms. Elliot 239 folio 904, painted by Mohammad Hossein Herawi at Shiraz (1581). This use of the drum was noted by Sakata in the Wakhan region of northern Afghanistan (1980a, 32). It is also current in Tajik Badakhshan (John Morgan O'Connell, personal communication).

14. The miniatures are (respectively) Ms. Elliot 194 folio 676, in Turkmen style with Indian retouching (1500–1501), and Ms. Elliot 239 folio 913, painted by Mohammad Hossein Herawi at Shiraz (1581) reproduced as Fig. 1 in this article.

15. Baily found that in western Afghanistan the Sufis performed *zikr* (also called *jahr*) with several singers and no musical instruments. At the Chishti *khaneqah* (Sufi lodge) in Kabul musicians played all instruments of Afghan classical music, with rhythm from tabla drums and large percussion stones identified by Slobin as *qairáq* (1976, 277).

16. The frame drum is termed *dáireh* in all areas of Afghanistan except Badakhshan, a culturally distinct region overlapping Afghanistan and Tajikistan. There it is termed *daff* (Sakata 1980a, 31; van den Berg, personal communication). During his fieldwork (1967–68) Slobin estimated that most urban households in northern Afghanistan possessed a *dáireh* "to be taken down for festivities" (1976, 265). In Herat women always had access to a drum—either their own, or that of a neighbouring household. Frame drums were usually communal property, not individually owned. No reliable information about the distribution of musical instruments in Afghanistan is currently available, but as a result of decades of conflict and religious pressure against music they are certainly less common. In 2004 I observed that frame drums were less common in homes, and that people sometimes used imported frame drums.

17. Jat is a general derogatory term applied to a variety of different groups. Other terms are Gharibzadeh, Chelu, and Ghorbat (see Rao 1982; Baily 1988). Similar groups producing frame drums and sieves exist in a widespread area (e.g. the nomadic Kouli tribe of Iran, "kinsfolk of the gypsies" who specialize as sieve-makers, blacksmiths and tinkers (Wulff 1966, 234–6).

18. Slobin's statement still holds, and has been retained in the revised 2001 *Grove* article (Baily 2001).

19. The jew's harp (*chang/chang-qobuz*) is notable as a solo instrument of women in Central Asia (see Levin 1996, 155–6). In Afghanistan its use is confined to the north (Slobin 1976, 273–6). Sakata states: "Generally, the Afghans do not seriously consider the *chang* as a musical instrument. Instead, they feel that the jaw's harp is a toy or an instrument of amusement for girls and women. Indeed, most of the performers are female" (1980b, 144). In the 1960s, when Lubtchansky recorded a solo on jew's harp, the male Uzbek performer was very embarrassed, saying only women and children play the instrument (Lubtchansky n.d.).

20. In Herat male Chelu musicians play it to accompany dancing by their women, who are prostitutes (Baily 1988, 34). Another outsider group who used the drum before the civil war were fully grown semi-transvestite eunuchs (*isák*), marginalised by virtue of their gender. They behaved in ways that were considered deeply shameful and "unmanly," wearing long hair, make-up and women's shawls, drumming and singing comic verses in the street as they collected tips from passers-by. They frequented an area of Kabul's old city near Darwaze Lahori, by the bus and lorry depot. Some worked as tea-house waiters, and they possibly also offered services of a sexual nature. Thanks to Nabi Misdaq for this information.

21. Marriage in Afghanistan is not necessarily patrilocal, but Qur'anic laws of divorce and inheritance prescribe patrilineality. For further details on marriage, see Doubleday (2005) and Tapper (1991).

22. See my article on frame drums and life-cycle ceremonies in Afghanistan (Doubleday forthcoming).

23. New Year festivities are a widespread and ancient feature of the Persianised world. The city of Persepolis in southern Iran was built as a site for New Year rituals. In Afghanistan Ali's shrine at Mazar-i Sharif, near Balkh, is the national focus of New Year festivities. His cult is syncretised with that of Anahita, goddess of the Oxus river, a major deity extolled in the Avesta. She had a celebrated shrine at Balkh where "licentious rites" were performed in her honour (Rahimi 1977, 24; Lee 1996). In the late 1960s, at New Year, Slobin noticed heaps of frame drums being sold around the central square of Ali's shrine (1976, 265). The drum skins were painted in red and green with a symmetrical flowering tree of life symbol common in women's embroidery (see Paiva and Dupaigne 1993).

24. In *Three Women of Herat* I gave Zainab Herawi the pseudonym Shirin, but when I visited Herat in 1994 her children urged me to reveal her true identity, since she is now unfortunately dead.

25. In Afghanistan possession by *jinns*, known as *maraz* ("the illness"), is a state of mental and nervous distress especially found among women. See Doubleday (2005, 101–14,128–34).

26. The dance mirrors the mythical descent to the Underworld of the goddesses Inanna and Ishtar (see Wolkstein and Kramer 1983; Pritchard 1975). At each of the seven gates of the Underworld, she sheds an item of personal adornment. The biblical story of Salomé's aphrodisiac dance for King Herod may be a derogatory remodelling of this myth and

its ritual, casting Salom– as a wicked temptress. The dancer's name, Salomé, may refer to Ishtar's "dance of welcome" (*shalom*: Hebrew for "peace," used as a welcome greeting) (Buonaventura 1983, 18).

27. In contrast with modern connotations of "prostitution," Ishtar's female temple servants had high status. Hammurabi's code of laws gave them privileges (Long 1992, 132–3).

28. These are: two Gypsy *ghawazee* in Cairo, with a male *daff* player (nineteenth-century drawing, p. 7); a troupe of Egyptian female dancers accompanied by eight women musicians, one playing a frame drum (nineteenth-century French lithograph, p. 36); some Cairene bare-breasted *ghawazee*, accompanied by a veiled female *daff* player and male lutenist (1762, p. 40); transvestite buffoon boy dancers accompanied by male musicians including three frame drum players (Turkish miniature, p. 50); Turkish *chengi* (female dancer) accompanied by a female frame drum player (p. 57); Samia Gamal, renowned Arab dancer of the 1950s, accompanied by three male frame drummers (still from cinema film, p. 99).

29. The female professional musicians of Herat with whom I worked were not prostitutes, but they were labelled as such.

30. Silverman states that the frame drum (*def, daire*) has been associated with "Balkan Muslim Rom female performers for at least a hundred years and probably longer" (2003, 120). The "frame drum couple" is one of the three principal Balkan Gypsy ensemble types (Pettan 1996, 38). In Greece, Yiftoi Gypsy musicians use frame drums; deep-seated prejudice was directed particularly against their women's "libidinous" dance (Brandl 1996, 26–27). A large Rom community in Skopje, Macedonia, make and play frame drums, and perform a "sexually provocative dance" called *chochek* (Silverman 1996, 66, 69). For information on gender, Rom performers and frame drums in the Balkans, see Silverman 2003 and Pettan 2003.

31. Fatima Gailani is the daughter of Pir Gailani (a former resistance leader) and a political force in her own right. Her information is reliable, backed up by my own observations and recorded interviews in Pakistan. Thanks to Anthony Hyman for drawing my attention to her article.

32. Levin reports a similar case in northern Tajikistan. When he touched a male *baxshi* healer's frame drum, the owner angrily told him he had sinned by touching the drum without washing himself or saying a special prayer: the drum would have to be reconsecrated (Levin 1996, 243).

33. For an illustration of calligraphy on a Kurdish Sufi drum, see During (1994, back cover). These Kurdish Sufis apply the same numerological symbolism to percussive chains added to their drum. Another example of physical modification to frame drums occurs in Morocco, where Sufis remove snares from the *bendir*, seeking to avoid their "sensual effect" (Langlois 1997, caption to Plate 21).

34. Redmond founded this group, and since the early 1990s has been teaching the history of frame drums from the point of view of "goddess spirituality." See her chapter Thirteen ("Giving Birth to Ourselves") for an account of the group's female-centred ritualised performances (Redmond 1997). Judy Piazza is another U.S. frame drum teacher promoting New-Age spirituality.

35. It is unclear whether by "just as happily" Reinhard means that the women do not mind men making prior claims on the instruments, or whether they play just as proficiently on trays. Any musician prefers to play a good instrument.

36. See for instance, this quotation from a French article in the Gazette des Beaux Arts, 1860: "Male genius has nothing to fear from female taste. Let men of genius conceive of great architectural projects, monumental sculpture, and elevated forms of painting. In a word, let men busy themselves with all that has to do with great art. Let women occupy themselves with those types of art they have always preferred, such as pastels, portraits or miniatures" (quoted in Parker and Pollock 1981, 1).

37. In parts of Arabia male professional musicians welcome honoured guests and heroes in highly visible public arenas. For instance, in Bahrain heroic pilots were greeted by a public ensemble of frame drums and cylindrical drums (McMillan and Stanfield 1995, 23).

38. Hassan quotes Salim al-Tikriti (1973, 156–7): "At Tikrit, when there is a lack of rain, the mullahs, adherents of the brotherhoods and the population meet after the Friday [communal] prayer. They make a popular procession out of the village, beating the *daff* and singing poems, begging God to grant his grace in the form of rain."

39. In the case of Balkan Muslim Rom female performers' use of frame drums, Silverman states that links with the sacred do not appear to apply (2003, 140 3n).

40. Taboos protecting "sacred flutes" have much to do with secrecy and deception. For instance, see Koskoff's discussion of Gourlay's work (Koskoff 1989, 13, citing Gourlay 1975).

41. The relationship between gender and musical instruments is examined fully in a forthcoming publication (Doubleday ed.), which contains theoretical discussion and individual case studies.

References

Ahmed, Leila. 1992. *Women and Gender in Islam: Historical Roots of a Modern Debate*. New Haven and London: Yale University Press.

Alexander, David, and Pat Alexander. 1973. *The Lion Handbook to the Bible*. Oxford: Lion Publishing.

Alloula, Malek. 1986. *The Colonial Harem*. Minneapolis: University of Minnesota Press.

Anderson, Warren/Thomas J. Mathieson. "Cybele." In *The New Grove Dictionary of Music and Musicians* (2nd ed.), edited by Stanley Sadie, Vol. 6:797. London: Macmillan Press.

Atanassov, Vergilij/Veronica Doubleday. 2001. "Daira." In *The New Grove Dictionary of Music and Musicians* (2nd ed.), edited by Stanley Sadie, Vol. 6:842–3. London: Macmillan Press.

Baghban, Hafizullah. 1977. The context and concept of humor in Magadi theater. PhD Diss. University of Indiana.

Baily, John. 1988. *Music of Afghanistan: Professional Musicians in the City of Herat*. Cambridge: Cambridge University Press.

———. 1996. "Using Tests of Sound Perception in Fieldwork." *Yearbook for Traditional Music* 28:147–3.

———. 2001. "Afghanistan." In *The New Grove Dictionary of Music and Musicians* (2nd ed.), edited by Stanley Sadie, Vol. 1:182–90. London: Macmillan Press.

Beck, Loi,s and Nikki Keddie, eds. 1978. *Women in the Muslim World*. Cambridge: Harvard University Press.

Blades, James, and Robert Anderson. 1984. "Frame Drum." In *The New Grove Dictionary of Musical Instruments*, edited by Stanley Sadie, Vol. 1:793–4. London: Macmillan Press.

Brandl, Rudolf M. 1996. "The 'Yiftoi' and the Music of Greece. Role and Function." *The World of Music*, 1:7–32.

Buonaventura, Wendy. 1983. *Belly Dancing*. London: Virago Press.

Campbell, Kay Hary. 2002. "Women's Music in the Arabian Peninsula." In *The Garland Encyclopedia of World Music, Vol. 6: The Middle East*, edited by Virginia Danielson, Scott Marcus, and Dwight Reynolds, 695–702. New York and London: Routledge.

Christensen, Dieter. 2002. "Musical Life in Sohar, Oman." In *The Garland Encyclopedia of World Music, Vol. 6: The Middle East*, edited by Virginia Danielson, Scott Marcus, and Dwight Reynolds, 671–84. New York and London: Routledge.

Cirlot, J. E. 1971. *A Dictionary of Symbols*. London: Routledge.

Cohen, Judith. Forthcoming. "'This Drum I Play': Women and Frame Drums in Portugal and Spain." In *Sounds of Power: Musical Instruments and Gender*, edited by Veronica Doubleday.

DeVale, Sue Carole. 1989. "Power and Meaning in Musical Instruments." In *Music and the Experience of God*, edited by David Power, Mary Collins and Mellonee Burnim: 94–110. Edinburgh: T & T Clark.

Dick, Alastair. 1984. "Daph." In *The New Grove Dictionary of Musical Instruments*, edited by Stanley Sadie, Vol. 1: 545–6. London: Macmillan Press.

Doubleday, Veronica. [1988] 2005. *Three Women of Herat*. London: I.B. Tauris.

———. 2000. "Music and Gender in Afghanistan." In *The Garland Encyclopedia of World Music, Vol. 5: South Asia: The Indian Subcontinent*, edited by Alison Arnold, 812–16. New York and London: Garland Publishing.

———. 2002. *Afghanistan: Female Musicians of Herat*. Audivis/Unesco compact disc with booklet (D8284). Paris: Naïve Distribution.

———. Forthcoming. "Frame Drums and Female Life-Cycle Ceremonies in Afghanistan." In *Sounds of Power: Musical Instruments and Gender*, edited by Veronica Doubleday.

Doubleday, Veronica (ed.) Forthcoming. *Sounds of Power: Musical Instruments and Gender*.

Doubleday, Veronica, and John Baily. 1995. "Patterns of Musical Development among Children in Afghanistan." In *Children in the Muslim Middle East*, edited by Elizabeth Warnock Fernea. Austin: University of Texas Press.

During, Jean. 1991. *The Art of Persian Music*. Washington DC: Mage Publishers.

———. 1993. "Daf(f) and Dayera I." In *Encyclopaedia Iranica*, edited by Ehsan Yarshater, vol. VI, fasc 6:560–62. Costa Mesa: Mazda Publishers.

———. 1994. *Kurdistan: zikr et chants soufis*. Paris: OCORA Radio France. Booklet accompanying compact disc.

———. 2002. "The Symbolic Universe of Music in Islamic Societies." In *The Garland Encyclopedia of World Music, Vol. 6: The Middle East*, edited by Virginia Danielson, Scott Marcus, and Dwight Reynolds, 177-88. New York and London: Routledge.

Edwards, J. Michele. 1991. "Women in Music to ca. 1450." In *Women and Music: A History*, edited by Karen Pendle, 8–28. Bloomington and Indianapolis: Indiana University Press.

Farmer, Henry George. 1929. *A History of Arabian Music*. London: Luzac.

———. 1931. *Studies in Oriental Musical Instruments*. London: Reeves Press.

———. 1938. *Studies in Oriental Musical Instruments*. Second Series. Glasgow: The Civic Press.

Fohrer, Georg. 1973. *Hebrew and Aramaic Dictionary of the Old Testament*. London: SCM Press.

Gailani, Fatima. 1996. "Once-Proud Freedom Fighters Brought Low." *South*, September issue. London.

Gibb, H. A. R., and J. H. Kramers, eds. 1961. *Shorter Encyclopaedia of Islam*. Leiden: Brill and Luzac.

Gourlay, Ken A. 1975. *Sound-Producing Instruments in Traditional Society: A Study of Esoteric Instruments and Their Role in Male-Female Relations*. Port Moresby: New Guinea Research Unit, The Australian National University.

Graham-Brown, Sarah. 1988. *Images of Women: Portrayal of Women in Photography of the Middle East 1860–1950*. London: Quartet Books.

Hamam, Abdul Hamid. 1996. "The Roots of Bedouin Singing." Unpublished manuscript of paper presented at 2nd meeting of the Study Group for Music of the Arab World, ICTM, Oxford.

Hanna, Judith Lynne. 1988. *Dance, Sex and Gender: Signs of Identity, Dominance, Defiance, and Desire*. Chicago and London: University of Chicago Press.

Hassan, Schéhérazade Qassim. 1980. *Les Instruments de Musique en Irak et leur rôle dans la société traditionelle*. Paris-La Haye-New York: Mouton Editeur and Ecole des Hautes Etudes en Sciences Sociales.

Henderson, Isobel. 1957. "Ancient Greek Music." In *The New Oxford History of Music: 1, Ancient and Oriental Music*, edited by Egon Wellesz, 336–403. London: Oxford University Press.

Jargy, Simon. 1971. *La Musique Arabe*. Paris: Presses Universitaires de France.

Jenkins, Jean. 1977. *Musical Instruments*. London: The Horniman Museum.

Joseph, Suad, and Susan Slyomovics, eds. 2001. *Women and Power in the Middle East*. University of Pennsylvania Press: Philadelphia.

Kerimova, Taira, 1996. *Women's love and Life: Female Folklore from Azerbaijan*. Leiden: PAN Records. Booklet accompanying compact disc.

Kilmer, Anne Draffkon. 2001. "Mesopotamia." In *The New Grove Dictionary of Musical Instruments*, edited by Stanley Sadie, Vol. 16:480–7. London: Macmillan Press.

Koskoff, Ellen. 1989. "An Introduction to Women, Music, and Culture." In *Women and Music in Cross-Cultural Perspective*, edited by Ellen Koskoff, 1–23. Urbana and Chicago: University of Illinois Press.

Langlois, Anthony. 1997. "Rai on the Border: Popular Music and Society in the Maghreb." Ph.D. dissertation. The Queen's University of Belfast.

Larousse Encyclopedia of Mythology. 1959. London: Paul Hamlyn.

Lawler, Lillian B. 1965. *The Dance in Ancient Greece.* Middletown: Wesleyan University Press.

Lee, Jonathan. 1997. "Poppies, Poles and the Paranormal; the New Year Festivals at Mazar-i Sharif, Afghanistan." Unpublished lecture for The Society for South Asian Studies, London.

Levin, Theodore. 1996. *The Hundred Thousand Fools of God: Musical Travels in Central Asia.* Bloomington: Indiana University Press.

Levy, Reuben. 1957. *The Social Structure of Islam.* Cambridge: Cambridge University Press.

Long, Asphodel P. 1992. *In a Chariot Drawn by Lions: The Search for the Female in Deity.* London: The Women's Press.

Lubtchansky, J. C. n.d. *Afghanistan et Iran. Collection du Mus– de l'Homme.* Paris:Vogue. Sleeve notes to LP.

Lutkehaus, Nancy C. 1998. "Music and Gender: Gender in New Guinean Music." In *The Garland Encyclopedia of World Music, Vol. 9: Australia and the Pacific Islands*, edited by Adrienne L. Kaeppler and J.W. Love, 245–6. New York and London: Garland Publishing.

McKinnon, James W., and Robert Anderson. 2001. "Tympanum." In *The New Grove Dictionary of Music and Musicians (2nd edn.)*, edited by Stanley Sadie, Vol. 26:17–18. London: Macmillan Press.

McMillan, Peter, and James L. Stanfield. 1995. "The Vimy Flies Again." *National Geographic*, 187/5 (photo and caption p.23).

Mays, James L., ed. 1968. *Harpers' Bible Commentary.* San Francisco: Harper and Row.

Meyers, Carol. 1993. "The Drum-Dance-Song Ensemble: Women's Performance in Biblical Israel." In *Rediscovering the Muses: Women's Musical Traditions*, edited by

Kimberley Marshall, 49–67. Boston: Northeastern University Press.

Montagu, Jeremy. 1984 "Tof." In *The New Grove Dictionary of Musical Instruments*, edited by Stanley Sadie, Vol. 3:603. London: Macmillan Press.

Morris, R. Conway, and Cvjetko Rihtman. 1984. "Def." In *The New Grove Dictionary of Musical Instruments*, edited by Stanley Sadie, Vol. 1:552–3. London: Macmillan Press.

Morris, R. Conway, and Cvjetko Rihtman, Christian Poché/Veronica Doubleday. 2001. "Daff." In *The New Grove Dictionary of Music and Musicians* (2nd ed.), edited by Stanley Sadie, Vol. 6:832–4. London: Macmillan Press.

Nettl, Bruno. 1983. *The Study of Ethnomusicology: Twenty-Nine Issues and Concepts.* Urbana: University of Illinois Press.

Nicholson, R. A. 1978. *Rumi: Poet and Mystic.* London: Unwin Paperbacks.

Ochshorn, Judith. 1990. "Ishtar and Her Cult." In *The Book of the Goddess Past and Present*, edited by Carl Olsen, 16-28. New York: The Crossroad Publishing Company.

Olsen, Miriam Rovsing. 2002. "Contemporary Issues of Gender and Music." In *The Garland Encyclopedia of World Music, Vol. 6: The Middle East*, edited by Virginia Danielson, Scott Marcus, and Dwight Reynolds, 299–307. New York and London: Routledge.

Paiva, Roland, and Bernard Dupaigne. 1993. *Afghan Embroidery.* Paris: UNHCR and Musée de l'Homme.

Parker, Rozsika, and Griselda Pollock. 1981. *Old Mistresses: Women, Art and Ideology.* London: Pandora.

Pettan, Svanibor. 1996. "Gypsies, Music, and Politics in the Balkans: A Case Study from Kosovo." *The World of Music* 38(1):33–61.

———. 2003. "Male, Female, and Beyond in the Culture and Music of Roma in Kosovo." In *Music and Gender: Perspectives from the Mediterranean*, edited by Tullia Magrini, 287–305. Chicago: The University of Chicago Press.

Picken, Lawrence. 1975. *Folk Musical Instruments of Turkey.* Oxford: Oxford University Press.

Poché, Christian. 1984a. "Duff." In *The New Grove Dictionary of Musical Instruments*, edited by Stanley Sadie, Vol. 1:616–17. London: Macmillan Press.

———. 1984b. "Mazhar." In *The New Grove Dictionary of Musical Instruments*, edited by Stanley Sadie, Vol. 2:625–6. London: Macmillan Press.

———. 1984c. "Riqq" In *The New Grove Dictionary of Musical Instruments*, edited by Stanley Sadie, Vol. 3:250–51. London: Macmillan Press.

Pritchard, James B. 1975. *Ancient Near East: An Anthology of Texts and Pictures.* 2 vols. Princeton: Princeton University Press.

Qureshi, Regula. 2001. "Pakistan." In *The New Grove Dictionary of Music and Musicians* (2nd ed.), edited by Stanley Sadie, Vol. 18:917–25. London: Macmillan Press.

Radice, Betty. 1971. *Who's Who in the Ancient World.* London: Penguin Books.

Rahimi, Fahima. 1977. *Women in Afghanistan.* Liestal: Stiftung Bibliographica Afghanica.

Rao, Apurna. 1982. *Les Gorbat d'Afghanistan: Aspects économiques d'un groupe itinérant "Jat."* Paris: Institut Français d'Iranologie de Teheran.

Redmond, Layne. 1997. *When the Drummers Were Women: A Spiritual History of Rhythm.* New York : Three Rivers Press.

Reinhard, Kurt and Ursula. 1969. *Turquie.* n.p.: Paris.

Reinhard, Ursula. 1990. "The Veils are Lifted: Music of Turkish Women." In *Music, Gender, and Culture*, edited by Marcia Herndon and Susanne Ziegler, 101–13. Wilhelmshaven: Florian Noetzel Verlag.

Robins, Gay. 1993. *Women in Ancient Egypt.* London: British Museum Press.

Robson, James. 1938. *Tracts on Listening to Music.* London: The Royal Asiatic Society.

Rouget, Gilbert. 1985. *Music and Trance: A Theory of the Relations Between Music and Possession.* Chicago: University of Chicago Press.

Roy Choudhury, M. L.1957. "Music in Islam." *Journal of the Asiatic Society* 23(2):43–102.

Sakata, Hiromi Lorraine. 1980a "Afghan Musical Instruments: Drums." *Afghanistan Journal* 7(1):30–32

———. 1980b. "Afghan Musical Instruments: Chang." *Afghanistan Journal* 7(4): 144–45.

———. [1983] 2002. *Music in the Mind: The Concepts of Music and Musician in Afghanistan.* Washington and London: Smithsonian Institution Press.

Sawa, Suzanne Meyers. 2002. "Historical Issues of Gender and Music." In *The Garland Encyclopedia of World Music, Vol. 6: The Middle East,* edited by Virginia Danielson, Scott Marcus, and Dwight Reynolds, 293–8. New York and London: Routledge.

Schimmel, Annemarie. 1975. *Mystical Dimensions of Islam.* Chapel Hill: The University of North Carolina Press.

———. 1994. *Deciphering the Signs of God.* Edinburgh: Edinburgh University Press.

Sered, Susan Starr. 1994. *Priestess, Mother, Sacred Sister: Religions Dominated by Women.* New York and Oxford: Oxford University Press.

Shiloah, Amnon. 1995. *Music in the World of Islam: A Socio-Cultural Study.* Aldershot: Scolar Press.

———. 2001. "Arab Music II: Folk Music." In *The New Grove Dictionary of Music and Musicians* (2nd ed.), edited by Stanley Sadie, Vol. 1:824–33. London: Macmillan Press.

Silverman, Carol. 1996. "Music and Power: Gender and Performance among Roma (Gypsies) of Skopje, Macedonia." *The World of Music* 38(1):63–76.

———. 2003. "The Gender of the Profession: Music, Dance, and Reputation among Balkan Muslim Rom Women." In *Music and Gender: Perspectives from the Mediterranean,* edited by Tullia Magrini, 119–45. Chicago: The University of Chicago Press.

Slobin, Mark. 1976. *Music in the Culture of Northern Afghanistan.* Viking Fund Publication in Anthropology No 54, Tucson: University of Arizona Press.

———. 1980. "Afghanistan." In *The New Grove Dictionary of Music and Musicians,* edited by Stanley Sadie, Vol. 1. London: Macmillan Press.

Stobart, Henry. 1994. "Flourishing horns and enchanted tubers: music and potatoes in highland Bolivia." *British Journal of Ethnomusicology* 3: 35–48.

Tapper, Nancy. 1991. *Bartered Brides: Politics, Gender and Marriage in an Afghan Tribal Society.* Cambridge: Cambridge University Press.

Teeter, Emily. 1993. "Female Professional Musicians in Pharaonic Egypt." In *Rediscovering the Muses: Women's Musical Traditions,* edited by Kimberley Marshall, 68–91. Boston: Northeastern University Press.

Tikriti, Salim al-. 1973. "Takalid wa a'raf min talla'far." [Traditions et coutumes de Talla'far] *al-turath al-sha'bi,* 4, 151–18.

Touma, Habib Hassan. 1977. *La Musique Arabe.* Paris: Buchet/Castel.

———. 1996. The Music of the Arabs (expanded edition). Portland Oregon: Amadeus Press.

Urkevich, Lisa. 2001. "Saudi Arabia." In *The New Grove Dictionary of Music and Musicians (2nd edn.),* edited by Stanley Sadie, Vol. 22:224–8. London: Macmillan Press.

Vermaseren, Maarten J. 1977. *Cybele and Attis: The Myth and the Cult.* London: Thames and Hudson.

Williams-Forte, Elizabeth. 1983. "Annotations of the Art." In *Inanna, Queen of Heaven and Earth: Her Stories and Hymns from Sumer,* by Diane Wolkstein and Samuel Noah Kramer, 174–99. New York: Harper & Row.

Wolkstein, Diane, and Samuel Noah Kramer. 1983. *Inanna, Queen of Heaven and Earth: Her Stories and Hymns from Sumer.* New York: Harper & Row.

Wosien, Maria-Gabriele. 1974. *Sacred Dance: Encounter with the Gods.* London: Thames and Hudson.

Wulff, Hans E. 1966. *The Traditional Crafts of Persia.* Cambridge: The M.I.T. Press.

Ziegler, Susanne. 1990. "Gender-Specific Traditional Wedding Music in Southwestern Turkey." In *Music, Gender, and Culture,* edited by Marcia Herndon and Susanne Ziegler, 85–100. Wilhelmshaven: Florian Noetzel Verlag.

Part IV

Globalization and Glocalization

8

On Redefining the "Local" Through World Music

Jocelyne Guilbault

Why is Defining the "Local" a Major Preoccupation Today?

Since the early 1980s, much literature in the social sciences has sought to explain the processes involved in the restructuring and transformation of the political and economic world order.[1] Within this framework, many critics have emphasized the globalization of culture and, correspondingly, the cultural industries and new technologies involved in the process of change. What interests me, as an ethnomusicologist who has been involved mainly with the study of local communities, is how the status of the "local" has been transformed within contemporary societies, but also why and for whom it has become vitally important to redefine it today. In this paper, I will use the phenomenon of "world music" as a case in point to assess the primacy of this question in the ongoing politics of popular musical culture.

It is no coincidence that the question of defining the local has become such a pressing issue in the 1990s, not only for small and industrially developing countries but also for traditionally dominant cultures. The globalization process of the 1980s has aroused fears worldwide, with varying reasons for different people, depending on their position in the scale of power and empire. For dominant cultures, the move towards a fundamentally delocalized world order articulated around a number of scattered production and distribution centres has imparted the fear that their traditional monopoly over the world financial and industrial system is being threatened (Robins 1989, 148).[2] In relation to the music industry, the importance given by the intellectuals to defining the local can therefore be connected to a growing concern that this change in the power structure has led to the fragmentation of the dominant traditions' well-established markets and, consequently, to a redefinition of their relationships with other cultures.[3] One of the results of a decentralized record production and distribution and hence of a more diversified global market is that popular musics such as rock, which have been dominant so far, can no longer be seen as "more central and less ethnically or racially specific than any other form" (Straw 1991, 372). The ethnicization of the mainstream forms of musics that had become almost synonymous with the so-called "global culture" can be viewed as both a sign and recognition that their historically privileged position is being challenged by the emergence of many other musics as well as networks of production and distribution. The current preoccupation in the traditionally dominant cultures with defining the

137

local can therefore be interpreted as a manifestation of the crisis occasioned by the repositioning of dominant cultures among themselves as well as with the "others."

The question of defining the local for small and industrially developing countries has come from at least two profoundly contrasting, albeit interrelated, perspectives. For some, it has come as a reaction linked with the fear of losing cultural identity in the face of worldwide homogenization. For others, defining the local has been perceived as an opportunity to redefine and promote local identity. In the context of decentralized production and distribution, this issue has been regarded as a cultural and political necessity. It has also sprung from an economic interest and opportunity to promote difference and to take advantage of the world market now more easily available thanks to the greater access to new technologies and polylateral distribution networks. In both cases, however, the effect of trying to define the local has been subversive, causing people to question the significance of the opposition global/local, as it has been understood mainly in small, industrially developing countries. The tendency to equate dominant cultures with global culture because they have become the common denominator in many spheres of activity is being reviewed in light of the fragmentation of many markets, including that of music. Global culture is now thought of as contested terrain where there are only locals engaged in a battle over transnational markets.

The Battle of the Locals

The two contrasting perspectives on the global/local nexus has generated two types of actions, one directed to the protection, the other to the promotion of the local cultural capital and identity. The fear of losing local identity has been transformed for a number of politicians and social activists into a new interest in developing public policy to promote local, traditional cultures and, in some cases, in creating various protectionist measures against the invasion of foreign media programs by satellites.[4] This growing interest in public policy already figured prominently in Wallis and Malm's exemplary study of twelve small countries (1984). In the 1990s these concerns now occupy central stage and dominate conference themes of organizations involved in the study of small, industrially developing countries, for example, the theme of the Caribbean Studies Association's 18th annual meeting in May 1993, "Caribbean Public Policy: Preparing for a Changing World," and recent publications featuring titles such as "Music in the Dialogue of Cultures: Traditional Music and Cultural Policy," edited by Max Peter Baumann (1991).

Although these efforts have been largely concerned with promoting as well as protecting the local, other measures and actions have tried to support and develop ways to enter and participate more actively in the international markets. Governmental projects and private associations in many small, industrially developing countries including those in the Caribbean have sponsored workshops or long-term courses to train their own people in developing, outside the traditional professional and organizational cultures of the nation-state, the appropriate skills to deal with globalization in many sectors, including the music industry. New categories of professionals in these milieus have emerged, including, for example, international copyright lawyers along with managers and distributors involved with the international markets.

One way of interpreting these changes is to say, as has often been the case, that those who could be identified here as the "small locals" have simply assimilated the tools of the dominant traditions—hence the thesis of the greying of cultures. The other possibility, which I prefer, is to see,

> homogenization and differentiation not as mutually exclusive features of musical globalization...but as integral constituents of musical aesthetics under late capitalism. Synchronicity, the contradictory experience of the universal market-place alongside proliferating neo-traditional codes and new ethnic schisms, is the key signature of the postmodern era (Erlmann 1996, 469)

Within this perspective, the appropriation by the small locals of the skills and resources of the dominant traditions must be seen as part of the necessary strategy (or as the necessary condition) for differentiation to emerge within the realm of commodity aesthetics. As Erlmann aptly remarks, "homogeneity and diversity are two symptoms of what one is tempted to call the Bennetton syndrome; the more people around the globe purchase the exact same garment, the more the commercial celebrates difference" (Erlmann 1996, 469).

By way of illustration, examining the case of world music is particularly revealing. The term "world music" is a label with such ambiguous references that a typology of the various kinds of music it groups together would be necessary in order to understand its multifaceted meanings. Even then, however, no consensus would be reached: depending on the country, distributors, record-shop owners, and music journalists, the social, political, or demographic position of certain minority groups in a given country, the category of "world music" would vary in content and include various sets of musical genres.[5] In this paper, I am referring only to what could be regarded as a subset of world music, that is, popular musics that have emerged in the 1980s; that are mass-distributed worldwide yet associated with minority groups and small or industrially developing countries; that combine local musical characteristics with those of mainstream genres in today's transnational music-related industry;[6] and that have reached the markets of industrialized countries (cf. also Rijven 1989)—in essence, musics such as *zouk*, *rai*, and *soukous*. Within this framework, world music is associated with a specific time—its time of emergence (the 1980s)—and to specific conditions, in this case, the distinctive features of that decade's political and economic scene, including the breakup of the communist block; the resurgence of many ethnic groups; the realignment of various communities and the formation of new alliances; increasing problems of multiculturality and polyethnicity; the consolidation of the global media system; and the reconfiguration of the world economic order with a more fluid international system—all marking the end of bipolarity. It is also associated with particular groups of people, defined more in relation to their racial affiliations, their group's economic position in the world economic order, their culture (in the sense of value system), and their traditional geographic space, that is, the location where these groups have been traditionally living, than in terms of gender, generation, or class.

These denotations still seem to persist for world-beat music journalists and radio announcers, as well as for many of its listeners, despite the current claim in academia that "contemporary world music does not emanate from locally circumscribed peasant community or artisan's workshop . . . but the ubiquitous nowhere of the international financial markets and the Internet" (Erlmann 1996, 475).[7] I would argue here that, while people from small and industrially developing countries take part in the new global culture, they can also choose to be in and out of this "space we all inhabit, irrespective of whether we find ourselves in the migratory or in the stationary mode" (Erlmann 1996, 476), they can also choose to be in and out of this specific transnational culture or only partially in it.[8] As will be discussed further, there is not only one transnational culture in the postmodern era, but several, which are, depending on the sector of activity or historical time and context, "usually more marked by some territorial culture than by others" (Hannerz 1990, 244).

The world musics to which I am referring illustrate par excellence how people from small and industrially developing countries have established in and out, border-zone relations with the transnational record-industry culture deeply marked by the dominant traditions. On the one hand, world music takes advantage of the skills and resources of the dominant traditions: it appropriates the latest technology and know-how in its production, marketing, and distribution and features many of the musical characteristics of the mainstream musics heard on the global market. By doing so, it uses a kind of lingua franca, if not understood, at least recognized by everyone. At the same time, however, world musics such as *zouk*, *rai*, and *soukous* juxtapose musical characteristics of a particular culture without any attempt to blend these elements with those of the dominant musical traditions—with the result that the output of the small locals is still clearly identifiable. The result of these strategies of composition—and here one really can use the word "strategies"

to refer to the conscious choice of musical elements made by these musicians, as was attested by field work on *zouk*[9]—has meant greater access to the music market controlled by the dominant traditions, as most commentators have been quick to point out. What has been acknowledged less often, however, is the fact that this new access to the markets of industrialized countries, designating the connection traditionally referred to as center/periphery, has constituted one of the venues, although not the only venue, by which world musics have developed commercial value and public recognition.

Except for rare cases such as the *lambada*, the emergence of world musics on the international market cannot be said to be tributary to the blind acceptance or/and promotion of something different by the dominant media. On the contrary, most musicians from small and industrially developing countries have experienced great difficulty in getting their musics played on the "big" channels. For example, until 1987 the French media (with the exception of "Libération" and "Actuel") ignored the leading *zouk* group, "Kassav"—even after it had performed in 1986 before an audience of some 300,000 at the Pelouse de Reuilly in Paris (see Figure 8.1). The reasons given for this absence of media coverage could be interpreted as a translation of the malaise caused by the breakdown of formerly well-established colonial-inspired broadcasting categories and the consequent forced changes of rapport with the others. In reference to "Kassav," for example, a French journalist commented sarcastically on her compatriots:

> It seems they were too "tan" for the Champs-Elysees. On NRJ (Nouvelle Radio Jeune], Creole is still considered no better than static. They weren't oppressed enough to make it into the pages of *Résistance*. And to pass muster at *Mosaïque*. you need to be a genuine immigrant. Until further notice, Kassav is French, given that they are Antilleans. (D. Elizabeth 1987)

For "Kassav," however, there was little doubt: according to Gene Scaramuzzo, most of the interviewed members of the group were convinced that "this refusal to legitimize an Antillean identity separate from France [was] behind the media's downplaying of zouk" (Scaramuzzo 1986, 31). Whatever the reasons, whether political or economic (the fear of the market fragmentation already discussed), the attitudes of the dominant media changed through force of circumstance. Musicians from small and industrially developing countries received some attention after succeeding in highly visible venues. After 1987 for instance, "Kassav"'s series of sold-out Zenith concerts in Paris compelled the French media to acknowledge the group's huge success and subsequently *zouk* productions in general.

In fact "Kassav"'s success, like that of many other minority groups, has come about gradually by relying first on its compatriots at home and in diaspora. In the same way, to continue with "Kassav," the group's popularity in Paris has grown out of the support of West Indians in exile, African immigrants, and other minority groups. Its success was initially achieved horizontally, as it were, with the "small people," as opposed to vertically (climbing the ladder) with the help of the "big people" in power—in this case, the French.[10] "Kassav" has secured its position by creating a relatively autonomous space with minority groups despite the indifference and at times animosity of the French media—a space on which it has focused, in the words of the group's founder, Pierre-Edouard Décimus "to show that things can happen, outside France's realm of influence." The promotion of Antillean music by and for other "small people," he added, is a new way to assert itself vis-à-vis world political and economic powers.

Two important points follow from this example. One demonstrates how the music industry can no longer be conceived of in terms of the center/periphery theory, based on the principle of bilateral market.[11] World musics are an ideal illustration of how they are connected to polylateral markets.[12] From another perspective, and this is my second point, the musicians of world musics also show that they are cosmopolitans who function in and out, at will, of what has been traditionally

Figure 8.1 The zouk group "Kassav" Reuilly in Paris.

perceived as the totalizing "system," that is, the system controlled by the dominant cultures. Over the juxtaposition of elements from their traditional music, they have adopted the musical language of the dominant traditions and play that card commercially to enter the industrialized countries' networks. At the same time, they have also established connections with other musical cultures and music markets, in this instance by emphasizing some of the distinct musical characteristics akin to theirs or else by forming new alliances with other minority groups occupying similar positions in the world political and economic order. The acknowledgement of these new networks and market spaces does not negate the complete commodification of musical performance that is ubiquitous in the market place and through which these new contacts have been made in the first place. Rather it shows how the central role of the dominant traditions is now deemphasized through these polylateral exchanges and new markets. From the small and industrially developing countries' perspective, defining the local within the new practices just outlined refers far more to choices motivated by political allegiances, cultural bonds, or economic necessities than to genealogical heritage or the sharing of a particular geographic location.

In the dominant traditions, the fear caused by market fragmentation and the change in relations with other cultures has led them to resort to old strategies in order to reinforce their control and power over emerging sociopolitical, cultural, and economic destabilizing forces. The creation of the label world music is itself very telling. For an ethnomusicologist, the use of the term is certainly not new. What is new, however, is the way it has been appropriated in the 1980s initially by eleven independent record companies in Britain and then by multinational labels in campaigns to promote non-Anglo-American pop music artists. By using this label in record stores, "the public would have an accessible section where they could find the records of [these] artists" (Rijven 1989, 216). The fact is, as Simon Hopkins argued in the notes to the compact disc "World Music: Songs from the Global City:"

There's seldom been a more confusing, arbitrary or universally detested a marketing term as the WM-words, and of all the arguments against it, this one seems the strongest: if all it takes for a record to end up in the world music rack is for it to come from Brazil, France, Iceland or in short, anywhere that the Queen's English isn't the first language, then the term is—let's be blunt about it—a meaningless load of crap. (Hopkins 1991)

This, I would argue, is why the label is in fact so telling.

On the one hand, it openly encapsulates a very wide range of new musics and, by so doing, succeeds more easily in controlling a market that had so far remained untapped and uncircumscribed by the dominant music industry. This label, in effect, has served as a means of recuperation and appropriation of popular musics that have developed "outside," as it were, the traditional channels of the Anglo-American industry. While helping to expand the economic market of the dominant cultures, the label world music, which Erlmann describes as "the mesmerizing formula for a new business venture, a kind of shorthand figure for a new—albeit fragmented—global economic reality with alluring commercial prospects" (Erlmann n.d., 8), could be thought of as an attempt to banalize difference by placing all these non-Anglo-American musics under the same rubric.[13] This would indeed reflect the post/neo-colonial tradition, which continues to be based on the notion of a bilateral market, conceived in terms of us and them, center/periphery, superculture/subcultures, transcendent versus ethnic cultures.

It is symptomatic that, at the mass media level, in the industrialized countries, radio programming perpetuates the rigid categories of colonial times right into the postmodern era. In 1992 radio broadcasting in France and Holland still tends to isolate non-Anglo-American pop music artists from the mainstream, elite pop stars. Whether they are played on the main radio stations, periphery radios (in France) or illegal radios (in Holland) where they receive the greatest amount of airplay, musics such as *zouk*, *rai*, or *soukous* are still ghettoized in specific programs. In many ways, the label "world music" has thus reinforced the divide between so-called mainstream Anglo-American popular musics and non-Anglo-American musics by being used as a catch-all category and placed in the margins of the dominant music industry.

These broadcasting policies and practices in industrialized countries stand in sharp contrast with the more recent developments on radio stations in small and industrially developing countries and reflect the very different interests and goals that are at stake in the two cases. In the small Creole-speaking countries of the Caribbean, for example, *zouk's* international success has played a major role in the deghettoization of Antillean music in local radio programming, particularly in the French Antilles, where it is no longer confined to special programs. Since 1989 Antillean music has competed with other international musics on the hit parade; on Guadeloupe's "Radio Caraïbe International," for instance, it appears as part of a new program appropriately called "Melting Pot." This program publicly recognizes *zouk's* international value and, at the same time, frees Antilleans to express other musical tastes. As Guadeloupean political scientist Eric Nabajoth explained, it shows how *zouk's* international success has helped Antilleans to lose their inferiority complex and to feel comfortable in competing with others on the market (personal interview, 20 April 1990).

In the case of the dominant traditions, however, at the individual level, "elite pop artists," as Steven Feld remarked,

are in the strongest artistic and economic position in the world to freely appropriate what they like of human musical diversity, with full support from record companies and often with the outright gratitude of the musicians whose work now will appear under a new name. (1988a, 36–37)

Music appropriation is certainly not unique to artists from the dominant traditions, but what is clear is that according to Feld, "the flow of products and the nature of ownership is differentiated by market valuation factors" (1988a, 37):

When James Brown breaks down complex African polyrhythms and incorporates them into dense funk/soul dance tracks, we don't speak of a powerful Afro-American star moving in on African musical turf. Ten years later, when Fela Anikulapo Kuti seizes the essence of the James Brown scratch guitar technique and makes it the centerpiece of his Afro-Beat, we don't speak of a powerful African star moving in on Afro-American turf. The economic stakes in this traffic are small, and the circulation has the revitalization dynamic of roots. But when the Talking Heads move in on both James Brown and Fela Anikulapo Kuti and use scratch, funk, Afro-Beat and jùjú rhythm as the basic grooves for *Remain in Light*, something else happens. The economic stakes—however much attention is drawn to the originators as a result—are indeed different, the gap between the lion's share and the originator's share enlarged, and the discourse of race and rip-offs immediate and heated. (Feld 1988a, 37)

This example clearly illustrates that world music has come to be increasingly located in issues of power and control "because of the nature of record companies and their cultivation of an international pop music elite with the power to sell enormous numbers of recordings" (Feld 1988a, 37). While world music has attracted Anglo-American musicians to its new materials, products, and ideas, it has been kept, as much as possible, at a comfortable distance from the main channels of promotion and distribution.

World Music and the Creation/Confirmation of Space

For the small and industrially developing countries, world music has in many ways contributed to the redefinition of the local. For one, it creates considerable stress in the countries of origin by underscoring how its relations with the international market reformulates local traditions and creative processes.[14] As it emphasizes the workings of the world political economy at the local level, world music renders the definition of the "we" as a site of difference more problematic for the locals. It challenges in fact the traditional way of thinking about the "we" as a self-enclosed unit by highlighting its relational character.[15]

At another level, world musics have contributed to some degree to the repositioning of the local cultures to which they are associated, by being part of a world movement that advances the desire of every nation not only to be recognized but also to *participate* in the workings of global economics and power. In this connection, *zouk* provides a case in point. The apprenticeship of "Kassav"'s Antillean musicians in the French recording industry—from recording-studio high technology, to marketing techniques, to acquiring the know-how to attract sponsorship and develop a star image—has ironically led them to conquer this same market. "Kassav," as well as—eventually—other *zouk* groups and singers, has indeed become such a dominant force in the French music business that it has convinced French authorities of its competitive strength on the international market. After having been segregated socially, culturally, and economically for years within the French system, Antillean artists not surprisingly felt a sense of victory in the choice of an Antillean female artist (Joelle Ursull) to represent France at the 1990 Eurovision competition.[16]

In its contribution to the redefinition of the local, world music, as mentioned earlier, faces a double bind. On the one hand, in order to assert a distinct local identity within the dominant system, musics such as *zouk*, *rai*, and *soukous* are forced to a great extent to use the dominant system's language (its technology, for instance).[17] In the process, they necessarily take on some of the characteristics of the system from which they aim to distinguish themselves. On the other hand, as Louise Meintjes points out (1990, 68), "to regulate and incorporate subordinate groups, the dominant class is forced to reformulate itself constantly so that its core values are not threatened. In reformulating itself it necessarily takes on some features of the subordinate groups that it suppresses."[18]

To regulate and incorporate subordinate groups in the music industry, the dominant cultures have, as we discussed earlier, created a label. This in itself has helped confirm their power to define the "others" and to level their differences and means of differentiation by framing them in a single category. In this sense, world music has been treated more as an additional commodity to market and control than as an agent of change in the redefinition of the status or position of the dominant cultures in the music industry. At the same time, while many world musics may have seemed to confirm the central value of the mainstream language of popular musics, they have paradoxically attracted the attention of elite pop artists and enabled them to explore new aesthetics. World music seems far ahead of other fields in its use of active social forces that are diverse and contradictory as agents of change along with its reliance on both local and international forces in shaping local identities. Although world music may have triggered a subtle transformation of the power centers in the music industry, it remains to be seen whether it will succeed in fostering the acceptance of world differences without parallel shifts in political and economic systems.

Notes

1. I am most grateful to the Social Sciences and Humanities Research Council of Canada for sponsoring this research. I want also to express my warmest thanks to Stan Rijven and Marcia Rodrigues for their stimulating comments and support. This is a revised version of a paper presented at the International Colloquium of IASPM held at Carleton University, Canada, 30 October 1992.
2. The threat felt by the dominant cultures of losing their monopoly over the music industry can be connected with at least two factors, the first associated with the creation of new and commercially important music markets outside of the traditional channels of production and distribution. The means to produce records in small and industrially developing countries have existed since at least the 1960s. What is new and what can be seen as a threatening force, however, is the polylateral networks of distribution that have emerged in the 1980s among minority groups. "Kassav," for example, produced by the independent Antillean producer Georges Debs, had already achieved fame not only in the West Indies but also in France and in French Africa and had important commercial value before it signed contracts with CBS. The second factor can be related to the shift of power among the dominant cultures themselves, which Reebee Garofalo illustrates in describing some of the profound structural changes in the ownership of the transnational music industry: "Only one of the top five transnational record companies—WEA (Warner Brothers/Elektra/Atlantic), a division of Time-Warner—remains in U.S. hands, and in 1991, Time-Warner entered a partnership agreement with Toshiba and C. Itoh to the tune of $1 billion. Further, with its $6.6 billion purchase of MCA in 1990, which included Geffen Records and Motown, Matsushita has also made a bid for a share of the international marketplace. To the extent that the United States is identified as the main imperialist culprit in the exportation of pop and rock, it must be noted that the United States is no longer the main beneficiary of the profits" (Garofalo 1992, 6).
3. This is reflected, for instance, in the social sciences, particularly in anthropology, where debates over the changes in relations with other cultures have led to a critical examination of how ethnographic authority has been assumed and "displayed" in scholarly writings. Cf., for example, Clifford 1983, Clifford & Marcus 1986, Geertz 1988, Marcus & Fisher 1986, to name only a few.
4. The notion of "traditional" cultures has become increasingly problematic in relation to the new emphasis placed on the globalization of culture. Whether invented or not, I take the term "traditional" cultures in Hobsbawm's sense, that is, as "a set of practices, normally governed by overtly or tacitly accepted rules and of a ritual or symbolic nature, which seek to inculcate certain values and norms of behavior by repetition, which automatically implies continuity with the past. In fact, where possible, they normally attempt to establish continuity with a suitable historic past" (Hobsbawm 1983, 1). Within this framework, it should be noted that "traditional" cultures are in fact defined from an ideological point of view and are consequently subject to redefinition locally as new political orientations arise. For a thorough discussion of an example in Guadeloupe, cf. Lafontaine 1983.
5. In this regard, it is interesting to note, for example, that in the United States, where there is an important Latino population, *salsa* is usually not considered world music (because it is no longer perceived as foreign), whereas in Britain, with a considerably smaller Latino population, the same genre is included.
6. The musical characteristics of mainstream genres that are commonly integrated with musical languages and instruments of non-Western origin typically include the use of instruments such as the electric bass and guitar, as well as synthesizers, along with the adoption of harmonic progressions based on the Western classical tonal musical language.
7. The emphasis on geographic space to identify a world-music group or singer is, according to Dutch music journalist Stan Rijven, deeply influenced by the pop music practice in the West, which always focuses on "localizing" the music, by identifying its place of origin (e.g., the Manchester scene, Prince from Minneapolis) and the year it was released (personal communication, December 1992).
8. In this connection, see Clifford's insightful article "Traveling Cultures" (1992), in which he skillfully brings out the complexities of traveling cultures and border-zones relations.
9. Cf. Guilbault (1993), in particular chapters 2 and 8. It should be noted that, while many features of world music are in effect selected after conscious choices made by the musicians or managers (from the kind of harmonic language featured

to the way they dress), not every aspect of the music is consciously decided. The process of Westernization has long been integrated, so that the use, for example, of the electric guitar, has simply become part of the soundscape.

10. On popular music as alternative communication, see Martins (1988). It should be noted that, when I refer to "Kassav"'s success as having been initially achieved horizontally, with the "small people," I do not mean to imply that the horizontal connections among "small people" have been in themselves without hierarchies and without internal competitions. An Antillean group is not received the same way as a Latino group in an African community in Paris. The expression "horizontal connections" is used here to highlight the polylateral networks and markets among small people that have been so far largely ignored in popular-music studies.

11. For a thorough discussion of this subject, cf. Chambers 1992.

12. Cf., for instance, Pacini Hernandez 1993, in which she describes the polylateral markets that link the Spanish Caribbean.

13. In their stimulating article "World Beat and the Cultural Imperialism Debate" (1990), Andrew Goodwin and Joe Gore refer to Stuart Cosgrove, who has pointed out that "for many World Beat fans in the West, what is offered is exoticism—world music sounds as aural tourism." On this issue, the two authors perceptively comment: "Here we confront the problem of the construction of an undifferentiated, usually African, 'Other'. In merely inverting the interpretation of an Africa or the Orient that remains undifferentiated, do contemporary World Beat and rap culture notions of globalism actually help to reproduce ethnocentric ways of seeing (and hearing) the world?" (Goodwin & Gore 1990, 76–77).

14. This subject has received considerable attention in relation to co-optation: cf. Frith 1987; Garofalo 1987; Vila 1989; and Randel 1991. On the interrelations of the international and local markets and their implications for musical aesthetics and politics, cf. Coplan 1985; Feld 1988b; Manuel 1988; Meintjes 1990; Turino 1988; and Waterman 1990a, 1990b.

15. On this issue, cf. Clifford & Marcus 1986; Cohen 1985; Marcus & Fisher 1986; Grenier & Guilbault 1990; Rabinow 1986; Rosaldo 1980; Turino 1990, and Waterman 1990b.

16. Eurovision is an annual song contest in which many European states and a few other countries around the world take part.

17. Keil noted the same politics at work when he observed: "In class society the media of the dominant class must be utilized for the style to be legitimated (1985, 122).

18. This quotation from Meintjes was inspired by Stuart Hall's article "Culture, Media and the 'Ideological Effect'" (1979). Hall's analysis of the dialectic situation is echoed by many other writers, cf., for example, Garofalo, 1987, 89.

References

Baumann, Max Peter (ed.). 1991. *Music in the Dialogue of Cultures: Traditional Music and Cultural Policy.* Intercultural Music Studies 2. Wilhelmshaven: Florian Noetzel.

Chambers, Iain 1992. "Travelling Sounds: Whose Centre, Whose Periphery?" *Popular Music Perspectives* 3:141–6.

Clifford, James. 1983. "On Ethnographic Authority." *Representations* 2:118–46.

———. 1992 "Traveling Cultures." In *Cultural Studies*, edited by Lawrence Grossberg et al., 96–116. New York: Routledge.

———, and George E. Marcus. 1986. *Writing Culture: The Poetics and Politics of Ethnography.* Berkeley and Los Angeles: University of California Press.

Cohen, Anthony P. 1985. *The Symbolic Construction of Community.* New York: Ellis Horwood.

Coplan, David. 1985. *In Township Tonight! South Africa's Black City Music and Theatre.* London: Longman.

D., Elizabeth. 1987. "Kassav." *Actuel* (91):93–6, 176.

Erlmann, Veit. 1996. "The Aesthetics of the Global Imagination: Reflections on World Music in the 1990s." *Public Culture* 8(3):467–87.

Feld, Steven. 1988a. "Notes on World Beat." *Public Culture Bulletin* 1(1):31–7.

———. 1988b. "Aesthetics as Iconicity of Style (Uptown Title), or (Downtown Title) 'Lift-Up-Over Sounding': Getting into the Kaluli Groove." *Yearbook for Traditional Music* 20:74–113.

Frith, Simon. 1987. "The Industrialization of Music." In *Popular Music and Communication*, edited by James Lull, 52–77. Newbury, CA: Sage Publications.

Garofalo, Reebee. 1987. "How Autonomous is Relative: Popular Music, the Social Formation and Cultural Struggle." *Popular Music* 6(1):77–92.

———. 1992. *Rockin' the Boat: Mass Music and Mass Movements.* Boston: South End Press.

Geertz, Clifford. 1988. *Works and Lives: The Anthropologist as Author.* Stanford, CA: Stanford University Press.

Goodwin, Andrew, and Joe Gore. 1990. "World Beat and the Cultural Imperialism Debate." *Socialist Review* 20(3):63–80.

Grenier, Line, and Jocelyne Guilbault. 1990. "'Authority' Revisited: the 'Other' in Anthropology/and Popular Music." *Ethnomusicology* 34(3):381–98.

Guilbault, Jocelyne. 1993. *Zouk: World Music in the West Indies.* Chicago: University of Chicago Press.

Hall, Stuart. 1979. "Culture, Media and the 'Ideological Effect'." In *Mass Communication and Society*, edited by J. Curran, M. Gurevitch, and J. Woolacot, 315–48. London: Sage Publications.

Hannerz, Ulf. 1990. "Cosmopolitans and Locals in World Culture." In *Global Culture: Nationalism, Globalization and Modernity*, edited by Mike Featherstone, 237–52. Newbury Park, CA: Sage Publications.

Hobsbawm, Eric. 1983. "Introduction: Inventing Traditions." In *The Invention of Tradition*, edited by E. Hobsbawm and Terence Ranger, 1–14. Cambridge: Cambridge University Press.

Hopkins, Simon. 1991. "World Music: Songs from the Global City." Insert notes accompanying *The Virgin Directory of World Music* compact disc VDWM1.

Keil, Charles. 1985. People's Music Comparatively: Style and Stereotype, Class and Hegemony." *Dialectical Anthropology* 10:119–30.

Lafontaine, Marie-Céline. 1983. "Le Carnaval de l'autre': A propos d' 'authenticité' en matière de musique guadeloupéenne, théories et réalités." *Les temps modernes*, May, 2126–73.

Manuel, Peter. 1988. *Popular Musics of the Non-Western World: An Introductory Survey*. New York: Oxford University Press.

Marcus, George E., and Michael M. J. Fisher. 1986. *Anthropology as Cultural Critique: An Experimental Moment in the Human Sciences*. Chicago: University of Chicago Press.

Martins, Carlos Alberto. 1988. "Popular Music as Alternative Communication: Uruguay. 1973–82." *Popular Music* 7(1):77–94.

Meintjes, Louise. 1990. "Paul Simon's Graceland, South Africa, and the Mediation of Musical Meaning." *Ethnomusicology* 34(1):37–74.

Pacini Hernandez, Deborah. 1993. "A View from the South: Spanish Caribbean Perspectives on World Beat." *The World of Music* 35(2):48–69.

Rabinow, Paul. 1986. "Representations Are Social Facts. Modernity and Post Modernity in Anthropology". In *Writing Culture: The Poetics and Politics of Ethnography*,.edited by J. Clifford and G. E. Marcus, 234–61. Berkeley and Los Angeles: University of California Press.

Randel, Don Michael. 1991. "Crossing Over with Rubén Blades." *Journal of the American Musicological Society* 44(2):301–23.

Rijven, Stan. 1989. "Introduction." *Popular Music* 8(3):215–19.

Robins, Kevin. 1989. "Reimagined Communities? European Image Spaces, Beyond Fordism." *Cultural Studies* 3(2):145–65.

Rosaldo, Michelle Z. 1980. "The Use and Abuse of Anthropology: Reflections on Feminism and Cross-Cultural Understanding." *Signs* 5(3):389–417.

Scaramuzzo, Gene. 1986. "Zouk: Magic Music of the French Antilles." *Reggae and African Beat* 5(4):27–31.

Straw, Will. 1991. "Systems of Articulation, Logics of Change: Communities and Scenes in Popular Music." *Cultural Studies* 5(3):368–88.

Turino, Thomas. 1988. "A Short History of Andean Music in Lima: Demographics, Social Power, and Style." *Latin American Music Review* 9(2):127–50.

———. 1990. "Structure, Context, and Strategy in Musical Ethnography." *Ethnomusicology* 34(3):399–412.

Vila, Pablo. 1989. "Argentina's Rock Nacional: The Struggle for Meaning." *Latin American Music Review* 10(1):1–28.

Wallis, Roger, and Krister Malm. 1984. *Big Sounds from Small People: The Music Industry in Small Countries*. New York: Pendragon Press.

Waterman, Christopher Alan. 1990a. *Jùjú: A Social History and Ethnography of an African Popular Music*. Chicago: University of Chicago Press.

———. 1990b. "Our Tradition is a Very Modern Tradition." *Ethnomusicology* 34(3):367–80.

9

The Canned Sardine Spirit Takes the Mic

Marina Roseman

Old Man Pungent: The Temiar Spirit Medium

Old Man Pungent, a Temiar spirit medium in the community of Kengkong in the forest of peninsular Malaysia, was known for his biting humor, ascerbic wit, brazen stance. By the time I arrived in 1982 to his highland Temiar village far upstream on the River Berok, he had heard from lowland village relatives about my plans to study, observe, and record Temiar healing ceremonies. Old Man Pungent, or *Taʔ Acuj*, had also heard about my tape recorder and microphones; indeed, on trips to Malay market towns on the forest's edge, he'd seen Malay pop singers on television, singing into their mics. Master performer that he was, he'd watched them playing to their audiences through this cone-shaped device that sucked the animated voice up and spewed it back out. Though wary it might steal the head soul that flows into voice as animated spirit, this ribald medium also saw in the microphone another potential prop for his show, a new form of engagement with co-participants and, perhaps, with the larger world of those from 'beyond the forest' (*gɔb*).

And so, after a period of my living, talking, working, singing, dancing with the villagers of Kengkong, when the villagers finally gave me the go-ahead to tape a ceremony, Old Man Pungent had some idea of what he was getting into. For several nights previous, curing ceremonies had been held for a young woman suffering from feverishness, stomach cramps, and diarrhea. Old Man Pungent had been attending to her together with another healer of the village, *Taʔ Rəgəəl*, whose name recalled the *Rəgəəl* tree, home of a *barɔh* bird, that fell one day across his path. He had brought the tree trunk home to become part of his house structure, and from that time was known as Old Man *Rəgəəl*. Together, in curing ceremonies, while singing songs given to each of them during dreams, the two men would be calling upon their spirit familiars for assistance in curing.

In preparation for the ceremony, I strung up one of my microphones from the round wooden rafters of the thatched, bamboo dwelling where the healing ceremony was to be held. This mic was suspended over the area where female chorus members, respondents to each song phrase the medium sings, sit before a log placed on the floor, beating pairs of bamboo-tube stampers in percussive accompaniment. The floor, made of bamboo slats lashed together and suspended about eight feet off the ground, reverberates with the beat of bamboo tubes and the movements of dancers: thus,

147

the need for suspension. I used another microphone to pick up the voices of the mediums moving about, singing, talking, ministrating to clients. Tonight, with the focus on healing, I was told that less people would be dancing. Hopeful that the floor would thus be more stable tonight, I placed the second microphone on a small stand on the lashed, bamboo-slat floor.

With hearth lights flickering low to comfort shy spirits arriving from near and far, and leaves filling the house with the fragrance of the forest to the spirits' delight, Old Man Pungent began to alternate chanting, to bring the illness out of the young woman's body, with yelps to startle the illness into disengaging from her body. Blowing the cool, refreshing liquid flowing with song from his spirit familiar into the patient's body, he then sucked out a splinter of wood that, he later explained, came from a tree near where she'd been gathering wild vegetables deep in the forest. The splinter had entered her stomach, pulled upon her heart-soul, and brought on her illness. With a sharp clap of his hands, he sent the illness back into the forest from whence it had come. A disgruntled chorus member jokingly complained: "Oh, you sent it in my direction!" Another participant countered: "No, he's sent it up into the ceremonial leaf ornaments hanging from the rafters."

Old Man Pungent then began to sing a song that he'd received, like the previous chant, in a dream from the spirit of the Durian fruit tree, while Old Man Rəgəəl took over the task of blowing, sucking, chanting, and ministering directly to the patient. In a show of bravado, Old Man Pungent picked up the microphone and sang directly into it. I scrambled to adjust the recording volume, while he proceeded to hold the mike, manipulating it as surely as a seasoned television performer. He was a man of the forest, but not about to be upstaged by other performers wherever they might hail from; rather, this new prop would serve his spirit guide, who sang through him and joked with participants, unfazed by the technologies of recording.[1]

Later, when Old Man Rəgəəl began to sing, an implicit challenge was in the air. Both mediums, having heard recordings of Temiar spirit songs broadcast by the Orang Asli ("Aboriginal") Broadcast Unit of Radio-TV Malaysia, knew singers who had been recorded and survived without suffering the illness of soul loss that might follow when the head-soul is disengaged in vocalization. But holding this implement of voice-grabbing itself, the microphone, was another step altogether. Not willing to seem less bold than his fellow medium, Old Man Rəgəəl now seized the mic from its stand. As he sang, his hand began to tremble, and the trembles shook his body. "Rəwaay haa?!" a chorus member called out, concerned for the state of his head soul. But Old Man Rəgəəl signaled to me that he wanted to continue, and he did, singing until the trembling in his body lessened, then ceased.

The Temiars, a small-scale riverine society of approximately 12,000 Austroasiatic-speaking hunter-gatherers and horticulturalists, today are fighting for their lives, land, and livelihood as a minority population in the Malaysian nation-state.[2] So often, as anthropologists and ethnomusicologists, we document the ways in which people accommodate changes in their social and physical environments. In this instance, however, I was reminded how the process of fieldwork itself brings new things, experiences, and concepts into a community. Even as I documented spirit songs and practices, the spirits were responding to my presence. Often, the spirits would sing about me, ask about my recording paraphenalia, even give me nicknames. The two healers I was working with were aware of my position as medium and mouthpiece, sending their gifts, their accomplishments, their songs, into wider arenas. We had talked about how my books and recordings of their songs and practices might help make them more visible and respected by those from "beyond the forest." These healers, knowing the risks of new technologies, also perceived their advantages. And, as consummate performers, neither was willing to be upstaged by the other. And so, even while I was content to let the microphone sit on its stand, recording from a "safer" distance, these two mediums, inhabited by their spirit familiars, took the mic in hand.

Temiars have long lived at the nexus of the local and the global, experiencing and responding to interactions ranging from those with precolonial Malay lowland court cultures, to the British colonialists arriving in the eighteenth- and consolidating their powers in the nineteenth centuries, to the Japanese Occupation during World War II and its postcolonial aftermath. In this article, I suggest that Temiar spirit mediums are mediators and song ceremonies are sites for mediating social change. Songs, received during dreams from the animated spirits of entities with whom Temiars have interacted during daily life, encapsulate and reproduce the continuity of a cosmological system while they incorporate the radical social, environmental, and political changes Temiars have undergone from precolonial times through to the present global economy. Individual experience is collectively shared in community-wide song ceremonies. Individual songs, performed live in ceremony and often broadcast by Radio Television Malaysia's Orang Asli Broadcast Unit, become the public culture of these indigenous forest people as they grapple with displacement and stake their place in the nation-state. From songs received from fresh river fish spirits to those from canned sardines, I trace a trajectory of musical and religious vitality amidst environmental devastation and social reorganization in the Malaysian rainforest. Through their musical and spiritual practices, I suggest, Temiars craft their dance of survival.

Sacred "Otherness"

Dream songs have long provided Temiars a site for mediating encounters with their *forest* environment (Roseman 1991). They use this space to incorporate the knowledge and power of "*out-forester*" (*gɔb*) peoples and commodities, as well. Temiar dream song receipt is based in an ethnopsychology that posits multiple soul components that may become detached and animated as "spirit." During dreams, usually the head- and sometimes the heart-soul component of both dreamer and beings he or she might encounter become temporarily detached. Taking imaginal form as miniature human beings, dreamer and spiritguide proceed to communicate. A song taught to the dreamer, as soul-component vocalized, becomes a channel for reestablishing contact with that spirit during

Figure 9.1 Abilem Lum (center) sings a song received from a spirit of the Annual Fruit Trees (nɔŋ tahon). Female chorus members respond vocally, while playing pairs of bamboo tubes in percussive accompaniment. Young men (right) dance beneath ceremonial leaf ornaments strung from rafters. Photo by the author.

nighttime, housebound ceremonies (see Figure 9.1) The spirit designates fragrant leaves, dance steps, and other performance parameters that will be recreated ceremonially to activate its presence in the human realm. The spirit, Temiars say, is able to see far above the forest canopy; made present in the shaman's song, it brings its extensive knowledge and perspective to bear upon human problems.

The Temiar world is one in which the constituting of self and community is based on a never-ending dialectical incorporation of that which is outside, be that spirits, other humans, neighboring forest peoples, non-foresters, or colonials. This process of dialectical incorporation, negotiated musically, destablizes and decenters as much as it controls and contains.[3] From that space above the rainforest canopy, Temiars now receive dream songs from airplanes and parachute drops as they do from birds, from wristwatches as well as pulsing insects. Foreign peoples and things are socialized in dreams, brought into kinship relations as spirit familiar "child" to the Temiar dreamer as "parent." Strange people, things, and technologies become humanized, even Temiar-ized, their potentially disruptive foreign presence now tapped for use as a spirit familiar in ceremony.

I first became aware of the potential for spirit songs to mediate relations not only with the forest environment, but with those from beyond the forest, when I began to record songs in the genre received from the water-dragon spirit, the Indic *naga* transformed into Temiar *daŋgah*. Temiars conceive of themselves as "forest peoples" (*sɛnʔɔɔy beek*) who live "upstream" in contradistinction to those from beyond the forest (*gɔb*), who live "downstream," "toward the marketplace." The rivers, flowing from the deep forest upstream to the marketplaces downstream, connect the two domains. *Səlombaŋ* was received by a medium living on the River *ʔembɛɛw*, as the waterdragon spirit made its way from the deep forest upstream to the headwaters and, eventually, the ocean, during the Great Floods of 1926. The song texts of *Səlombaŋ* have a greater number of Malay words, though the spirit still arrives looking like a forest person.

The genre termed *Pɛhnɔɔh gɔb* has an even greater number of Malay words in the song texts, and incorporates a performance format reminiscent of Malay spirit ceremonies, in which a drummer-interlocutor asks questions of the medium. The characteristic Temiar performance format of interactive choral response is dropped in "Malay-style" ceremonies, while the spirit guide arrives in Malay dress. These ceremonies, Temiar healers contend, are particularly useful for illnesses coming from the rivers and the earth, or illnesses like tuberculosis and malaria, which Temiars historically associated with "outforester" or foreign influence. Forest genres, on the other hand, are useful for illnesses coming from the trees, fruits, forest landforms and inhabitants.

In these spirit songs and practices, Temiars map their historical and geographic experiences in cosmological terms. And with these practices, they formulate strategies for responding to the diverse effects of forest and marketplace upon their health and well-being, incorporating both the energies of the forest upstream and the marketplace downstream into their therapeutic armory.

The Gombak Tunnel

While *Pɛhnɔɔh gɔb* and *Səlombaŋ* instituted *new* musical and spirit genres, "outforester" entitites were also incorporated into *existing* genres. One of these is a song received from the Spirit of the Gombak Tunnel.

Long after the Japanese Occupation of Malaysia during World War II ended in the early 1940's, the Japanese presence continues to echo in Temiar memories and reemerge in Temiar experience. In the 1960's, while working for the Department of Orang Asli Affairs at the Orang Asli Hospital built in Gombak, a Temiar medium and healer, Ading Kerah, rode on a motorcycle with his friend through an uncompleted roadworks project, a tunnel through a mountain that would eventually link the Gombak road with Pahang. The immigrant Japanese and Korean roadworkers, now once again transforming the landscape, recalled for Ading Kerah the tremendous historical upheavals wrought during World War II and the subsequent Emergency, both of which Temiars term, "the Japanese War." In 1982, Ading Kerah, living at that time in Menrik on the Berok River, recounted his experience in the Gombak Tunnel:

That one, I dreamt of a Japanese worker. That was from inside the tunnel on the Gombak boundary. A high mountain, source of one of the tributaries of the Pahang river; they were making a hole, a tunnel, where they were making a highway.

So in the beginning, there was a friend of mine, Semai, named Bah Aring. He had a motorcycle. At that time, they were still working on the tunnel, Japanese and Korean workers. That tunnel had two "troops" working on it.

My friend, he invited me to go hunting with our blowpipes, to go after some game. So we went, and I brought my blowpipe, my poison darts in their bamboo case. We got onto the motorcycle. My friend asked me, "Which road shall we take?"

"Let's take the old road," I answered. So we set out.

We arrived at the 16-mile marker above Gombak, and my friend said to me, "We'll cut off here onto the new road." Straightaway, there we were, taking the new road, the big new highway.

We arrived at the border of Gombak. At that time, the Japanese and Koreans still hadn't finished building. So the electric lights were not connected yet; it was still dark. We met a guard and asked him, "Can we take this route?" He answered, "Yes, but it's dark."

We entered the tunnel. It was still a dirt road. They hadn't yet tarred it. We reached the middle of the tunnel. Water was dripping inside that tunnel: water, fluid essence of the rocks, maybe, I'm not sure. The water dropped, pulling, on the crown of my head. It made my body as cold as ice, until I was shivering, my body shaking.

We arrived on the Pahang side, and I said to my friend, "Let's go back. I don't want to go further, I can't stand it. I feel like I'm sick."

He asked me, "What's the matter, why are you so cold?"

I told him, "Inside the tunnel, water dripped onto the crown of my head."

So we headed back, taking the old road; I refused to go on the tunnel road. We were going back, and reached the 17-mile marker above Gombak. At that point, there was a Chinese-built road. I was feeling a little better, not as cold any more. So I said to my friend, "Let's go onto this road, and blowpipe some game." He drove the motorcycle not more than a half an hour when it turned over and we fell. We fell well, we weren't hurt, and the motorcycle wasn't ruined. But the engine wouldn't start. We started back, pulling the motorcycle along to the main road. We brushed off the motor, cleaned it, and it came back to life. We headed straight home, never got to do any hunting. We went on home.

That night, I dreamt. I dreamt of a Japanese worker, a young man, with a long thinnish body, quite handsome. He admonished me: "What were you doing in the Gombak Tunnel? According to the rules, if it's not ready, you shouldn't enter!"

I answered, "Forgive me, sir, I didn't know."

"That's all right then," he said. If you want to know my name, the name of the one who holds the tunnel, I, who am the essence of the tunnel, ʔɛsmureey is my name."

He asked me about my wife. "Do you have a wife, do you have children?"

I answered him, "Sir, I have a wife and six children." Another one was still inside her stomach, you see.

He answered, "Did you know your wife has given birth?"

I responded, "No, I didn't know. It's been a while that I've been posted here, away from my family."

He answered, "Your wife, she has given birth to your child, last night, a girl. Being that this is so, it would be better if I gave her a name. You can call your child ʔamʔ səmureey."

That's the origin of the sacred place, the Gombak Tunnel.

Images of development and modernization—the tunnel through the mountain, the tarred road, the motorcycle—are conjoined here with material and conceptual markers of the Temiar way of life, the blowpipe and the hunt, the spiritual fluid of the rocks, the crown of Ading Kerah's head (location of the head soul). Their confluence erupts in momentary misfortune and loss: Ading Kerah's perception of illness that passes, the motorcycle accident that doesn't cause permanent damage. A successful game hunt eludes this Temiar pair, traveling the highway on their motorcycle holding blowpipes.

The disjuncture between out-forester and forest technologies and cultures is bridged, however, through dream and song. In his dream, Ading Kerah is informed of the rules: wait until the tunnel is finished, do not enter the mountain in its half-raw, half-reconstructed state. The powers of mountain formation and roadwork confront one another; spirit water flows from the gashes made in the mountain's interior. Ading Kerah has unknowingly entered this fray. But from this clash of cultures and technologies, Ading Kerah receives the gift of song from the essence of the tunnel, and the "true name" of the tunnel. Should Ading need to tap into this circuit of power to heal the sick or prevent illness in his community, he sings the song. The tunnel's name, embedded in his song text and given to his child, helps him evoke the spirit of the tunnel.

The song that emerges, unlike those of *Pɛhnɔɔh gɔb* or *salɔmbaŋ* discussed earlier, does not invoke a new genre. Rather, the Gombak Tunnel Spirit expresses himself within the quintessential forest genre *Taŋgaay*, a genre that encompasses the spirits of flowers, mountains, and other forest beings. The tunnel takes its place with other spirit songs of mountains and landscape in a musical map that places it with "things above ground" in the Temiar experiential universe. Yet the melodic contour of the first song phrase is not nearly as flat as those of *Taŋgaay* in the Perolak/Betis area. For Ading Kerah, with kinship ties from the state of Perak to Lombak headwaters of the Betis River, sings *Taŋgaay* in a style affected by his current location in his wife's village of Menrik, along the Berok River.

The more expansive tonal range in his Gombak Tunnel song emerges from geographical and demographic proximity of the Temiars in the Menrik area to the Semai, another "forest people" or aboriginal group dwelling nearby in the Cameroon Highlands, Pahang, and Perak. What Temiar term their "Semai-style" of singing, or *Gamok*, predominates among the Temiars of the upper Berok river, where the singer Ading Kerah is living at this time. Songs of the *Gamok* genre exhibit a melodic contour that descends and ascends with ease through a range extending from a fifth above to a fourth below the tonal center, rendering an expansive open melodic sound quite different from the more constrained format of *Taŋgaay*.[4] The Gombak Tunnel song partakes of this influence, simultaneously negotiating relationships with out-forester Japanese and with other forest peoples, the Semai, while remaining within the constraints of the Temiar genre *Taŋgaay*.

Ading Kerah incorporates the strange by transforming its essential being into a spirit guide (or, the strange incorporates him by giving him a song to which he can relate). The words and melody given by the Spirit of the Gombak Tunnel are nested within the rhythm of the bamboo tubes, symbolically embedded within the familiar pulsation of the rainforest soundscape and the human heart (Roseman 1991, 168ff). The Temiar world was dramatically transformed during Japanese Occupation and subsequent Emergency, yet the musical response to this "change" is not expressed here in the transformation of formal ceremonial parameters. Rather, in this case, it is found in the *intentional use* of already existing religious practices and discursive structures to encompass altered circumstances. Ading Kerah cushions the shock of the "uncanny" by embedding new phenomena in familiar dynamic processes of dream song composition, performance practice, instrumentation, and musical structure. The strangeness is in the familiarity.

Figure 9.2 Song of the Canned Sardine Spirit, by Angah Busu (T91 OR31-2).

Spiritualizing Commodities: The Canned Sardine Song

Low population density and a semi-nomadic settlement pattern constitute some of the survival techniques that Temiars have developed in relation to their forest ecology. In small settlements along the tributaries of major rivers, they are dispersed geographically and demographically so as

Figure 9.2 Song of the Canned Sardine Spirit, by Angah Busu (T91 OR31-2), *continued.*

not to overtax forest resources, including fish, game, water, and land. Yet in the interests of "national security," "national integration," and "development," many Orang Asli have been relocated into large, permanent regroupment settlements. Gradually losing their indigenous subsistence base, they have become increasingly dependent on their participation in the cash economy. Yet the economic base they are encouraged to redevelop, usually as arboriculturalists, peasants or rubber smallholders, is undermined by their landlessness. Under Malay Constitutional Law, the aboriginal peoples of the peninsula are not allowed to own land; they are corporate tenants on lands that can be granted or removed from aboriginal reserve status. Even as they try to restructure

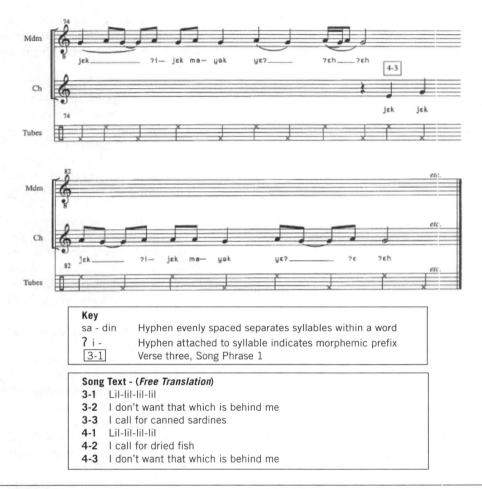

Key

sa - din	Hyphen evenly spaced separates syllables within a word
ʔ i -	Hyphen attached to syllable indicates morphemic prefix
3-1	Verse three, Song Phrase 1

Song Text - (*Free Translation*)

3-1 Lil-lil-lil-lil
3-2 I don't want that which is behind me
3-3 I call for canned sardines
4-1 Lil-lil-lil-lil
4-2 I call for dried fish
4-3 I don't want that which is behind me

Figure 9.2 Song of the Canned Sardine Spirit, by Angah Busu (T91 OR31-2), *continued*.

economically in new circumstances, regroupment projects may be moved again, and their efforts at reestablishing themselves come to naught.

Given the concentrated populations and low acreage of regroupment projects, rivers quickly become overfished, game depleted. Forest resources like rattan and the palm leaves used to thatch roofs are gathered more quickly than they can be replenished. Those fish that do survive the effects of population densification struggle in waters polluted by rainforest devastation of ancestral lands from which Temiars have since been removed in the name of national development and progress. Increasingly, Temiars augment their diets with foods bought in the marketplace downstream, or from petty entrepreneurs who brave the logging roads with their four-wheel drive vehicles, selling the new staples of Temiar life. Tea, sugar, canned milk, canned sardines, dried noodles, dried fish: these are items that can survive the transport and storage necessitated when commodities move from cities and towns into the forest.

Upstream toward the source of the Betis River in 1991, while recording during a spirit ceremony ending a mourning period, I heard a song received by *Taʔ ʔameŋ* from the Dried Fish and Canned Sardine Spirit. *Taʔ ʔameŋ*, also known by his Malay name Angah Busu, was the "representative headman" in Barong, one of several closely-located renegade settlements formed by Temiars who had thus far refused to join regroupment projects. As he sang, his spiritguide expressed its desires.

It didn't desire the "things behind it, in the past," or the forest leaves and root incense that a forest spiritguide might call for. Rather, it requested market goods, singing: "I don't want those behind me/I call, call, call, calling for canned sardines//I call, calling for dried fish/Don't lag behind me" (see Figure 9.2).

The catchy tune and contemporary subject matter combined to produce a hit, and I often heard younger singers throughout the area singing this song during return trips in 1992 and 1995. The Canned Sardine Spirit arrived in the musical genre *Poŋgeey*, associated with the spirit of a chrysanthemum flower species that grows in clearings around Temiar houses. These flowers, tended as "flowers of field and settlement," are taxonomically juxtaposed with "flowers of the jungle." The healing powers of the Dried Fish and Canned Sardine Spirit are thus given a place within the Temiar social and spatial universe, marked by their arrival in the *Poŋgeey* genre associated not with the jungle, but with "the settlement." Schizophonic displacement is contravened by a Temiar poetics of emplacement.

I do not intend to posit an unmediated Temiar "local" or "traditional" self against which the global is experienced. Rather, in the imaginary space of dreams and healing ceremonies, Temiars have developed cultural frames of reference for interpolating themselves in relation to ever-expanding spheres of "otherness": from other Temiars, to forest, to non-forest entities. Dream songs constitute a site for mediating the interpenetration of difference and similarity fundamental to Temiar cultural productions of personal and social identities, be they delineated along the axis of human/non-human, forester/out-forester, male/female, above ground/below ground. These sites have been called upon as Temiars incorporate ever-wider spheres of influence, maintaining their position as agents transforming the world even as they are transformed by it.

Increasingly, I am coming to believe that Temiars project that which they both fear and desire onto their spiritguide song-givers, in a classic act of what is called "introjection" in the psychological literature. Temiars project the cultural possibilities and coveted things outforester Others carry onto spirit familiars, who are often imaged as cross-sexual objects of desire: women dream of spirits arriving as handsome young men, men dream of shapely female adolescents and children. Spirit figures appear as miniatures, homunculi, small enough to be intimate but not intimidating. And they give songs which empower the dreamer-composer with long-range vision, geographic mobility, and knowledge to counter the illness and misfortune brought into the forest from Other exotic places: the "marketplace" downstream, as well as the "deeper jungle" upstream. Through this complex interpolation of fear, fantasy, desire, and mutuality, Temiars deal with their Others.

Spirit practices—these imaginative and performative realms of dream and song—are critical sites for the engagement of local peoples with global processes. Spirit songs sung to effect individual healings address, as well, the physical and spiritual health of a social group traumatized by loss of land and resources. The songs of the Gombak Tunnel Spirit and the Canned Sardine Spirit will be used in ceremonies for help in healing, or for the many other uses to which dream song ceremonies are directed: to trace important moments in the agricultural cycle; to welcome or sendoff travelers; to mark a mourning period's end; or to celebrate the experience of dancing, trancing, and singing with the spirits. Singing these songs, Temiars engage the spirits of modernity for their own purposes.

In their dream songs, Temiars draw the spirits into history through the power of expressive culture. Animated signs absorb the crash of disjunctured pasts and presents in Temiar ceremonial performance. Community members exploit the ability of motions and odors, musical sounds and glimmering colors to cross temporal and ontological boundaries, transcend geographic and cosmological space, polyphonically signal multiply-layered identities, and phenomenologically resituate experience.[5]

In her impressive comparative study of America's global cities, entitled *New York, Chicago, and Los Angeles* (U. Minnesota, 1999), Janet Abu-Lughod brings to the study of globalization the historical depth of a scholar whose previous work, entitled *Before European Hegemony: the World*

System A.D. 1250–1350 (Oxford University Press, 1989) traces the political, economic, and cultural flows intra- and extra-regionally linking Asia, the Middle East, and Europe. She compares New York, Chicago, and Los Angeles to extract both the nature of the global engagement and transregional influence that marks them as "global cities," and the historical, geographic, political and social specificities that shape New York as distinctively New York, Chicago as Chicago, and Los Angeles as Los Angeles.

It is this attentiveness to on-the-ground cultural and historical specificities held in productive tension with a clear recognition of overarching forces impinging on the local from "the beyond" (be that the Other, the Sacred, the National, the Global), in the first place; conjoined with an attentiveness toward individual and social constructions of reality held in productive engagement with recognition of the brute consequences of state and global intrusions on local lives, in the second, that I would hope our ethnographies of musical experience and spirit practices might bring to globalization studies.

On the one hand, I am impressed by the resilience of Temiar ethnopsychology and cosmology, which is able to engage the spirits of foreign things and people within an indigenous discursive system of power and knowledge, thereby retaining some modicum of agency. On the other hand, I am concerned that such shamanistic incorporation of the Outforest Other might presage an ideological acceptance of material disenfranchisement as Temiars focus upon the flash of a spiritguide's beauty, rather than mobilizing to resist their material losses. Yet I have come to see this ability to grasp a spirit's healing song from those people, things, and technologies that have so thoroughly assaulted their material resource base as an act of social suturing, an art of survival, a technology for maintaining personal and social integrity in the face of nearly overwhelming odds.

Thomas Csordas has written compellingly about the notion of Otherness and the constitution of the sacred self. "The sacred is an existential encounter with Otherness that is a touchstone of our humanity. It is a touchstone because it defines us by what we are not—by what is beyond our limits, or what touches us precisely at our limits" (1994, 4–5). "This sense of otherness," he argues, "is phenomenologically grounded in our embodiment." In spirit song performances, at the juncture—and disjuncture—of person and world, substance and energy, self and other, Temiars transmute their experiences with non-forester Others, transfixing the global in the local. Spiritualizing intrusive commodities and technologies, they simultaneously dis-inscribe themselves from "outforest" agendas, and are reinscribed in outforester visions of the future.

Acknowledgments

Field research with Temiars of Kelantan and Perak in 1981–1982,1991,1992,1995, and 1997 has been conducted under the auspices of the Social Science Research Foundation, Asian Cultural Council, Wenner Gren Foundation for Anthropological Research (Grant No. 4064), National Science Foundation (BNS81-02784), and Research Foundation of the University of Pennsylvania, with additional travel funds provided by Universiti Sains Malaysia and Malaysian Air Lines (1991). Analysis and writing were furthered by a Guggenheim Foundation Fellowship (1996–97), Professional in Residence Fellowship from the Annenberg School for Communications at University of Pennsylvania (1996–97), and the National Endowment of the Humanities (2000). My gratitude to these institutions; to my sponsors at the Cultural Centre of Universiti Malaya, the Department of Sociology and Anthropology at Universiti Kebangsaan Malaysia in Bangi, Selangor, and the Muzium Negara (National Museum, Kuala Lumpur); and to the Orang Asli Broadcast Unit at Radio-TV Malaysia, whose staff shared their extensive knowledge with me. Temiars and other Orang Asli have been wise and patient teachers, hosts, and friends; so too, several Malaysian families have graciously provided urban home bases. This article has been enriched by panel discussions at annual meetings of the American Anthropology Association 2000 (Marjorie Balzer, panel organizer), the Society for the Anthropology of Religion 2000 (Laurel Kendall, panel organizer), and Society for Ethnomusicology 1998 (Marina Roseman and Laura Larco, co-organizers); ongoing presentations and conversations with David Howes and the members of the Concordia Sensoria Research Team at Concordia University; and our *The World of Music* volume editor, Ron Emoff.

Notes

1. This recording, from the initial chanting through the surge in volume when *Ta Acuj* takes the microphone in hand, can be heard on Band 10 of the compact disc, *Dream Songs and Healing Sounds: In the Rainforests of Malaysia* (Smithsonian Folkways Recordings SF CD 40417,1995).

2. See Dentan et al. 1997, Nicholas 2000.
3. Piot (1999, 23) argues similarly for the Kabre of Northern Togo. Noting that spirit communication is fraught with ambiguity and uncertainty, he contends that so-called "traditional" Kabre "villagers" are cosmopolitan, "if by cosmopolitanism we mean that people partake in a social life characterized by flux, uncertainty, encounters with difference, and the experience of processes of transculturation."
4. A transcription of Temiar singing influenced by Semai-style singing can be found in Roseman 1991, Figure 9.3. Examples also occur in Roseman 1995a (Bands 1,10, and 12).
5. A growing literature addresses the ways in which spirit practices and expressive culture encompass the often disconcerting experiences of modernity; see, for example, Comaroff and Comaroff 1993; Barwick, Marett and Tunstill 1995; Mageo and Howard 1996; Benjamin 1996; Ferzacca 1996; Roseman 1996; Kendall 1996; Erlmann 1999; Buenconsejo 1999; Feld 2000; Samuels and Connor 2000; and Howes 2003.

References

Abu-Lughod, Janet. 1989. *Before European Hegemony: The World System A.D. 1250–1350*. Cambridge: Oxford University Press.

Abu-Lughod, Janet. 1999. *New York, Chicago, Los Angeles*. Minneapolis: University of Minnesota Press.

Agawu, Kofi. 1995. "The Invention of 'African Rhythm.'" *Journal of the American Musicological Society* 48(3):380–395.

Anderson, Benedict. 1991/1983. *Imagined Communities: Reflections on the Origin and Spread of Nationalism*, Rev. ed. London, New York: Verso.

Appadurai, Arjun. 1996. *Modernity at Large: Cultural Dimensions of Globalization*. Minneapolis: University of Minnesota Press.

Attali, Jacques. 1977. *Noise: The Political Economy of Music*. Brian Massumi, trans. Minneapolis: University of Minnesota Press.

Averill, Gage. 1997. *A Day for the Hunter, A Day for the Prey: Popular Music and Power in Haiti*. Chicago: University of Chicago.

Barwick, Linda, Allan Marett, and Guy Tunstill. 1995. *The Essence of Singing and the Substance of Song: Recent Responses to the Aboriginal Performing Arts and Other Essays in Honour of Catherine Ellis*. Sydney: University of Sydney.

Benjamin, Geoffrey. 1996. *Rationalisation and Re-enchantment in Malaysia: Temiar Religion 1964–1995*. Department of Sociology Working Papers No. 130. Singapore: National University of Singapore.

Benjamin, Walter. 1999. *The Arcades Project*. H. Eiland and K. McLaughlin, trans. Cambridge: The Belknap Press of Harvard University Press.

Bhabha, Homi K. 1994. *The Location of Culture*. New York: Routledge.

Blacking, John. 1978. "Some Problems of Theory and Method in the Study of Musical Change." *Yearbook of the International Folk Music Council* 3:91–108.

Buenconsejo, José. 2002. *Songs and Gifts at the Frontier: Person and Exchange in the Agusan Manobo Possession Ritual, Philippines*. New York: Routledge.

Campbell, Donald. 1997. *The Mozart Effect*. New York: Avon Books.

Casey, Edward S. 1996. "How to Get from Space to Place in a Fairly Short Stretch of Time?" *In Senses of Place*, edited by Steven Feld and Keith Basso, 13–52. Santa Fe, NM: School of American Research Press.

Caygill, Howard. 1998. *Walter Benjamin: The Colour of Experience*. New York: Routledge.

de Certeau, Michael. 1984. "Walking in the City". *In His Practice of Everyday Life*. Berkeley, Los Angeles: University of California Press.

Clifford, James. 1997. *Routes: Travel and Translation in the Late Twentieth Century*. Cambridge University Press.

Comaroff, John, and Jean Comaroff. 1992. *Ethnography and the Historical Imagination*. Boulder, CO: Westview Press.

Comaroff Jean, and John Comaroff. 1993. "Introduction." In *Modernity and Its Malcontents: Ritual and Power in Postcolonial Africa*, edited by Jean and John Comaroff, xi–xxxvii. Chicago: University of Chicago Press.

Conner, Linda H., and Geoffrey Samuel, eds. 2000. *Healing Powers and Modernity: Traditional Medicine, Shamanism, and Science in Asian Societies*. Westport, CT: Greenwood Publishing Group 19.

Cooper, Frederick, and Ann Laura Stoler. 1997. *Tensions of Empire: Colonial Cultures in a Bourgeois World*. Berkeley: University of California Press.

Coplan, David. 1994. *In the Time of Cannibals: The Word Music of South Africa's Basotho Migrants*. Chicago: University of Chicago.

Csordas, Thomas J. 1994. *The Sacred Self: A Cultural Phenomenology of Charismatic Healing*. Berkeley: University of California Press.

Dates, Jannette L., and William Barlow, eds. 1993. *Split Image: African Americans in the Mass Media*. Washington, DC: Howard University Press.

Dentan, R. K. 1992. "The Rise, Maintenance, and Destruction of Peaceable Polity: A Preliminary Essay in Political Ecology." In *Aggression and Peacefulness in Humans and Other Primates*, edited by J. Silverberg and J. P. Gray, 214–70. London: Oxford University Press.

Dentan, R K., and Ong Hean Chooi. 1995. "Stewards of the Green and Beautiful World: A Preliminary Report on Aboriculture and Its Policy Implications." *Dimensions of Tradition and Development in Malaysia*, edited by Rokiah and Tan Chee-Beng. Kuala Lumpur: Pelanduk.

Dentan, R. K., K. Endicott, A. Gomes, and M. B. Hooker. 1997. *Malaysia and the Original People: A Case Study of the Impact of Development on Indigenous Peoples*. Boston: Allyn and Bacon.

Densmore, Frances. 1934. "The Songs of Indian Soldiers during the World War." *Musical Quarterly* 20:419–25.

Ellis, Catherine J. 1980. "Aboriginal Music and Dance in Southern Australia." In *New Grove Dictionary of Music and Musicians*, Vol 1, edited by S. Sadie, 722–28. London: Macmillan.

Erlmann, Veit. 1999. *Music, Modernity, and the Global Imagination: South Africa and the West.* Oxford: Oxford University Press.

Feld, Steven. 1990. *Sound and Sentiment: Birds, Weeping, Poetics and Song in Kaluli Expression.* Philadelphia: University of Pennsylvania.

———. 2000. "Sound Worlds." In *Sound,* edited by Patricia Kruth and Henry Stobart, 173–200. Cambridge: Cambridge University Press.

Feld, Steve, and Keith Basso, eds. 1996. *Senses of Place.* Santa Fe: School of American Research Press.

Ferzacca, Steve. 1996. *In this Pocket of the Universe: Healing the Modern in a Central Javanese City.* Doctoral dissertation, Department of Anthropology, University of Wisconsin, Madison. Ann Arbor, MI: University Microfilms.

Frith, Simon. 1996. *Performing Rites: On the Value of Popular Music.* Cambridge: Harvard University Press.

Fox, Aaron. 1992. "The Jukebox of History: Narratives of Loss and Desire in the Discourse of Country Music." *Popular Music* 11:53–72.

———. 1993. "Split Subjectivity in Country Music and Honky-Tonk Discourse." In *All that Glitters: Country Music in America,* edited by George H. Lewis. Bowling Green: Bowling Green State University Press.

Geertz, Clifford. 1973. *The Interpretation of Cultures.* New York: Basic Books.

Giddens, Anthony. 1991. *Modernity and Self-Identity: Self and Society in the Late Modern Age.* Stanford: Stanford University Press.

Gilroy, Paul. 1993. *The Black Atlantic: Modernity and Double Consciousness.* Cambridge: Harvard University Press.

Guilbault, Jocelyne et al. 1993. *Zouk: World Music in the West Indies.* Chicago: University of Chicago Press.

Gupta, Akhil, and James Ferguson, eds. 1997. *Anthropological Locations: Boundaries and Grounds of a Field Science.* Berkeley; Los Angeles: University of California Press.

Hall, Stuart. 1994. "Cultural Identity and Diaspora." In *Colonial Discourse and Post-colonial Theory: A Reader,* edited by

——— et al., eds. 1992. *Modernity and its Futures.* Cambridge: Polity Press.

Patrick Williams and Laura Chrisman, 392–403. New York: Columbia University.

Hayward, Philip, ed. 1998. *Sound Alliances: Indigenous Peoples, Cultural Politics and Popular Music in the Pacific.* London: Cassell.

Hirsch, Eric, and Michael O'Hanlon, eds. 1995. *The Anthropology of Landscape: Perspectives on Place and Space.* Oxford: Clarendon Press.

Howes, David. 2003. *Sensual Relations: Engaging the Senses in Culture and Social Theory.* Ann Arbor: University of Michigan Press.

Kartomi, Margaret J., and Stephen Blum. 1994. *Music-Cultures in Contact: Convergences and Collisions.* Basel, Switzerland: Gordon & Breach.

Keane, Webb. 1997. *Signs of Recognition: Powers and Hazards of Representation in an Indonesian Society.* Berkeley: University of California Press.

Keil, Charles, and Steven Feld. 1994. *Music Grooves: Essays and Dialogues.* Chicago: University of Chicago Press.

Kendall, Laurel. 1996. "Korean Shamans and the Spirits of Capitalism." *American Anthropologist* 98(3):512–27.

Kroodsma, Donald E., and E. H. Miller. 1982. *Acoustic Communication in Birds.* New York: Academic Press.

Lavie, Smadar, and Ted Swedenburg, eds. 1996. *Displacement, Diaspora, and Geographies of Identity.* Durham, NC: Duke University Press.

Leary, John D. 1995. *Violence and the Dream People: The Orang Asli in the Malayan Emergency, 1948–1960.* Monographs in International Studies; Southeast Asia series, 95. Athens: Center for International Studies, Ohio University.

Lipsitz, George. 1994. *Dangerous Crossroads: Popular Music, Postmodernism and the Poetics of Place.* London: Verso.

Lomax, Alan. 1968. *Folk Song Style and Culture.* Washington: American Association for the Advancement of Science.

Lornell, Kip, and Anne K. Rasmussen. 1997. *Musics of Multicultural America: A Study of Twelve Musical Communities.* New York: Schirmer.

Loomba, Ania. 1998. *Colonialism/Postcolonialism.* New York: Routledge.

Mageo, Jeannette M., and Alan Howard, eds. 1996. *Spirits in Culture, History, and Mind.* New York: Routledge.

Merriam, Alan P. 1967. *Ethnomusicology of the Flathead Indians.* Chicago: Aldine Press.

Moyle, R.M. 1979. *Songs of the Pintupi: Musical Life in a Central Australian Society.* Canberra: Australian Institute of Aboriginal Studies.

Myers, Fred. 1991. *Pintupi Country, Pintupi Self: Sentiment, Place, and Politics among Western Desert Aborigines.* Berkeley: University of California.

Nettl, Bruno. 1983. *The Study of Ethnomusicology: Twenty-nine Issues and Concepts.* Urbana: University of Illinois Press.

———, ed. 1978. *Eight Urban Musical Cultures: Tradition and Change.* Urbana: University of Illinois Press.

Nicholas, Colin. 2000. *The Orange Asli and the Contest for Resources: Indigenous Politics, Development and Identity in Peninsular Malaysia.* Copenhagen, Denmark: International Work Group for Indigenous Affairs (IWIGA).

Pacini Hernandez, Deborah. 1995. *Bachata: A Social History of a Dominican Popular Music.* Philadelphia: Temple University Press.

Parmentier, Richard J. 1987. *The Sacred Remains: Myth, History, and Polity in Belau.* Chicago: University of Chicago Press.

Payne, Katharine B., W. R. Langbauer Jr., and E. M. Thomas. 1986. "Infrasonic calls of the Asian elephant (*Elephas maximus*)." *Behavioral Ecology and Sociobiology* 18:297–301.

Pemberton, John. 1994. *On the Subject of "Java."* Ithaca, NY: Cornell University Press.

Piot, Charles. 1999. *Remotely Global: Village Modernity in West Africa.* Chicago: University of Chicago.

Povinelli, Elizabeth A. 1993. *Labor's Lot: The Power, History, and Culture of Aboriginal Action*. Chicago: University of Chicago Press.

Rachagan, S. Sothi. 1990. "Constitutional and Statutory Provisions Governing the Orang Asli." In *Tribal Peoples and Development in Southeast Asia*, edited by Lim Teck Ghee and Albert G. Gomes, 101–11. Kuala Lumpur Department of Anthropology and Sociology, University of Malaya.

Rauscher, Fraces H., Gordon L. Shaw, and Katerine N. Ky. 1995. "Listening to Mozart Enhances Spatial-Temporal Reasoning: Towards a Neurophysiological Basis." *Neuroscience Letters* 185:44–7.

———, ———, Linda J. Levine, Eric L. Wright, Wendy R. Denis, and Robert L. Newcomb 1997. "Music Training Causes Long–Term Enhancement of Preschool Children's Spatial Temporal Reasoning." *Neurological Research* 19:208.

Reyes-Schramm, Adelaide. 1990a. "Ethnic Music, the Urban Area, Ethnomusicology." *Sociologus* 29(1):1–21.

———. 1990b. "Exploration in Urban Ethnomusicology: Hard Lessons from the Spectacularly Ordinary." *Yearbook for Traditional Music* 14:3–20.

Richards, Douglas G. 1985. "Biological Strategies for Communication." *IEEE Communications Magazine* 23(6 June):10–8.

Rose, Dan. 1987. *Black American Street Life: South Philadelphia, 1969–1971*. Philadelphia: University of Pennsylvania Press.

Roseman, Marina. 1983. "The New Rican Village: Artists in Control of the Image-making Machinery." *Latin American Music Review* 4(1):132–167.

———. 1991. *Healing Sounds from the Malaysian Rainforest: Temiar Music and Medicine*. Los Angeles: University of California Press; Sydney: Oceania Publications.

———. 1995. *Dream Songs and Healing Sounds: In the Rainforests of Malaysia*. Smithsonian/Folkways Recordings SF CD 40417 (compact disc).

———. 1996a. "Pure Products Go Crazy: Rainforest Healing in a Nation-State." In *The Performance of Healing*, edited by Carol Laderman and Marina Roseman, 233–269. New York: Routledge.

———. 1996b. "Decolonizing Ethnomusicology: When Peripheral Voices Move in from the Margins. In *Aflame with Music: One Hundred Years of Music at the University of Melbourne*, edited by B. Broadstock et. al., 167–89. Melbourne: Centre for Studies in Australian Music.

———. 1998. "Singers of the Landscape: Song, History, and Property Rights in the Malaysian Rain Forest." *American Anthropologist* 100(1):106–21.

Schafer, R. Murray. 1977. *The Tuning of the World*. New York: Knopf.

Seeger, Anthony. 1987. *Why Suyá Sing: A Musical Anthropology of an Amazonian People*. Cambridge: Cambridge University Press.

Slobin, Mark. 1993. *Subcultural Sounds: Micromusics of the West*. Hanover. Wesleyan University Press.

Steedly, Mary Margaret. 1993. *Hanging without a Rope: Narrative Experience in Colonial and Postcolonial Karoland*. Princeton, NJ: Princeton University Press.

Stewart, Kathleen. 1996. *A Space on the Side of the Road*. Princeton, N.J.: Princeton University Press.

Sumarsam. 1995. *Gamelan: Cultural Interaction and Musical Development in Central Java*. Chicago: University of Chicago Press.

Tan Sooi Beng. 1993. *Bangsawan: A Social and Stylistic History of Popular Malay opera*. Singapore: Oxford University Press.

Taylor, Timothy D. 1997. *Global Pop: World Music, World Markets*. New York and London: Routledge.

Thomas, Nicholas. 1994. *Colonialism's Culture: Anthropology, Travel and Government*. Princeton, NJ: Princeton University Press.

Tsing, Anna. 1993. *In the Realm of the Diamond Queen: Marginality in an Out-of-the-Way Place*. Princeton, NJ: Princeton University Press.

Turino, Thomas. 1993. *Moving Away from Silence*. Chicago: University of Chicago Press.

Turner, Victor. 1967. *The Forest of Symbols: Aspects of Ndembu Ritual*. Ithaca, NY: Cornell University Press.

Wallerstein, Immanuel. 1974. *The Modern World-System: Capitalist Agriculture and the Origins of the European Word-Economy in the Sixteenth Century*. New York: Academic Press.

Waterman, Christopher. 1991. *Jùjú: The Social History of an African Popular Music*. Chicago: University of Chicago.

Wild, Steve A. 1987. "Recreating the Jukurrpa: Adaptation and Innovation of Songs and Ceremonies in Warlpiri Society." In *Songs of Aboriginal Australia*, edited by M. Clunies Ross, T. Donaldson and S. Wild, 97–120. Sydney: Oceania Publications.

Wiora, Walter. 1965. *The Four Ages of Music*. New York: Norton.

Wolf, Eric. 1982. *Europe and the People Without History*. Los Angeles: University of California Press.

Wolters, Oliver W. 1982. *History, Culture, and Region in Southeast Asian Perspectives*. Singapore: Institute of Southeast Asian Studies.

Temiar Field Collection Materials

Roseman Field Collection T95 OD5.2 [Temiar 1995 Original DAT Tape No. 5, item 2]

Roseman Field Collection T95 OD7 [Temiar 1995, Original DAT Tape No. 7]

Roseman Field Collection T81/82 OR84.3 [Temiar 1981/1982 On original Reel-to-Reel Tape No. 84 item 3]

10

A Musical Instrument Travels Around the World
Jenbe Playing in Bamako, West Africa, and Beyond

Rainer Polak

The *jenbe* (*jembe, djembé*)[1] is a goblet-shaped drum. Local traditions of *jenbe* playing in rural areas exist mainly among Manding-speaking groups in northern Guinea and southern Mali, around the section of the river Niger between the towns of Faranah, Guinea and Koulikoro, Mali (see Charry 2000, 196, map 8). The *jenbe* has spread further in the course of the urbanization of the former colony, *Afrique Occidental Français*, and later as a result of the formation of the independent states of Guinea, Mali, Ivory Coast, Senegal, and Burkina Faso. Important contemporary centers of *jenbe* traditions, notably Conakry, Bamako, Abidjan, Dakar, and Bobo Dioulasso, are not situated within the core area of rural *jenbe* playing but rather are adjacent to it (see Figure 10.1).

Three Contexts of *Jenbe* Playing

Jenbe drum ensemble music has been performed in the context of local dance and drum events with communal and family celebrations for centuries. *Jenbe* players are specialists who use knowledge handed down from tradition, personal competence, privately owned instruments (for the most part), and their own labor and creativity in individual performances. They play only when engaged for a specific occasion, and, in the urban centers, earn their living in this way. Professional music practice in West Africa is often associated with distinct social groups of griots (called *jeli* in Bamana and other Manding languages) who act as oral historians, praise singers, social mediators, celebration and popular musicians, etc. *Jenbe* playing, however, does not belong to the practices more or less exclusively belonging to the griots. It is a free profession in urban West Africa.[2]

Since the late 1950s, the *jenbe* has been integrated into the ballet programs of both private and state-sponsored (communal, regional, and national) folkloric ensembles in West Africa. Unlike any African musical instrument before it, the *jenbe* also has gained international standing in recent decades. International tours of national ballet companies have introduced the *jenbe* to the rest of

2824. - Voyage du Ministre des Colonies à la Côte d'Afrique - KONAKRY
Place du Gouvernement à l'Arrivée

Figure 10.1 Jenbe players (left bottom) at the French colonial minister's reception in Conakry. Photo: Fortier 1908. From CD-Rom Atlas du Patrimoine n°4, West African Postcards (1895–1930), file number 20. Reprinted with the kind permission of Philippe David, Images & Memoire, Paris.

the world. Since the mid-1980s concerts and CDs featuring *jenbe* music, classes for (and playing by) amateur drummers, and the exportation of the instrument have all led to an unparalleled boom in Europe and North America.

The following will outline local family celebrations, folkloric state ballets, and the international market for percussion music as they are present as different contexts of *jenbe* music in the Malian metropolis, Bamako.

Drum and Dance Events in Urban Family Celebrations

Local drum and dance events in Bamako are hosted in the context of so-called transition rites. At life-cycle events such as the Islamic naming of a newborn child, a circumcision, or a wedding, family members organize festive days or evenings. They invite their larger circle of relatives, the neighborhood, colleagues, and all those who pass by and want to stay to watch or participate. These celebrations, in addition to involving the consumption of plenty of food and the ritual exchange of goods, are marked by drum and dance events. Weddings consist of one or two evening receptions preceding the main event (*denba-tulon*) in honor of the bride's honorary mothers (*denbaw*),[3] who organize and finance the festivals and the celebration during the actual wedding day. Of all local celebration engagements of Bamako professional drummers, weddings make up more than 80 percent.[4]

Until well into the 1960s, celebrations featuring *jenbe* music in Bamako represented urban extensions and transformations of ethnically, regionally, or locally specific rural traditions.[5] Only those who had been accustomed to dancing to the *jenbe* before having migrated to Bamako continued to do so in the city. Today families of very diverse social backgrounds and ethnic and regional origins promote *jenbe* celebrations. Among them are Manding speakers such as the Maninka, Bamana, Wasulunka, and the Khasonka, in addition to members of about a dozen groups from the north of Bamako and from neighboring countries. Only about one-third of the demand for work of professional *jenbe* drummers in Bamako takes place among the Maninka and Wasulunka, two groups that had already known the *jenbe* as a central part of their rural entertainment practices. Some families residing in Bamako organize *soirées dansantes* with popular music, or drum and dance celebrations with ensembles other than *jenbe* players, according to their specific ethnic or regional backgrounds. Yet, many today prefer the *jenbe* irrespective of whether they had known the *jenbe* as part of their former rural tradition.

There may be, at the same time and for the same occasion, one *jenbe* ensemble and another celebration music ensemble, for instance, a Fulbe flute, fiddle, and calabash percussion ensemble. Both ensembles then will play either in turn or simultaneously, though occupying different spaces: normally the "ethnic" party will perform inside the compound walls and the *jenbe* party outside in the street. Sometimes they will even perform together, that is, if the hosting family forces them to do so. Such a forced pairing will sometimes turn out fine, but sometimes it will result in rather strange musical clashes. At any rate, rivalries and arguments between the ensembles are to be expected. In such cases, it is evident that the *jenbe* meets the younger females' desire to dance and to amuse themselves together with their local neighbors, friends, and colleagues, while elder family members feel better entertained and represented by music showing close ties to their original traditions.[6]

Since independence, *jenbe* playing has become an integral part of a supra-ethnic, local culture of Bamako. The style and repertoire of *jenbe* drumming in the metropolis is different from rural *jenbe* traditions. If a master drummer from the rural Maninka land comes to Bamako, he will start out like an apprentice and play only accompanying parts for a couple of months. One speaks of *bamakòfòli*, the "music of Bamako," as distinct from, for example, *maninkafòli*, "music of the Maninka." The Bamako repertoire and style of *jenbe* celebration music represents a tradition of its own. It is a recent urban tradition that builds on, fuses and recreates different sources.

Figure 10.2 Jeli Madi Kuyate and the author performing at a drum and dance event in Bamako on a denkundi (Islamic naming ceremony). Photo: Barbara Polak 1991.

State Ballets as National Folklore

Both in the context of local celebrations and of African ballet,[7] drummers, singers, and dancers interact to create a common performance. However, in ballet playing the drummers have to meet demands for a type of interaction quite different from that of the celebration context. The characteristic quality of celebration music is to allow everybody to participate in the common performance with his or her individual contribution in the form of dancing, singing, or other activities (cf. Knight 1985, 68, 83; Charry 2000, 195, 198). The sequence of events always has to be established and adjusted to meet the needs of the participant's movements in the course of a performance. Any spontaneous intervention may decisively influence the interaction. Role distinction between performers and audience is not especially marked and is further nuanced by role switching: anyone may become the focus of public attention for the limited time span when he or she takes the initiative. The drummers alone play a role that is not easily nor regularly performed by non-specialists.

In contrast to this, in ballet performance role distinction between audience and performers is far more rigid. The repertoire is condensed, arranged into pieces, made uniformed and preestablished (cf. Keita 1957, 207f; Charry 1996, 68). It artistically blends elements of different sources into a new aesthetic whole. Choreographic and musical arrangements have to be developed in formal rehearsal. By contrast, celebration music does not contain a situation of practice other than the actual performance.

The phenomenon of West African state ballet originally started with the French colonial administration, which aimed to integrate African theatre into their African civil servants' curriculum during the 1930s. Among the graduates of the Ecole Normale William Ponty (near Dakar), many became leaders of the later independence movement who brought the idea and practice of African theatre back to their home countries (Cutter 1971, 248ff; Hopkins 1965, 163f). One leader so influenced was Modibo Keita, who in the 1950s was the mayor of Bamako and who later became the first president of the Republic of Mali. In the 1950s, the colonial administration established a system of *centres culturels*, whose main purpose was to establish the practice of African theatre in a hierarchical system of local, regional, and territorial competitions; the All-French-West-Africa finale was held in Dakar (Traore 1957; Hopkins 1965, 164; Cutter 1971, 263ff; Skinner 1974, 292f).

The independence movement *Rassemblement Democratique Africain* adopted the system of cultural competitions from the colonizer, and in 1958, together with other international youth organizations, held a French West African-wide "Festival de la Jeunesse d'Afrique" in Bamako that included athletic and theatrical competitions.[8] After independence, the national states of Guinea and Mali immediately adopted the hierarchical system of athletic and cultural competitions on a national level.[9] Moreover, African ballet, together with *ensembles instrumentales* and *orchestres modernes*,[10] was institutionalized as national folklore[11] in the form of so-called "national ballets." State-owned national ensembles recruited artists as civil servants into permanent troupes to meet the state's demand for public representation. State ballets staged the folklore of the nation, or that of a region or other administrative sub-unit. They intended to construct the identities of these entities and to present them to the citizens, to foreign representatives, and to the world public in general (see Hopkins 1965 and Cutter 1967, 1971, 244–88). State ballets have been crucial to the building of African national identities after independence in the late 1950s and 1960s; the first and foremost among these were those developed under socialist leadership, as in Guinea and Mali.

The state ballet in Bamako today exists mainly in the form of the state-run *Ballet National du Mali*, which is perceived to be the "national troupe." Since its official founding in 1962, this permanent ensemble has operated with *jenbe* ensembles as its main musical element. In contrast, the other two categories of official troupes work mainly either with the griots' instruments and genres (*Ensemble Instrumental National*) or with Western instruments and popular genres (*Orchestre National A* and *B* and *Orchestre Badema*). The national ballet has enjoyed high prestige in Mali

Figure 10.3 Jeli Madi Kuyate, jenbe player with the Ballet National du Mali since 1966. Photo: private coll. Kuyate.

and abroad, and, like other state ballets, it has also served as a springboard for those members who have wanted to make it in the international market. However, it offers a very small number (only four or five) of salaried official positions for drummers as national artists. These positions, though poorly paid, are much sought after. Sedu Keita, a younger drummer in the group I study with, had been taking part in daily rehearsals and performances for four years without being paid in the vain hope of being eventually rewarded with an official position. Finally he changed strategies and joined a commercial pop band instead.

In 1991 the Malian one-party state crumbled and with it, its cultural policy. The national ballet, which had been suffering from reduced state sponsoring of national folklore since the end of the socialist regime in 1968, was further limited in its resources and role as keeper of a national culture.[12] The budget cuts instituted by the new democratic governments, however, had an even more drastic impact on another institution of the cultural policy sector. They terminated the cultural competitions that between 1962 and 1990 had been introducing and integrating many youths to the practice of folkloric ballets on local, regional, and national levels.[13] Since this state system was cancelled in 1991, commercial cultural competitions and privately and NGO-sponsored ballet projects have thus far not been able to make up for this loss. *Jenbe* players in Bamako especially complain about this because the multitude of competing ballets of the sub-groups of the state party and of higher educational institutions had constituted a great demand for drummers to be hired and paid for longer periods of time each year.

International Markets

In Europe and North America, a market has existed since the mid-1980s for concerts and CDs with percussion based on *jenbe* music. Yet even more striking than this is the extent of instrument sales, *jenbe* classes, and amateur-playing taking place in the industrialized countries in the 1990s. The *jenbe* is about to replace the Afro-Cuban *conga* in the West as the most widespread drum played without sticks but with bare hands. It has actually surpassed Ghanaian drum and dance genres within the international scenes of "Afro" and percussion and dance enthusiasts. The leading industrial percussion manufacturers (Remo, Meinl, LP, Afro-Percussion, etc.) began producing *jenbew*, and educational institutions have begun to invite private teachers to give instruction in *jenbe* playing.

The *jenbe* playing in recording studios, concert stages, drum and dance workshops, and schools, does not simply consist of "traditional" repertoires and styles of local African celebration music. The arrangement techniques and transformations developed in the ballet context form a constituent part of the mediation process of *jenbe* music in the West. Among these are, for example, signal phrases marking the beginnings or endings of pieces or prearranged rhythmic changes, the enlargement of ensembles with accompanying instruments and parts, and the canonization of a standard repertoire. As dancing is mostly left out and the focus is shifted further toward the music, for instance its arrangements and the lead drummer's role, *jenbe* percussion music represents a third *jenbe*-related genre, after celebration music and ballet music.

Many African *jenbe* players in the international scene have concentrated their business relationships mainly in one Western country. Some aspects of the *jenbe* market, however, show a tendency towards internationalization. Instructional books are being translated into English to possibly serve beyond national markets.[14] These materials and CDs are produced and distributed internationally. The Internet provides quite a lot of advertisement and public relations web-sites for international (African and non-African) players, teachers, and traders. The Internet also carries different sorts of related information, for instance, collections of notations, discographies, and discussion lists. The most successful of all *jenbe* players in the West, Mamady Keïta, may also be seen as the personification of the tendency towards the internationalization of *jenbe* practice. He has established educational institutes in Brussels, Paris, Munich, Washington, Tokyo, and other cities. These private drumming schools are run by accredited local teachers and are centrally coordinated, for instance in terms of occasions when the master visits, or online advertisement from a central server.

Conakry has been the major center for the internationalization of *jenbe* culture. Abidjan and Dakar, too, have played important roles in this process. Even if it has been catching up during the past five years or so, Bamako is lagging somewhat behind the other metropolises in terms of personal, cultural, and economic integration into the international market and *jenbe* scene. Nevertheless, the international *jenbe* market in Bamako is effective in a variety of ways. Some dozen drummers who have been successfully working abroad for more than just one concert tour (and through this have "made it" in the eyes of their colleagues) stay in town. For some or even most of them, their return stay in Bamako is only for a limited duration. They already have arranged for their next jobs abroad, or at least hope to do so as soon as possible. Moreover, non-Africans frequently come to Bamako and stay some days, weeks, or even months, for training as *jenbe* players. One finds all levels of accomplishment, from beginners to professionals. Most Bamako *jenbe* players make plans or just dream of single, repeated, or permanent possibilities (concerts tours, teaching seasons, emigration); they want to work in some country of the whites, or the rich world, as they tend to perceive it.

The number of drums produced for export in Bamako is many times greater than that for local demand. Quite a few local drummers earn extra income by assembling instruments to be exported as either pieceworkers or sub-contractors. As performers and especially as teachers, many international drummers have direct sales prospects at their disposal and run some sort of export business (see Figure 10.4).

Figure 10.4 Manufacture of jenbe bodies for export-traders in Bamako by woodworker/entrepreneur Isu Kumare and his workers and apprentices. Photo: Polak 1998.

Drum ensemble music is almost completely absent from the local cassette market in Bamako (see Charry 1996, online version). Yet *jenbe* music is listened to from cassettes, particularly by the drummers themselves. Even though small in numbers, those cassettes, which are brought in mainly as souvenirs by international drummers to Bamako from Europe or, more recently, from the U.S., have made most local drummers familiar with the repertoire and style of international *jenbe* percussion music.

A Chronological View

Local drum and dance celebrations, the state ballet, and *jenbe* percussion in the industrialized countries each deserve more attention as social institutions, cultural forms, and genres of artistic expression than space here permits. This article will follow the outline already given, focusing on the relationships and possible interactions between these three contexts of *jenbe* drumming.

This section takes a chronological perspective. Local drum and dance celebrations, folkloric ballets, and international *jenbe* percussion came into being successively and, in part, grew out of one another. Repertoires that had been practiced previously in the context of local celebrations were re-worked and integrated into the basis of practice for the state ballets. Through their many concert tours abroad, the ballet companies introduced *jenbe* music and musicians to the world.[15]

Many of the early protagonists and contemporary *jenbe* stars of the northern hemisphere started out as local village drummers and later were recruited by regional and national ballet groups. Years of work in these ballets have introduced them to industrialized countries, and, with time, they established contacts and eventually permanent business relationships.[16]

The biographies of most Bamako drummers born before 1970 generally reflect his chronological development. They had spent their youth as farmers and local celebration drummers in the countryside and originally migrated to Bamako not for the purpose of becoming musicians, but to seek a form of "normal" employment as characterized by earning fixed monthly wages. But the demand for celebration drumming and periodical ballet engagements combined to offer the prospect of a decent income. Eventually they preferred this to other jobs then available to male youths, such as selling iced water or ice cream in the streets, pushing hand-lorries, driving mule-carts, washing cloth, or doing a restaurant's dishes. Since the decline of state ballet in the 1990s, their perspectives for other jobs in addition to festivals have been connected with the international market.

Since the mid-1980s, many Bamako-born youths, then about fifteen years old, have been flooding into the *jenbe* business as apprentices and eventually, some five or ten years later, as professionals in their own right. A considerable number of these no longer hold celebration music to be the field of basic socialization into the drumming culture and profession, but instead are trying to head directly toward the international market.

Let me cast two sidelong glances onto some other musical genres in order to emphasize the point that the nationalization of formerly local cultural forms has in prominent cases actually pre-conditioned and catalyzed their internationalization and commercialization. First, I shall draw on other Malian (and greater francophone West African) musical genres for one example. The autobiography of the all-round musician Sorry Bamba shows the progression of his work in the fields of local dance music in the 1950s, state-sponsored ballet and *orchestre* musics in the 1960s and 1970s, and in international Mande pop music in the 1980s and 1990s. The international pop music careers of interpreters of the Mande guitar and harp traditions (Charry 1994) and of Malian female singers (Duran 1995, Diawara 1996, Schulz 2001) would not have been possible without their tenure with the regional and national *orchestres* and *ensembles* founded after independence.

Second, we have an example from another continent. There is one more instrument from the formerly "non-European" musical genres besides the *jenbe* that has spread to the industrialized countries on a strikingly large scale, namely the Australian *didjeridu*. This instrument, too, has developed from an object used by one ethnic group and in specific contexts only to the emblem of a greater, i.e., pan-Aboriginal ethnicity, and later on to a national symbol (namely of Australia), before it began its journey around the world.[17]

Capitalism generates a permanent demand for new cultural forms that are to be commercialized. Until now cultural forms could only originate in local contexts, although they are able to spread globally (Spittler 2000). In most cases contacts between the world market and local culture are mediated through certain institutions or agencies.[18] The examples given here (*jenbe*, Mande pop music, and *didjeridu* booms in the West) all show the national state to be one instance of this effect. This is especially the case with the cultural policies of West African states after their independence, states which have turned out to be mediating agents between local cultures and the world music market. Even more than this: in the context of official Malian and Guinean institutions, cultural forms have been isolated and rearranged, and now are being further developed and successfully marketed on the international scene.

One outcome of this is that the market for African *jenbe* players in Europe and America today is to a considerable extent supplied by former national ballet drummers who personally have shaped the processes that now fit and embody their careers and their playing styles and repertoires. In contrast, for the great majority of local *jenbe* players in Bamako (or even more so for those from the countryside), going to the land of the whites for commercial success will remain but a dream.

Nationalization preceding, mediating, and conditioning the globalization of local culture is expected and, as indicated by the Australian example, widespread. Yet, there is more to the specific case than this rather conventional wisdom. First, there is a paradox. Politicians and artists of independent African states in the 1960s longed for international respect and acceptance of their nationalist and Africanizing ways. Yet the successful consequences of their political activities, for instance worldwide *jenbe* playing and the marketing of West African music, actually happened to take place by meeting the formerly colonizing system's demands for cultural forms to commercialize. This is of some irony, especially regarding the decidedly anti-colonial and anti-capitalist stance of most West African cultural policies in the 1960s. And since the African states that produced this culture have ended up in permanent economic decline and dependence, for many of their "national" artists who did not start an international career, this irony tastes bitter. Secondly, there are some questions concerning the triumphant advance of the *jenbe* that remain unanswered.

Unanswered Questions

How did it come to be that the *jenbe,* of all African instruments, is now played in so many classes and enjoys such a vogue among amateur drummers in Europe and North America? Why not, for instance, the bridge-harp *kora* or the xylophone *bala*? These instruments too, through LPs and CDs and international concert tours of Malian and Guinean ballet groups, ensembles, and individual artists, have fascinated a worldwide audience.

Merely referring to an exoticism that definitely plays a role in the spread of the *jenbe* (and the *didjeridu*) in the West, does not sufficiently explain this growth of popularity. Perhaps in industrialized and highly mechanized societies there is a specific desire for the physical experience of beating a skin with the bare hands. There could also be a desire for beating a drum that—like most membranophones—is of very limited tonal qualities but instead has rich timbral qualities. Certainly, the powerful and brilliant sound of the *jenbe* is an important factor in its worldwide popularity. However, the expectations and experiences of beginning drummers who attend classes or buy a *jenbe*, like many other aspects of its striking international spread, have yet to be empirically researched.[19]

Besides Guinean and Malian former national drummers, some *jenbe* players who had not spent much time in state ballet ensembles entered the European scene at an early stage. Fodé Youla and his *jenbe*-based percussion ensemble Africa Djolé marked the beginning of the *jenbe* boom in Germany with a now legendary concert and workshop in Berlin (see "Africa Djolé," 1978 disc). It is an astonishing fact that only one year before Africa Djolé's breakthrough in Germany, Youla published a recording in Paris that does not contain a single note of *jenbe* playing (Youla 1977 disc). Instead, all solos are played on a much lower-tuned drum. The cover photo shows a drum with a calf-hide head, perhaps an instrument from Youla's home region in lower Guinea. However, Youla had already perfected the song repertoire and percussive arrangement techniques that he would later employ with Africa Djolé. With Africa Djolé, Youla switched to the *jenbe* and added an extra *jenbe* soloist. This different instrument, with its greater soloistic and expressive qualities, was just what the German Afro-percussion and dance scene was waiting for.

Adama Dramé and then Soungalo Coulibaly have been pioneering various aspects of the *jenbe* markets in France and Switzerland since 1984 and 1986, respectively.[20] Both are residents of Bouaké in the Ivory Coast. They came to this city from Burkina Faso and Mali, respectively, as labor migrants. They live in a country whose economy is the strongest in francophone West Africa and whose non-socialist cultural policy never promoted the state ballet as part of national folklore to the extent that Guinea and Mali did. Both musicians had mainly performed as urban, commercial celebration drummers in different cities in Burkina Faso, Mali, and the Ivory Coast before having been hired to tour Europe. After having completed their first tours abroad, both continued to work in the local celebration context and at the same time have set up their private performance groups for future tours (see Dramé and Senn-Borloz 1992).

As mentioned in the introductory section of this article, in Abidjan, Bamako, Bobo Dioulasso, Conakry, Dakar, and many other cities in the Ivory Coast, Mali, Burkina Faso, Guinea, and Senegal, commercial *jenbe* playing constitutes a free profession. This profession generally is based on demand in the urban celebration culture; it is manifest in a distinct milieu of urban *jenbe* players who meet this demand. It might be a rather conventional wisdom that nationalization may precede, mediate, and condition the globalization of a formerly local cultural form. But how did it come to be that the *jenbe*, of all the Manding (and greater Western Sudanic) musical instruments—and there are plenty—arrived on the celebration and entertainment scene of so many West African cities with such success in the course of the twentieth century? A linear historical perspective of subsequential developments which—even if the insights it offers are far-reaching—is not sufficient to approach this question.

The Making of a Globalized Instrument

To this point I have roughly differentiated local Bamakoian, national Malian, and international Western levels of professional *jenbe* practice as three distinct social institutions and cultural forms: drum and dance festivals organized by families, folkloric ballets sponsored by the West African states, and percussion music demanded by specific segments of the world market and specific institutions of Western societies. These institutions and genres, however, are far from forming closed social or musical systems. On the contrary, the simultaneity of their existence in one place, and the overlapping practice of one group of agents of one social milieu in two or all three of the named contexts, allows for interaction. Zanetti (1996, 174), for instance, reports on the impact of state ballet drumming in Guinea:

> Rapidement, leur musique devient modèle pour tous les jeunes jembefola [*jenbe* players]; le vocabulaire rhythmique du ballet, assimilé et rejoué dans les fêtes traditionelles, entre alors dans le bagage indispensable à l'apprentissage de l'instrument, et se répand rapidement dans toute la zone d'influence mandingue.

The object of this central section of the article is to show that, within only a few years, repercussions of the international and national *jenbe* practices can have significant effects on local celebration music. Taking into account such repercussions of the more recent institutions and genres onto the seemingly "older" and more "traditional" celebration music implies a view of tradition that includes cultural change and allows some degree of constant change to be at the heart of any process of handing down music in time (cf. for instance Nettl 1983, 172–186, and 1996).

In an ongoing process, international percussionists borrow from the national ballet drummers, or from their own experiences as ballet drummers; ballet drummers borrow from the local celebration drummers—or from their own experiences as former or even as current local drummers. At the same time, drummers working mainly in local festivals borrow consistently from their national and international colleagues, or from their own experiences in these contexts. Thus it becomes quite possible that elements or traits that had been borrowed by the local level from the national and international levels later on get borrowed again and recycled into the subsequent practice of the ballet ensembles and percussionists. The effecting processes of selective interaction and feedback can be of considerable complexity. Yet because of the limitations of research and for the sake of clarity and illustration, I will rely on one relatively simple and obvious example of feedback that has occurred within the field of instrument construction and change in sound.

The model of the typical Bamako *jenbe* has been subject to considerable change in the course of the past fifteen years. Its drum body has decreased in size: the average drumhead diminished in diameter from about 35–38 cm to 30–35 cm. The tension of the skinhead has increased, and the pitch has risen. Each tone that is produced by one stroke has decreased in duration (i.e., has become of shorter decay). The sound with the highest and sharpest timbre,[21] the so-called "slap," has especially gained in brightness and pithiness within the overall sound of the larger instrumental ensemble. The base of the wooden shell has become narrower and conically tapered towards the bowl. This again has sharpened the distinctiveness of its three main timbres, while instruments with rather broad, cylindrical bases have a certain portion of the bass timbre that generally overlaps the tone and slap timbres, no matter what the striking technique. The overall sound of a Bamako *jenbe* today is more concise, sharply contoured, cleaner, dryer, and thinner than it used to be.[22]

One crucial element in the construction of the *jenbe* is the mode of mounting the skin onto the shell. The following will focus in some detail on the recent change in this technical function and its possible relations to different aspects of practice, i.e., acoustical sound, the work of instrument-making, and playing style.

In Bamako, as elsewhere in West Africa, it was common practice until well into the 1980s to sew the skin onto a strap made of several braids of leather cord that ran around the drum shell tightly below the upper edge of the bowl.[23] Apart from the wooden shell, all components of the drum originally were made of different kinds of animal skin: the skin, the sewing cord, the aforementioned strap, another strap that was wrapped and sewn into the edge of the skin for reinforcement, the tensioning cord, and a third strap around which the tensioning cord turned at the lower edge of the bowl (for an illustration of this technique, as applied with partly different materials, see Figures 10.5 and 10.6). This type of *jenbe* can reach and steadily maintain the amount of skin tension necessary to produce the right sounds only if assembled with the greatest of care and generous use of materials. In most cases, however, the skin of such a *jenbe* has to be heated over an open fire immediately before being played. The tension thus reached will start to decrease within the following fifteen to thirty minutes. Thus, one is obliged to repeat the procedure of making a fire and heating the skin every half hour, or every hour at the minimum.

I will describe two changes in the mode of head fixing in *jenbe*-making in Bamako: the introduction of new materials and the appropriation of a new technique.

Industrial Materials

Having taken residence in New York City in the early 1970s, the Guinean-born Ladji Camara came to be the first freelance *jenbe* player and teacher of renown outside Africa. Abdulai Aziz Ahmed, an African American from New York City who in the early 1970s was among the first pupils of Ladji Camara, has said:

> When I first saw Ladji's drum, it was tied with a couple of different kinds of cord, telephone wire, and lacing went in all directions. That was the way it was. He did not care about what it looked like. Over there (Africa) they used whatever was available. (Sunkett 1996, 145)

In the 1950s, it became common practice to twist thin iron wire around the bowl instead of leather cord in order to produce the braided straps. The lower straps were replaced by solid iron rings of four or five mm. In Bamako during the 1970s, tensioning cords of leather had been superseded by strong, 4- to 6-mm nylon cords. Thin synthetic cord had replaced leather string for sewing.

Jenbe construction invokes high demands on a tensioning cord material that does not easily break under high tension. Nylon cord of more than 4 millimeters fulfills these demands. In the context of *jenbe* construction, it actually breaks only after heavy abrasion that occurs only in the course of several, even up to a dozen, head changes. Leather cord, in contrast, often breaks, sometimes

Figure 10.5 Jenbe with sewn-on head. The tensioning cord is made of nylon; the sewing cord is of synthetic fiber, too. Photo: Polak 1998.

even in the process of its first tensioning. This obliges one to make additional knots, which not only takes extra effort in itself but adds toilsome work while threading the cord in the process of tensioning or tuning the drum. Iron wire and nylon cord are reusable, i.e., they do not have to be completely replaced with each skin change, as was the case with the organic materials. Moreover, the industrial materials are available in cities, whereas more specialized sorts of animal skin for the sewing and tensioning cords are not.[24]

In the countryside, every possible way of mixing the most divergent materials is still in common usage today. However, the new industrial materials have replaced the older ones in the practice of urban professional drummers because of technical and economical advantages concerning the aspects of tensile strength, durability, and availability. Still, until the 1980s, the technique of sewing on the skin to one reinforcing and one tension-transmitting leather strap had not yet been subject to structural change as a result of using these new materials. The constituent parts were still assembled in the same way, and the components have continued to fulfill the same functions as before.

A New Technique

Fastening of the skin by sewing can be replaced by wedging the skin between two solid iron rings. The iron is bent around the upper edge of the bowl by hand and fashioned into a ring by welding.

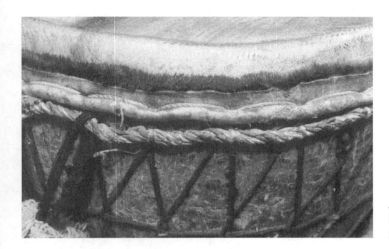

Figure 10.6 Detail of instrument shown in Figure 10.5.

Two such rings are made. One iron ring is wedged into the edge of the skin. This inner "flesh" ring performs a function similar to that of the former leather head band. Loops of nylon cord are knotted on the second iron ring. The tension cord runs through the loops. The tension applied to the cord is transmitted to the loops around which the cord turns, and thus to the tension-transmitting ring. Only when the tension-transmitting ring is pulled down does it wedge the skin between itself and the reinforcement ring, so that the tension is transmitted to the skin.[25] Once tensioned, this upper "head" ring and the loops together perform much the same function as the former leather stitching cord (see Figure 10.7).

The importance of the rings has increased in that they now multifunctionally serve both as tension transmitter and reinforcement (as before), and as two counterparts of a clamp that holds the skin. The following refers to instruments assembled with this clamp technique using iron rings and synthetic cord as "iron *jenbe*." By contrast, "leather *jenbe*" designates instruments constructed with the sewing technique irrelevant of the materials used; these could be leather or leather mixed with wire and nylon cord. These are translations of the Bamana terms, *nègè jenbe* (iron *jenbe*) and *nfòsòn jenbe* (leather strap *jenbe*), and follows their indigenous usage.

Clamp techniques for holding drumheads are commonly used worldwide and applied in the construction of lug-tensioned drums, for instance in marching drums, drum sets, and in industrially produced *conga* and *bongo* drums. The clamp technique employed to tune *jenbe* skins with two iron rings in combination with cord lacing was developed in the 1970s. Some sources suggest that this happened first in the U.S.A. and Europe, where drummers of the Guinean, Malian, and Senegalese national ballets, other drummers from West Africa, and African-American and European percussionists met. Ahmed (1998) even presents a detailed genealogy that claims to identify the definite origin of the iron *jenbe*:

> When I first saw djembes like Ladji's, the heads were sewed on all with rope, no iron rings. In Senegal they were done with wire and pegs. It was Chief Bey [an African-American professional percussionist] who developed that technique. He taught his godson Richard Byrd, who taught me. Richard fixed Ladji [Camara's] first drum with iron rings. I taught brothers in Chicago, principally Moshe Milon and the brothers who were in the Sun Drummers. Moshe shared this with Famoudou [Konaté] and now it is everywhere.

During the 1970s, the iron *jenbe* might have reached Dakar and Abidjan as the expected standard for an export drum.[26] Yet, it is equally possible that artisans in Dakar or Abidjan had developed the iron *jenbe* independently. It is not my goal here to define the exact origins of the iron *jenbe*.

Figure 10.7 A contemporary Bamako jenbe with rings made of 6-mm steel reinforcing bar (re-bar). Photo: Polak 1997.

It is however of interest that the new technique was adopted from its original context of the early globalizing *jenbe* scene into local *jenbe* practices in the West African interior.

In Bamako, the first iron *jenbe* appeared in the early 1980s.[27] At this time, the change to the iron *jenbe* in Dakar and even more so in Abidjan was already in an advanced state, if not almost complete.[28] *Jenbe* players returning from work as migrants in Abidjan and from the international tours of the national ballet ensemble had brought the first samples of iron *jenbew* along. The following describes the introduction of the iron *jenbe* into local practice from the perspective of the professional *jenbe* drummers of Badialan, which is a *quartier populaire* in the western part of Bamako.

In 1983 Kasim Kuyate, then about twenty-seven years old, was just about to purchase the materials for assembling the first *jenbe* of his own. He had previously seen iron *jenbew* only in photos of people returning from Abidjan. At his first sight of an actual iron *jenbe*, he decided to make his own drum according to this shining example. However, even though as a griot he was interested and had some general competence in making handicrafts, he failed to deduce the exact procedure for mounting an iron *jenbe* in all its subtleties from the mere inspection of a completed sample.

Nothing really came out of it. All the others [namely the other drummers of the Western part of town] have seen it, but nobody else tried himself, or followed my example. After one or two years [of trials and errors] I gave up. (Interview, Bamako, January 1998)

It was not until 1986 or 1987 that Kuyate returned to the problem. He reports:

I finally learned the right way [to prepare the materials and assemble an iron *jenbe*] from François [Dembele]. (. . .) also some white people came along by this time, from Abidjan, they came to him, and some had their iron *jenbew* with them. Only shortly before we [drummers of western neighborhoods Badialan and Bolibana] got them, they had them in Medina Kura [eastern/central neighborhood]. (Interview, Bamako, January 1998)

In the early 1980s François Dembele was among the leading *jenbe* players with the *Ballet National of Mali*. Drummers from other parts of Bamako also consider Dembele to have been the forerunner of the iron *jenbe* in the city of Bamako. For example Moussa Traore (1999, n.p.), who originally is from an eastern suburb of Bamako and now resides in the United States, reports that he first saw an iron *jenbe* in 1984 with François Dembele at a rehearsal of the national ballet ensemble. Dembele himself states that he became acquainted with the iron *jenbe* in the U.S.A. during a concert tour of the national ballet; he recalls seeing it for the first time with members of the Guinean national ballet (interview, Bamako, March 1998). No more than five years were to pass before, at the end of the 1980s, all *jenbe* players in Bamako had adopted the clamp technique with solid iron rings from the milieu of the national ballet and other drummers with foreign contacts.

When Bamako drummers discuss the iron *jenbe*, the time before its coming is hailed as "the good old days" in one special respect. During the short rests that occurred from time to time during the course of a performance because one had to retune the drum, the musician enjoyed a break from the strenuous work of playing. For while a drummer was obliged to kindle a small fire and heat the drumhead, the playing came to a halt without causing the dancers and singers to complain. Today, in contrast, it is not rare for drummers to have to play continually for two or three hours, and other participants are immediately affronted if the drummers stop for whatever reason.

One decisive argument, however, is in favor of the iron *jenbe*: it is far easier to change the skin of an iron *jenbe* than by using the finicky and tiresome sewing technique. In Bamako, *jenbe* players change the skins of their instruments because of wear and tear every one to three months, if not earlier, when it is damaged or does not sound right. From an interview with Kasim Kuyate (Bamako, January 1998): "The iron *jenbe* pleased me. It does not take much work to assemble and it does not damage the skin [as stitching does]." The iron rings and nylon cord certainly cost money but require less care. It saves much time that some of the nylon and iron elements can be reused as components without being taken apart, for instance the loops of cord on the upper and lower tension rings that form the eyelets for the tension cord.

The new clamp technique had an impact on musical practice that is more far-reaching than simply that of easing instrument construction. Most importantly, wedging the skin between the rings used as clamps does not damage the skin, i.e., it does not create predetermined breaking points. The clamp technique thus removes the decisive limiting factor of tension application. It allows for the enormous tension that today is commonly applied to goat skinheads and nylon cords.

Instrument Making and Musical Practice

Today, large *jenbew* are considered impractical. Given the fact that urban professional drummers quite often have to play marching or standing upright with the instrument strapped around their waist or over one or both shoulders for several hours, this stands to reason. Beyond that, however, instrument size and tuning are related to stylistic identity: large *jenbew* tuned low are today associated with the staid and mature, but old-fashioned, style of the elders. One certainly could moderately tension and tune an iron *jenbe* low. With the exception of some elders, however, nobody does so. Here, more than practical reason is clearly involved; this is a culturally valued interpretation. This fact becomes even more obvious when seen from the older drummers' perspective. The older drummers despise the youngsters' small and high-pitched *jenbew*. They identify their former pupils' instruments with the present (allegedly spoiled and corrupt) musical style, which is characterized by faster tempos, larger ensembles and more unrestrained ornamentation.

Yamadu Dunbia and Kasim Kuyate, who both have been performing professionally in Bamako for decades, agree that only with large and low-tuned *jenbew* is one able to practice what they consider orthodox, or "normal" style, as they say in Bamako. Indeed, from time to time older drummers would lower the tension and pitch of a *jenbe* tuned too high with a handful of water rubbed into the skin. Younger drummers would never lower the tension of a drum. To many of them, the idea of an over-tensioned *jenbe* does not even seem to exist.

Yet the cultural, generationally distinct evaluation of different styles does not directly determine an individual's actions. Rather than being deducible from a stylistic or cultural system, action always takes place in the field of (often conflicting) interaction between cultural norms and values, practical reason, and personal intentionality. The following example may show that individual action means dealing with these aspects. Since his youth, the old Dunbia (born between 1917 and 1920) has been playing mainly in small ensembles consisting of one *jenbe* and one accompanying drum. Perfectly suitable for this task are large, low-tuned *jenbew*, with their colorful and evocative[29] sound. Indeed, Dunbia owns two large *jenbew* of more than 37 cm in diameter. Yet one has to add that Dunbia has retired long ago; now he plays only very sporadically. He makes part of his earnings by renting his instruments out to younger drummers who often complain about their size, poor technical state, and low tuning. Kuyate was born around 1954 and represents the middle generation. Still, he actually has a very small *jenbe* of his own. This might be partly explained by the fact that he, in contrast to Dunbia, has experienced the trend towards larger ensembles, now at least three and commonly four or five drummers, faster tempos and longer periods of non-stop playing. This trend partly derives from the ever-increasing influence of ballet playing on celebration music in Bamako since the 1960s.[30] When in 1997 and 1998 an ensemble consisting of Dunbia, Kuyate, a twelve-year-old apprentice and myself performed a dozen or so engagements, both of the older performers felt fortunate to have my rather small and light *jenbe* of 34 cm with us. This was especially the case when our feet and public transport (which presents difficulties in Bamako) had to take us to another end of the city. Thus, pragmatic considerations and cultural approval or disapproval prove to be flexibly assessed, parallel criteria in evaluating instruments (see Figure 10.8).

Without a doubt, however, there are unambiguous differences between the generations in making use of the possibilities inherent in the iron *jenbe*. In the view of younger drummers, extremely tensioned *jenbew* are nothing but the norm. The playing of tightly tuned skins results in calluses all over one's palm, and eventually in permanent deformations of the hand. Many younger drummers hold this to be an emblem of their profession, and they are proud of it. In emergencies, that is, in cases of sores or chapped skin, they play with taped fingers.

Their elders, who have been playing on looser skins all their lives, are exposed to this damage to a significantly lesser extent. They see calluses as protection against harm, but not as a positive sign or value of musicianship. From their point of view, the degree of drum skin tension commonly applied today both causes cracks on the player's palms and degrades the quality of *jenbe* sound.

The ideal of high-tuned *jenbe* is nothing new. Even in the days of the leather strap *jenbe*, drummers used to try new ways of fastening the drumhead with the objective of reaching the highest possible tension. When wire and nylon were introduced, some drummers for example only selectively employed the new materials and left some parts of the leather as they were formerly made. They preferred this material, taking advantage of its ability to contract, when wet processed, while drying.

Figure 10.8 The late Kati Namori Keita (ca. 1927–1999), owner of the instrument shown in Figure 10.5 and soloist of sound sample 1, was among the dozen prominent drummers who in the 1960's and 1970's shaped the Bamako style of jenbe playing. He was held to be the last professional drummer in Bamako who refused to accept the iron jenbe. Photo: Polak 1998.

The iron *jenbe*, however, has served as a new and necessary precondition for the radical realization of a formerly limited ideal. This solution to an older problem had been used to an extreme. New contexts such as large ensembles and playing inside halls or in recording studios has created new needs for which the new *jenbe* sound is appropriate. Nevertheless, the rationalization of one aspect (high tension creating higher pitch and concise sounds) impairs others, as for instance a loss of mellowness and brightness of sonority.

Market Integration and Cultural Change

By the end of the 1990s, all of the approximately twenty professional *jenbe* players in Badialan, Bamako, had previously worked as celebration drummers. Of these, seventeen had been, or still were, members of ballet troupes, for the most part state ballets, two of which were NGO-sponsored and one private. The majority of these musicians had already taught foreigners.[31] About half of them had worked in the instrument export business. None of them, however, had stopped working at family celebrations at any time. Two drummers from Badialan have had considerable regular income in addition to celebration employment: Jeli Madi Kuyate (see Figures 10.2 and 10.3) has been employed with the *Ballet National* and has held the official status of a civil servant for three decades. Drisa Kone has worked as a *jenbe* player and a teacher in Europe for several months each year between 1991 and 1998. Nevertheless, they too have always continued to practice and to identify themselves, at least partly, as celebration drummers.

The demand for work for *jenbe* players is differentiated and is located on different local, national, and international levels. To the local agents working as drummers in Bamako, however, these different sources of demand appear as parallel and simultaneous sectors of the local job market. Almost every individual serves several markets in order to diversify and add to his sources of income; nobody can afford to take the risk of concentrating exclusively on only one of the various drum-related sources of income. Thus, everybody learns to meet the standards of the different markets to the highest degree possible. The three sectors for work for *jenbe* players in Bamako—namely local festivals, state ballet ensembles, and the international market—support one and the same group of agents. Urban professional drummers are differentiated by specialization only gradually and to a limited extent.

The technique of fastening skins between iron rings used as clamps is an example of a repercussion from national and international music practices onto local practices. National and international traditions partly developed out of local practices and later—but not necessarily much later—reaffected these local practices. About fifteen years ago, the spread in popularity of the iron *jenbe* in Bamako began in the city center, where one finds the prominent intermediary institutions and current meeting places of Bamako-based musicians, international agents, and consumers or representatives of music markets.[32] In the course of only a few years (between about 1985 and 1990), the iron *jenbe* gained acceptance and almost complete prevalence over the leather-strap *jenbe*. The material in common use nowadays is a 4- to 7-mm round iron or steel reinforcing bar which is rather easily available in Bamako, as in all urban centers where buildings are constructed of concrete. At the same time the iron *jenbe* has just started to spread little by little in the countryside where round iron, welder's shops, and strong nylon cord have been hard to find until now, and are even harder to pay for. In the early 1990s, when the iron rings had only been in use for a short time, drummers still used to heat their iron *jenbew* above a small fire of cardboard. This passed out of use within a couple of years. Today, Bamako drummers take advantage of the possibilities of the new technique with more skill. When readjustment of the tension is necessary during a performance (which is now more rarely and less systematically the case), this is accomplished with a few powerful blows to the upper iron ring. To this end, one simply takes the pestle from the closest grain mortar that is at hand in every compound; some drummers even carry an iron hammer with them.

The iron *jenbe* has turned out with time to be a pre-condition for the globalization of *jenbe*. It was only the solid and steady method of attaching drumheads with the clamp technique that is relatively easy to do, which made possible and practical the massive spread of the *jenbe* in industrialized countries in the 1990s. Only since Bamako drummers have adopted, learned to use and master this technique have they been able to successfully meet the standards of the international market—as their colleagues from Abidjan, Conakry, and Dakar had started to do years before them.

Jenbe players in West African cities, Europe, and America have all eventually committed themselves to the same technique of skin fastening. This obvious homogenization of instrument making applies foremost to its technical aspect and only to a lesser extent to its conceptualization. In one respect, the interpretations of the iron *jenbe* by Africans and non-Africans diametrically oppose each other. For the Bamako drummers, the iron *jenbe* represents the "modern" *jenbe* in contrast to the ancient model of the leather-strap *jenbe*; for Europeans and Americans the iron *jenbe* is the "traditional," if not "African," *jenbe* as opposed to industrially produced, lug-tensioned instruments. However, this divergent conceptualization and the resulting misunderstandings do not hinder the two parties to effectively interact via the world market on quite a large scale.

The example of instrument making as featured in this article shows that interaction between local, national, and international markets and artistic genres can be advantageous for the economic and cultural vitality of a local musical tradition. Drummers in Bamako have made an international technique their own and have profited from this feedback, both practically and economically. The transformation and revaluation of a formerly rural celebration music to a national folklore and later to an internationally admired art has generally contributed to upgrading its status in the judgment of the Bamakoian population. It has contributed to its integration into the local culture of the metropolis of the Republic of Mali, while other genres and instruments have disappeared in the urban context. Local culture, its utilization by national cultural politics, and its international commercialization are thus closely related.

The artistic and professional vitality of urban *jenbe*-playing in West Africa—especially in the metropolises, where the local and the national have merged since independence—predated and preconditioned its recent globalization. Yet today it continues to flourish, and that only since the instrument began to travel around the world. Even drummers of citywide renown find it increasingly difficult to survive in Bamako nowadays if they do not get jobs on the global market.

Jenbe players of the middle and elder generations steadily and sometimes aggressively complain about the cultural and aesthetic depreciation of *jenbe* making and playing in the course of its intensified integration in local and global markets. Zanetti (1996) seems to adopt and restate such value judgments of musical change. On the one hand he admires the art and great tradition of the Guinean national drummers, and on the other, he tends to condemn the commercialization of this art as producing stylistic and repertory-related decadence in urban drumming. All agents in the *jenbe* culture put the blame on one aspect and grant fame to another, that is, they oppose commodification and support cultural authenticity. It is evident, however, that the elder drummers, no less than the younger ones, follow both musical and economic interests. Professionalization, nationalization, and commercialization of urban *jenbe* playing in West Africa have been going on as integrated and ambivalent processes since the 1960s, when those elder drummers who are now complaining were in their youth and were creative. Their denial of any quality in present *jenbe* playing is due in part to their wish to exclude their younger rivals from the market, or to their disappointment over the fact that their own share of that market has dwindled over the years.

Acknowledgments

My fieldwork in Mali in 1997/98, and archive work in Paris was funded by the German Research Council (*Deutsche Forschungsgemeinschaft, DFG*) in the context of a post-graduate program, "Cross-cultural Relationships in Africa," at the University of Bayreuth (1996–1999).

I wish to thank my research partners, namely the drummers from Badialan, Bamako, and their families, who with patience, grace and dignity have been letting me participate in their lives and "observe" them since 1991 (Yamadu Dunbia, Jeli Madi Kuyate, Fasiriman Keita, Kasim Kuyate, Jaraba Jakite, Drisa Kone, Madu Jakite, Sedu Balo, Sedu Keita, Draman Keita, Vieux Kamara, and others). I am also grateful to the Malian and European drummers Namori Keita, Moussa Traore, Madu Faraba Sylla, Bala Samake, François Dembele, Stephan Rigert, and Uhuru, for talking to me and expanding the limits of a case study. Finally, my thanks go to Ulrich Bauer, Tom Daddesio, Jeremy Chevrier, Chris Johansen, and Eric Charry, who read drafts of this text and offered corrections and comments.

Notes

1. My spelling of this instrument name follows the conventional spelling of the Bamana (French: Bambara) and the closely related Maninka (French: Malinké) languages in Mali. Accordingly, my marking the plural of the noun *jenbe* with the suffix w as "*jenbew*" does conform with the Malian convention.
2. Knight (1984) has established the distinction between griots and drummers and their respective social spheres, cultural attributes, and musical practices in Manding society. Duran (1995) and Modic (1996) describe styles and institutions of professional or semi-professional music practice of Malian females of non-griot origin; drawing on these case studies, Hale (1998, 235–37) discusses the relationship of griots' and non-griots' professional or semi-professional musicianship. In the past, the social group of "blacksmiths" (Bam. *numu*) was associated with the instrument (see also Charry 2000, 199, 213f).

3. A bride's honorary mother or mothers are recruited from among her older female relatives. The bride's birth mother cannot function as honorary mother at the same time; often, the birth mother's sisters or cousins function as honorary mothers.

4. My research assistant, Madu Jakite, collected statistical data between March, 1997, and March, 1998. These data comprise date, place, occasion, organizer, players, instruments used, and repertoire played, of 356 local celebration engagements performed by *jenbe* players from Badialan, a *quartier populaire* in western Bamako. About ten lead drummers, or a total of twenty-five professional drummers (among them Madu Jakite), belong to the studied group.

The qualitative research upon which this article is based was completed in Bamako (and selectively in the *cercles* of Kangaba, Kolokani, and Banamba) in 1991, 1994, 1995, 1997, and 1998. Much stress was laid on participation in the work of the studied people, that is, my development and practice as a celebration drummer. Over the years, I took part in about 150 performances as a player and observer.

5. Cf. Meillassoux 1968, 86–112.

6. Cf. Modic (1996, 82, 114) for cases of parallel engagement of Bamana musicians and *jenbe* players in Bamako.

7. The French word *ballet* in Mali has both the meaning of the organizing institutions, performing ensembles, and the genre of folkloristic dance drama. Its synonyms *troupe folklorique* or *ensemble folklorique* refer to the institutions and ensembles, whereas (Bam.) *catiri* signifies the artistic genre; the latter is a loan word from French *théâtre*. The semantic field of the English term "ballet" includes the type of action meant here, i.e., a theatrical entertainment in which ballet dancing and music are combined with scenery, costumes, and narrative elements.

8. Ballet and theatre troupes from eight territories of French West Africa (i.e., all but Mauritania) took part. The program reads as follows: "*presentation–nuit d'acceuil–danse folklorique–grand bal–bal populaire*" [opening day]; "*rencontre–conférences–échanges culturels–competitions sportives et culturelles–théâtre–manifestations folkloriques–bal populaire*" [second through fifth days]; "*kermes enfantine–échanges culturelles–rencontres diverses–adieu–grand bal–bar frais–danses folkloriques–feu d'artifice*" [sixth and last day] (Festival Afrique 1958, 1–8).

9. See Traoré 1957, Festival Afrique 1958, Hopkins 1965, Cutter 1967, 1971, 244–88, and Meillassoux 1968, 69–72.

10. See Charry (1994, 32, and footnote 25) for the West African usage of *ensemble* and *orchestre* which, like *ballet*, signify both institutions and musical genres.

11. See Keita (1957), the most influential of all West African ballet directors, for an emic ("authenticity") and Mark (1994) for an etic ("intentional construction of identity") justification for using the term "folklore" to designate West African ballet.

12. This generally enhanced the increasing commercialization of the expressive arts in Bamako; see Schulz 2001.

13. The national finales of the cultural competitions in Bamako were labeled *Semaine artistiques, culturelles et sportives de la Jeunesse* from 1962 to 1968, and *Biennale artistique* from 1970 to 1990. They each had been prepared by qualifying contests (*Inter-quartier, Inter-commune, Inter-regionale*) several months in advance. For recent developments in Malian cultural policy, see Schulz 2001.

14. Blanc (1993) originally wrote in French and Ott (Konaté and Ott 1997) in German; both have been translated into English. Billmeier and Keïta's book (1999) is trilingual.

15. Even the first world tour (1962 through 1964) of the *Ballets Africains de la République de Guinée* (compare 1964-disc) counted over fifty performances in the cities of five continents.

16. For instance Famoudou Konaté (formerly first *jenbe* player of the *Ballets Africains de la République de Guinée*), Mamady Keïta (formerly *Ballet Djoliba*, a second Guinean national ballet), Maré Sanogo, and François Dembele (both formerly *Troupe Folklorique National de Mali*, later called *Ballet National du Mali*).

17. I here rely on Nettl (1996), who interprets the specialized literature.

18. The significant role of electronic media in the development and distribution of "world music" is obvious; Youssou N'dour, Ladysmith Black Mambazo, and Oumou Sangare were at the top of the African cassettes market before they were "discovered" by the Western cultural industry in 1984, 1986, and 1989 (respectively) through CDs and world music festivals. See Diawara (1996) for the Mande case and Erlmann (1994) for a critical analysis of the hegemonial structure underlying the world music market.

19. It would be of interest to compare the *jenbe* boom with other globalized performance arts, for instance *didjeridu* playing, tango and oriental dance, and with new spiritual movements that have occurred in Westernized countries.

20. Dramé was the first to develop a regular output of LPs and later CDs (see discography) and an individual style of solo playing; Coulibaly successfully integrated *jenbe* playing into larger instrumental (including non-percussion) ensembles of Mande "neo-traditional" and Mande-based world music (see discography; cf. Zanetti 1996).

21. A skilled *jenbe* player is able to produce tones of definable and distinct sonoric qualities. The three main timbres are called "bass," "tone," and "slap" in the international musician's jargon. A dark bass timbre is produced by striking the drumhead with the entire palm of one's hand; the full-tone timbre is produced by striking the skin at its outer edge with the underside of one's fingers; the sharp slap timbre results from striking the head at its outer edge but with only the underside of each finger's first joint touching the membrane.

22. See Appendix : Sound samples on the Internet.

23. Compare Schaeffner (1990, 85–86) and Zemp (1971, 41) for descriptions of the sewing technique to fasten a *jenbe* membrane. A photo of a *jenbe* of 1938 with sewn-on membrane (Ponsard n.d., Coll. Musée de l'Homme, Paris, file number D.84.1026.493) is reprinted in Charry 2000, fig. 26. Another possibility to fasten a *jenbe* membrane is to simply nail the skin onto the drum body. On the organology and classification of West African drums, see Meyer (1997).

24. Availability was also the main reason for replacing a variety of skins to make *jenbe* heads (for instance antelope-skins, *Cephalophus grimmia* and *Tragelaphus scriptus*) with only goat skin in the urban and international contexts.

25. See Blanc (1993, 66–72) and Meyer (1997, 29–32) for more detailed descriptions and illustrations.

26. Ahmed states: "Little by little, the drums that came over [imported from Africa] started to have metal rings on them" (quoted in Sunkett 1996, 145).

27. An example from another center of urban *jenbe* playing in the savannah, Bouak!, Ivory Coast, confirms this date: On the first LP by Adama Dramé (1984a–disc; recorded in 1978 in Bouaké) one can hear the marked decrease in pitch of the drum even during the course of a single piece; this is typical' for a sewn and fire-heated *jenbe*. The cover photo shows Dramé playing a *jenbe* carefully and regularly assembled with the sewing technique using a new, strong nylon cord. Starting with Dramé's second LP (1984b–disc), his *jenbe* sound had become markedly higher and more steady in pitch, as is typical for the iron *jenbe*.
28. Personal communications with the *jenbe* players Stephan Rigert (Switzerland) and Uhuru (Germany).
29. Dunbia as well as Kuyate are specialists in playing for spirit possession cults; in this context the sound of large and low-tuned *jenbew* is evocative in a literal sense as it is provoking the spirits to appear, or to induce a trance. This is held to be difficult with a very tightly tuned *jenbe*; in allusion to this, "old-style" *jenbew* are sometimes labeled "spirit *jenbe*" by Bamako drummers.
30. A change in instrument construction and sound similar to the one described had taken place years before in Guinea. An agent and observer in the Guinean-French *jenbe* scene simply deduces this from the context of state ballets: "*Le son guinéen s'est épuré par les années de travail au sein des ballets qui pouvaient regrouper une dizaine de percussionnistes. Par nécessité, le son devait être clair, sec et précis, parfaitement défini*" (Kokelaere and Saïdani 1995, n.p.).
31. These foreigners mainly came from France, Austria, Germany, Holland, Spain, the U.S., and Canada. Among them were musicians, development project workers, tourists and researchers, namely Eric Charry, Wesleyan University, Clemens Zobel, EHESS, Paris, and the author.
32. In addition to the *Ballet National* and the cultural competitions/festivals already mentioned, the *Carrefour des Jeunes* and the *Institut National des Arts* are of outstanding importance. The drummers from parts of Bamako neighboring the city center are more closely oriented toward the international market than others; the international market, analogously, influences the ones from the outer districts less. The neighborhood of Badialan has resulted from the westward extension of Bamako in the 1950s and early 1960s (see Villien-Rossi 1966 and van Westen 1982). This case study thus is typical of the social milieu and musical practice of urban professional *jenbe* playing as it has developed in Bamako since the 1960s.

References

Anon., ed. 1958. "Festival Afrique." *Organe du Premier festival de la jeunesse d'Afrique*, 6.–11.9.1958 (8 issues, no. 1 of 22 July, 1958; suspended with the end of the festival).

Ahmed, Abdulai Aziz. 1998. "Re: How to build a relationship of trust." *Djembe–l* (e-mail discussion list; djembe-l@u.washington.edu, 07 July 1998. Archived on the Internet at: http://www.escribe.com/music/djembe/index. html?mID=42518; September 2000.

Bamba, Sorry. 1996. *De la tradition à la World music*. Paris: Harmattan.

Billmeier, Uschi, and Mamady Keïta. 2000. *Ein Leben für die Djembé – Traditionelle Rhythmen der Malinke; A Life for the Djembé – Traditional Rhythms of the Malinke; Un vie pour le Djembé – Rythmes traditionels des Malinké*. Engerda: Arun.

Blanc, Serge. 1993. *Le tambour Djembé*. Lyon: Editions Maurice Sonjon.

Charry, Eric S. 1994. "The Grand Mande Guitar Tradition." *The World of Music* 36(2):21–61.

———. 1996. "A Guide to the Jembe." *Percussive Notes* 34(2):66–72.

———. 2000. *Mande Music: Traditional and Modern Music of the Maninka and Mandinka of Western Africa*. Chicago; London: The University of Chicago Press.

Cutter, Charles Hickman. 1967. "The Politics of Music in Mali." *African Arts* 1(3):38–39, 74–77.

———. 1971. *Nation-building in Mali*. Ph.D. dissertation, Los Angeles, University of California:

Dagan, Esther A. 1993. *Drums. The Heartbeat of Africa*. Montreal: Galerie Amrad African Art Publications.

Delafosse, Maurice. 1912. *Haut-Sénégal-Niger*. Paris: Larose.

Diawara, Mamadou. 1996. "Le griot mande à l'heure de la globalisation." *Cahiers d'Etudes Africaines* 144:591–612.

Dramé, Adama, and Senn-Borloz, Arlette. 1992. *Jeliya: Être griot et musicien aujourd'hui*. Paris: Harmattan.

Duran, Lucy. 1995. "Birds of Wasulu: Freedom of Expression and Expression of Freedom in Popular Music of Southern Mali." *British Journal of Ethnomusicology* 2:117–42.

Erlmann, Veit. 1996. "The Aesthetics of the Global Imagination: Reflections on the World Music in the 1990s." *Public Culture* 8:467–87.

Hale, Thomas A. 1998. *Griots and Griottes: Masters of Words and Music*. Bloomington: Indiana University Press.

Hopkins, Nicholas S. 1965. "Le théâtre moderne au Mali." *Présence Africaine* 53:162–93.

Huet, Michel, and Fodeba Keita. 1954. *Les hommes de la Danse*. Lausanne: Editions Clairefontaine.

Joyeux, Charles. 1924. "Etude sur quelques manifestations musicales observées an Haute-Guinée Française." *Revue d'Ethnographie* 17:170–212.

Keita, Fodeba. 1957. "La danse africaine et la scène." *Presence Africaine* 15:202–209.

Knight, Roderic C. 1974. "Mandinka Drumming." *African Arts* 7:24–35.

———. 1984. "Music in Africa: The Manding Contexts." In *Performance Practice. Ethnomusicological Perspectives*, edited by Gerard Béhague, 53–90. Westport, CT: Greenwood Press.

Kokelaere, François, and Saïdani, Nasser. 1995. "90: Les années Djembé." *Djemb'Info. Le carrefour belge de la Percussion et de la Danse de l'Afrique de l'Ouest* (Web site), http://www.prag masoft.be/djembe/articles/Annees90/index.html, May 1999.

Konaté, Famoudou, and Ott, Thomas. 1997. *Rhythmen und Lieder aus Guinea*. Oldershausen: Institut für Didaktik populärer Musik.

Mark, Peter. 1994. "Art, Ritual, and Folklore. Dance and Cultural Identity among the Peoples of the Casamance." *Cahiers d'Etudes Africaines* 136:484–563.

Meillassoux, Claude. 1968. *Urbanization of an African Community: Voluntary Associations in Bamako*. Seattle: University of Washington Press.

Meyer, Andreas. 1997. *Afrikanische Trommeln. West- und Zentralafrika*. Berlin: Veröffentlichungen des Museums für Völkerkunde Berlin.

Modic, Kate. 1996. *Song, Performance and Power: The Bèn Ka Di Women's Association in Bamako, Mali*. Ph.D. dissertation, Bloomington: Indiana University Press..

Nettl, Bruno. 1983. *The Study of Ethnomusicology. Twenty-nine Issues and Concepts*. Urbana: University of Illinois Press.

———. 1996. "Relating the Present to the Past. Thoughts on the Study of Musical Change and Culture Change in Ethnomusicology." *Music and Anthropology* 1 (Electronic journal): http://www.muspe.unibo.it/period/MA/index/number1/nettl1/ne1.htm; March 2005.

Polak, Rainer. 2004. *Festmusik als Arbeit, Trommeln als Beruf. Jenbe-Spieler in einer westafrikanischen Großstadt*. Berlin: Reimer.

Schaeffner, André. 1990. *Le sistre et le hochet. Musique, théâtre et danse dans les sociétes africaines*. Paris: Hermann.

Schulz, Dorothea Elizabeth. 2001. *Perpetuating the Politics of Praise: Jeli Singers, Radios, and Political Mediation in Mali*. Köln: Köppe.

Spittler, Gerd. 2000. "Lokale Vielfalt oder globale Uniformität?" In *Interkulturelle Beziehungen und Kulturwandel in Afrika*, edited by Ulrich Bauer, Henrik Egbert, and Frauke Jäger, 239–51. *Beiträge zur Globalisierungsdebatte*. Frankfurt a.M: Peter Lang Verlag.

Sunkett, Mark. 1995. *Mandiani Drum and Dance: Djimbe Performance and Black Aesthetics from Africa to the New World*. Tempe, AZ: White Cliffs Media.

Traoré, B. 1957. "Le théâtre negro-africaine." *Présence Africaine* 15:180–201.

Traore, Moussa. 1999. "Re: Mali Foli." Private e-mail message, 2 May 1999.

Villien-Rossi, Marie-Louise. 1966. "Bamako, capitale du Mali." *Bulletin de l' IFAN*, Serie B 1(2):249–380.

Westen, A. C. M. van. 1995. *Unsettled: Low-income Housing and Mobility in Bamako, Mali*. Utrecht: Koninklijk Aardrijkskundig Genootschap and others (dissertation, University of Utrecht).

Zanetti, Vincent. 1996. "De la place du village aux scènes internationales: l'évolution du jembe et de son repertoire." *Cahier de Musiques Traditionelles* 9:167–188.

Zemp, Hugo. 1971. *Musique Dan. La musique dans la pens!e et la vie sociale d'une société africaine*. Paris: Mouton.

Appendix A: Annotated Discography

This appendix lists sound recordings of *jenbe* playing. The focus of selection and annotation is historical relevance. The catalogue is subdivided into decades according to the time of the recording.

1930's

Various artists. 1966. *Traditions: Afrique Occidentale/Soudan Français*. Radio France Internationale/Archives Radiophoniques. "Nya foli," "Sene foli," "Samory war song": songs, *bala*, and *jenbe* drum ensemble, probably from southeastern Mali.Recorded in 1931 at the colonial exposition, Paris. Digital reprint of 78-rpm shellacs, *Bibliothèque National Français* (*BNF*), Paris, file number PDC 12.000272.3.

Various artists. 1991. *African Music*. Folkways Cassette Series 08852 [first ed. 1957]. A1, "War song": *bolon* (quasi-bridge harp), drum ensemble (probably with one *jenbe*). Recorded 1933 in Bankoumana (cercle of Kangaba, southern Mali) by Laura Boulton/ Strauss West Africa expedition.

1950's

The ethnomusicologist Gilbert Rouget (*Musée de l'Homme*, Paris) traveled to the Kankan area in upper Guinea in 1950 and 1952. Twelve tracks of his recordings represent the earliest documented corpus of *jenbe* music. The recordings of 1950 have been published on various discs:

Koroma, Jean et Mamadu Koroma. n.d.. *Saramoriba*. Africavox (78-rpm shellac) A 100–1. AX 10, "Chant pour la danse avec tambour": two *jenbew*.

Various artists. 1956. *African Music From The French Colonies*. Columbia World Library of Folk and Primitive Music (33-tpm LP) KL 205. A9, "Drum duet": two *jenbew*.

Various artists. n.d.. *Koukou; Allah ye oube ouro*. Africavox (78-rpm shellac) GT-8. AX 64 and 65, "Water-drums": song, two *jenbew*, and one pair of *ji-dunun* (water-drums).

Various artists. 1959. *Pondu Kakou. Musique de Société Secrète–Côte d'Ivoire, Dahomey, Guinée*. Contre-point (33-rpm LP) MCV 20141. B6, "Batterie malinke: *mosso bara*": two *jenbe*; B9, "Danse de femmes: *mosso bara*": song, two *jenbe*.

Rouget's six *jenbe* recordings of 1950 have not yet been republished. But his six recordings of 1952 that were first published on various shellacs in 1952 were re-released on LPs in 1972 (*Musique Malinke*, Vogue LDM 30113; *Musique d'Afrique*

Occiden-tale, Vogue LDM 30116), were pirated in 1995 (*African Tribal Music and Dances*, Laserlight digital CD 12179), and finally published on the following CD:

Various artists. 1999. *Guinée. Musique des Malinké*. Le chant du monde (CD) CNR 2741112. Two *jenbe* players perform duets and accompany song, flute, and *ji-dunun* in the following pieces: #15, "Call the mothers", #16, "Water drum (*ji dunu*)", #17, "Water drums and women's chorus–women's dance", #18, "Two drums–Drumming for *moso don*, women's dance", #19, "Song for bird mask (*koma*)", #20, "Women's drum–moso *bara*". The solo drum is a leather strap *jenbe*, while the smaller accompanying *jenbe* has its head nailed on.

1960's

Les Ballets Africains. 1964. *Les Ballets Africains*. Bel Air (LP) 411043. Live recording of the *Ensemble National de la République de Guinée*. A1, "Soko"; A3, "Minnuit": *ensemble instrumentale* music with interludes (one minute each) of *jenbe* drum ensemble music. B6, "Finale–Tam-tam Africain": exotic soundscapes (cries, rattles, animal sounds, etc.), two-and-a-half minutes of *jenbe* ensemble playing. The *jenbe* rhythm consists of several sequences of dense and overlapping *échauffements*, i.e., the musical equivalent of solo dancing. Archived at *BNF*, Paris, file number B 72 000175. Famoudou Konaté plays the lead *jenbe* on this and on the following recording.

Ballets Africains de la République de Guinée. 1967. *orgie de rhythme…orgie de couleurs*. Syliphone (LP) SLP 14. Bl, "Initiation": drum ensemble music. Within this track (totaling 4 tracks), the *jenbe* forms the interludes between the main parts lead by the *krin* (slit drum). The *jenbe* ensemble rhythm is based on *suku/furasi fòli*, a Maninka rhythm originally associated with the celebrations held during the night before circumcision (*furasi*), and nowadays popular at all drum/dance occasions. Archived at BNF, Paris, file number B 70 000953.

Excursus on the *Ballets Africains*

The *Ballets Africains* was formed in 1947 in Paris by the playwright, director, and choreographer, Fodeba Keita. The original line-up comprised artists of West African, Central African, and Caribbean origin. The repertoire of drum and dance events did not play an important role in the early years of the *Ballets Africains*. All 78-rpm shellac discs that the *Ballets* recorded in Paris during the late 1940s and early 1950s consist of *orchestre moderne* and *ensemble instrumentale*. Not a single one, however, contains any *jenbe* playing. For instance, the Ballet's legendary homage to Bamako—"A Bamako, les filles sont belles"—is a song sung in standard French, set in a *rumba* rhythm, and orchestrated with guitar, *tumba*, and *claves* (Ballets Africains de Keita Fodeba, [n.d., ca. 1947], *L' Afrique de demain/Bamako*. Chant du Monde 728 [archived at *BNF*, Paris, file number C 012226]).

Keita's many performances of the early 1950s too are mainly set for guitar (*orchestre moderne*) and *kora*, *bala*, and *flute* (*ensemble instrumentale*) music; only exceptionally are some parts set for drum ensemble music. In one piece, however, Fodeba Keita reveals his fascination with the integrative capacities of drum/dance events. This piece, called *Noel de mon enfance*, is completely set in "*rhythme de tam-tam*". It describes Keita's experience of a village celebration, in which the locals and the French representatives of the colonial power merge in communal action—he speaks of a "holy communion"—and transgress, or at least for a moment forget, the borders of cultural otherness and dependence (Keita 1950, 44–47).

In 1953, the *jenbe* player Ladji Camara joined Keita's Ballets Africains and pioneered the tie of *jenbe* music and African ballet that later would prove so close and successful. The *jenbe* traditions of the region of Kankan in northeastern Guinea, where both Keita and Camara come from, later became most influential in the development of a national Guinean, and recently of an international, *jenbe* style. In 1958, Keita's troupe was appointed the national ballet of the first independent state of francophone Africa, the République de Guinée. This marked a remarkable transformation, considering the international and intercultural origin of the troupe in Paris. *Jenbe* music apparently had a specific role in the 1960s programs of the Ballets Africains. It filled only some minutes of a program; as an interlude and finale, however, it represented a conspicuous and essential element of the show. Although the music of the two LPs listed above is mainly modern guitar and *ensemble instrumental* music, the covers and supplements show exclusively folkloristically costumed dancers and drummers.

In 1958, the Ballets Africains performed at the Festival d'Afrique in Bamako; in the festival newspaper (*Festival Afrique* 3, n.p.), a lengthy excerpt of Fodeba Keita's programmatic text "Les hommes de danse" (Huet and Keita 1954, 8–15) was reprinted. In 1958 and 1959, almost every West African independence movement leader of importance visited Conakry and was welcomed with the impressive spectacles of the Ballets Africains at the airport and evening receptions at conference halls. The national ballet of Guinea took the role of a prototype for the Malian and other West African national ballets. From the 1960s onwards, the Guinean national ensemble, with its lead drummer Famoudou Konaté (who had replaced Ladji Camara), has been among the leading mediators of the spread of the *jenbe* outside West Africa.

Various artists. n.d.. *African Rhythms and Instruments, Vol. I*. Lyrichord, LYR (CD) 7328. These recordings feature the national folklore of various African states as performed at the *Première Festival Panafricaine*, Algiers, 1969. The Troupe Folklorique (national ballet) of Mali plays three pieces: 4, "xylophone, percussion and female voices"; 5, "drums and rattles"; and 6, "kono." No. 4 is the ballet's version of a Maninka *jenbe*-rhythm called *menjani*. No. 5 is misleadingly edited: the first 80 seconds of this piece belong to piece *menjani* (no. 4). Only after one-and-a-half minutes does the rhythm *ngonba* begin, a genre of southeastern Bamana. This rhythm originally is played with Bamana drums of the *bòn* type, but was transposed to the *jenbe/dunun* ensemble by the national ballet. The players of pieces no. 4 and no. 5 are Brèm Kuyate–*bala*, Maré Sanogo–*jenbe*, Madu Faraba Sylla–*jenbe*, Bala Samake–*jenbe*, Tindo Jakite–*jenbe*, Sèginè Koita–*dunun*, Seran Kanute–*dunun-ba*, and Sungalo Sacko–*tama* (interviews with Jeli Madi Kuyate and Bala Samake,

2/2000). No. 6, *kònò*, features a Bamana rhythm from the region of Segu representing a bird mask. This piece is not performed with a *jenbe* as lead drum, but with a Bamana drum of the *bòn* type, played by Zani Diabate.

Various artists. 1969. *Djungdjung*. Love records LR (LP) 12. A6, "Dance rhythm": two *jenbew*, one *dunun*. This is the earliest *jenbe* recording from Bamako. It features the rhythm *sunun* played by members of the national ballet, Madu Faraba Sylla-*jenbe*, Tindo Jakite-*jenbe*, and Sègine Koita-*dunun* (identified by Jeli Madi Kuyate and Madu Faraba Sylla, 2/2000).

Various artists. n.d.. *Epic, Historical, Political and Propaganda Songs of the Socialist Government of Modibo Keita (1960–68)*. Albatros (LP) VPA 8327. B2, "You must be courageous": song, flute, *dunun*, *jenbe*.

Various artists. n.d.. *Escale en Guinée*. Path! (LP) CPTX 240746 [ca. 1963/64]. Al, "Gloire à P.D.G. [*Parti Démocratique Guinéen*]": *bala*, *bolon*, *jenbe*.

Various artists. n.d.. *The Music of the Dan*. UNESCO Collection/Bärenreiter Musicaphon (LP) BM 30 L 2301. A3, B10, B11, B12: two *jenbe*-like drums, one five-drum-set, song, trumpets (horns).

Various artists. n.d.. *Musique du Mali. Vol. 2*. Melodie (2 CDs) DK 053. CD1, # 6, "Baaralaw": song, one *jenbe*, guitar. Performed by the regional troupe of Kayes (not of Bamako, as is wrongly maintained in the liner notes).

Various artists. n.d.. *Percussions de Côte d'Ivoire*. Alvarès (LP) C488. Bl: two *jenbe*-like drums, one set of five small goblet-shaped drums.

Various artists. 1961. *Sons nouveaux d'une nation nouvelle: la République de Guinée*. Tempo LP 7008. B3, "danse du feu": one *jenbe*, one *dununba*, one *tama*; performed by the ballet troupe of the region of Kankan.

1970's

Africa Djolé. n.d.. *Live: The Concert in Berlin '78*. Free Music Production, FMP (CD) 1. The first, and very popular recording of completely *jenbe/dunun*-based music on the European market.

Camara, Ladji. 1979. *Africa, New York*. Lyrichord, LYR (CD) 7345. The first *jenbe* recording on the U.S. market; recorded in 1975 in New York City.

Dramé, Adama/Mondet ed. 1984a. *Rhythms of the Manding*. Grem, DSM (LP) 042. This recording of 1976–78 (first published in 1979, Phillips, UNESCO collection 6586 042) features the earliest field recordings of urban *jenbe* celebration music. Two tracks of *jenbe* solo playing anticipate much of Dramé's later developments of virtuosic *jenbe* percussion.

Youla, Fodé. 1977. *Soleil de Guinée*. Sonodisc (LP) SAF 500531.

Various artists. n.d.. *Biennales du Mali. Arts et culture Vol. 1*. Sono Disc (CD) SD40. No. 6. "Ne bè taa maliba la/Sa ka fisa ni malo ye": song, choir, Bamana–*bala*, *dununba*, *jenbe*; performed by the Troupe folklorique régionale de Bamako. This disc contains recordings of the 1970 (not 1980, as is wrongly maintained in the liner notes) finale of the Malian cultural competitions. Most of the tracks were previously published (*Les meilleurs Souvenirs de la première Biennale artistique et culturelle de la Jeunesse* [1970], Bärenreiter Musicaphon (LP) BM 30 L 2651; *Mali* n.d.' Radio France Internationale/Archives Radiophoniques ARC 12).

1980's

Africa Djolé. 1980. *Kaloum*. Free Music Production (LP) FMP/SAJ-26.

———. (n.d). *Basikolo-Ne-Ne*. Free Music Production FMP (CD) 44.

Coulibaly, Soungalo. 1988. *Na ya*. (cassette; no label/number; produced in France). Some of Coulibaly's arrangements of Malian repertoire on this cassette have re-entered the tradition of celebration music in Bamako since then.

Dramé, Adama. 1984. *Traditions*. Auvidis (LP)AV 4510.

———. 1987. *Grand maitres de la percussion: tambour djembe*. Auvidis (LP, CD) B6126.

Keïta, Mamady and Sewa Kan. 1989. *Wassolon*. Fonti Musicali (CD) FMD 159.

Various artists. 1981. *Kora, Balafon et Percussions du Senegal*. Arion (LP) ARN 33602. A1, "Introduction à la fête" [rhythm *wolosodòn*], A3, "danse de fête" [rhythm *dansa*]: three *jenbe*, one *dunun*.

Various artists. 1987. *Musik der Senufo*. Museum fur Völkerkunde Berlin, MC (LP) 4.

Various artists. 1987. *Guineé. Les Peuls du Wassolon*. Ocora (CD) HM 83.

1990's

Ballets Africains de Papa Ladji Camara, Les. 1994/95 (*no title*). Lyrichord LYR(CD)7419.

Ballets Africains, Les. 1991. *Les Ballets Africains de la République de Guinée*. Buda (CD) 82513-2.

———. 1994. *Silo*. Buda (CD) 92579-2.

Coulibaly, Soungalo. 1992. *Percussion and Songs from Mali*. Arion, ARN-64192.

———. 1999. *Dengo*. Djinn Djow Productions (no label number).

Dramé, Adama. 1992. *Mandingo Drums*. Playa Sound (CD) PS 65085.

Doumbia, Abdoul. 1995. *Abdoul Doumbia*. (CD) AKD 95.

Kante, Mamadou. 1994. *Drums from Mali*. Playa Sound (CD) PLS 65132.

Keita, Mamady. 1992. *Nankama*. Fonti Musicali (CD) FMD 195.

———. 1995. *Mogobalu*. Fonti Musicali (CD) FMD 205.

———. 1996. *Hamanah*. Fonti Musicali (CD) FMD 211

———. 1998. *Afo*. Fonti Musicali (CD)FMD215.

———. 2000. *Balandugu Kan*. Fonti Musicali (CD) FMD 218.

Konaté, Famoudou et al. 1991. *Rhythmen der Malinké*. Museum für Völkerkunde Berlin (CD) MC 18. Field recordings of urban celebration music from Conakry; studio recordings. Konaté's *jenbe* playing expertise plus the high standards of an ethnomusicological recording edition make this CD the most outstanding production of *jenbe* music of the 1990s.

———. 1998.*Guinée: Percussions et chants Malinké*. Chants du Monde/Buda 92727-2.

Rhythms of Mali. 1995. *Drums of Mali*. DJ (CD) 1001. Baco Djicorn Djenne

Sidibe, Mamadou. 2000. *Village Djembe Drumming*. MP3.com (CD) 48139.

Traoré, Moussa. 1999. *Mali Foli*. Talking Drum Records TD (CD) 80108.

Various artists. 1996. *The Mali Tradition. The Art of Jenbe Drumming*. Bandaloop (CD) BLP 001. [Re-edited 2005 as Sapatillo SPCD001]

Various artists. 1997. *Dònkili-Call to Dance. Festival Music from Mali*. Pan Records PAN (CD) 2060.

Various artists. 1999. *Bamako Foli. Jenbe Music from Bamako (Mali)*. [Re-edited 2005 as Sapatillo SPCD002]

Appendix B: Musical Examples

Sound samples are available on the Internet at http://www.uni-bamberg.de/ppp/ethnomusikologie/wom003. htm#Sound%20Examples. The aim of the sound samples is to make audible the change of sound of the Bamako *jenbe* that came along with the change of instrument making and style analyzed in the article. All samples feature the same rhythm. The players, who all play their own instruments, belong to different generations of the same tradition in Bamako.

Sound Sample 1:

Namori Keita (*jenbe*), born around 1927, and Fasiriman Keita (*dunun*) play rhythm *sunun* in a studio-like setting in Namori Keita's compound in Kati, close to Bamako. Namori Keita performs on his low tuned leather *jenbe* (see Figure 10.5) that is about 36 cm in diameter. His warm and "breathing" –as one says in Bamana–*jenbe* sound, playing style, and drum patterns are representative of the 1960s and 1970s. Recording: Polak 1998.

Sound Sample 2:

Jaraba Jakite (*jenbe*), bom around 1953, Madu Jakite (*jenbe*). Solo Samake (*dunun*), and Fasiriman Keita (*dunun*) play the rhythm *sunun* at a wedding celebration in Bamako. Soloist Jaraba Jakite plays a rather high tuned iron *jenbe* of about 36 cm in diameter. His roaring and hissing sound is typical of the celebration drummers of Bamako in the 1980's. Recording: Polak 1994.

Sound Sample 3:

Draman Keita (jenbe), Sedu Keita (jenbe), Vieux Kamara (dunun) und Lansina Keita (dunun) play the rhythm sunun in a studio-like setting in Bamako. All players were born between 1966 and 1974. Draman Keita and Sedu Keita both play extremely high tensioned jenbew of only 28–30 cm in diameter. The dry and high pitched sound of jenbew like these is much appreciated by the younger generation of drummers who are setting the tone in Bamako since the 1990's. Recording: Polak 1998.

Part V

Media, Technology, and Technoculture

11

Mozart in Mirrorshades
Ethnomusicology, Technology, and the Politics of Representation

René T. A. Lysloff

Time travel is perhaps one of the most widely encountered themes in science fiction and, in the cyberpunk sci-fi story "Mozart in Mirrorshades" (Sterling and Shiner 1985), the idea of changing history is given an ironic postmodern twist. In this irreverent tale of the collision of European highbrow and American lowbrow cultures, time is not a single thread running from the past through the present and into the future. Instead it is malleable, with infinite possibilities: changing the past simply creates an alternative thread of time while our own remains unaffected. Thus, time travelers could do whatever they wanted, altering and corrupting the past without the danger of a temporal paradox or some other threat to their own present. In such a scenario, history itself is the object of economic exploitation and expansion, offering a virtually limitless supply of natural and cultural resources while also providing an abundance of cheap industrial labor as well as a vast market for inexpensive and disposable manufactured goods. In a nutshell, the past becomes the future's third world.

To summarize the story, Mozart's life is radically and irrevocably altered with the arrival of rapacious time-traveling technocrats (ostensibly from America's near future). With their considerably superior technology and scientific knowledge, the time travelers proceed to extract the natural and cultural resources of 1775 Europe. In two years, they build several gigantic petrochemical refineries with pipelines reaching oil reserves throughout the planet, bringing their own heavy equipment from the future and employing local labor from the past. In exchange, they offer cheap manufactured goods, commodifiable technology, and limited scientific knowledge to the natives. The past thus becomes "modernized" with electricity, electronic gadgetry, mass media, popular culture, and twenty-first-century fashion.

Along with many other young natives, Mozart is profoundly influenced by the media technology and popular music brought by the time-travelers. Indeed, he falls in love with the musical possibilities of the future and manages to purchase various kinds of electronic audio equipment. Listening to the radio and numerous cassette tapes acquired from the time travelers, he quickly teaches himself the rock idiom. Discarding his powdered wig, velvet waistcoat, and knee breeches, Mozart now sports a bristling hedgehog haircut, faded jeans, camo jacket, and mirrored sunglasses.

As a hashish-smoking rock musician, Mozart is soon the rage of Salzburg. One of his concerts is described in the story as follows: "Minuet like guitar arpeggios screamed over sequenced choral motifs. Stacks of amps blasted synthesizer riffs lifted from a tape of K-Tel pop hits. The howling audience showered Mozart with confetti stripped from the club's hand-painted wallpaper" (ibid., 229).

Indeed, Mozart enjoys far greater success in the hi-tech popular music scene than he does seeking court or church patronage with his more traditional compositions. In any case, the many pieces he was to have written later in his life are now already available on commercial cassette tapes. Furthermore, he learns from the history books provided by one of the time travelers that, for him, classical music is a far too dangerous profession and pursuing it would assuredly mean his own eventual death in poverty. As a clever young man, Mozart thus modifies his musical interests to alter the course of his own destiny. In the end, "Wolf" as he is now called, is given a "green card" and allowed to emigrate to the future where his music has already hit the charts.

Music and Technoculture

I use "Mozart in Mirrorshades" to illustrate an aspect of culture that has been largely ignored by ethnomusicologists. Although the general issue of cultural imperialism was introduced several decades ago, it was as recently as 1986, when this story first appeared, that music scholars (mostly those specializing in popular music) were beginning to discuss in earnest the global impact of Anglo-European mass media and popular culture. Yet, most of these studies have tended to focus on the software of media technology (that is, the "industry" and its products).[1]

While remaining within the general discussion of cultural imperialism, I want to shift attention toward the widely distributed electronic hardware of media technology: the radios, microphones, amplifiers, cassette tape recorders, stereo systems, CD players, and so forth, that are now so much a part of our everyday lives that it would be difficult to imagine being without them. At this point I want to introduce the term "technoculture" and define it according to several essays by Andrew Ross (see, for example, Ross and Penley [1991] and Ross [1991]). Ross argues that the recent media and information technologies have given rise to new communities and forms of cultural practice. The term *technoculture*, according to him, describes social groups and behaviors characterized by creative strategies of technological adaptation, avoidance, subversion, or resistance. Furthermore, Ross argues that "it is important to understand technology not as a mechanical imposition on our lives but as a fully cultural process, soaked through with social meaning that only makes sense in the context of familiar kinds of behavior" (1991, 3). Technology, then, is not simply the social and personal intrusions of big science made manifest; it also permeates and informs almost every aspect of human experiences.

"Mozart in Mirrorshades" brings this argument closer to home. With a postmodern juxta-position of nostalgia for the past and cynicism about the future, old world tradition and "brave new world" technoculture are brought into direct conflict in the body of Mozart. The story thus dramatizes the often adversarial relationship between technology and culture, particularly the new media technology and what is considered "traditional" culture. Extending Ross's concept of technoculture further, I want to argue that changing technologies implicate cultural practices and epistemologies involving music—and not only popular music. It is important to note that, even while we may deny its power over us, electronic technology is rapidly becoming the primary means through which we experience music. Increasingly, the CD or cassette (or phonograph) recording is no longer supplemental to the experiencing of live musical performance. More often than not, it is the reverse: mediated performance has now become the originating source for experiencing a given music. Furthermore, a great deal of music is now more commonly conceived with this same audio technology in mind, created to be experienced through the home stereo or the radio rather than through live performance. As Paul Théberge argues, "electronic technologies and the industries that supply them are not simply the technical and economic context within which 'music' is made, but rather, they are among the very *preconditions* for contemporary musical culture, thought of in its broadest sense, in the latter half of the twentieth century" (1993, 151; my emphasis).

Thus, because of the far-reaching implications of musical technoculture, we must consider a broad spectrum of practices and epistemologies—not only techno-musical sub- and countercultures, but behaviors and knowledges ranging from traditional institutions on the one hand to contemporary music scholarship on the other. By examining technocultures of music, we can overcome the conventional distinction, even conflict, between technology and culture, implicit especially in studies of "traditional" musics in the field of ethnomusicology.

Representing the Other

Common sense tells us that technology, rather than being part of our lived experience, only mediates it. Until recently, this view has been apparent in much of the ethnomusicological literature and the various recording methods used to represent the soundscape of the musical Other. Ethnomusicologists are allowed, even encouraged, to use technology in research, bringing to the field cameras, cassette tape players (or now, digital audio recorders), microphones, handycams, and so on. Upon return from the field, we listen to our material on our stereos, view it on our VCRs and color televisions, and write about it on our personal computers. Some researchers edit, analyze, and recontextualize recorded material with sophisticated electronic studio equipment. Others, if their recordings are marketable, might even distribute their field materials through commercial record companies. We might say, then, that technology privileges researchers, distancing them from the object of research—whether musical or human—and allowing them to control it. Indeed, the sound document becomes a true object: isolated from the noisy chaos of real life in the field it becomes analyzable, frameable, manipulable, and ultimately... exploitable.

The technologically privileged position of the ethnomusicologist is largely assumed in the literature. After all, the history of ethnomusicology is closely linked to the history of audio recording. Writing on "field technology" in the widely used graduate textbook, *Ethnomusicology: an Introduction,* Helen Myers complains about the declining standards of recording in the field: "In the 1990s we face the danger that professional ethnomusicologists, by opting for convenience, are preserving the sights and sounds of music of our time on domestic equipment designed originally as dictation machines or for amateur enthusiasts to make home movies" (1992, 84). Myers continues by asserting that pedestrian recordings, presumably made with mediocre equipment, result in "equally pedestrian standards of writing" (ibid.). This privileging of recording technology and the curatorial positioning of ethnomusicology was not lost on Richard Middleton, who viewed it as "yet another result of the colonial quest of the Western bourgeoisie, bent on preserving other people's musics before they disappear, documenting 'survivals' or 'traditional' practices, and enjoying the pleasures of exoticism into the bargain" (1990, 146). After noting that ethnomusicologists focus almost exclusively on the music of "Oriental" high cultures and folk or "primitive" societies, he continues with the following critical observation: "The primary motives for ethnomusicological exoticism, then, obviously lie in value judgments about 'authenticity' in musical culture" (ibid.).

Indeed, assumptions about Western technological preeminence and scientific know-how—rooted in past colonialist notions of social (and even racial) superiority—invest ethnomusicology with the authority to validate a given music. Yet, in practice, evaluation of musical authenticity generally is informed by the need for both ethnographic legitimacy and aesthetic interest.[2] The whole matter becomes politically charged when it is applied to recorded musical Others: that is, the argument that an "authentic" performance is a good thing often becomes conflated with the idea that a good performance *sounds* "authentic." The technologically privileged ethnomusicologist is thus caught in a web of conflicting notions of aesthetics, ethnographic truth, acoustical reality, cultural legitimacy, and specific intellectual interests. Consider the following passage from the same essay by Helen Myers:

> The ethnomusicologist's concern for context should extend even to recording techniques. In fieldwork, it is essential to remember one is recording not only a sound source but also its context, the sound field. The ethnomusicologist's dream of placing all the performers in a professional recording studio (often done by national cultural institutes at great expense) robs the performance of its natural ambiance: audience, traffic, animals, conversation, discussion, cooking, eating, drinking—life. (1992, 53)

In this passage, an aesthetics of authenticity blurs with a quasi-anthropological discourse on contextualized realism. The researcher must decide between the musicological "purity" of studio production and the ethnological "realism" of the field recording in a "natural" setting. My point here is not to debate the merits of one kind of recording over another but to problematize the ethnomusicologist's position *vis-à-vis* audio technology—and to suggest the implicit and often contested notions of authenticity and authority related to such technology when recordings are read as cultural "texts."

On the other hand, when "natives" use electronic devices or enjoy mediated performances, technology is now considered intrusive and often rendered invisible by the researcher. An example of this is a documentary film made several years ago of Javanese shadow theater. The film crew insisted on the use of an oil lantern, instead the usual electric lamp, for purposes of "authenticity." Another example took place in the 1970s, when a researcher recorded Javanese court gamelan music in Yogyakarta and Surakarta for a commercial recording company. The researcher did not place microphones in such a way to feature the female vocalists, as Javanese engineers usually do in studio recordings and radio broadcasts, but, instead, placed them in such a way that the vocal parts remained simply another layer in the complex texture of traditional Javanese music—according to current American views of "authentic" gamelan sound—rendering invisible any suggestion of electronic amplification of the female voice. This romanticized notion of "authenticity," along with the concurrent hostility toward technological intrusion, is not far from the kind of view held by fans of folk music who booed at Bob Dylan when he "went electric" in 1966. As Simon Frith notes in reference to popular music, "the implication is that technology is somehow false or falsifying," that it is "unnatural" (creating artificial presence in performance) "alienating" (coming between performers and their audiences) and somehow "opposed to art" (emptying musical performance of creativity and expressiveness) (1986, 265–66). This may explain why ethnomusicologists have, at least until very recently, been reluctant to concern themselves with mass-mediated and experimental or contemporary musics. Even as we use media technology in our everyday lives, we may often fail to recognize that these devices—the radio, the stereo system, the television—have all become heavily loaded with ideological and cultural baggage. It is especially easy to forget that across cultural boundaries technology can take on different meanings and be used in entirely new contexts. For example, while the radio might be dismissed in the West as an alienating and consumer-driven medium of culturally-drained post-capitalist corporate society, it has another set of meanings in the Islamic world where it is used to broadcast the call to prayer and maintain traditional ethnic and religious community in modern urbanized settings.

From Schizophonia to Plunderphonics

New technology has elevated sound reproduction beyond realism into a kind of audio hyper-reality. New digital recording and editing techniques in fact now allow us to create acoustical environments that could not possibly exist in live contexts—but which, nonetheless, seem real. While earlier media technologies have extended our eyes and ears, the new digital technologies are now extending the imagination—and, in turn, the imagination itself is, to a large extent, determined by the mass media that employs these new technologies. The issue of authenticity becomes further problematized in this age of what Dick Hebdige calls "versioning" (1987, 12–6). In other words, the recording is no longer the end-product in the documentation of musical performance; it is now only a particular version, open to expropriation, remix, resequencing, and recontextualization.

This leads us to another issue in technoculture. The discussions surrounding cultural imperialism have tended to focus on the influence of Western mass media on the music of the Other (See, for example, Goodwin and Gore [1990] and Laing [1986]). Unique traditions and practices, some believe, will eventually disappear in a process of cultural graying out in the globalization of mass media and communications technology. (For more on cultural gray out see Lomax 1968 and 1977.) The discussion becomes more complex and problematic, however, with the advent of digital technology. It is no longer simply a matter of the impact of such media *on* the musical Other but also what media are taking *from* and doing *with* world music—that is, how media are *re*-presenting the Other. Through the magic of digital technology, traditional musics captured on earlier sound recordings are now available as source material for new recombinant musical forms. Thus, the technological innovations that first resulted in schizophonia—the separation of sound from its originating source—continue to be further developed, leading to another technocultural phenomenon, what John Oswald calls "plunderphonics" (1992, 116–125)—the art and compositional prerogative of audio piracy.[3]

When Murray Schafer introduced the term schizophonia over two decades ago, he intended it to be a "nervous" word because audio technology "creates a synthetic soundscape in which natural sounds are becoming increasingly unnatural while machine-made substitutes are providing the operative signals directing modern life" (1980, 91). Inspired by the word schizophrenia, the term is meant to raise anxious questions about the impact of audio technology not only across cultures but within our own culture. Plunderphonics is also a nervous word, perhaps. On the one hand, it questions the idea of ownership and the notion that acoustic materials, such as sound samples used to inspire composition, could themselves be considered compositions (Oswald 1992, 116). While a piece of music, a performance, or even a melody may be legally protected from copyright infringement, should the same laws be used to protect individual tones or rhythms, or even timbres? As audio technology becomes more sophisticated and interactive, the line between rightful ownership and legitimate creative appropriation grows increasingly blurred. On the other hand, unique soundscapes and musical traditions of the world are now routinely becoming compositional grist for commodity culture, open to versioning. Most of us are aware of past debates over musical projects by Paul Simon, David Byrne, and Mickey Hart as well as other popular music artists who have found themselves in the ambiguous role of being both curators and exploiters of world music.

An example of versioning is a recent popular recording by the 1996 grammy award-winning ambient techno group called Deep Forest. In their eponymous 1992 album, the music of the Pygmies (more correctly known as the Mbuti people) of the Ituri Forest in Zaire became transformed into an industrialized dance music known as techno. Instead of simply appropriating Pygmy music, the group uses digital technology to create what appears to be a collaborative effort with the Pygmies in a larger transcultural project. Sampled and sequenced songs of the Pygmies are melodically and rhythmically incorporated into the overall musical texture throughout the album. Overall, the result is impressive but troubling. In the title track ("Deep Forest"), over thick, synthesized Western harmonies, a deeply resonant male voice intones: "somewhere—deep in the jungle—are living some little men and women—they are our fossils—and maybe—maybe they are our future." In another track called "Night Bird," traditional Pygmy singing is seamlessly layered over environmental sounds, lush drawn-out New Age-like harmonies, and a driving ambient-techno-dance beat.

In the liner notes, the members of Deep Forest attempt to contextualize their project in a romantically phrased and somewhat garbled rhetoric of global ecology and endangered cultural practices (Sanchez 1992):

> Imprinted with ancestral wisdom of the African chants, the music of Deep Forest immediately touches everyone's soul and instinct. The forest of all civilizations is a mysterious place where the yarn of tales and legends is woven with images of men, women, children, animals and fairies. Not only living creatures, but also trees steeped in magical powers. Universal rites and customs have been profoundly marked by the influence of the forest, a place of power and knowledge passed down from generation to generation by the oral traditions of primitive societies. The chants of Deep Forest, Baka chants of Cameroun, of Burundi, of Senegal and of Pygmies, transmit a part of this important oral tradition gathering all peoples and joining all continents through the universal language of music. Deep Forest is the respect [for] this tradition which humanity should cherish as a treasure which marries world harmony, a harmony often compromised today. That's why the musical creation of Deep Forest has received the support of UNESCO and of two musicologists, Hugo Zempe and Shima Aron [sic], who collected the original documents.

Here, as in the recording itself, the Pygmies are unknowing collaborators in an Orientalistic narrative of cultural exoticism commodified through the trope of musical universalism, of authentically "primitive" animism colonized by New Age mysticism, and of primal nature salvaged through high technology. Note the discursive strategy of invoking UNESCO along with the names of scholars Hugo Zemp and Simha Arom (whose names are both misspelled in the original text) to add academic and political authority to the project. In these textual and musical narratives, Pygmies disappear into what Donna Haraway calls "a political semiotics of representation."

> Permanently speechless, forever requiring the services of a ventriloquist, never forcing a recall vote, in each case the object or ground of representation is the realization of the representative's fondest dream.... The effectiveness of such representation depends on distancing operations. The represented must be disengaged from surrounding and constituting discursive nexuses and relocated in the authorial domain of the representative. Indeed, the effect of this magical operation is to disempower those ... who are 'close' to the now-represented 'natural' object.... The represented is reduced to the permanent status of the recipient of action, never to be a co-actor in an articulated practice among unlike, but joined, social partners. (1992, 311)

In the case of Deep Forest, the musical and texted narratives "speak" for the expropriated and muted Pygmies, disempowering them as discursive objects but, at the same time, enrolling them as rhetorical allies and passive musical collaborators. With Western state-of-the-art technology, the artists and producers have positioned themselves as curators of a docile Pygmy culture—they even vow to donate part of their profits to "The Pygmy Fund" and urge their fans to do the same—and high-tech plunderphonia is now justified in the names of global ecology and cultural preservation. Everyone is happy! The Pygmies are the recipients of post-colonial Western concern and munificence, the recording artists and producers gain fame and fortune, and the listener is transformed into a social activist through the simple act of consumption.

Deep Forest defines itself not as a band but as "a concept, a state of mind." Meditative music like that of Deep Forest and romantic sentiments toward disappearing ecology and peoples are usually the domain of New Age artists and aging rock stars. Indeed, it is astounding that such ideas are found on this album considering that the Deep Forest project arose out of the Euro-American urban techno-dance scene. One can hardly imagine a community further removed from traditional culture and the concerns of rainforest ecology. Yet recordings like Deep Forest, with an emphasis on soothing and often exotic sound sculptures, are increasingly popular among techno fans. Such recordings are identified as "ambient" techno, intended originally as music for cooling down from the hypnotic effects and physicality of techno rave events and dance clubs. Generally, world music is now part of the technological "primitivism" of both New Age and techno ambient music, both often appropriating the musical Other for exotic, meditative sound sculpturing. Another album, entitled *Ethnotechno* (1993, Wax Trax! Records Inc.), is made up of a collection of various techno-music artists combining sampled world musics with a synthesized techno beat. In the liner notes, the compiler, Scott Taves, defines ethnotechno as "ethnology and technology" and the collection is described as: "World musics and ancient cultures interface with state of the art music machines in the electronic underground. Nothing too precious or academic will be allowed here. A global outlook and a lust for futuristic groove is the bottom line. Welcome to Ethno-Techno, Sonic Anthropology Volume 1."

In this case, the artists are not presented as advocates for endangered cultures and ecologies but as travelers in a rich world of musical diversity made accessible through the technology of digital sampling. There is no moralizing over disappearing forests and musical traditions. Instead, the "authentic" sounds of traditional world music are incorporated into the technological artificiality of synthesizer and drum machines to create "sonic anthropology" where the listener can "travel" to exotic acoustical spaces. On the cellophane wrapper is a sticker stating, "75 minutes of pan-global electro bliss." The various cuts, similar to the Deep Forest project, employ non-Western sampled sounds and music in new compositions but with the original material left recognizable to the untrained ear. That is, a listener with basic world music background will likely be able to identify, for example, the Tuvan throat-singing in the piece "Alash (When I Graze My Beautiful Sheep)" by Juno Reactor.[4] The pleasure of listening to recordings like these is not in cultural advocacy, despite the rhetoric of the Deep Forest project; nor is it to provide the listener with a kind of "authentic" aesthetic experience, as with many New Age music compositions employing world musics and/or natural sounds. Instead, the pleasure of such techno ambient music lies in the technological artifice itself—in "natural" sounds (and music) being made "un-natural" through sequencing in the context of synthesized rhythms and sounds.

Digital sampling is also heard increasingly in non-Western popular music. In Indonesia, for example, digital technology and sampled sound-bytes from American television, radio, and pop music, are often used in sometimes ingenious and startling ways. Technology often carries a different, often ambiguous, set of meanings, usually related to the fear of Westernization and secularization (particularly in Islamic societies) along with a desire for modernization. In Javanese shadow theater performances in the region of Banyumas, musicians sometimes use a Casio keyboard in addition to the gamelan, for creating sound effects to accompany action scenes. Interestingly, they refer to this as *musik* (referring to Western music) to distinguish it from the music of the gamelan (known as *krawitan*). In Indonesian popular music, sampled sounds and high-tech musical instruments are used in the creation of a recent sub-genre called *disco-dangdut*. What identifies the parent genre, *dangdut*, is the instrumentation (featuring an Indian tabla-like sound), the musical influence from both Indian film music and American rock, and most importantly, the stressed fourth and first beats in a four-beat meter. Disco-dangdut continues to have most of these characteristics but with a faster beat along with the addition of synthesized sound and digital sampling. Particularly interesting is the playful use of sampled material, usually voice sounds (ranging from simple vocables to whole phrases as well as hissing and sighs), to add a complex texture of interlocking vocal parts—very much like the traditional practice of *senggakan* (non-texted vocal calls) in rural gamelan music performance. In this case, technology has provided local artists with the means for redeploying traditional ideas in new musical contexts.

Audio Simulacra

For better or worse, sampling technology has stimulated a great deal of creativity among artists throughout the world who are becoming as much sound engineers as they are musicians; in appropriating acoustic material from both near and far away, such artists enhance and expand the sound possibilities of their own compositions and reinscribe new meanings over past traditions. Sold in compact disk or cassette tape format, new recordings are increasingly conceived and produced with stereo high-fidelity audio technology in mind and range from exact reproductions of natural soundscapes and other found sounds to complex compositions made up of sequenced or otherwise digitally-manipulated sound and music samples combined with the synthesizers and studio-performed acoustical instruments. Many such recordings often employ remixed and resequenced sounds appropriated from other recordings, making it difficult to trace or even recognize the originating source material. They range from exact but selective reproductions of natural soundscapes (or virtual sonic realities) to complex compositions made up of sequenced or otherwise digitally-manipulated sound samples combined with the music of synthesizers and studio-performed acoustical instruments. Such recordings are true simulacra—perfect copies whose originals never existed. Examples of musical simulacra are abundant in particular genres of popular music" hip-hop, reggae, techno, and ambient, to name some.[5]

In the field of ethnomusicology, one of the best known examples of audio simulacra is the now familiar *Voices of the Rainforest* recorded by Steven Feld in Papua New Guinea and released by Rykodisc in 1991. Like the time travelers in "Mozart in Mirrorshades," Feld came to New Guinea with state-of-the-art technology, not to exploit the Kaluli but to study their music. Using pioneering field-recording and studio-editing techniques, Feld provided a superb compact disk of a "typical" twenty-four-hour day in the life of the Kaluli, made up equally of both environmental sounds and local musical performance. However, with the use of superior audio technology both in the field and later in the studio, Feld was able to intervene in Kaluli reality by omitting the sounds of…technology. Feld admits that his recording presents a rather unusual soundscape day, "one without the motor sounds of tractors cutting the lawn at the mission airstrip, without the whirring rhythms of mission station generator, washing machine, or sawmill. Without the airplanes taking off and landing. or the local radios…, or cassette players with run-down batteries.…And without the recently intensified and almost daily buzz of helicopters and light planes…" (1991, 137 and later in Feld and Keil 1994).

Feld himself addresses the representational politics behind his recording, posing the troubling question of whether "Voices" is a deceptive or romanticized portrait of the Kaluli soundscape. He answers that it is a highly specific portrayal, "a sound world that increasingly fewer Kaluli will actively know about and value, but one that increasingly more Kaluli will only hear on cassette and sentimentally wonder about" (ibid.). Feld's dilemma is in fact now (or soon will be) the dilemma of *all* ethnomusicologists. Evoking the cyberpunk story I described earlier, the ethnomusicologist, with his enlightened attitudes toward technology and ecology, and his romantic views of the native, has become the sympathetic "time-traveler" who brings the irrevocably changed Mozart recordings of his own never-to-be created symphonies. Indeed, like the cyberpunk Mozart, the Kaluli are nostalgic for a lost past that, as a result of the impact of technology, can now only be vicariously experienced *through* technology.

Conclusions

One of the reasons I especially enjoyed the story "Mozart in Mirrorshades" was the ambiguous ending. From one perspective, Mozart could be seen as a tragic figure, his destiny as the world's greatest classical composer preempted by the arrival of the exploitative time-traveling technocrats.

From this perspective, we might view the advent of technology with the kind of suspicion and cynicism found among thinkers like Neil Postman, who see a growing "technology" that slowly but inexorably empties the world of symbolic meaning, replacing it with the free-floating signs of advertisements and fashion (1993). The post-colonial era might be viewed as a time of *virtual* colonization: traditional cultures are not protected under current copyright laws and their musics (and other practices and knowledges) are thus open to electronically-based commercial colonization by the first world mass media. Indeed, it is a time when an entire name for a people and their practices could become appropriated to signify a computer networking program and registry (as, in fact, is the case of "Java" and "Gamelan," now copyrighted by EarthWeb LLC and Sun Microsystems).

However, Mozart might also be understood as a kind of hero or trickster. Adapting to the reality of his situation he cleverly manages to avoid imminent death in poverty and even become a wealthy rock star of the future. Thus, ethnomusicologists might learn several lessons from the story: (1) that the "native" is not necessarily a naive and passive recipient of media technology; (2) that media technology may be *especially* empowering for those people with little or no political and economic power; (3) that people may use media technology in radically new and surprising ways, and infuse it with meanings specific to such use; and (4) the social meanings associated with particular technologies often change as these technologies traverse cultural boundaries.

Using the story as a twisted allegory we might conclude that the media technologies are far from neutral. Nor are they ever fully controlled by any single constituency. They are sites of continuous social and political struggle—in the realm of world music, the struggles are acted out in terms of cultural ownership, musical authenticity, and intellectual authority. While it is true that media technologies were developed in the interests of industry and corporate profit, and for the purposes of domination and exploitation (Penley and Ross 1991, xii), they are also becoming more standardized, accessible, and widely disseminated—and the corporate control over their use increasingly decentralized.[6] In other words, although the media technologies may be a facet of larger hegemonizing and homogenizing forces, their accessibility and availability provide people with more means to cope with, even to resist or subvert those same forces.

In this article, I have proposed some new understandings of musical culture where the concept of "culture" itself is radically reconfigured in terms of ever-expanding, increasingly sophisticated media and informational technology. What we need is an ethnomusicology of technoculture, the ethnomusicological study of such reconfigured cultures. My purpose is to break from past conventions of examining only folkish or high art "traditions" of music. As world music (whether popular or folk or high art) becomes increasingly implicated in the globalization of advanced audio technologies, the field of ethnomusicology will have to adapt to changing ideas of musical authenticity, cultural representation, and intellectual authority. It will be the work of the ethnomusicologist to analyze and explain the cultural negotiations involved with the global intersections of traditional musics, popular desires, and technological possibilities.

Notes

1. One of the earliest studies to address music and technology specifically is Keil 1984 (reprinted with a brief postlude by the author in Feld and Keil 1994).
2. See, for example, Bruno Nettl's remarks (1983, 316), "The concept of the 'authentic' for a long time dominated collecting activities, became mixed with 'old' and 'exotic' and synonymous with 'good.'"
3. Oswald coined the term in 1989 when he named his now-outlawed album *Plunder-phonics*, a recording made up of various, often parodic, manipulations of music by well-known performers and composers ranging from Michael Jackson, the Beatles, and Dolly Parton to Stravinsky and Beethoven. Although his sources were scrupulously credited and copies of the album were not sold but simply given away, Oswald was threatened with a lawsuit by the Canadian Recording Industry Association. In the end, he was forced to stop distribution and destroy all remaining copies. He now uses the term to refer to the problems of musical creativity in the age of electronic (digital) reproduction.
4. The Tuvan throat-singing was sampled off the Smithsonian-Folkways recording, *Tuva: Music from the Center of Asia.*
5. For a detailed discussion of hip-hop technoculture, see Rose 1994.
6. For a fascinating discussion of the media technologies, particularly in relation to the recording industry in India, see the Introduction to Peter Manuel's important work, *Cassette Culture* (1993).

References

Clifford, James. 1988. *The Predicament of Culture.* Cambridge: Harvard University.
Druckrey, Timothy, and Bender, Gretchen. 1994. *Culture on the Brink: Ideologies of Technology.* Seattle: Bay Press.
Feld, Steven. 1991a. "Voices of the Rainforest." *Public Culture* 4(1):131–140.
———. 1991b. "Voices of the Rainforest." Liner notes of audio recording, compact disk. Rykodisc: RCD 10173.
———. 1994. "Notes on World Beat." *Public Culture* 1(1):31–37.
———, and Keil, Charles. 1994. *Music Grooves.* Chicago: University of Chicago.
Frith, Simon. 1986. "Art Versus Technology: the Strange Case of Popular Music." *Media, Culture & Society* 8(3):263–279.
Hebdige, Dick. 1987. *Cut 'n' Mix.* New York: Comedia.
Hollinger, Veronica. 1991. "Cybernetic Deconstructions: Cyberpunk and Postmodernism." In *Storming the Reality Studio*, edited by Larry McCaffery. Durham, NC: Duke University Press.
Keil, Charles. 1994. "Music Mediated and Live in Japan." In *Music Grooves*, by Charles Keil and Steven Feld. Chicago: University of Chicago. First published in 1984 in *Ethnomusicology* 27(1):91–96.
Laing, David. 1986. "The Music Industry and the Cultural Imperialism Debate." *Media, Culture & Society* 8(3):331–341.
Lomax, Alan. 1968. *Folk Song Style and Culture.* New Brunswick: Transaction Books.
———. 1977. "Appeal for Cultural Equity." *Journal of Communication* 27(2):125–139.
Manuel, Peter. 1993. *Cassette Culture: Popular Music and Technology in North India.* Chicago: University of Chicago.
Myers, Helen, ed. 1992. *Ethnomusicology: An Introduction.* New York: W.W. Norton.
Oswald, John. 1992. "Plunderphonics." In *Cassette Mythos*, edited by Robin James. Brooklyn, NY: Autonomedia.
Penley, Constance, and Ross, Andrew, eds. 1991. *Technoculture.* Minneapolis: University of Minnesota.
Postman, Neil. 1993. "The Great Symbol Drain." In *Technopoly: The Surrender of Culture to Technology.* New York: Vintage Books.
Price, Sally. 1989. *Primitive Art in Civilized Places.* Chicago: University of Chicago.
Reynolds, Simon. 1990. *Blissed Out: the Rapture of Rock.* London: Serpent's Tail.
Rose, Tricia. 1994. *Black Noise.* Hanover and London: Wesleyan University Press.
Ross, Andrew. 1991. *Strange Weather: Culture, Science, and Technology in the Age of Limits.* New York: Verso.
———. 1992. "New Age Technoculture." In *Cultural Studies*, edited by Lawrence Grossberg, Cary Nelson, and Paula Treichler. New York: Routledge.
Sanchez, Michel. 1992. "Deep Forest." Liner notes to audio recording, compact disk. Celine Music/Synsound (manufactured by 550 Music):BK 57840.
Schafer, R. Murray. 1980. *The Tuning of the World.* Philadelphia: University of Pennsylvania.
Sterling, Bruce, and Lewis Shiner. 1985. "Mozart in Mirrorshades." In *Mirrorshades: the Cyberpunk Anthology*, edited by Bruce Sterling. New York: Ace Books.
Taves, Scott. [1993]. "Ethnotechno." Liner notes to audio recording, compact disk. Wax Trax! Records, Inc. (manufactured and distributed by TVT Records): TVT 7211–2.
Théberge, Paul. 1993. "Random Access: Music, Technology, Postmodernism." In *The Last Post*, edited by Simon Miller. Manchester: Manchester University.

12

Technology and the Production of Islamic Space
The Call to Prayer in Singapore

Tong Soon Lee

In almost every Islamic community today, the loudspeaker, radio and television have become essential in the traditional call to prayer, a remarkable juxtaposition of high media technology and conservative religious practice. The loudspeaker simply extended the purpose of the minaret, that towering section of the mosque where the reciter traditionally stood to perform the call to prayer, his voice reaching the surrounding Islamic community. Until recently, in Singapore, this community was located relatively close to the mosque in homogeneous contexts. In the early 1970s, however, as a result of urbanization and resettlement programs that accompanied the process of industrialization in Singapore, the amplified call to prayer became a source of conflict in the emerging reinterpretation of social and acoustical spaces. By focusing on the use of the loudspeaker and radio in the Islamic call to prayer in Singapore, my paper explores the intricate, and sometimes stormy, relationship between technology and the spatial organization of social life. I want to argue that media technology is not necessarily closely associated with popular culture, but can be inextricably bound to so-called "traditional" forms of expressive cultures, in this case, the religious institution of Islam.[1]

Adhan—The Islamic Call to Prayer

The Islamic call to prayer, otherwise known as the *adhan* (or *azan*), is recited five times a day from every mosque to inform Muslims of the prayer times, namely *Subuh* (before dawn), *Zuhur* (noon), *Asar* (late afternoon), *Maghrib* (after sunset), and *Isyak* (evening).[2] For Muslims, the *adhan* is sacred. As a social phenomenon, the *adhan* unifies and regulates the Islamic community by marking the times for prayer and creating a sacred context that obligates a specific religious response. Upon hearing the *adhan*, Muslims are obliged to put aside all mundane affairs and respond to the call physically and spiritually. Indeed, the *adhan* is seen as a microcosm of Islamic beliefs as it "covers all essentials of the faith" (Fiqh us-Sun-nah at-Tahara and as-Salah 1989, 95). Furthermore, the *adhan* symbolizes the presence and blessings of God when it is recited in celebratory events such as births or during calamities.

While the towering minaret of the mosque serves as a physical landmark that signifies the sacred center of the local Islamic community, the call to prayer is a "soundmark" (Schafer 1994, 10), regulating the daily life of each Muslim. In this way, the Islamic community may be identified along acoustic lines, that is, "the area over which the muezzin's voice can be heard as he announces the call to prayer from the minaret" (ibid., 215).[3] In broader cultural terms, the call to prayer is iconic of the social identity of Muslims.

In Singapore today, the recitation of the *adhan* in every mosque is amplified through the use of loudspeakers. In addition, a pre-recorded version of the *adhan* is broadcast over the radio.[4] There are two radio stations in Singapore that broadcast programs in Malay, namely Warna 94.2 FM and Ria 89.7 FM. However, the *adhan* is broadcast only on Warna 94.2 FM, as it caters solely for the Malay/Islamic community.[5] Its broadcast is entirely in Malay while Ria 89.7 FM mixes both English and Malay, and plays mainly popular music in both languages. There is no television broadcast of the *adhan* in Singapore, but the Islamic community is able to receive a broadcast over the Malaysian television channels, Malaysia being directly to the north of Singapore.[6] The old mosques in Singapore, particularly those built before 1975, had their loudspeakers placed outwards, toward the community surrounding the mosque.[7] After 1975, however, the loudspeakers in what is called the "new generation mosques" (Majlis Ugama Islam Singapura 1991) were re-directed toward the interior.[8]

Negotiating Islamic Space

For much of the decades after 1959, when Singapore was granted self-government in domestic affairs by the British Colonial Office, the emphasis of the ruling People's Action Party, or PAP, was political consolidation, industrialization, economic expansion and urbanization, within the general discourse on nation-building (Chua 1995a). Such political motivations engendered the urbanization and resettlement project, formalized in 1967.[9] Since then, "the fate of rural Singapore was sealed" as there were "massive changes in Singapore's cultural and physical landscape" (Sequerah 1995, 186). The emphasis was on the construction of new "satellite" towns with public, high-rise apartments constituting the core residential area, surrounded by industrial estates and served by expressways. As a result, rural settlements were gradually demolished to make way for these developments (Wong and Yen 1985; Chua 1995b; Seet 1995; Sequerah 1995).[10]

During the post-World War II period until Singapore's political independence in 1965, the bulk of the population lived in urban villages and rural *kampungs* (Chua 1995b, 227).[11] The population distribution in the rural contexts was largely characterized by ethnic divisions, each forming relatively homogeneous communities.[12] The population in Malay *kampungs* was largely Muslim and predominantly Malay, with Islam regulating "the pulse of *kampung* life" (Seet 1995, 209).[13] Each *kampung* would usually have a mosque or *surau*—a sanctified space used for religious gatherings—headed by a religious leader (known as the *imam*), who led prayer meetings and arbitrated on matters related to the Islamic faith (Seet 1995).

In the urbanization process, the removal of burial grounds and places of worship caused anxiety among all ethnic groups (*Straits Times* 1 Aug 1974; *Berita Harian* 7 Jun 1974a, 7 Jun 1974b, 13 Jun 1974). Muslim leaders from PAP made numerous public addresses to the Islamic population, urging them to accept and adapt to a modern, urban environment. Muslims in Singapore were urged to "discard some of their age-old 'adat' [customs] to make way for progress" (*Straits Times* 22 Dec 1973, 24 Dec 1973, 11 Aug 1974, 26 Oct 1974). [14]

One of the most important issues highlighted in their speeches was the assurance that the clearing of religious buildings did not apply to the Islamic community alone, but also affected Chinese and Indian temples, as well as Christian churches. The following observation extracted from a newspaper article (*Berita Harian* 11 Jun 1974) reveals the sentiments of several Islamic organizations toward this issue, expressed during a meeting held on 1 June 1974 (hereafter referred to as the Meeting), out of which a petition was drawn and sent to the former Prime Minister Lee Kuan Yew, [15] "They were of the opinion [that] efforts were already undertaken [by the government] to destroy the freedom of Islam in our Republic." [16] Muslim leaders emphasized that the removal of religious sites "has only been resorted to when absolutely necessary and unavoidable. In no way can this be represented as being done only against the Muslim places of worship." Furthermore, they affirmed that the government "had already publicly announced... that in the process of urban renewal and development, adequate sites would be [re]served for a temple, a mosque, and a church in each of the new towns." In addition, the government has provided generous subsidies to the Islamic community in the purchase of sites for the building of mosques in these towns (*Straits Times* 18 Jul 1974a).[17]

It was pertinent for Muslim leaders to assure the Islamic community of the impartial attitude of the government toward religious and ethnic issues, in a country that emphasizes intercultural harmony. Nevertheless, the relocation of religious sites and the subsequent issue involving the use of loudspeakers for *adhan* recitation had evoked larger social issues concerning Malays in Singapore, as I will elaborate below.

Adhan and the Islamic Soundscape

Accompanying the altered landscape, from a localized, rural setting marked by ethnic homogeneity, to a more urbanized and multiethnic environment, was a transformation in the organization of social space. Muslims were relocated in closer proximity to other ethnic groups and, at the same time, further from one another and from the mosque. Once exclusive to Islamic rural communities, the sacred acoustic environment of the amplified call to prayer was now "inhabited" by non-Muslims. In other words, the urbanization process had brought about a diffusion of close-knit and homogeneous ethnic communities into newly organized, heterogeneous, multiethnic communities. Muslims now inhabit high-rise apartment complexes, with other ethnic groups and religious followers as close neighbors. These high-rise apartments are microcosms of a multicultural environment that the government constructs in the process of nation-building, with quotas set on the percentage of each ethnic community living in each neighborhood.[18]

In the new context, sound production from traditional practices was sometimes regarded as "intrusive" to members not involved in those events. The new, urbanized resettlement, therefore, also resulted in new regulations concerning these practices, one of which was the legislation of the anti-noise pollution campaign in August 1974. This campaign affected not only the Islamic call to prayer, but also public and religious activities by other ethnic communities. How, then, did the anti-noise pollution campaign affect the Islamic community?

Between May and July 1974, as part of the noise abatement campaign, the government and Islamic organizations in Singapore decided to re-direct the loudspeakers of the mosques inward, where it originally faced the exterior of the mosque. Newspaper reports published during this period showed that this decision infuriated a section of the Islamic population, thereby creating conflicts between the government and members of the Islamic community. This conflict arose because of their misconceptions that the government had planned to ban the use of loudspeakers for the call to prayer, thus threatening the very core of Islamic religious practice. A newspaper report on the Meeting notes that "[i]n the view of the participants of this meeting, efforts were being made by the authorities to suppress Islam, contain its growth, and restrict the freedom of its followers when they came to know that mosques in this country would no longer be allowed to use microphones. Some even went so far as to allege that this was an effort to put a stop to the muezzin's call to prayers"

(*Straits Times* 10 Jun 1974). Reversing the direction of the loudspeakers toward the interior of the mosque under the pretext of the noise abatement campaign was not favorably received. A Muslim journalist asked "why should the ... loudspeaker ... be directed inwards the mosques—wouldn't that be diverting from the reason for azan—to call others to prayer?... Can the azan that lasts a minute be considered noise and a disturbance to others?" (*Berita Harian* 24 May 1974).[19]

The Islamic community was urged to understand the necessity of reducing noise pollution in the new environment and to support the implementation of the noise abatement campaign (*Straits Times* 23 Jul 1974). More important, newspaper reports emphasize that the campaign was not directed solely at the Islamic call to prayer, but also applied to various activities of all ethnic communities and social institutions, including "Chinese opera, funeral processions, church bells, Chinese and Indian temples, music during weddings, record shops and places of entertainment ... the recitation of pledges in schools and school sports" (*Berita Harian* 14 June 1974b).[20]

The Singapore Muslim Assembly and the Singapore Muslim Action Front were two organizations that filed petitions to the government concerning issues that arose out of the urbanization program, among which was the controversy surrounding the use of loudspeakers in mosques for the call to prayer (*Straits Times* 18 July 1974a, 18 July 1974b, 24 July 1974; *Berita Harian* 2 June 1974, 14 June 1974b). Indeed, the Singapore Muslim Assembly noted that the Meeting was "a direct result of the controversy surrounding the use of loudspeakers by mosques to call the faithful to prayers" (*Straits Times* 24 Jul 1974).

Muslim leaders from the ruling government, however, accused both the Singapore Muslim Assembly and the Singapore Muslim Action Front for their "Divisive Folly" (*Straits Times* 18 Jul 1974b). The two Islamic groups were said to have submitted their petitions on Muslim matters (referring to the issues emerging out of the urbanization program) to the Singapore Government to coincide with the Islamic Foreign Ministers' Conference in Kuala Lumpur (Malaysia), held during the period from 21 to 25 June 1974. Without waiting for the government's response, they distributed copies of their petition to the public as well as to the participants at the conference to "discredit Singapore before the foreign delegates" on a "frequently exploited" issue—the "suppression of Malays in Singapore" (*Straits Times* 18 Jul 1974a).[21]

The issue concerning the use of the loudspeakers for the Islamic call to prayer reflected larger historical and socio-political matters pertaining to the Malays in Singapore. In Singapore, where the majority of the Malay population is Muslims, matters pertaining to the Islamic faith are very often bound with ethnic concerns. In addition, Singapore was part of the Malaysian Federation from 1963 to 1965 and for historical and political reasons, its constitution recognizes Malays as the indigenous population and Malay as the national language.[22] This historical alliance with Malaysia had "given Singapore's minority Malay population a sense of its own interests and political significance as a community in the larger regional picture" (Chua 1995a, 18). Furthermore, as a "Chinese enclave in the Malay sea" (ibid., 108),[23] the government is concerned with religious harmony and inter-ethnic relations, particularly between the Chinese—constituting the majority of the country's population as well as in the ruling political party—and Malay. In such a context, the Singapore government was circumstantially impartial in handling the problems that emerged from the urbanization program. It is important to note that this conflict indicates the central, but sometimes ambiguous place of media technology in the Islamic call to prayer, in a country that takes pride in ethnic and religious plurality.

After discussions with the government, Islamic organizations agreed to (1) reduce the amplitude of loudspeakers in existing mosques, where they remain facing outside, (2) re-direct loudspeakers toward the interior of new mosques to be built in the future and (3) broadcast the call to prayer five times a day over the radio, which previously only transmitted the sunset calls. Using the radio played an important role in resolving this conflict that resulted from the use of loudspeakers in the new, urbanized context. Compared to the loudspeaker, the radio is a different form of media technology that was well-adapted to the new spatial organization.

Mediating the Islamic Community

In the rural context, it was possible to define the Islamic community in Singapore as, borrowing Murray Schafer's terminology, an "acoustic community" (1994, 214–217), a community characterized by the acoustic space within which the call to prayer could be heard. In the new, urban environment, however, it became difficult to maintain the Islamic acoustic community because the environment had become larger and more interspersed with non-Muslims.

In the modern, multiethnic context of Singapore, the concept of the Islamic community had suddenly become a matter of fluid boundaries and contested public space. Roger Friedland and Deirdre Boden (1994, 33) emphasize that "individuals, organizations, and societies construct space and time in the way they do *because* of the meanings they impart to them" (emphasis in original). In this way, we might understand all sounds as cultural phenomena, with socially imbued meaning. The sacredness of the call to prayer is an Islamic cultural construct, yet, at the same time, it can be as much a noise hazard to the majority of non-Muslims in Singapore, as Chinese street operas might be to the non-Chinese population.

Nevertheless, creating a sacred acoustic space to define community is crucial to an Islamic people struggling to affirm their cultural viability and maintain the social borders distinguishing their community in relation to the larger, non-Islamic environment. In urbanized societies, such borders are fluid, ambiguous and usually tenuous. Electronic mediation of the call to prayer in the transformed environment provides the means to reclaim the acoustic space that once identified the Islamic community during its rural past. Paraphrasing Arjun Appadurai (1990, 17), who is himself paraphrasing Walter Benjamin, I would call this the work of culture production in an age of electronic mediation.[24] In the rural past, the amplified call to prayer defined a physical space through the acoustical phenomenon, that, in turn, defined the Islamic sacred and social space. The radio, however, superseded the loudspeaker in the new urban environment, taking over its role as a tool for culture production and also redefining the concept of community.

Presence/Absence of the Community

Regardless of the physical distances that separate Muslims from the mosque and from each other, they now remain a community—an imagined community (Anderson 1991)—defined in relation to the radio transmission of the call to prayer. Through the use of radio, the extended and separated profiles of Muslims in the urban environment now formed uninterrupted acoustic space, and resultantly, a unified, social and religious space. It is the radio, rather than the physical proximity of a mosque, that facilitates the cohesion of the Islamic community and maintains its identity within the larger, urban context of Singapore. Indeed, the radio is sometimes revered as a symbol of God's presence, outside the locale of the mosque.

Friedland and Boden (1994, 23) note that "the immediacy of *presence* is extended by humans, first through language, [and] now through technology" (emphasis in original). The far-reaching presence, or absence, created by technology, implies the existence of extended spatial relationships between the sound-producer and its recipient. The amplified call to prayer creates an immediate Islamic presence for a larger, more dispersed community. However, the reorganization of social space in Singapore has made it necessary for Muslims to reinterpret their tools of culture production and adapt to changes in social space.

At the same time, the media itself brought about new spatial and social relationships (Berland 1992). In retrospect, broadcasting the call to prayer over the radio appeared to ease the conflict. The radio is one form of electronic mediation that was well adapted to individuated users, such as the relocated and dispersed Islamic population; it simultaneously separates and reunites listeners in differentiated and expanded spaces (ibid., 46). Electronic mediation creates a dialectical relation between *presence* and *absence*. The *absence* of shared physical space among Muslims in Singapore does not affect their religious and socio-cultural identity, because of the *presence* of shared acoustic space created through radio transmission.

Mediating Culture Production

Schafer (1994, 165) notes that "all acoustic communications systems have a common aim: to push man's voice farther afield ([and] to improve and elaborate the messages sent over those distances." But we can see that in the case of Singapore, the use of media technology has had larger social implications that concerned culture production and the easing of intercultural tensions. It is, therefore, not an exaggeration to note that the reorganization of social space in Singapore during 1960s and 1970s resulted in an increased dependence on technology to maintain cultural identities. The "new" Islamic context—defined by the electronic broadcast of the *adhan*—facilitates a mediation between technology, space, and social identity, as Islamic identity is "technologically articulated with the changing spatiality of social production" (Berland 1992, 39) in Singapore.

The conflict over the use of loudspeakers in the call to prayer suggests that the technologically aided production of Islamic culture is closely linked to the politics of religious and ethnic expression. The call to prayer does not merely inform Muslims that it is time to pray, it is a statement that says "we" are Muslims. As Arjun Appadurai (1990) notes, the process of culture production in changing spatial contexts has become a matter of identity politics.[25] He further suggests that communications technology has relativized spatial dimensions in the contemporary world, and in such a context, social agents identify and align themselves along different axes.[26] The use of electronic mediation is an example of an axis that constitutes the heart of this identity politic, where Muslims seek to maintain their past in the present, their historical construction of religious and cultural expression through the call to prayer in the larger, secularizing environment. The controversy reflects, as it continues to generate, an awareness of the inextricable relationship between technology and Islamic identity.

Miniaturizing Reception

Performing the call to prayer from the minaret had assumed the collective, physical proximity of the Islamic community that surrounds the mosque. However, broadcast over radio, the call to prayer has become decentralized; the mosque is no longer the exclusive source from which the call to prayer is recited. In other words, what was previously an inclusive, community-wide tradition has now become decentralized and individualized, reduced to an almost personal, private act of worship.

Compared to the loudspeaker, the radio may be seen as a "miniaturization" (Chow 1993) in the broadcast of the call to prayer. This altered mode of transmission requires, and is required by, a change in the form of reception and a concept of an "imagined community." In the spatially reorganized, urban and multiethnic context, Islamic culture production through the call to prayer is now a matter of choice, of consciously creating newly localized and homogeneous acoustic sites through radio transmission, sites which are linked by commonalities of the Islamic culture. Listening to the call to prayer via the radio reunites each member of the Islamic community and creates an abstract communal Islamic space without the encroachment of non-Islamic social spaces. In this way, the individuated listener is the context for electronic mediation and at the same time, a product and process of the technological articulation of Islamic identity in a new spatial context.

Although the personal and almost private act of listening to the call to prayer separates the individual listener from the larger community, "miniaturizing" the call to prayer, to paraphrase Rey Chow (1993, 398), makes its listeners aware of the impending presence of Muslims as well as non-

Muslims in Singapore. This altered state of reception of the call to prayer through the radio—the increased frequency of broadcast and listening in "miniaturized," individualized spaces—offers the Islamic community a means of cultural self-production within the collective, non-Islamic context of Singapore. This new form of reception of the call to prayer over the radio suggests that the "collective," both Muslims and non-Muslims, is not necessarily an "other," but a mundane and imagined part of the Muslim "self" that can be brought to *presence*, or relegated to *absence*, at the switch of a button. The radio provides its listeners the power and the "ability to control the timing and spacing of human activities and thus the 'locales' of action" (Friedland and Boden 1994, 28). In terms of technology, Muslims are thus able to play an active part in their decision to participate in the imagined Islamic community.

While the government organizes, controls, and provides urban *places* through its resettlement program, the communities of people construct their own *spaces* through their practices of living (Fiske 1992), in this case, constructing and maintaining an Islamic space through the use of electronic mediation. In this sense, then, "space is a practiced place" (de Certeau 1984, 117). While media technology may be a facet of the larger corporate and culture industry, usually dismissed as an alienating medium in the West, it is reconfigured as a "fully cultural process" (Ross 1991, 3) within the Islamic community in Singapore. In this way, "technology . . . is not simply the social and personal intrusions of big science made manifest; it also permeates and informs almost every aspect of human experiences" (Lysloff 1997, 208).

An important aspect of broadcasting the call to prayer (as well as other forms of religious speeches, *Qur'an* readings and news of the Islamic community) is the redefinition of the listening context (Berland 1992, 41) that, in turn, enlarges the Islamic community. In Singapore, women do not usually attend prayers in the mosque, while men are obliged to do so. In this case, the radio may be seen as the main (if not the only) vehicle of maintaining the religious and social identity of women (and those unable to go to the mosques) through the broadcast of the call to prayer. While the mosque serves as a structural space that facilitates group identity largely among men, the radio constructs a larger Islamic community through its airwaves and includes women. In this way, by "drawing new types of listeners" (ibid.), media technology reconfigures the concept of Islamic community. Technology becomes a tool through which women affirm their status within the Islamic community. In terms of the physical proximity of the mosque, women are generally displaced from the community. However, in an electronically mediated context, women are not only involved in the Islamic community, but are positioned equally with men, in terms of their reception of the Islamic call to prayer.[27]

Conclusion

Past critics of mass media and technology have argued that these electronic forms are part of a larger culture industry that induces social alienation and passive reception, empties meaning from life, and is controlled by a dominating and oppressive power (Adorno and Horkheimer 1993; Postman 1993; Keil and Feld 1994). In Singapore, however, the use of the radio broadcast in the call to prayer demonstrates how a community actively employs media technology to maintain collectivity in a pluralistic society; media technology here affirms religious and cultural identity and is absolutely important in the work of Islamic culture production. We might say that Muslims are "traditionalizing" media technology, and that they are defining its social significance. Broadly speaking, modem media technologies have become part of the social process in contemporary cultures, in which new uses are defined by different social groups with different needs and interests. In response to critics of media technology, then, I quote Paul Théberge (1993, 152), who asserts that "the ultimate significance of any technological development is . . . neither singular, immediate nor entirely predictable."

Radio broadcast of the call to prayer creates what Schafer (1994, 90) calls schizophonia, "the split between an original sound and its electroacoustical transmission or reproduction." Schafer intended the term to be "a nervous word" (ibid., 91) and indicates his anxiety of the impact of sound technology on the sound environment. However, I have argued that, for the Islamic community in Singapore, the radio has been indispensable in their efforts to maintain cultural identity.

To my knowledge, recordings of the call to prayer (for purposes other than radio broadcast) are discouraged in Singapore—perhaps for the same reasons that the *Qur'an* is not translated into other languages—and live recitation is the accepted norm. What this suggests is an importance placed on the ephemerality of live performance, that the act of recitation is as sacred as the text itself.[28] Why, then, had it become acceptable for the call to prayer to be broadcast over the radio? Such schizophonic technology seems to run counter to conservative Islamic views of sacred performance. Nevertheless, Islamic leaders in Singapore seemed to be convinced that the benefits of media technology outweigh the costs, whatever they are, and that modernization does not necessarily lead to secularization. It is interesting to note that broadcasting the call to prayer has, for better or worse, produced an aesthetics for "good" versions of *adhan* recitation. An *adhan* reciter whose version is chosen by the Islamic Council of Singapore to be broadcast over the radio, is revered as a good and skillful reciter, whose interpretation is commended or even modeled upon by other reciters.

Media technology has played an important role in the situation I have just described, making the abstract principles of "space" immediate and tangible, creating an arena that offers possibilities for conscious acts of negotiation among ethnic groups that are divided in cultural and religious experiences. Where one form of media technology had created conflicts, another eased community disputes and created an environment of multicultural tolerance. It is important to remember that discourses about the meaning of space and value of technology are always socially and culturally constructed, and that these issues are among numerous ever-changing constructs that constantly get articulated, modified and transformed on multiple fronts, including the field of ethnomusicology.

Notes

1. An earlier version of this paper was presented at the Fortieth Annual Meeting of the Society for Ethnomusicology, 19–22 October 1995, Los Angeles, California. This paper is an extension of my Master's thesis. *Musical Processes and Their Religious Significance in the Islamic Call to Prayer* (University of Pittsburgh, 1995). Fieldwork research for my thesis was done in Singapore from May to July 1994. I am grateful to René T. A. Lysloff and Bell Yung for their invaluable criticisms and insights, and to Goh Bong Sue and Noridah Moosa for their assistance. The writing of this paper was assisted by the Tan Kah Kee Foundation Postgraduate Scholarship and the International Dissertation Field Research Fellowship of the Social Science Research Council and the American Council of Learned Societies.
2. The exact prayer times, or *Waktu Sembahyang,* for each time period differ slightly throughout the year. In Singapore, the prayer times are published in a pamphlet by MUIS (Majlis Ugama Islam Singapura), the Islamic Council of Singapore.
3. *Muezzin* (or *mu'adhdhin*) refers to the *adhan* reciter.
4. The broadcast is sometimes used by *muezzin* in their respective mosques as an indicator to begin the call to prayer.
5. The majority of the Malay population in Singapore is Muslims, that is, followers of the Islamic faith.
6. Regarding television broadcast in Singapore, the two major channels are in English (the first language in Singapore) and Mandarin (since Chinese constitutes the majority of the Singapore population). There is no channel catering specifically for the Malay community. Malay programs are usually featured together with programs in Tamil (the native language of the majority of Indians in Singapore).
7. It is difficult to ascertain when loudspeakers were used to amplify the call to prayer in Singapore. Recollections of several elderly Muslims suggest that the use of loudspeakers probably began in the early 1950s. Prior to that, the *kentung*, a wooden, cylindrical idiophone, usually placed in the mosque, was struck to summon Muslims in the community for prayers. In such situations, the *adhan* would be recited after the congregation arrived.
8. In 1975, a Mosque Building Fund Scheme was established by MUIS. Under this scheme, all Muslims can make monthly contributions toward the building of a mosque in the newly developed, urbanized housing estates (Majlis Ugama Islam Singapura 1991).
9. The project was known as the Ring Concept plan, with an emphasis on "the progressive urbanization of Singapore's landscape" (Sequerah 1995, 186).

10. See Chua 1995b for a critical discussion on how the concept of nostalgia (for the rural past) is appropriated in contemporary Singapore as a form of social critique of the present.
11. "Kampung" (or "kampong") is a Malay word referring to "village." "Kampung" and "village" are often used interchangeably. However, as in this case, "kampung" sometimes suggests a more rural setting, in contrast to the village, which connotes a more urbanized context.
12. The three largest ethnic groups in Singapore are the Chinese, Malay and Indian. Two other prominent groups are the Eurasians and Peranakans. Chua (1991) delineates two distinct types of villages in Singapore, namely, the Chinese and Malay villages.
13. It is important to note that not all Malays in Singapore are Muslims, and that the Islamic community comprises members of other ethnic groups such as Indians and Chinese.
14. "Adat" refers to the traditional or customary cultural practices of the Malays.
15. See *Straits Times* 5 June 1974, 10 June 1974, and *Berita Harian* 2 June 1974, 11 June 1974, 20 June 1974, for descriptions of the meeting. These Islamic organizations petitioned against the demolition of religious buildings and burial sites, as well as the noise abatement campaign that regarded the amplified call to prayer as "noise."
16. Extracted and translated from a newspaper article written by Haji Muda Baru, a participant at the gathering, who was expressing his views on the meeting. He was directing his disappointment at MUIS for their apparent apathy toward the removal of burial grounds and religious sites.
17. Extracted from a speech by then Minister of Social Affairs Mr. Othman Wok.
18. See Chua 1995a, 124–146 and Lai 1995, 121–134.
19. Extracted and translated from a newspaper article by Mohd Guntor Sadali.
20. See *Berita Harian* 14 Jun 1974a for further discussions. See *Straits Times* 20 July 1974, 25 July 1974, 26 July 1974, 6 August 1974 for reports on how the noise abatement campaign affected Chinese street opera performance.
21. Extracted from a speech by then Minister of Social Affairs Mr. Othman Wok.
22. The lyrics of the National Anthem of Singapore are in Malay.
23. Singapore is situated at the south of Peninsular Malaysia and is surrounded by the islands of Indonesia.
24. Appadurai paraphrased Walter Benjamin's "The Work of Art in the Age of Mechanical Reproduction" (1969, 217–252) as "The Work of Reproduction in an Age of Mechanical Art."
25. Appadurai uses the term "-scapes" to describe such spatial fluidity.
26. See also Appadurai 1996.
27. The final chapter of my Master's thesis explores the religious experience through the Islamic call to prayer, drawing mainly on Victor Turner's (1995) ideas on liminality, antistructure, and *communitas*.
28. Indeed, Benedict Anderson (1991, 12–19) concedes that the cultural system of distinct religious communities (such as Islam) was imagined largely through the medium of the sacred language and script (such as classical Arabic).

References

Anderson, Benedict. 1991. *Imagined Communities: Reflections on the Origin and Spread of Nationalism.* London and New York: Verso. Originally published in 1983.

Appadurai, Arjun. 1990. "Disjuncture and Difference in the Global Cultural Economy." *Public Culture* 2(2):1–24.

———. 1996. *Modernity at Large: Cultural Dimensions of Globalization.* Minneapolis: University of Minnesota Press.

Adorno, Theodor, and Max Horkheimer. 1993. "The Culture Industry: Enlightenment as Mass Deception." In *The Cultural Studies Reader*, edited by Simon During, 29–43. London and New York: Routledge.

Benjamin, Walter. 1969. "The Work of Art in the Age of Mechanical Reproduction." In *Illuminations*, edited by Hannah Arendt and translated by Harry Zohn, 217–252. New York: Schoken Books, Originally published in 1955, Frankfurt, Germany: Suhrkamp Verlag.

Berland, Jody. 1992. "Angels Dancing: Cultural Technologies and the Production of Space." In *Cultural Studies*, edited by Lawrence Grossberg, Cary Nelson, Paula Treichler, 51–55. New York: Routledge.

Chua, Beng Huat. 1991. "Modernism and the Vernacular: Transformation of Public Spaces and Social Life in Singapore." *Journal of Architectural and Planning Research* 8(3):203–221.

Chua, Beng Huat. 1995a. *Communitarian Ideology and Democracy in Singapore.* New York and London: Routledge.

———. 1995b. "That Imagined Space: Nostalgia for Kampungs." In *Portraits of Places: History, Community and Identity in Singapore*, edited by Brenda S. A. Yeoh and Lily Kong, 222–241. Singapore: Times Editions Pte Ltd.

Chow, Rey. 1993. "Listening Otherwise, Music Miniaturized: A Different Type of Question about Revolution." In *The Cultural Studies Reader*, edited by Simon During, 382–402. London and New York: Routledge.

de Certeau, Michel. 1984. *The Practice of Everyday Life*, translated by Steven Rendall. Berkeley; Los Angeles: University of California Press.

Fiqh us-Sunnah at-Tahara and as-Salah. 1989. "The Call to Prayer (*Adhan*)." In *As-Sayyid Sabiq* [Purification and Prayer], vol. 1. Translated by Muhammed Sa'eed Dabas and Jamal al-Din M. Zarabozo, 95–104. Indianapolis: American Trust Publication.

Fiske, John. 1992. "Cultural Studies and the Culture of Everyday Life." In *Cultural Studies*, edited by Lawrence Grossberg, Cary Nelson, Paula A. Treichler, 154–173. New York and London: Routledge.

Friedland, Roger and Deirdre Boden. 1994. "NowHere: An Introduction to Space, Time and Modernity." In *NowHere: Space, Time and Modernity*, edited by Roger Friedland and Deirdre Boden, 1–60. Berkeley; Los Angeles: University of California Press.

Keil, Charles and Steven Feld. 1994. *Music Grooves: Essays and Dialogues.* Chicago and London: University of Chicago Press.

Lai, Ah Eng. 1995. *Meanings of Multiethnicity: A Case-Study of Ethnicity and Ethnic Relations in Singapore*. New York: Oxford University Press.

Lysloff, René T. A. 1997. "Mozart in Mirrorshades: Ethnomusicology, Technology, and the Politics of Representation." *Ethnomusicology* 41(2):206–219.

Majlis Ugama Islam Singapura. 1991. *New Generation Mosques and Their Activities Bringing Back the Golden Era of Islam In Singapore*. Singapore: Majlis Ugama Islam Singapura.

Postman, Neil. 1992. "The Great Symbol Drain." In *Technopoly: The Surrender of Culture to Technology*, 164–180. New York: Vintage Books.

Ross, Andrew. 1991. *Strange Weather: Culture, Science, and Technology in the Age of Limits*. New York: Verso.

Schafer, R. Murray. 1994. *The Soundscape: Our Sonic Environment and the Tuning of the World*. Rochester, Vermont: Destiny Books. Originally published as *The Tuning of the World* in 1977, New York: Knopf.

Sect, K. K. 1995. "Last Days at Wak Selat: The Demise of a Kampung." In *Portraits of Places: History, Community and Identity in Singapore*, edited by Brenda S. A. Yeoh and Lily Kong, 202–221. Singapore: Times Editions.

Sequerah, Pearl. 1995. "Chong Pang Village: A Bygone Lifestyle." In *Portraits of Places: History, Community and Identity In Singapore*, edited by Brenda S. A. Yeoh and Lily Kong, 180–201. Singapore: Times Editions.

Théberge, Paul. 1993. "Random Access: Music, Technology, Postmodernism." In *The Last Post: Music after Modernism*, edited by Simon Miller, 150–182. Manchester: Manchester University Press.

Turner, Victor W. 1995. *The Ritual Process: Structure and Anti-Structure*. New York: Aldi-ne De Gruyter. Originally published in 1969, Chicago: Aldine Publishing Company.

Wong, Aline K., and Stephen H. K. Yen, eds. 1985. Housing a Nation: 25 Years of Public Housing in Singapore. Singapore: Maruzen Asia for the Housing Development Board.

Newspaper Articles

From Straits Times *(Singapore)*

"Adat That No Longer Applies." 22 December 1973:7.
"Discard 'Adat' Call: Malay Groups Agree." 24 December 1973:10.
"Muslim Team Appointed to Send Memo to Lee." 5 June 1974:23.
"Need for Clarification on Noise Pollution and Call to Prayers: Translation of an Editorial from Bertta Harian, Jun 7." 10 June 1974:13.
"Politicians Exploiting Religious Issue—Bid to Smear Government: Othman." 18 July 1974a:l, 17–18.
"Divisive Folly." 18 July 1974b:10.
"Clamp on Noise from Wayangs." 20 July 1974:11.
"Let's Throw Our Weight behind Anti-Noise Move." 23 July 1974:8.
"We're Not So Foolish: Muslim Groups." 24 July 1974:11.
"Noise Control: Wayangs Seek Deposit Cut." 25 July 1974:5.
"Of Funeral Rites and Noise Wayangs." 26 July 1974:12.
"Muslims Won't Be Affected by Government Cremation Plan." 1 August 1975:5.
"Plea for Cut in Wayang Fees." 6 August 1974:5.
"Mattar: Urban Renewal a Must for Progress." 11 August 1974:5.
"Face Problems Squarely' Call to Muslims." 26 October 1974:13.

From Berita Harian *(Singapore)*

"Adakah tindakan itu sengaja bertujuan hendak menghina? [Is the Action Intended To Be Disrespectful?]." 24 May 1974:4.
"Badan 15 orang dibentuk untuk uruskan masaalah Islam [A Body of 15 Formed To Handle Islam's Woes]." 2 June 1974:10.
"Rumah2 ibadat yang terjejas [Houses of Worship Jeopardized]." 7 June 1974a:l, 8.
"Pembangunan semula: Penerangan perlu diberi [Redevelopment: An Explanation Must Be Given]." 7 June 1974b:4.
"Perjumpaan badan2 Islam: Sikap MUIS dikesali [Gathering of Islamic Bodies: MUIS Attitude Regretted]." 11 June 1974:4.
"Resolusi mengenai ganti tapak mesjid sudah dipinda [Resolution on the Replacement of Mosque Site Has Been Amended]." 13 June 1974:1.
"Jangan lekas marah sebelum pelajari tiap persoalan sedalam-dalamnya [Do Not Be Quick to Anger before Studying in Detail Every Issue]." 14 June 1974a:4.
"Pertemuan badan2 Islam dan Pemerintah dianjur untuk Pemerintah dianjur untuk atasi masaalah yang mereka hadapi [Meeting of Islamic Bodies and Government to Overcome Problems Confronting Them]." 14 June 1974b:4.
"Kecewa dengan sikap 'iepas tangan' MUIS terhadap soal bersama [Disappointed with the 'Washing of Hands' Attitude of MUIS Regarding the Issue of Togetherness]." 20 June 1974:4.

13

Acting Up, Talking Tech
New York Rock Musicians and
Their Metaphors of Technology

Leslie C. Gay, Jr.

Relationships between popular musics and technology, while commonly acknowledged in music scholarship, often have been limited to discussion of these musics as dependent upon large, complex industries whose ability to produce and reproduce a product is technologically based.[1] Only recently have technologies been scrutinized as lived and experienced, not just as the annoying tape noise in the background of daily life but tied to familiar and persistent cultural practices.[2] I argue here that technologies emerge in intentional linguistic and behavioral processes for rationalizing and dividing the world (see Penley and Ross 1991; Ross 1991) for local New York City rock musicians.

The close relationship between electronic technologies and the very concept of popular music in this century is affirmed each time we pick up an electric guitar, watch MTV, or purchase a compact disc. Thus it is not surprising that knowledge of music technologies and how to exploit, adapt, and resist them is essential to communities of rock musicians in New York and elsewhere. Technologies also become bound to tropes within the lives of rock musicians and central to their existence as rockers. These tropes—specifically metaphors—are intricate, with patterns and meanings continually reformed through the social and technological encounters of musicians. Most explicitly for New York rock musicians, technologies and technological adaptations are tied to cultural practices that authenticate musicianship while signaling alliances and alienation among musical and social groups. Moreover, new technological adaptations allow for reconfigurations and new alignments of power for women rock musicians.

This article is based on field research with rock musicians primarily between 1986–1990 and the summer of 1992; the research includes participant observation, key informant interviews, and the analysis of published primary texts important for rock musicians in New York, like local zines and the *Village Voice*. "Local" musicians are those who live and work primarily in the environs of New York City. However, as Akhil Gupta and James Ferguson have argued, facile definitions of "local" based on assumptions equating physical space and culture fail to acknowledge the complexities of contemporary life and the "local" as a social construction (1992). Thus, while a geographic definition of New York rock musicians is necessary here to address the technological issues, rock musicians in New York, as musicians elsewhere, cannot be explained solely by their placement, nor easily by self-identified aspects of common ethnicity (usually "white"), shared age range (broadly 18–35), gender (often male), or social and economic backgrounds ("middle class") (see Gay 1993).

Defining New York rock musicians through their performance styles proves equally problematic. Rock bands refer to themselves and are discussed in the New York press with a wide range of terminology. These terms extend from music stylistic labels—such as "rock," "guitar rock," "garage band," "hardcore," "post core," "heavy metal," "slash metal" and so on—to general terms of "alternative" and "underground" rock. Individuals of local rock bands hesitate to label or classify their own music, and often distance themselves from broad labels used in the press or in marketing recordings. If pushed to do so, rather than just giving a simple stylistic label to explain the kind of music they perform, they prefer to give an exposé on the various better-known bands, or songs, which are influential or in some way similar to their group or their work. The common denominator among New York rock bands is their adherence to performing "original" music, that is, playing music composed by the band rather than covers of other musicians' recordings. Rock musicians, however, do see New York as consisting of several musical "scenes," each with a hard-to-define rock style, associated clubs, and bands. The strongest distinctions are drawn between "normal" rock bands and "indie" bands. Normal rock, which consciously emulates the music of major recording labels and "Top-40" radio, flourishes in clubs such as the Continental Divide and McGoverns. Indie bands, whose styles build from 1970s punk, prevail in clubs such as CBGB on the Bowery and Maxwell's in Hoboken.

Identification with the concept of indie occurs because rock musicians and their bands have recordings released by independent labels or, just as importantly, they "adhere to the idea" presented by indies (Alan Lickt, personal communication 1992). The term "indie," short for independent recording label, while commonly used in popular music scholarship, is problematic. It is consistently used to describe a company with limited production and distribution, whose products are built around a restricted number of music styles or genres. However, for rock musicians and some fans in the United States, indies—while often regional in character, concerned with the music and bands from one city or area of the country—are often national in reputation. Of singular importance for rock musicians is that independent labels are managed by their peers, fellow musicians and local music aficionados, who are approachable and interested in their music. Indies thus offer an accessible avenue to record a band's music. These companies gain further significance because they are viewed as more likely to create recordings that reflect an individual band's musical aesthetics, unconstrained by the "commercial" concerns of larger companies. These indie rock ideals about the importance self expression found among many New York musicians intersect with their concerns about technology and its use.

"Too Many Knobs"

At the 305 Bar, a Chinese restaurant turned rock club near New York's Port Authority Bus Terminal, a rock musician friend criticizes another guitarist's performance by saying that he has "too many knobs between the guitar and the amp's speaker" (Jimbo Walsh, personal communication 1989). This statement refers to the highly processed guitar sound the performer had created with his considerable electronic gear: electric guitar, amplifier, rackmounted digital-delay reverb and a battery of effects pedals linked through a few feet of cables. My friend later explained that "every electronic thing adds some muck to the sound and deteriorates the fidelity, hindering the directness of the 'feel' of the guitar" (Walsh, personal communication 1994).

At the heart of the critique was a problem of obstructing musical communication. For many New York rockers, fewer knobs—less processing of the musical sound—yields a more direct, more "real," communication between musician and audience. Throughout the period of my field research, this axiom was commonly held by New York's largest constituency of local rock musicians, those identifying themselves with indie record labels. This relationship between technology and communication extends to music a common metaphor of language communication, the "conduit metaphor," which acts as a "preferred framework for conceptualizing communication" in English, according to linguist Michael Reddy (1993, 165). I will return to this point after a brief review of pertinent linguistic theories and their use here.

Image Schemata and Metaphor

Ethnomusicology once headily embraced the application of linguistic theories to discuss and theorize about musical practices. The results of this disciplinary mix are inconclusive, with the enthusiasm for applying linguistic operations to music often falling short of projected aims (see Feld 1974; Powers 1980). More recently Robert Walser argues that the lack of fit between linguistic theory and musical practice stems from a friction between ethnomusicology's broad interests in culture and the "very satisfying intuitions we gain from ethnography, listening to music, and performing it" on the one hand ,and the dominant philosophical tradition, which informs much linguistic theory, that takes "the understanding of all meaning as abstract and propositional" (Walser 1991, 118). Walser (ibid.) suggests Mark Johnson's linguistic theory of image schemata, which connects meaning with patterns of activity, as an alternative as it offers a better fit for ethnomusicology, showing image schemata to be central to meaningfulness (Johnson 1987). "In order for us to have meaningful connected experiences that we can comprehend and reason about," Johnson states, "there must be pattern and order to our actions, perceptions, and conceptions. *A schema is a recurrent pattern, shape, and regularity in, or of, the ongoing ordering activities.* These patterns emerge as meaningful structures for us chiefly at the level of our bodily movements through space, our manipulation of objects, and our perceptual interactions" [emphasis original] (1987, 29). Importantly, metaphor links these patterns of bodily activity to language, behavior, and musical practice.

The importance of metaphors in the conceptualization of musics and musical behaviors has been established in ethnomusicology, especially in the work of Steven Feld with the Kaluli of Bosavi, Papua New Guinea (1982a; 1982b). Metaphors, as used in this work, are not just poetic figures of speech in which something is represented in the terms of another, but are essential to these musicians' "ordinary conceptual system," as George Lakoff and Mark Johnson argue, fundamental to both thought and action (1980, 3). George Lakoff argues elsewhere that metaphor must be viewed as more than mere figure of speech, a point that warrants reinforcement. He states that "the locus of metaphor is not in language at all, but in the way we conceptualize one mental domain in terms of another. The general theory of metaphor is given by characterizing such cross-domain mappings. And in the process, everyday abstract concepts like time, states, change, causation, and purpose also turn out to be metaphorical" (1993, 203).

Musicianship

Metaphor and image schemata, the patterns of performance and their connection to specific technological adaptations, create meaning for New York rock guitarists. Michael Reddy's general metaphor cited above—communication as a conduit—applied to the musician's statement "too many knobs between the guitar and the amp's speaker" integrates several metaphors for music: (1) musical ideas, and their associated meanings, are objects (ideas are objects); (2) musical "gestures" are containers (sounds are containers); and (3) communication is sending. Thus musical objects, held in the sound-performance containers created through guitar performance, move through the physical conduit of the electronic patch cords, through the sound-effects equipment, to the amplifier, and ultimately via sound waves to the audience. The activities of performance and the linear course formed by the physical connections between musician, instrument, and audience form image schemata that reinforce the communication as conduit metaphor—in effect, evidence of its actuality.[3]

The configuration of the components along musicians' physical and metaphorical conduits and their musical result are of foremost concern for rockers. A musician's rig—the assembled musical equipment—and the ability to make music with this array of electronic technologies constitute an important part of the collective lore of rock musicians. Such lore and associated activities have deep connections with the context in which rock musicians develop their performance skills. It begins with listening to and imitating rock recordings, acquiring an initial repertory and a sense of what constitutes good rock sound, what Stith Bennett in his study of rock "copy" bands in Colorado calls a "recording consciousness" (1980, 126). This lore is refined through a musician's experiences in rock bands. Rock bands are special institutions for rock musicians, a theme I have advanced elsewhere (1991). Publicly bands are a collective of individuals united in music performance, a ritual that, among other things, legitimatizes its members as rock musicians. However, in their numerous hours of rehearsal, bands also function as educational forums, as rock master classes where musical techniques are developed and skills are honed through interaction with the other musicians of the bands (Gay 1991, 63–187).

Musical instruments are, in one sense, "technological extensions to the sound producing capabilities and kinetic expressions of the human body" (Gay 1997). The ability to manipulate this technology in a culturally relevant manner is essential to performance and musicianship. For rock musicians, this importance is especially emphasized. Although often overlooked in definitions of musicianship, the knowledge base and skills necessary to create this music hold few rivals in technological complexity (c.f. McClary 1989, 79). The control of the distortion (and thus timbre) of the guitar, for instance, requires sophisticated reconstructions of Marshall "combo" amplifiers to create "hot-wired" amps that attenuate the amount of electronic signal sent to the speakers with a "power soak" while overdriving the amp's tubes, making them overheat in order to increase distortion but not volume (Jimbo Walsh, personal communication 1994). Yet rockers continue to manage the distance of their musical conduit, concerned, even skeptical about the use and misuse of technology. "I've just gotten my own little distortion box now to use for effect, a Turbo-Rat," states Rich Turnbull. "I just want that extra little crunch or kind of growl to a particular sound. And I don't really use it that much. Only when I have a particular little lead part that I might want to stand out a little bit. Because I think you can really over-rely on [effects] boxes. And you know, you see bands and there's a guitarist that's got six things lined up in a row and he spends more time stomping on his different pedals and everything" (personal communication 1989).

A musician's dependence upon technologies to communicate and to authenticate musicianship is verified by the circumstances of singers within rock bands. Singers who are not also instrumentalists have limited authority in the creation of a band's music, often restricted to the role of spectator. That is, despite their importance during performance in communicating directly with an audience, in delivering a band's verbal message through song lyrics and in fronting the band between songs, singers almost inevitably find themselves excluded from the otherwise inclusive and hands-on composition process of rock songs. Tellingly, singers have virtually no status within the social structure of a band: as "singers" they are not regarded as "musicians" (Gay 1991, 145–186, 208–225).

Though a musician's gear is the topic of endless deliberation and concern, the measure of musical skill and social status is not found solely in technological configurations, but also in their musical use. Technical skill and musicianship for most New York rockers is not just, say, playing fastest, or loudest, or even the most "artfully," but demonstrating authority over the technology by making it less an extension to one's body than part of the body itself. The rock guitarist critique of "too many knobs" and the communication-as-conduit metaphor that began this discussion suggests that the closer the musical instrument is to becoming part of body the better, for the "feel" of the guitar connects directly to the "feeling," the meaningful content, communicated by the musician. Shorten the conduit, enhance the communication. Musical expression, then, obstructed by the technology, rather than controlled by the musician, not only obscures communication with an audience but also disconnects the musical instrument from the rocker.[4]

The importance of the unity between the musician and technology is seen in the way rockers define themselves and others in relation to musical sound. Musicians commonly say they seek to create unique sound signatures through the configurations of their equipment, often making more of the technologies than performance style. Tim Harris, of the band Antietam, links the accomplishments of his partner Tara Key with this factor. "Tara's really developed her setup," Tim says, "... [with] a Mesa Boogie amp and a Jazz Chorus running on stereo at the same time with a certain figuration of pedals and a Les Paul guitar ... she gets a real distorted sound that's pretty *recognizable Tara*" (personal communication 1992; my emphasis).

Thus for rockers the concept of "musician" is a culturally defined construct that merges technology and performance. In an extreme view, tethered to his or her equipment, dependent upon the technology to communicate, recognized by its "voice," not able to function—a nonmusician—without its support, the rock musician exists as cyborg, a hybrid of human and machine.

Affiliation and Alienation

For any constellation of technologies there is a myriad of possibilities in its control and musical use. The musical adoption of technologies rarely occurs as straightforwardly as manufacturers intend. Musicians routinely transform or circumvent the original design of an instrument or component to suit needs or preferred concepts of sound. Hot-wired Marshall amps allow highly distorted guitar sound at lower volumes, something not envisioned by the manufacturer, but effective musically, and in New York City less offensive to unsympathetic neighbors or rock rehearsal-studio managers concerned with noise pollution ordinances.

The proper musical use and meaning of technology are contested matters, with one musician's obstruction of communication another's enhancement. Just as the technologies that transmit the guitarist's electronic signals metaphorically connect the musician to the audience and signifies categories of communication—open, obstructed, real, deceitful, and so on—they also connect one musician to others of similar caste while segregating these rockers from other groups. The disagreement on musical sound—"too many knobs between the guitar and the amp's speaker"—thus disassociates one guitarist from the other. In such rituals of daily life, technologies help define difference for musics, musicians, and audiences.

New York rock bands exist in an inordinately competitive world; Rich Turnbull of the band Big Fence compares his band's struggles to a fierce Darwinian fight for survival within a food chain of competing rock bands (Gay 1991, 54; Turnbull personal communication 1989). In this world, difference, in music-sound or performance-style, real or feigned, prevails as an important means to make yourself and your band noticed among the hundreds active in the city. Considerations of difference illustrate rock musicians' sense of their locality more broadly too. Among local New York rock musicians, for whom live performance is a more significant expressive mode than recordings, genre distinctions are technological and visual as well as aural. Guitarists who claim musical allegiance to Eric Clapton or Jimi Hendrix, for example, view the use of a Fender Stratocaster with a Marshall amp as "the eleventh commandment from God," while Telecasters are associated with a "country-twang thing" (Jimbo Walsh, personal communication 1994).

Larger contrasts in cultural adaptations of technologies convey different social domains and their respective musical forms. "If it sounds good without electricity, it's probably pop," Alan Lickt, of the band Love Child, says. "If you need the band it's probably rock," he adds, neatly dividing his musical terrain by technology (personal communication 1992). Other aspects of technology further distinguish rock music from other forms.

While there are significant counter-responses among local New York rockers, for many rap music often seems uninteresting, nonmusical, or just invisible despite its strong presence in New York. Rap and hip-hop music unfolds in Tricia Rose's book *Black Noise* as a vigorous and often contentious blend of African-American poetic and musical traditions and the "contemporary technological terrain" of the urban United States (1994, 63).[5] The "human beatbox" effects, "robot dancing," and electro-boogie of early hip-hoppers also present distinct responses to socioeconomic restrictions to technologies (see Toop 1984). Moreover, rap's polyphonic, multivocal expressions, today largely dependent upon digital sound-sampling and multitracking technologies from the recording studio, are far removed from the performance traditions and technological transformations favored among most New York rock musicians, who situate music creation in rock clubs rather than recording studios.

While rap and hip-hop musicians literally "play" the instruments of the studio, manipulating the digital samplers, sound mixers, and so forth, rock musicians often view the studio and its inhabitants as threatening, not necessarily part of their domain. Making recordings is an important activity for rock musicians, one that offers the potential for even more control of a band's sound. But the studio challenges these musicians with foreign technologies, new performance practices, and, often, unfamiliar studio personnel (Gay 1995). Among many rock musicians in New York, movement into the studio context and the use of its technologies represents the first step toward the "commercialization" and depersonalization of their music.[6]

Alignments of Power

The dependence upon technologies to create the rock "voice" matched against the objectives of better communication—to have less technology, "fewer knobs"—reaffirms that control of technologies is at the core of any definition of musicianship for rockers. That control, and with it power, is so centered suggests that while technologies are often restrictive in their cultural use, new technological configurations offer prospects for redistributions of power. Marked illustrations of such restrictions and redistributions occur for women rock musicians around piano keyboard and bass guitar technologies, respectively.

Rock music in New York centers on the electric guitar and related technologies. For most local rockers, keyboard instruments connect with musics outside rock: to classical music, through piano lessons as a child and the perceived weightiness of this instrument's repertory, or to the synthesizer-oriented sound of nationally-known dance and pop music. Keyboard instruments, moreover, are often seen as "girly," in part because the majority of keyboardists in New York are women. Keyboard instruments correspond for rockers to notions of pretentious art music or characterless commercial music, with women keyboard players regarded as nonrockers, nonmusicians, or worse, ornaments to the band's performance.[7] Mavis Bayton makes similar points in a study of women rockers in the United Kingdom (1989). Bayton describes social constructions that define specific music technologies as "masculine" and restrictive to women rock musicians. Building upon the work of Linda Dahl (1984) and Harold Abeles and Susan Porter (1978), Bayton maintains that "instruments are gender stereotyped... that both musicians and non-musicians share a sexual classification scheme, in which, for example, drums and most horns are seen as 'male,' whilst flute, violin and clarinet are seen as 'female'" (1989, 122).[8] Rock musicians in New York operate with similar stereotypes.

For many women musicians these instrument-based notions of "maleness" and "femaleness" remain active even as they confront and resist them as restrictions to their own ambitions as musicians. Carla Schickele, a woman bass player in New York, shows this conflict bluntly by stating: "it's probably pretty sexist of me, but it's a stereotype in my mind of like the guitarist's girlfriend who wants to be in a band but doesn't really know how to play anything, so they get her a whole synthesizer and she just plays one note. I've seen millions of bands where there's just a girl who plays a couple of different notes but it doesn't add anything to the music and doesn't seem to have any point other than her looking good on stage. That annoys the shit out of me" (personal communication 1992). For Schickele, the use of technology to falsify musicianship, or for other extra-musical purposes, is an affront to her own musicianship.

For women guitarists, sex-role stereotyping remains a factor that often colors their experiences with rock music technologies. Bayton reports that joining a band is often a woman's first experience with guitar amplification. "I think there is a tendency for us still to be scared of equipment: the 'black-box-with-chrome-knobs' syndrome," an unidentified woman guitarist in Bayton's study says. "I've obviously become very familiar with what I do but *I still don't feel physically as at one with my equipment* as I think most men do…It took me a year before I turned my volume up," she adds (1989, 303; my emphasis).

Yet despite the continuance of such stereotypes and consequent restrictions, women do have less derogatory and more empowering manifestations in New York rock. "Girly" keyboardist or "band ornament" are only two categories within a wide range of women's experiences. To say today that rock music equates simply with male-domination is a cliche and not wholly true for the context of New York. At one extreme there are women keyboard players in restricted positions, such as Pilly of the band Hide the Babies, who reveals her status when she states: "overall [I have] mixed feelings about keyboards and keyboard players…I mean, I would love to be a guitar player….I used to really try to solo like a guitarist" (pers.com. 1989). At another extreme there is Louise Parnassa, who for almost a decade booked bands at New York's seminal rock club, CBGB. Louise, as she is always called, is omnipresent for New York rockers and all powerful within the domain of the club. Both revered and vilified for her control of access to performance at the club, her office phone number remains "secret knowledge" even though it is known by most New York rockers.[9] Within these extremes, women in rock are engaged in an ongoing discourse about who and what they are.

Earlier I joined the notion of the cyborg with the social construction of the musician, drawing performer, performance, and technology together. In so doing, I borrowed the concept from Donna Haraway's article "A Cyborg Manifesto." Haraway uses the cyborg as "a condensed image of both imagination and material reality" to illustrate radical, historical transformations for women and feminism. "There is nothing about being 'female' that naturally binds women," Haraway writes. "There is not even such a state as 'being' female, [it is] itself a highly complex category constructed in contested sexual scientific discourses and other social practices" (1991, 155). While this concept highlights the significance of technologies for musicians generally, it also reveals the constructed and contested nature of women rock musicians. One construction that has transformed women's experience in rock has occurred around bass guitar technologies.

The bass guitar, a powerful instrument at the foundation of New York rock sound and essential to a band's performance, remains less consequential to a band's overall sound than the electric guitar, which has become an icon of rock. Tied broadly to rock and popular musics within the United States and beyond, the guitar acts as an aural and visual standard that embodies a range of musics and associations. Its associations range from that of swaggering heavy metal guitarists with their emphasis on power and control (Walser 1993) to the extremes of many punk rock musicians and their intentionally "incompetent" anarchic guitar sound and riotous performance (Laing 1985; Wicke 1987) all within a interpretive dialectic with experiences of earlier guitarists, especially African-American blues and rhythm and blues performers. Most local New York guitarists reject extremes of guitar performance and simplistic reductions that equate rock music with the guitar alone. Rather they stress the musical sound and performance of the whole ensemble, celebrating the band over the individual, and consciously constructing songs that highlight group contribution (Gay 1991, 188–226). Yet the guitar remains the dominant sound of New York rock: it conveys a band's most prevalent sound color. "Just being the only instrument that's doing any sort of melody…," guitarist Billy Zuckerman grumbles, "I've got to carry pretty much all the color of the sound. You can't fuck up. The audience will hear it" (personal communication 1989).

The bass guitar, however, holds musical functions important to the ensemble, in "playing more structural parts" (John Neilson, personal communication 1992) and in "moving the rhythm forward through time" (Robert Dennis, personal communication 1989).Some musicians view it as a more difficult instrument than the guitar: Lin Culbertson argues "in some ways it's harder, 'cause you have to be so steady, you have to be so locked in, where [with] guitar [there] is so much more freeform" (personal communication 1992). Still, for many musicians the guitar prevails over all else, and the bass appears less attractive and less important. Thus, bassists generally find themselves less politically powerful than guitarists within a band's social structure (Gay 1991, 145–168).

The social deemphasis of the bass by musicians makes it more accessible, and in particular more available to women. "At that time [when I began playing bass]," says Carla Schickele, "it was still relatively rare...to have a female bass player. So guys would really be thrilled about the whole gimmick part of it, but really wouldn't be expecting you to be able to play very well.... [and] I really couldn't play very well [at first]..." (personal communication 1992). Playing bass thus can become an important entry point for woman musicians into rock bands.[10] The bass guitar is also an instrument without negative associations for women, allowing for new configurations of meanings and relationships. Many musicians, men and women, find a powerful calling as a bassist. "I always feel more comfortable in a supporting role," says Dave Reddy. "I'm not sure what it is about me, but I don't like being out front" (personal communication 1989). For some women this aspect emerges as especially important: "You're in the back and are keeping things under control, you're not in the spotlight," contends bassist Sue Garner. "It's not like you have to be the [obnoxious] lead guitar player doodling around" (personal communication 1992).

Women's displays of technological control over the bass demonstrate their musicianship within rock bands and marks them as more than just "girly" or "ornament." Moreover, if musical instruments are conceived as part of the body in a cyborgian construction of musician, then instruments also augment a musician's sense of self. Carla Schickele, for instance, sees the bass as a "direct infusion into rock 'n' roll" that distances her from traditional "women's music," while extending her musical possibilities. There "is the wonderful juxtaposition between a low, gravelly bass sound and...a higher register voice" she says, adding, "I want to be able to sing stuff down there and I can't do it, so at least I can get down there on an instrument" (personal communication 1992). Sue Garner holds a similar view, linking bass performance with her own sexuality: "The fact that our voices are higher...there's something that feels really sexy about getting to play those really low things, you know, having that kind of low frequencies" (personal communication 1992).

In the best sense of Haraway's term, women bass players are musical cyborgs. While men often initially accept women bassists as a "gimmick," as Garner and Schickele's statements make clear, women exploit, adapt, and transform the technology and its cultural meaning for themselves. Thus technologies and their social reconfigurations offer a means for undermining stereotypes and changing alignments of power. If, as George Lakoff argues, metaphor relates one mental domain in terms of another, mapping experience and meaning from one familiar domain to one less familiar (1993, 203), then the woman-as-bass-player construction acts as a visual/aural metaphor upon which women access social power by drawing on the musical importance of the bass guitar.

Summary and Conclusion

Andrew Ross argues that technologies must be understood "not as a mechanical imposition on our lives but *as a fully cultural process,* soaked through with social meaning that only makes sense in the context of familiar kinds of behavior" (1991, 3). Cultural practices tied to technologies cannot be predetermined, nor can specific cultural adaptations and transformations be predicted. The relations between technologies and their cultural use are complex and interrelated, with uses and meanings constructed and contested through the discourse of daily lives, through image schemata and metaphorical shifts. For rock musicians in New York, such cultural processes are explicit and crucial.

Technologies wielded faithfully to culturally delineated practices draw social insiders together and celebrate certain social groups while excluding and restricting others. For New York rockers several levels of this sort of discourse occurs, from individual musicians seeking distinct signature sounds, to dividing the world into social groups and their respective musical forms, such as rock contrasted with rap. Moreover, while technological adaptations are often restrictive and regressive, culpable in perpetuating the stereotype of "girly" keyboard players in New York rock, new adaptations offer possibilities for reconfiguration, exploited to challenge prevailing alignments of power within social groups. The important presence of women bass players in rock exemplifies such a reconfiguration for women rock musicians.

Essential for musical communication, and perceived metaphorically as a kind of musical conduit, technologies connect a musician to his or her audience while, in effect, collapsing the technology and musician into a single entity. Such constructions of musician and musicianship, however, go beyond the domain of rock in New York. With musical instruments and performance practices viewed as technological adaptations, all musicians are constructs, heavily dependent upon the exploitation and control of technologies. Certainly today most vocalists would be included in this construction of musician, given the pervasive use of electronic reinforcement and enhancement of the voice within a wide range of performance contexts and genres, even for those deemed "folk" and "traditional."

Although not concerned directly with relationships between musical instrument and musician, Mark Dery questions what is "natural" to the body (1996). His copious examples—ranging from genetic engineering to cosmetic surgery and including everything from synthetic knee joints and heart pacemakers to breast implants and body piercings—point out ways in which people and machines merge. Dery's arguments show that such mergers, such technological reconfigurations of the body, have begun to define our existence. Yet reflection upon these complex relationships between people and machines, technologically based image schemata—sometimes fiercely invasive to the body, other times innocuous, often shrouded by cultural bias, and always saturated with meaning—has scarcely begun.

The relationship between musician and instrument, the merging of musical self with musical machine, seems especially mundane compared with Dery's biotechnical examples. Musicians do not exist solely, at least not yet, in some virtual reality or through a scientist's genetic engineering or a surgeon's medical implants or a writer's "cyberbole" (ibid., 247). The technological "unnaturalness" of the performance artist Stelarc and his skewered body hanging from an East Village building (ibid., 151–169) contrasts sharply with the "naturalness" of musician with instrument, whether a rock guitarist, a concert violinist, or a *voudoun* drummer. Yet the technological adaptations necessary for these musicians—the merging of musician and musical instrument—are more significant than those adaptations illustrated by Dery, representing more widespread and pervasive practices. Despite this fact, the culturally-based, technological transformations necessary for music performance scarcely warrant mentioning in most scholarship.

Ethnomusicology has mostly ignored cultural processes tied to technological adaptations or simply rejected newly adapted technologies as threats to canonized older ones.[11] Even Charles Keil, who has called for the ethnomusicological study of music technologies, often decries the use of newer technologies and the "technologized" performance practices of many musicians (1994). Keil, however, too easily dismisses many technological adaptations as "mechanical" contrivances dictated from above, in conflict with the on-the-ground interactive performance practices among ensembles, smoothing the out-of-timeness and out-of-tuneness of the participatory discrepancies (ibid., 96,107). The emphasis on technological control presented here, however, shows rock musicians engaged, even preoccupied, with maintaining their own sense of musical participation, not abandoning their selves to technologies solely conceived by someone else, but adapted and adopted to suit themselves and their music performances. For these musicians, rather than constraining musicianship, rock music technologies and their proper use encourage and validate it.

The technological adaptations for rock musicians thus argue against simplistic views of technologies as peripheral, neutral, or necessarily adverse to musical practices. Whether traditional or inventive, "natural" or "artificial," plugged-in or not, technologies mediate musical performance. Technologies, and the metaphors in which they are culturally secured, must not be invisible to ethnomusicologists.

Notes

1. An earlier draft of this paper was read at the joint convention of the Society for Ethnomusicology and the American Folklore Society, University of Wisconsin-Milwaukee, October 22, 1994. I wish to thank Rachel Carlson, Jimbo Walsh, Janna Saslaw, Janet Sturman, and the Journal's referees, whose careful reading and comments helped me shape and improve this article.

   While such technology studies offer insights into relationships between technologies and social consequence, their analytical frame delineates broader research objectives or significantly different theoretical directions than the present study. For example, Steve Chapple and Reebee Garofalo link technological developments and reconfigurations to broad expansions and contractions of popular music production as part of a struggle for market control by transnational corporations (1977); Stephen Struthers likewise places his emphasis on capital constraint in the development of recording technologies and minimizes human action in technological adaptations and innovations within the recording studio (1987); and Peter Wicke sees post-Beatles rock music as a product of specific, historically unique technological transformations wrought by the mass media of the 1960s (1982, 232).

2. Studies concerned directly with music technologies as lived and experienced exist not as a well focused research stream, but rather as a meandering flow with varying perspectives. For example, in an early ethnography of rock musicians in the United States Stith Bennett limits his examination of technological adaptations to cataloging rock instrument types and contrasting non-electric musical instruments—those dependent solely on "human muscular manipulation" to produce sound—with electric instruments, which give more control over sound and on a greater than human scale (1980, 50). Looking at the recording studio, Edward Kealy ties popular music production broadly to the historical development and adaptation of new recording technologies and to changing practices of recording engineers (1990 [1979]). On the other hand, Antoine Hennion assumes technological adaptations to be neutral to the organization of recording-studio personnel and the construction of meanings for a record-buying public (1990 [1983]). In more recent ethnographic research on women rock musicians in the United Kingdom, Mavis Bayton describes social relations that define specific technologies as "masculine" and restrictive to women musicians, a point to which I will return (1989). Important to my research here too are Robert Walser's study of heavy metal musicians, which takes technological innovations as crucial to heavy metal sound and social meanings (1993), and Tricia Rose's work with rap and hip-hop which, like Walser's work, views music technologies as cultural objects imbued with meanings through their use (1994; Dery 1994). Andrew Goodwin's seminal article despite its importance in arguing the ramifications of digital technologies for music-making, fails to extend to the level of musicians' experiences (1990 [1988]). Rather Goodwin builds up from Walter Benjamin's concept of aura to discuss changes in technologies and concepts of creativity. Peter Manuel similarly draws upon Benjamin and Theodore Adorno (1993). Not to discount the value of this research and its concern for the social implications of new technologies, Manuel's focus remains strongly tied to the cassette as a micro-medium artifact, an agent of affirmation or opposition by social groups. Such artifactual approaches, as Carolyn Marvin argues, "foster the belief that social processes connected to media logically and historically begin with the instrument... [with new media] presumed to fashion new social groups... from voiceless collectivities and to inspire new uses based on novel technological properties" (1988, 4–5). Similarly, the focus of my work here shifts from the artifacts "to the drama in which existing groups perpetually negotiate power, authority, representation, and knowledge with whatever resources are available" (ibid.).

3. Metaphors, as George Lakoff and Mark Johnson show, plot one domain of experience and meaning in terms of another. To make this clear, I follow the structure "target-domain is/as source-domain" established by Lakoff and Johnson (1980).

   For the musical version of this metaphor, musical gestures and the meanings they carry are viewed as limited to musical sound. Other aspects of performance, such as its context, fall outside this metaphor. As with Lakoff and Johnson's analysis, in the common usage of the communication-as-conduit metaphor ideas/meanings are independent of context and speaker (ibid., 11). For discussion of the communication as conduit metaphor's non-musical use see Reddy 1993 and Lakoff and Johnson 1980, 11.

4. This notion conflates the communication as conduit metaphor with several other related metaphors. Lakoff contends that concepts of quantity encompass at least two metaphors in the English language: "more is up, less is down" and "linear scales are paths." The latter, he states, "maps the starting point of the path onto the bottom of the scale and maps distance traveled onto quantity in general" (Lakoff 1993, 213–214). Rock musicians, and possibly others too, reconfigure and invert this complex of metaphor of quantity to refer to quality as well: if "linear scales are paths," and (1) good musical communication is the goal (purposes are destinations); (2) a musician's gear is at the heart of musical communication (means are paths to destinations); and (3) "too many knobs," the length of the conduit, affects communication negatively (difficulties are impediments to motion towards the destination), then distance-is-degradation (see also ibid., 220).

5. Other authors have pointed to a specific relationship between African-American culture and technology. Mark Dery sees a kind of "Afrofuturism" that draws upon black language, history, music, and myth to redefine technologies as liberating to African-Americans rather than restrictive. Noting the work of a few writers, painters, filmmakers, and musicians, Dery includes in this grouping Jimi Hendrix's *Electric Ladyland,* George Clinton's *Computer Games,* Herbie Hancock's *Future Shock,* the work of Sun Ra's Omniverse Arkestra, and much of Lee "Scratch" Perry's dub reggae (1994, 182).

6. Within academia, Steven Feld's notion of schizophonia—the dislocation of music from its producers—resonates with rock musicians' views about the effect of the recording studio (1994b; see also Schafer 1977). Further, Simon Frith's discussion of the industrialization of music corresponds to the views of many rock musicians in New York. Frith sees "multinational leisure corporations" as historically controlling access to technologies to "colonize" those musicians who lack access and to misuse technologies to misrepresent music performance (1988).

7. Constructions of meaning that equate women keyboardists with their instruments are presented through Johnson's image schemata. Similarly, Steven Feld uses the phrase "interpretive moves" to connect meaning to experience and behavior (1994a). For Feld, meaning is constructed by drawing upon the backgrounds of performers and listeners, their knowledge, experience, and attitudes. They organize "what the sound object or event is and what one feels, grasps, or knows about it" (ibid., 89). It is through the associational and reflexive moves of New York rock musicians that they mark keyboards and women performers negatively as "girly." This interpretation is not new, nor is it restricted to New York rock musicians: women and the piano have long associations in the United States and Europe. Arthur Loesser states that "the history of the pianoforte and the history of the social status of women can be interpreted in terms of one another" (1954, 267). Mary Burgan further argues that, for women in nineteenth-century England, the piano functioned as "an emblem of social status" providing "a gauge of a women's training in the required accomplishments of genteel society" (1989, 42). As with rockers in New York, such relationships and their meanings are often derisive. Judith Tick, for instance, sees the "piano girl" represented "in genre paintings or popular illustrations of the early nineteenth-century artists, in the literary world of music criticism, and in the polemical world of cultural feminism... [as] the archsymbol of the dilettante" musician (1986, 325).

8. Bayton argues further that those trained first in classical music, often as pianists, must overcome a "crises of technical confidence" when they discover that classical music training helps little with rock music. This training helps perpetuate a social structure in which "the (male) composer is exalted while the individual (female) player has low status" (1989, 240).

    In an ethnographic analysis of rock musicmaking in Liverpool, Sara Cohen does not confront the role of women keyboardists isolated from women musicians generally. She does state that "The women... involved in the Liverpool music scene were mostly backing singers and non-instrumentalists.... Even female instrumentalists usually found that they were not treated as equal members of the band by their male counterparts and were ignored during conversations and decision-making" (1991, 206).

9. In Roman Kozak's book *This Ain't No Disco* Louise Parnassa claims that Hilly Kristal, CBGB's owner, books the bands, while she acts as its business manager (1988, 129). New York rockers, however, doubt such statements. At the least, Louise acts as a gatekeeper between bands and Hilly Kristal, and limits access to the club.

10. "[T]he presence of women in rock has been surprising the unobservant virtually since the music was invented," writes Ann Powers, yet the sheer number of women involved, the variety of "visions" now available to women rockers, and their impact upon rock music has increased dramatically within the last ten years (1994). Significant in this change are women bass players, such as Tina Weymouth of the 1970s band the Talking Heads.

11. While not discerned as culturally-based technological adaptations in the sense used here, studies of musical instruments and their junctions to cultural practices have been important for ethnomusicology. As examples, see John Baily's study of the Herati *dutâr* of Afghanistan (1976), Thomas Turino on the *charango* of Canas, Peru (1983), or Judith Becker's study of the *gamelan* in Java (1979). Moreover, John Baily's research, among others, on the cognition of performance and the ways in which "music making involves patterned movement in relationship to the active surface of a musical instrument" (1985, 237) does show the importance of technological adaptations in relationship to music performance (see also Baily 1989).

References

Abeles, Harold F., and Susan Yank Porter. 1978. "The Sex Stereotyping of Instruments." *Journal of Research in Music Education* 26(2):65–75.

Baily, John. 1976. "Recent Changes in the Dutâr of Herat." *Asian Music* 8(1):29–63.

———. 1985. "Music Structure and Human Movement." In *Musical Structure and Cognition,* edited by P. Howell, I. Cross and R. West. London: Academic Press.

———. 1989. "Principles of Rhythmic Improvisation for the Afghan Rubab." *Bulletin of the International Council for Traditional Music, UK Chapter* 22:3–15.

Bayton, Mavis. 1989. "How Women Become Rock Musicians," Ph.D. Diss. The University of Warwick, Warwick, United Kingdom.

Becker, Judith. 1979. "Time and Tune in Java." In *The Imagination of Reality,* edited by A. L. Becker and A. A. Yengoyan. Norwood, NJ: Ablex.

Bennett, H. Stith. 1980. *On Becoming a Rock Musician.* Amherst: University of Massachusetts Press.

Burgan, Mary. 1989. "Heroines at the Piano: Women and Music in Nineteenth-Century Fiction." In *The Lost Chord: Essays on Victorian Music,* edited by N. Temperly. Bloomington: Indiana University Press.

Chapple, Steve, and Reebee Garofalo. 1977. *Rock 'n' Roll Is Here to Pay: The History and Politics of the Music Industry.* Chicago: Nelson-Hall.

Cohen, Sara. 1991. *Rock Culture in Liverpool: Popular Music in the Making.* Oxford: Clarendon Press.

Dahl, Linda. 1984. *Stormy Weather: The Music and Lives of a Century of Jazzwomen.* New York: Pantheon Books.

Dery, Mark. 1994. "Black to the Future: Interviews with Samuel R. Delany, Greg Tate, and Tricia Rose." In *Flame Wars: The Discourse of Cyberculture,* edited by M. Dery. Durham, NC: Duke University Press.

———. 1996. *Escape Velocity: Cyberculture at the End of the Century.* New York: Grove Press.

Feld, Steven. 1974. "Linguistic Models in Ethnomusicology." *Ethnomusicology* 18:197–217.

———. 1982a. "Flow Like a Waterfall." *Yearbook for Traditional Music* 13:22–47.

———. 1982b. *Sound and Sentiment: Birds, Weeping, Poetics, and Song in Kaluli Expression.* Philadelphia: University of Pennsylvania Press.

———. 1994a. "Communication, Music, and Speech about Music." In *Music Grooves: Essays and Dialogues,* by C. Keil and S. Feld. Chicago: The University of Chicago Press.

———. 1994b. "From Schizophonia to Schismogenesis: On the Discourses and Commodification Practices of 'World Music' and 'World Beat.'" In *Music Grooves: Essays and Dialogues,* by C. Keil and S. Feld. Chicago: University of Chicago Press.

Frith, Simon. 1988. *Music for Pleasure: Essays in the Sociology of Pop.* Cambridge: Polity/Blackwell.

Gay, Jr., Leslie C. 1991. "Commitment, Cohesion, and Creative Process: A Study of New York City Rock Bands." Ph.D. Diss., Columbia University.

———. 1993. "Rockin' the Imagined Local: New York Rock Musicians in a Reterritorialized World." In *Popular Music—Style and Identity,* edited by W. Straw, S. Johnson, et al. Montreal: Centre for Research on Canadian Cultural Industries and Institutions.

———. 1995. "From Technodependency to Technophobia: One Case for New York City Rock Musicians—or—The Luddite within Us All." Paper read at Preconference Symposium: Music and Technoculture, Annual Meeting, Society for Ethnomusicology, October 18, 1995, Los Angeles.

———. 1997. "Musical Instruments." In *Folklore: An Encyclopedia of Forms, Methods, and History,* edited by T. A. Green. New York: ABC-CUD.

Goodwin, Andrew. 1990 [1988]. "Sample and Hold: Pop Music in the Digital Age of Reproduction." In *On Record: Rock, Pop, and the Written Word,* edited by S. Frith and A. Goodwin. New York: Pantheon.

Gupta, Akhil, and James Ferguson. 1992. "Beyond 'Culture': Space, Identity, and the Politics of Difference." *Cultural Anthropology* 7(1):6–23.

Haraway, Donna J. 1991. "A Cyborg Manifesto: Science, Technology, and Socialist-Feminism in the Late Twentieth Century." In *Simians, Cyborgs, and Women: The Reinvention of Nature,* edited by D. J. Haraway. New York: Routledge.

Hennion, Antoine. 1990 [1983]. "The Production of Success. An Antimusicology of the Pop Song." In *On Record: Rock, Pop, and the Written Word,* edited by S. Frith and A. Goodwin. New York: Pantheon.

Johnson, Mark. 1987. *The Body in the Mind: The Bodily Basis for Meaning, Imagination, and Reason.* Chicago: University of Chicago Press.

Kealy, Edward R. 1990 [1979]. "From Craft to Art: The Case of Sound Mixers and Popular Music." In *On Record: Rock, Pop, and the Written Word,* edited by S. Frith and A. Goodwin. New York: Pantheon.

Keil, Charles. 1994. "Participatory Discrepancies and the Power of Music." In *Music Grooves: Essays and Dialogues,* by C. Keil and S. Feld. Chicago: University of Chicago Press.

Kozak, Roman. 1988. *This Ain't No Disco: The Story of CBGB.* Boston: Faber and Faber.

Laing, Dave. 1985. *One Chord Wonders: Power and Meaning in Punk Rock.* Milton Keyes: Open University Press.

Lakoff, George. 1993. "The Contemporary Theory of Metaphor." In *Metaphor and Thought,* edited by A. Ortony. Cambridge: Cambridge University Press.

———, and Mark Johnson. 1980. *Metaphors We Live By.* Chicago: The University of Chicago Press.

Loesser, Arthur. 1954. *Men, Women, and Pianos: A Social History.* New York: Simon and Schuster.

Manuel, Peter. 1993. *Cassette Culture: Popular Music and Technology in North India.* Chicago: The University of Chicago Press.

McClary, Susan 1989. "Terminal Prestige: The Case of Avant-Garde Music Composition." *Cultural Critique* 12:57–81.

Marvin, Carolyn. 1988. *When Old Technologies Were New: Thinking about Electric Communication in the Late Nineteenth Century.* Oxford: Oxford University Press.

Penley, Constance, and Andrew Ross. 1991. "Introduction." In *Technoculture,* edited by C. Penley and A. Ross. Minneapolis: University of Minnesota Press.

Powers, Ann. 1994. "When Women Venture Forth." The *New York Times,* Sunday, October 9, 1994, 32 H, 39 H.

Powers, Harold S. 1980. "Language Models and Musical Analysis." *Ethnomusicology* 24:1–60.

Reddy, Michael. 1993. "The Conduit Metaphor." In *Metaphor and Thought,* edited by A. Ortony. Cambridge: Cambridge University Press.

Rose, Tricia. 1994. *Black Noise: Rap Music and Black Culture in Contemporary America.* Hanover, NH: Wesleyan University Press.

Ross, Andrew. 1991. *Strange Weather: Culture, Science, and Technology in the Age of Limits.* London: Verso.

Schafer, R. Murray. 1977. *The Tuning of the World.* New York: Knopf.

Struthers, Stephen. 1987. "Recording Music: Technology and the Art of Recording." In *Lost in Music: Culture, Style, and the Musical Event,* edited by A. L. White. London: Routledge & Kegan Paul.

Tick, Judith. 1986. "Passed Away Is the Piano Girl: Changes in American Musical Life, 1870–1900." In *Women Making Music: The Western Art Tradition 1150–1950,* edited by J. Bowers and J. Tick. Urbana: University of Illinois Press.

Toop, David. 1984. *The Rap Attack: African Jibe to New York Hip Hop.* Boston: South End.

Turino, Thomas. 1983. "The Charango and the *Sirena*: Music, Magic, and the Power of Love." *Latin American Music Review* 4(1):81–119.

Walser, Robert. 1991. "The Body in the Music: Epistemology and Musical Semiotics." *College Music Symposium* 31:117–126.

———. 1993. *Running with the Devil: Power, Gender, and Madness In Heavy Metal Music.* Hanover: Wesleyan University Press/University Press of New England.

Wicke, Peter. 1982. "Rock Music: A Musical-Aesthetic Study." *Popular Music* 2:219–243.

———. 1987. *Rock Music: Culture, Aesthetics, and Sociology.* Cambridge: Cambridge University Press.

Part VI
Nationalism and Transnationalism

14

The Sonic Dimensions
of Nationalism in Modern China
Musical Representation and Transformation

Sue Touhy

Confucius said, "In putting at ease those above and governing the people, nothing is better than ritual. In altering customs and changing habits, nothing is better than music."

Quoted by Kong Yingda (574–648), *Liji zhengyi*[1]

Introduction

Over two thousand years ago, Marquis Yi displayed the character and power of the state of Zeng through a magnificent set of bronze bells. About five centuries later, scholar-officials in the Imperial Office of Music collected popular songs to assess the attitudes of the empire's subjects; two millennia after that, twentieth-century scholars in the Folksong Collection Bureau searched for the voice of the people of the new Republic of China (ROC). In the 1930s, urban Chinese voices sang rousing choral pieces in rallies held to mobilize the nation against foreign invaders; and in a remote Communist base area, musicians revised folksongs to awaken the peasants to the nation's plight and to their own suffering. Fifty years later, citizens throughout the People's Republic of China (PRC) woke up daily to loudspeakers playing "The East Is Red," which was followed by music to accompany the nation's morning calisthenics. And annually since the PRC's founding in 1949, a musical variety show has dominated National Day ceremonies in Tiananmen Square, simulcast on China Central Television (CCTV) since the 1980s.

Are these random musical incidents connected only by their geographic coincidence? I argue they form a piece, a monumental piece composed through the discourse and practices of twentieth-century musical nationalism that link them to each other within the organizational form of the Chinese nation. The vocabulary and contexts of the nation, in turn, reconfigure musical discourse and practice; new terms such as *minzu* (nation, nationality, race) label pieces in music books, and performances occur within designated national spaces.[2] Two-thousand-year-old song anthologies become models for collating the nation's current diversity, concerts commemorate earlier social-political movements, and national media daily broadcast a musical synchronicity that sonically encompasses the country in a staggering array of musical styles. Thus, the dimensions of twentieth-century musical nationalism are vast, spatially covering the width and breadth of the territory, and temporally spanning from the ancient past through the future and from morning through night. The sonic dimensions are at once vernacular, traditional, modern, and international, and they come together in a national soundtrack of epic proportions.

My claim of musical expansiveness stands in sharp contrast to particular prescriptive pronouncements and state-legislated restrictions on music in the PRC over the last fifty years. At times, the state has rejected the Chinese past and the foreign as musical sources unsuitable for its citizens, and official ideologies have rigidly defined categories of music that are or should be representative of the Chinese people. But sounds banned one year have been celebrated the next at state ceremonies in the nation's capital. Understanding the processes of musical nationalism requires a broad perspective of the time, people, and music under examination.

Conventional definitions often limit national music to that consciously composed using "native" characteristics. A standard dictionary of Western music history locates musical nationalism as a nineteenth-century movement "based on the idea that the composer should make his work an expression of national and ethnic traits, chiefly by drawing on the folk melodies and dance rhythms of his country and by choosing scenes from his country's history or life" (Apel 1975, 564).[3] And, as a few examples that follow will demonstrate, similar concepts have guided some discussions of twentieth-century Chinese composition. Here, however, I argue that the process of musical nationalism is not a matter of isolating a distinctive sonic-cultural emblem; the national cannot be heard as a timbral or structural feature inherent in musical sound. Instead, this analysis takes into account music associated with the nation through conscious design or the coincidence of circumstance. Links between music and the nation are forged, sometimes unintentionally, through the contextualization of music within the framework of the nation—its conceptualization, vocabulary, and structures. Nationalism may scoop up everything in its musical path, forward and backward, as music is repeatedly linked to the nation and performed within its sites.

This essay sketches out the broad dimensions of musical nationalism to examine the mutually transformative process of making music national and of realizing the nation musically. In the construction and reconstruction of the Chinese nation in different guises and under different political ideologies throughout the twentieth century, music has served as an expressive form of representation and as an experiential form of organization. It not only has symbolically represented nationalists' conceptions of the nation but also has provided contexts for the nation's people to participate actively in their performance. Musical eclecticism, thus, arises in part from the diversity of the people it is intended to represent and from the different aims of those striving to organize the national redefinition. Operating within ideological frameworks as diverse as the musical styles, nationalists have provided different musical answers to questions of what is Chinese and what should be national. The term "nationalists" here broadly refers to twentieth-century national leaders (and aspiring leaders), musicians working in national movements, and others involved—by inclination or occupation—in public discourse directed toward defining the musical nation and its future.

Although discussions of nationalism may be phrased in various terms and I have learned much from a variety of writers on nationalism (such as Benedict Anderson, Partha Chatterjee, and Eric Hobsbawm), here I look at nationalism as a transformative process intent on changing the ways in which people think of themselves and their relations with others and on fostering attachments to the nation. I focus particularly on what Clifford Geertz has described as the attempts to create the broader ties of nationalism, which involves the transformation of preexisting ties and identities into national ones.[4] When pulled into national arenas, local music may bring with it preexisting associations. But its meanings transform within the avowedly national contexts of performance as prior attachments to the musical sounds are transposed to affiliations to the national idea that they perform. The sounds—and, theoretically, the identities associated with them—then collapse into the national frame to be heard and felt as national.[5]

Geertz characterizes the images of nationalist ideologies as "cultural devices designed to render one or another aspect of the broad process of collective self-redefinition explicit, to cast essentialist pride or epochalist hope into specific symbolic forms, where more than dimly felt, they can be described, developed, celebrated, and used" (1973, 252). Chinese nationalists—of various periods and political affiliations—build upon preexisting musical associations to represent a broader identity. But I argue that certain qualities of music make it more powerful than the image in "altering customs and habits." Musical forms act as symbolic expressions of order and musical performances as active means of organizing people, drawing upon widespread beliefs that music can stir as well as depict emotions, can create as well as represent community. Going beyond the image or text, music adds a performative dimension—an active means by which to experience the nation, by which to feel and act national.

Such a broad sweep of time requires both generalization and selection, but attention to the vast dimensions of twentieth-century musical nationalism is needed to situate the growing number of studies of particular periods and genres in relation to ideological trends.[6] I have selected several cases as particular instances of the more general practices, discourse, and sounds of musical nationalism. Most of the examples deal with vocal music and folksong (as a complement to the literatures on instrumental and theatre forms), and many illustrate the tensions involved in constituting the nation musically. Although drawing material primarily from the PRC, this article takes into account other political configurations to which that nation has been connected, including imperial China. "Sound Ideas from a National Musical History" provides a brief historical background on concepts of the role of music in society and highlights models from the past that have been used repeatedly over the last fifty years. "Searching for the Right Voice" then examines twentieth-century debates about whose voice should represent the nation's people. Finally, "Music as Organizational Forms" concentrates on the organization of people through the social and participatory nature of musical performance and its on-going reproduction in the media.

Sound Ideas from a National Musical History

The identity of the nation stands in relation to perceived others, and the musical past is among the "others" engaged by twentieth-century nationalists. They construct broad temporal ties, representing the nation as an historical entity and as the legitimate heir to the Chinese empire and "its" territory. The terms "Chinese music history" and "the imperial past" are contemporary rhetorical constructions, of course. I use them here, keeping in mind that previous cultural-political entities were not always unified under an imperial order nor were they necessarily "Chinese" in the senses in which that term (and the national system) is understood today. Music history offers models for twentieth-century paradigms for the relations between music, politics, and identity. We may write today of the long history of Chinese state attention to music because this history is as much modern as it is historical. This section looks at sounds and ideas from the past that have been woven explicitly into the fabric of the present as historical precedents for contemporary action and as twentieth-century manifestations of the continuity of Chinese musical thought.

Filtering the past through contemporary ideological aims, musical nationalists have sifted through history just as carefully as they have made selective use of the foreign and local. In the PRC, for instance, cultural leaders in the 1960s—emphasizing the music of workers, peasants, and soldiers—criticized much of the musical past as feudal remnants of the ruling classes. The late 1970s, however, reopened the past for prudent musical mining. "Our legacy of national music is the product of two- or three-thousand years of class society.... Some represents the reactionary music culture of oppressing classes; some represents the progressive music culture of the oppressed classes"

(ZGYSYJY 1983, 4). Even the music of "oppressing classes" found a place in music textbooks and, by the late 1980s, became a part of the nation's music history to be performed in reenactments of imperial ceremonies for tourists.

Just as it encompasses the diversity of contemporary music cultures, musical nationalism sweeps the musical thought of the millennia into a unified frame of "Chinese music history," bringing music of diverse groups and states into the national fold by excavating their archaeological remains from the soil within the contemporary territorial boundaries. After their discovery in 1978, the bronze bells of Marquis Yi of the state of Zeng (ca. 433 BC) were displayed in national museums, and musicians in the 1990s performed music—reconstructed Tang dynasty pieces from the seventh century and the "Ode to Joy" reconceptualization of Beethoven's Ninth Symphony—on their reproductions. Although many consider nationalism to be a parochial movement and national music to be "a contradiction of what was previously considered one of the chief prerogatives of music, i.e., its universal or international character" (Apel 1975, 564), in practice both can be quite universalizing.

In twentieth-century China, much musical discourse takes no pains to hide music's associations with political goals. According to many authors, the musical-political connection is a continuation or revival of earlier Chinese philosophies. Although arguing that a multitude of structures and philosophies shape the actions of modern Chinese intellectuals, Barbara Mittler convincingly demonstrates the conceptual power of twentieth-century appeals to the melding of politics and music within the "Chinese tradition" (1997, 44–45; 38–55). Wu Yuqing identifies perspectives from the ancient past that guide contemporary practices, especially the idea that music "serves as a slave and appendage of government . . . [and] artistic method submits to political requirements" (1994, 968, 969). According to Wu, brought into the twentieth century, the traditional Ruist view of music "puts musical sociology (yinyue shehuixue) and musical political science (yinyue zhengzhixue) at the center of its framework," emphasizing the social and political functions of music (1994, 963).[7]

Like most scholars, Wu cites the Yue Ji (Record of Music) as a primary source for ancient theory.[8] Among the principles brought from the imperial past into twentieth-century discourse are related notions of music as an expression of identity and of the character of the state, the transformative power of music on society, and the correlation of musical and social form in the realization of order. Early anthologies such as the Shijing (Book of Songs) divided music according to states, and it is written repeatedly that Confucius (551–479 BCE) could discern a state's character by hearing its music. Moreover, music influences behaviors; just as some music embodies ethical qualities that ensure proper conduct and emotion, other music leads to licentious behaviors and results in social disorder.[9] Music and ritual are essential to the smooth running of human affairs, and the order of music could be used to effect the order of the empire. At the establishment of a new dynasty, for example, the bells were tuned in order to restore harmony to music and society.

Although I have come across no mention of retuning bells at recent Chinese Communist Party (CCP) conferences, the government of the PRC continues to display its power musically. Nationalists of all sorts have used music as a tool in the organization of China in the form of a nation. After the dissolution of the imperial system, most leaders saw the nation-state as the only viable model for China's future in light of the international proliferation of nation states, including those whose armies occupied Chinese land. For much of the four decades following the establishment in 1912 of the ROC, China was weakened by foreign and civil wars. Musicians and cultural leaders struggled for national transformation, often guided by the real fear that the as-yet-to-be-realized nation tottered on the verge of extinction. China needed a national anthem to rally the people in concerted action.[10]

Basic motifs in early musical nationalism included structuring musical activities through mass education and through a high level of organization (and reorganization) aimed toward broad-scale dissemination of ideas. To communicate their diverse ideas musically, early nationalists were practical and eclectic. Some of the same musicians who participated in the Folksong Collection movement (est. 1919) also reformed traditional Chinese music and assimilated foreign music (Wong 1991). The Society for the Promotion of National Music (Guoyue gaijinshe; est. 1927) encouraged "on one hand, taking the inherent spirit of China and, on the other hand, accommodating the foreign tide in order to break a new path" (ZGDBKQS 1989, 246).[11] When the very concept of nation was new, educators taught school songs (*xuetang yuege*)—a genre influenced by Japanese military and children's music and music taught by Christian missionaries (Stock 1995; Wong 1984)—in the newly organized public school system. Songs such as "Freedom" ("Ziyou"), "Man of China" ("Zhongguo nan'er"), "Song of the Ancestral Homeland" ("Zuguoge"), "Love One's Country" ("Aiguo"), and "The Yellow River" ("Huanghe") were composed to teach people what a "nation" consists of—its territory, people, and principles—and their role within it. And lyrics to "The Bitterness of Foot-binding" ("Chanzu ku") and "Strive for Women's Rights" ("Mian nuquan") educated people about their fellow nationals, their past suffering and their position in the new society.

Two of Xian Xinghai's cantatas musically link the national spirit with the nation's territory and struggle.[12] His "September Eighteenth Cantata" ("Jiu-yi-ba dahechang") commemorates the Japa-nese seizure of Chinese territory in 1931 and centers on the theme of heroism and martyrdom; and the massive "Yellow River Cantata" ("Huanghe dahechang") was sung by people struggling in the early 1940s and continues to be sung today. In 1995 a chorus of ten thousand people performed the cantata in a concert commemorating the fiftieth anniversary of China's triumph in the War of Resistance against Japanese invasion. The Yellow River is a persistent musical theme and often a metaphor for the nation, its beauty, power, and hardships. A contemporary evaluation credits Xian's eclecticism: "With the Yellow River as the background [the "Yellow River Cantata"] enthusiastically praises the glorious history of the Chinese nationality (*Zhonghua minzu*) and the persistent strug-gling spirit of the Chinese citizens (*renmin*); it bitterly criticizes the cruelties of the oppressors and the torment suffered by the Chinese people" (ZGDBKQS 1989, 729). Hoping to nourish a sense of belonging and concern, nationalists pulled on the nation's musical heartstrings.

The musical activities of the Chinese Communist Party (CCP), concentrated in rural areas during the late 1930s and 1940s, influenced the development of state policies in post-1949 PRC (Holm 1991; Kraus 1983; Tuohy 1988). A key strategy entailed forming core groups of music workers who undertook labor-intensive, face-to-face work at the grassroots level to encourage the people to participate in the society CCP leaders were in the process of formulating. At the Lu Xun Arts Academy in Yan'an (est. 1938) musicians revised local folk music with new ideological content, then brought it back to the people to disseminate, and organized musical troupes of all types to popularize the new music of the socialist state. The Party developed "a range of new ritu-als and ritual-like observances designed to involve the masses as participants in public life and to give expression to the values of New Democracy" (Holm 1984, 32). As Ellen Judd demonstrates, in the cultural redefinition in the 1940s, the performing arts offered the peasantry a "persuasive presentation of a new conception of the world" (Judd 1986, 31). With its central principle that art should be based on, reflect, and serve "the people," Mao Zedong's 1942 *Yan'an Talks on Literature and Art*—became the key strategic document.[13]

Socialist construction remained central in the musical rhetoric of the PRC, even as ideologies varied. In the 1960s, the slogan of the "three-izes"—revolutionize, nationalize, popularize (*gemin-ghua, minzuhua, dazhonghua*) music—guided official musical activities, and after the 1962 meet-ing of the CCP Congress, the theme of class struggle dominated (ZGYSYJY 1983, 1; Zhou Yang 1960; Miao Ye 1994). Most acknowledge the Cultural Revolution (c. 1964–1974) which followed as a devastating time for the nation's music and people; a limited number of model works, a few revolutionary songs, and recitations of quotations from Mao's *Red Book* played repeatedly, to be memorized and embodied.

In 1978, rebuilding the nation after the ravages of the Cultural Revolution began with meeting after meeting of cultural leaders who criticized mistakes of the recent past and suggested models for musical reconstruction ("Shenru jieping..." 1978). The Cultural Revolution (particularly Jiang

Qing and the Gang of Four) received most of the blame for cultural and musical chaos, but leaders also criticized earlier activities such as the 1958 folksong movement (ZGWYYSJ 1980, 333; Tao Yang 1981). Political and cultural leaders encouraged music workers to "correctly understand the relationship between art and politics" and repeated phrases such as "sift through the past to bring forth the new," "build on the traditional legacy of Chinese civilization," and "use foreign things to serve China" (quoting from Jia Zhi's speech at the 1979 Congress of Chinese Literature and Art Workers in ZGWYYSJ 1980, 336; see also Wang Yunjie 1983). To signal the government's support of changes in artistic policy, speakers included the nation's top leaders—Deng Xiaoping and Hu Yaobang (themselves only recently "rehabilitated")—and leaders in the People's Liberation Army, Women's League, the Communist Youth League, and in the Culture, Education, and Propaganda ministries. A flurry of publications followed as national music textbooks and anthologies were revised "to reflect the new period" (Wang Huihe 1984; Wang Jiachen 1984; Zhang Wen 1981; ZGMJWYYJH 1980; ZGYSYJY 1983).

While leaders, musical aesthetics, and perspectives of the nation changed over time, each decade offered its own conditions for attending to national musical construction and each provided models used by succeeding generations. The musical reorganization happened quickly and varied in its particulars, but among the national music movements over the last one hundred years, few questioned the *idea* of a Chinese nation; instead, the questions focused on what kind of a nation it was to be and which people were to represent it.

Searching for the Right Voice

Nationalist movements throughout the world devote a portion of their energies to the "voice of the people." The real or ideal vox populi conveys new national messages in vocal music performed in national contexts. In China much debate has centered on the questions of which voice of the people is the "right" one and which vocal qualities and forms best express the spirit of the nation. Joined with the "to the people" campaigns in the early twentieth century, song movements embraced two missions: to learn from and to teach the people. These missions reflect a tension found throughout the century in the dual goals of representing and transforming the people.[14]

When musical activists searched for the people's voice, they found vocal diversity; no one voice represented the nation as a whole, let alone met their goals for a national future. Because defining the voice of the people is tantamount to defining the nation, the activists had different opinions as to what such a voice should sound like. Should the nation's voice be an urban sound from the metropolitan coast or a rural sound from the inland provinces? Were the people to sound traditional, or modern, or "futuristic"—an ideal sound of a Chinese people united in the future? Some advocated maintaining a Chinese "essence" from the past, only to be countered by those arguing China needed a new, stronger voice to meet both nationalist and popular demand.[15]

Ideological issues combined with practical problems implicated in the nationalist process generally. If music was to foster national ties, nationalists needed a voice understandable to a broad range of people; moreover, they needed music to perform in the new national arenas. They came up with fascinating solutions that revealed the tension between the music they found and that which they needed. First, they could represent existing musical diversity by selectively preserving music they discovered but displaying it uniformly. For example, the musics featured in national day ceremonies might be performed in dissimilar styles (often revised for national consumption) and sung in distinctive languages (often translated into national speech), but difference was expressed within a unified national frame. Secondly, nationalists could create a unified voice through a process of vocal and perceptual transformation—that is, by modifying the voices of China and changing perceptions of particular styles so that people would hear them as national and as "mine/ours." Despite the intricacies of different views, the basic requirements for a national voice could be boiled down to one Chinese people could understand and accept as their own. Most musical activists have measured acceptability by the criteria of popularity, championing music popular among or capable of becoming popular (popularizable) among the people.

Folk music in particular has been discursively presented as "among the people" (*minjian*), but making it a national vocal symbol required musical and perceptual revisions among the very people leading the cause. Gu Jiegang, a historian who worked to reformulate the nation's history and destiny, wrote of the songs collected during the 1920s Folksong Collection movement: "It never occurred to me [before] that such verses were meritorious enough to put into print" (Ku Chieh-kang 1931, 67). The struggle to recognize the value of folk music itself is historicized as Duan Baolin refers back to the practices of two thousand years ago to counter those who derided the twentieth-century practice of collecting folksongs: "They do not know that the *Book of Songs* (Shijing) and Yuefu poetry they worship so much cannot be separated from folksongs" (1982, 118).

Through design or circumstance, musical nationalists heard and composed music in and for diverse contexts. Many composers based in metropolitan centers drew upon folk collections but also went to the factories to listen to urban workers, assimilating their music into foreign musical forms to compose Chinese popular and art music. The composer Nie Er wrote songs such as "The New Female" ("Xinnuxing," 1934, based on music sung by female factory workers), the "Pioneers" ("Kailu xianfeng"), and "The Great Road" ("Daluge," 1934) that became popular through their dissemination in feature films, records, and social-political movements (Tuohy 1999). Though newly composed, these songs met the criteria of popularizable. In the late 1930s, the Japanese invasion forced many musical leaders to the inland provinces where it was expedient to listen to the peasants rather than the urban proletariat—a musical move that paralleled an ideological shift in the CCP—and to emphasize recomposed local folk music, often in the form of choral arrangements.[16]

Most national institutions and media in need of music were carried out on a mass scale and/or were directed toward the masses. The 1930s social-political movements, aimed at mobilizing the masses to act as one against a foreign enemy, required music to foster concerted mass action. Unable to find preexisting Chinese musical forms for these new contexts—thousands singing together in rallies and demonstrations—movement leaders advocated new vocal music that would be "taken up by the people."

> It does not matter if they [the songs] are of low or high quality; all that matters is that they [the people] want to accept the task of national salvation and accept the songs of the progressive composers. . . . If we use orchestral music or instrumental songs in the present movement, their function will be nil; therefore, only if we create popular collective music can the masses be awakened and can we organize their force. (Sha Mei 1936, reprinted in Xiao Fang 1987, 235)

Mass political demonstrations required marching music, so musicians assimilated the musical marches of foreign nations and taught them to the people as Chinese within national movements.

Apart from needing music, public institutions and media functioned as educational settings through which to transform perceptions about the nationalness of vocal styles and to train the nation's singing voice. Schools provided vocal training; songs were also taught in the neighborhood cultural stations and through the mass media. In the 1980s newspapers published a "weekly song," written in Chinese and using a simplified notation system; television and radio programs then played that song at specified times each day throughout the week—a truly multimedia form of mass musical education. At times the dominant strategy appears to have been to make music popular and to create a "voice of the people" by sheer repetition. But the issue, if not always the reality, of "popular" and "popularizable" continued throughout the century and can be seen in recent efforts to modify traditional vocal styles like Peking Opera in order to accommodate popular demand.

Issues associated with the musical voice paralleled those of the spoken voice. Like their musical counterparts, those involved in national speech movements faced a nation of hundreds of Chinese "regional dialects" (not to mention languages of minority nationalities)—many of them mutually unintelligible—from which to construct a standard speech for national communication. Leaders hoped a common language would not only make it possible for members of the nation to understand each other but also to transform local, regional, and ethnic loyalties into national ones (DeFrancis 1950). Vocal music proved to be a vehicle for the dissemination of national standard speech, and that speech became the dominant language of the national musical voice. Except in those situations where dialects or minority languages were retained to accommodate local sentiment or to represent the nation's diversity (and/or authenticity), the lyrics of music in films, large-scale rallies, and schools have been sung in national speech. With the language problem more or less solved, the next question was determining which vocal quality should be used to sing it.

A discourse that could label as "national" any musical form with longevity in the Chinese territory and acceptance by the Chinese masses explained the nationalization of local, ethnic, and foreign vocal qualities. According to Miao Ye (1994, 1013–14), European traditional vocal arts (*Ouzhou de chuantong changfa*) "have sown new seeds in the territory of our country's several-thousand-year-old traditional vocal music...and by the 1930s and 1940s gradually developed as one part of the Chinese vocal arts tradition." Once assimilated into the musical lives of the Chinese people, the foreign could perform national functions as suggested in the pronouncement of the 1957 Nationwide Conference on Vocal Music Education: "Since entering China, the traditional European singing method has undergone a long period of development and already has begun the process of combining with Chinese national artistic tradition; it has been welcomed by the masses (*qunzhong*), has performed positive functions in the revolutionary struggle and socialist construction, and already has become a new form in Chinese musical life" (originally published in *Renmin yinyue* [People's music], 1957, no. 3; quoted in Miao Ye 1994, 1019). Whether using traditional European or Chinese vocal methods, singers can "give expression to national characteristics" (Miao Ye 1994, 1025).

The foreign retained its foreignness under certain conditions such as those immediately following the establishment of the PRC. One of the first problems addressed by the newly formed Communications Office of Musical Issues (Yinyue wenti tongxunbu) was "the singing method problem," nicknamed the "native soil" versus "foreign" vocal debate. According to Miao Ye, from a

> purely academic standpoint, most agreed that we should assimilate the best qualities of both....But in the particular situation, this [solution] was obstructed by the influence of the political atmosphere....Some west European countries were still hostile forces, therefore, something stained with the association of 'foreign' (referring to western Europe but not including east European countries that were at the time socialist) could be troublesome. (1994, 1015)

Musical leaders tried out various solutions to such vocal problems, sometimes to the detriment of their careers. The debates related as well to the general dichotomy of professional (the specialist, associated with a dominant intellectual elite) versus amateur (the people, masses).

The public discourse in the 1980s and 1990s about popular music and the singer Cui Jian illustrates how these issues of voice mixed together in practice.[17] One genre Cui Jian sang was Northwest Wind (*Xibeifeng*), a genre rhetorically and musically connected to regional Chinese folk music styles and, in some people's ears, in distinction to foreign ones. Thus, when they heard him sing Northwest Wind, some listeners attributed his rough vocal quality to music "based in the people." Others, however, attributed it to foreign influence because Cui Jian also sang rock 'n' roll (*yaogun yinyue*). Such seemingly small terminological intricacies and the flexibility of musical representation took on additional significance when representation of the nation's revolutionary heritage was at stake. Some state leaders, listening to lyrics about the Long March and Chinese "folk scenes," thought Cui's music was patriotic; others did not, and he was banned from the stage. As Mittler points out, however, "the right explanation at the right time was and is vital to politicians (and composers) in China" (1997, 62). The discourse about Cui Jian shifted once again when the state needed him only a few months later as a star performer to represent Chinese popular music in an international sports spectacle.

Music as Organizational Form

As it represents the nation's people, music also organizes those people, and their actions return to organize music—a mutual transformation that occurs through the ever-present vocabulary and structures of the nation-state. Representatives of the nation's people perform in national day celebrations; musicians compose for national movements and collect songs for national anthologies; and a musical soundtrack coordinates the nation's daily activities. Each setting offers potential for the reconceptualization of musical meaning and identity. Scholars have argued persuasively that identities are constructed through discourse, institutions, and actions that pervade our daily lives.

Neither transparent nor inherent, a Chinese national identity is a flexible one created within situated social-musical interaction; nationalism is not a passive construction but an active one. If music is a performed metaphor of the transformation to national identities, it is also performed for and by those whose identities are at issue. People practice their parts in groups and enact the abstract concepts of working in concert, of a nation made of parts contributing to a whole. The redundancy of symbolic representation and experiential action, in live social contexts and reproduced in the media, contributes to the musical modulation of identities.

We have seen several instances where musical representation collapsed into or expanded upon other identities (self- or other-defined)—ethnic, socialist, historical, gender—through structures that made national identities primary. But as James Fernandez reminds us, "Humans organize their social worlds into domains of belonging and . . . a great deal of human life is spent in maintaining, arranging, or rearranging these domains" (Fernandez 1986, 265 and xii). Cross-cutting categories at all levels, local to national, have organized Chinese people and music. If one strategy for creating broader national ties collapses identities and another expands on preexisting affiliations, the third strategy disrupts previous patterns of social interaction and creates new forms of identity, some of which are decidedly not national (but also subject to collapsing and expanding strategies). In this section I will focus on three types of organization that combine these strategies: the social organization of people through musical groups, the reorganization of the national music canon, and the musical organization of human action.

Though the 1930s musical activist Sha Mei worried that previous movements were undeveloped because they "lacked rational organization," we can see the full force of musical organization applied early this century in the wartime movements mentioned above. First, musicians and educators organized into small groups; these groups then organized people to take action and effect change—musical and non-musical—in the Singing for Resistance Against Japan and National Salvation Movement (*Kangri jiuwang geyong yundong*). From 1935 to 1937 in Shanghai alone, they established twenty formal music organizations with multiple subunits and initiated Masses Singing Societies (Minzhong geyonghui) that performed National Defense Music (Guofang yinyue) in schools and in the countryside (Sha Mei, in Xiao Fang 1987, 236; see also Huo Tuqi 1936, Wang Huihe 1984, 120, Xiao Fang 1987, 243–45, and Zhou Weizhi 1936).

The Chinese Nationwide Singing World Resist the Enemy Society (Zhonghua quanguo geyongjie kangdi xiehui; est. 1938) joined in mass demonstrations that spread to other parts of the country. In 1936, five thousand people sang in a Shanghai assembly to raise funds for the movement; and in October, a concert held in Northwest China raised funds to "relieve the people in stricken areas" (*zhenzai yinyuehui*). Music educators launched nighttime schools for female workers on the urban coast and organized the musical work of social-political transformation in the inland provinces.[18] These groups ranged in size from small-scale factory troupes to mass-scale societies and provided structures for organized social action and new terms of identity, such as "progressive composer" or participant (or martyr) in national survival.

Throughout the twentieth century, institutional structures and discourse have linked to the national cause myriad groups formed for nonmusical reasons as well. Agricultural collectives, neighborhood associations, women's leagues, and sports teams have become sites for the construction of identities and for musical organization. The People's Liberation Army sponsors its own musicians, as do local factories and "masses cultural centers." Since the early 1950s, the Ministry of Culture and other government offices have sponsored centers for education, the arts, and entertainment—"masses stations" in villages and cultural palaces in large cities. Identified by their "unit" (work, leisure, or place affiliation), people practice together, establishing new forms of interaction with their fellow members.

In an apparent contradiction, however, much of the national is organized through the local. Although parallel local organizations exist throughout the country and perform together (or against each other) in national festivals, local loyalties remain strong and are represented in national movements. Video footage from early twentieth-century mass demonstrations and from 1989 demonstrations in Tiananmen Square alike show people marching together in their groups and displaying their local and work affiliations on huge placards: "Nanjing University," "Beijing No. 1 Bicycle Factory," and so on.

New song compilations appear daily to meet the performance needs of these many organizations; many of them come out in multiple and multimedia formats and are reproduced in multiple venues. During 1995, the fiftieth anniversary of the end of the Japanese War, concerts of music from the 1930s and early 1940s were held throughout the country as tapes and songbooks were published for individuals and local groups. Audio tapes such as "Choice Songs of the War of Resistance Against Japan" ("Kangri zhanzheng gequ jingxuan"; Beijing chubanshe, 1995) and "Go Forcefully to Cut off the Heads of the Foreign Invader Devils" ("Dali xiang guizi toushang kan qu"; Yunnan yinxiang chubanshe, 1995) consist primarily of movie theme songs that also were sung in the wartime and revolutionary movements throughout the twentieth century, including those composed by Xian Xinghai and Nie Er (mentioned above). The same year a series of karaoke videos appeared in conjunction with the nationwide karaoke competition organized by the Ministry of Culture in 1995.

Along with old "standards" and new compositions, compilations of minority and regional folk musics draw from nationwide collection projects that began in the 1920s and continue to be conducted systematically through the 1990s. Compilers arrange anthologies according to different organizational principles—province, region, nationality, and genre—and follow common practices of identifying each song by the nationality and place name of the singer or song (and, less frequently, the singer's gender and the year of collection). Thus, depending on its published context, one song may be enlisted as a province's representative local product or as an expression of regional or ethnic spirit, and it becomes a part of the Chinese musical canon as each group contributes its song to the national musical anthology.

These national anthologies generate a reformulated canon of the nation's music—a canon that reflects the rhetoric of national inclusiveness. This "new" canon spotlights musical forms said to have been left out of the orthodox musical tradition of the empire. Such omissions include the music of previously underrepresented groups: folk music of China's peasants, popular songs of urban dwellers, women's musical forms, and songs by those in the territory's margins (physical or political). The canon contextualizes these preexisting or new classifications of music and people as national. Songs promoting new roles for women stand alongside songs about "other national issues," and the folksong from Hu'nan and the Tibetan epic become at once regional and ethnic symbols of national music. The inclusion of music of underrepresented groups, particularly of China's fifty five officially recognized national minority groups, intends to reflect the "multinational family of the Chinese nationality" and the official ideology of a unified multinational country.

This reformulated canon, moreover, plays in contexts explicitly labeled as national—often by the groups it is meant to represent—in performed enactments of a new national order. Nationally coordinated collection projects of the 1950s, 1980s, and 1990s have produced volumes of folksongs for every county, province, and municipality in the PRC, with the "best," or "most representative" songs making their way into the national anthology. National sites for performances range from Spring Festival variety shows broadcast on CCTV, government ceremonies, and national competitions. Festivals and programs such as "National Arts Week" (again based on earlier models like the first Nationwide Music Week in 1956) occur at the local level but are coordinated nationally.

National festivals and radio broadcasts form a national stage, real and metaphorical, constructed in modern China. And upon this stage musical troupes, many of them government funded, perform as representatives of their particular groups and of the rich musical heritage of the nation (Tuohy 1988). In performance, the representation is both socially constituted and displayed through the mass nature of the ceremony. The festivities surrounding the 35th anniversary of the founding of the PRC serve as an example of a repeated, multiple-venue, and multimediated grand display event.[19] In the capital of the PRC in front of Tiananmen and the vast array of dignitaries (themselves representatives of various groups), musicians from across China performed the music of "their" group or region. The diversity of people performing at the entrance to the Forbidden City testified to the transformation from ancient "feudal" times—when performances of the orthodox ceremonial music of the empire were confined to the emperor and a ruling elite—to the present imagination of inclusive representation and equality. These musical groups played simultaneously up and down Chang'an Street, bound together through at least three interpretive frames: first, of the parade; second, of the celebration of the nation; and third, of the television broadcasts of both carried through the nation and to overseas Chinese communities.

Indeed, as another form of national stage the mass electronic media reproduce these processes, blurring the lines between local and national. Local radio broadcasts surround the national news and music from other parts of the nation. These local songs and reports are heard as selections on the nationally syndicated programs "Folksongs of China," "All Over the Country," and "Frontiers of the Homeland." The weekly televised travelogues "Across China" and "The Great Territory of the Homeland" regularly broadcast feature spots on minority and folk musics; even when it is not the feature story, music accompanies the visuals of "Chinese scenes."

Once organized, the people and the music serve as symbols that represent the defined features of particular identities. Village cultural centers hold competitions in which their representatives are chosen to be sent on to the next highest level and ultimately to the national stage. The selected songs and performers are labeled as typical representatives of places and genres—the best crystallizations a group has to offer for national music competitions. In her analysis of local festivals, Beverly Stoeltje examines the dual process by which a person becomes a sign and then performs that sign (1988, 221–22), a theory that can be usefully extended to the Chinese national stage. Here the individual musician travels to the nation's capital as a living symbol of his or her group or region; while on the national stage, the musician is representative of and performs a particular identity and its representative music. Moreover, the musician returns to his or her locale replete with plaques and ribbons, as a national representative and is displayed as such in the village.

On the other hand, government attempts to create, or at least to display, unity through nationally orchestrated competitions often reinforce loyalties to non-national groups. Ethnic, local, and provincial groups—many of which were earlier organized or reconceptualized by the state—all have at stake more than their musical sounds. When it was announced that a Gansu-province singer won the 1990 nationwide popular song competition, articles appeared the next day in Tianjin city newspapers. Tianjiners, who had thought they had the competition in the bag, were even more incensed that the winner came from the "provinces" and a "backward" one at that. Those in Gansu, a province that usually fared well in folk or minority competitions, celebrated as the province took its place in the national popular music scene. On one hand, the celebrations and the complaints were carried out vehemently in municipal and provincial terms, which are simultaneously terms of the nation and might be explained as arguments among siblings using the metaphor of the big national family. On the other hand, they illustrate real tensions of "local nationalisms" and native place loyalties which the state works to quell (Ma Yin 1989, 21). As always there are forces and identities, old and new, other than nationalism at work.

Perhaps the most unique organizational form can be found in the national loudspeaker system that produced, in a very real sense, a national soundtrack. The dominance of loudspeaker programs—controlled locally but under overall national orchestration—has declined, although they still could be heard in work places and government units, particularly in rural or remote areas in the 1990s. Prior to the 1990s, however, loudspeakers were mounted on the sides of public buildings, in trains, and in nearly every collective work or residential center. A site of musical performance and discourse, loudspeaker programs organized the nation's activities. They broke up the day into aurally marked temporal units that followed a schedule: morning wake-up music, exercise music, national and local news; more exercise music later in the day, lunch announcements; silence during the "rest period," and so on. Portions of the daily schedule varied according to local conditions; in Xinjiang, where the sun rises later and where more minority nationalities live than in central China, the time schedule was adjusted and more minority music performed. But no matter where one was in the PRC, one could wake to the sound of "The East Is Red" and work out to the sound of a female announcer singing out repetitions ("one, two, three....") to the same piece of music every day. The pervasiveness and musical diversity of this national system were extraordinary. I remember seeing atop a solitary pole on a deserted dirt road in the Gobi desert a loudspeaker from which was played "Bess, You Is My Woman Now" (from George Gershwin's *Porgy and Bess*). The loudspeaker system reflected another state attempt to orchestrate the actions of the citizenry and to solidify national affiliations. And like the other forms of musical organization, this national aural soundscape was a pervasive and sustained performance of everyday life.

Conclusions

Countless other examples would serve equally well to illustrate the broad processes of musical nationalism that have accompanied the transformation of China. Indeed, that is my point. They are repeated, reproduced, reorganized, and interrelated day by day in diverse settings, working together to portray the temporal and spatial dimensions of the nation. They give concrete form to the abstract concepts of the unity, historical longevity, national destiny, and order of the nation through a soundtrack that permeates the daily life of citizens throughout the PRC. These musical activities function as performances of the social imaginary, "the creative and symbolic dimension of the social world, the dimension through which human beings create their ways of living together and their ways of representing their collective life" (Thompson 1984, 6).

These sonic forms give us a wealth of materials central to the process of nationalism as well as alternative methods with which to analyze them. With the primacy of language metaphors so common in cultural analyses, the nation has been essentialized in linear terms.[20] By privileging in our analyses the metaphor of the "master narrative of the nation-state," scholars have discovered or created coherent stories. But as Benjamin Lee has suggested, other forms of "publicness" are available besides print, and we may look for different dynamics in the "multimediation of mass publicity" (Lee 1993, 171). Within the new performance arenas of the twentieth century—the mass song assembly, school music courses, and national electronic media—the voices of new identities can be heard in concert with other voices.

In musical performance, citizens do not merely "read" the nation; they see, hear, and participate in it. The metaphorical "voice of the people" can be heard as a real, embodied voice. It might even be your voice, your body. But this is a system in which many voices, sometimes dissonant ones, are heard and through which the dissonant may be framed as consonant. The aesthetics used to judge whether they form a coherent piece, whether the correct vocal quality is being used and whether the voices are in harmony are in constant flux. If, as many have suggested, there is a master narrative of the nation, there is also a national soundtrack, one with multiple tracks laid down by producers with different aesthetic and ideological aims—and with some tracks out of their control.

Of course, at issue are questions about whose "social imaginary" is being performed, who composes it, and who believes it. Certainly the official ideology of the Chinese nationality (*Zhonghua minzu*) and its parallel in the ever-changing national musical canon does not always play out in practice nor in the minds of the citizens to whom it refers. While some may have explicit national goals, nationalists (or government officials) are not a consensual body; at any one point in time, the state has not supported much of the music mentioned here. Much music unintentionally becomes implicated in the nationalist process, a process which at times appears to be out of control—at least out of the control of a particular individual or coherent group. Attention to these coincidental multiple processes helps resolve the apparent contradiction between the broad dimensions of musical nationalism—inclusive by design or coincidence—and the exclusive practices of particular groups and periods (including restrictions on what constitutes the national in national music).

Prasenjit Duara writes of the difficulties of rescuing history from the nation-state and of seeking alternative forms through which to conceptualize history. Of course alternative frames for the interpretation of music exist. Many call Chinese popular music "Western," and it is disseminated through multinational marketing structures. Groups labeled by the PRC as national minorities are configured in alternative forms (many of which are national as well), and music used to reinforce a non-PRC identity. And the term "Chinese music" extends to music far outside the boundaries of the PRC (or the ROC) to overseas communities.

But even alternative or oppositional voices often make their point through the national frame, asking not "Is there an alternative to the nation?" but rather "What and who is representative of the nation?" and "Who gets to represent it?" And they call upon the same musical sounds, strategies, and sites to put forward their ideas. Filmmakers Chen Kaige and Zhang Yimou use Peking Opera, urban popular music, and rural folk music from the 1930s in such films as *Yellow Earth* (*Huangtudi*) and *Red Sorghum* (*Honggao-liang*) to provide the national "roots" or "people's voice." In Tiananmen Square in 1989 we heard demonstrators concerned with China's future (and labeled by the state as antinational) perform the "Ode to Joy," "The East is Red," "The Internationale," music from earlier social-political movements, contemporary Chinese rock music, and regional folksongs.

The temporal ties of national music history, the national voice, and the musical organization of the nation operate as central strategies in the representation of the broader ties of nationalism and its musical modulations of identity. On one hand, we can hear tremendous diversity and creativity in the music performed within the physical and conceptual frames of the nation. But the national frame itself, at least at the end of the twentieth century, is still a tight one. Its structure is reinforced by claims to past continuity, by widespread notions that nationality is the natural human grouping and primary cultural determinant, and by the international context of nations that make composing a nation and a national anthem a requirement. Can we imagine PRC athletes stepping up to receive their gold medals at Olympic ceremonies in an atmosphere of silence?

Notes

1. Translated by Cook (1995, 3). The quote also exemplifies the long-term intertextuality of Chinese texts; it is Kong Yingda's seventh-century quotation, attributed to Confucius and taken from the "Yiwen zhi" chapter ("a reworking by Ban Gu [32–92 AD] of the *Qi lue* of Liu Xin [ca. 53 BC–23 AD]") of the *Hanshu* (Cook 1995, 19, 76). I would like to thank the many colleagues who have offered valuable suggestions on drafts of this paper, particularly Du Yaxiong,

Robert Eno, Michael Herzfeld, Ke Yang, Ellen Koskoff, Beverly Stoeljte, Ruth M. Stone, Jeffrey Wasserstrom, Rubie Watson, and Zhang Yingjin.

2. "*Minzu*" may refer to particular nationalities or to the "Chinese nationality" (all nationalities living in the nation; Zhonghua minzu). *Minzu yinyue* (national music) is used most often in the PRC rather than "*guoyue*" a term used earlier in the century and today in the ROC. The *Indiana East Asian Working Papers Series on Language and Politics in Modern China*, edited by Jeffrey Wasserstrom and Sue Tuohy (distributed by the East Asian Studies Center, Indiana University), offers articles on shifting meanings of keywords of the Chinese revolution; see also Wang Lie 1983.

3. The Chinese music encyclopedia similarly associates musical nationalism with nineteenth-century European Romanticism, but the entry for the "school of nationalist music" (*minzu yue pai*) does not cover Chinese music (ZGDBKQS 1989, 457–59); "national music" (minzu yinyue) is discussed under the heading of Chinese music.

4. Geertz 1973, 259–63. He also calls this process "lumping," and "the aggregation of independently defined, specifically outlined traditional primordial groups into larger, more diffuse units whose implicit frame of reference is not the local scene but the 'nation'—in the sense of the whole society encompassed by the new civil state" (1973, 306–7).

5. Such mutually transformative processes occur through many modalities. Wu Hung 1991, focusing on architecture and monuments, demonstrates how activities staged in the frame of Tiananmen Square transform the square's meanings and vice versa. See also Rubie Watson 1995 and Lau 1995–96.

6. A small sample includes Brace 1991, Chao 1995, Guy 1999, Jones 1992, Kagan 1963, Lau 1995–96, McDougall 1984, Mittler 1997, Schimmelpenninck 1997, Stock 1996, Wong 1984, and other studies cited throughout this article; a more comprehensive list of relevant references, particularly those written by Chinese scholars of the periods in question, can be found in Tuohy 1988. Apart from primary and secondary written sources, contemporary materials are drawn from ethnomusicological fieldwork I conducted in the PRC during 1983–85 and in the summers of 1990, 1993, and 1995.

7. Wu calls this an instrumentalist philosophy in which the moral, practical, and didactic functions of music are overdetermined (1994, 964, 968). Although Wu uses "Ruist" ("Confucian"), the term seems to point more broadly to a cluster of political-philosophic traditions; and, although he defines *Zhongguo xiandai yinyue sichao* (literally, "Chinese modern music ideological trend") specifically as the leftist ideological trends of the 1960s and 1970s, he seems to allude more broadly to ideological practices in modern China.

8. The *Record of Music* was written no later than the Western Han (the second and first centuries B.C.E.) and took material from the Warring States period (403–221 B.C.E.); many consider it "to be the single most influential work on music in the Chinese tradition.... [It] continued to exert a great and inescapable formative influence on much of subsequent Chinese musical thought" (Cook 1995, 11). On early Chinese music philosophies, see also DeWoskin 1982, von Falkenhausen 1993, Zhao Feng 1983. ZGYSYJY 1994. Joseph Lam's 1998 book provides a richly detailed explanation of the realization of Confucian ideals within both music theory and ritual enactment during the Ming.

9. The music of the states of Zheng and Wei constitute "the standard example of licentious music" in classical texts: "The music of Zheng and Wei is the music of a chaotic age. It borders on dissoluteness (*man*).... The administration was disorganized, the people dispersed" (quoted from the *Record of Music* and translated in Cook 1995, 33, 32).

10. The PRC national anthem is a more recent arrangement of "The March of the Volunteers" ("Yiyongjun jinxingge") written by Nie Er and Tian Han in 1935 for a feature film; it was released on record and sung in political rallies during the 1930s. Many English-language works analyze different conceptions of the state and of China's future at the time; see Duara (1995, Grieder 1981, and Schneider 1971).

11. This idea—maintain the Chinese spirit or essence while borrowing foreign techniques and ideas—was widespread during the decades before and after the fall of the Qing dynasty. Discussions of national music (guoyue) were set within a vigorous debate on national studies and culture generally. The period's musical mix is described in ZGDBKQS (1989, 880–87) and Wang Huihe (1984); *Zhongyang yinyue xueyuan* (1987) contains over four hundred songs from the period, public school music, masses songs (*qunzhong gequ*), and choral works.

12. Xian Xinghai (1905–45) worked in urban centers and in the CCP-organized rural music institutes. He also composed "National Salvation Army Song" ("Jiuguojun ge"), "March of the Youth" ("Qingnian jinxingqu"), and "Children of the Homeland" ("Zuguo de haizimen"); see Kraus (1989). Other composers wrote commemorative pieces for earlier movements such as Lu Ji's "Song in Remembrance of the May Fourth Movement" ("Wusi jiniange," 1939). Many well-known musicians of the 1930s and 1940s died rather young and became commemorative martyrs in PRC music history.

13. See McDougall 1980 for a good English-language translation. Along with the earlier *Record of Music*, the *Yan'an Talks* is one of the most frequently cited works on the relations between music, politics, and society.

14. English-language works such as Hayford 1990, Hung 1985, and Schneider 1971 cover these social-political movements. Duan Baolin 1982 describes the establishment of the Folksong Collection Bureau, and Zhong Jingwen 1980 examines the Bureau's association to the May Fourth and New Literature movements.

15. Similar arguments have plagued the discussion of "national form" in music, literature, politics, and so on; see Cheek 1984, Holm 1991, 43–86, Mittler 1997, 269; 282–85, and Yung 1989. Guan Lin 1984 is an edited volume of articles on national style in vocal music.

16. Many songs of this period became "standards" in revolutionary anthologies of the 1950s and 1960s and patriotic anthologies of the 1980s and 1990s. The mass chorus, often sung in four-part harmony, was a typical form of the war-time movements and in later twentieth-century Chinese vocal music. The Central Musical Troupe (Zhongyang yuetuan). Central Broadcasting Musical Troupe (Zhongyang guangbo yuetuan), and Folksong Choral Group (Minge hechangdui; a multi-nationality group formed in 1952 as part of the Central Music and Dance Troupe) have become famous for their choral performances.

17. These issues are far more complex, of course, and names of and varying perspectives toward genres changed over time; see Brace 1991, Jones 1992, and Steen 1996.

18. Musicians and cultural leaders established small schools, training centers, and musical troupes such as the Gansu Youth Japanese War of Resistance Troupe in 1937 in the more remote Northwest region. While there, they collected and revised music to stimulate anti-war sentiment and to propagate new ideologies (Zhang Yaxiong 1940 [1986]).

19. The same can be said of any other National Day ceremony. In the PRC that year, I was able to keep track of the discourse and preparations leading up to the festival. On October 1, however, I was unable to go to Beijing because of severe travel restrictions (meant to keep people out of the capital) and, like most others in the nation, watched the Beijing ceremony on CCTV and participated in live events at the local level in Tianjin (most national-level activities in the PRC are carried out simultaneously in local contexts). The public square in Tianjin—somewhat of a local equivalent to Tiananmen Square—reproduced much of what was occurring in Beijing, albeit on a smaller scale.

20. Language metaphors have dominated the literature of nationalism studies, with a particularly strong emphasis on the written word in analyses of China. Benedict Anderson cites historical China as a sacral culture "imaginable largely through the medium of a sacred language and written script" (Anderson 1991, 13); see also Benjamin Lee 1993 on the centrality of the printed word in Chinese studies. Others, from Confucius down to scholars of the present, however, have pointed to the connections among music, ritual, and power in Chinese philosophies and state practices, a topic discussed briefly above. For a discussion of the equal importance of the enactment of symbolic forms in ritual, see also James Watson 1992.

References

Anderson, Benedict. 1991. *Imagined Communities: Reflections on the Origin and Spread of Nationalism*. Rev. ed. London: Verso.

Apel, Willi. 1975. *Harvard Dictionary of Music*, 2nd rev. ed. Cambridge, MA.: Belknap Press of Harvard University Press.

Brace, Tim. 1991. "Popular Music in Contemporary Beijing: Modernism and Cultural Identity." *Asian Music* 22(2):43–66.

Chao, Nancy Hao-Ming. 1995. "Twentieth-Century Chinese Vocal Music with Reference to Its Development and Nationalistic Characteristics from the May 4th Movement (1919) to 1945." Ph.D. diss., University of California, Los Angeles.

Cheek, Timothy. 1984. "The Fading of Wild Lilies: Wang Shiwei and Mao Zedong's *Yan'an Talks* in the First CCP Rectification Movement." *Australian Journal of Chinese Affairs* 11:25–58.

Cook, Scott. 1995. "*Yue Ji—Record of Music*: Introduction, Translation, Notes, and Commentary." *Asian Music* 26(2):1–96.

DeFrancis, John F. 1950 [1972]. *Nationalism and Language Reform in China*. Reprint ed. New York: Octagon.

DeWoskin, Kenneth J. 1982. *A Song for One or Two: Music and the Concept of Art in Early China*. Ann Arbor: University of Michigan Center for Chinese Studies.

Duan Baolin. 1982. "Cai Yuanpei xiansheng yu minjian wenxue" [Professor Cai Yuanpei and folk literature]. In *Minjian wenxue lunwenxuan* (A collection of articles on folk literature), edited by Zhongguo minjian wenyi yanjiuhui yanjiubu, 117–33. Changsha: Hunan renmin chubanshe.

Duara, Prasenjit. 1995. *Rescuing History from the Nation: Questioning Narratives of Modern China*. Chicago: University of Chicago Press.

Fernandez, James W. 1986. *Persuasions and Performances: The Play of Tropes in Culture*. Bloomington: Indiana University Press.

Geertz, Clifford. 1973. *The Interpretation of Cultures: Selected Essays*. New York: Basic Books.

Grieder, Jerome B. 1981. *Intellectuals and the State in Modern China*. New York: Free Press.

Guan Lin, ed. 1984. *Shengyue yishu de minzu fengge* (The national style in vocal arts). Beijing: Wenhua yishu chubanshe.

Guy, Nancy. 1999. "Governing the Arts, Governing the State: Peking Opera and Political Authority in Taiwan." *Ethnomusicology* 43:508–26.

Hayford, Charles W. 1990. *To the People: James Yen and Village China*. New York: Columbia University Press.

Holm, David. 1984. "Folk Art as Propaganda: The *Yangge* Movement in Yan'an." In McDougall 1984, 3–35.

———. 1991. *Art and Ideology in Revolutionary China*. Oxford: Clarendon Press.

Hung, Chang-tai. 1985. *Going to the People: Chinese Intellectuals and Folk Literature, 1918–1937*. Cambridge, MA: Harvard University Press.

Huo Tuqi [Lu Ji]. 1936. "Lun guofang yinyue" (On national defense music). *Sbenghuo zhishi* (Life Knowledge) 12 (April).

Jones, Andrew F. 1992. *Like a Knife: Ideology and Genre in Contemporary Chinese Popular Music*. Ithaca, NY: East Asia Program, Cornell University.

Judd, Ellen R. 1986. "Cultural Redefinition in Yan'an China." *Ethnos* 1(2):29–51.

Kagan, Alan L. 1963. "Music and the Hundred Flowers Movement." *Musical Quarterly* 49:417–30.

Kouwenhoven, Frank. 1997. "Barbarian Pipes Forever: Some Thoughts on Chinese Culture and Nationalism." *CHIME* 10–11:3–7.

Kraus, Richard Curt. 1983. "China's Cultural 'Liberalization' and Conflict over the Social Organization of the Arts." *Modern China* 9:212–27.

———. 1989. *Pianos and Politics in China: Middle-Class Ambitions and the Struggle over Western Music*. New York and Oxford: Oxford University Press.

Ku Chieh-kang [Gu Jiegang]. 1931. *The Autobiography of a Chinese Historian: Being the Preface to a Symposium on Ancient Chinese History (Gushipian)* (1926). Trans. Arthur W. Hummel. Leyden: E.J. Brill.

Lam, Joseph Sui Ching. 1998. *State Sacrifices and Music in Ming China: Orthodoxy, Creativity, and Expressiveness*. Albany: State University of New York Press.

Lau, Frederick. 1995–96. "Individuality and Political Discourse in Solo *Dizi* Compositions." *Asian Music* 27(1):133–52.

Lee, Benjamin. 1993. "Going Public." *Public Culture* 2:165–78.

Ma Yin, ed. 1989. *China's Minority Nationalities*. Beijing: Foreign Languages Press.

McDougall, Bonnie S., ed. 1980. *Mao Zedong's "Talks at the Yan'an Conference on Literature and Arts."* Ann Arbor: University of Michigan Press.

———, ed. 1984. *Popular Chinese Literature and Performing Arts in the People's Republic of China*. Berkeley: University of California Press.

Miao Ye. 1994. "Xin Zhongguo shengyue biaoyan yishu de fazhan (1949–1989 nian)" (The development of vocal performing arts in New China, 1949–1989). In ZGYSYJY, 1012–29.

Mittler, Barbara. 1997. *Dangerous Tunes: The Politics of Chinese Music in Hong Kong, Taiwan, and the People's Republic of China since 1949*. Wiesbaden: Harrassowitz Verlag.

Schimmelpenninck, Antoinet. 1997. *Chinese Folk Songs and Folk Singers: Shan'ge Traditions in Southern Jiangsu*. Leiden: Chime Foundation.

Schneider, Laurence A. 1971. *Ku Chieh-kang and China's New History: Nationalism and the Quest for Alternative Traditions*. Berkeley: University of California Press.

"Shenru jieping. . . ." 1978. "Shenru jieping Sirenbang xiuzheng zhuyi wenyi luxian, chedi susheng Sirenbang zai wenyi luxian de liudu" (Thoroughly expose and criticize the Gang of Four's revisionist line in literature and art and liquidate its pernicious influence). *Gansu wenyi* (Gansu arts and literature) 7:4–5.

Steen, Andreas. 1996. *Der Lange Marsch des Rock 'n Roll: Pop- und Rockmusik in der Volksrepublik China*. Hamburg, Munster: Lit-Verlag.

Stock, Jonathan P.J. 1996. *Musical Creativity in Twentieth-Century China: Abing, His Music, and Its Changing Meanings*. Rochester, NY: University of Rochester Press.

Stoeltje, Beverly. 1988. "Gender Representations in Performance: The Cowgirl and the Hostess." *Journal of Folklore Research* 25:219–41.

Tao Yang. 1981. "Guanyu 1958 nian minge de pingjia wenti" (Problems concerning the appraisal of the 1958 folksongs). In Wang Wenhua, vol. 1, 307–316.

Thompson, John B. 1984. *Studies in the Theory of Ideology*. Berkeley: University of California Press.

Tuohy, Sue. 1988. "Imagining the Chinese Tradition: The Case of Hua'er Songs, Festivals, and Scholarship." Ph.D. dissertation. Indiana University, Bloomington.

———. 1999. "Metropolitan Sounds: Chinese Film Music of the 1930s." In *Romance, Sexuality, Politics: Cinema and Urban Culture in Shanghai*, edited by Yingjin Zhang, 200–21. Stanford: Stanford University Press.

von Falkenhausen, Lothar. 1993. *Suspended Music: Chime-Bells in the Culture of Bronze-Age China*. Berkeley: University of California Press.

Wang Huihe. 1984. *Zhongguo jinxiandai yinyueshi* (A history of modern Chinese music). Beijing: Renmin yinyue chubanshe.

Wang Jiachen, ed. 1984. *Xinshidai de ge: Gequxuan* (A collection of songs of the new period). Beijing: Xinhua chubanshe.

Wang, Lie. 1983. "The definition of 'nation' and the formation of the Han nationality." *Social Sciences in China* 4(2):167–88.

Wang Yunjie. 1983. "Jicheng er bu juni chuantong xingshi; chuangxin er bu tuoli minzu fengge" (Carry forward traditional forms without being rigid; create new works without leaving national style). *Yinyue yishu* (Musical arts) 15(4):82–86.

Wang Wenhua, ed. 1981. *Minjian wenyi jikan* (A collection of articles on folk arts). Shanghai wenyi chubanshe.

Watson, James. 1992. "The Renegotiation of Chinese Cultural Identity in the Post-Mao Era." In *Popular Protest and Political Culture in Modern China*, edited by Jeffrey Wasserstrom and Elizabeth Perry. Boulder, CO: Westview Press, 67–84.

Watson, Rubie. 1995. "Palaces, Museums, and Squares: Chinese National Spaces.: *Museum Anthropology* 19(2):7–19.

Wong, Isabel K.F. 1984. "*Geming gequ*: Songs for the Education of the Masses." In McDougall 1984, 112–43.

———. 1991. "From Reaction to Synthesis: Chinese Musicology in the Twentieth Century." In *Comparative Musicology and Anthropology of Music: Essays in the History of Ethnomusicology*, edited by Bruno Nettl and Philip V. Bohlman, 37–55. University of Chicago Press.

Wu, Hung. 1991. "Tiananmen Square: A Political History of Monuments." *Representations* 35:84–117.

Wu Yuqing. 1994. "Ruxue chuantong yu xiandai yinyue sichao" (The Ruist tradition and the ideological trend in modern music). In ZGYSYJY, 962–78.

Xiao Fang, ed. 1987. "*Yi'er jiu*" *yihou Shanghai jiuguohui shiliao xuanji* (The Shanghai national salvation assemblies after the December 9th movement: A collection of historical documents). Shanghai: Shanghai shehui kexueyuan chubanshe.

Yung, Bell. 1989. *Cantonese Opera as Creative Process*. Cambridge: Cambridge University Press.

Zhang Wen. 1981. "Xinminge yundong yu minjian wenxue" (The new folksong movement and folk literature). In Wang Wenhua, vol. 1, 293–306.

Zhang Yaxiong. 1940 [1986]. *Hua'erji* (Collection of hua'er). Revised ed. Beijing: Zhongguo wenyi chubanshe.

Zhao Feng, ed. 1983. *Yue Ji lunbian* (A collection of articles on the Record of Music). Beijing: Renmin yinyue chubanshe.

Zhong Jingwen. 1980. "Wusi qianhou de geyaoxue yundong" (The folksong study movement around the time of the May Fourth movement). In ZGMJWYYJH, 1, 389–405.

[ZGDBKQS] Zhongguo dabaike quanshu yinyue wudao bianji weiyuanhui, ed. 1989. *Zhongguo dabaike quanshu: Yinyue wudao* (The Chinese encyclopedia: Music and dance). Beijing: Zhongguo dabaike quanshu chubanshe.

[ZGMJWYYJH] Zhongguo minjian wenyi yanjiuhui, Shanghai fenhui, ed. 1980. *Zhongguo minjian wenxue lunwenxuan, 1949–1979* (An anthology of articles on Chinese folk literature, 1949–1979). 3 vols. Shanghai: Shanghai wenyi chubanshe.

[ZGWYYSJ] Zhongguo wenyi yishujie lianhehui, ed. 1980. *Zhongguo wenxue yishu gongzuozhe disici daibiaodahui wenji* (Collected works from the Fourth Congress of Chinese Literature and Art Workers). Chengdu: Sichuan renmin chubanshe.

[ZGYSYJY] Zhongguo yishu yanjiuyuan yinyue yanjiusuo, ed. 1983. *Minzu yinyue gailun* (An outline of national music). Revised edition. Beijing: Renmin yinyue chubanshe.

[ZGYSYJY] Zhongguo yishu yanjiuyuan yinyue yanjiusuo, ed. 1994. *Yinyuexue wenji* [Collection of articles in musicology]. Ji'nan: Shandong youyi chubanshe.

Zhongyang yinyue xueyuan, ed. 1987. *Zhongguo Jinxiandai yinyueshi jiaoxue cankao ziliao* (Reference materials for the study of Chinese modern music history). Beijing: Renmin yinyue chubanshe.

Zhou Weizhi. 1936. "Guofang yinyue bixu dazhonghua" (National defense music must better develop a mass nature). *Shenghuo zhishi* (Life Knowledge) 12 (April).

Zhou Yang. 1960. "Women shehui zhuyi wenxue yishu de daolu" (The path of socialist literature and art). In *Zhongguo wenxue yishu gongzuozhe disanci daibiao dahui wenjian (Documents from the third national congress of literature and art workers), edited by Zhongguo wenxue yishujie lianhehui, 18–71. Beijing: Renmin wenxue chubanshe.*

15

Russia's New Anthem and the Negotiation of National Identity

J. Martin Daughtry

National anthems are often thought to embody the ideologies and collective self-images of the nations to which they are attached; anthems are, in the words of one historian, the "collective voice" of nations (Eyck 1995, xx). This view is complicated somewhat by the fact that ideologies and collective self-images are subject to the conflicting and ever-changing interpretations of groups and individuals within nations and as such are always conditional, contestable, and fluid. For this reason it is perhaps more productive to regard an anthem not as the static reflection of a monolithic ideology but rather as a polysemous text through which national identity is constantly being negotiated. Occasionally these negotiations break down; when the disparity between a nation's collective self-image (as interpreted by popular consensus or dictatorial whim) and its anthem's immanent range of meanings becomes too great, the anthem is often revised or removed. (To take an example from Russian history, no amount of creative interpretation could reconcile "God Save the Tsar" with the identity of a post-tsarist Russia, so the Provisional Government of 1917 was forced to discard it.) While this phenomenon commonly accompanies changes of regime, moments in which state symbols are changed during regimes are more rare, and as such provide a particularly productive point of entry into discourses on national identity. The much-publicized "national anthem crisis" in Russia in late 2000 was one such moment.

Old Melody, New Anthem

On December 25, 2000, Russian President Vladimir Putin signed a controversial law entitled "On the National Anthem of the Russian Federation." For most of the preceding decade, the Russian national anthem had been "Patriotic Song," an instrumental piece written by the nineteenth-century composer Mikhail Glinka. The new law replaced this piece with the melody of its immediate predecessor, the anthem commonly known as "Unbreakable Union."[1] Composed by a Soviet general, with lyrics written by a children's poet and personally edited by Joseph Stalin, "Unbreakable Union" had served as the national anthem of the Soviet Union for 46 years, from the middle of World War II through the end of perestroika. Soon after the law was signed, a new set of lyrics for the anthem was proposed and swiftly ratified. By New Year's Day 2001, the old melody of the Soviet

243

anthem had gained a new identity as "Russia, Our Holy Power," the second post-Soviet anthem of the Russian Federation.[2]

The movement to reinstate the Soviet anthem melody sparked a range of public reactions in Russia in the weeks leading up to and immediately following the passage of the new legislation. From the floor of the Parliament, politicians gave fiery speeches, alternately hailing and denouncing the proposed anthem. Newspapers published daily updates and impassioned editorials. "Itogi," a primetime TV news magazine on Russia's main independent network, devoted an entire hour-long broadcast to the issue.[3] Thousands of private citizens voiced their opinions on the Internet and in street demonstrations. Fascinated by the magnitude of the public uproar over a piece of music—and unable to travel to Russia to observe it firsthand—I engaged in several months of "virtual fieldwork," collecting and interpreting a large number of postings from individual and mass-media Web sites.[4] Most of these texts reflected two fundamentally opposed positions in the anthem discourse.[5] A plurality of Russians appeared to view the rehabilitation of the Soviet anthem melody as a positive move, one that allowed Russian citizens to take pride in their past and honor the considerable accomplishments of the Soviet Union, not least of which was its decisive role in the defeat of fascism in World War II. A smaller but much more vociferous group regarded the anthem as an unprecedented affront to the millions who suffered and died under Stalin and an ominous sign of a future return to the authoritarian policies of the Soviet era. According to most estimates, each of these groups comprised tens of millions of people. Never before in Russia's history had the meaning of a piece of music been contested so passionately. In the present article I chronicle this conflict and situate it within (1) the twentieth-century history of national anthems in Russia, and (2) the ongoing struggle to determine Russia's national identity.

Musical Nationalism and National Anthems

Musical expressions of nationalism have emerged as a central area of ethnomusicological inquiry in the last decade.[6] One area that has largely escaped our attention, however, is the articulation of nationalist agendas within precomposed orchestral works that employ European tonal conventions—i.e., "Western classical music"—the broad category into which most national anthems appear to fit (Boyd 2001). Despite our oft-heralded willingness to study all of the world's musical communities, we continue to be largely content to leave the analysis of Western classical music to our colleagues in musicology.[7] Western musicologists, for their part, have tended to equate musical nationalism exclusively with nineteenth-century European Romantic elites who, influenced by the work of German writer Johann Gottfried von Herder, began collecting folklore and incorporating it into art music settings in order to express a distilled musical sense of "Russianness," "Hungarianness," etc. (Taruskin 1996, 9–11). In the past several years, a number of musicologists (led most notably by Richard Taruskin [1996; 2001]) have problematized this narrow view of musical nationalism. Nonetheless, for the time being at least, when discussing compositions like the Russian national anthem it seems prudent to mention that the definition of musical nationalism as a nineteenth-century Romantic phenomenon is not implied.

For the present study, our picture of musical nationalism may attain greater clarity if we delineate two of the possible modes in which it is often articulated within Western orchestral and choral music. These modes are roughly equivalent in scope to the *species* and *genus* categories of scientific classification, and I have provisionally assigned the adjectival forms of those words to them. Through this lens, the nineteenth-century Romantic composers of Herderian bent can be considered producers of *specific* musical nationalism, i.e., music in which local folk elements (or Orientalized facsimiles thereof) are employed to impart the flavor of a particular ethnicity or nation. The majority of the world's national anthems, by contrast, index nationhood in quite a different way: by adhering to musical conventions established by their European predecessors.[8] In other words, we ascribe a nationalistic aspect to these pieces because they sound familiarly "anthemic." This type of musical nationalism can be called *generic* in the sense that it references nationalism as a supranational category, as a *genus* (or, given that we are dealing with music, as a *genre*).

In his insightful essay on anthems in the revised *New Grove Dictionary*, Malcolm Boyd singles out two compositions as providing the generic foundation for the majority of the world's anthems. "God Save the King/Queen," widely considered the oldest of all national anthems, has been a model for many anthems in Europe and the former colonies. This piece, with its "stately rhythmic tread and...smooth melodic movement" is the archetype for the anthem-as-hymn (Boyd 2001, 655). Indeed, in many languages (including Russian) the word for national anthem is borrowed from the Latin *hymnus*, thus underlining the extent to which anthems are seen as quasi-sacred vehicles praising either the monarch or the state itself. As Boyd further notes, an alternative to the anthem-as-hymn model is the anthem-as-march exemplified by the "Marseillaise" of the French Republic. This rousing martial piece, with its characteristic alternating dotted-eighth and sixteenth notes and double instance of ascending perfect fourths, has proven highly influential.[9] I will return to these two archetypes later, as each has inspired more than one national anthem in Russia's history. In the meantime, it is sufficient to acknowledge that most anthems—including all of Russia's[10]—participate in a largely European tradition of nationalist cultural products, a tradition that has been somewhat peripheral in musicological and ethnomusicological inquiry.[11]

Performance and Affect

Within this tradition, anthems can be distinguished from other cultural products such as flags and emblems in that they are performed, and usually performed collectively. Benedict Anderson, in one of his rare digressions into music, muses on the peculiar power of collective performance:

> There is a special kind of contemporaneous community which language alone suggests—above all in the form of poetry and songs. Take national anthems, for example, sung on national holidays. No matter how banal the words and mediocre the tunes, there is in this singing an experience of simultaneity. At precisely such moments, people wholly unknown to each other utter the same verses to the same melody. The image: unisonance. Singing the "Marseillaise," Waltzing Matilda, and Indonesia Raya provide occasions for unisonality, for the echoed physical realization of the imagined community.... How selfless this unisonance feels! If we are aware that others are singing these songs precisely when and as we are, we have no idea who they may be, or even where, out of earshot, they are singing. Nothing connects us all but imagined sound. (1991, 145)

Thus, anthems are used to generate a collective sentiment among the members of the groups who sing them. This mildly altered state, which Anderson calls "unisonance" and James Porter refers to as "ideological euphoria" (1998, 185) is not wholly unrelated to the ecstatic state achieved in many ritual situations. Take for example the healing songs of the Tumbuka of Northern Malawi, as described by Steven Friedson: "[m]any...Tumbuka relate the music to the batteries in radios.... One produces electricity through chemical reactions, the other produces heat through music and dance. Both are technologies in the sense that they are cultural means...of controlling energy for utilitarian purposes" (1998, 280). Tumbuka healing songs produce the heat necessary to cure a patient; an anthem produces the heat needed to affect the nation's birth and/or constant regeneration through the imaginations of its citizenry (cf. Anderson 1991). In this way, both genres can be seen as technology "in Heidegger's (1977[1993]) sense: a technology that reveals a world" (Friedson 1998, 280–81).

The heat that anthems generate is often so valued by state authorities that laws are enacted to regulate their performance (Mach 1994, 61). A recent presidential decree in Russia provides a current example of state control over anthem performance. The decree prescribes the audience's behavior when the national anthem is performed:

> During official performances of the State anthem of Russia those present are to listen to it standing, men without headgear. In the event that the performance of the anthem is accompanied by the raising of the State flag of Russia, those present are to turn to face the flag.... Any performance or use of the anthem in violation of this law, and also disrespect expressed toward the anthem will be subject to prosecution in accordance with the legislation of the Russian Federation. ("Zakonodatel'stvo" 2001)[12]

This legally enforced ritual dimension of anthems elevates them above the level of mere propaganda. The role that anthems play in coordinating the collective act of imagination that generates and maintains national identity gives them a special cultural status.

The Origin of "Unbreakable Union"

In the Soviet Union of 1943, power to confer such unique status on a piece of music rested solely in the hands of the General Secretary of the Communist Party, Joseph Vissarionovich Stalin. In the summer of that year, Stalin voiced his desire to replace the existing national anthem, the "Internationale," with a new anthem to inspire and invigorate the war-weary country. A contest was announced. Two young army officers, Sergei Mikhalkov (b. 1913), who had been a writer of children's poems before the war, and his friend, the poet Garol'd El'-Registan (b. 1924), collaborated on a set of lyrics. Amidst scores of submissions, their entry caught Stalin's eye. Before approving the lyrics, however, Stalin demanded a number of alterations. What follows is an excerpt from Mikhalkov's account of his first face-to-face meeting with this most intimidating editor. "In the dark vestibule between the doors we mechanically cross ourselves and cross the threshold of the state office. It is 10:30 p.m. . . . Directly across from us the Leader himself is standing with a piece of paper in his hands. We greet him: 'Hello, Comrade Stalin!' . . . 'Familiarize yourselves with this! 'he says sharply [handing them the paper with his corrections]. 'Do you have any objections? The most important thing is to preserve these thoughts. Is this possible?' " (Mikhalkov 1998, 6). Stalin made a number of changes in the lyrics before approving them. He then convened a commission to decide what melody best fit the text. Several famous composers, including Shostakovich, Prokofiev, and Khachaturian, submitted entries. Ultimately, however, the melody that pleased Stalin most was the tune that the lyricists had in mind when they wrote the text: "The Anthem of the Bolshevik Party" ("Gimn partii Bol'shevikov"), composed by the founder of the Red (later Soviet) Army Song and Dance Ensemble and a prolific composer of patriotic music, General Alexander Aleksandrov (1883–1946). In keeping with the martial ethos of the time, this piece adhered to the anthem-as-march model, closely resembling the "Internationale" and, to a certain extent, the "Marseillaise." Stalin decreed that Aleksandrov's piece and the "Internationale" switch places: the "Internationale" was re-designated as the official Anthem of the Bolshevik Party, while Aleksandrov's composition, with Mikhalkov and El'-Registan's lyrics, became the national anthem. The new anthem, which begins with the words "Unbreakable Union" ("Soyuz nerushimyi"), was given its first official performance on January 1, 1944 (see Figure 15.1).[13]

Stalin's decision to retire the "Internationale" in favor of "Unbreakable Union" provides us with a snapshot of his personal negotiation between official Marxist doctrine and Stalinist *realpolitik* (Marx 1945; Vihavainen 2000, 75–77). According to Marx, the nation-state is a manifestation of bourgeois culture that will ultimately be surmounted by a united proletariat. This sentiment

#	English Translation	Transliteration
	Verse 1:	
1	An unbreakable union of free republics	*Soyúz nerushímy respúblik svobódnykh*
2	Has been eternally welded together by great Russia.	*Splotíla navéki velíkaya Rus.*
3	All hail the united and mighty Soviet Union,	*Da zdrávstvuet sózdanny vólei naródov,*
4	Created by the will of the people!	*Yedíny, mogúchi Sovétski Soyúz!*
	Refrain 1	
5	Glory to our free fatherland,	*Slávsya Otéchestvo náshe svobódnoe,*
6	The reliable bastion of the peoples' friendship!	*Drúzhby naródov nadyózhny oplót!*
7	May the Soviet banner, the people's banner	*Známya sovétskoe, známya naródnoe*
8	Lead us from one victory to the next!	*Púst ot pobédy k pobéde vedyót!*
	Verse 2	
9	The sun of freedom glowed through the storm	*Skvoz grózy siyálo nam sólntse svobódy*
10	And the great Lenin illuminated our path.	*I Lénin velíki nam pút ozaríl.*
11	Thus Stalin has raised us, to be loyal to the nation,	*Nas vyrastil Stálin – na vérnost naródu,*
12	To work, and to do great deeds, he has inspired us.	*Na trúd i na pódvigi nás vdokhnovíl.*
	Refrain 2	
13	Glory to our free fatherland	*Slávsya Otéchestvo náshe svobódnoe*
14	The reliable bastion of the peoples' happiness!	*Shástya naródov nadyózhny oplót!*
15	May the Soviet banner, the people's banner	*Známya sovétskoe, známya naródnoe*
16	Lead us from one victory to the next!	*Púst ot pobédy k pobéde vedyót!*
	Verse 3	
17	We cultivated our army in battle,	*My ármiyu náshu rastíli v srazhényakh,*
18	We will wipe all despicable invaders from our path!	*Zakhvátchikov pódlykh s dorógi smetyóm!*
19	In battle, we decide the fate of future generations,	*My v bítvakh resháem sudbú pokoléni,*
20	We will lead the way to the glory of our fatherland!	*My k sláve Otchíznu svoyú povedyóm!*
	Refrain 3	
21	Glory to our free fatherland	*Slávsya Otéchestvo náshe svobódnoe*
22	The reliable bastion of the peoples' glory!	*Slávy naródov nadyózhny oplót!*
23	May the Soviet banner, the people's banner	*Známya sovétskoe, známya naródnoe*
24	Lead us from one victory to the next!	*Púst ot pobédy k pobéde vedyót!*

Figure 15.1 Lyrics of the 1944 Version of "Unbreakable Union."

is expressed directly in the "Internationale," the Soviet translation of which begins: "Arise, you who have been stamped with a curse: the entire world of the hungry and the slaves! . . . We will destroy this world of violence and then build a new world, [where] he who was insignificant will be all-powerful!" Stalin, who at the time was indisputably the world's most prominent Marxist, acknowledged the utility of creating a strong Soviet *national* identity: it was easier to convince soldiers to die for an imagined Soviet "fatherland" than for the more abstract ideal of international communism. In this sense, "Unbreakable Union" was the Soviet Union's first "nationalist" national anthem. The first verse of the lyrics establishes the image of a unified Soviet nation, albeit a Russified one ("eternally welded together by great Russia"). Additionally, several semantically loaded terms that contribute to this image are repeated throughout the lyrics. These include the Russian words for "union" (*soyuz*); "freedom/free" (*svoboda/svobodnoye*); modern and archaic words for "fatherland" (*otechestvo, otchizna*), and the pithy word "*narod*," which can be translated variously as "people," "folk," or "nation." All of these words either coincide with or are semantically linked to a small body of terms that some political scientists have labeled "key concepts of [Russian] nationalism" (Chulos and Piirainen 2000, 9). The tension between the nationalist impulse and the internationalist character of Marxism was maintained to one degree or another throughout the history of the Union, but never was it felt more strongly than during the Stalinist era.

A Change in Lyrics and in Ideology: "Unbreakable Union" After Stalin

Soon after Stalin's death in 1953, the lyrics to "Unbreakable Union" were removed by Nikita Khrushchev as part of his denunciation of Stalin and the cult of personality that had surrounded him. The anthem remained officially wordless for over twenty years, throughout Khrushchev's reign and well into that of his successor, Leonid Brezhnev. In 1977, the search for a politically acceptable alternative to the Stalin-infused text finally ended. That year, the co-author of the original lyrics, Sergei Mikhalkov, completed work on a revised set that matched more closely the Party's conception of the post-Stalinist Soviet Union (see Figure 15.2).

The 1977 version is printed on the left. Lines removed from the 1944 version are printed in italics on the right. The lines that replaced them are printed in bold on the left. The second and third refrains of the 1944 version were omitted from the 1977 version, in which the refrain is simply repeated.

#	1977 Version (English translation and transliteration)	1944 Version lines that were changed (English translation)
	Verse 1	
1	An unbreakable union of free republics *Soyúz nerushímy respúblik svobódnykh*	
2	Has been eternally welded together by great Russia. *Splotíla navéki velíkaya Rus.*	
3	All hail the united and mighty Soviet Union, *Da zdrávstvuet sózdanny vólei naródov,*	
4	Created by the will of the people! *Yedíny, mogúchi Sovétski Soyúz!*	
5	*Refrain:* Glory to our free fatherland, *Slávsya Otéchestvo náshe svobódnoe,*	
6	The reliable bastion of friendship among the peoples! *Drúzhby naródov nadyózhny oplót!*	
7	The Party of Lenin, the strength of the people *Pártiya Lénina, síla naródnaya*	*May the Soviet banner, the people's banner*
8	Will lead us to communism's triumph! *Nas k torzhestvú kommunízma vedyót!*	*Lead us from one victory to the next!*
	Verse 2	
9	The sun of freedom glowed through the storm, *Skvoz grózy siyálo nam sólntse svobódy*	
10	And the great Lenin illuminated our path. *I Lénin velíki nam pút ozaríl.*	
11	He lifted the peoples to the right cause, *Na právoe délo on pódnyal naródy,*	*Thus Stalin has raised us, to be loyal to the people*
12	And inspired us to labor and to do great deeds! *Na trúd i na pódvigi nas vdokhnovíl.*	
	REPEAT REFRAIN:	
	Verse 3	
13	In the victory of the eternal ideas of communism *V pobéde bessmértnykh idéi kommunízma*	*We cultivated our army in battle,*
14	We see the future of our country, *My vídim gryadúshee náshei straný,*	*We will wipe all despicable invaders from our path!*
15	And to the red banner of our glorious fatherland, *I krásnomu známeni vólei otchízny,*	*In battle, we decide the fate of future generations,*
16	We will always be selflessly faithful! *My búdem vsegdá bezzavétno verný!*	*We will lead our fatherland to glory!*
	REPEAT REFRAIN:	

Figure 15.2 Comparison of the 1944 and 1977 Lyrics to "Unbreakable Union."

In addition to expunging all references to Stalin, Mikhalkov's new lyrics significantly increased the salience of Lenin. The "great deeds" that Stalin inspired in the 1944 version (line #12) were attributed to Lenin in the 1977 version. And the climax of the refrain (line #7), which had previously foregrounded "the Soviet banner, the people's banner," was altered to "the Party of Lenin, the strength of the people." Also, the third stanza's commitment to victory through war ("In battle, we decide the fate of future generations"), relevant in 1944 but less so in 1977, was replaced with an affirmation of triumph through superior ideology ("In the victory of the eternal ideas of communism/we see the future of our country"). These changes can be read as part of the broad effort to erase the mistakes of the Stalinist era from the country's consciousness, and to provide a revised national image in which the lionized persona of Lenin, the country's founding father, eclipsed the personae of its present leadership. This new version of "Unbreakable Union" remained the national anthem of the Soviet Union until its demise.

A New Anthem for a New Nation: Glinka's "Patriotic Song"

The events leading up to the disintegration of the Soviet Union in December 1991 have been exhaustively documented and analyzed, and do not need to be repeated in detail here. It is sufficient to recall that by 1990 Boris Yeltsin had become the factual leader of the Russian Republic, which at that point was still nominally part of the USSR.[14] At some point during that year, it was brought to Yeltsin's attention that the Russian Republic was the only Soviet republic lacking its own anthem. According to musicologist Alexander Belonenko, the Russian president solved this problem "very quickly, in the traditional Russian manner":

> I unfortunately don't know who his advisor was, but somehow [Mikhail Glinka's] "Patriotic Song" ("Patrioticheskaya pesnya") was proposed....I was told that, [when the piece was officially played], Boris Nikolayevich [Yeltsin] stood up, everyone stood up. . . . Well, basically, with that volitional move it was decided that Glinka's song had become the anthem. (Rezunkov 2000)

That a work by Glinka should be chosen surprised no one. The historical setting of his first opera and his penchant for adapting Russian folk melodies in his compositions had earned Glinka a reputation as "the father of Russian musical nationalism" (Frolova-Walker 1998, 341–42, 350; Taruskin 1997, 25–47). Moreover, "Patriotic Song" exhibited the "stately rhythmic tread and . . . smooth melodic movement" of the anthem-as-hymn model that produced "God Save the King/Queen" and "God Save the Tsar." It was not the most obvious candidate among Glinka's works, however; the popular and majestic chorus from the epilogue to his opera A Life for the Tsar (Zhizn' za tsarya) had long been regarded as "Russia's second national anthem" (Rezunkov 2000), and had been proposed as a possible successor to "God Save the Tsar" back in 1917. Nonetheless, the die had been cast by Yeltsin, and two years after Russia became a sovereign nation, the Parliament ratified "Patriotic Song" as the Russian Federation's official national anthem.[15]

The Glinka anthem lacked lyrics, and submissions began pouring in from all over the country. However, ten years and over six thousand submissions later, the Russian government remained unable to agree upon a suitable text for "Patriotic Song." In the meantime, factions within the Russian Parliament had begun to question the appropriateness of the Glinka anthem, with some Communists and their allies advocating a return to the rousing strains of "Unbreakable Union" and others suggesting that a new piece be composed.

The most widely-reported indictment of "Patriotic Song" came from members of "Spartak Moscow," Russia's flagship soccer team. In an open letter sent to newly-elected President Vladimir Putin in the summer of 2000, the team urged him to find a set of lyrics for Russia's wordless anthem. According to several reports, the players felt that the lack of a "proper anthem" to sing at matches was affecting their morale and performance (Yablokova 2000). Similar complaints were voiced by Russian gold medal winners at the 2000 Olympics, who felt embarrassed to be the only ones whose lips did not move as their national anthem was performed at the awards ceremonies (McLaughlin 2000).[16]

A nationwide poll conducted on November 13, 2000, revealed that only fifteen percent of the Russian people supported the Glinka anthem ("Majority" 2000). Ostensibly in response to the popular discontent demonstrated by the poll and by letters such as those from the Spartak soccer team and the Olympic athletes, President Putin established a government commission charged with examining a number of options (including adopting a new anthem, writing lyrics to the Glinka melody, or resurrecting the Tsarist or Communist-era anthem melodies) and proposing a solution to the anthem crisis. He also made it known that he personally preferred Aleksandrov's "Unbreakable Union" melody over all others. The commission examined eight possible anthems, including a popular patriotic film tune from the 1930s, "My Native Country is Vast" ("Shiroka strana moya rodnaya"), and a song submitted by the perennial Russian pop superstar Alla Pugacheva. But, given the popularity and influence of Putin's administration, it was no great surprise when the commission announced its recommendation to reinstate Aleksandrov's melody (minus the Soviet lyrics, of course). The irony of this choice—replacing an anthem criticized for its lack of lyrics with a piece from which the lyrics had been stripped—was described by one critic as bordering on the absurd (Chudakova et al. 2000, 7). Nonetheless, the change was made official on December 8, 2000, when the lower house of the Parliament (the Duma) voted for the anthem, with 381 in favor and 51 opposed. Three weeks later, after Putin had signed the Duma resolution into law, the Duma approved a new set of lyrics, based largely on a version submitted by none other than Sergei Mikhalkov, now 87, the author of the original Stalinist lyrics of 1943 and the de-Stalinized revision of 1977. Much of Mikhalkov's first submission was rejected, apparently due to the fact that he had taken much of the first stanza from an ode to Stalin he wrote in the 1940s ("V novy vek so stalinskim gimnom" 2000). His lyrics were then altered by a government-organized committee. The official version, titled "Russia, Our Holy Power" ("Rossiya, svyashchennaya nasha derzhava"), reads as shown in Figure 15.3.[17]

#	English Translation	Transliteration
	Verse 1	
1	Russia, our holy power,	*Rossíya svyashénnaya násha derzháva*
2	Russia, our beloved [or "favorite"] country!	*Rossíya lyubímaya násha straná!*
3	A mighty will and great glory	*Mogúchaya vólya, velíkaya sláva*
4	Are your achievement for all time!	*Tvoyó dostoyánie na vsé vremená!*
	Refrain	
5	Glory to our free Fatherland	*Slávsya Otéchestvo náshe svobódnoe*
6	An age-old union of fraternal Peoples	*Brátskikh naródov soyúz vekovói!*
7	The People's wisdom, given by our ancestors—	*Prédkami dánnaya múdrost naródnaya*
8	Glory to you, country! We are proud of you!	*Slávsya straná! My gordímsya tobói!*
	Verse 2	
9	From the southern seas to the Polar regions	*Ot yúzhnykh moréi do polyárnovo kráya*
10	Our forests and fields have spread out.	*Raskínulis' náshi lesá i polyá.*
11	You are the only one on earth! You are unique—	*Odná ty na svéte! Odná ty takáya -*
12	Protected by God, our native land!	*Khranímaya Bógom rodnáya zemlyá!*
	REPEAT REFRAIN	
	Verse 3	
13	A wide space for dreams and for life	*Shiróki prostór dlya mechty i dlya zhízni*
14	Are opened for us by the coming years.	*Gryadúshie nam otkryváyut godá.*
15	Our faithfulness to the Fatherland gives us strength.	*Nam sílu dayót násha vérnost' Otchízne.*
16	So it was, so it is, and so it always will be!	*Tak bylo, tak ést i tak búdet vsegdá!*
	REPEAT REFRAIN	

Figure 15.3 Lyrics to "Russia, Our Holy Power."

One could criticize these lyrics for a number of banal phrases ("so it was, so it is, and so it always will be"; "you are the only one on earth") or for the almost comic alteration between formal, inflated language ("a mighty will and great glory are your achievement for all time") and language displaying what could be described as a New Age sensibility ("a wide space for dreams and for life are opened to us by the coming years"). Nonetheless, on the surface at least, the image of Russian national identity that is evoked by these lyrics could hardly be more different than the one created by the Soviet anthem. All overt references to the atheist Socialist state and the pursuit of communism are gone; in their place are lines describing Russia as "a holy country… protected by God." The personae of Lenin and Stalin are replaced by the anthropomorphized country, which is addressed directly using the familiar second person pronoun, "*ty*." The future of the country no longer promises "the victory of the eternal ideas of communism"; rather, it will bring "a wide space for dreams and for life." Critiques of poetic value aside, it would appear that the new lyrics provide an image of a radically new nation for Russians to imagine into existence. As a result, one might expect that the reactionaries would have more cause for outrage than the progressives. Of course, this was not the case: the Communists and other parties aligned with the government enthusiastically supported the anthem, while the liberals denounced it with one voice. In the final section of the present article I analyze several reasons—some obvious, others less so—why this occurred. Before doing so, however, let us examine in some detail the two principal positions in the conflict.

The December 2000 Discourse on a New Russian National Anthem

The cursory history above demonstrates the extent to which national anthems can be implicated in the advancement of new national ideologies. It seems that an important, even indispensable, way to erase the ideology of the past, be it the Tsar's or Stalin's or Yeltsin's, is through song. To pick up the metaphor of music-as-technology once again, the "heat" generated by Russia's twentieth-century anthems was used to encourage and coordinate numerous revisions of national sentiment. However, an anthem's heat is not all-powerful; no piece of music can fully divest citizens of their individual agency, forcing them to participate in the creation of a nation the character of which they despise. This fact is made abundantly clear by the widespread and vociferous protests that erupted in reaction to the Parliament's decision to reinstate the Soviet-era melody in December 2000. By examining a number of these reactions I hope to demonstrate that, as a technology designed to "reveal a world" of national unity and cohesion, the new anthem's effectiveness was weakened both by internal flaws and external schisms.

Having lost all of its sovereignty—and no small amount of its sway—over Eastern Europe, Central Asia, the Caucasus, Ukraine, Moldova, Belarus and the Baltics, Russia's geographic borders have shrunk to their smallest point in centuries. Numerous conflicts, of which Chechnya has been the most bloody, have challenged Russia's authority within its official borders during its first decade of independence. On the world stage Russia's severely attenuated stature has earned it the ignominious label of "former superpower." Domestically, the standard of living for the bulk of the population is low, life spans are short, suicide rates are high, clinical depression is rampant. It was in the context of these statistics that the Parliament voted to bring back the melody of the Soviet anthem. Some analysts interpreted the decision as an attempt to ameliorate Russia's troubled present by evoking the grandeur of its Soviet past. Others read an additional, more sinister motive into the reappearance of the Soviet anthem melody—revanchism—and launched vocal protests as a result.

The active supporters of Aleksandrov's anthem consisted primarily of Communists and pro-government politicians. The most vocal detractors comprised liberal politicians and the majority of the so-called "cultural intelligentsia." Significantly, and not at all surprisingly, politicians and members of the cultural elite on both sides of the conflict often claimed to speak on behalf of the largely silent "Russian people."

Politicians

For the months of November and December 2000, the anthem was a central issue of debate among politicians; every major Russian political figure voiced an opinion. This debate underscored the ideological divide that separates the Russian left (e.g., Communists and Putin's "Unity" coalition) from its moderate right (e.g., the Western-leaning "liberal" parties). President Putin, the most influential supporter of Aleksandrov's anthem, made the following comments in a televised address to the country:

> Recently, particularly heated discussions have surrounded the anthem, the former Soviet anthem composed by Aleksandrov. You and I know the results of the opinion polls—an overwhelming majority of Russian citizens prefer precisely this melody. It is difficult to disagree with the logic that not every question can be decided by the arithmetical majority. But let us not forget that in this case we are talking about the majority of the people ["narod"]. In the final analysis, these State symbols are being proposed for that very narod. I will admit the possibility that the narod and I are making a mistake. But I want to appeal to those who are not in favor of this decision. I ask you to refrain from dramatizing the situation and erecting insurmountable barriers, from burning bridges and splitting society yet again. If we agree that it is unacceptable to use the symbols of past epochs, including the Soviet epoch, then we must admit that entire generations of our countrymen—including our mothers and fathers—lived useless, senseless lives, that they existed for naught. I cannot agree with that, not with my head, not with my heart. (Putin 2000)

Putin's speech was a finely crafted piece of persuasive rhetoric. In equating his position with the unequivocal will of the Russian people ("I will admit the possibility that the narod and I are making a mistake"), he implied that all dissenters are outsiders, separated from the narod, extremist agitators who hope to destroy the unity of Russian society. This rare nationally-televised appearance demonstrates the high priority that the anthem held for Putin; it also points to his realization that opposition to the new anthem was formidable. For one of the first times, Putin found himself publicly pitted against his mentor, former President Boris Yeltsin. (Yeltsin, who had handed the presidency to Putin on New Year's Eve, 1999, was the very person who retired "Unbreakable Union" a decade earlier.) On December 6, 2000, Yeltsin gave an interview containing his most overt criticism of Putin's policies to date: "I am categorically opposed to the return of the anthem of the USSR as our state anthem . . . I associate the anthem with only one thing: [Communist] Party Congresses, at which the power of Party bureaucrats was confirmed and strengthened" ("Interv'yu" 2000). Yeltsin avowed that the return of the anthem merely confirmed his belief that he should have outlawed the Communist Party in 1991.

Back on the other side of the political fence, the ruling coalition of the Communist and Unity parties actively lobbied for the rehabilitation of the Soviet anthem melody. In the words of Prime Minister Mikhail Kasyanov, "The Soviet [anthem's] melody is easy to remember. It sent 'goose bumps' down my body when I was in the army." The Glinka anthem does not generate a "shivering thrill. It's not very vivid . . . and therefore does not 'hearten'—as any good anthem should" (Lambroshini 2000a, translator unknown).

Kasyanov's comment was typical of the pro-Aleksandrov camp, which tended to cast its praise of his melody in experiential rather than ideological terms (e.g., "Unbreakable Union" is a rousing piece of music). Indeed, as the December 8 Duma vote demonstrated, the "shivering thrill" was a partisan experience: the *Yabloko* Party and the Union of Right Forces (*Soyuz Pravykh Sil*, or SPS), the two most liberal Parliamentary factions, voted against the new anthem, and the parties' luminaries denounced it *con brio*. Grigory Yavlinsky, leader of the Yabloko Party, labeled the decision "a signal of where our society is heading. It shows what we should expect in the near future. It is revealing—it takes away any illusions in regard to the short- and mid-term policy of this country's leadership." Boris Nemtsov, leader of the SPS Party, echoed this position, calling the decision a "major political mistake...that is going to reverberate for a long time" (in Lambroshini 2000b). Nemtsov also made a novel proposition that he said would remedy the damage inflicted by the proposed anthem. He announced that he and his party would support the return of Aleksandrov's anthem if the government agreed to remove Lenin's corpse from the Mausoleum on Red Square and convert the notorious red granite structure into a "Memorial Complex in Memory of the Victims of the Political Turmoil of the Twentieth Century, Dedicated to All Who Died as a Result of the Revolution, the Civil War, and Political Repression." This provocative proposition was followed by an overtly satirical one: the SPS Party proposed as lyrics to Aleksandrov's anthem those given in Figure 15.4, thus, according to some accounts, forcing the Parliament to formally debate their merits on the floor.

Several lines of the proposed lyrics are copied directly from the official 1977 text (e.g., lines 18, 20, 21), but their placement creates an ironic inversion of their original meaning. Other lines from the 1977 text are altered satirically (e.g., lines 5, 8, 13). There is no public record of the extent to which the Duma deputies appreciated the irony of the SPS lyrics. It is not in the least surprising, however, that neither of the SPS propositions found much support during the voting process. Putin's

#	English Translation	Transliteration
	Verse 1	
1	From sea to sea, spreading out freely	*Ot mórya do moray raskínulas vólno*
2	Is a country of businesslike and active people!	*Straná delovykh i aktívnykh lyudéi!*
3	In free Russia the peoples are satisfied,	*V svobódnoi Rossíi naródy dovólny,*
4	Living under the wing of liberal ideas!	*Zhivyá pod krylóm liberálnykh idéi!*
	Refrain 1	
5	Glory to you, our open society,	*Slávsya ty óbshestvo náshe otkrýtoe,*
6	[Clearing a] broad path for investment!	*Dlyá investítsi shiróki prokhód!*
7	The rapid development of a hard currency market	*Rýnka valyútnovo bystrorazvítie*
8	Will lead us to the triumph of globalism!	*Nás k torzhestvú globalízma vedyót!*
	Verse 2	
9	The tsars and "gen-secs" [General Secretaries] didn't destroy the *narod,*	*Tsarí i "genséki" naród ne slomíli,*
10	And we've swept communism's ashes from our feet!	*I prakh kommunízma stryakhnúli my s nóg!*
11	Our rights and freedoms have inspired the people,	*Pravá i svobódy naród okrylíli,*
12	We labor honestly and pay our taxes!	*My trúdimsya chéstno i plátim nalóg!*
	Refrain 2	
13	Glory to the peoples' private property,	*Slávsya naródnaya sóbstvennost chástnaya,*
14	The reliable guarantee of human rights!	*Práv chelovéka nadyózhny garánt!*
15	We will build such a beautiful life	*Zhízn my postróim takúyu prekrásnuyu*
16	That every emigrant will come back to us!	*K nám vozvratítsya lyubói emigránt!*
	Verse 3	
17	In the friendly accordance of labor and capital	*V soglási'i drúzhnom trudá s kapítalom*
18	We envision the future of our country,	*My vídim gryadúshee náshei strany,*
19	And to the right-leaning ideas of our native liberals	*I k právym idéyam rodnýkh liberálov*
20	We will be selflessly faithful!	*My búdem vsegdá bezzavétno verný!*
	Refrain 3	
21	Glory to our free Fatherland,	*Slávsya Otéchestvo náshe svobódnoe,*
22	The reliable bastion of monetarism!	*Monetarízma nadyózhny oplót!*
23	Russia, distinctive and multinational	*Rús samobytnaya, mnogonaródnaya*
24	Will provide the world with a lesson in liberalism!	*Míru urók liberálny dayót!*

Figure 15.4 SPS Party's Proposed Lyrics for the Russian Anthem.

coalition won the day, and Aleksandrov's composition with Mikhalkov's new text was adopted by a margin that reflected party lines.

The Cultural Intelligentsia

In contrast to Russia's politicians, who split into two camps regarding the anthem, the cultural intelligentsia—a group comprising musicians, artists, academics, literary figures and critics—was more unified in its response. It overwhelmingly opposed the anthem, with many well-known figures pledging to engage in civil disobedience by remaining seated when it was performed.[19] Like the liberal politicians, the cultural intelligentsia regarded Aleksandrov's anthem as a step toward Soviet revanchism and as an affront to those who suffered under the Soviet regime. Unfettered by any restrictions of political prudence, however, they expressed themselves even more forcefully than their representatives in government.

Below I present, with minimal further comment, a number of excerpts from open letters to President Putin written and signed by several dozen highly prominent members of the cultural intelligentsia. These quotes illustrate their objections to Aleksandrov's melody and hint at the passionate nature of these objections. I have printed in bold sections that are particularly relevant to the analytical section of this article that follows.

> To once again blare **an anthem of Stalinist origin**...which is now equipped with "democratic" words, is a cynical and shameless gibe directed at the long-suffering...narod; it is a kind of moral sadomasochism on a national scale. (Chudakova et al. 2000, 21)

> The venture to return the music of the former Soviet anthem to national use arouses in us disgust and protest...This melody is one of the most vivid symbols of a past epoch. **No new text can erase the words that are firmly attached to Aleksandrov's music**, words that glorify Lenin and Stalin...Millions of our fellow citizens will never respect this anthem, which violates their beliefs and insults the memories of the victims of Soviet political repressions. ("Muzyka" 2000)

> We [the members of the Russian PEN Club] have tried to bring to the attention of the powers-that-be that this **"music of totalitarianism,"** this symbol of an epoch of violence and terror offends the feelings of many citizens of this country, infringes upon the freedom of their conscience and, in our view, **destroys the fragile societal harmony that existed up until recently.** We call on you, the President of all Russians, and not on the majority or the minority, to re-evaluate the devastating effects of this decision before you sign an order that will surely estrange [many] Russian citizens and serve for many as a sign that the democratic transformation of our country is defunct. (Chudakova et al. 2000, 34)

> **The decision to accept the melody of the Soviet anthem will split society into two pieces.** While some listened to it with tears of pride in their eyes, [the performance of the anthem] caused the eyes of others to fill with totally different tears—from the memory of the monstrous lawlessness created in the name and at the order of **a state, whose ideology has become imprinted in these words and sounds.** (Chudakova et al. 2000, 46)

> The restoration of the Stalinist anthem doesn't unite society, but rather places a cross upon [i.e., kills] the younger generation's faith in their elders. During the past ten years of democracy, Russia has seen the birth of a generation of free people, for whom the Stalinist regime is the most dark, cruel and shameful period in the thousand-year history of the country. **No**

verbal plastering will hide from the new Russia the sinister essence of the GULAG. The mass graves at Kolyma and Katyn' will stir at the sound of "thus Stalin has raised us." (Chudakova et al. 2000, 20)

The cultural intelligentsia protested the anthem with vehemence. Their fear that the new anthem was a harbinger of a future return to authoritarianism resonated with the questioning attitude many outside Russia had adopted vis-à-vis Putin's vision for the country.[20] Many of their subsequent statements argued that Russia's true national identity was connected with its ability to break with the patterns of Stalinism rather than repeat them. Significantly, the appearance of the new, politically progressive lyrics did not quell these critics. My goal in the next sections of this article is to understand why this was the case.

Re-Intoning the New Russian Anthem

Earlier, I gave a brief interpretation of the apparent ideological messages presented by the lyrics of the "Unbreakable Union" and "Russia, Our Holy Power." But if the recent societal uproar has demonstrated anything, it is that any lyrical analysis that ignores the melody is entirely missing the point. If the lyrics were of primary concern, then replacing Mikhalkov's 1977 text with his 2000 one would have quieted the criticism or at least redirected it toward the character of the new lyrics. However, it is clear that those who opposed the anthem were much more concerned about its melody than its text.

Within this stormy discourse, and despite their divergent positions, both sides appeared to operate from a number of common assumptions about the nature of music. First, all parties clearly demonstrated a belief that music itself (as distinguished from lyrics) can serve as a powerful signifier, one which is capable of overwhelming the referential potential of the lyrics. Second, all agreed that once signification has been attached to a melody, it cannot be removed completely or with ease. The opposing sides disagreed only about the content of that signification. For those in favor of the return of Aleksandrov's composition, the melody was infused with profoundly positive political and social connotations. (Indeed, if these connotations were in danger of being superseded entirely by the anthem's new context, there would be no reason to fight for it.) For the dissenters, on the other hand, the music is, and, according to their statements, *always will be* infused with the evils of a corrupt regime. The disagreement over the anthem's semantic content demonstrates a third tenet that is a corollary to the second: namely, that music's meanings are ascribed to it by communities of listeners. While the rhetoric of the protesters tended toward the absolute (e.g., "no new text can erase the words that are firmly attached to Aleksandrov's music") the attitude that both camps tacitly assumed was that "music means what I say it means!": there can be no meaning in music without an audience to generate it.

Russian musicologists enjoy the interesting luxury of having a single term that encompasses precisely these three tenets. In his 1947 volume, *Musical Form as Process, Book 2: Intonation*, musicologist Boris Asaf'ev (1884–1949) introduced the concept of "intonation" (*intonatsiya*), which subsequently assumed a prominent position in the discourses of Russian musicologists and ethnomusicologists alike (Zemtsovsky 1997). In Asaf'ev's use "intonation" refers to a complex and dynamic phenomenon that comprises a musical gesture or combination of gestures, its performance, and the semantic charge (i.e., the meaningful content) that the gesture carries. This charge is ascribed to the musical gesture by the historically situated group of performers and listeners that produce and receive it. The process taking place in today's Russia resembles what some Russian musicologists have called *re-intoning* (*pere-intonirovanie*): "in a changed social situation a musical form has to be intoned differently in addressing new listeners. The new intonation…causes a shift in the meaning; *but something of the original meaning is bound to be retained*" (Monelle 1992,

279 in a discussion of Zak 1982, emphasis added). This idea runs parallel to a number of recent ethnomusicological writings, from Peter Manuel's extended account of recycled melodies in India (Manuel 1993, 131–52) to Thomas Turino's discussion of "semantic snowballing" in Zimbabwe (Turino 2000, 175).

Using this homegrown terminology, the pro-anthem camp might argue that the anthem melody has already been successfully re-intoned by the community of Russian citizens who have been articulating it since January 2001. This fresh intonation retains a positive glow of the earlier Soviet-era intonation, an aura of greatness and history, but it is essentially new in that it trumpets the ideals of the 2000 lyrics. The opposition, by contrast, would claim that the powerful fusion of music and ideology in "Unbreakable Union" cannot be re-intoned at all as long as those who remember its original context are still living. In fact, as many of the open letters to the President state, Aleksandrov's melody continues to be haunted by the words "Stalin has raised us" from the original 1944 lyrics (Chudakova et al. 2000, 20, 25, 35). Thus, according to some Russians, the 1977 attempt at re-intoning the anthem for a post-Stalinist Soviet Union was a failure. Indeed, even some of the anthem supporters agree that they will hear the old lyrics when they sing the new ones.

The Interaction of Text and Melody

When I first read the quotes of those who claim to hear the Soviet lyrics even as they are singing the new anthem, I attributed this to the peculiar power of human memory and to the individuals' desire to remember the old lyrics, whether to feed their nostalgia or to stand witness to the perceived evils of the past. After closely examining "Unbreakable Union" and "Russia, Our Holy Power," however, I suspect that two structural factors contribute to the "stickiness" of the old lyrics and thus complicate any attempts to re-intone Aleksandrov's melody. First, despite the fundamental differences of their surface ideological messages, the lyrics to "Russia, Our Holy Power" evoke the lyrics of "Unbreakable Union" on the lexical level. All of the central terms that are present two or more times (and thus emphasized) in "Unbreakable Union" can be found in the new lyrics: "union" (soyuz), "freedom" (svoboda), "fatherland" (otechestvo/otchizna), and the ubiquitous "nation/folk/people" (narod). If we bracket the obligatory references to Lenin and communism in the 1977 version, we can say that this collection of semantically loaded terms forms the conceptual foundation of both the Soviet lyrics and the new lyrics. Two words here are particularly evocative of the old anthem. The word for "union" (soyuz) is familiar to all in its original context, as one half of "Soviet Union" (Sovetskii Soyuz). Also, one of the words for "fatherland" (otchizna) is archaic, and is rarely seen in contemporary Russian outside the context of the Soviet anthem. Although the new lyrics ostensibly describe a different "union" and a new post-Soviet "fatherland," the Soviet history of this collection of words is hard to ignore. Nowhere is this effect more apparent than in the first line of the new refrain, "Glory to our free fatherland," which is copied verbatim from "Unbreakable Union."

Additionally, the way the new lyrics align with the melodic contour of Aleksandrov's composition contributes to the evocation of the old anthem. This problem is best illustrated at the climax of the refrain, the moment when the old lyrics seem to adhere most stubbornly to Aleksandrov's notes. The anthem's musical peak arrives with a cymbal crash on the heels of a dramatic crescendo over eight beats. The melodic climax that follows is signaled by the piece's loudest, longest, highest-pitched note, which initiates an extended progression to the final cadence.[21] In Mikhalkov's 1977 text, the anthem's musical climax coincides with the words "the Party of Lenin" (*Partiya Lenina*)—arguably the most important two words in the lyrics. They constitute the nominative subject of a phrase that crystallizes the message of all three verses. This phrase, which begins at the climax and continues to the final cadence six bars later, sums up the official Soviet ideology perfectly: "The Party of Lenin, the strength of the people, will lead us to communism's triumph."

The power of this musical moment is generated in part by the fact that the textual and musical climaxes exactly coincide.

In "Russia, Our Holy Power," by contrast, the musical climax is accompanied by the first part of a subordinate clause in the instrumental case: "by our ancestors given" (*predkami dannaya*). Making allowances for the Russian language's flexible word order, we can translate the full phrase as, "the people's wisdom, given by our ancestors" (*predkami dannaya mudrost' narodnaya*). This cryptic phrase, which technically constitutes a sentence fragment, has been criticized in the press as "filler," and "nonsensical"; one critic stated that the phrase "the people's wisdom" "begs for alteration" (Il'in 2001). He may have been referring to the easy act of textual vandalism that could be achieved by replacing the word *mudrost'* (wisdom) with its rhyming partner, *glupost'* (stupidity), thus creating the sarcastic message, "the people's stupidity, given by our ancestors." For these reasons, it appears safe to predict that the strong phrase "Party of Lenin, strength of the people, will lead us to communism's triumph" will not be easily erased by the awkward "the people's wisdom, given by our ancestors. Glory to the country. We are proud of you!"

Conclusion

Over the last twenty years or so, ethnomusicologists have proven very successful at demonstrating how music can serve as a vehicle for meaning and how that meaning is determined by historically situated communities and thus subject to change over time. Moreover, in our postmodern world of free-floating signifiers, examples abound of the ease with which musical works can be appropriated and resignified, both cross-culturally and within a single community. The concepts of intonation and re-intoning remind us that musical gestures often retain traces of the meaning that was originally ascribed to them. The present case demonstrates that, for some communities at least, these traces can be strong enough to prevent re-intonation altogether.

My brief musical analysis suggests that the structural weakness in the fusion of melody and lyrics in "Russia, Our Holy Power" (which sets the piece in stark contrast with the more artfully fused "Unbreakable Union") may be one of the factors inhibiting its re-intonation. The ethnographic section of this paper suggests another factor: the fundamental ideological fault line that runs between the political majority and the cultural elite in contemporary Russia. By documenting these clashing positions, I hope to have demonstrated the extent to which the anthem is not a static reflection of Russian national identity but rather a fluid and polysemous text, subject to multiple, conflicting readings. Russian national identity is currently being negotiated through these readings. The cultural intelligentsia's interpretation of the anthem constituted the most vocal and passionate criticism of the Soviet period, and consequently the most emphatic support of Russia's fledgling democracy, in years. At the same time, the overwhelming support of the anthem by the government and a plurality of Russia's 146 million citizens is powerful evidence of a widespread nostalgia for the Soviet period, and proof of Putin's political mandate. Under these volatile conditions, the future of the new anthem is unclear. As of this writing, a recording of the new anthem is broadcast every day at 6:00 a.m. and midnight on government radio and television stations; the process of re-intoning the anthem through repetition in a new context has begun. Further ethnographic work will be necessary to determine the degree to which this process is successful.

Acknowledgments

I would like to thank Timothy Rice for his insightful comments on and criticism of earlier drafts of this article. Izaly Zemtsovsky has shown great patience in discussing with me the Russian concepts that I employ here, for which I am particularly grateful. I would also like to thank Philip Bohlman, Emily Daughtry, Nancy Guy, Bruno Nettl, A. Jihad Racy, Helen Rees, and Tony Seeger for their valuable comments and encouragement during various stages of the writing process.

Notes

1. The federal law regarding the anthem and a copy of the official piano reduction can be found on the Russian government's Web site: http://www.gov.ru/main/symbols/gsrf4_1.html (20 May 2002).
2. The anthem law was part of a legislative packet that also confirmed the Russian tricolor as the state flag, the double-headed eagle as the state emblem, and reintroduced the Soviet "victory flag" (the red banner without the hammer and sickle that was raised over the Reichstag at the end of World War II) as the flag of the Russian armed forces. Due to space limitations, I will not discuss these other state symbols here, except to say that they were all much less controversial than the anthem.
3. In the months since this article was written, the independent network, NTV, was subject to a hostile takeover by Gazprom, a powerful government-dominated corporation. Gazprom ousted the board of directors, installing a new board of company loyalists. As a result, the network lost a large degree of its autonomy, and a number of journalists, including Yevgeny Kiselyov, the anchor of "Itogi," moved to the last remaining independent network, TV6, in protest. In January 2002, this network too was liquidated. Critics of President Putin's administration read these events as evidence of Putin's desire to reinstate Soviet-era control over the press. For these critics, as this article discusses below, the appearance of "Unbreakable Union" was further proof of Putin's revanchist intentions.
4. I have collected over a hundred articles from the Russian and Anglophone press, written in anticipation of and reaction to the rehabilitation of the Soviet melody and the new lyrics. In addition, I have monitored a number of personal webpages that discuss the event, and collected over a dozen open letters, addressed to President Putin or the Parliament and signed by prominent Russian citizens. (Many of the open letters and press articles were subsequently published in Chudakova et al., 2000.)
5. Of course, I do not mean to imply that everyone in Russia was a member of one camp or another; apathy and ironic laughter were not uncommon reactions to the anthem change, if my Russian friends are at all representative. For the purposes of this analysis, however, the data have forced me to abandon my distrust of binary oppositions and acknowledge that the conflict itself was essentially two-sided.
6. In the 1990s, for example, the journal *Ethnomusicology* published about twenty articles focusing on music and nationalism. Many of these works have used nationalism as a framing device in studies of the popular music of a particular region (e.g., Meintjes 1990; Waterman 1990; Averill 1994; Manuel 1994). Others have explored nationalism's relevance in the discourse surrounding traditional or "folk" music styles (Yang 1994; Buchanan 1995; Davis 1997; Goertzen 1998; Scruggs 1999; Sugarman 1999). Discussions of nationalism can also be found in recent dissertations and books on traditional and/or popular musics by Donna Buchanan (1991), Timothy Rice (1994), Christopher Goertzen (1997), Helen Rees (2000) and Thomas Turino (2000).
7. See Nettl 1995 for an exception to this statement.
8. According to Boyd, exceptions to this model are exceedingly rare: "[f]or anthems independent of the European tradition one must look mainly to Eastern countries such as Myanmar, Japan, Tibet and Sri Lanka, whose anthems rely strongly on folk music and sometimes call for indigenous instruments and are accompanied by formal gestures" (2001, 655).
9. For example, over seventy of the world's extant national anthems begin with an ascending perfect fourth from dominant to tonic. Both the current Russian anthem and the "Internationale" begin in this manner.
10. In the twentieth-century history of national anthems in Russia, only one example of specific musical nationalism has been seriously considered. In 1917, after the tsar had been overthrown but before the Bolsheviks came to power, the leadership of the Provisional Government suggested that an arrangement of "Ey ukhnem" (the "Song of the Volga Boatmen") be designated the national anthem. This proposal was still on the table when the Bolsheviks triumphed in the October Revolution. They quickly designated a Russian-language version of the "Internationale" as the national anthem of the newly-formed Soviet Union.
11. Works on national anthems from both sides of the disciplinary fence include two major compendia (Nettl 1967; Reed and Bristow 1993); a substantial number of individual anthem histories (e.g., Sonneck 1914; Aguilera 1958); articles by Mach (1994), Byerly (1998), and Guy (2002); and Boyd's recent entry in the revised *New Grove Dictionary* (2001). While hardly inconsequential, this body of scholarship is dwarfed by the combined works on specific nationalism by musicologists and works on nationalism in oral and popular musics by ethnomusicologists.
12. Unless otherwise noted, I have translated all of the Russian sources that appear in this paper (e.g., the anthem lyrics, open letters, and quotations from Russian scholarly works, the Russian government, and the Russian press).
13. Recordings of "Unbreakable Union" and the "Internationale" can be found at the Skazka, Russian Society of Trondheim Web site: http://www.skazka.no/anthems (13 November 2002). A note on transliteration: Throughout the body of this article and in the references, I have used a modified version of the Library of Congress transliteration system that, while not exactly standard, maintains a consistent correlation to the letters of the Russian alphabet, thus enabling Russian speakers to reconstruct the original. When transliterating the various anthem lyrics, however, I felt that the need to convey their pronunciation outweighed the need for graphic accuracy. I therefore have used a radically simplified system that is geared to give non-Russian speakers a rough idea of the sound of the words. This system is basically phonetic, with the following exceptions: when the letter "o" is stressed ("ó") it sounds somewhat like the long "o" in "oath." If it is unstressed, its sound is somewhere between the "o" in "bother" and the "o" in "other." Also, the letter "e" is pronounced roughly like the "ye" in "yellow." The letter "y," when combined with another vowel, acts like the "y" in "you." When alone, it sounds somewhat like the "i" in "sit" would if placed farther back in the throat.
14. Yeltsin was elected speaker of the Supreme Soviet of the Russian Republic in May 1990. On June 12, 1990, he was elected president of the Russian Republic, which at that point was a sovereign member of the Soviet Union. In December 1991, after the Union was dissolved in the wake of a failed coup, Yeltsin was automatically made president of the newly-formed Russian Federation. For an excellent history of the disintegration of the Soviet Union and the formation of the post-Soviet states, see Suny 1997.
15. A recording of "Patriotic Song" can be found at the Skazka, Russian Society of Trondheim Web site: http://www.skazka.no/anthems (20 May 2002).

16. This position is weakened slightly by the fact that, as of 1993, the following seven countries had wordless national anthems: Kuwait, Mauritania, Qatar, San Marino, Somalia, Spain, and the United Arab Emirates (Reed and Bristow 1993).

17. Several Russian critics have argued that Pavel' Ovsyannikov's official arrangement of "Russia, Our Holy Power" is bombastic and in bad taste. Indeed, the differences between Ovsyannikov's arrangement and Aleksandrov's arrangement of "Unbreakable Union" are striking. They would make an interesting subject for a comparative study along the lines of Nancy Guy's (2002), which treats individual performances of the Taiwanese anthem as separate "utterances," in Bakhtin's sense. For the purposes of this paper, however, I have chosen not to deal with the differences in arrangements, as most of the public debate of the new anthem's merits took place before "Russia, Our Holy Power" was ever performed. A recording of "Russia, Our Holy Power" can be found at the official Web site of the Russian Federation Administrative Bodies: http://www.gov.ru:8104/main/symbols/gsrf4_5.html (20 May 2002).

18. These lyrics were apparently composed by an SPS Party member, one S. Sidorov. In addition to Sidorov's satirical lyrics, former Prime Minister Yevgeny Primakov submitted a more serious set that he composed. Outside the Parliament, private citizens have flooded the Internet with proposed lyrics. I have collected over forty verses set to Aleksandrov's melody, the most recent of which was posted on the Internet on May 10, 2001.

19. The cultural intelligentsia's unity was not absolute: on December 6, 2000, a group of fourteen cultural figures of modest stature wrote an open letter to the Parliament in support of the return of Aleksandrov's anthem. The authors called the decision "very timely" and acknowledged that "it would be naïve to think that there is a decision that would please everyone" ("Chetyrnadtsat' " 2000). In addition, prominent filmmaker Nikita Mikhalkov, son of Sergei Mikhalkov, announced that he supported his father's lyrics. However, it is clear that the vast majority of the intelligentsia opposed the decision.

20. See for example the following article in the *Time Europe Daily*: http://www.time.com/time/europe/webonly/europe/2000/12/anthem.html (20 May 2002). Many in the Western mainstream press appeared more amused than alarmed with the anthem crisis. See for example this article by CNN: http://www.cnn.com/2000/WORLD/europe/08/02/russia.anthem/ (20 May 2002).

21. For a multimedia example illustrating the musical peak of "Unbreakable Union" and "Russia, Our Holy Power," please see the "multimedia appendices" section of the journal *Ethnomusicology*'s webpage, or navigate directly to: http://www.ethnomusicology.org/publications/Daughtry.htm.

References

Aguilera, M. 1958. *Historia del himno nacional de Colombia*. Bogota.

Anderson, Benedict. 1991. *Imagined Communities: Reflections on the Origin and Spread of Nationalism*. Revised edition. London: Verso.

Asaf'ev, Boris. 1947. *Muzykal'naya forma kak protsess, kniga vtoraya: intonatsiya* (Musical Form as Process, Book 2: Intonation). Moscow: Gosudarstvennoye Muzykal'noye Izdatel'stvo.

Averill, Gage. 1994. "*Anraje* to *Angaje*: Carnival Politics and Music in Haiti." *Ethnomusicology* 38(2):217–47.

Boyd, Malcolm. 2001. "National Anthems." In *The New Grove Dictionary of Music and Musicians*, 2d ed., edited by Stanley Sadie, vol. 17, 654–55. New York: Grove's Dictionaries.

Buchanan, Donna A. 1991. "The Bulgarian Folk Orchestra: Cultural Performance, Symbol, and the Construction of National Identity in Socialist Bulgaria." Ph.D. dissertation. University of Texas (Austin).

———. 1995. "Metaphors of Power, Metaphors of Truth: The Politics of Music Professionalism in Bulgarian Folk Orchestras." *Ethnomusicology* 39(3):381–416.

Byerly, Ingrid Bianca. 1998. "Mirror, Mediator, and Prophet: The Music *Indaba* of Late-Apartheid South Africa." *Ethnomusicology* 42(1):1–44.

"Chetyrnadtsat' [deyatelei kul'tury...podpisali otkrytoye pis'mo v zashchitu Putina i muzyki Aleksandrova]" (Fourteen Cultural Figures...Signed an Open Letter in Defense of Putin and Aleksandrov's Music). 2000. *Polit.ru*, 6 December 2000. http://www.polit.ru (29 January 2001).

Chudakova, M. O., A. R. Kirilkin and E. A. Toddes, eds. 2000. *Za Glinku! Protiv vozvrata k sovetskomu gimnu: sbornik informatsionnykh materialov* (For Glinka! Against a Return to the Soviet Anthem: an Anthology of Informational Materials). Moscow: Yazyki Russkoi Kul'tury.

Chulos, Chris and Timo Piirainen, eds. 2000. *The Fall of an Empire, the Birth of a Nation: National Identities in Russia*. Aldershot, England: Ashgate.

Davis, Ruth. 1997. "Cultural Policy and the Tunisian *Ma'luf*: Redefining a Tradition." *Ethnomusicology* 41(1):1–21.

Eyck, F. Gunther. 1995. *The Voice of Nations: European National Anthems and Their Authors*. Westport, Connecticut: Greenwood Press.

Friedson, Steven. 1998. "Tumbuka Healing." In *Garland Encyclopedia of World Music, Vol. 1, Africa*, edited by Ruth M. Stone, 271–83. New York: Garland.

Frolova-Walker, Marina. 1998. "'National in Form, Socialist in Content': Musical Nation-Building in the Soviet Republics." *Journal of the American Musicological Society* 51(2):331–71.

Goertzen, Christopher. 1997. *Fiddling for Norway: Revival and Identity*. Chicago: University of Chicago Press.

———. 1998. "The Norwegian Folk Revival and the *Gammeldans* Controversy." *Ethnomusicology* 42(1):99–127.

Guy, Nancy. 2002. "'Republic of China National Anthem' on Taiwan: One Anthem, One Performance, Multiple Realities." *Ethnomusicology* 46(1):96–119.

Heidegger, Martin. 1977[1993]. "On the Question Concerning Technology." In *Basic Writings*, rev. ed., edited by David Farrell Krell, translated by William Lovitt, 307–42. San Francisco: Harper San Francisco.

Il'in, A. S. 2001. "Otzyv na tekst gimna Rossii avtora S. Mikhalkova" (Reaction to the Text of the Russian Anthem Authored by S. Mikhalkov). *Forum/Moskva/Rossiya*. http://www.forum. msk.ru/files/010118120847 html (20 March 2001).

"Interv'yu" (Interview with former President Boris Yeltsin). 2000. *Komsomolskaya Pravda*, 6 December 2000. http://www. kp.ru (12 December 2000).

Lambroshini, Sophie. 2000a. "Russia: Search for a Suitable Anthem Goes On." *Radio Free Europe/Radio Liberty*, 24 October 2000. http://www.rferl.org/nca/features/2000/10/24102000194810.asp (8 December 2000).

———. 2000b. "Russia: Duma Votes To Reinstate Soviet Anthem." *Radio Free Europe/Radio Liberty*, 8 December 2000. http://www.rferl.org/nca/features/2000/12/08122000151346. asp (8 December 2000).

Mach, Zdzislaw. 1994. "National Anthems: The Case of Chopin as a National Composer." In *Ethnicity, Identity and Music: The Musical Construction of Place*, edited by Martin Stokes, 61–70. Oxford: Berg Publishers.

"Majority [of Russians Inclined to Revive USSR Anthem]." 2000. *Pravda*, 13 November 2000, translator unknown. http://english.pravda.ru/society/2000/11/13/871.html (29 January 2000).

Manuel, Peter. 1993. *Cassette Culture: Popular Music and Technology in North India*. Chicago and London: University of Chicago Press.

———. 1994. "Puerto Rican Music and Cultural Identity: Creative Appropriation of Cuban Sources from Danza to Salsa." *Ethnomusicology* 38(2):249–80.

Marx, Karl. 1945. *The Communist Manifesto*, Authorized English Translation. New York: New York Labor News Co.

McLaughlin, Daniel. 2000. "Stalin's Favorite Makes Anthem Shortlist." *Reuters*, 24 November 2000. http://198.3.103.147/news/r/001124/10/odd-anthem-dc (24 November 2000).

Meintjes, Louise. 1990. "Paul Simon's Graceland, South Africa, and the Mediation of Musical Meaning." *Ethnomusicology* 34(l):37–74.

Mikhalkov, Sergei. 1998. "*Gimn Sovetskogo Soyuza*" (Anthem of the Soviet Union). *Zavtra: Gazeta Gosudarstva Rossiskogo* 14(227). http://zavtra.ru/cgi/veil/data/zavtra/98/227/ 71_all.html (4 April 2001).

Monelle, Raymond. 1992. *Linguistics and Semiotics in Music*. Chur, Switzerland: Harwood Academic Publishers.

"Muzyka [sovetskogo gimna vyzyvayet otvrashcheniye u tvorcheskoi intelligentsii]" (Music of the Soviet Anthem Arouses Disgust in the Cultural Intelligentsia). 2000. *Lenta.ru*, 5 December 2000. http://www.lenta.ru/russia/2000/12/05/izvestia/culture.htm (29 January 2001).

Nettl, Bruno. 1995. *Heartland Excursions: Ethnomusicological Reflections on Schools of Music*. Urbana: University of Illinois Press.

Nettl, Paul. 1967. *National Anthems*, 2d edition, translated by Alexander Gode. New York: Frederick Ungar Publishing Company.

Porter, James. 1998. "Music and Ideology." In *Garland Encyclopedia of World Music, Vol. 8: Europe*, edited by Timothy Rice, James Porter, and Chris Goertzen, 184–90. New York: Garland.

Putin, Vladimir. 2000. Televised appearance on "Itogi," 10 December 2000. http://www.ntv.ru/itogi/index.html (10 December 2000).

Reed, W. L. and M. J. Bristow, eds. 1993. *National Anthems of the World*, 8th edition. London: Cassel.

Rees, Helen. 2000. *Echoes of History: Naxi Music in Modern China*. New York: Oxford University Press.

Rezunkov, Victor, moderator. 2000. "*Gimn i vlast': khronika tshcheslaviya*" (The Anthem and Power: a Chronicle of Vanity). Interview on *Radio Svoboda*. http://www.svoboda.org/programs/otb/2000/obi.25.asp (28 January 2002).

Rice, Timothy. 1994. *May It Fill Your Soul: Experiencing Bulgarian Music*. Chicago: University of Chicago Press.

Scruggs, T. M. 1999. "Let's Enjoy As Nicaraguans': The Use of Music in the Construction of a Nicaraguan National Consciousness." *Ethnomusicology* 43(2):297–321.

Sonneck, Oscar George Theodore. 1914. *The Star-Spangled Banner*. Washington, DC: U.S. Government Print Office.

Sugarman, Jane. 1999. "Imagining the Homeland: Poetry, Songs, and the Discourses of Albanian Nationalism." *Ethnomusicology* 43(3):419–58.

Suny, Ronald Grigor. 1997. *The Soviet Experiment: Russia, the USSR, and the Successor States*. New York: Oxford University Press.

Taruskin, Richard. 1996. "Introduction." *Repercussions* 5(1 and 2), special issue: "Nationalism in Music." Richard Taruskin, guest editor, 5–20.

———. 1997. *Defining Russia Musically: Historical and Hermeneutical Essays*. Princeton: Princeton University Press.

———. 2001. "Nationalism." In *The New Grove Dictionary of Music and Musicians*, 2d ed., edited by Stanley Sadie, vol. 17, 689–706. London: Macmillan.

Turino, Thomas. 2000. *Nationalists, Cosmopolitans, and Popular Music in Zimbabwe*. Chicago: University of Chicago Press.

"V novy vek so stalinskim gimnom" (In a New Century with the Stalinist Anthem). 2000. *Polit.ru*, 2 December 2000. http://www.polit.ru/fullnews.html/date=2000–12–02 (20 December 2000).

Vihavainen, Timo. 2000. "Nationalism and Internationalism: How Did the Bolsheviks Cope with National Sentiments?" In *The Fall of an Empire, the Birth of a Nation: National Identities in Russia*, edited by Chris J. Chulos and Timo Piirainen, 75–97. Aldershot, England: Ashgate Publishing Ltd.

Waterman, Christopher. 1990. "'Our Tradition is a Very Modern Tradition': Popular Music and the Construction of Pan-Yoruba Identity." *Ethnomusicology* 34(3):367–80.

Yablokova, Oksana. 2000. "Anthem Dispute Shows House Divided." *The Moscow Times*, 21 November 2000. http://www.themoscowtimes.com/stories/2000/11/21/011.html (12 December 2000).

Yang, Mu. 1994. "Academic Ignorance or Political Taboo? Some Issues in China's Study of Its Folk Song Culture." *Ethnomusicology* 38(2):303–20.

Zak, Vladimir. 1982. "On the Melodies of Popular Song." *Popular Music* 2:91–111.

"Zakonodatel'stvo [o gosudarstvennykh simvolakh]" (Legislation on State Symbols). 2001. *Vesti.ru*. http://www.vesti.ru/printged/976276205.html (1 February 2001).

Zemtsovsky, Izaly. 1997. "An Attempt at a Synthetic Paradigm." *Ethnomusicology* 41(2):185–205.

16

"Mezanmi, Kouman Nou Ye?
My Friends, How Are You?"
Musical Constructions of the Haitian Transnation

Gage Averill

In 1990, Haitian President Jean-Bertrand Aristide appointed Farah Juste, a well-known political singer from Miami, to be the representative to the government from the *Dizyèm Depatman* (10th Department),[1] a neologism for the Haitian *dyaspo* or *dyaspora* (diaspora). Aristide hoped to draw on the resources, talents, and investment potential of the diaspora to rebuild insular Haiti.[2] By appointing a singer as its representative, Aristide recognized the leading role of musicians in constructing and sustaining a notion of a Haitian nationhood *lòt bò dlo* (across the water).

The transnational character of the Haitian diaspora was impressed on me in my first interview on the subject of Haitian music. The director of the Haitian American Chamber of Commerce in Miami interrupted our conversation to listen intently to the daily broadcasts from Haiti over one of the 60 Haitian radio programs in Miami. Many experiences like this led me to question how immigrants variously "belonged" to Haiti and the United States and how Haitian popular music, which circulated freely in the diaspora and at home, articulated this sense of dual belonging. For these reasons, I borrowed the transnational "tour" by Haitian musicians as the spatializing metaphor for my own doctoral dissertation research (Averill 1989a).

Haitian populations overseas correspond to the most restrictive criteria for diaspora status (Safran, 83) except for a lack of consensus over the question of returning to the homeland. Among Haitians, individual outlooks on this vary considerably, and they vary in the aggregate over time. I argue that the increasingly transnational character of the population, the rise in circular migration patterns, and the increased possibilities for regular electronic and physical contact render this question—and to some extent the stability of the concept of diaspora—obsolete. The lives of many Haitians come to resemble Haitian commercial music in at least one critical aspect: they are increasingly suspended in the new transnational space between nation state and diaspora.

Haitians conceive of themselves as a people twice displaced, a diaspora within a diaspora. They are descendants of Africans who were displaced by the slave trade, who then reconstituted themselves into a new multi-ethnic African nationality (and nation state), and who were dispersed again by poverty and political turmoil. Paul Gilroy correctly stresses that the African diaspora, now conceived within four nodal points—the Caribbean, the United States, Europe, and Africa—forms a larger context for cultural exchange (157). In the Haitian case, immigrants relate intimately not only to a host society, the society they left behind, and the Haitian diaspora, but to another transnational entity, the African diaspora, finding commonalities with this larger entity.

The process by which transmigrants conceive of a homeland and incorporate it into daily life has emerged as a critical topic in diasporic studies. Mark Slobin has advocated more attention to how diasporas and homelands communicate and influence each other. Citing both Gold and Anderson, Slobin (64) stresses the importance in immigrant communities of the concept of the "mother country" and challenges researchers to investigate it more fully in all of its dimensions. Despite the circumstances that encouraged emigration, many Haitian exiles hold nostalgic views of home that have been amplified by the time and distance away from Haiti; reinforced by the indignities of immigrant life and encounters with American racism and xenophobia; and focused by reflexive and purposeful activity of politicians, journalists, and artists (especially musicians). This article examines the musical linkages between transmigrants and their homeland, tracing the ideological changes in this notion over time. It also investigates how the transnational circulation of Haitian popular music has helped to configure new postnational social spaces and social relations that span homeland and diaspora. I find that both the musical process (the circulation of transnational musics) and the discursive products (especially musical texts) have served to construct transnational Haitian identity.

"When You're in the White's Country": Migration and Nostalgia

Transnational labor migration from Haiti results from an interdependent set of political and economic factors. In the 30 years after the election of François Duvalier (1957), nearly a million Haitians—approximately 15% of the island nation's population—fled Haiti. Nearly half—more than 400,000—settled in New York City (Laguerre, 169–70; Stepick, 1; Glick Schiller et al., 184).

Three distinct waves of emigration from Haiti commenced with the exodus of political refugees from the traditional mulatto elite in the period surrounding Duvalier's election. A second wave included a large number of middle-class educators, merchants, professionals, civil servants, and students, and crested in the 10 years after Duvalier assumed the title of "*président à vie*" (1965) as economic opportunities for the middle class dried up and state-sponsored terrorism increased. With the decline in environmental, economic, and political life in the countryside (for example, appropriation of lands by Duvalier's Chefs de Section and his militia, the Tonton Makout-s), Haiti's peasants began to pool savings and sell their belongings to buy passage for family members on ships sailing illegally to the United States. Economists have debated the benefits to Haiti, if any, of this out-migration.[3]

The common distinction between economic and political refugees is of little help in understanding the Haitian situation. The longevity of the "predatory state" (Lundahl 1979, 297) has convinced many Haitians that economic progress is impossible.[4] The predatory or parasitic state is a product of core-periphery relations. Dupuy finds that a "triple alliance" of the dictatorship, bourgeoisie, and US interests has perpetuated problems of underdevelopment and immiseration (211). Dewind and Kinley point out that foreign assistance to Haiti has, paradoxically, worsened conditions in the countryside, increasing internal and external migration.

Disincentives to migrate include attachments to home, family, culture, and the "mother country." Romantic nationalism thrives in Haitian expressive culture, especially in works dealing with exile. One of Haiti's most famous *méringues*,[5] "Souvenir d'Haïti" (Memory of Haiti), is a turn-of-the-century treatise on the pain of exile. For generations, it has served composers as a source of nostalgic images of Haitian foods, women, climate, and culture (I include only the chorus and the second verse below; all translations are mine):

Ayiti cheri, pi bon peyi pase *ou lanpwen*	Haiti my dear, there's no better country
Fòk mwen te kite w poum te *kap konprann valè w*	I had to leave you to understand your worth
Fòk mwen te manke w pou m *te k ap apresye w*	I had to lose you to be able to appreciate you
Pou m santi vrèman tout sa *w te ye pou mwen*	In order to truly feel all that you were to me
Lè w nan peyi blan	When you're in the white's country
Ou gen youn vye frèt ki pa *janm bon*	There is a constant, despicable cold
E toutlajounen ou blije boule *chabon*	And all day you have to burn charcoal
Ou pa kap wè klè otan syèl la *ret andèy*	You can't see clearly with the sky covered
E pandan si mwa tout *pyebwa pa gen fèy*	And for six months, the trees have no leaves

Even at that time, with only a tiny fraction of Haiti's intellectual and economic elite overseas, the alienation of exile already helped to frame the idea of a homeland. Three quarters of a century later, with a large fraction of Haiti's population abroad, lead singer Ti-Manno (Roselin Antoine Jean-Baptiste) of the Haitian band D.P. Express constructed the homeland in hospitable terms that contrasted with the alienated and atomized customs of *letranje* (the foreign world):

Mwen pa pral mouri nan peyi *etranje*	I'm not going to die in a foreign country
Mennen m ale lakay-mwen...	Lead me to my country...
Nan peyi-m m ap tounnen	I'm coming back to the country
Nan ti peyi-m sa, se la mwen *gen manman*	In my little country, I have my mother
Nan ti peyi-m sa, se la mwen *gen ti sè*	In my little country, I have my little sister
Nan ti peyi-m sa, se la si m *tonbe ma leve*	In my little country, if I fall I can get up
Nan ti peyi-m sa, se la si m *grangou m manje*	In my little country, if I'm hungry, I eat
Nan ti peyi-m sa, se la si m *malad y a trete*	In my little country, if I'm sick, they treat me
	(SUP 111)

Responding to the loneliness and nostalgia of its diasporic audience, the band Skah Shah sang the following song in 1971:

Maten-an, mwen leve je-m *louvri*	In the morning I get up and open my eyes
Gen youn doulè chita sou kè- *mwen*	There's a sadness that sits on my heart
Mwen sonje peyi mwen, Ayiti *cheri!...*	I miss my country, Dear Haiti!...
Moun lakay pense m erèz	Folks at home think I'm happy
Lè m pa ekri yo kritike	When I don't write, they criticize me
San yo pa konnen se kè-m	Without realizing that my heart

K ap rache nan Nouyòk…	Is breaking in New York…
Mezanmi, nou pa ban m	My friends, you don't give me
nouvèl, o!	any news of you!
Mezanmi, kouman nou ye?	My friends, how are you?
	(SS 201)

One Haitian-American woman, who was 12 years old and living in Haiti at the time that this song came out, told me, "When I heard that song, I cried and cried, and I remember saying to myself that I was *never, never* going to leave my country. But look at me now!" (Pierre-Louis). As this example points out, popular song texts about migration formed a discourse on migration that informed personal and family decisions.

"When All the Musicians Were Flying"

Given musical opportunities in the diaspora, Haiti lost much of its musical talent in the space of little over a decade. These were the years "*lè tout mizisyen tap vole*" (when all the musicians were flying, i.e., emigrating). Haitian musicians were more likely than the population as a whole to approximate the ideal actors predicated by equilibrium theories of migration. Musicians were able to cross national borders with relative ease and did so quite often. They were thoroughly aware of pay differentials and relative economic opportunities in various locales. Many musicians lived their lives as urban semi-nomads—bachelors who spent much of their young lives touring. Finally, because the bands could expect to return to Haiti on tours (once the members received green cards), the break with home seemed less irrevocable. Musicians settled in concentrations of Haitian immigrants, seeking access to weekend club and party engagements.

Few musicians were political refugees in the strict sense, as they were seldom direct targets of political repression in Haiti. However, many chafed under the arbitrary restrictions on freedom of expression, interference from Tonton Makout-s in economic matters (i.e., skimming profits from concerts), command performances for Duvalierists, and the periods of terror when few people went out at night to hear music. Thus, the economic migration of musicians ultimately encompassed political realities.

The majority of Haitians in the United States in the 1960s had left Haiti during the era of the big bands, before the peak of popularity of *konpa* and the rock-oriented *mini-djaz*.[6] Of the few Haitian bands in New York in this period, most were patterned on the big-band format. In 1968, the first *mini-djaz* formed in New York; a descendent of Haiti's early *mini-djaz*, Ibo Combo, it retained the Ibo Combo name. When the *mini-djaz* Shleu-Shleu toured New York in 1970, the great majority of the band remained in the city. Soon after, a version of the Haitian *mini-djaz* Tabou Combo reorganized in New York with many of the original performers:

When we broke up in 1970 [in Haiti]…we had no intention of re-forming the group. I wanted to play soccer, and when I came here, I went to Chicago to work and study. Kapi, Jean-Claude, and Herman started playing because a lot of people had heard of Tabou Combo in New York and a lot of the Haitians wanted to party. They sent us some pictures and it seems they had a pretty good crowd. They call me up and say, "Hey, what are you doing there?" So I came to New York, and some new guys were there. (Interview: Joseph)

As personalities whose fame had spread to the diaspora through record sales and tours, musicians often came to their new communities with patronage networks already in place and promoters willing to help them with residency permits and relocation. Three years after Tabou Combo, a second incarnation of Shleu-Shleu also emigrated, adopting the name Skah Shah.

We had a contract with a guy named Georges Francis. He knew about the band because we were making albums and were really hot in Haiti. They didn't have anything here except Tabou Combo because Original Shleu-Shleu was going down, and they needed something else. We got B-2 work contracts. The union is supposed to sign it here—they have to accept it first before you come. You have to get contracts with the nightclubs you're going to play, and you show them the ad and everything. If you saw what we were making in Haiti, it was good. But when we got here, it was better than good. (Interview: St. Victor)

The Cap Haitian band, Les Diables Bleu (The Blue Devils), was also aided in their emigration by a producer intent on marketing the band in the diaspora:

We came to the United States when the Mayor of Miami invited us to play at an international festival, and after that the guys didn't want to go back. We had a contract to go to the Dominican Republic, but we didn't go. We called Marc Duverger [a New York-based record producer] from Miami and say we want to stay. He asks if we are sure and we say "yes!" So he paid for our tickets to New York because he wanted a band that could compete with Skah Shah. (Interview: Morisseau)

Bands without papers were limited to domestic travel. For engagements in Paris or the French Antilles, bands hired substitute musicians with green cards. As it became increasingly difficult for Haitians to get US travel visas, some music producers engaged in a profitable side-business of putting together fake bands, recording and promoting a single, and then arranging a tour and securing visas so that the entire group could get out of Haiti. These groups disbanded on arrival or soon after fulfilling their contractual responsibilities. Many legitimate bands also broke up after arrival due to economic pressures. Musicians saw jobs and *maryaj rezidans* (marriage for residence purposes) as the primary means of obtaining a green card, and both made it difficult to continue playing in a *mini-djaz*.

The band split after a year—maybe less than a year—after we got here. Some guys went to Chicago, some went to Miami. They split because everyone is after a job and they go where they can find a job. That was very tough. No one is what you can call very legal here … getting a green card and everything. They had to work for it in any way. They had to take a lawyer, some get married, some work for it and get it after a while, so it was that kind of a situation—pressure! (Interview: Morisseau)

Rituals of Return in the Koloni

Early Haitian immigrants typically referred to these communities as *koloni-s* (colonies), a term that implied a mass of people living in close proximity but with little social cohesion (Buchanan, 173). First wave immigrants were deeply concerned with the political situation in Haiti; most viewed themselves as temporary migrants in the United States and planned to return to Haiti after the overthrow of Duvalier. Social prejudice derived from insular Haiti guided behavior in the new environment, revealing the deep divisions of class and race among Haitian immigrants. When possible, upper-class Haitians moved out of lower-class neighborhoods like Bedford Stuyvesant or the Flatbush area into Queens or out of the city entirely to places like Rockland County. The Queens–Brooklyn dichotomy came to represent a new dividing line between *lelit-la* and *piti pèp-la* (elite and the "small people").

As in Haiti, *mini-djaz* played for all classes, but almost always within class-segregated contexts. Haitian nightclubs in the diaspora each had a certain class as their target clientele, and these class-based distinctions were maintained by ticket prices and targeted advertising (such as the use of mailing lists). The goal was to keep persons considered *moun dezòd* (unruly people or troublemakers) out of the clubs meant for *moun byennelve* ("proper" people):

> The big places here used to have 1,000, 2,000 [people in attendance] but they used to have fights and that's no good. They used to shoot too! You go out with your wife or girlfriend to enjoy yourself, and you end up running! People are sending out tickets now like they used to do in Haiti—in advance. You have a mailing list and you send out an invitation. (Interview: St. Victor)

Class divisions, fear of the INS, and deep political divisions among exiled political figures mediated against Haitians organizing along ethnic lines in the early phase, as Glick Schiller has pointed out, but it is an exaggeration to assume that "early Haitian arrivals avoided any collective activity" (Basch et al., 188). Rather, the collective activity took place in private at Friday night church socials or in rented ballrooms and clubs.

> We had our own club in New York *in a Chinese restaurant* and we called it Club Camaraderie. That's the name of a famous private club in Haiti at that time where families took their kids for special parties in the afternoon, and at night time, they return their families home and they go out by themselves. (Interview: Tavernier)

As this example points out, Haitian immigrants attempted to reproduce their spatially and temporally bounded experience of home in their recreational activities. Many in the generation that left Haiti around 1970 patronized the diaspora's *mini-djaz* as a re-immersion in homeland culture. Nightclubs, restaurants, and dance halls catering to Haitian audiences reproduced the names of well known clubs in Haiti (e.g., Club Camaraderie, Canne à Sucre, Cabane Créole, La Bacoulou, Djoumbala, and Château Royale) to foster a sense of familiarity, to invoke the ambience of the original, to reassuringly texture the new environs with features drawn from the old, and thus to help ease the transition into the new environment. Reputation is a kind of symbolic capital that helps to transport into the diaspora residual merchant-client networks and patronage systems. Michel Laguerre observed a similar pattern in New York Haitian businesses in general (93). For producer Fred Paul, immigrant nostalgia sparked his career choice:

> I said to myself, "It's funny that every Haitian in America is still eating like they were in Haiti … they have to get their rice and beans every day, they have to get their plantains every day, and they still buy either Haitian music or they buy…all those Spanish acts that they always knew. It's funny." So I said, "That's the business I'm going to go into." (Interview: Paul)[7]

Haitian bands in the States preserved cultural capital through symbolic references to earlier groups in Haiti, immediately establishing credibility, history, and audience in the diaspora. The New York Haitian newspapers of the early 1970s published advertisements for groups bearing the name of bands in Haiti attached to diaspora signifiers: Gypsies de Queens, Gypsies de New York, Les Fantaisistes de New York, Les Fantaisistes de Montréal, and others. A survey that appeared in Haiti's *Superstar Magazine* traced the attendance problems of New York's Haitian nightclubs to factors including nostalgia for the old bands and a variety of fears in the new setting:

> What are the causes? Why are they deserting the Haitian dances? The responses line up along seven axes: 50% declare that the music has changed, that it is has suffered from too closely embracing American music. You find this first group chiefly among the older adults

(55 or more years old). "Only the Weber Sicots, the Nemours, and the Jazz des Jeunes could bring me out to a Haitian dance" said Tony Mayas. 20% don't go out anymore because of the too-frequent fights, hooligans, and other accidents of which one risks being the victim. 2% of Haitians in New York find the price of a dance too high: $10 to $12 a head in inflationary times. 3% fear the INS and denunciations by other Haitians. 5% of Haitians go to the dances only on special occasions (the arrival of a mini-djaz or orchestra from Haiti such as D.P. Express, Bossa Combo, Gemini Express, Coupé Cloué, or Tropicana). ("Pourquoi la majorité," 4; translated from French)

Voluntary associations of all kinds sprang up in the diaspora, sponsoring musical events that evoked strong connections to the homeland. Regional associations held fund-raising parties for their localities of origin in Haiti—often on the Patron Saints' Day associated with the town or region—and hired *mini-djaz* for the entertainment. Youth groups sponsored fashion shows (with music) and *bals*. Sporting clubs contracted with *mini-djaz* to play awards ceremonies and post-game celebrations. Political organizations sponsored programs with speeches and music. Variety shows, called *spèktak* or *gala* (often with political overtones), became a staple for the politicized Haitian community, and these inevitably concluded with a *mini-djaz*. In this way, Haitian bands participated in community organization and were the core around which community-building events and "rituals of return" were constructed. The political music of this period was largely focused on overthrowing the Duvalier dictatorship.

"We're on the Edge of a Machete": *Konminote* and Crossover

Collective definitions of Haitians *lòt bò dlo* evolved noticeably over time, a feature of Haitian social life documented and theorized extensively by Nina Glick Schiller and her collaborators (Glick Schiller et al.; Glick Schiller and Fouron; Basch et al.). The growing use of the term *konminote* (community), rather than *koloni*, coincided with the organization of Haitians along "ethnic" lines in their host society to confront common problems such as the stigmatization of Haitians as politically violent, impoverished Vodou practitioners. Efforts to organize the population along ethnic lines stressed a new concern for local conditions, urban US politics, and their doubly oppressed minority status (marginalized as blacks and as foreigners). A strong sense of victimization is found in many songs by political or *angaje* performers, including the following by Atis Endependan (Independent Artists):

Kounye a menm lan tout peyi
    w ale
	Today, in any country to
	    which you go

Ou jwenn yon bann Ayisyen
    an egzil…
	You'll find a lot of Haitians in
	    exile

Kèlkeswa kote n ye	No matter where we are
Se klè nou lan manchèt	It's clear we're on the edge of a machete
	(Paredon P-1031)

Atis Endependan was one of a number of political cultural organizations that were promoting the use of Creole (as opposed to the elite language, French) and Haitian peasant culture in the diaspora. The *angaje* (*engagè*, political) music movement, also known as the *chanson patryotik Ayisyen* (Haitian patriotic song) developed a strategy directed toward the immigrants' national *and* ethnic predicaments (Averill 1994). Political singer Ti-Manno, in exile in the United States by 1981, criticized Haitian class stratification at home and in the United States (New York and Boston) in the song "Nèg Kont Nèg" (Black Against Black):

Nèg Kwins di l pa kanmarad	Queens people say they're not comrades
Nèg Bwouklin	With Brooklyn folks
Nèg Petyonvil di l siperyè	Petionville people say they're superior
Nèg Kafou	To Carrefour folks
Nèg Kanbwij di l pa kanmarad	Cambridge guys say they're not friends
Nèg Dòches	Of Dorchester guys
Nèg Potopwens di l pa annafè	Port-au-Prince folk say they'll have nothing to do
Ak nèg pwovens	With provincials

(CRLP 8016)

In this stage of diasporic development, popular music had a particularly clear-cut dual inter- and intracommunity function. Music reinforced ethnic boundaries, forming a sonic *antouraj* (fence around the *lakou* or extended family compound), within which—at the table, on the dance floor, at school parties, at fashion shows—the Haitian population transacted their business and reconstituted a corporate sensibility. Popular music also functioned at the boundaries to represent the community to others, sometimes situationally extending the boundaries to include other segments of the African diaspora: Caribbean peoples, black Americans, Creole speakers, etc. A host of venues for presentation, communication, and negotiation across ethnic boundaries has developed since the 1960s, when ethnicity and pluralism took on new importance in US cities. Multiethnic festivals like Caribbean Carnival (on Eastern Parkway in Brooklyn) and multi-ethnic venues (e.g., the dance club, Sounds of Brazil in New York) function in this manner—a means by which the music serves as a point of contact between subcultures in the United States or between a subculture and whatever concept of a hegemonic mainstream is operant at the time.

Haitian musicians attempted to maximize market success by responding to multiple audiences (or potential audiences). They created rituals of return—nostalgic immersions in the culture left behind—for the Haitian community, especially first generation immigrants who retained strong attachments to the homeland while simultaneously tailoring musical products for crossover success by emulating stylistic and structural elements of other subcultural musics as well as mainstream commercial musics of the host country. This challenged musicians to balance the demands of their existing patronage networks (within an ethnic group of origin) with potential patronage from outside the group. I should stress that it is not only the diasporic bands that are subjected to these pressures, but that these influences operate systemically throughout the transnational Haitian music market.[8]

To broaden their appeal, Haitian musicians used the introductory sections to *konpa* songs as explorations of other African diasporic styles (e.g., *salsa, reggae, funk*), which were then followed by the song and dance sections in a *konpa* rhythm. Tabou Combo dropped this type of introduction for reasons that reveal the influences to which they were responding:

We used to start the introduction with a lot of brass or whatever, then the singer would sing. We'd start the *kata* [*konpa* drum set rhythm] in the break. We don't do that anymore. They were playing a lot of Tabou albums in the discotheques and we noticed that the deejays always started playing the songs in the middle because the introduction wasn't that important. So now we start the beginning very hot. We kept a few breaks so the deejays could mix from one Tabou song to another from break to break. We were very hot in the discos because we were easy to mix. (Interview: Joseph)

We spent the whole summer of '77 rehearsing, preparing a demo in English for Benny Ashburn, who was [managing] the Commodores. He was very much interested in Tabou Combo. He was trying to put us on the Motown label which would have been a very big break for us. At that time, the Commodores were expanding, going up, and unfortunately that didn't work out for us. That was the main reason why we introduced horns in the band. (Interview: Andre)

Tabou Combo patterned their logo, costumes, and album art of the period after that of the Commodores. Groups like Parliment-Funkadelic, Earth Wind & Fire, Commodores, and Tower of Power influenced other New York *mini-djaz* like Djet-X and System Band, both of which adopted the space-age, futuristic semiotics of the earlier groups. The interest in black funk and soul groups arose in part because of their similarity to Haitian *mini-djaz* in group size, structure, and musical resources and in part because of the ideological bridges linking key populations of the African diaspora.

These crossover strategies and efforts by a group like Tabou Combo constitute a phenomenon distinct from the processes of cultural assimilation and Americanization. The influences that came to play were circulating primarily within the African diaspora, as *konpa*, *soca*, reggae, salsa, r&b, funk, jazz, *soukous*, *zouk*, and other African diasporic genres tugged at their stylistic boundaries. Far from obliterating "Haitianness," musicians exploited the "mark" of ethnic difference while modifying (sometimes situationally) elements of style, content, and performance practice (especially those considered necessary to meet presumed standards of non-Haitian markets) to expand patronage networks beyond a Haitian audience.

"Wise People in the Courtyards": *Dyaspora* and *Dizyèm Depatman*

As the struggle against the Duvalier dictatorship intensified throughout the mid 1980s, interest in island politics was renewed. Leaders in the diaspora increasingly used the term *dyaspo* or *dyaspora* (diaspora) to promote identification with the Haitian nation and with a political agenda incorporating both the U.S. *and* Haitian political situation. This ideological development of the diaspora is evident in two songs sung by Farah Juste, the singer mentioned in the opening sentence of this article. The two songs, "Dyaspora" and "*Dizyèm Depatman*," were recorded four years apart, the former just after the fall of Duvalier and the latter just after the inauguration of Aristide. In the former, the scattering of Haitians throughout the world is mourned as a tragedy for the Haitian people. The song lyrics link the development of a diaspora to the machinations of foreign countries and private voluntary organizations that control development and humanitarian aid in Haiti (Anglade, 68–71; Dewind and Kinley). In the later song, Juste chronicles the participation of the diaspora in transnational politics with a decidedly positive spin to the existence of a diaspora.

Yo bay Meriken yo zòn nò-a	They give the Americans the North Zone
Yo bay Kanadyen yo zòn sid-la	They give the Canadians the South Zone
Yo bay blan Fwanse-yo tout plaj	They give the white French the beaches
Yo pap gade sa Desalin te kite pou pèp-la	They're not protecting what Dessalines kept for us
Ou jwenn Ayisyen nan Bahamas	You find Haitians in the Bahamas
Ou jwenn Ayisyen nan Sen Domeng…	You find Haitians in the Dominican Republic
Ayiti fin tonbe yon diaspò	Haiti ends up becoming a diaspora
	(Michga M-019)

Lamoun Nouyòk leve kanpe	New York Haitians are standing up
Moun Bwouklin tranble…	In Brooklyn, they're like an earthquake…
Ayisyen Monreyal yo se moun total	Montreal Haitians are an incredible people
Yo pran lari ni gen fredi, lanèj, ak lapli…	They take to the streets in cold, snow, and rain…
M konnen gen granmoun	I know that there are wise people
Nan lakou dizyèm depatman yo	In the "courtyards" of the 10th Department
Ann fè yon rasanbleman	We're working together
Voye Ayiti monte…	To make Haiti better…
Pa kite peyi a nan boutèy	Don't keep our country in a bottle
	(No catalog number)

The lyrics *"gen granmoun nan lakou"* ("there are wise people in the courtyard / at home") refer to a well-known Vodou song that questions whether there are such people anymore. Juste provocatively employs the intimate and local form of social organization (the *lakou* or courtyard, around which extended family residences are arranged) as a metaphor for the immigrant communities, rendering notions of community and nation less abstract and more organic. Haitian newspapers have, in recent years, increasingly referred to immigrant communities with the identifier *"lakou"* (Lakou Miyami or Lakou Monreyal). In Juste's latter song, the transnational dispersion of Haitians becomes a resource and a social force for rebuilding Haiti.

In the months immediately following the exile of Baby Doc and his family, almost all commercial recordings emanating from the diaspora contained at least one *angaje* song about developments in Haiti. From the exile of Duvalier until the September 1991 Army coup supported by the bourgeois elite, former political refugees had much freer access to Haiti. Unrestricted travel to (and around) Haiti was possible during most of this period for anyone with a passport and money. Family members returned home with gifts, and diaspora residents vacationing at home brought earnings for a hard-strapped and de-touristified economy. Haitian-American radio stations and programs rebroadcast insular news programs and Haitian newspapers from the diaspora gained wider circulation on the island. Encouraged by the emergence of the Lavalas movement of Father Jean-Bertrand Aristide in Haiti, Haitians in the United States became increasingly radicalized vis à vis Haitian struggles in the United States, marching against AIDS stigmatization, boycotting grocery store discrimination, pressuring the INS for better treatment of Haitian immigrants, etc. Subcultural pride as an immigrant group in the United States (and the willingness to organize around immigrant issues) was—in the Haitian case—tied to pride in the political process on the island.

Aristide believed that the *Dizyèm Depatman* could form an important source of cash and expertise for his campaign and for the country, and he envisioned the involvement of many Haitian-American technocrats to help rebuild Haiti. Despite some indications of personal resentment of diaspora Haitians and their American mannerisms, many Haitians shared the optimism about the new incorporation of Haitians abroad into the affairs of the country. Singer Masterdji (Georges Lys Herard) urged diaspora Haitians to help build a "Road to Paradise" or "Chimen Paradi":

Yo diaspo, yo rezidan, poutan	They're diaspora, resident aliens, but
Pa kwè yo bliye kote yo soti	Don't think they've forgotten their roots
Ni poukisa y ap travi di	Nor why they're working so hard
Kòm tan vin pi bèl	As the times get better
Yo deside pran zèl	They decide to take wing
Pou jambe dlo	To cross the water

Pou wè nèg Pòtòprens	To see the folks in Port-au-Prince, to see
Sa k te kembe nan provens, fanmi-yo	What's happened in the provinces, their families
Men nan men, nan tout rakwen	Hand in hand, in every corner
Pou y al plante lakonesans	They'll plant understanding
	(Bwa Patat Records 90001)

Video technology played an interesting new role in transnational consciousness. For many years, performances by diaspora-based Haitian folkloric troupes had maintained a sentimental link with insular Haitian traditions for diaspora Haitians (Wilcken). Suddenly freed to travel throughout the country, diaspora Haitians returned with video cameras to capture *fèt patwonal* (patron's day festivals) in their home towns, important Vodou ceremonies, *rara* bands, and carnival in Port-au-Prince. Cheap copies of these videos found their way onto shelves in Haitian stores throughout the diaspora. Those unable to travel were now able to purchase the videos in Brooklyn stores. I believe that the decline in the fortunes of Haitian folkloric troupes noted by Wilcken was hastened by the ability of diaspora residents to consume the "real (mediated) thing" through video folklore.

Conclusion

The emergence of a Haitian diaspora is the single most defining feature of Haitian political economy in the past three decades. It is itself an artifact of a globalization spurred on by the global aims of transnational capital. Diasporas everywhere intensify issues of identity. Arjun Appadurai argues that "[i]n the postnational world we see emerging, diaspora runs with, and not against the grain of identity, movement, and reproduction" (423). The strongly imagined connections to homeland and nation that emerge in populations with attenuated connections to both, suggest that new varieties of nationalism are being birthed from the corpse of the integral nation state.

The Haitian music industry and its circulation of expressive commodities has been organized transnationally from its inception. Throughout the history of a Haitian diaspora, the recording industry linked diasporic and insular Haitians as a "community-of-taste," sharing a system of music production and consumption, with the circulation of musical commodities helping to bridge the distances created through migration. The transnational Haitian music market thus functioned as a "disembedding mechanism" (Giddens, 53) by which social relations were constructed outside of the realm of face-to-face encounters and localized contexts. The flow of audio and video cassettes, LPs and CDs—like radio broadcasts and rebroadcasts, affordable air travel, mailed remittances, and circular migration—has shrunk the cultural distance between New York, Miami and Port-au-Prince.

That music moves through space and diminishes in intensity with distance from a point of origin has been a crucial link to understanding its role in demarcating ritual space, in signalling power and authority, and in identifying communal celebratory spaces. Mediated through markets and broadcast media circulating within a transnational *system* of musical production and consumption, music functions to similar ends but on a far vaster scale, marking, signifying, and constructing transnational spaces and the identities that form within them. Music, it appears, may be the trans-national medium par excellence, defining social spaces as it moves through them.

In the diaspora during the 1960s and early 1970s, Haitian bands provided the contexts around which immigrants gathered for some of their most important collective rituals. Nostalgic song lyrics and the deliberate evocation of premigrational musical styles helped immigrants to imagine a homeland and to reconstitute elements of it in their new environment. As local considerations came to the foreground, immigrant musicians confronted these issues in texts, and at the same time mastered multiple musical codes to pitch musical products at diverse audiences, especially to other African diasporic communities.

Haitian popular music—in its transnational organization and circulation—anticipated and intensified transnational consciousness, helping to create, encourage, and sustain a culture that connects Haiti and the United States. Popular music has been an important component of the connective tissue of the Haitian transnation.

Notes

The first part of the title of this article refers to lyrics from the song "Haïti" by Skah Shah, 1974 (*Haïti* SS 201) that discuss systems for communication between diaspora and homeland, an issue of central importance in this article.

1. There are nine major political-administrative units (*dèpartements*) in insular Haiti. Thus, a reference to a 10th unit implies a fictive extension of the Haitian state to encompass its expatriates.
2. This is an instance of a generalized pattern recognized by Safran (93) in which homeland governments "exploit diaspora sentiments" in key host societies for their own political purposes. The Haitian diaspora has provided a continuous flow of remittances to families left behind, and these remittances constitute a significant percentage of the Haitian gross national product.
3. In equilibrium theories, population movements result from disequilibria in income and resources between regions or countries, and restore equilibrium through their movement. This approach effaces the political roots of disequilibria between Haiti and the U.S. (Stepick, 338). Lundahl has argued that no equilibrium is reached in the Haitian situation because migration itself contributes to a downward socio-economic-environmental spiral that he calls "cumulative causation" (*Haitian*, 39, 42–43). Equilibrium models marginalize the role of economic, cultural, political, and institutional barriers to migration in the country of origin as well as resistance to immigration on the part of the magnet country. Dependency theorists maintain that this flow of human resources from the periphery to the core is a critical product of core-periphery dynamics, working to the benefit of the core through a process financed by the migrants themselves (Locher, 327).
4. Analysts of Haitian history and political economy agree that Haitian governments have typically answered to a small fraction of the population, have functioned to siphon customs receipts and taxes from the peasantry, and have returned little of value to the public in the form of infrastructure or services. "Kleptocracy" is a term that has had some currency in this literature (Fass, 2). In the same spirit, Michel-Rolph Trouillot has titled his book *Haiti, State Against Nation*.
5. The *méringue* is a traditional Haitian couple dance that originated in the hybridization of European figure dances and Central African social dances sometime after Haitian independence. There are rural and urban forms, but the best known is the urban elite parlor dance or *méringue lente* (Averill 1989b).
6. *Mini-djaz* refers to a kind of band that became popular in Haiti in the mid-1960s. In contrast to the dance bands of the 1940s, '50s, and early '60s (called *djaz*, a creolization of the American term "jazz"), they were smaller and younger, and utilized electric instruments. Their repertoires were eclectic and transnational from the start, including Haitian *konpa*-s along with Latin *boleros*, imported rock tunes, and Brazilian *bossa novas* (Averill 1993).
7. Nearly all of the major Haitian producers from the late 1950s on have been based in the diaspora. Joe Anson (Ibo Records), Marc Duverger (Marc Records), Fred Paul (Mini Records), Jerome Donfred (JD Records), René St. Aude (St. Aude Records), Giroboam Raphael (Geronimo Records), and Melodie Makers have all been headquartered in the US. Interestingly, most albums were—and still are—recorded in Haiti (the 24-track Audiotek studio is the studio of choice), but the tapes are then taken to the U.S. to be mixed or mastered.
8. Juste-Constant underestimates the global context and transnational system of music circulation in his work on Haitian immigrant musicians in Montreal. The changes he notes taking place in the music (i.e., more improvisation, which he ascribes to the presence of Canadian nationals in the immigrant bands) can be found in music produced *in Haiti* in the mid-1960s. My own research suggests that none of the changes noted by Juste-Constant are due to immigrant status per se and certainly not to acculturation. Acculturation, with its directional arrow of cultural change, does not account for the ongoing, dynamic feedback between source and host societies in migration, nor for the increased identification with homelands that develop in diasporas. I prefer models emphasizing competitive strategies and intentional social praxis.

References

Anderson, Benedict. 1983. *Imagined Communities: Reflections on the Origins and Spread of Nationalism*. London: Verso.

André, Yvon. 1987. "Kapi." Personal interview. 10 Aug.

Anglade, Georges. 1982. *Atlas Critique d'Haïti*. Montreal: Groupe d'Etudes et de Recherches Critiques d'Espace, Département de Géographie, Université du Québec à Montréal et Centre de Recherches Caraïbes de l'Université de Montréal.

Appadurai, Arjun. 1993. "Patriotism and Its Futures." *Public Culture* 5:411–30.

Atis Endepandan. 1975. *Ki Sa Pou-N Fè?* Paredon P-1031.

Averill, Gage. 1989a. "Haitian Dance Band Music: The Political Economy of Exuberance." Diss. University of Washington.

———. 1989b. "Haitian Dance Bands, 1915–1970: Class, Race, and Authenticity." *Latin American Music Review* 10: 203–35.

———. 1993. "*Toujou Sou Konpa*: Issues of Change and Interchange in Haitian Popular Dance Music." *Zouk: World Music in the West Indies*, Jocelyne Guilbault et al. Chicago: University of Chicago Press.

———. 1994. " 'Se Kreyòl Nou Ye' (We're Creole): Musical Discourse on Haitian Identities." *Music and Black Ethnicity: The Caribbean and South America*, edited by Gerard H. Béhague. New Brunswick: Transaction Publishers.

Basch, Linda, Nina Glick Schiller, and Christina Szanton Blanc. 1994. *Nations Undone: Transnational Projects, Postcolonial Predicaments and Deterritorialized Nation-States*. Langhorne: Gordon and Breach.

Buchanan, Susan Huelsebus. 1982. "Scattered Seeds: The Meaning of the Migration for Haitians in New York City." Diss. New York University.

Dewind, Josh, and David H. Kinley III. 1988. *Aiding Migration: The Impact of International Development Assistance On Haiti*. Boulder; London: Westview Press.

D.P. Express. 1979. *David*. Superstar Records, SUP 111.

Dupuy, Alex. 1989. *Haiti in the World Economy: Class, Race, and Underdevelopment Since 1700*. Boulder; London: Westview Press.

Fass, Simon M. 1990. *Political Economy in Haiti: The Drama of Survival*. New Brunswick: Transaction Publishers.

Giddens, Anthony. 1990. *The Consequences of Modernity*. Stanford: Stanford University Press.

Gilroy, Paul. 1987. "*There Ain't No Black in the Union Jack*": *The Cultural Politics of Race and Nation*. Chicago: University of Chicago Press.

Glick Schiller, Nina, and Georges Fouron. 1990. " 'Everywhere We Go, We Are in Danger': Ti Manno and the Emergence of a Haitian Transnational Identity." *American Ethnologist* 17:329–47.

Glick Schiller, Nina, et al. 1987. "All in the Same Boat? Unity and Diversity in Haitian Organizing In New York." *Caribbean Life in New York City: Sociocultural Dimension*, edited by Constance Sutton and Elsa M. Chaney, 181–201. New York: Center for Migration Studies of New York.

Gold, Gerald, ed. 1984. *Minorities and Mother Country Imagery*. St. John's: Memorial U of Newfoundland.

Joseph, Jean-Yves. 1988. "Fanfan Ti-Bòt." Personal interview. 24 June.

Juste, Farah. *Fò Dimenche*. Michga Records, M-019.

———. *10èm Department*. No catalog number.

Juste-Constant, Vogeli. 1990. "Haitian Popular Music in Montreal: The Effect of Acculturation." *Popular Music* 9:79–86.

Laguerre, Michel S. 1984. *American Odyssey: Haitians in New York City*. Ithaca/London: Cornell University Press.

Locher, Uli. 1984. "Migration in Haiti." *Haiti—Today and Tomorrow: An Interdisciplinary Study*, edited by Charles R. Foster and Albert Valdman, 325–36. Lanham: University Press of America.

Lundahl, Mats. 1979. *Peasants and Poverty: A Study of Haiti*. London: Croom Helm.

———. 1983. *The Haitian Economy: Man, Land, and Markets*. New York: St. Martin's.

Master Dji. 1990. *Pòlitik Pa M*. Bwa Patat Records, 90001.

Morisseau, Guesley. 1988. "Ti-Gous." Personal interview. 19 May.

Paul, Fred. 1991. Personal interview. 9 Nov.

Pierre-Louis, Martine. 1989. Personal communication. 8 Feb.

"Pourquoi la majorité des Haïtiens a New York ne fréquentent plus les bals haïtiens??? " 1983. *Superstar Magazine* 16:4.

Safran, William. 1991. "Diasporas in Modern Societies: Myths of Homeland and Return." *Diaspora* 1:83–99.

Skah Shah. 1971. *Haïti*. SS 201.

Slobin, Mark. 1993. *Subcultural Sounds: Micromusics of the West*. Hanover: Wesleyan UP/UP of New England.

Stepick, Alex, et al. 1984. "The Roots of Haitian Migration." *Haiti—Today and Tomorrow: An Interdisciplinary Study*, edited by Charles R. Foster and Albert Valdman, 337–349. Lanham: University Press of America.

St. Victor, Jean Michel. 1988. "Zouzoul." Personal interview. 1 July.

Tavernier, José. 1989. Personal interview. 12 Feb.

Ti-Manno. *Sort Tiers Monde*. Chancy Records, CRLP 8016.

Trouillot, Michel-Rolph. 1990. *Haiti, State Against Nation: The Origins and Legacy of Duvalierism*. New York: Monthly Review Press.

Widmaier, Mushi. 1988. Personal interview. 22 July.

Wilcken, Lois. 1991. "Music Folklore Among Haitians in New York: Staged Representations and the Negotiation of Identity." Diss. Columbia University.

17

"Indian" Music in the Diaspora
Case Studies of Chutney in Trinidad and in London

Tina K. Ramnarine

Chutney is a contemporary Indian-Caribbean musical genre that displays influences from diverse sources. Whereas some musical elements can be traced to India and can be analysed as examples of musical retention or preservation, others have emerged as a result of musicians interacting in the pluricultural contexts of the Caribbean. Chutney musicians draw upon ideas from Indian folk traditions, devotional songs and film music, as well as from calypso, soca and rap. Although chutney draws upon traditions (mainly those of wedding celebrations) which came to the Caribbean with the first indentured labourers from India, the first public performances of this genre took place in Trinidad as recently as the late 1980s. Some efforts had been made to introduce the music into the public arena during the 1970s (for example, through the performances of the chutney singer, Sundar Popo), but these did not attract large audiences. Chutney shows are also presented, and are gaining increasing popularity, in London, New York and Toronto—metropolitan centres in which Indian-Caribbeans have settled. There are some musicians in India who perform chutney, having incorporated Caribbean popular forms into their repertories; Manuel (1995, 217) names the duo Babla and Kanchan. Their largest audiences, with regard to chutney, are nonetheless in the Caribbean—in Trinidad, Guyana, and Surinam, places with significant Indian-Caribbean populations.

Although tradition is often perceived as stemming from and having close ties to particular localities, the relationship between tradition and place is questioned when a single tradition is maintained, developed and changed by people in several different geographic contexts. With which place can a tradition like chutney be associated? India, the Caribbean, or the urban centres around the world which have become "home" to Indian-Caribbean communities? Consideration of human mobility, and of migrants as carriers of traditions to different places, has expanded the commonly adopted ethnomusicological frame of reference of studying music in its cultural context in a specific geographic location. The shift in emphasis has led to questions about the survival of elements of tradition in new contexts, and the ability of music to retain its identity away from the culture from which it sprang (Reyes-Schramm 1990). Although recent ethnographic accounts have examined music and musicians in the context of migration from rural to urban centres (e.g., Stokes 1992, Turino 1993), much research remains to be carried out on the topic of music-making in the diaspora. Projects tracing the roots of African music in the New World (Herskovits 1947, Levine 1977, Small 1987, Alleyne 1988) provide models for similar undertakings in the field of Indian music in the diaspora. Yet the complexity of music-making in diasporic contexts lies in the immense variation between different examples. For example, over 150 organisations were interviewed for the anthology *Klangbilder der Welt*, produced by the International Centre for Comparative Musicology, a study which revealed an enormous "range of approaches and histories of formation, activity, and stylistic choice" among what Slobin calls the "diasporic intercultural networks" found in Berlin (Slobin 1993, 66).

The main aim of this paper is to draw attention to a tradition which, despite its prevalence in the Caribbean and amongst Indian-Caribbean communities around the world, has received scant attention in ethnomusicological literature. This is in contrast to writings on music in India itself, which have a long history with a particular abundance of theoretical treatises. British colonial writings on Indian music in India are also plentiful and include descriptions of art and folk traditions (see Myers 1993a, Jairazbhoy 1993). There is also a growing literature on Caribbean music: recent studies include Manuel's general text on Caribbean music (1995), Guilbault's ethnography of zouk (1993), and Cowley's historical account of the development of calypso (1996). Writings on Indian-Caribbean music, however, are scarce (major exceptions being the works of Myers 1993b and Desroches 1996). References to chutney are even rarer. The main sources include press reports, Constance's (1991) book in which chutney is mentioned in relation to calypso and Ribeiro's (1992) examination of chutney. One of the earliest references is found in Ahyoung's dissertation, where mention is made of women's songs known as "chatni" (1977, 73), more commonly known today as "chutney." (I have chosen here to follow contemporary convention.)

There are three main reasons for the paucity of material relating to chutney, one of which is indeed the general lack of documentation on Indian music in the Caribbean. The second is that chutney as public performance is a recent phenomenon. Although it is well-known in the Caribbean and in Latin America, it has not yet established its presence in the market of world music. In Britain, for example, commercial cassettes of chutney (produced in the Caribbean and in the USA) are not readily available and can only be bought from private vendors. Third, chutney draws upon a tradition which was performed by women for audiences of women at private gatherings such as *mathkor* (pre-wedding celebrations) and at the birth of a child. Knowledge of *mathkor* was, and still is, passed on orally. Women's traditions are often difficult for ethnographers to access (Koskoff 1989). Yet this is not a secret tradition. The lack of empirical data and historical research is also a reflection on the general inattention paid to the experiences of Indian-Caribbean women (Poynting 1987).

The processes whereby the music and dance of *mathkor* came to be incorporated and represented in the popular genre chutney is a topic of my current research and will only be mentioned briefly in this paper. My main concern here is with chutney as contemporary music. Myers (1993b) and Manuel (1995) do mention chutney as an emerging popular genre, but more detailed descriptions and analyses of this tradition as public performance are only now being undertaken. In on-going research projects in the Caribbean, the tradition is being analysed in terms of "counter-nationalist discourses" and in relation to issues of gender (Kirk Meghu, personal communication 1995). A documentary film by Karen Martinez, "Chutney in Yuh Soca," examines the tradition as one in the process of "douglarisation," a Trinidadian expression coterminous with Hannerz's "creolisation" (1987). That music can be interpreted in diverse and contrasting ways, as illustrated by these approaches, makes it a potentially powerful area of discussion in public debate. Although research on chutney has barely begun, all kinds of claims are already being made for it. In surveying recent press reports on the Trinidad Carnival, February 1996, it is clear that chutney means different things to different people. One view is that it is an "Indian" tradition, and that recent chutney songs give the first indications of a movement of a people "to lay claim as authentic Indians in Trindiad and Tobago" (Ken Parmasad, cited in Alexander 1996). Another view is that it is not quite Indian and does not reveal the real musical wealth of India's musical traditions which are also available to Indians in the Caribbean (Ravi-Ji 1996). Chutney's emergence as a popular genre is interlinked with issues of the place, status and changing roles of Indians in the Caribbean. In discussions of these issues, the emphasis has been placed on "ethnicity" and "culture."

In this paper I shall interpret chutney shows as cultural performances which comment—through song texts in particular—on the experiences of a people in the diaspora. In the Caribbean, the diasporic context has become the new homeland. Performances of chutney create a sense of relatedness for performers and audiences, and affirm a specific ethnic and cultural identity. I shall argue that, as a tradition which has developed in a diasporic context, chutney emerges not as an Indian but as a specifically Indian-Caribbean form of expression. The spelling "chutney" rather than "chatni" is itself an identification of the genre as Indian-Caribbean, not Indian. The argument is pursued by examining chutney in Trinidad and in London, and by tracing, albeit briefly, the history of chutney from women's tradition to popular genre. A concern with ethnicity forms part of the complex relations that exist between different ethnic groups in Trinidad. The song text, particularly the calypso text as a well-established form of social commentary, has been a medium for exploring these dynamics, characterised both by dissension and by solidarity (see Deosarran 1987). Discussions about the preservation and mixing of cultures in chutney have been fuelled by the incorporation of African-Caribbean musical elements, for example, calypso rhythms. Such musical interaction, and the debate it inspires, are of course central to the interpretation of chutney as an Indian-Caribbean tradition. I do not wish to dwell on the dynamics between different ethnic groups in Trinidad, or indeed in London, here, but I shall draw attention to the mobility of "cultural elements" in discussing both the movements of people and chutney song texts. The focus, however, will be on chutney as an expression of an Indian-Caribbean identity: an identity which is expressed in the song texts by references to kinship systems, cultural practices and objects and the experience of migration.

Indentureship and the Emergence of an Indian-Caribbean Identity

The interlinking of place discussed here (Trinidad and London) is related to interlinking histories. Caryl Phillips observes that much British history is little known, "not least because much of it took place in India, Africa and the Caribbean" (quoted by Jaggi 1995). The historical forces which brought together Indian, British and Caribbean elements must be taken into account in tracing both the formation of an Indian-Caribbean identity and the development of the chutney tradition. Referring to chutney as a tradition in itself calls for some kind of historical account. Following Glassie's definition of tradition as "a temporal concept, inherently tangled with the past, the future, with history" (1995, 399), chutney can be perceived as a tradition because it looks back to the past, to folk songs which came from India and which women continued to perform in the Caribbean. As a popular genre it also looks to the future. It is a tradition which may eventually become part of the phenomenon of World Music. In tracing the development of chutney and the emergence of an Indian-Caribbean identity, we can begin by considering population movement from India to the Caribbean following British imperial policies to replace the workforce on sugar cane estates in particular.

Both in Britain and in the Colonies themselves, the question of labour dominated discussions on the future of the West Indian sugar plantations, following the emancipation of slaves in 1838. The colonial Caribbean cane-sugar industry, with the labour of African slaves, had expanded to such an extent during the eighteenth and nineteenth centuries that what had once been a rare commodity had become a daily consumer product (Mintz 1985). But after 1838 the emancipated slaves deserted plantation agriculture on the terms and conditions prescribed by the planters and by the British government, unwilling to work "for their former masters, for wages instead of lashes"

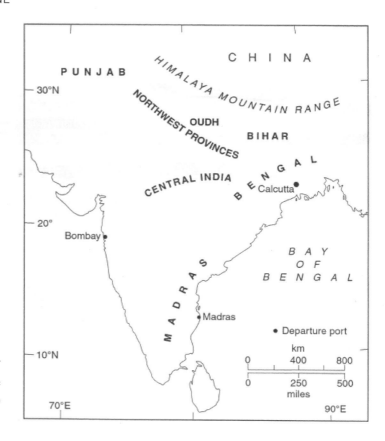

Figure 17.1 Sketch map of India showing the places of origin of Indian indentured laborers who traveled to the Caribbean.

(Williams 1962, 86). To maintain the colonial plantation system of sugar production, labourers were recruited from other parts of the Empire. Between 1838 and 1917, more than half a million Indians (mostly from the Northwest Provinces of Uttar Pradesh and Bihar) were taken to the Caribbean as indentured (contracted) labourers, changing the whole population pattern in the West Indies (see Figure 17.1 and Figure 17.2)

British recruiters in India told prospective labourers that "they would be going to Chini-dad (land of sugar) or that Fiji was a place just beyond Calcutta" (Samaroo 1987, 28). Indian labourers, neither realising the journey which lay ahead of them nor understanding the contracts which they signed, saw indentureship as a way of escaping harsh economic conditions and hunger, and anticipated an easier life in new lands. Some of them did not sign contracts: they were simply kidnapped. The system of indentureship, strikingly similar to the system of slavery which preceded it, was criticised in turn and gave rise to anti-indenture campaigns.

The first ship transporting Indians to Trinidad, the *Fath Al Razak*, landed in Port of Spain in 1845 with 217 Indians aboard. Their contracts initially lasted for a period of five years after which they could work for a further five years in order to claim a free return passage to India. When indentureship was abolished in 1917, less than a quarter of the Indian labourers returned to their homeland. Most of them decided to exchange the passage to India for a grant of land, for as Cudjoe observes, "so much had the quality and reality of their experience changed that there was really no home to which they could return" (Cudjoe 1985, 19). "Chinidad" had become Trinidad. Today, Indians as an ethnic group form nearly half of the island's population. Yet it is not a homogeneous group, for the Indians came from different regions, spoke different languages and dialects, were members of different castes, and brought a variety of cultural practices with them.

Figure 17.2 Sketch map of Trinidad showing places referred to in the text.

Examples of the retention of cultural elements from India to Trinidad have been located in kinship systems, village structure and religious rituals (Klass 1961), and in clothing, food and language (Lowenthal 1972). The majority of indentured labourers came from the northern provinces of Uttar Pradesh and Bihar where Bhojpuri, was spoken. The Bhojpur tradition, therefore, which had produced religious heroes such as Rama, Krishna and Buddha, as well as the *Ramayana* and the *Mahabharata* epics, became dominant in Trinidad.

The preservation of religious ideals and the celebration of religious festivals were significant in maintaining a sense of ethnic and cultural identity. Music has continued to play an integral role in religious rituals. Traces of ritual music can be found in some chutney songs. As well as the preservation of traditions, new ideas imported from India (including religious movements and figures) are absorbed by Indian-Caribbean populations. Films (subtitled in English) have been imported from India since the 1940s and have made an important contribution to the chutney style. Also, since the 1940s several dancers from India—including Rajkumar Krishna Persad, Sat and Mondira Balkaransingh, and Pratap and Priya Pawar—have held workshops and classes in Trinidad teaching the classical *Odissi* style and Punjabi, Gujerati, Bihari and southern Indian folk dances.

The demise of certain traditional practices was equally significant in the formation of an Indian-Caribbean identity. Language and the feudal caste system broke down. In Trinidad, labourers from different castes, from Brahmins (high caste) to Chamar (low caste), lived next to each other in the barracks and worked together in the cane-fields. English, which had been established as the official language of British India by 1835, emerged as the common language which enabled Indians in the Caribbean to communicate with each other and with the rest of the populace. The experience of indentureship in Trinidad led to the development of a sense of ethnic solidarity which has been somewhat ironically characterised by Sam Selvon as "East Indian Trinidadian West Indian" (Selvon 1987, 21). Here is a statement of ethnic identity which demonstrates allegiances to India as the ancestral country of origin, to the Caribbean island Trinidad which is "home," and to the Caribbean region in general. By drawing on elements from different traditions, chutney reinforces these loyalties and affirms the identity of Indian-Caribbeans as Caribbean people of Indian origin.

Even where commentators assert that the tradition is Indian, the assertion is made in a context in which being "Indian" serves both to remind Indian-Caribbeans of their ancestry and to further local political debates and interests.

Chutney in Trinidad

Given that chutney is said to have its origins in the celebration known as *mathkor*, a predominantly female mode of expression, special attention must be accorded to the role of women in Indian-Caribbean society. Patterns of family structure were affected during the period of indentureship by the scarcity of female labourers. Working on the sugar plantations, women gained a certain independence which was, however, compromised by their continuing scarcity. Women were expected, in some cases compelled, to marry at a young age and did not have the same educational opportunities as men.

Reference to *mathkor* is found in Ramnath's (n.d.) book on Indian culture written for Indian-Caribbean people who, the author explicitly stated, seemed to be forgetting the "true meanings" of many of the rituals which they continued to perform. Ramnath (n.d., 97–98) describes and explains the meaning of *mathkor* as part of the Aryan Hindu Sanatanist[1] wedding ceremony (Figure 17.3) as follows:

> Mathkor literally means dirt digging…This pujan [religious ceremony] is the honouring of Mother Earth from whence all physical things have their beginnings. On the afternoon just before the pundit [priest] performs the first ceremony to commence the wedding…the mother [both the bride's and the groom's] along with close relatives and friends go to a place where the intended ceremony will be performed. The spot must be free from refuse or waste

Figure 17.3 An Aryan Hindu Sanatanist Wedding Ceremony in Trinidad.

matter, preferably near a river, lake or pond...On this spot the mother takes clean water brought with her or water from the river or pond so long as the water is clean. She must use her right hand and sprinkle the water on the spot...After washing her hands she takes water again from a bronze goblet or *lota* and sprinkles the spot again. This time the significance is that the spot is being made pure or cleansed.

...The mother will thank Mother Earth who had blessed and afforded her this great opportunity to have a child who is to be married...During the time when the mother is performing her rituals, lady relatives and friends beat drums, and dance to appropriate songs to Mother Earth and other deities.

Vertovec also refers to the *mathkor* ceremony, describing the dances as "highly suggestive" (1993, 203). Such a description is reminiscent of those I encountered with regard to chutney. The following comment is typical of those I came across during informal conversations with women in south Trinidadian villages: "Today you find a lot of men going to hear the chutney shows. The dancing is a bit, you know, 'vulgar'. The women shake up the waist and I think that is why a lot of men go—to see the dance."

As well as dance, drums such as the *dholak* and *tassa* (Figure 17.4) play an important role in *mathkor* and also in contemporary chutney, as seen in these two accounts by women in a south Trinidad village:

"I remember my sister's wedding. I was only a child at the time. My aunt gave me a lot of money because it would have been my turn next to get married. The day before the wedding all the women came to our house and we all went down to the river. We always went to the river O. They were singing, dancing and playing drums. They put saffron on my sister's forehead and painted her hands...."

Figure 17.4 Heating tassa drums for a wedding in Trinidad.

"I saw when the neighbour opposite was going to get married. All the women dressed in their saris started singing and dancing outside the house. They were going to the river. Some of them were playing the drums. I could have gone but I was in the shop...."

Mathkor, as women's pre-wedding celebration, with the ritual bathing, the drumming, singing and dancing, can be traced to cultural practices in India. The *dholak*, for example, is still played as a domestic instrument in the north of India. The use of the drum by women in Trinidad seems to be a continuation of a tradition "depicted in Mughal and provincial court sources, where it was played by the women of the palace to accompany birth and wedding songs and sometimes also dance" (Dick 1984, 562). The importance of going to the riverside in the accounts above is paralleled by the widespread practice in India of pre-wedding ritual bathing, the *ban*. There are similarities between the pre-wedding celebrations in India and in Trinidad, but the important points here are first, that wedding songs constitute "a major part of India's folksong tradition" (Wade 1980, 150), and second, that they are sung by women. The songs are "rich in documentation about family lineage" (ibid.). Whatever the social restrictions, then, Indian-Caribbean women who continued these performances played a vital role in celebrations marking the expansion of the family, and were the carriers of musical traditions, folksong in particular. These are some of the traditions that chutney singers draw upon today.

Searching for parallel practices between Indian and Indian-Caribbean populations seems to point to earlier performances of chutney in Trinidad (drawing on the folksongs of *mathkor*) as preserving tradition. Yet the tradition has changed. Chutney shows today usually feature a solo singer (male or female) with a backing band. They are held in formal performance contexts: in halls and theatres. In addition to the continued use of the *dholak*, the traditional chutney ensemble includes a *dhantal* (an idiophone struck with a horseshoe shaped beater that has become significant as a marker of Indian-Caribbean identity, Ramnarine 2001, 63–68) and harmonium (Figure 17.5). The instrumentation often also includes guitars, keyboards and drum machines. Members

Figure 17.5 A chutney ensemble. Left to right: dholak, harmonium, dhantal.

of the audience, particularly women, invariably get up to dance at these shows. In short, changes lie in new conceptualisations and treatment of folksong, so that this is now a musical repertory to which men can turn as well as women; in performance contexts, from the riverside as part of ritual to the stage as entertainment; and in the music itself, from the singing, clapping and drumming of women to a more varied instrumentation including the use of electronic instruments and of male voices. One reason for rapid change in the tradition (from women's performance to popular genre) is suggested by Manuel who writes that "the flowering of the chutney scene has paralleled the increased movement of East Indians away from rural sugar plantations and into the urban mainstream" (Manuel 1995, 218). The changing status and role of Indian-Caribbean women has also contributed to rapid musical change.

In a study of Indian music in Felicity, a village in North Trinidad, Myers writes: "Indian music is different things to different people. For the younger generation it refers especially to Indian film songs, for the older to the traditional Bhojpuri folk songs, and for practically everybody to temple songs, such as bhajan and kirtan. For all, it means a repertory with texts in an Indian language" (1993b, 235). Despite the emphasis on language (noteworthy, for many Indian-Caribbeans have little knowledge of the languages of their forebears), many contemporary chutney song texts are in English with a few Hindi words added. Sometimes a Hindi text intermingles with its English translation. The use of English is significant for two main reasons: it is the language of today's Indian-Trinidadian population, and Trinidadians from a non-Indian background find chutney more accessible than, for example, Indian religious songs. Yet this is not the English of the coloniser, it is the Indian-Caribbean adaptation of the language (see Cudjoe 1985, Mahabir 1985).

As I have already indicated, the attitudes of audiences towards chutney are varied. In addition to questions about the origin and musical value of chutney, it is also a tradition which, for some people, represents the Indian response to calypso. For others it is simply good party music. Some dislike chutney because it is music with too much "wining" (dancing) and "jamming" (partying). For an article in the *Trinidad Guardian* in 1996, school children were asked why they thought that chutney had been so popular during the carnival celebrations that year. Here are some of their comments:

Maurisa Ramsingh: "I think its popularity is due to the 'coalition' government because this represents the coming together of two races [African and Indian]. Chutney has now become a major force in uniting the two races."

Patel Grant: "It is popular because of the continued pattern in which Stalin [a calypsonian] won the Calypso Monarch competition last year with Sundar Popo [a chutney singer]."

Simon Williams: "...it represents a coming together of two cultures."

Richard Payle: "I think that chutney has become popular because the calypsonians of East Indian descent have brought forward their culture, and because of this the other races have adopted what the Indian calypsonians have brought forward." [Cited in *Trinidad Guardian*, 17.ii.96, 9, no author given]

These are commentaries on the political significance of chutney, on the interaction between calypso and chutney—and on a more general level between "two cultures"—and on issues of ethnicity and the role played by music in society. In contrast to speculations about the Indianness of chutney, these school children do not posit a simple opposition between chutney and calypso. Instead, they stress musical interaction.

Although Myers noted "a conspicuous absence of acculturation between East Indian and Creole music" (1980, 150) less than two decades ago, contemporary chutney is indeed a popular genre with roots in both India and Africa, which has developed in the pluricultural contexts of the Caribbean. The rhythm of "chutney soca" has been described as "totally indigenous" (Baptiste 1993, 39). Parallels can be drawn between chutney and calypso on the basis of song competitions, the celebratory aspects of the music with an emphasis on dancing and on parties, a focus on the singer, and the range of topics addressed by the texts of the songs. Moreover, there is evidence of increasing interaction between chutney and calypso musicians with the participation of chutney artists in carnival and in the calypso tents, and with the entry of African-Caribbean musicians into chutney competitions. The second annual National Chutney Monarch competition (1996), modelled on calypso ones, was approved by chutney and calypso organisations: the National Association of Chutney Artists of Trinidad and Tobago, the Trinbago Unified Calypsonians Organisation, the Ministry of Community Development, Culture, and Women's Affairs, and the Carnival/Cultural Judges Association of Trinidad and Tobago. Chutney and calypso, therefore, are not performance events exclusive to a specific ethnic group. The use of the term "chutney soca" is evidence of the influence of calypso, and it is sometimes used to describe the genre (as it has been presented in the public arena).

Processes of acculturation, borrowing and incorporation as a result of culture contact in a pluricultural context can be traced in the development of chutney as an Indian-Caribbean tradition. If it is a tradition which has been both preserved and changed in Trinidad, popular and folk music in India has also undergone adaptation and change in interaction with other musical influences. This is particularly true of Indian film music. In its early stages Indian cinema "borrowed extensively from Hollywood and European productions," but it has developed as "a home-grown domestic entertainment form guided by indigenous aesthetics and conditions" (Manuel 1988, 173). This is not, then, a mere imitation of Western cinema, just as chutney is not simply a reproduced Indian tradition. The emphasis in film music has been on producing simple and catchy tunes, and this in turn has influenced regional folk music. Links between chutney and Indian popular musical forms, via the film industry, can be noted here. In addition to being the dominant category of popular music in South Asia, film music also reaches audiences throughout the Indian diaspora. Diatonic melodies to which Western styles of harmonisation can be added, as well as the combination of Indian instruments such as the *dholak* and the *tabla* (drum pair) with Western ones, are characteristic of both popular forms in India (Manuel 1988, ch. 7) and in the Caribbean.

The notion of musical revitalization is also pertinent to the analysis of chutney. As well as imported film music, Indian musicians and religious leaders who teach Indian classical music (in particular) have travelled to Trinidad. Some of the most influential figures have included the Hindu missionaries from the Bombay-based Arya Samaj reformist movement, who visited Trinidad during the 1920s; Professor Adesh, who has visited repeatedly since the 1960s and has now set up a religious movement in addition to teaching North Indian classical music; and the Sai Baba religious movement introduced in 1974 (see Myers 1993b, 238–9). Devotional music hitherto unknown in Trinidad has been introduced through such movements. Indian communities in Trinidad have looked to such figures for ideas as to what is truly Indian, and their comments about Indian-Caribbean culture in relation to the "parent" one have stimulated debates about authenticity. Tracing the development of chutney is further complicated by such exchanges, for some Indian elements, then, are not examples of retention at all, but are new ideas which are incorporated in constructing a Caribbean "Indianness."

Song Texts

Many chutney song texts are repetitive. The structure is usually alternating verse and chorus. I have selected some examples which highlight the ways in which chutney texts create a sense of relatedness, of belonging, firstly by exploring the experiences and every-day concerns of Indian-Caribbeans, and secondly by the naming of specific places—in the Caribbean or elsewhere with large Indian-

Caribbean populations (in the following examples, Guyana, Trinidad, the USA, Canada and the Trinidadian villages Penal and Sangre Grande). Some of these song texts centre around themes of marriage and courtship. These are the themes with which women, in private contexts, must have been concerned on such occasions as preparing a bride for a wedding. A thread of continuity is thus provided, with the transition of chutney from private to public spheres, through its narrative content. The song texts are those of some of the most successful chutney singers. These include Sundar Popo, one of the first musicians to bring chutney to a wider audience during the 1970s, Anand Yankaran, Drupatee Ramgoonai, and from the village Fyrish in Guyana, Terry Gajraj.

Example 1: Sundar Popo (JMC[2] cassette JMC-1113, 1995), "Indian arrival"

> The *Fatel Rozack* [common spelling of *Fath Al Razak*] came from India
> with me *nanee* [maternal grandmother] and me *nana* [maternal grandfather]
> and some landed here.
>
> They brought with them their language, Urdu and Hindi,
> their culture: Hosein, Phagwa, Ramlila and Divali.
>
> ...Like brother and sister
> in the boat they came, singing and playing their tabla.
> Remember 1845, the 13th of May
> 225 immigrants who landed on that day.
>
> Early every morning, the bells ring louder
> to labour agriculture so their children wouldn't suffer,
> sugar cane, cocoa, coconut, rice and banana.
>
> Together with me *agee* [paternal grandmother]
> and me *agaa* [paternal grandfather],
> labour was cheap but food was cheaper
> watch *penga* [money] come for flour
> and *penga* come for rice
> cent and a half for sugar
> and everything was nice.

This song was released in the year when Indians were celebrating 150 years in Trinidad. Sundar Popo provided a well-known account of Indian migration to Trinidad and the labourers' experiences on the plantations, referring to the *Fath Al Razak*, sugar cane and other agricultural pursuits. This was one of the chutney songs composed in celebration of "Arrival Day."

Example 2: Anand Yankaran (JMC cassette JMC-1112, 1996), "Guyana kay dulahin"

> *Guyana kay dulahin* [bride (or daughter-in-law) from Guyana]
> come to Trinidad
> I want to be your *dulaha* [bridegroom].

In this song text the bridegroom appeals for a bride not from India but from another Caribbean island. Through marriage, kinship ties are thereby strengthened between Indian-Caribbeans from Trinidad and Guyana, at the same time as they are weakened between the Caribbean and the ancestral homeland, India. On the other hand, the continued use of kinship terms such as *dulaha* and *dulahin* is one of the clearest examples of preservation of language.

Example 3: Terry Gajraj (cassette recording, 1994), "Guyana Baboo"

> Me come from de country they call Guyana
> land of de bauxite, de rice and sugar...
> Singing in the US and Canada
> I am coming back man, back to Guyana...
> I am coming back, back to Guyana
> to find me a *dulahin* for this *dulaha*.

Whereas Indians began migrating to the Caribbean in 1838, a more recent Indian-Caribbean migration to the United States and to Canada began during the 1980s. Terry Gajraj is a chutney singer whose lyrics draw upon his experiences in Guyana. The description of Guyana as the land of rice and sugar reminds the listener of plantation agriculture, which has been so important for the island economy and which played a pivotal role in transporting Indian populations to the Caribbean. Having migrated to a diasporic context which is home to Indian-Caribbean communities (North America), the singer as the protagonist in this song nonetheless emphatically identifies himself with the Caribbean through repetition of the phrase "I am coming back." He intends to find a bride from the Caribbean, thereby strengthening his affiliation to Guyana (as in example 1) by kinship ties. Again, the kinship terms *dulahin* and *dulaha* are used.

Similar sentiments are expressed in other chutney texts. The use of other kinship terms (*nanee*, grandmother; *bhowji*, sister-in-law), references to food (*baiganee*, an aubergine snack; chutney; rice; *dhal*, lentils) and to instruments (*tassa*, drum) are other representations of common experiences. Calypsonians draw upon a similar kind of imagery in texts dealing with Indian-Caribbean themes. One of the most well-known is the love song produced by the eminent calypsonian Mighty Sparrow (Example 4).

Example 4: Mighty Sparrow (BLS cassette BLS-1015, 1992), "Marajhin"

> I will tell you true
> the way I feel for you
> I'll do anything to make you happy
> so if you think it's best
> to change me style of dress
> I will wear a *caphra* [cotton suit] or a *dhoti* [cloth wrapped around waist]
> I'll give you a modern *jupa* [wooden house] down in Penal
> and I'll change my name to Rooplal or Sparrowlal
> I could learn to grind *masala* [spice] and *chunka-dhal* [lentils]
> and jump out of time to sweet pan for carnival.

Drupatee Ramgoonai describes musical interaction in the Caribbean as follows:

Example 5: Drupatee Ramgoonai (1989), "Indian soca"

> Indian soca, sounding sweeter,
> hotter than a *chulha* [stove];
> rhythm from Africa and India,
> blend together is a perfect mixture.

Example 6: Sundar Popo (JMC-CT 1082, 1994), "Phoulourie"

> CHORUS: *phoulourie bina chutney* [a spicy snack without chutney] *Kai say banee* [that's all I'm preparing].
>
> VERSES: I went Sangre Grande
> to meet Lord Harry...
> I beating my drum
> and I singing my song
> the only thing I missing
> is my bottle of rum...
> Me and my darling
> was flying in a plane
> the plane catch a fire
> and we fell inside the cane...
> Jack and Jill went up the hill
> to fetch a pail of water
> Jack fell down and broke his thumb
> and Jill came tumbling after.
> Little Jack Horner
> Sat in a corner
> eating his Christmas pie...

Many different themes are raised in this song. Sangre Grande, phoulourie chutney, the drum, the bottle of rum, the cane—these are all images of local village life. The plane is today's way of travelling. By falling back into the cane, the singer does not leave his familiar environment. Even in travelling to other places, the singer carries the experience of the sugar cane fields with him.

In contrast to Manuel's observation that "most of Trinidad's musical vitality and cultural dynamism has developed in spite of rather than because of British rule", and that the island "remains host to a number of distinctly non-English music traditions" (1995, 184), the inclusion of the nursery rhymes in Sundar Popo's chutney song is an example of those cultural elements which have been absorbed in the tradition as a result of historical circumstance and interaction between people from diverse places. London, like Trinidad, is host to many diverse traditions from around the world, of which chutney is just one.

Chutney in London

During the 1950s and 1960s, Caribbeans were recruited to fill the post-war labour shortage in the "mother country" (Britain). The descendants of Indian migrants to the Caribbean undertook a second migration, again in response to British policy. Although many of those who made the journey are Caribbeans of Indian descent, an Indian-Caribbean identity is still scarcely recognised in Britain. The experience of emigrating to a country which—despite ties on imperial, political and economic levels—did not feel like a homeland, brought issues of identity to the forefront. Questions of ethnicity and culture resurface in a new geographic context. Indian-Trinidadians in London were, until 1962 with the colony's independence from the empire, British citizens, yet visible "others" who maintained strong affiliations to the Caribbean, and who had a connection, from the more distant past, with India. The Race Equality Policy Group of the London Policy Unit was the first local authority department to recognise an Indian-Caribbean community, appointing an officer

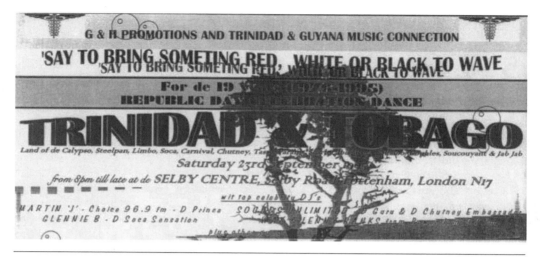

Figure 17.6 Promotional poster for a chutney show in London. Reproduced by kind permission of S. Rambaran.

to liaise with community representatives in 1986. An Indo-Caribbean Cultural Association was set up in 1988. That the existence of the community is nevertheless little known is not surprising given that for many Indian-Caribbeans a sense of belonging to a particular community is largely achieved through maintaining links with other Indian-Caribbeans, with friends, relatives, friends of friends and so on. Community events are infrequent. The occasional chutney performances, with singers from the Caribbean, provide one of the few opportunities for a group expression of identity. The promotional posters for these events reveal some of the symbols of that identity. These include steel band, soca, parang and chutney (Figure 17.6).

That such performances are organised at all is evidence of the links that are maintained between London's Indian-Caribbean community and the Caribbean. Chutney shows began to be organised in London soon after chutney singers entered the arena of public performance in the Caribbean, largely due to the efforts of Suresh Rambaran, who established G and H Promotions. As one of the first promoters of chutney music in London, he organised some performances as charity events to raise money to send to Trinidad. In general, however, the performances have not been profit-generating and have been organised because of Rambaran's personal interest in contemporary Indian-Caribbean music (Suresh Rambaran, personal communication). Before these public musical performances, the main medium for exploring issues of identity was through literature; indeed, a preoccupation with delineating identities is apparent in the writings of many Indian-Caribbean authors. In his opening address to the conference on East Indians in the Caribbean (1979), Selvon commented (1987, 17):

> I wrote a story once which was based on fact, about a Trinidad Indian who couldn't get a room to live in because the English landlord didn't want people from the Westindies, only bona fide Indians from the banks of the Ganges. So my boy posed as a true-true [real] Indian and got the room... But truth is even stranger than fiction, for when I applied to the Indian High Commission in London for a job, I was told that I was not an Indian because I came from Trinidad and was not born in India.

As a tradition which has developed in diasporic contexts, drawing upon diverse cultural and musical elements, chutney too is a reflection of the variety of identities adopted by individuals. This is true on a more general level in considering Caribbeans in the diaspora and their musical choices. Manuel writes that "a typical New York West Indian may have various overlapping ethnic self-identities, for example, as Trinidadian, as West Indian, as Black, and . . . as American. Musical tastes reflect these intersections, as young West Indians grow up enjoying rap and R&B as well as the Sparrow in their parents' record collections" (1995, 209–10).

Diversity in musical choices and overlapping identities are general features of what Slobin (1993) terms the "intercultural network" in his survey of the ways in which music travels to different parts of the world. Taking into account the musical biographies of individuals is one way of probing the workings of an intercultural network. As an example, consider the musical biography of the Guyanese singer Terry Gajraj, who migrated to the USA during the 1980s. With his recording "Guyana Baboo" (1994), Gajraj became one of the best-selling recorded Indian-Caribbean singers. Traditional "Indian" elements have been transmitted to him through the family from one generation to another. His father taught him to play the accordion, the harmonica and the guitar. He learnt some Hindi and singing from his grandfather, who was a *pundit* (Hindu priest). By the age of six, Gajraj was performing at his family's *mandir* (temple). The music of ritual and the traditions transmitted through the family have been combined with other musical influences. He later freelanced with soca groups (the Original Pioneers and Melody Makers) and performed at weddings, fairs, and estate dances. In 1989, like many other young Caribbeans seeking their fortunes, he moved to the USA, where his recording career was launched due to a fortunate set of circumstances and chance meetings. During the 1990s he was invited to perform in the calypso tents at the Trinidad carnival. His own evaluation of his chutney style is that he blends Indian songs with influences from soca, reggae and rap. From his base in New York he travels to different performance venues, including different cities in the USA and in Canada, the Caribbean (as a chutney singer and as a calypsonian) and London. The diverse influences which we find in the musical biography of this singer are those that constitute the tradition of chutney as well.

A performance given by Terry Gajraj in London in 1995 attracted approximately 400 people—a good turnout, according to the organisers. The venue was a school hall which had been hired for the evening. Beer from the Caribbean and Indian food like *roti* (a type of bread) and chicken curry was sold. Chutney in London, unlike in the Caribbean or amongst the Caribbean community in New York, is a little-known music which barely attracts audiences beyond the Indian-Caribbean community. The best-known Asian musical genre in Britain is bhangra, the music of "British Asian youth culture" (Baumann 1990), which emerged during the 1970s. Through bhangra, a re-invented Punjabi folk tradition which developed in London and in the Midlands, the Punjabi sphere of influence extends to other South Asian communities in Britain, the USA and Australia. Whether audiences are small or large, both chutney and bhangra are examples of popular musical genres which have developed in the diaspora, which cross many geographic, political and cultural boundaries and which are performed in urban centres like London. Both forms reveal influences from diverse sources. Bhangra musicians in London and in the Midlands, like chutney musicians in Trinidad, have looked to African-Caribbean models of musical expression. Yet bhangra as a re-invented and re-contextualised tradition is rooted in a folk tradition from a defined region—the Punjab. By contrast, the origins of chutney beyond the Caribbean are difficult to trace. Bhojpuri traditions may be dominant among the Indian-Caribbean population, but elements incorporated from different regions in India together with those from local contexts in the Caribbean also contribute to chutney.

Conclusions

Exchanges between travellers, and experiences in the New World, led to the development of new traditions and identities as soon as the first indentured labourers from India undertook the journey over the *kala pani* (black water) to Trinidad. Sometimes the language of alienation and grief is used in song texts of migrants (as Stokes 1992 describes in relation to southeast Turkish migrants in Istanbul). Such use is not often found in contemporary chutney texts. Instead, themes of courtship and marriage are prevalent and seem to have their origin in the performance of chutney in private, initiatory contexts as the status of a woman changed to that of a bride or a mother. Recent changes in the tradition—the move from private to public performance, the entry of male performers and the increasing links between chutney and other Caribbean musical genres—all have a political importance. The arrival of chutney at the forefront of popular culture has coincided with the Indian-Caribbean ascent to political power, which culminated with the election of an Indian-Caribbean prime minister in Trinidad. Chutney shows create a sense of relatedness between Indian-Caribbeans via the use of what are perceived to be Indian elements from the ancestral homeland. These elements are a cultural heritage on one hand, and on the other, the result of a continuing interaction with India.

Yet chutney is an Indian-Caribbean tradition. Chutney singers incorporate the musical procedures of other, better-known Caribbean traditions, and aim to reach as wide an audience as possible. An Indian-Caribbean identity is affirmed amidst the contrasting claims made about the tradition. Whether the tradition is described as an authentic Indian one, or whether it is perceived as the result of musical interaction in the Caribbean, debates regarding chutney occur in the context of asserting an Indian identity in the Caribbean, not in India. The debate is about protecting Indian culture in the Caribbean from other powerful influences on one hand, and on the other, about celebrating the Indian contribution to the diverse cultural life of the Caribbean. The political significance of chutney, which I have only touched upon here, partly accounts for the vast differences in the reception of the tradition in Trinidad and in London. In Trinidad, chutney is now another established popular genre. In London, it is hardly known outside the relatively small Indian-Caribbean community. Performances are advertised to, and attended by, members of that community.

I have described chutney as hitherto predominantly female traditions performed in private and rural contexts (such as *mathkor*), which have been transformed into a popular genre enjoying current favour. Difficulties in tracing its history are paralleled by those in attempting to trace the genealogical histories of Indian-Caribbean families. Oral testimonies are vital in the study of Indian-Caribbean experiences. Yet these are incomplete and reflect the subjective experience of the narrator. V.S. Naipaul eloquently expresses the uncertainties as follows: "In our blood and bone and brain we carry the memories of thousands of beings. We cannot understand all the traits we have inherited. Sometimes we can be strangers to ourselves" (1994, 9). The attempt both to trace the history of, and to uncover the sources which contribute to, chutney is informed by more than a general ethnomusicological interest in the origins and history of different traditions (Brailoiu 1984, Blum et al. 1993). The memory of chutney as a hitherto female tradition performed on specific occasions is central to the interpretation of the tradition I have pursued here. Women's performance of chutney (music and dance) was a celebration of the extension of the family. It was part of the rites in which new kinship ties were established through a marriage or a birth. Contemporary chutney shows create a sense of a wider kinship whereby people are linked by ties (historical, political and cultural) which extend beyond the family to the community. Even if members of that community remain unknown to each other, they share a common inheritance. This is a sense of relatedness which is expressed by men as well as by women, and which encompasses Indian-Caribbean communities around the world. If in the diasporic context described here, London, chutney is still only really known to members of a specific community, it is nevertheless a tradition which may ultimately join other ones, including the better-known Trinidadian calypso and steel band, jostling for audiences and funding on the World Music stage.

Epilogue

Since this paper was originally published, almost a decade ago, chutney has indeed become established as a popular Caribbean tradition that finds a place on the World Music stage. Chutney performers have also begun to undertake tours in India. These include the group, Ram Khilwan and Troupe, Rikki Jai (a winner of both the Chutney Soca Monarch and National Chutney Monarch titles) and currently, as this goes to press, a group managed by the music promoter, Ajeet Praimsingh, D'Bhuyaa Saaj Troupe. Chutney musicians continue to experiment with a variety of musical techniques and to appear in Carnival. The tradition has attracted substantial research interest since the mid-1990s. Myers (1998) and Manuel (2000) devote chapters to chutney. Many of the ideas presented in this paper were elaborated in my own ethnography of this tradition (2001). Chutney, as an example of Indian diasporic musical practice, continues to inspire researchers, for example Niranjana (2005). Re-reading this paper, I am aware that it contributed to research trends expanding ethnomusicological approaches that had hitherto been largely concerned with locally bounded, or at least locally studied, traditions. More recently, though, I have been adding some important nuances to, even revising, some of the ideas presented here, questioning, in particular, some of our taken for granted assumptions about "ethnicity," "identity" and "culture" (see Ramnarine 2004). It seems that the study of music in the diaspora still holds much potential for prompting ethnomusicologists to further consider long cherished paradigms in pursuit of more profound understandings of music and creative processes in human life.

Notes

1. For an explanation of Sanatanism, as well as of the Arya Samaj movement mentioned below, see Vertovec 1992, 57–61 and chapter 4.
2. JMC is Jamaican Music Connection, a record label based in New York; BLS Records (example 4) is based in the Virgin Islands.

References

Ahyoung, Selwyn E. 1977. *The Music of Trinidad*. Unpub. B. A. dissertation, University of Indiana.
Alexander, G. 1996. "Chutney Adds its Spice to our Cultural Evolution." *Trinidad Guardian* 11, 2.
Alleyne, Mervyn. 1988. *Roots of Jamaican Culture*. London: Pluto Press.
Baptiste, Rhona. 1993. *Trinitalk: A Dictionary of Words and Proverbs of Trinidad and Tobago*. Port of Spain: CISS.
Baumann, Gerd. 1990. "The Re-invention of Bhangra: Social Change and Aesthetic Shifts in a Punjabi Music in Britain." *The World of Music* 32(2):81–98.
Blum, Stephen, Philip Bohlman, and Neuman, Daniel, ed. 1993. *Ethnomusicology and Modern Music History*. Chicago: Chicago University Press.
Brailoiu, Constantin. 1984. *Problems of Ethnomusicology*, ed. and trans. A. L. Lloyd. Cambridge: Cambridge University Press.
Constance, Zero Obi. 1991. *Tassa, Chutney and Soca: The East Indian Contribution to Calypso*. Trinidad: San Fernando.
Cowley, John. 1996. *Carnival, Canboulay and Calypso Traditions in the Making*. Cambridge: Cambridge University Press.
Cudjoe, Selwyn R. 1985. "Foreword." In *The Still Cry: Personal Accounts of East Indians in Trinidad and Tobago during Indentureship (1845–1917)*, edited by Noor K. Mahabir, 9–33. Tacarigua: Calaloux Publications.
Dabydeen, David, and Brinsley Samaroo, eds. 1987. *India in the Caribbean*. London: Hansib.
Deosarran, Ramesh. 1987. "The 'Caribbean Man': A Study of the Psychology of Perception and the Media." In *India in the Caribbean*, edited by D. Dabydeen and B. Samaroo, 81–117. London: Hansib.
Desroches, Monique. 1996. *Tambours des Dieux: Musique et Sacrifice d'origine Tamoule en Martinique*. Montreal: Harmattan.
Dick, Alastair. 1984. "Dholak" In *New Grove Dictionary of Musical Instruments*, edited by Stanley Sadie, 562. London: Macmillan.
Glassie, Herbert. 1995. "Tradition." *Journal of American Folklore* 108 (430):395–412.
Guilbault, Jocelyn et al. 1993. *Zouk: World Music in the West Indies*. Chicago: University of Chicago Press.
Hannerz, Ulf. 1987. "The World in Creolisation." *Africa* 57.4:546–59.
Herskovits, Melville J., and Frances. S. Herskovits. 1947. *Trinidad Village*. New York: A.A. Knopf.
Jaggi, Maya. December 1995. "Their Long Voyage Home." *The Guardian* 29.
Jairazbhoy, Nazir. 1993. "India." In *Ethnomusicology: Historical and Regional Studies*, edited by Helen Myers, 274–93. London: Macmillan.
Klass, Morton. 1961. *East Indians in Trinidad: A Study of Cultural Persistence*. Illinois: Waveland Press.
Koskoff, Ellen, ed. 1989. *Women and Music in Cross-cultural Perspective*. Urbana and Chicago: University of Illinois Press.
Levine, Lawrence W. 1977. *Black Culture and Black Consciousness: Afro-American Folk thought from Slavery to Freedom*. Oxford: Oxford University Press.
Lowenthal, David. 1972. *West Indian Societies*. Oxford: Oxford University Press.

Mahabir, Noor K. 1985. *The Still Cry: Personal Accounts of East Indians in Trinidad and Tobago during the Period of Indentureship (1845–1917)*. Tacarigua: Calaloux Publications.

Manuel, Peter. 1988. *Popular Musics of the Non-Western World: An Introductory Survey*. Oxford: Oxford University Press.

———. 1995. *Caribbean Currents: Caribbean Music from Rumba to Reggae*. Philadelphia: Temple University Press.

———. 1995. *East Indian Music in the West Indies: Tn-singing, Chutney, and the Making of Indo-Caribbean Culture*. Philadelphia: Temple University Press.

Martinez, Karen. 1996. *Chutney in Yuh Soca*. Filmakers Library. Video, 36 mins.

Mintz, Sydney. 1985. *Sweetness and Power: The Place of Sugar in Modern History*. London: Viking.

Myers, Helen. 1980. "Trinidad and Tobago." In *New Grove Dictionary of Music*, edited by Stanley Sadie, 146–50. London: Macmillan Press.

———. 1993a. "The West Indies." In *Ethnomusicology: Historical and Regional Studies*, edited by Helen Myers, 461–71. London: Macmillan Press.

———. 1993b. "Indian, East Indian and West Indian Music in Felicity, Trinidad." In *Ethnomusicology and Modern Music History*, edited by Stephen Blum, Philip Bohlman and Daniel Neuman, 231–41. Urbana and Chicago: University of Illinois Press.

———. 1998. *Music of Hindu Trinidad: Songs from the India Diaspora*. Chicago and London: University of Chicago Press.

Naipaul, V. S. 1994. *A Way in the World*. London: Heinemann.

Niranjana, Tejaswini. 2005. "Mobilizing India: Music and Ethnic Identity in Trinidad." Paper presented at the seminar, Remembered Rhythms, Delhi, February 2005.

Poynting, Jeremy. 1987. "East Indian Women in the Caribbean: Experience and Voice." In *India in the Caribbean*, edited by D. Dabydeen and B. Samaroo, 231–63. London: Hansib.

Ramnarine, Tina K. 2001. *Creating Their Own Space: The Development of an Indian-Caribbean Musical Tradition*. Barbados, Jamaica, Trinidad and Tobago: University of West Indies Press.

———. 2004. "Music in the Diasporic Imagination and the Performance of Cultural (Dis)placement in Trinidad." In *Island Musics*, ed. K. Dawe. Oxford and New York: Berg, 153-170.

Ramnath, Harry. 1976. *India Came West*. Marabella: Ramnath.

Ravi-Ji. February 1996. "Neglecting Real Musical Wealth." *Trinidad Guardian* 11:13.

Ribeiro, Indra. 1992. *The phenomenon of chutney singing in Trinidad and Tobago: the functional value of a social phenomenon*. Unpub. B. A. dissertation, University of West Indies, St. Augustine.

Samaroo, Brinsley. 1987. "Two Abolitions: African Slavery and East Indian Indentureship." In *India in the Caribbean*, edited by D. Dabydeen and B. Samaroo, 25–41. London: Hansib.

Schramm, Adelaida R. 1990. "Music and the Refugee Experience." *World of Music* 32(3):3–21.

Selvon, Sam. 1987. "Three into One can't go—East Indian, Trinidadian, Westindian." In *India in the Caribbean* eds. D. Dabydeen and B. Samaroo, 13–24. London: Hansib.

Slobin, Mark. 1993. *Subcultural Sounds: Micromusics of the West*. Hanover, N.H.: Wesleyan University Press.

Small, Christopher. 1987. *Music of the Common Tongue*. London: Calder.

Stokes, Martin. 1992. *The Arabesk Debate: Music and Musicians in Modern Turkey*. Oxford: Clarendon Press.

Turino, Thomas. 1993. *Moving Away from Silence: Music of the Peruvian Altiplano and the Experience of Urban Migration*. Chicago: University of Chicago Press.

Vertovec, Steven. 1992. *Hindu Trinidad: Religion, Ethnicity and Socio-economic Change*. London: Macmillan.

Wade, Bonnie. 1980. "India." In *New Grove Dictionary of Music and Musicians*, edited by Stanley Sadie, 147–58. London: Macmillan.

Williams, Eric. 1964. *History of the People of Trinidad and Tobago*. London: Andre Deutsch.

Part VII

Place and Embodiment

18

The Embodiment of Salsa
Musicians, Instruments, and the Performance of a Latin Style and Identity

Patria Román-Velázquez

This paper examines the construction of Latin American identities in London as embodied and narrated by salsa musicians.[1] Salsa is the name given to describe a specific musical practice that was initially associated with the Spanish Caribbean populations of Puerto Ricans and Cubans in New York City. As a result of the process of communication, initially between Cuba,[2] Puerto Rico and New York, and later with other South American countries such as Venezuela and Colombia, salsa soon became associated with a pan-Latin identity. Subsequently, salsa has become part of the visible presence of Latin American cultural practices[3] in many countries around the world such as Britain, France, Germany, Holland, Ireland, Japan, Norway, Spain and Switzerland among others.[4] This is not to say that salsa and Latin America directly correspond in a straightforward way, but that these are related through processes of continuity and transformation.

I am particularly interested in how salsa signifies a sense of Latin identity through instrumentation and musicians' performance. The embodiment of salsa is proposed as a way of theorizing about how body and music are articulated to communicate a particular Latin cultural identity in salsa music clubs in London. In work elsewhere I have discussed how salsa music is embodied by dancers and disc jockeys (Román-Velázquez 1996), here I concentrate on musicians. I pay particular attention to the way in which body and music are informed by specific ideas of gender, sexuality and ethnicity. This method of approaching salsa music is an attempt to understand the interrelation between body and music in a specific setting.

To pursue this, first, I engage with two theoretical explanations: one which considers the relationship between body and music, and one which considers the cultural construction of bodies in the sense in which bodies are not neutral biological essences. Second, and based on interviews conducted with musicians whilst doing ethnographic research in salsa music clubs in London, I explore the discourses through which musicians thought of instruments in terms of certain ethnic characteristics. I also pay attention to how musical identities are embodied during musicians' performance through the use of the voice and in particular Spanish language. I highlight how such ideas operate to construct a particularly gendered and sexualised musical Latin performance. Finally, I shall note how the musicians' actions involve an interaction with the dancers during which particular codes and conventions of performance style are drawn on as signifiers of salsa and Latinness.

The Relationship Between Music, Bodies and Places

The embodiment of salsa is approached as a two-fold process whereby bodies are experienced through music, when present, and whereby music (again, when present) is experienced through our bodies (Williams 1965; McClary 1991). In relation to this issue Raymond Williams has written that,

> Rhythm is a way of transmitting a description of experience, in such a way that the experience is recreated in the person receiving it, not merely as an "abstraction" or an "emotion," but as a physical effect on the organism—on the blood, on the breathing, on the physical patterns of the brain. (1965, 40)

Drawing on Williams, Susan McClary has argued that this way of understanding music considers the way in which "sound waves are assembled in such a way as to resemble physical gestures," and that, "we as listeners are able to read or make sense of them, largely by means of our lifelong experiences as embodied creatures" (1991, 24). McClary has also argued that our bodies are experienced through music in the sense that emotions and feelings are often more acute through listening to music and the way music has the "ability to make us experience our bodies in accordance with its gestures and rhythms" (ibid, 23). As McClary has recognised, the interrelated experience of bodies and music is mediated through genre specific codes and through specific social contexts and other socially constructed meanings that are recognised by listeners.

This perspective is important for my argument as it demonstrates that musical sounds (melodies, rhythms, etc.) are "symbol systems" (Tagg 1990) encoded in quite specific historical circumstances and are both deliberately encoded and decoded to produce social meanings (McClary 1991). As McClary explains,

> For music is not the universal language it has sometimes been cracked up to be: it changes over time, and it differs with respect to geographical locale. Even at any given moment in place, it is always constituted by several competing repertories, distributed along the lines of gender, age, ethnic identity, educational background, or economic class. (ibid., 25)

The relationship between body and music is not exclusively related to corporal movements and rhythms, but to specific cultural practices and social meanings. As I have no musicological knowledge to study how specific tones, rhythms and timbres come to be related to the bodily experience of music, it is the cultural construction of the body in its relation to salsa musicians in London that I am interested in exploring. In particular, I am interested in how specific body practices come to be associated with notions of "Latinness."

This paper is concerned with the cultural construction of the body in relation to salsa; a body that is "Latinised," and recognised as such by participants, through cultural practices informed by gender relations and discourses about sexuality. As Jeffrey Weeks (1986, 1992) has argued, ideas about gender and sexuality do not correspond to any natural biological essence (as was once thought) but to sexed bodies as these are culturally constructed.[5] In this sense, Weeks argues that sex "refers both to an act and to a category of person, to a practice and to a gender" (1986, 13) in the way in which specific physical characteristics associated with being female or male are often assumed to have a connection with specific erotic behaviours (1986). Thus, sexuality is as much a historical construction as it is a cultural construction (Weeks 1986, 1992). Gender, thus, refers to "the social condition of being male or female, and sexuality, the cultural way of living out our bodily pleasures and desires" (Weeks 1986, 45). Hence, there is no intrinsic relationship between sexed bodies, gender and sexuality, as these are culturally constructed, communicated and experienced.

Issues of ethnicity are also closely related to my explanation about the construction of Latin identity through musical practices. This relationship was highlighted by the musicians I interviewed in terms of their experience of being labelled with an ethnic category that was associated with assumptions and beliefs about an ethnicised body and musical competence. Ethnicity often becomes an issue in situations where cultural contact creates barriers to processes of transformation, particularly when it is asserted that due to ethnic characteristics certain people can, or cannot, engage in particular practices and activities. Musicians in London were trying to break with fixed notions about the relationship between body, ethnicity and musical competence. However, they were still having to confront assumptions about the relationship between their ethnic background and the instruments they played, either because they were Latin or because they were not Latin. Musicians in London (Latin Americans and non-Latin Americans) were engaging in musical practices which can be seen as an attempt to negotiate and transform the experience of what Stuart Hall (1991) has referred to as "old and new identities, old and new ethnicities." Here, the old "ethnic identity" refers to a Latin music as located in Latin America, the new ethnicities and identities refers to the possibilities which occur as salsa music is made and remade in London.

By emphasising the cultural construction of ethnicised, gendered and sexualised bodies I also attempt to highlight that "Latin" is not a fixed category, but open to change and transformation, whilst acknowledging its continuity. This, because Latin American identities are heterogeneous and constituted out of the interaction between the different groups that came into contact through processes of colonisation (Chanady 1994). As salsa is remade in different parts of the world, so particular Latin identities are constructed and communicated in salsa clubs in London, yet these are not totally new. As Stuart Hall (1995) has also argued, the relationship between cultural identities and places should be understood through the processes whereby meanings are constructed. Thus, even when a specific cultural identity develops in relation to specific places, such as the salsa clubs, an unfixed relationship between cultural identities and places can still be maintained due to the way in which Latin cultural practices are experienced in different ways across the world.

The argument that cultural identities are not fixed to a place of origin has more resonance when thinking of those musicians who perform salsa, who may have no direct, or indirect, link with Latin America in terms of kinship or place of birth. In this respect ideas about Latin identity do not correspond to pre-given bodies in any essentialised way. Thus, this approach rejects the notion of a biologically inherited or "natural" link between body and music, and proposes one which is constructed through specific practices. Thus this paper contributes to an understanding of cultural identities as always in the process of formation. Although here I only explore the relationship between body and music in a particular time in London, it is important to bear in mind that the interrelation between body and music is not something that transcends any historical discourse.[6] Thus, salsa is still, despite processes of globalisation, fixed to notions of Latinness and it is this issue that musicians have to confront as performers of Latin music.

Cultural Identities and Musical Instruments

Instruments are used in completely different ways in different types of music; not only in producing melodies or rhythms, but also in the ways instruments are used as part of musicians' performance. The way for example, the bass guitar is played in rock is different to the way it is played in salsa. The rock bass sound tends to stick to the beat following the bass drum, whilst in salsa it "swings across" the bars of the music and has been described as the "anticipated bass" (Manuel 1985). The bass guitar is also used differently during the performance. For example, the movements and performance of the bass player in rock music is completely different to that of the bass player in salsa music. The exaggerated jumping movements of the rock bass player across the stage makes the salsa bass player seem steady and calm in comparison, which is not necessarily the case. I am only using this contrast as an extreme example to demonstrate how instruments are used to perform different musical styles and in doing so musicians are enacting particular cultural identities.

Although it seems an obvious statement, playing an instrument requires a body for it to be played, and to play musical instruments certain bodily positions and postures need to be learnt (McClary 1991). This raises a number of issues connected to the presence of culturally constructed bodies and the way the performance of instruments are not only connected to genre specific codes and musical skills, but also to wider discussions about the way in which cultural identities are actually made and remade in relation to particular practices and places.

Salsa is based on a 3/2 or 2/3 rhythmic pattern that is called "la clave," which is the basic "matrix" through which all rhythms interweave. The instruments are not necessarily played on the bars of each beat as in rock music and this particular method of playing music has sometimes been ethnicised in the way it is often attributed to African-related musics, and contrasted with European notation.[7] However, as Philip Tagg (1989) has argued, distinctions between African and European music are often based on essentialist ideas about music and people and often racist stereotypes and assumptions. Paul Gilroy (1993) has also made reference to this issue when pointing out that racism has often resulted in blacks being thought of as more "authentic" in terms of musical and sexual expression of the body, whilst Europeans have often been associated more with the mind and less spontaneous types of musical performance. In a similar way Latin Americans, in this research, were often referred to as more natural as musical performers. Salsa is particularly interesting here because as a musical form it combines elements which, according to musicological research, derive equally from African rhythms and European melodic patterns (Roberts 1985; Boggs 1992; Alvarez 1992). Because of this, salsa has been portrayed as a "flexible" musical style that can be accommodated to a range of other musical practices and forms.

Despite assumptions about a "natural" Latin affinity for dance and rhythm, in playing salsa, as in dancing, the rhythms have to be learnt. Playing salsa is a learning process that requires a great deal of musical perception and practice. For example, Kay, an English trumpet player for the group *Salsa y Aché*, explained,

> I did a lot of the transcriptions from the original recording and first of all I was writing them down in the wrong time signature; I was writing them in 2/4 and then I learned it was in 4/4. I had to learn about the rhythms and how that actually applies to Latin music in general. It was a matter of playing more and more and playing with other musicians and getting into the style. This music is quite new to me. I have been in this band for five years and that is the time I have been playing salsa. So I did not grow up with it, as Oscar for instance.[8]

Playing music, as Kay mentioned, is part of a broad learning process. Although she first tried to approach the rhythms in terms of her formal training in classical European notation, she had to learn how the rhythms actually worked by practising and listening to the music.

This point was elaborated by Mark, an English piano player for *Picante Band*, who was trained for classical music. He explained that,

> ...there is a myth that musicians with certain training cannot play properly other rhythms, but it is a matter of training. I would like to see those things breaking down....I learned how to play Latin music by listening to records, assimilating a lot and then by playing....There are elements in notation that you can not notate, actually something similar happens to European music. Rhythms are different because they are phrased in a different way.[9]

However, Oscar, a Colombian timbale player for *Salsa y Aché*, whom Kay mentioned as "growing up with the rhythm," commented on his learning process:

> It started when I was a kid. My family was here (England) and they sent me a radio to Colombia when I was about nine years. I was fiddling around and that is how I found the sound, what is called salsa, Latin music. I started to listen.... Slowly this fever grew into me and I wanted to be a musician. When I was sixteen I came to London, and ... I said that I wanted to dedicate myself to be a musician. About a year after I bought some bongos, went to see Roberto Pla. When I saw him I was so impressed by him, and I said I was going to play the timbales. I bought a very cheap second hand one, I started to ask people how to play. From Colombia I had some knowledge about the sounds because I used to see the local band. But I did not know the names for how they were used, which concepts they used for different types of music. So, I started to learn all that slowly. Basically, I started to play with small groups. But I did not know much and every one started to push me aside because I did not know as much as them. I did not let that put me down. I always kept persisting.... I kept on asking and bothering people to teach me. The more I was playing the better I was getting and I still practice a lot with my sticks.[10]

Oscar does not have a formal preparation in music like most of the salsa musicians I interviewed. His training has been different and he has learned how to play salsa in England, not in Colombia. I have quoted him extensively because he challenges the myth that being "Latin" involves having a natural sense of the rhythm and highlights the importance of place for learning a musical practice. These three musicians have approached salsa in a similar way, but from different standpoints:

Kay and Mark had a formal preparation and started understanding, translating and playing the rhythms, and Oscar was first exposed to the music, then started understanding the rhythms through listening and practising. My point here is that these three musicians mentioned their exposure and approach to music as the key influence for playing salsa in London. Musical perception, rather than ethnic background, is the key point for understanding and playing a musical practice like salsa.

However, here it is also important to highlight that Oscar first listened to salsa in Colombia through a radio that was sent to him from England, and that it was at the age of sixteen that he travel to London, where he learnt how to play salsa. Thus, place becomes an important site for understanding, approaching and learning musical practices. Their musical perception may have been very different if Oscar, Mark or Kay had been trained or learnt in, for example, Colombia. These musicians would have come into contact with different ways of playing music, different sounds and performing experiences. By saying this I do not want to imply that one is more authentic than the other, but that specific local music practices have an impact on an individual's access to salsa and how it is heard, approached and played, and, as in London, on the way that salsa is made and remade in every location it travels to. Thus, places are important sites for the meeting and exchange of different cultural practices and possible cultural transformations.

Although both Latin American and British musicians acknowledged that playing salsa is a learning process, still this association between instruments, rhythms and ethnicity persists. The ethnic background of musicians is usually considered among musicians in terms of the instruments they play. The percussion instruments are used in salsa to create rhythm whilst the brass sections are used more for creating melodies. Among the musicians I spoke to informally and interviewed it was often pointed out that those playing the percussion instruments, creating the rhythms, were usually Latin Americans, whilst the British would usually play the instruments creating melodies. For example, Kay said, "it tends to be that most of the horn players are English and the rhythm players are Latin and the singers are Latin. So there aren't many Latin horn players."[11] Nina, the saxophone player for *Salsa y Aché*, also supported this comment: "you tend to get percussion players and singers who are Latin. There is a trumpet player who is Cuban and he is very good, but most of them are percussion players."[12] There is a tendency to "ethnicise" certain rhythms and instruments around certain myths about musical and cultural characteristics that conform to fixed ideas about Latins having the rhythm and Europeans having the melody.

Re-making Latin Music in London

There can be at least three ways in which this division—that of certain instruments considered to be more "Latin" than others—has been gradually broken down, whilst contributing to the re-making of a Latin musical identity. First, there were British musicians playing percussion instruments. Second, economic aspects and practical considerations were having an impact on some of the bands' instrumentation. And, third, whilst non-Latin American musicians were learning to play Latin music, so Latin musicians were also having to adapt their playing to perform in a different place outside Latin America.

In the first place, British musicians were also playing percussion instruments. For example, Dave, an English musician, plays the bongo for *La Clave*, Hamish, of Scottish background, plays the congas for *Salsa y Aché* and Mark is the piano player for *Picante Band* (the piano in salsa is used firstly for rhythm and only for melody as a secondary aspect). These three musicians rejected the notion of a relationship between ethnicity and instruments.

Dave, who spent a year in New York, mentioned that in England his ethnic background was less of a problem because there are not that many salsa players, but of playing in New York he said:

> Over there, because there are so many Latin musicians, it is more difficult to be accepted. I mean, it is just that people are not used to hearing or seeing non-Latin people playing that kind of music. Of course they don't believe that is possible.... That was not a problem here because there is not that many Latin musicians, so at that level any musician playing that kind of music was going to be accepted.[13]

For Hamish, who has been playing congas for over ten years, there is no relationship between ethnic background and being able to play certain instruments or music, although he accepted that these preconceptions exist: "It is harder to be accepted if you are playing African or Latin music if you are not from that culture, I have come across that certain times. But most of the time it is your capabilities regardless of your ethnic background.... Some people have preconceptions but I try to ignore that and do the best I can."[14]

Mark, for example, accepted that such ideas might have come about as a result of cultural exposure and upbringing, but explained that, as in language, there is no fixed relationship between ethnicity and playing music:

> I think that with a lots of things, like linguistic things, which I think a lot of the phraseology in music has a similarity with, I suspect that it is largely environmental. Say, in other words, if you are to take somebody from China at birth and bring them up in Cuba, well they grow up talking Spanish with a Cuban accent or a Cuban way and if they become musicians they will undoubtedly play that way. They would not mysteriously grow up playing Chinese music. I think that is like the whole question of race, I think we tend to overestimate its importance. It does get overestimated. I don't think the pigment in your skin really makes a lot of difference to how you phrase music; it's more likely to be with whom you have been playing, like who have you been listening to will affect the way you speak. If you have been speaking Spanish all your life and you come to England and live in east London you would undoubtedly acquire English that has elements of east London way of talking, and people do.[15]

These three musicians are not only breaking beliefs that those instruments used to create rhythms can only be played by Latin Americans, but were also making reference to the relationship between music, playing certain instruments and ethnic background as one that is culturally constructed. This is an issue that they have had to reflect on as a result of their experience of playing Latin music as non-Latin people. Their ethnic background is questioned by others who still conform to essentialist ideas about Latin identity and musical competence for playing percussion instruments.

The second aspect influencing the re-making of salsa music in London that was mentioned by musicians was related to economic issues and to the practicalities of playing salsa in London. Playing music involves dealing with a number of economic constraints and practical considerations, as has been pointed out in previous ethnographic studies of jazz musicians (Becker 1966). These have often been written about from the perspective of how these constraints limit the musicians' performance, here I want to stress the way they result in the transformation and re-making of a Latin musical identity. One of the most notable economic constraints I found was related to the payment of musicians, particularly because salsa bands can usually have between six and twelve musicians. As Kinacho, a Colombian trumpet player, said about this:

> A salsa band needs a minimum of five people in the rhythm section, three or four in the brass, the singer and any other. Then, you are talking about eleven or twelve people and who is going to pay for that now? We are six or seven and we have a good sound. We can charge more or less enough and still pay the musicians well. The cost of living here is high.... Technology is there and I use it. Some people criticise us because of the machines, but I go for technology and believe in it.... As I told you before we have to pay rent, insurance and petrol. For that reason I welcome technology.[16]

Kinacho made reference to the number of musicians as a constraint for gaining work in clubs where the costs for the owners were higher due to the number of musicians. One way he found to get around this was to use "the technology," by this he means the electronic synthesizers and drum machines that can simulate very closely the sound of other instruments both alone and playing together. This has been a controversial issue amongst many musicians since these instruments have become widely available at a low cost. Although simulating the sounds of other instruments they are changing the character of musical performance. By using this type of technological device, bands of six to eleven musicians, such as *Palenque*, could also perform as trios, with a "big band sound."[17] This not only guaranteed constant work for some of the musicians of the band, but also a change in the character of live performance.

A third way in which musicians have challenged beliefs about a natural Latin musical performance and contributed to the re-making of Latin music in a different place is through the way that Latin American musicians have had to change their musical style to deal with different local circumstances. Here I shall give the example of Roberto Pla, a timbale player who was a professional musician in Colombia where he played for ten years with Lucho Bermudez's band and who now in Britain directs his own band, *Roberto Pla's Latin Jazz Ensemble*. When he first arrived in Britain, in 1978, he did not start playing as a musician straight away but a year and a half later. Roberto mentioned that he first had to deal with the "cultural shock" of the new surroundings.[18] As part of that process of adaptation he used to see a local salsa band of British musicians called *Cayenne*, one of the first Latin bands in London. Out of his interaction with the musicians he started playing with them. However, this did not just happen spontaneously, as he narrated,

> I had a very limited knowledge of English, and those guys were stars. I never had the break for a dialogue with them, until this one day when they were playing at the Royal Free Hospital. That day I had drunk a few beers and said to myself "I am going to play with these people." They were playing an incredible jam (improvisation) session. I was talking to this woman

next to me, her name is Linda Taylor and she is a famous singer, but I did not know that at the time, and I started to simulate a drum "solo" with my mouth. And this woman said: "Hey, you can do that, why don't you get up there and play." So, I had another pint and then I said to her, "Well I am going to play for you." I left to the stage, I went to the timbale player and said to him "please lend me your instrument. Can I play?" He says, "No, ask the leader." So, I asked the leader, "Can I play the timbales?" He says, "No." But he looked at me and he said, "Play the maracas." So I picked up the maracas and started playing the maracas and they all smiled. I said, Bingo. So, I went back to the timbales and asked him, "Can I play the timbales?" and he was "No, no, no." And I basically took the stick and started playing and then everyone started smiling, you know. Then I took a solo…and the next day I was offered a place in the band. I did not have drums. They bought them for me, and my life changed.[19]

When he started playing with *Cayenne* he had to change his style, as he recalled:

I had to change my style in order to survive. It was an education. In the process I was learning to play percussion in the way that they can digest it. I had to adapt to what they were doing, just to work. I enjoyed it because the music is interesting, but at the same time I was thinking about what I must do to play what is really close to my heart. Eventually we formed a band and came to work in a rhythm section. Today I am really proud of my education, playing next to *Cayenne* because these guys are really good, they are professional musicians.[20]

The process of re-making Latin music in London was signified in the name of one of the first bands that Roberto Pla founded, which was called *Sonido de Londres* (The London Sound). Whilst Roberto found it enjoyable and developed a new style to the one he was used to, as he indicated, at first the change was forced on to him "to survive." This type of constraint (the need to please audiences and hence employers and maintain work) is not always thought of in such positive terms. In Becker's (1966) study of dance musicians in the United States in the 1950s he pointed out how musicians resented the way that their freedom to follow their favourite styles and patterns of performance was constrained by the expectations of audiences and requirements of owners. This was sometimes mentioned to me by those musicians who wanted to play music that was more than something to dance to. For example, when talking about composing music for the *Palenque Band*, Kinacho said:

We try to do commercial music, music to dance. We are thinking of the dancers. Our compositions are for the English public rather than the Latin one. It is difficult to get into the English medium, if you are singing in another language.…To achieve a recording here it is very difficult, and competing with bands from Colombia and Puerto Rico is almost impossible. For now we focus on working commercially and in stimulating people to dance.…The music is for the feet, for the head very little. There are interesting lyrics, but most of them are superficial and simple. The people are interested in a simple thing that they can dance and move to.…We are in a country in which the cost of life is high, we have to pay rent, insurance, petrol. Then we have to "sell out" making that music.[21]

Kinacho mentioned language as a constraint and felt that it would be a waste of effort to compose a poetic song in Spanish because the lyrics would not be understood and hence fail to communicate to most of the audience. These examples show the different responses of musicians to constraints—some feeling that there are new opportunities for new styles, some feeling that what they produced was being compromised by economic constraints and the language. However, in both examples, the economic constraints have led to the creation of different musical styles and performances: in the case of Kinacho by introducing technological devices that allowed him to perform with a small band, and in the case of Roberto in developing a Latin—jazz fusion style. In both cases the changes were also adopted because they would appeal to English audiences.

These last points raise two issues that I will discuss in the next section. First, the way that bands interact with dancers. Second, most of the musicians introduced in this section were male, and here a further dimension is added by the way that discourses of gender have an impact on musical performance.

Body, Voice and Language in Creating a Latin Musical Performance

In this section I pay particular attention to how a gendered and sexualised Latin musical identity is being performed by musicians. One of the ways that a Latin musical identity is established is by the use of Spanish language. However, as English audiences might not always understand the language, the lead singers need to develop particular ways of interacting with participants at these clubs. In this section I will be discussing how a particular Latin identity is established through the use of the voice and through musical performances.

Salsa songs contain an improvisation session which is called the "soneo." The composer of salsa knows this and takes it into consideration when composing by allowing for improvisation (Quintero-Rivera, 1998). Thus, musicians can improvise for as long as they can maintain it, and as long as they can come back and join with the rhythm of the band. Whilst musicians improvise, dancers are also encouraged to improvise. However, this does not simply involve the dancers responding to the musicians, it also involves musicians responding to the dancers' reactions. During these prominent interactions a relationship is established and maintained through dance movements, verbal expressions and visual gestures made by both dancers and musicians. This in-teraction between bands and dancers took a particular characteristic and dynamic in London. As I mentioned earlier, the use of drum machine synthesizers have had an impact on live performance. This can be particularly noticeable during an improvisation section due to the way in which the drum machine is set to rhythm patterns and sounds that cannot be easily changed during a live performance. Thus, the musicians often have to follow what has been prearranged. This can have an impact on the interaction of musicians who may not be able to engage as fully in the "dialogic" experience of playing together on the stage. But it can also have an impact on the interaction between dancers and musicians as this develops through a series of exchanges and responses to changing rhythmic patterns.

In live performances in London, musicians expect to have dancers and not "spectators." For example, Kinacho mentioned, "For me, as a musician on the stage, the most important thing is to see people dancing, and dancing it as it should be danced."[22] Hence, one of the central ways in which the interaction between musicians and dancers is established is through dance. However, the level of activity varies greatly depending on the different clubs and particular situations on any given night. One way in which musicians established a relationship with dancers was by dancing with the audience. For example, Kinacho often maintains the interactive relationship with the audience by dancing with them. When recalling one of his first performances in London's Latin clubs, Kinacho said: "First people used to come to watch the band....I used to stop playing and go to the dance floor and start to dance with someone....Even now, last week when playing in *Cuba Libre* I danced."[23] Hence, one way of interacting is by dancing with the audience as in the case of Kinacho.

Another element that had an impact on live performances was the use of Spanish language by the lead singer. When no one was dancing the lead singer would often ask people to dance. When this was the case the lead singer would address the audience in English, though Spanish was the language usually used to address dancers. As an example, I recall from my observations at *Club*

Bahia when Lino Rocha, on that day the lead singer for *La Explosión*, said after the first number to which no one danced: "Well now you have seen what the band looks like, now you can dance," then "Well we have seen couples numbers one and two, now we want to see couples three, four, five and six and so on."[24] The relationship between dancers and musicians is established from the very beginning of the performance. However, the lead singers rarely talk in English, unless they need to make people dance. The lyrics of the songs will always be in Spanish and it was usually during the improvisation session that the singer would address dancers in Spanish. Lino Rocha commented on how he feels about this particular issue when he is on stage:

> It depends on the people, if they give me more I give them more. As most of the public is English, I don't know, but sometimes it is difficult for me to think that they can feel the music because they cannot understand the language. Can you imagine, singing salsa in Spanish in an English speaking country. However, I have heard and people have told me that they can feel the music and that it has nothing to do with the language but with what they capture of me. In this sense it has to do with how I feel it with my heart and how I express it with my face and body.... Also, people tell me that they like the way I sing because I have a bit of 'soul' in my voice.[25]

Thus, even when, most of the time, the language used is Spanish, as Lino mentioned, his gestures and body movements are an important component of his performances as these are, in some instances, the signs through which people understand the music. Whilst language cannot be quickly learnt, an understanding of the visual and musical codes of various types of music has been encouraged by the distribution of videos and television broadcasts and by touring musicians. Thus, body movements and gestures are important during the interaction between dancers and musicians and, as with language, these signify Latinness in the way in which these body movements and expressions are part of the performance of a salsa band and at the same time performed by a Latin American person. In the above quote Lino also emphasised another issue, that is, the use of the voice as in soul music.

This last issue relates to how people recognise, associate and identify a genre specific sound, such as soul, through the voice of the singer. In a recent article, Simon Frith has pointed out the importance of the voice for musicians and audiences in either creating, interpreting or challenging genre specific codes. In reflecting on "electronic voices" he highlights the importance of the voice as the "sound of a body." In relation to this he states that even when voices are heard through a telephone, radio or recording,

> ... we assign them bodies, we imagine their physical production. And this is not just a matter of sex and gender, but involves the other basic attributes as well: age, race, ethnicity, class; everything that is necessary to put together a person to go with a voice. And the point to stress here is that when it comes to the singing voice all such readings have as much to do with conventional as with "natural" expression, with the ways in which in particular genre singing voices are coded not just female, but also young black, middle class, etcetera. (1995, 6)

Frith addresses the importance of the voice for popular music, not only in terms of genre specific codes but also specifically in relation to age, race, ethnicity, class and gender. This leads me to discuss the use of the voice in salsa music as it was mentioned by the musicians interviewed. In what follows I will be referring to the voice as it signifies "Latin" and as gendered, as these were the issues that the musicians I interviewed mentioned as having an impact on salsa music performances.

The lead singer occupies a prominent position in salsa bands and as the lyrics of salsa are in Spanish, the language ability of a singer is an important consideration when a band is contracting singers. Singing and improvising in Spanish were considered important signifiers of a "Latin" musical identity. As I have already mentioned, salsa bands in London have both Latin American and British musicians. However, bands often seek a Latin American lead singer. For example, Daniela, who is an English female musician, narrated her experience when auditioning to be the lead singer for one of the salsa bands in London:

> When I did that audition…one of the things they were worried about was my ability to improvise in Spanish. They wanted a Latin person, although my Spanish was not bad. I am sure there were those prejudices.…My Spanish is quite good, and you don't have to say that much with improvisation, when you think about it, it is always the same line.[26]

Daniela, who then formed the band *Salsa y Aché*, thought language was a strong factor influencing the decision for her not to be accepted as the lead singer, even when she had been learning Spanish for over eight years and considered herself to be fluent in Spanish.[27] However, what was questioned was her ability to improvise in the Spanish language. Although improvisation is included as an integral part of a salsa composition, there is more to the issue than what Daniela referred to as repeating "the same line." The lead singer should be able to respond to, and contribute to, the exchange and interaction between musicians on stage and dancers. Thus, improvisation involves more than the formal composition of lyrics, but the subtle use of the voice and intonation as an instrument when interacting with musicians and dancers. As an example, Héctor Lavoe might have used "the same line" on many occasions, but he was considered to be one of the greatest improvisers of salsa. Thus, improvisation goes beyond issues of language.

However, the use of Spanish language is a central element through which a sense of Latinness is conveyed. This point relates to more complicated debates than I can discuss here, but I do want to point out certain issues which I think are relevant for further discussion of this subject. As I mentioned earlier, salsa developed from the blending of different musical practices that came into contact in New York City and this mixture of musical patterns and rhythms is considered particularly important for enabling the later movement, development and transformation of salsa around the world. However, if on the musical side salsa has been able to mix and blend with different local styles (whether in Colombia or London), it has not been able to go beyond the language barrier. Whilst other genres such as rock and rap are sung in many different languages, salsa is still predominantly sung in Spanish. It is worth highlighting that Willie Colón, an important contributor to "classic" New York salsa during the 1970s, composed and sung in Spanish, even though his first language was English (Quintero-Rivera, 1998). More recently, Nora the vocalist with *Orquesta de la Luz*, a Japanese salsa band, sung in Spanish whilst not understanding the language beyond the band's song lyrics. For Willie Colón, a "Newyorican"—a U.S.-born Puerto Rican—to compose and sing in Spanish was a political statement in the United States during the 1970s. For Nora singing in Spanish involved adhering to the conventions of the genre. Although there have been a few attempts to record salsa with the inclusion of English lyrics (by artists such as David Byrne or La India), only one band have successfully challenged the Spanish dominance of salsa lyrics, that of Africando, from Senegal, who sang much of their first album (*Vol 1, Trovador*) in Wolof.

The use of the voice was mentioned as an important element for salsa musicians in London, not only in terms of being able to sing in Spanish, but also in having the intonation. For example, Kay, a trumpet player for *Salsa y Aché*, who together with the other horn players sing the choruses to their songs commented: "As far as the singing goes, I studied some Spanish so I know what I am singing about most of the time; but I have had to work on the accents and getting the intonation."[28] On this particular subject Daniela added, "I think the melody is important, if you can sing a diverse amount of melodies, then the words do not matter so much. I think it is the musical aspect that matters more."[29] Hence, Spanish language and the specific use of the voice are important elements through which "Latinness" is conveyed, thus contributing to a Latin musical identity.

The use of Spanish language and the use of the voice are particular "sounds of a body" (Frith 1995) and this is often a male Latin body as the use of the voice in salsa was also referred to through a gendered discourse. In general, salsa has been dominated by males and this was mentioned as having consequences for how voices were being used in the music.[30] Most musicians and singers are males, and as Daniela pointed out "Most of the salsa voices are high register male voices. I think they prefer hearing that, than a woman singing. There is a shortage of singers. There seem to be more women singers than men, but it seems to be that it is the men who are called."[31] During the year of the research, for example, Lino Rocha was also the lead singer for *La Clave*, *Tumbaito* and *Pa'lante* confirming what Daniela referred to as a male voice preference in salsa music.

In relation to the choruses of *Salsa y Aché*, Kay commented, "This band is quite different because we all sing the chorus as well, which is all female voices. That is quite unusual and most of the songs we do the chorus of are male voices, so sometimes getting the keys is quite difficult. But we are getting used to it."[32] According to these female musicians, salsa has also been gendered through being associated with male voices, although in recent years more females have begun to play salsa.

All the comments discussed above were made by female musicians and this highlights another issue, that of gender in musical performances. Although in London women were playing salsa and creating a space to perform, their gender was emphasised as part of the identity of a band. To discuss this issue I will focus on *Salsa y Aché*, a band of eleven members of whom six are women.

Daniela published an advert in *City Limits* to form a band, which would later became *Salsa y Aché*. Most of the respondents were women, even though the advert did not specify any particular sex. The fact that most of the respondents were women, as Daniela acknowledged, indicated that there were women musicians interested in playing salsa, and who had simply not had the opportunity. After a year of rehearsing, *Salsa y Aché* started to perform and they built on the fact that most band members were women and made that part of the identity of the band.[33]

Salsa y Aché promote themselves as an "eleven piece Latin dance extravaganza with an all-women horn section" in promotional leaflets and in magazine advertisements. As Kay mentioned, "This band has a woman brass horn section and we always put that on the publicity. I don't know whether that is a good thing or not, I do not know what people expect by that.... I think they expect you to be sexy."[34] The women in *Salsa y Aché* dressed in miniskirts and initially attempted to move the "all-women horn section" to the front of the stage, in contrast to other salsa bands where it is conventionally at the back. Musically, this did not work and they discontinued it.[35] In this case, sexuality and gender are linked in that a particular act is expected from a gendered body and this affected the band's performance. First, as it was unusual to have so many women in a salsa band this aspect was emphasised by presenting the women in the foreground. This was then stopped for musical reasons. Second, and related to this, women were expected to be "sexy" in addition to playing instruments, which again affected the presentation of the band's performance.

Related to this issue, Luz Elena, the director of *Conjunto Sabroso*, a band which started performing in November 1994, criticised the notion that in most salsa bands women were expected to dress in miniskirts. She said that if a band is to have women then the sexual aspect is foregrounded and it becomes almost impossible to wear any alternative to miniskirts and to challenge what she called the "sexy performance" required in some bands.[36]

It was often the case that some of the male-dominated bands, when inviting any women, required that they perform as dancers or singers in the chorus. Whilst women are often found in this position in Afro-American and Anglo-American popular music (Steward and Garratt 1984), these practices are also informed by Latin "machismo." As Eldin Villafañe has written: "This complex of values known as machismo above all speaks of a family structure where authority is vested in the male head of the family, and where a particular definition of masculinity emphasises physical and sexual prowess" (1994, 157).

The point here is that in musical performances women are expected to be sexy through dressing codes and through the movement of the whole body and to display a particular "Latin" type of female sexiness. It is not that men are not being sexy. Machismo could be just as much a constraint. However, men are also playing instruments and being "sexy" is foregrounded and emphasised for women in a different way to men. Although Luz Elena formed *Conjunto Sabroso* in an attempt to change these expectations of gender and sexuality, what I want to highlight from these examples is that in the performance of salsa music gender is linked to sexuality in terms of what is expected from female musicians. Also, as a Colombian woman, she had to negotiate her space in salsa bands by confronting fixed ideas about Latin female identity. Whilst it is important to stress that this male domination in music is not particular to salsa but to other genres of popular music, I have attempted to demonstrate that relations of gender and sexuality contribute to the construction of a particular "sexy" female body as an expectation which then becomes part of a "Latin" musical identity.

Summary

I have attempted to contribute to debates about the body and music through a discussion of how the performance of salsa constructs a particular sense of Latin identity through the bodies of musicians. The embodiment of salsa is proposed as a way of theorising about how body and music are articulated to communicate a particular Latin cultural identity. In considering the relationship between body and music, I have stressed the cultural construction of bodies in the sense in which bodies are not neutral biological essences.

Salsa clubs in London have provided a focus for studying the construction of Latin identities as embodied and communicated by performing salsa musicians and how this is informed by specific codes of gender, sexuality and ethnicity. Throughout this essay I have argued that the embodiment of salsa develops through specific practices whereby instruments, performance techniques, vocal sounds, bodily movements and ways of dressing are encoded and experienced as part of a particular Latin identity.

I also explained how the existence of essentialist beliefs about a natural Latin body and musical abilities, although a constraint, were challenged by musicians who are making "Latin" music. First, by the involvement of non-Latin musicians in playing salsa, whose practices challenged assumptions about a "natural" relationship between bodies, places and music. Second, through the participation of Latin American musicians and the new styles developing from the interaction between musicians and from having to adapt to different local circumstances. Finally, I mentioned how technological devices, sometimes used to solve practical economic problems, were contributing to the re-making of a Latin music performance and identity in London. I also indicated how the use of both Spanish and English language and the involvement of women in salsa music making were also contributing to a type of salsa and Latin performance.

However, whilst musicians have been challenging the idea of essential links between ethnicity, bodies and instruments, the practices through which salsa is embodied have continued to present limitations and expectations for women according to their sexed bodies. Particular expectations about the practices of gender and sexuality became an issue for women in relation to body movements, the use of the voice and instrumental performance. In this paper, focusing on the performance and participation of musicians in the micro setting of a club, I have suggested that women's place in salsa clubs has to be negotiated in relation to what is expected from sexed bodies. This leads me to conclude that unequal relations of power are directly experienced and embodied through gender relations and practices of sexuality and in turn operate as a micro politics of the body.

Notes

1. This essay is based on research carried out in London's salsa clubs during 1993–94. A version of this chapter appears in *The Making of Latin London: Music, Place and Identity*, Ashgate, 1999, and in my Ph.D. thesis, "The construction of Latin identities and salsa music clubs: An ethnographic study," University of Leicester, 1996.

2. In the case of Cuba, this communication stopped after the Cuban Revolution, particularly after the missile conflict of 1962 and the trade embargo enforced by the U.S. administration.

3. I am drawing from Raymond Williams' (1981) conceptualisation of culture. In this sense it refers to material and symbolic practices. Material, as it is used in anthropology, to refer to a whole way of life; and symbolic, as in cultural studies, in that it refers to culture as "the signifying system through which a social order is communicated, reproduced, experienced and explored" (Williams 1981, 13). Cultural practices, thus, refer to the activities through which a culture is constituted.

4. Research about salsa in these countries is still very small, however some introductory articles have been published. Cintha Harjadi has recently finished a research project on salsa in Amsterdam. The original research is written in Dutch, a short version was published in English as part of the proceedings of the *Popular Music Studies in a Dutch Perspective* Conference. Also published is the article "Salsa comes to Europe" by Solothurnman (1988), 4. This article is about salsa musicians in Switzerland. Research on salsa in Japan is currently being developed by Shuhei Hosokawa (1995).

5. The body as socially constructed has been addressed in Judith Butler (1990), Chris Shilling (1993), Mike Featherstone et al. (1991), Pasi Falk (1994) and also the journal *Body and Society* edited by Featherstone and Turner, March 1995 onwards.

6. Historical research on the relationship between bodies and music has been discussed by Quintero-Rivera (1998). His research explores the relationship between music, class and ethnicity in the Caribbean, with particular attention paid to Puerto Rico. The book includes a chapter on the body in which he explores historical-sociological material about dance etiquette and its relationship with class, race and gender.

7. Different styles of popular music have sometimes been discussed in terms of distinctions between 'Afrocentric' and 'Eurocentric' styles, for example, Stephens (1991).

8. Personal interview with Kay, 27 April 1995.

9. Personal interview with Mark Donlon, 16 December 1993.

10. Personal interview with Oscar, 27 April 1995.

11. Personal interview with Kay, 27 April 1995.

12. Personal interview with Nina, 27 April 1995.

13. Personal interview with Dave Pattman, 27 April 1994.

14. Personal interview with Hamish, 27 April 1995.

15. Personal interview with Mark Donlon, 16 December 1993.

16. Personal interview with Fernando (Kinacho) Suárez, 1 July 1994. "Nosotros nos apoyamos en la electrónica, en la tecnología. Podemos prescindir de ciertos elementos de la banda. Para tener una banda de salsa mí'nimo se necesitan cinco personas en lo que llaman el rhythm session, tres o cuatro personas en el brass, el cantante y otro. Entonces ya estas hablando de unas once o doce personas y ¿quién va a pagar eso ahora? Nosotros somos seis o siete y sonamos bien. Podemos cobrar más o menos y pagarle a la gente bien. La vida aquí se ha puesto muy costosa.... La tecnología está ahí y yo la uso. Hay gente que nos critica, 'ah que máquinas'. Yo voy con la teconología, yo creo en la tecnología.... Como dijimos antes hay que pagar renta, seguro y gasolina. Por eso que viva la tecnología."

17. Personal interview with Fernando (Kinacho) Suárez, l July 1994.

18. Personal interview with Roberto Pla, 16 November 1993.

19. Personal interview with Roberto Pla, 16 November 1993. The first part of this fragment was in Spanish, when he introduces the voice of the singer he continues in English. The part in Spanish follows: "El inglés mío era limitado y los muchachos en verdad son estrellas. Nunca hubo un 'breaquesito' para tener un diálogo. Hasta que un día estaban tocando en Royal Free Hospital, y ese día me tomé un par de cervezas y dije yo voy a tocar con esta gente. Ellos estaban tocando un jam session increible. Había una muchacha que se llama Linda Taylor que es una cantante famosa y no lo sabía y yo estaba hablando con ella y comencé a hacer un solo de tambores con la boca (simula) y la muchacha dice: 'Hey, you can do that,'..."

20. Personal interview with Roberto Pla, 16 November 1993.

21. Personal interview with Fernando (Kinacho) Suárez, 1 July 1994. "Tratamos de hacer música comercial que sea música para bailar. Estamos pensando en el bailador. Nuestras composiciones son un poco, demasiado creo pensadas en el público inglés que en el público latino. Es difícil meterse en el medio inglés, cantando en otro idioma.... Lograr una grabación aquí es muy difícil y muy remota y competir con las bandas de Colombia o Puerto Rico es casi imposible. Nosotros, por ahora nos dedicamos comercialmente a trabajar y a hacer bailar a la gente.... La música es dedicada para los pies, la cabeza muy poco. Hay letras interesantes, pero la mayoría de las letras son muy banales, muy sencillas. A la gente le interesa una cosa sencilla para bailar y poderse mover.... Estamos en un país en donde la vida cuesta, hay que pagar renta, hay que pagar seguro, gasolina. Entonces nos toca vendernos haciendo esa música."

22. Personal interview with Kinacho, 1 July 1994. "Para mí como músico en el escenario lo más importante es ver la gente bailando, y bailando bien como se debe bailar."

23. Personal interview with Kinacho, 1 July 1994. "Primero la gente venia a ver.... Yo dejaba de tocar, me bajaba y me ponía a bailar con alguien... Inclusive todavía, la semana pasada salí a bailar en el Cuba Libre."

24. From observations, *Club Bahia*, whilst playing for *La Explosión* band, 18 March 1994. Lino Rocha a Venezuelan singer officially for *La Clave*, unofficially for *La Explosión*, *Pa'lante*, *Tumbaito* and any other band who needs a singer temporarily.

25. Personal interview with Lino Rocha 25 March 1994. "Depende de la gente. La gente me da más y yo le doy más. No sé, es que la mayor parte del público son ingleses y a veces creo que es difícil que ellos sientan la música porque no entienden la lengua. Imagínate, cantando salsa en español en un país que es inglés. Según lo que he oído y me han comentado ellos de todas maneras lo sienten, que no tiene nada que ver con la lengua sino con lo que ellos captan de mí. En el sentido de cómo lo siento con el corazón y cómo lo expreso en la cara y el cuerpo... También me dicen que les gusta mi manera de cantar porque tengo un poco de 'soul' en la voz."

26. Personal interview with Daniela, 27 April 1995.
27. Personal interview with Daniela, 27 April 1995.
28. Personal interview with Kay, 27 April 1995.
29. Personal interview with Daniela, 27 April 1995.
30. Vernon Boggs acknowledges that salsa has been dominated by males. However, in his edited book *Salsiology* (1992) he writes a chapter in which he discusses the influence and participation of women in salsa bands.
31. Personal interview with Daniela, 27 April 1995.
32. Personal interview with Kay, 27 April 1995.
33. Personal interview with Nina, 27 April 1995.
34. Personal interview with Kay, 27 April 1995.
35. From observations at Bar Tiempo, 5 November 1993. When I met the band I mentioned this incident to corroborate my observations.
36. Informal conversation with Luz Elena, 27 April 1995.

References

Alvarez, Luis M. 1992. "La presencia negra en la música puertorriqueña." In *La Tercera Raíz: Presencia Africana en Puerto Rico*, 20–31. San Juan, P.R.: Centro de Estudios de la Realidad Puertorriqueña : Instituto de Cultura Puertorriqueña.

Becker, Howard S. 1966. *Outsiders. Studies in the Sociology of Deviance*. London: Free Press of Glencoe.

Boggs, Vernon. 1992. *Salsiology*. New York: Greenwood Press.

Butler, Judith. 1990. *Gender Trouble: Feminism and Subversion of Identity*. London: Routledge.

Chanady, Amaryll. 1994. "Latin America Imagined Community and the Postmodern Challenge." In *Latin American Identity and Constructions of Difference*, edited by A. Chanady, ix–xvi. Hispanic Issues vol.10. Minneapolis & London: University of Minnesota Press.

Falk, Pasi. 1994. *The Consuming Body*. London: Sage Publications.

Featherstone, Mike, and Bryan S. Turner. 1995. "Body and Society: An Introduction." *Body and Society*, 1(1):1–12

Featherstone, Mike, Mike Hepworth, and Bryan S. Turner, eds. 1991. *The Body: Social Process and Cultural Theory*. London: Sage Publications.

Frith, Simon. 1995. "The Body Electric." *Critical Quarterly* 37(2):1–10.

Gilroy, Paul. 1993. *The Black Atlantic: Modernity and Double Consciousness*. London: Verso.

Hall, Stuart. 1991. "Old and New Identities, Old and New Ethnicities." In *Culture Globalization and The World System: Contemporary Systems for the Representation of Identity*, edited by Anthony D. King, 41–68. Binghamton, NY: Dept. of Art and Art History, State University of New York at Binghamton.

———. 1995. "New Cultures for Old." In *A Place in the World? Places Cultures and Globalization*, edited by Doreen Massey (Milton Keynes), 175–214. New York: Open University; Oxford University Press.

Harjadh, C. 1994. "Salsa in Amsterdam. Development and Adaptation of a Latinamerican Music Old Dance Style." Paper presented at the Popular Music Studies in a Dutch Perspective Conference, Melkweg, Amsterdam 24 October, 30–36.

Hosokawa, S. 1995. "'Salsa no tiene frontera': Orquesta de la Luz or the Globalization and Japanization of Afro-Caribbean Music." Manuscript.

Manuel, Peter. 1985. "The Anticipated Bass in Cuban Popular Music." *Latin American Music Review* 6(2):249–61.

McClary, Susan. 1991. *Feminine Endings: Music, Gender and Sexuality*. Minneapolis: University of Minnesota.

Quintero-Rivera, A.G. 1998. *Seis, bomba, danza…sonata: Salsa y Control! Sociología de la música tropical*. México: Siglo Veintiuno Editores.

Roberts, J.S. 1985 [1975]. *The Latin Tinge. The Impact of Latin American Music on the United States*. New York:

Román-Velázquez, Patria. 1996. "The Construction of Latin Identities and Salsa Music Clubs in London: An Ethnographic Study." Ph.D. Thesis, Centre for Mass Communication Research, University of Leicester.

Román-Velázquez, Patria. 1999. *The Making of Latin London: Salsa Music, Place and Identity*, Aldershot: Ashgate.

Shilling, Chris. 1993. *The Body and Social Theory*. London: Sage Publications.

Solothurnman, J. 1988. "Salsa Comes to Europe." *Jazz Forum* 113:48–51.

Stephens, Gregory. 1991. "Rap Music's Double-voiced Discourse: A Crossroads for Interracial Communication." *Journal of Communication Inquiry* 15(2):70–91.

Steward, Sue, and Sheryl Garratt. 1984. *Signed Sealed and Delivered. True Life Stories of Women in Pop*. London: Pluto Press.

Tagg, Philip. 1989. "Open Letter: 'Black Music', 'Afro-American Music' and 'European Music.'" *Popular Music* 8(3):285–98.

———. 1990. "Music in Mass Media Studies." In *Popular Music Research*, edited by K. Roe and V. Carlsson, 103–14. Gothenburg: NORDICOM-Sweden.

Villafañe, Eldin. 1994. "The Liberating Spirit: Toward a Hispanic American Pentecostal Social Ethic." In *Barrios and Borderlands: Cultures of Latinos and Latinas in the United States*, edited by Denis Lynn Daly Heyck, 152–58. New York and London: Routledge.

Weeks, Jeffrey. 1986. *Sexuality*. London: Routledge.

———. 1992. "The Body and Sexuality." In *Social and Cultural Forms of Modernity*, edited by Robert Bocock and Kenneth Thompson, 219–66. Oxford : Polity Press.

Williams, Raymond. 1965. *The Long Revolution*. London: Chatto and Windus.

———. 1981. *Culture*. London: Fontana.

19

Dueling Landscapes
Singing Places and Identities in Highland Bolivia

Thomas Solomon

Recent research in ethnomusicology and popular music has drawn attention to the close relationships between music, place, and identity. That "music and place" has become an important new focus of research is evident from the numerous recent publications on the topic, including edited volumes (Leyshon, Matless and Revill 1998; Stokes 1994b; Whiteley, Bennett and Hawkins 2004), monographs (Bennett 2000, Forman 2002, Mitchell 1996), special issues of journals (e.g., *Popular Music* vol. 19, no.1 in 2000), and even a textbook (Connell and Gibson 2003) on the topic, not to mention a plethora of individual journal articles, book chapters, and conference special sessions or whole conferences (Ivade 1994) dedicated to this theme. Some of this work uses the terms *place* and *space* as metaphors similar to Foucault's (1972, 51–52) concept of "site" as a field or space where power relationships are played out; other writers use the terms more literally, grounding their analyses ethnographically in people's concrete experience of lived physical landscapes (cf. Feld 1996a, 1996b).

Among the insights generated by this new scholarship is the idea that musical performance serves as a practice for place-making. This follows the understanding that music does not simply "reflect" pre-existing cultural structures, but rather musical performance is a social activity through which culture is created, negotiated, and performed (Seeger 1987). The presentational aspect of much musical performance makes it particularly useful for the public construction of identities; musical performance events, as bounded entities in time, serve to focus group consciousness on the issues they raise, including relationships between selves and places. As Stokes suggests, "The musical event... evokes and organizes collective memories and present experiences of place with an intensity, power and simplicity unmatched by any other social activity" (1994a, 3).

That musical performance is a practice for constructing identity is now an ethnomusicological commonplace. That it can also be a practice for constructing *place* may not seem so obvious at first. Geographers and anthropologists working on the cultural construction of place have recently explored how places are not simply pre-existing backdrops for activity, but rather are actively made and imagined by people through social processes (Bender 1993b; Feld and Basso 1996; Hirsch and O'Hanlon 1995; Rodman 1992). A place-oriented ethnomusicology would thus explore how musical performance is a social practice for place-making.

In this paper I explore some ways in which musical performance may embody identity and ground it in place. By *embodiment* I mean how musical sound gives physical presence to identity, making it phenomenologically real to those involved in the events here described. My data come from fieldwork during 1993 in the *ayllu* (ethnic group based on kinship networks and dwelling in a traditional territory) of Chayantaka, an indigenous people of highland Bolivia.[1] I argue that for Chayantaka, musical performance is a practice for embodying community identity, inscribing it on earthly landscapes as well as in the landscapes of the mind.

The Chayantaka live in forty-five indigenous peasant communities spread out over an area of approximately 140 square miles in the eastern range of the Bolivian Andes, at an altitude of between 10,000 and 14,000 feet above sea level. Chayantaka territory lies mostly within the province of Bustillo, in the northern part of the Bolivian *departamento* (state) of Potosí. They subsist on potatoes, corn, and other grains, and raise llamas, sheep, and goats.[2]

It may seem an obvious point to make, but it is important to point out that for Chayantaka, a "community" (*comunidad*) is not just a settlement, but also the people who live there, as well as the fields and pastures around the settlement that belong to them. For Chayantaka, the people of a community, as a social body, are inseparable from the landscape where they live. In this paper I trace out the theme of the musical imagination of place-identity from two ethnographic directions—an analysis of spatial patterns created by the purposeful movement of groups of musicians through space, and a discussion of how singers deploy community names and descriptions of community landscapes in song texts. In conclusion I argue that for Chayantaka, musical performance is a practice that emplaces and embodies community identities in very specific ways.

Carnival Visits and Inter-Community Networks

In the central Andes, south of the Equator, Carnival comes not in spring but in fall, and is a celebration of first fruits (Harris 1982, 57; Rasnake 1988, 242). Different ritual activities take place each day of the week-long Carnival celebration. In Chayantaka communities, Tuesday and Wednesday of Carnival week are the days for *wisitas* (from Spanish *visitar*), visits to other villages. On these days *kumparsas*, small bands of unmarried boys and girls in their teens and early twenties, rove constantly from one community to another to play music and visit with friends. Roles in musical performance are gendered—boys play stringed instruments called *charangos* while girls sing verses in the Quechua language. Upon arrival in a community, the kumparsa heads to the house of friends or relatives. The residents invite them inside to the house's patio, where the group plays a song genre called *wayñu*, especially associated with Carnival. The owner of the house offers the players *chicha* (corn beer) and the group performs again for a while before moving on to another house within the community. After visiting several houses in this way, the group then moves on to another community, usually one within a walk of an hour or two. Wherever they happen to find themselves at nightfall, they stay, usually playing music all night in someone's house, until they set off for another community in the early morning.

This moving about from one community to another has a practical aspect. Since the rule for marriage is community exogamy—one must marry someone from a different community than one's own—the wisitas allow young people from different communities to come into contact with each other in a socially sanctioned way. Carnival is the ideal time to begin romantic relationships, and from the perspective of the young people involved, the primary goal of the wisitas is to meet potential marriage partners, or maintain liaisons already begun during earlier fiestas. Since the kumparsas are constantly moving about, boys and girls are just as likely to meet on the paths between communities as in the communities themselves. Girls may leave their community's kumparsa to join a group from another community in order to be with a boy to whom they are attracted.

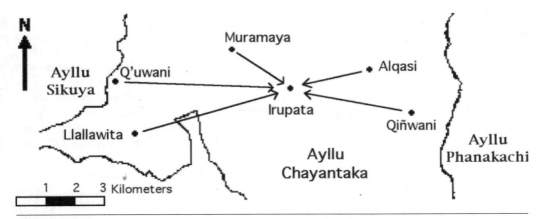

Figure 19.1 Relative locations of communities whose kumparsas visited Irupata during Carnival in 1993.

Boys may also leave their group to tag along with another group that includes a girl they would like to court. These two days, when young people are not supervised by adults, provide the ideal opportunity for the *suwanakuy*, the act of stealing a girl away and bringing her home to one's own community, thus beginning the marriage process (Carter 1977).[3]

The way the kumparsas criss-cross Chayantaka territory also has the effect of constructing a network of inter-community relationships. Each performing group visits several communities during a very short period of time, and any one community will be visited by kumparsas from several different communities. For example, on Tuesday of Carnival week in 1993 the community of Irupata was visited by performers from the communities of Llallawita, Muramaya, Alqasi, Qiñwani, and Q'uwani (see Figure 19.1).

The itinerary of a kumparsa from any particular community is unique, but the itineraries of kumparsas from nearby communities overlap. While it would be impossible for any one group to visit more than a few communities within a radius of several kilometers over this two-day period, the cumulative effect of so many groups doing this simultaneously, with overlapping itineraries throughout the entirety of Chayantaka territory, is the articulation of a network of relationships between all forty-five Chayantaka communities. The roving kumparsas collectively inscribe Chayantaka territory as a network of inter-community relationships by marking out the domain within which operates the marriage rule of community exogamy.[4]

Collectively performing music in another's community is a way of musically inscribing that place with the community identity of the performers. In the case of the Carnival visits, performance is a way of announcing the community identity of the performers to potential social allies, a declaration of intent to solidify the inter-community network by establishing kin ties through marriage. Performers musically construct their place-based identity, establishing relationships between people and places through the performance of Carnival songs.

One specific way Chayantaka performers explicitly invoke their community affiliations during the Carnival visits is by naming their community or describing its landscape in the texts of the songs they sing. In the next two sections I consider these songs.

Community Names

As elsewhere in the Andes, Chayantaka community names typically describe some aspect of the landscape of the community they name. Consultants were able to give a Quechua, Aymara, or sometimes Spanish etymology for most community names. For example, in the name of the community Chayanta Qalqala, *chayanta* is Aymara for tin. *Qalaqala* is a reduplication of the Aymara word *qala*, "rock"; the reduplication gives the meaning "many rocks." The community's name thus refers to a cluster of boulders containing visible tin deposits on a slope along one side of the main settlement of the community.

Plant names are particularly common in Chayantaka toponyms. Chayantaka community names frequently consist of a plant name with the Aymara suffix *-ni*, denoting possession: *x-ni* = "place that has the plant *x*." Examples of this include the names of the communities of Qiñwani (*qiñwa* = *Polylepis incana*, a kind of tree),[5] Tuturani (*tutura* = *Scirpus totora*, a water reed), and Q'uwani (*q'uwa* = *Lepidophyllum teretiusculum*, an aromatic herb).

A community's name may describe not the landscape of its main settlement, but some other notable aspect of the surrounding lands that belong to the community. For example, the name of the community of Lusarita derives from the Spanish word *losa*, meaning large slabs of rock with smooth, flat sides. There is a large rocky area containing exfoliated slabs of this kind within the territory of this community, but not visible from the main settlement itself.

Most of the toponyms in the region are in Aymara, reflecting that Aymara is the original language of the area, with Quechua intruding only recently (Albó 1980; Hosokawa 1980; Howard-Malverde 1995). But due to the overlap between Quechua and Aymara vocabularies, especially in words for the names of plants and landforms, young people who spoke Quechua and no Aymara had no problem explaining to me some old toponyms from their region. But in the case of many Aymara toponyms that use vocabulary not shared with Quechua, younger consultants from the southern-most part of Chayantaka territory, where Quechua has all but replaced Aymara, were often unable to provide etymologies. When I asked them the meaning of these names, they would invariably suggest I ask an older person (*awilu*, from Spanish *abuelo*, lit. "grandfather"), who would know more Aymara and probably be able to explain them. If the names of places provide a framework for experiencing them (Basso 1984, 25; Tilley 1994, 18–19), then young people's loss of fluency in Aymara thus has important implications for their experience of landscape. The differential distribu-tion of knowledge of Aymara results in a differential ability to interpret toponyms in that language, including even the name of one's own community. With their etymologies forgotten, the names literally become disembodied from the landscape. Even if the meanings that connected them more specifically to the landscape are no longer understood, community names do, however, still index the community as a social body.

It is for this latter reason that community names are prominent in song texts. In Carnival songs singers often invoke their community's name, most commonly in the following formulaic verse, where N. is the name of the community:

Quechua text	English gloss
Jamushayku, chamushayku [refrain]	We're coming, we're arriving [refrain]
Comunidad N. [refrain]	The community of N. [refrain]

The verse can be set to most any Carnival song melody, and typically includes line-ending refrains consisting of nonsense syllables such as "ay siway" or the names of girls or plants such as "Sarita" or "sausisita." The choice of refrain varies between communities and with the personal preferences of the singers. Musical Examples 19.1 and 19.2 illustrate some of the variety among the melodies with which performers from different communities sing this verse.[6]

Communities may relocate their main settlement, moving it to another site within the com-munity's land. For example, when the rocky slope that was the site of the main settlement of the community of Lusarita began to weaken and give way, and houses were in danger of sliding down the mountainside, the people of the community decided to move the settlement to a nearby flat space.

Jamushayku, chamushayku   We're coming, we're arriving
Comunidad *Pata Pata*   The community of *Pata Pata*

Musical Example 19.1 Community-naming formula as sung by a group from the community of Pata Pata.

Jamushayku, chamushayku   We're coming, we're arriving
Comunidad *Muramaya*, chulita   The community of *Muramaya*, girl
Margarita   Margarita

Musical Example 19.2 Community-naming formula as sung by a group from the community of Muramaya.

While the site for a community's main settlement may change, the community name usually remains the same. This can sometimes lead to a situation in which the community's name, while evocative of the old settlement site, no longer describes the landscape of the new site. For example, the name of the community of Irupata is formed from *iru* (*Stipa papposa*, a variety of the hardy, spiny grass that grows in upper elevations throughout the Andes) + *pata* ("high place"), meaning "a high place where iru grows." The main settlement of this community was in the past located in a place where iru grew in abundance. But the community has moved its main settlement twice in living memory, most recently in the late 1970s. The current site of the community's main settlement is a flat plain where no iru grows, so the name Irupata does not really describe the current landscape of the community. Names such as these that refer to the landscapes of previous settlements help evoke the community's history for people interested in knowing that history and transmitting it, but they are not as evocative for many young people who grow up in a landscape very different from that which their community's name describes.

While people may be able to provide etymologies for most community names when asked, in everyday practice people do not give much thought to the etymologies of these toponyms.[7] Since community names may refer to landscape features of settlements abandoned many years past, and young Quechua speakers may not know the significance of many Aymara toponyms, it would seem that while community names still evoke the social body of the community, for many young people these toponyms are not always as evocative of the landscape. In these cases the ability of names to facilitate identification with landscape may not seem strong. But data on another set of names young Chayantaka use to refer to their communities indicates that language is indeed useful as a resource for identification and the creation of affective bonds with landscape. It is to these names that I now turn.

Community Nicknames

In addition to everyday toponyms, Chayantaka have another category of names they use to refer to their communities. These names appear only in song texts. While very similar in form to community toponyms, they are not toponyms *per se*. These names always consist of two Quechua words of two syllables each. As in many toponyms proper, the words describe specific geographical features such as mountains, rivers, or plants found in the landscape of the community. Chayantaka have no word to collectively name these descriptions, but recognize that they are different from the everyday names of communities, which may be used both in songs and in everyday speech. Because of the affectionate way these landscape descriptions are used in song texts, I refer to them here as "nicknames."

The nicknames' consistent form of two terms joined together allows for a dimension of contrast between the nicknames of different communities. The two words in combination refer to some unique feature or combination of features in the landscape of the singers' home community which would not be found in any other Chayantaka community. Nicknames for different communities may share one of the two terms, but the other term must be different. For example, the nickname of the community of Irupata is *ch'iki pampa*, "plain of *ch'iki* grass," while the nickname of Berenguela is *layu pampa*, "plain of clover." While the nicknames of both communities contain the word *pampa* ("plain"), they are distinguished by the contrasting terms *ch'iki* and *layu*, two different kinds of vegetation. A similar overlap/contrast can be observed in the nicknames for the communities of Wayt'i and Pata Pata, *sunch'u mayu* ("river that passes by *sunch'u* flowers") and *ch'alla mayu* ("river with sandy banks"), respectively.

Some communities may have more than one such nickname, describing different aspects of the community's landscape. Table 19.1 summarizes the community nicknames I collected during my fieldwork in 1993.

Singers most commonly use community nicknames in a very specific way, inserting them into formulaic verses known by singers from all Chayantaka communities. The most common formula has two variants, in which N. is the community nickname:

Variant 1:

Ch'uluy watuy laychu laychu	Tassel of my knitted cap, swaying
[refrain]	[refrain]
N.-smá walaychus [refrain]	We N.-s are real rascals! [refrain]

Table 19.1 Geographic Nicknames of Some Communities of Ayllu Chayantaka

Community	Nickname	Gloss
Irupata	ch'iki pampa	plain of *ch'iki* grass
Berenguela	layu pampa	plain of clover
Llallawita	llallaw q'asa; luma k'uchu; kinsa churus	ravine between twin mountain peaks; corner in the mountain; three *churus* (strips of land formed by the confluence of rivers)
K'utimarka	k'uchu paku	*paku* grass in the corner
Muramaya	sausi mayu; wirta mayu	river that passes by a weeping willow; river that passes by a garden
Wayt'I	sunch'u mayu	river that passes by *sunch'u* plants
Lusarita	sunch'u kinra	slopes where *sunch'u* plants grow
Pata Pata	ch'alla mayu	river with sandy banks
Ch'uxñuma	mayu pata	sloping land above the banks of a river
Changarani	uray mayu	river down below
Jist'arata	wayra q'asa	windy ravine

Variant 2:

Ujantitay laychu laychu [refrain]	My scarf, swaying [refrain]
N.-smá walaychus [refrain]	We N.-s are real rascals! [refrain]

The meaning of these verses requires some explication. In the first variant, *ch'ulu watuy* refers to the long tassels (*watu*, from Spanish *guato*) hanging from the earflaps of the knitted caps (*ch'ulu*) that men wear. In the second variant, *ujantita* (from Spanish *bufanda*) is the long knitted scarf that girls wear draped over their shoulders or around their necks, and that boys wear hanging from their belts down the sides and backs of their legs. *Laychu* indicates a back and forth motion; the reduplication *laychu laychu* indicates a continued swaying back and forth, as might happen with these garments while one is dancing. *Walaychu* means vagabond, rogue, or quick-witted person; here the singers use the term in a humorous, self-deprecating way appropriate to the frame of sexual play created in Carnival song performance, so I have translated it as "rascal."

The first line of these formulaic verses, while evoking the dancing and singing of the performance occasion, also sets up the rhyme completed in the second line, which contains the two-word landscape description. The second term of the landscape description is always in the plural, even though normally a landscape description by itself would appear in the singular; the complement of the landscape phrase is another plural noun, *walaychus*. Quechua allows deletion of the verb "to be" in certain contexts; the deleted verb here is understood to be *kayku*, meaning "we are," making the subject of the sentence the singers themselves, as well as, by implication, the other members of their community. The grammatical structure of the line thus indicates that the singers are identifying themselves, in a playfully self-deprecating way by calling themselves rascals, with the landscape itself that they describe, hence the use of the plural form of the nouns. As in the case of the formula for naming the community, these lines also usually have short nonsensical refrains at the end. I will now consider a few actual instances of the use of community nicknames in these verses.

Figure 19.2 View of the community of Irupata during the rainy season, showing its grassy plain.

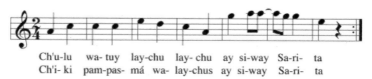

| Ch'u-lu | wa-tuy | lay-chu | lay-chu | ay si-way | Sa-ri- ta |
| Ch'i- ki | pam-pas- má | wa- lay-chus | ay si-way | Sa-ri- ta |

Ch'ulu watuy laychu laychu
  ay siway Sarita
Ch'iki pampasmá walaychus
  ay siway Sarita

Tassel of my knitted cap, swaying,
  ay siway Sara
We *plains* of *ch'iki* are real rascals,
  ay siway Sara

Musical Example 19.3 Formula for singing community nicknames, as sung by a group from the community of Irupata.

The main settlement of the community of Irupata, as mentioned above, is located on a large plain. During the rainy season this fertile plain turns very green with potato fields and a type of grass known as *ch'iki* (probably *Acicarpha procumbens*) (see Figure 19.2). The nickname for Irupata describes this landscape as a *ch'iki pampa*, literally "plain of *ch'iki*." Singers from Irupata used this nickname in the verse transcribed in Musical Example 19.3.

The most common nickname for the community of Llallawita requires somewhat more explanation. The main settlement of this community is located at the base of a small mountain. This mountain has two peaks, one higher than the other, separated by a shallow ravine or saddle (see Figure 19.3). The shape of this mountain is likened to a *llallawa*, any vegetable or fruit, but especially a potato, that has grown deformed, appearing to be two fruits grown or stuck together[8] (see Figure 19.4).

The name of the higher and larger of the two peaks of the mountain is Jach'a Llallawa ("Big Llallawa" in Aymara); the name of the smaller, lower peak is Jisk'a Llallawa ("Little Llallawa"). The name of the community itself is the diminutive form of *llallawa*, referring to the small twin-peaked

Figure 19.3 The main settlement of the community of Llallawita, at the base of a small mountain with two peaks.

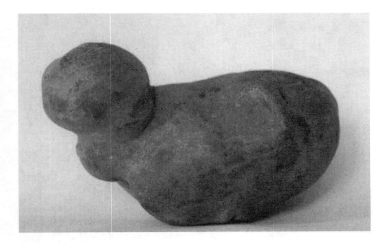

Figure 19.4 A llallawa potato.

mountain as a whole. But the community's most common nickname, *llallaw q'asa*, describes the settlement's landscape even more specifically. For the first term, the final vowel of *llallawa* is elided, reducing the word to two syllables so that it will fit within the rhythmic format of Carnival song melodies; the second term *q'asa* refers to the saddle or shallow ravine between the two peaks of the mountain. The settlement itself of Llallawita is slightly tucked into one end of this ravine, so the description *llallaw q'asa*, literally "ravine between the twin peaks," precisely locates the settlement within the landscape of the mountain. One example of the use of this nickname by singers from Llallawita is transcribed in Musical Example 19.4:

U- jan-ti- tay lay-chu lay- chu   si-way sau- si-si-   ta
Lla-llaw q'a-sas-má wa-lay-chus   si-way sau- si-si-   ta

Ujantitay laychu laychu
   siway sausisita
Llallaw q'asasmá walaychus
   siway sausisita

Tassel of my scarf, swaying,
   siway weeping willow
We *llallawa ravines* are real rascals,
   siway weeping willow

Musical Example 19.4 Formula for singing community nicknames, as sung by a group from the community of Llallawita.

Community nicknames may describe not the landscape of the main settlement itself, but nearby places within the territory of the community. The main settlement of the community of Muramaya is located in a small flat space above a ravine through which runs a small river. Muramaya's nickname *sausi mayu*, however, describes a point where the river (*mayu*) passes by a weeping willow tree (*sausi*, from Spanish *sauce*, "willow") (see Figure 19.5). The "river" itself, actually a small stream channeled on one side by a stone wall, is dry in this photo because at the time I took it the water was being diverted further upstream for irrigation.

This nickname appeared in a verse, transcribed in Musical Example 19.5, performed by a kumparsa from Muramaya during a Carnival visit to the community of Irupata in 1993.

Figure 19.5 The place described as sausi mayu, "river passing by a weeping willow tree," near the settlement of Muramaya.

U- jan- ti- tay lay- chu lay- chu   si- way sau-   si- si-   ta
Sau-si   ma-yus-má   wa- lay- chus   si- way sau-   si- si-   ta

Ujantitay laychu laychu siway
   sausisita
Sausi mayusmá walaychus
   siway sausisita

My scarf, swaying, siway
   weeping willow
We *weeping willow-rivers* are real rascals,
   siway weeping willow

Musical Example 19.5 Formula for singing community nicknames, as sung by a group from the community of Muramaya.

The above examples show how singers from three different communities can sing the same formulaic verse, each using a different tune, and each plugging into the verse a description of the landscape around their own home community. The singers identify themselves with their respective landscapes, embodying their community identity in their land in the act of singing the verse.

By using the plural form of the nickname the singers not only invoke the landscape, but specifically identify themselves with the landforms described; embedded within the second line of the verses is the proposition "we *are* the [grassy plain, ravine between the peaks, river running by the weeping willow, etc.]."

The nicknames discussed here appear only in song texts. People from the community of Irupata, for example, would not say "I am from *ch'iki pampa*" in everyday conversation; they would simply use their community's common everyday name. This raises a question for understanding nicknames and the way they are used: Why do singers use these nicknames specifically in *songs*? The answer, I think, lies in *who* is doing the performing: young unmarried men and women.

The verses discussed above suggest that young people's identification with their community landscapes is enabled much more evocatively through the use of nicknames than by using everyday community toponyms. Moving far beyond simple reference, the nicknames embody physico-social landscapes of lived experience. It is significant that these nicknames are in the Quechua language, not Aymara. Young Quechua speakers invent these nicknames in order to evoke their experience of their home landscapes. Desiring to construct their identity in terms of the land they know and live on, and sensing that many old Aymara toponyms—in a language they do not understand—do not satisfy this need, they invent new names to use in songs. Important here is the fact that nearly all the Quechua nicknames I collected are used by singers from communities whose common everyday name is in Aymara.

In Chayantaka society, as among many Andean peoples, one is not fully socialized into one's community until one has married and had children (Albó and Mamani 1980, 287; Brush 1977, 138; Carter 1977, 178; Isbell 1978, 81). Young people represent the potential for the continued existence of the community, but adults do not recognize them as equal partners with a voice in community affairs until they have actually proven this potential through socio-biological reproduction. Several times during my fieldwork I witnessed unmarried young men attempt to make contributions to community discussions, only to be told by adults to be quiet, that they could not participate in the decision-making process because they were not married and thus lacked the experience necessary to partake in community governance. One arena where young people are more freely able—and even encouraged—to express themselves is musical performance. Song texts are thus important vehicles for young people for publicly making statements about who they think they are. The nicknames that young people invent appear in song performance because that is one of the primary media that young people have for self-expression within the community (other such media include weaving and knitting).[9]

Folklorist Kent Ryden has argued that "sense of self becomes inextricably linked to the physical components of a place, or to participation in place-bound ways of life..." (1993, 64). While Ryden writes in terms of individual experience, this argument can also apply to collective senses of identity. For young Chayantaka musicians, landscapes become central as sites for imagining collective identities. Sense of self and sense of place are intimately connected—perhaps better described as a "sense of place-self"—and individuals' shared sense of place-based identity becomes the basis of a sense of community.

Dueling Landscapes

During the Carnival visits described earlier in this paper, two or more musical groups from different communities often encounter each other while visiting the same house. In these situations, the groups often simultaneously perform different songs in a kind of duel, called *takipayanaku* in Quechua (Solomon 1994). Each group tries to play louder and longer than the others. The verses described above are especially important in these informal competitions, especially when the young people are staying up all night playing after a day of performing and drinking. In this context each group may limit its singing to one or two verses repeated over and over, typically verses naming their community or the above formulas with their community's nickname. As each group sings its landscape, asserting its identity, the twin implications are "My community's landscape is more beautiful than yours," and "We're better than you." Textually, the duel is constructed in terms of the landscapes themselves, which embody collective identities at the community level.

Singers thus constantly refer to the names of their communities and describe their landscapes. To sing community toponyms (to a lesser extent), and to sing the community landscape descriptions in the nicknames (to a greater extent) is to call the social body of the community into being, embodied not just in the people themselves, but in the landscape of the settlement and surrounding land: to be from Irupata is to *be* the grassy plain; to be from Muramaya is to *be* that place where the river passes by the weeping willow tree. This is not just an overly literal interpretation on my part of the metaphors of these song texts. These verses are the discursive expressions of a native theory of the essence of identity embodied in place—a kind of ethno-phenomenology of place-self.

At this point I would like to anticipate some problems the reader may perceive in my analysis here. There may seem to be a certain *literalness* of identity—a too-easy correspondence between "community" and "identity," and an emphasis on collective identities to the exclusion of other kinds of identity, such as individual, biographical identity. Concurrently, I have also focused here on a very *texted* kind of identity—a specifically discursive construction, recoverable from linguistic data in what appears to be a very transparent way. In response to these criticisms, I would respond that the literalness and textedness of identities discussed here come out of young Chayantakas' own concern with textually constructing their identity—one might almost contend that they obsess on discursive self-definition, at least in their song texts. Chayantaka choose carefully the words of their songs, and as the song texts discussed above show, when they sing, they sing about who they are in a very explicit way, in terms of collective identities. Chayantaka Carnival songs are not a vehicle for overt individual biographical statements; they are a collective vehicle for the construction of communal identities.

The Sound of Place/The Place of Sound

Throughout this paper I have discussed Chayantaka communities as places discursively imagined in song texts. But communities would not figure so prominently in songs if they were not already sites of intense feeling outside the heightened contexts of fiesta performance. The sensuousness of everyday life is closely tied to the experience of places, including community settlements. An anecdote from my fieldwork may convey the evocative power communities as places have for Chayantaka.

Once two of my field assistants from the community of Irupata accompanied me on a two-day visit by foot to another community in order to interview instrument makers and take photographs of places mentioned in the texts of songs we had transcribed and translated together. The rainy season had begun a few weeks earlier, and while the rain was fortunately light during most of our trip, at one point on the first day we were caught outside in a hailstorm with nowhere to take refuge. I used my large-framed backpack to protect myself from the pelting of the small hailstones—which stung as they struck the exposed skin of my face and neck—but my companions had no protection other than some large bushes which they crouched under. The following day, near the end of our three-hour walk back home, the plain of Irupata, green with grass and fields of recently sprouted potato plants, came into view as we passed over the top of a rise. One of my companions spontaneously commented, "There's no place more beautiful in Ayllu Chayantaka than the plain of Irupata after the rains have started, when it's so green." My companion's pride and affection for the landscape of his community was typical of the way people talked about their places. After getting caught in the hailstorm the previous day, and sleeping the night before in wet clothes in a stranger's house in an unfamiliar community, the sight of home, a place that embodied years of accumulated experiences, aroused intense emotion in him. The plain's greenness signaled the presence of life—not just the growing plants, but the people that planted them. The beauty of the place evoked the complex of social relationships that sustained the community there.

This kind of deeply felt sentiment toward a place is an example of what geographer Yi-Fu Tuan (1974) calls *topophilia*, the affective bonds people have with places. For Chayantaka, topophilia comes from the accumulated daily experiences of socially organized agricultural work—planting, tending the fields, harvesting. The sensuousness of everyday agricultural life is manifest in such mundane events as making a *wathiya* (earth-oven) out of the very dirt of the field in which one is working, and cooking in it and having for lunch the same potatoes one dug out of the earth only an hour before.

Chayantaka landscapes are thus not just visual—they are also tactile, and full of smells, tastes, and sounds.[10] The land embodies the deeply felt everyday experiences of carrying on agriculture and pastoralism, the work of which is collectively accomplished through reciprocal networks of kin relationships. "Experience, memory, and feeling combine with the physical environment to push peaks of human meaning above the abstract plain of space" (Ryden 1993, 40); "Sense of place literally begins with the senses" (Hufford 1987, 16).

Throughout this paper I have referred to "Chayantaka *landscapes*," without specifically addressing the concept of *landscape* itself. Geographer Denis Cosgrove has traced the history of the idea of *landscape* and has described it as a particularly Western way of seeing the external world, an ideological construction intricately bound up with capitalism and directed toward "the control and domination over space as an absolute, objective entity, its transformation into the property of individual or state" (1985, 46; see also Cosgrove 1984; Relph 1981, 22–41; Williams 1973, 121–126; and the essays in Cosgrove and Daniels 1988). That the Western idea of landscape should be described as specifically a way of *seeing* is significant; Cosgrove argues that the visual concept of landscape was made possible by the development in painting of the realist technique of linear perspective to represent three-dimensional space on a two-dimensional surface.

Recent anthropological, geographical and musicological explorations of the interplay of the senses (Austern 2002, Bendix 2000, Howes 1991, Pocock 1993, Stoller 1989, Tuan 1993) critique this solely vision-based epistemology and call for the exploration of the roles of the other senses in the cultural patterning of perception. A similar point has been made in recent theorizing about landscape and place; Bender (1993a) and Tilley (1994) suggest that researchers should transcend the purely visual approach to landscape and investigate how place and space are experienced through all the senses. It is in this spirit that humanistic geographer Tuan (1993) writes of "landscapes of smell" and "landscapes of touch." Such an approach also allows for a cross-culturally more applicable concept of landscape as place-experience.

Writing more specifically about the realm of sound, musicologist and composer R. Murray Schafer (1977, 1985), building on Edmund Carpenter's and Marshall McLuhan's concept of "acoustic space" (1960), explores the soundscapes of different living environments. Feld (1996b) provides an ethnographic example of the interplay of the senses in the perception of space and place, emphasizing the sound of place and the place of sound among the Kaluli of Papua New Guinea. The Chayantaka data also point to a multi-sensory experience of landscape in which sound plays a major role. This is not to deny the visual impact of places on Chayantaka—recall the reaction of my companion as the settlement of Irupata came into view—but rather to argue that sight is not the only sense they use to emplace themselves as members of a community. In the performance of Carnival songs, community names and landscape descriptions, because they are *sung*, become vehicles for embodying self in place and place in self through sound.

While the focus here has been on song texts, singers also use other musical means to construct their communal identities. In a more comprehensive discussion of musical imaginations of place-identity (Solomon 1997), I consider how the timbre of instrumental ensembles, singing style, and even the choice of which instrument to play all serve to construct and evoke place-based identities. For example, one community was known for the distinctive timbre of its string ensembles, resulting from the players' choice of a particular combination of metal and nylon strings for their instruments. When I played for people excerpts from my field recordings, they could easily identify the community of origin of the players based on these kinds of aural cues.

When speaking Quechua, people explain the recognizable musical differences between communities by means of an aphorism I heard many times during my field research: "*Sapa lugar ujjina kustumbri tiyan*"—literally, "Each place has a different custom." This kind of discursive construction of the differences in expressive cultural practices between communities is common in the Andes. Schechter (1992, 2–3, 8–9), for example, describes a similar principle among the Cotacachi Quichua in Ecuador, who invoke the phrase "*cada llajta*" ("every community") when explaining what they perceive as the uniqueness of their own music in relation to the music of other communities and regions.

Performance As Embodiment and Emplacement

For Chayantaka, landscapes—the places themselves—are what Robert Plant Armstrong (1971) calls "affecting presences" (cf. Feld 1996a, 74). Since I am extending Armstrong's idea in a direction perhaps he had not intended, I should explain myself here. Armstrong proposed the term "affecting presence" as a replacement for "art object" in order to emphasize the processual nature of (1) how artists embody felt experience in creative works, and (2) how those who encounter these works feel the artist's experiences through the encounter. To say then that a place is an affecting presence is thus to recognize that (1) to *name* a place is to *call it into being* by identifying it as an entity separate from the surrounding space—in a sense, to *create* the place[11]—and that (2) to encounter a culturally defined place is to encounter the experiences and feelings of those who came before and made that place, and interpolate those experiences and feelings with one's own. Emplacement becomes inseparable from embodiment (Feld 1996b); the senses make places, and places literally make sense—they are cultural ways of organizing felt experiences of the environment. This idea is similar to the point Ryden is making when he writes that *sense of place* itself is a kind of genre, a "traditional attitude or stance vis-à-vis the physical world" (1993, 68).

As discussed above, for Chayantaka one of the primary ways places are made sensible is through sound. For Chayantaka, collectively produced sounds embody collective identities and poetically inscribe them in specific places. To say that sound *embodies* identity is to say that the very materiality of sound—its sensible qualities (Urban 1991)—makes tangible and feelingful the facts of social relationships between people who share similar sets of experiences; it is to say that sound objectifies the experience of sociality in a way that can be perceived by the senses—the physicality of tone and timbre, patterned in time to enable even further bodily participation through dancing.

Musical performance creates the social space for these acts of embodiment. For Chayantaka, musical performance is not just for one's self—it always occurs in the presence of people from other communities, whether during visits to their places, or at regional fiestas or music festivals to which people from many communities come. Performance occasions are the opportunities to call into being the social body and landscape of one's own community in front of representatives of other such communities. Performance creates the space for calling into being the differences that make a difference—the differences between communities. The medium of specifically *musical* performance—using the breath, mouth, and vocal cords to sing, or the breath or hands to play musical instruments—makes this emplacement/embodiment *sensible* in an aesthetically powerful way.

Notes

1. Fieldwork in Bolivia was supported in 1990 by a grant from the Tinker Foundation and in 1993–1994 by a Fulbright-Hays Doctoral Dissertation Abroad Fellowship. I presented material from this paper at the 1993 Reunión Anual de Etnología at the Museo Nacional de Etnología y Folklore in La Paz, Bolivia, at the 1994 annual meeting of the American Anthropological Association, and at an invited talk in the Columbia University Department of Music in October 1997. My thanks to those who commented on various written versions of these ideas and at the fora mentioned above, especially Tom Abercrombie, Steven Feld, Aaron Fox, and Richard Schaedel. This paper is adapted from portions of chapter six of my doctoral dissertation (Solomon 1997). Since the first publication of this article in 2000, I have continued to explore relationships between music, place and identity through a new research project on Turkish rap and hip-hop (Solomon 2005).
2. For basic information on Chayantaka ecology and social organization, see Flores Aguanta (1990, 1991), Kraft (1995), and Mendoza, Flores, and Letourneux (1994).
3. Stobart (2002b) describes similar courtship practices centering on musical ensembles during Carnival and other fiestas in Ayllu Macha, another indigenous group of northern Potosí, whose territory lies to the south of the Chayantaka.
4. The Chayantaka Carnival musical visits are part of a pan-Andean complex of musical rituals for boundary marking or place inscription. Examples of the use of music in these rituals abound in the Andeanist ethnographic literature; Allen (1988, 183, 201), Bourque (1994), Radcliffe (1990), Rappaport (1985, 32), Rasnake (1986) and Sallnow (1987) are only a few examples.
5. Botanical identifications are taken from De Lucca D. and Zalles A. (1992).
6. To facilitate reading and comparison, all transcriptions in this paper have been transposed so that the tonal center is *A*.
7. G. Martínez (1983b, 62) similarly notes that his Aymara consultants from Ch'uani (Camacho Province, Department of La Paz), when asked the meaning of a toponym, would often respond "It's just its name" (*sutikipuniw* in Aymara).
8. This term seems to be in use throughout the Aymara-speaking area. Van den Berg (1990, 145–146) summarizes the early colonial sources on the term *llallahua* as a term for odd-shaped fruits and vegetables, especially potatoes, including the chronicle of Polo de Ondegardo (ca. 1585) and an entry in the Aymara dictionary of Bertonio (ca. 1612). Contemporary ethnographers working in the *altiplano* area of Bolivia and Peru have also noted the special attention people give to misshapen potatoes (LaBarre 1948, 165, 176; Paredes 1976[1920], 126; Paredes Candia 1980, 217; Tschopik 1947, 518).
9. For a description of Chayantaka weaving techniques, see López, Flores, and Letourneau (1992).
10. In a series of papers based on his research in Ayllu Macha, to the south of the Chayantaka, Henry Stobart (1994, 1996a, 1996b, 2000, 2002a, 2002b) also discusses aspects of the relationship between music, the environment and the senses. Stobart's work and the Chayantaka case study discussed here are suggestive of some interesting similarities and contrasts between these two closely related Andean peoples, though an extended comparison of Stobart's work and mine is beyond the scope of this paper.
11. Compare Tuan's (1991) arguments about what he calls "language and the making of place" and Mugerauer's (1985) discussion of "the saying of the environment."

References

Albó, Javier. 1980. *Lengua y Sociedad en Bolivia 1976*. La Paz: Instituto Nacional de Estadística.

Albo, Xavier and Mauricio Mamani. 1980. "Esposos, Suegros y Padrinos entre los Aymaras." In *Parentesco y Matrimonio en los Andes*, edited by Enrique Mayer and Ralph Bolton, 283–326. Lima: Pontificia Universidad Católica del Perú, Fondo Editorial.

Allen, Catherine J. 1988. *The Hold Life Has: Coca and Cultural Identity in an Andean Community*. Washington: Smithsonian Institution Press.

Armstrong, Robert Plant. 1971. *The Affecting Presence: An Essay in Humanistic Anthropology*. Urbana: University of Illinois Press.

Austern, Linda Phyllis, ed. 2002. *Music, Sensation, and Sensuality*. New York: Routledge.

Basso, Keith H. 1984. "'Stalking with Stories': Names, Places, and Moral Narratives among the Western Apache." In *Text, Play, and Story: The Construction and Reconstruction of Self and Society* (1983 *Proceedings of the American Ethnological Society*), edited by Edward M. Bruner, 19–55. Prospect Heights, IL: Waveland Press.

Bender, Barbara. 1993a. "Introduction: Landscape—Meaning and Action." In *Landscape: Politics and Perspectives*, edited by Barbara Bender, 1–17. Oxford: Berg.

———, ed. 1993b. *Landscape: Politics and Perspectives*. Oxford: Berg.

Bendix, Regina. 2000. "The Pleasures of the Ear: Toward an Ethnography of Listening." *Cultural Analysis* 1. http://ist-socrates.berkeley.edu/~caforum/volume1/vol1_article3.html, accessed 19 February, 2005.

Bennett, Andy. 2000. *Popular Music and Youth Culture: Music, Identity and Place*. New York: St. Martin's Press.

Berg, Hans van den. 1990. *La Tierra no Da Así Nomás: Los Ritos Agrícolas en la Religión de los Aymara-cristianos*. La Paz: HISBOL-UCB/ISET.

Bourque, Nicole L. 1994. "Spatial Meaning in Andean Festivals: Corpus Christi and Octavo." *Ethnology* 33(3):229–243.

Brush, Stephen B. 1977. "Kinship and Land Use in a Northern Sierra Community." In *Andean Kinship and Marriage*, edited by Ralph Bolton and Enrique Mayer, 136–52. Washington, D.C.: American Anthropological Association.

Carpenter, Edmund and Marshall McLuhan. 1960. "Acoustic Space." In *Explorations in Communication*, edited by Edmund Carpenter and Marshall McLuhan, 65–70. Boston: Beacon Press.

Carter, W.E. 1977. "Trial Marriage in the Andes?" In *Andean Kinship and Marriage*, edited by Ralph Bolton and Enrique Mayer, 177–216. Washington, D.C.: American Anthropological Association.

Connell, John and Chris Gibson. 2003. *Sound Tracks: Popular Music, Identity and Place*. London: Routledge.

Cosgrove, Denis E. 1984. *Social Formation and Symbolic Landscape*. Totowa, NJ: Barnes and Noble Books.

———. 1985. "Prospect, Perspective, and the Evolution of the Landscape Idea." *Transactions of the Institute of British Geographers* 10(l):45–62.

Cosgrove, Denis E. and Stephen Daniels, eds. 1988. *The Iconography of Landscape: Essays on the Symbolic Representation, Design, and Use of Past Environments*. New York: Cambridge University Press.

Feld, Steven. 1996a. "Poetics of Place: Ecological and Aesthetic Co-evolution in a Papua New Guinea Rainforest Community." In *Redefining Nature: Ecology, Culture and Domestication*, edited by Roy F. Ellen and Katsuyoshi Fukui, 61–87. Oxford: Berg.

———. 1996b. "Waterfalls of Song: An Acoustemology of Place Resounding in Bosavi, Papua New Guinea." In *Senses of Place*, edited by Steven Feld and Keith Basso, 91–135. Santa Fe: School of American Research Press.

Feld, Steven and Keith Basso, eds. 1996. *Senses of Place*. Santa Fe: School of American Research Press.

Flores Aguanta, Willer. 1990. "Desestructuración y Pérdida de Identidad Étnica en el Norte de Potosí." In *Reunión Anual de Etnología, 1990*, 93–97. La Paz: Museo Nacional de Etnografía y Folklore.

———. 1991. "Breve Descripción Socio-económica del Ayllu de Chayantaka." In *Reunión Anual de Etnología, 1991*, 43–55. La Paz: Museo Nacional de Etnografía y Folklore.

Forman, Murray. 2002. *The 'Hood Comes First: Race, Space, and Place in Rap and Hip Hop*. Middletown: Wesleyan University Press.

Foucault, Michel. 1972. *The Archaeology of Knowledge*. New York: Pantheon Books.

Harris, Olivia. 1982. "The Dead and Devils among the Bolivian Laymi." In *Death and the Regeneration of Life*, edited by Maurice Bloch and Jonathan Parry, 45–73. Cambridge: Cambridge University Press.

Hirsch, Eric and Michael O'Hanlon, eds. 1995. *The Anthropology of Landscape: Perspectives on Place and Space*. Oxford: Clarendon Press.

Hosokawa, Koomei. 1980. *Diagnóstico Sociolingüístico de la Región Norte de Potosí*. La Paz: INEL.

Howard-Malverde, Rosaleen. 1995. "'Pachamama is a Spanish Word': Linguistic Tension between Aymara, Quechua, and Spanish in Northern Potosí (Bolivia)." *Anthropological Linguistics* 37(2):141–168.

Howes, David, ed. 1991. *The Varieties of Sensory Experience: A Sourcebook in the Anthropology of the Senses*. Toronto: University of Toronto Press.

Hufford, Mary T. 1987. "Telling the Landscape: Folklife Expressions and Sense of Place." In *Pinelands Folklife*, edited by Rita Zorn Moonsammy, David Stephen Cohen and Lorraine E. Williams, 13–41. New Brunswick: Rutgers University Press.

Isbell, Billie Jean. 1978. *To Defend Ourselves: Ecology and Ritual in an Andean Village*. Austin: University of Texas Press.

Ivade, Peter. 1994. "The Place of Music: A Conference." *Popular Music* 13(1):105–107.

Kraft, Karen Elaine. 1995. "Andean Fields and Fallow Pastures: Communal Land Use Management under Pressures for Intensification." Ph.D. dissertation (Anthropology), University of Florida (Gainesville). University Microfilms International, No.96l8721.

LaBarre, Weston. 1948. "The Aymara Indians of the Lake Titicaca Plateau, Bolivia." *Memoir Series of the American Anthropological Association* 68. Washington, D.C.: American Anthropological Association.

Leyshon, Andrew, David Matless, and George Revill, eds. 1998. *The Place of Music*. New York: The Guilford Press.

López, Jaime, Willer Flores, and Catherine Letourneux. 1992. *Lliqllas Chayantakas*. La Paz: Programa de Autodesarrollo Campesino PAC-Potosí and Ruralter.

Lucca D., Manuel de, and Jaime Zalles A. 1992. *Flora Medicinal Boliviana: Diccionario Enciclopédico*. La Paz: Editorial Los Amigos del Libro.

Martínez, Gabriel. 1983. "Topónimos de Chuani: ¿Organización y Significación del Territorio?" *Antropológica* 1(1):51–84.

Mendoza, Fernando, Willer Flores, and Catherine Letourneux. 1994. *Atlas de los Ayllus de Chayanta. Vol. 1: Territorios del Suni*. Potosí, Bolivia: Programa de Autodesarrollo Campesino, Fase de Consolidación.

Mitchell, Tony. 1996. *Popular Music and Local Identity: Rock, Pop and Rap in Europe and Oceania*. London: Leicester University Press.

Mugerauer, Robert. 1985. "Language and the Emergence of Environment." In *Dwelling, Place and Environment*, edited by David Seamon and Robert Mugerauer, 51–70. Dordrecht: Martinus Nijhoff Publishers.

Paredes, M. Rigoberto. 1976 [1920]. *Mitos, Supersticiones y Supervivencias Populares de Bolivia*. 5th ed. La Paz: Biblioteca del Sesquicentenario de la República.

Paredes Candia, Antonio. 1980. *Folklore de Potosí: Algunos Aspectos*. La Paz: Ediciones ISLA.

Pocock, Douglas. 1993. "The Senses in Focus." *Area* 25(1):11–16.

Radcliffe, Sarah A. 1990. "Marking the Boundaries between the Community, the State, and History in the Andes." *Journal of Latin American Studies* 22(3):575–94.

Rappaport, Joanne. 1985. "History, Myth, and the Dynamics of Territorial Maintenance in Tierradentro, Colombia." *American Ethnologist* 12(l):27–45.

Rasnake, Roger Neil. 1986. "Carnival in Yura: Ritual Reflections on *Ayllu* and State Relations." *American Ethnologist* 13(4):662–680.

———. 1988. *Domination and Cultural Resistance: Authority and Power among an Andean People*. Durham: Duke University Press.

Relph, E. 1976. *Place and Placelessness*. London: Pion Limited.

Rodman, Margaret C. 1992. "Empowering Place: Multilocality and Multivocality." *American Anthropologist* 94(3):640–656.

Ryden, Kent C. 1993. *Mapping the Invisible Landscape: Folklore, Writing, and the Sense of Place*. Iowa City: University of Iowa Press.

Sallnow, Michael J. 1987. *Pilgrims of the Andes: Regional Cults in Cusco*. Washington, D.C.: Smithsonian Institution Press.

Schafer, R. Murray. 1977. *The Tuning of the World*. New York: Alfred A. Knopf.

———. 1985. "Acoustic Space." In *Dwelling, Place and Environment: Towards a Phenomenology of Person and World*, edited by David Seamon and Robert Mugerauer, 87–98. Dordrecht: Martinus Nijhoff Publishers.

Schechter, John M. 1992. *The Indispensable Harp: Historical Development, Modern Roles, Configurations, and Performance Practices in Ecuador and Latin America*. Kent, OH: Kent State University Press.

Seeger, Anthony. 1987. *Why Suyá Sing: A Musical Anthropology of an Amazonian People*. Cambridge: Cambridge University Press.

Solomon, Thomas. 1994. "*Coplas de Todos Santos* in Cochabamba: Language, Music, and Performance in Bolivian Quechua Song Dueling." *Journal of American Folklore* 107(425):378–4l4.

———. 1997. "Mountains of Song: Musical Constructions of Ecology, Place and Identity in Highland Bolivia." Ph.D. dissertation (Anthropology), University of Texas, Austin. University Microfilms International, No.9803031.

———. 2005. "'Living Underground is Tough': Authenticity and Locality in the Hip-hop Community in Istanbul, Turkey." *Popular Music* 24(1):1–20.

Stobart, Henry. 1994. "Flourishing Horns and Enchanted Tubers: Music and Potatoes in Highland Bolivia." *British Journal of Ethnomusicology* 3:35–48.

———. 1996a. "*Tara* and *Q'iwa*—Worlds of Sound and Meaning." In *Cosmología y Música en los Andes*, edited by Max Peter Baumann, 67–81. Vervuert: Iberoamericana.

———. 1996b. "The Llama's Flute: Musical Misunderstandings in the Andes." *Early Music* 24(3):471–482.

———. 2000. "Bodies of Sound and Landscapes of Music: A View from the Bolivian Andes." In *Musical Healing in Cultural Contexts*, edited by Penelope Gouk, 26–45. Aldershot: Ashgate.

———. 2002a. "Interlocking Realms: Knowing Music and Musical Knowing in the Bolivia Andes." In *Knowledge and Learning in the Andes: Ethnographic Perspectives*, edited by Henry Stobart and Rosaleen Howard, 79–106. Liverpool: Liverpool University Press.

———. 2002b. "Sensational Sacrifices: Feasting the Senses in the Bolivian Andes." In *Music, Sensation, and Sensuality*, edited by Linda Phyllis Austern, 97–120. New York: Routledge.

Stokes, Martin. 1994a. "Introduction: Ethnicity, Identity and Music." In *Ethnicity, Identity and Music: The Musical Construction of Place*, edited by Martin Stokes, 1–27. Oxford: Berg.

———, ed. 1994b. *Ethnicity, Identity and Music: The Musical Construction of Place*. Oxford: Berg.

Stoller, Paul. 1989. *The Taste of Ethnographic Things: The Senses in Anthropology*. Philadelphia: University of Pennsylvania Press.

Tilley, Christopher. 1994. *A Phenomenology of Landscape: Places, Paths and Monuments*. Oxford: Berg.

Tschopik, Harry, Jr. 1947. "The Aymara." In *Handbook of South American Indians. Volume 2: The Andean Civilizations* (*Smithsonian Institution Bureau of Ethnology Bulletin* 143), edited by Julian H. Steward, 501–73. Washington: United Sates Government Printing Office.

Tuan, Yi-Fu. 1974. *Topophilia: A Study of Environmental Perception, Attitudes, and Values*. Englewood Cliffs: Prentice-Hall.

———. 1991 "Language and the Making of Place: A Narrative-Descriptive Approach." *Annals of the Association of American Geographers* 81(4):684–696.

———. 1993. *Passing Strange and Wonderful: Aesthetics, Nature, and Culture*. Washington, D.C.: Island Press.

Urban, Greg. 1991. *A Discourse-Centered Approach to Culture: Native South American Myths and Rituals*. Austin: University of Texas Press.

Whiteley, Sheila, Andy Bennett and Stan Hawkins, eds. 2004. *Music, Space and Place: Popular Music and Cultural Identity*. Aldershot: Ashgate.

Williams, Raymond. 1973. *The Country and the City*. New York: Oxford University Press.

Part VIII

Racial and Ethnic Identities

20

Native American Rap and Reggae
Dancing "To the Beat of a Different Drummer"

Neal Ullestad

From the mountains to the valley/From the deserts to the plains. To the deepest caves of ocean/I've traveled over a canyon again. Nothing more I can do/All alone and sometimes blue. I'll turn my radio on/My radio on.
>   *"I'll Turn My Radio On"—Walela*
>   —Rita and Priscilla Coolidge with Laura Satterfield

Following World War II and continuing into the 1980s, turning the radio on offered the random possibility of hearing Native American musicians and their songs in a popular format. There was Peter La Farge's popular hit "The Ballad of Ira Hayes," sung by Johnny Cash in the '50s;[1] Buffy Sainte-Marie in the '60s; and Rita Coolidge and Redbone in the 1970s and early '80s. It wasn't just college radio. And "mainstream" radio did so much more than obliquely feature Native American talents such as the Band's Robbie Robertson working with Bob Dylan. There was an openness in radio formats back then that's consciously avoided today in the mass-market-obsessed twenty-first century. Outside the limited range of certain community-oriented stations and about two dozen stations on or near reservations, the unfortunate reality is that turning the radio on today generally won't bring forth any of the new and innovative forms of Native American music (see Figure 20.1) currently available.[2]

In fact, even in the southwestern United States, where demographic concentrations of Native Americans, their sympathizers, and tourists create stronger markets for indigenous music and the wider range of music is more evident, many people are surprised to learn that today's Native American music is more than chants, drums, and flutes. Contemporary Native American music is rich and diverse, incorporating many tribally derived traditions, as well as popular and commercial forms and styles, including polkas, country music, folk, rock and roll, blues, jazz, rap, and reggae.

One reason people think primarily of chanting and drumming when they think about Native American music is that indigenous people, if they are represented in popular culture at all, are usually portrayed as part of our cultural past, not as part of our musical present. Innovative Native American music that exists today generally isn't afforded access to mass media to be able to draw a wide audience. In the face of marginalization by the mainstream, Native American musicians

Figure 20.1 At the microphone, Casper the Hopi reggae rapper at the Teva Spirit of Unity Festival in Phoenix, September 19, 1999. Photo Neal Ullestad.

experience two distinct poles of artistic expression: traditionalist and commercial/assimilationist. Rejecting the idea of having to choose between these two seemingly unbridgeable poles is a broad array of artists who combine the two approaches, those who work within the wide "in between" category, combining elements of traditional and commercial music, as well as traditional and contemporary themes. They are the focus of this article. Though largely unavailable on radio and television, this music is accessible in the form of compact discs and tapes across the country from large and small record companies, sometimes in music mega-stores, and regularly distributed out of the trunk of a musician's car to small local outlets, and at live venues.

In these times of change, times of confrontation at the levels of politics, sexuality, and religion—times of extreme uneven economic development—cultural transformation and exchange arise in wildly diverse places and spaces. Part of what makes popular music so complex is the fact that time and place are at times more dominant factors than the musician, listener, or message. Musicians encounter crossroads of time and place, and they sing of the relationship between the social world we are losing and that which is being built. Popular music can express anxieties as well as hopes for what lies ahead because it is a place of dreams. We are "carried away" by the music. Or, conversely, a recorded album or single is carried away in our shopping bag. Some dreams may be easily realized, others not.

We continue to see a massive cross-pollination of cultural forms around the world today. The global economy, dominated by transworld corporate monopolies, has brought together in the marketplace sounds and songs from Haiti and the United States, Australia and Jamaica, Japan, Germany, West and South Africa, Cuba and Colombia, Algeria and France, all with amazing results. The hybrids that emerge at these various crossroads illustrate wide-ranging historical traditions and developing trends. The rapid exchange of ideas, information, people, technology, and emotion in this modern world has very real effects on the music, even as the music itself generates its own very concrete effects. This article explores the work of specific artists who experiment with cultural, political, and social techniques of education and performance that are unique applications of traditional and modern musical expression.

These musicians stand at the crossroads, physically and culturally, a crossroads of ideas, images, and expressions from around the world that have "created new networks of identification and affiliation that render obsolete some traditional political practices and identities while creating complicated and complex new cultural fusions with profound political implications" (Lipsitz, 13). The choice of rap and reggae—still considered "outlaw" musics in many arenas—to express their ideas, implies that these artists are not rushing toward the mainstream.

The "in between" of these musicians, chosen for artistic, personal or economic reasons, is complicated by social and cultural struggles over location and displacement in both physical places and discursive spaces. Their music is a clear example of the process that George Lipsitz considers popular music's simultaneous undermining and reinforcement of our sense of place. Similar to other indigenous musicians around the world, such as Australian aborigines who experiment with calypso and reggae, or to indigenous Algerian rai music embraced by antiracists in France, these Native American musicians signify an intercultural, or, as Robin Kelley has called it, "polycultural" cooperation ("People," 5), not always found in popular music. The "in between" they represent can reflect both the experiences of these musicians and their strategic attempts to gain wider recognition.

After briefly documenting the diversity of contemporary Native American music, this article describes the work of five such Native American musicians. These artists combine contemporary elements of rap, reggae, blues, rock, and jazz with traditional sounds to produce hybrid music that is dynamic and challenging, and as often as not contains political themes as a prominent element. Distinct features of Native American traditional music forms are briefly contrasted here within a framework intended to direct attention to the effects of the intersection of four major factors articulated to make, disseminate, and enjoy popular music today: the artist, a live or recorded "product," the audience or consumer, and that "music industry" which mediates almost all relations between the other three. This music at the crossroads epitomizes the conflicts between the mainstream and its margins, in this case between modernity and tradition. An attempt is made to contextualize how most Native American music is available on compact disc and tape, yet is marginalized because it is most prevalently available "on the radio" or "on the shelves" only in isolated "tourist" areas or in the rapidly decreasing number of independent bookstores and music shops. This marginalization, an aspect of the national/ethnic/gender identity politics at the heart of so many cultural and social issues today, is also a result of specific choices made by these musicians to retain traditional elements in their artistic expression.

Native American Music in the USA Today

Briefly listing over a dozen Native American musicians who combine contemporary sounds with traditional ones helps to illustrate the wide diversity of indigenous music in the USA today. Out in the southwestern Arizona desert, members of the Redhouse Family express their own Navajo and Northern Plains musical traditions in Rope and Hoop Dances at certain venues, and perform café-rock in another; then join together to produce the polished straight-ahead jazz fusion found on the family's compact disc *Urban Indian*. Far from this most "cosmopolitan" of sounds thrives

R. Carlos Nakai's evolving explorations with Jackalope on *Weavings* and beyond a New Age jazz sensibility to symphonic arrangements quite ethereal in nature. While in some areas of the country the traditional drums and chants of the powwow and potlatch are drowned out now by Muzak in new casinos, Waila music—"chicken scratch" polkas of such performers as Southern Scratch (1994) and the Tohono Raiders (1985)—remains quite popular across certain reservations in the southwestern United States.

Joanne Shenandoah's opening performance of her song for peace entitled "America" at Woodstock '94, and contained on her compact disc *Once in a Red Moon* was a poignant, but not unlikely or atypical moment in an active native-folk-rock career most recently represented on her CD *Covenant*, that moves into dance and trance. Shenandoah has covered much new ground since she previously released a disc of children's music, and her more adult-oriented *Matriarch: Iroquois Women's Songs*. And while the "traditional rock" of Bill Miller is reminiscent of Bruce Springsteen, the country folk of Floyd Westerman has followed more in the path of Peter La Farge with his distinct drum beats in the 1950s and '60s. Westerman's work continues to reflect the direct influence of Bob Dylan, before his electronic turn, more similar to the path of Buffy Sainte-Marie and her more topical and edgy folk. Sainte-Marie's political presence has continued to be felt with the song "Bury My Heart (at Wounded Knee)" on her *Coincidence & Likely Stories* compact disc, as well as the compilation *In the Spirit of Crazy Horse: Songs for Leonard Peltier P.O.W.* More recently Saint-Marie had success with her 1996 albums *Up Where We Belong* and *Quiet Places*, and most recently with *Fire & Fleet & Candlelight* (1999 Vanguard).

In the hard rock arena John Trudell's poetic ventures, and experiments with spoken word, folk, and rock and roll over the past two decades have meant that a resilient talent was not lost to the desperation of drugs and alcohol that has plagued so many on and off reservations. And the militant "hardcore" rap of WithOut Rezervation once based in Oakland, California, and Btaka Brown from southern California have expressed Native American concerns and ideas in the music of much of today's youth: rap. Today, the Oklahoma-based Litefoot, and the artists around him, continue in a similar vein. But with the emergence of Joy Harjo and her "jazzy-tribal-reggae" band Poetic Justice, there was a new and vibrant expression of the energy released when musical languages communicate across roots cultures, a synergy only hinted at by the continued popularity of Jamaican reggae among the Hopi clustered around Culture Connection up near Kykotsmovi on Second Mesa. And, following somewhat in the footsteps of Redbone, who played at the first Earth Day in 1970 long before their hit "Come and Get Your Love" (1973/75), Red Thunder supported the release of their compact disc *Makoce Wakal* with their "Sacred Site Tour" accompanying the "alternative" rock artists of H.O.R.D.E. (Blues Traveller, Hootie & the Blowfish, Lenny Kravitz, etc.) in the summer and fall of 1996. More recently Casper Lomayesva, the Hopi singer, has become popular in reggae circles across the country. And finally, in Santa Fe, New Mexico, today, two other popular Native American musical acts, Robert Mirabal and his "alter-Native" rock and poetry, and Walela (Rita Coolidge together with her sister Priscilla and Laura Satterfield) are serving up new music in and around that Southwestern cultural center, now with favorable national audience and critical response. These represent more than a baker's dozen of the number of distinct musical sounds, styles, and techniques that spring from indigenous communities in North America as we concluded the twentieth century and now proceed in the twenty-first.

Poetry in Motion: Joy Harjo at the End of the Twentieth Century

> *Once we abandoned ourselves for television,*
> *the box that separates the dreamer from the dreaming...*
> *We found ourselves somewhere near the diminishing point of civilization...*
> "A Postcolonial Tale"—Joy Harjo (1996)

Meridel Le Sueur, beloved literary figure for nearly three quarters of a century, described Joy Harjo's award-winning poetry as opening a window "into awakening" (Harjo in *Mad* book cover). Others have called Harjo's work "breathtaking" and "miraculous" (ibid.). A professor of English at the University of New Mexico in the late '90s when she began putting her poetry to music, Harjo has gathered critical, scholarly, and popular acclaim for over two decades. Still her Native American roots appear to have "ghettoized" her work as far as the mainstream is concerned. In April of 1997 a *New York Times* article by Dinitia Smith entitled "The Indian in Literature Is Growing Up," seemed to hold the promise of increasing interest in Native American poetry, prose and music because their work is increasingly "hard edged, urban and pop oriented" (1). However, the reviewer emphasized the uniqueness rather than the universality of the new wave of Native American writers and did not address the way poets such as Joy Harjo speak to all citizens of the North American continent, not just for and of their "own people." With the breadth of her artistic scope, the depth of her heartfelt emotion, and the unflinching confrontation of hard truths, few would deny the extent of Harjo's universal creative achievement.

Joy Harjo was born in Tulsa, Oklahoma, in 1951. Her mother was of mixed Cherokee and French blood, and her Creek father was descended from a long line of leaders and speakers. A registered Muskogee member, Harjo studied in Santa Fe and Iowa City, and has taught at Arizona State University, the University of Arizona, and the University of Colorado at Boulder, in addition to the University of New Mexico. She began her academic career in drawing and painting; but, inspired by Leslie Marmon Silko, the noted Laguna Pueblo author, as well as Emily Dickinson, Harjo shifted her energies to poetry. She has now been working in the musical realm for nearly ten years. Her poems have been anthologized in several academic categories. And poems from her four early books of poetry—*She Had Some Horses, Secrets from the Center of the World, In Mad Love and War, and The Woman Who Fell from the Sky* (with an accompanying audio tape)—are contained on her first CD. These poems are sometimes gritty and tough, sometimes compassionate, and at others still, playful and witty. Often her poem titles preview what's to come: "Creation Story," "Fear Poem," "Mourning Song," and "A Postcolonial Tale," providing more than a hint of their content.

Interestingly enough, Harjo's work teaching at the University of New Mexico in Albuquerque paralleled her work coediting the W. W. Norton volume, *Reinventing the Enemy's Language: North American Native Women's Writing* with Gloria Bird. Over the same decade her interest in the soprano saxophone and reggae music found fulfilling fusion with her poetry. Just as Le Sueur combined a wide range of artistic activities (autobiography, fiction, journalism, and poetry spanning decades of her nearly century-long life), Harjo has not been satisfied to develop just one or two of her talents, but has pursued painting, writing, teaching, and, now, music. "Playing saxophone is like honoring a succession of myths...the myth of the saxophone...and Billie Holliday and John Coltrane" (Kallet, 119).

Prominent feminist poet and activist Adrienne Rich has described Joy Harjo's poetry as a "breathtaking complex witness" to "our mixed and fermenting end of century North American imagination" (Harjo *Woman* book cover). Based on "her world remaking language: precise, unsentimental" (ibid.), Joy Harjo lets us see our country and those who inhabit it in a bright light of illumination, not as some shadowy mythical construct that obscures or glorifies vast segments of our history.

Though her poetry reflects residual contradictions resulting from centuries of colonialism and racism, it also speaks to emerging geopolitical and economic realities. In her poetry, traditional understandings of place are merged with realities of displacement shared by so many today, such that she speaks of identity and identification beyond the boundaries of her own nation, and exhibits the increased importance of popular culture in the public sphere around the world. Her work is far more than a novel diversion from the Pop mainstream because she speaks powerfully for diasporic populations in ways that most of us can understand. Hers is a unique standpoint, carefully crafted from familiar words and phrases, yet telling tales that haven't been told so boldly, so confidently, if

Figure 20.2 Joy Harjo. Reprinted with permission from Mekko Productions.

at all. Harjo stands as a beacon for others by representing her own displaced people; by speaking for some of the first to experience displacement and extermination, quite literally; she now speaks to the rest of us in words and phrases we all recognize.

In the late '90s, touring in support of the CD *Letter from the End of the Twentieth Century*, Harjo gave radical new meaning to the idea of a poetry reading. Her "jazzy-tribal-reggae" band, Poetic Justice, explored a wide range of midtempo jazz, rock, and reggae music to accompany Harjo's poetic recitation, which gave way at crucial moments to her soprano or alto saxophone solos that soothe or soar as required by the moment. Reminiscent at times of Soul II Soul or Kenny G, and at other times Joshua Redman or Pharoah Sanders, Harjo's fervent desire to wed her poetry with reggae music grew from experiences in 1980s London, where dub poets such as Linton Kwesi Johnson, Mutabaruka, and Oku Onuora were creating an international stir in literary and musical circles alike. Seeing these other artists put their poetry to music planted a seed for her own band Poetic Justice to germinate, grow and blossom.

When asked why she left her teaching position at the University of New Mexico, Harjo explained that she "couldn't spend enough time on the music trying to work around an academic calendar" (interview with author 5 April 1997). She acknowledges the genuine effort required to work with a group of musicians to be able to achieve a "good performance." Her band Poetic Justice, a six-piece ensemble with veteran musicians from various traditional, jazz, rhythm and blues, and rock and roll backgrounds, also has East and West Indian influences from raga to calypso. The band members, John Williams and William Bluehouse Johnson on bass and rhythm guitars, Susan Williams

(John's sister) on drums and percussion, Richard Carbajal on lead guitar, and Frank Poocha on powwow drums and keyboards, are riveting on stage. In a live show in Tucson, Arizona, in February of 1998, Poocha playfully interacted with Harjo and other band members while dancing to the sultry, subversive sway of the reggae beat. Traditional sounds and chanting sometimes offer a counterpoint to rolling rhythms, at other times a reinforcement. At a pause in her poetry, Harjo weaves her saxophone into the mix, offering balm for the wounded listener or extra swing to promote a cathartic release.

According to Harjo, moving and rhythm began to play a significant part in the creation of her poetry with the publication and accompanying audio tape release of *The Woman Who Fell from the Sky* in 1994: "Putting a band together and performing the poetry changed my writing. I... began performing my poems rather than saying them. Performance became a storytelling event around the initial urge for the poetry" (Gonzáles, 18). On her compact disc *Letter from the End of the Twentieth Century*, the music alternately helps build emotions or soothes the harsh realities exposed by the lyrics. An example of the "simple" word-painting or "soundscape," as Harjo has called it, is heard on the title track. The story of a "casual murder" is retold on a cab ride, inspiring a wide range of speculation on the global social meaning of such an event. In Harjo's words the young murder victim looks down into the cell of his attacker:

He gives the young man his favorite name and calls him his brother.
The young killer is then no longer shamed but filled with remorse and cries all
the cries he has stored for a thousand years. ("Letter")

One cannot escape the uncompromising documentation of the European conquest and genocide practiced in the name of "manifest destiny" with "God on our side" when listening to the poetry on this compact disc. In "Fear Poem," Harjo does not shy away from confronting the horrible fear fostered by the brutality indigenous people faced at the hands of European conquerors:

I give you back to the white soldiers, who burned down my home, beheaded my children, raped and sodomized my brothers and sisters. I give you back to those who stole the food from our plates when we were starving. ("Fear Poem")

Yet, Harjo's joyous passion for life and her celebration of survival in the face of seemingly overwhelming odds go far beyond protest to the transcendence that is true art. In one of her most explicitly political poems about a woman murdered on the Pine Ridge Reservation in the 1970s, "For Anna Mae Pictou Aquash, Whose spirit is present here and in the dappled stars (For we remember the story and must tell it again so we may all live)," the "scene" set by the author is one of enormous beauty:

Beneath a sky blurred with mist and wind, I am amazed as I watch the violet heads of crocuses erupt from the stiff earth... ("Anna Mae")

The accompaniment of a gentle jazz-rock fusion lays the basis for Harjo to layer her own smooth soprano saxophone riffs. And the casual storytelling style employed makes the most horrifying verbal picture bearable. In conclusion, Harjo explains:

(It was the women who told me) and we understood wordlessly the ripe meaning of your murder.
    As I understood ten years later after the slow changing of the seasons that we have just begun to touch the dazzling whirlwind of our anger... ("Anna Mae")

Today, Harjo has taken a new turn with her 2004 CD, *Native Joy For Real*, where she shifts her musical style to a "song-chant-jazz-tribal" fusion that has been nominated for three Native American Music Awards, including best blues/jazz album. In exploring a different approach to her vocal art, performing blues, soft rock and ballads, Harjo's voice has been compared to such diverse artists as Suzanne Vega, Sade and Ann Wilson of Heart. As a published poet Harjo is unsurpassed in this group of Native American musicians, but she is not alone in this pursuit. John Trudell has also mined a similar, but quite distinct, vein for years.

Issues of Freedom and Justice

John Trudell's *Johnny Damas & Me* album (produced by Jackson Browne) was a 1994 musical highlight in many years of poetic work, and is an example of a process of fusing traditional sounds, values, and sensibilities with thought-provoking lyrics, this time with urgent rock and roll. Trudell was a Vietnam vet and an early American Indian Movement (A.I.M.) activist, who lost his wife and children in an arsonist's fire over two decades ago, and who has been putting his own poetry to music almost ever since. The blend of music on this album is genuinely innovative, midtempo rock and roll, with the Southern California sound of Jackson Browne, John Hiatt, and Don Henley predominating. But the chiming 12-string guitars of the Byrds are reprised, and the title cut is a hard rocking indictment of "Nazi Babylon," unleashing energy reminiscent of the Dils' punk rock agitprop:

> In the Nazi Babylon/ Ruthless and arrogant...
> using hatred as a shield, in the world where to give also means to take... ("Johnny Damas")

In "Rant & Roll" Trudell welcomes us to "Grafitti Land," where "All the rides are in your head. The ticket is what is thought. And what is said." He wants us to

> Rant & Roll, Heartspeak from the spirit.
> Say it loud so everyone can hear it.
> Say what you mean. Mean what you say.
> Rant & Roll, when you feel that way. ("Rant")

Further, Trudell is a true innovator when it comes to gender relations. Few other men express such heartfelt empathy toward women's daily struggles for dignity, equality, and survival. In "See the Woman" Trudell declares that "she survives all that man has done," metaphorically linking Mother Earth to a specific individual and to all women:

> See the woman spirit
> Daily serving courage with laughter.
> Her breath a dream
> and a Prayer. ("See the Woman")

There is a sense of loss of land and love and innocence that seems ever present, both poignant and passionate. Trudell told the activist journal *Cultural Democracy* in 1996 that he is consciously working to encourage more women-centered traditions of indigenous cultures in opposition to the straightjacket of commodity culture and its seemingly all-powerful patriarchal props. Says Trudell, "I'm trying to address the issue of gender conflict...[T]he basic distrust that has been programmed into the genders...hat's the most political thing that's ever been done, to turn male and female against each other...." For Trudell this happened "...with the emergence of the idea of a male dominator god. . . . [T]he notion of the male dominator god was that the earth was to be exploited, not to be lived with in harmony. But when the people were all praying and worshipping the Earth, that meant they respected the woman because she was the physical manifestation of the female earth. . . . [S]exism is deeply rooted in that attitude change about how one lives with the Earth" (Segel, 5).

In live performance, Trudell's band is a fascinating multicultural mix of young men, with the versatility of Gary Ray, Eric Eckstein, and Mark Schatzkamer providing a solid structure for him to explore his wide range of interests. The chanting and traditional sounds provided by Milton "Quiltman" Sahme in a September 20, 1997, show in Tucson, Arizona, were fully integrated into the overall sound. This isn't simply pop rock with drums and chants added. It's integrated rock and roll by a Native American with a multicultural band directed to anyone who will listen. In the Tucson benefit show for the Yoemem Tekia Foundation of the Yaqui Nation the audience was overwhelmingly indigenous people, even though the theatrical venue was a very unlikely place for a rock and rap show.

More recently Trudell released *Blue Indians* in 1999 and *Bone Days* in 2003. With material that spans nearly his whole writing career, *Bone Days* contains stirring calls-to-arms such as "Crazy Horse" and scathing indictments such as "Hanging on the Cross," but also such deeply felt reflections as "Undercurrent."

In a quite different approach to rock music in 1993 Robbie Bee released the *Reservation of Education* album with the Boyz from the Rez. This was a follow-up to his first release, *Rebel Rouzer*, on his father Tom Bee's label (Warrior/Sound of America Records), the label that releases the hard rock of the elder Bee's band XIT, and released Russell Means's first album *Electric Warrior*. These artists have been producing more traditional rock and roll for years. And they've all been influenced by rap and hard rock, as well as techno, acid jazz, dance music of various stripes, and industrial grunge and country.

Robbie Bee's second disc is the most light hearted of all these releases, with more rocking, even disco, dance beats, driving what he calls "pow wow hip hop" and "red house swing," which sometimes even sounds like a Babyface or Boyz II Men ballad. With biting sarcasm in "Looney Rooney," Bee targets racist commentary from CBS television's Andy Rooney on *60 Minutes*, brashly chanting to the beat of a throbbing bass groove:

> The bottom line is this man's absurd.
> He's just run, running off at the mouth,
> without even knowing what he's talkin' about . . .
> Looney Rooney, Looney Rooney.

Continuing in the same vein, Bee pulls no punches and makes the entire tirade a fun, danceable spoof that even Rooney might find amusing:

> You're seen on TV/putting down people and acting ugly.
> But you've become too big for your pants
> You have your own column. Now you have your own dance. ("Looney")

Often with an emphasis on education for "true democracy," Robbie Bee makes references to, and samples from, much of modern popular culture, especially western movies of all types. Distribution of this music has been facilitated by a large independent national firm, KOCH. Tom Bee told Dick Weissman, author of *The Music Business: Career Opportunities and Self-Defense*, that because of the arrangement with KOCH the Warrior/SOAR catalog is relatively widely available in major U.S. cities and therefore nearly 60% of sales are to non-Indians.[3] Interestingly enough, among the members of Robbie Bee's integrated band is a black man, Michael D, described in song lyrics as historically linked to previous "Ebony Warriors" such as Frederick Douglass.

Native American Rap and Hip-Hop

WithOut Rezervation (W.O.R. pronounced war) carved out a radical, urban approach to contemporary indigenous American issues which stands side-by-side with the boldest of conscious rappers such as Paris, Michael Franti and Spearhead, KRS-1, Tupac, Consolidated, Ice Cube and Chuck D. And though the very clear visibility of Native Americans in the mixed membership group Funkdoobiest was reflected self-consciously in some of their lyrics, all of W.O.R.'s members self-consciously trace their heritage to specific Native American nations, producing a much more roots-conscious effect, with Funkdoobiest more commercial/assimilationist than W.O.R. (but no less immersed in rap music).

Refusing the media-grabbing misogyny of artists such as Too Short, Lil' John, Snoop Dogg and so many others, the anger articulated by these three young men from the San Francisco Bay Area—whose roots are Paiute, Navajo, and Tohono O'odham—is directed at social structures that, among other things, leave many Native Americans filled with self-hate and alcohol. W.O.R. also target racist police and the trivialization of humanity embodied in sports team mascots such as the Chiefs, Braves, and Redskins. They chant in "Mascot":

> We don't want to be the whiteman's mascot.
> Don't want to be degraded and humiliated
> The "tomahawk chop" has got to stop
> We're nobody's mascot. So prepare for W.O.R.

Christopher Columbus is rightly singled out as a symbol for the conquering dominator mentality that has led to the slaughter and enslavement of so many non-European people. Columbus is

Figure 20.3 WithOut Rezervation (aka W.O.R.). From left: Corey Aranaydo (Tohono/Akimel O'odham), Kevin Nez (Diné), Chris LaMarr (Paiute/Pit River). Photo: Robert Doyle. Reprinted with permission from Canyon Records Productions.

criticized indirectly in "502 Years" and in the title track of the album, "Are You Ready for W.O.R.?," but he is mercilessly pilloried in "Was He a Fool?":

> Was he a fool? Or was he a hero? This is fact and not fiction.
> The true history of Christopher Columbus is that he did us native people
>   wrong.
> The mother fucker was lost. That makes him a zero in my book.
> Cause of the lives he took, cause of the land he stole. All of the hopes he
>   dulled…
> He didn't discover nothin'.

Themes of survival and self-respect predominate on the album *Are You Ready for W.O.R.?* with songs entitled "Defend the Territory," "Guilty Until Proven Innocent," and "Red, White & Blue." The laidback "Cali" style of hiphop mixes easily with traditional chanting and drumming on much of this album. But, with the militant anger of W.O.R. mixed up front, and a deep bass groove throbbing below the surface, the sound avoids the harsh "gangsta" stance, as well as the more frantic and boisterous styles of hip hop that can keep people from hearing the words. This band has something to say, and they want us to hear it.[4]

Similar to WithOut Rezervation, Btaka from southern California, integrated traditional chants and drumming into his rap music. This hip hop sound, again dominated by more hardcore background bass and beats, makes clearminded comments on the music industry, Btaka's own Pomo and Apache tribal identity and family relations, as well as the legacy of colonialism. Btaka Brown boasts of his independent challenge to major recording labels and points to his own perseverance and parental encouragement as crucial for his success. Again, the arrival of Christopher Columbus is cited as a turning point in the history of the Americas. In "Indian Life," Btaka can't understand the conqueror's motive:

> …I cannot place the meaning of life to discriminate against my race
> I don't understand but I'm trying to see/I've got to stay clear of the pain and
>   misery. (*Indian Roots*)

And then comes the direct confrontation with the colonial legacy of genocide. Btaka exclaims:

> Christopher Columbus killed for the land/
> He didn't take the time to try to understand!
> The ways and wisdom of Indian life. (*Indian Roots*)

Columbus started wars of conquest, assuming that the indigenous people of the Americas were "ignorant savages," little more than animals; Btaka strongly disagrees, and articulates a convincing argument for his opposing stance.

Again, similar to WithOut Rezervation, Btaka's lyrics on *Indian Roots* are notable for their lack of references to women. But on his first album, *Indian Funk*, he has more traditional love songs, in addition to his militant raps. However, he never steps over the line to demean women. Btaka follows the lead of other conscious rappers such as Paris and Wyclef, who tend to include a song "to the ladies," where wrongs are confessed or love professed.

W.O.R. and Btaka tend to follow in the footsteps of another storytelling musical tradition dominated by men, and also centered along the border between the U.S. and Mexico. In most "Mexicano" corridos, the corrido form itself, the majority of its practitioners, and the dominant subject matter for most documented and recorded corridos are male-centered and patriarchal in character.[5] Hip hop and rap are similarly dominated by male figures, poses, and themes, with notable exceptions such as Lauryn Hill, Queen Latifah, Salt 'n Pepa, and TLC; and these Native American rappers are following those conscious rappers who have gone before who have not felt a need to incorporate lyrics degrading to women.

Some Distinguishing Features of Native American Rap, Reggae, and Rock

The Native American musicians discussed here share similarities on a number of levels, including their music's oral traditions, its identity and political overtones, its spoken-word delivery, its dialectical combination of contemporary music and traditional sounds, and its strong connections to the southwestern United States.

Traditionally musical production has been at the center of the construction of Native American cultural identity. "... [S]ong was not simply self-expression. It was a magic which called upon the powers of Nature and constrained them to man's will. People sang in trouble, in danger, to cure the sick, to confound their enemies, and to make the crops grow. They sang as they fought and as they worked, all together" (Underhill, 5). Historically, Native American performer and audience shared implicit knowledge of language and ways of speaking and "seeing." Louis Owens has described the relationship by citing Tohono O'odham autobiographer Maria Chona: "The song is very short because we understand so much" (Owens, 12). For Owens, in the oral tradition "context and text are one thing.... The joy, the understanding, the language are all of a piece" (Owens, 13). For some, such music appears "apolitical" in the sense that it does not engage contemporary structures and practices of oppression but favors focusing on the preservation of traditional knowledge and skills. But such a focus is highly political in the context of the ever-present dominant dynamic of most contemporary cultural production which favors—and some would say worships—ahistorical and "revolutionary" newness or the total homogenization of today's consumer culture.

The five artists here do not shy away from political and social issues in their lyrics, particularly regarding the conquest of the Americas and the continuing discrimination against and harassment of indigenous people. Similar to such "conscious" rappers as Chuck D, Tupac Shakur, and Paris, who have offered "a window into, and critique of, the criminalization of black youth ..." (Kelley, *Race* 185), these artists are not simply chroniclers of events, they are activists and agitators as well. The music professes opinions about, and interest in, the broader social history of our country and the world, as well as a desire for justice that contrasts with the trivia of most pop and with the vulgarities of media-hyped sex and violence of many "gangsta" rappers. And this music has an edge that only "other" marginalized musicians tend to produce (since the mainstream ignores that which tends to offend anyone). The music is not afforded much airplay, or shelf-space because the musicians are "political" simply by their choice of material and by being socially aware of their community and environment; and the niche market they and most others here address, isn't large enough. Joy Harjo, like Trudell and WithOut Rezervation, asks to be heard when it comes to issues of social awareness and justice. These artists have made a choice to be more relevant to their own communities and sympathizers than to the broader consumer society. In this they follow a branch of the path previously paved by La Farge, Westerman, and Sainte-Marie.

But there is more than a radically unwavering and uncompromising use of language to document the traditions, as well as the injustice, of the past and present of Native American life. There is also the willingness to hope for the future, no matter how obliquely, or how hopeless the present may seem. As Joy Harjo explains in the concluding lines of "A Postcolonial Tale" on her first album, "Our children put down their guns when we did to imagine with us. We imagined the shining link between the heart and the sun. We imagined tables of food for everyone. We imagined the songs." Then a twist that encourages reflection: "The imagination conversely illumines us, sings with us, dances with us, drums with us, loves us" ("Postcolonial").

This points to another aspect of political identity formation and historical reflection found in these artists' music, a self-consciousness that has little in common with mainstream fantasy and delusions. There's no aggressively repeated "You did me wrong!" Rather, these musicians tend to accept personal responsibility. This music generates a recognition of identity formation explicitly. In "Be Brown," Btaka declares, "I'm brown and proud. And I'm proud of the skin I'm in" (*Indian Funk*). There are individual expressions of diverse emotions among these musicians. And the recognition of identity formation contains elements from which one may struggle to change oneself and confront others whose paths have proven to be self-destructive.

Joy Harjo pronounces a self-indictment simultaneous with her denunciation of colonial terror in "Fear Poem": "You have choked me, but I gave you the leash. You have gutted me, but I gave you the knife. You have devoured me, but I laid myself across the fire" ("Postcolonial"). Such blunt honesty can liberate or debilitate, but it leaves few untouched.

And the young rappers here confront head-on contradictions within indigenous communities, such as their brothers and sisters who are alcoholics. On WithOut Rezervation's "Dead Indian/To the Sell Outs," they rap to those who've "sold your soul to the Devil" by "not thinkin' but drinkin,'" while a reporter's voice in the background comes into focus explaining that on reservations, "the leading cause of death is alcohol related." In "Drinking Your Life Away," there is little question how Btaka feels about alcohol on the reservation: "You walk into a party /can't resist a beer, man. You pick up a forty/and you start drinkin'. You just don't understan' about the things you do...but it's killin' you" (*Indian Funk*).

The "fusion" undertaken by these artists certainly lends a new perspective to the potential of present and future currents in the hybrid mix that is popular music in the USA today. But while these artists embrace aspects of technology that tend to make mainstream pop a nonfolk form (sophisticated recording studios, modern musical styles, electronically amplified and modified voices and instruments), they simultaneously celebrate a folk belief in the essential role music plays in everyday emotional life and social events (lyrics expressive of the hopes, fears, and desires of "regular" working people, preservation of ancient rituals and languages that cannot but conflict with fashionable and "logical" knowledge, ideas, and sounds). A special creativity springs from the tension between certain Native American traditions and the modern musical conventions that dominate urban contemporary patterns and relations. There is a tension between "authentic," acoustic traditional sounds and digital modifications or reproductions such that the distance "from" the mainstream is pushed and pulled, and the "envelope" stretches and contracts such that there are times we witness links that bridge between the margins and the mainstream—the edge and the "middle of the road"—no matter how temporarily. This tension is little different from that in any situation of "crossover" potential, which can lead to charges of "sell out" or the "success" of a one-hit-wonder. The sound of these artists isn't "offensive" or "too exotic," nor are most of the lyrics. It is the self-conscious "stance" or standpoint, the attitude of the artist and the "place" they occupy in society that tends to keep the musicians considered here marginalized. They have consciously chosen to remain "in between" and not become fully assimilated or commercialized.

Finally, a physical concentration of indigenous populations, as well as their sympathizers and interested tourists, in certain southwestern states of the United States seems to be a contributing factor in the success of the Native American musicians cited here. This distinct region within what has been called the wider "Borderlands" or "La Frontera"—along the boundary stretching nearly 2,000 miles between the United States and Mexico, from Baja and California, through Arizona, Sonora, New Mexico, Chihuahua and Coahuila, Nuevo Leon, Tamaulipas, and up to Texas and Oklahoma (Weisman, xiii)—contains many indigenous people on land traditionally held by their ancestors. In fact, the frontier that extends hundreds of miles north and south along the border between the United States and Mexico—a "Red and Brown Frontier"—is crisscrossed by traditional boundaries and demarcations between many ethnic groupings large and small, some separations being geological and as fluid and natural as the arroyos heading toward the Rio Grande and Colorado Rivers; others being quite as unnatural as concrete-lined canals and riverbanks or the straight steel fences and walls that separate modern ranches and capitalist countries, still as full of holes as NAFTA environmental and labor regulations. La Frontera, the "Last Frontier" in a way that the so-called "West" never could be except in Hollywood, is more than a Borderland, more than "a vague and undetermined place created by the emotional residue of an unnatural boundary" (Anzaldúa, 3); it is a crossroads.

Interestingly, the crossroads metaphor (as discussed above) has been a recurrent theme in popular music since long before Robert Johnson penned his classic blues with that name. No doubt the ability to see in different directions and the freedom to choose what direction to take are key elements in this theme's resilience. Not only have Native Americans been driven onto reservations in La Frontera, in some cases on land ancestrally occupied for millennia, and at least for centuries; they have been invaded and overrun by Spanish, Mexican, Anglo, Irish, German, and Scandinavian, as well as Central and South American populations, who've crossed through and settled down in the course of historical development in the region. Also in the process of being relocated, those Native Americans displaced and dispersed from eastern and northern portions of the country have found some sense of stability in contact with older Pueblos and tribes that have not been torn so completely from their ancestral lands. The distinctive rock and roll and Chicano folk sound of East L.A.'s Los Lobos, and the hybrid mixes of Tex-Mex, Norteña, and Waila are only four of the distinct musical forms that have emerged spontaneously from "La Frontera" and continue to flourish along the border.

At such a cultural crossroads as "La Frontera," "Popular music has a peculiar relationship to the poetics and politics of place. Recorded music travels from place to place, transcending physical and temporal barriers. It alters our understanding of the local and immediate, making it possible for us to experience close contact with cultures from far away. Yet precisely because music travels, it also augments our appreciation of place" (Lipsitz, 3). As George Lipsitz further explains in his remarkable work *Dangerous Crossroads: Popular Music, Postmodernism and the Poetics of Place*, "Collisions occur at the crossroads; decisions must be made there. But the crossroads can also provide a unique perspective, a vantage point where one can see in more than one direction" (Lipsitz, 7–8).

Expressions of individual and national identity, for equality and justice within these borderlands of the North American continent—itself a crossroads of diverse cultures and streams of immigration—have become a part of the struggle to retain and survive on land that, in some cases, has never been militarily "conquered" by the white man. In this region indigenous American music survives with more success than elsewhere in either the United States or Mexico for various reasons. One is that La Frontera—the Red and Brown Frontier—is a place of interaction, indeed the crossroads described above, a space that simultaneously divides and unites two huge nation states. And in the space between the two most dominant formations, a plurality of cultures continues to thrive in many ways. Native Americans have found a more ambiguous and less antagonistic environment in which to carve out places and spaces for them to pursue traditional sounds as well as explore their modern ideas. Each of the artists considered here uses music to express struggles for indigenous identity, equality, and justice within the context of global hegemonic relations that define and constitute La Frontera, the Borderlands, perversely nurtured by the very forces competing to dominate it and the entire world.

In a situation in this Frontier similar to that occupied by some Native Americans, Louie Perez of the Los Angeles Chicano rock band Los Lobos explained in an interview in southern Arizona's *Border Beat* magazine: "Chicanos are always straddling the fence because they're not totally accepted on either side [of the border]. Americans and Mexicans both ask Chicanos, 'are you American or Mexican?' It's enough to make you feel displaced on both sides of the border. You can either grieve about it or find something liberating about it. I think we've found freedom in it . . . the freedom to say we don't belong anywhere, we belong to the universe" (Carvalho, 22). And so artists thus situated can become more receptive to different explanations, or even radical and unorthodox ideas.

Most Native Americans face a similar, although quite distinct situation in relation to the "land," property, and "place" as African Americans, Latinos, and the many other modern "refugee" and diasporic populations of today, from Africa and the Caribbean Islands to Southeast Asia. However, since not all Native American nations have been forcibly removed from their ancestral homelands, the concept of a Red and Brown Frontier can be useful if we are to assess the polycultural mix of the region. Many insights into such an approach are realized by looking to Paul Gilroy's formulation of a "Black Atlantic" and "double consciousness" in his attempts to show "how different nationalist paradigms for thinking about cultural history fail when confronted by the intercultural and transnational formation" (Gilroy, ix) of the vast dispersion of humanity that is the Black Diaspora—the decentered yet somehow cohesive centripetal forces that hold "together" all those who are of African heritage in the "new world." By shifting our understanding to apply a similar approach to La Frontera—the "Red & Brown Frontier"—where those of Native American heritage exist between and among many distinct peoples and different nations, a place "in between" nations where most Native Americans and Mexicans have been conquered and displaced by Europeans, but also where other Native Americans and Chicanos and Hispanics remain on the land where their ancestors have lived for centuries and even millennia, certain contradictions are more easily understood. But the predominant feature of the area is the borderline/boundary between undeniably "hostile powers in the global free-market" (Kermode, 24), notwithstanding the promises of NAFTA and its gaggle of continued supporters. The continuing, even escalating, political division of one country from the other means that the frontier will stay quite volatile.

The likelihood of creating a "dual consciousness" in any particular individual who has been displaced or has become a part of diasporic marginalization is strong in such an area. But the implications for an emergent "double" subject-position on identity politics in general and regarding solidarity on the progressive front in the so-called "culture wars," is limited again to the context, the conceptual knowledge, or what Walter Benjamin described as "heightened consciousness" (431) that may or may not accompany it.

Native Americans exist in two worlds, even those who choose self-consciously to "live" their lives in one or the other. WithOut Rezervation cite Chief Seattle with a pastiched overdub, declaring "You cannot walk both roads" ("Skin I'm In"). But they walk, to one degree or another, in "our" world nonetheless. And, self-consciously polycultural women such as Leslie Marmon Silko and Joy Harjo have challenged stereotypes of Native Americans as savages and illiterates and used their language in ways that tend to cross or transcend boundaries and borders, not reinforce them.

Conclusions

> Our Hopi reservation no stretch far and wide.
> It gives us sense of purpose, me say sense of pride.
> Religion and our culture help keep us strong.
> I'm proud of these people, that's why me sing this song.
> Just check the history books, it is not [just] what I say.
> The government, the policies they take my land away.
> > "Original Landlord"
> > —Casper (1997)

Music reflects the patterns, relations, and structures of identity at the center of our lives. What does this particular music say regarding those who exist in the middle of a major crossroads in our society, who epitomize the "postmodern" duality of living self-consciously in two worlds: traditional and modern? With their politics, hybrid culture, and simultaneous mainstream fascination/marginalization, the Native American musicians discussed herein "walk both roads," both contemporary and traditional. As they cross back and forth between cultures, crisscrossing identity, national, and ethnic demarcations, the forcible relocation and dispersion of their ancestors offers a form of "liberation" from certain rigid social constraints. The audience, too, is "liberated" in a sense because the hybridity to which the divergent populations are attracted touches so many others, though perhaps not to the degree that the musicians themselves would prefer. But the mixed or hybrid character taken on by the songs and genres reflects the continuing crises of Native American societies. Living in two worlds, but not really in either one, has significant political as well social, spiritual, and economic implications. As with most popular innovation, it is the smallest independent and individual recording labels that fill the desire for new indigenous music, despite the global industry's perpetual addiction to swallowing the stream of creative small producers who spring up between the hard edges of massive conglomerates (such form of growth imposed by the very narrowness of vision of the same corporate bureaucracies that stifle true diversity while claiming to embrace it, once the "rough edges" are knocked off).

But the perseverance of these musicians is a testament to popular music's fundamental role in identity formation in their lives and the lives of their audiences. The place they occupy is between two distinct cultural formations, traditional and modern. It has become clear that the identity of these artists tends to be quite political, primarily because of their contradictory location in modern society. It is also clear that the affinity of these musicians to the southwestern United States not only has an influence on the music, but also is much more than a demographic "coincidence." The broad deserts and high mesas of Arizona and New Mexico are about as marginal to the goings on in Los Angeles and New York corporate offices as can be imagined.

But an even more serious political element keeps music produced by Native Americans marginalized in the broader context—the fact that it reminds us of past and present treatment of the first inhabitants of the Americas and their descendants. Theirs is not a safe or "guiltfree" history and "innocent" past, offensive to no one, the history and past preferred by the pop mainstream when forced to address it. Studying these musicians, and others like them, in greater depth can offer insights into more general questions regarding culture, identity, and power.

Native American music, especially in the southwestern United States, can remain a dynamic element at the margins of pop by capitalizing on its place as part of the larger Borderlands region, the Frontier that is home to many indigenous people (both those who remain on the land of their ancestors and those who are displaced, dispersed, and dispossessed). The uniqueness of the border region, of the "Red & Brown Frontier"—La Frontera—will continue to be reflected in its music because of its place as a crossroads.

An ethical crossroads exists as well, where those who recognize this situation as they work in the music industry, in media, or in academia, ponder responsibilities that accompany our freedoms and rights. While emphasis can be placed on celebrating, preserving, and protecting that which is positive in past and present individual and collective efforts, thoughtful criticism must be raised over negative features of certain traditional relationships that are elitist, racist, and sexist, whether in academic, popular, or spiritual circles—revealing injustice and supporting corrective measures.

Finally, cooperation to create a new inclusive language of musical and social communication and analysis requires a real shift in current relations. True polycultural understanding requires the productive rupture of disciplinary boundaries, accompanied by a decentering of control that can help challenge specific positions of authority and, perhaps, restructure institutional and discursive relations from ones that sustain the status quo in favor of patriarchy and global corporate capital within academia and the industry, to more democratic ones.

The musicians discussed here exhibit only some of the emerging possibilities at the intersection of indigenous American traditions and pop rock, rap, blues and reggae at the beginning of the twenty-first century. In this new century, Casper the Hopi reggae rapper, with his Rastafar-ian-tinged-roots-style music, and whose second CD *Sounds of Reality* will soon be followed by a third, *Honor the People*, has gained a great deal of attention among reggae fans, and Joy Harjo and John Trudell continue to challenge us with the dedicated pursuit of their art. Litefoot was recently declared Hip Hop Artist of the Year at the Native American Music Awards, and now younger rap artists Shadoyze and Night Shield (in South Dakota), among a significant number of others, are gaining attention. Traditional Native American music has a supportive environment and home in La Frontera, a Red & Brown Frontier. And the artists described here build on that heritage and explore new ground; by merging their past with the present, they anticipate a fascinating vision of the future.

Notes

1. Peter La Farge, the adopted son of Oliver La Farge, influential Anglo Indian-affairs attorney, was an organizer for the Federation for American Indian Rights (F.A.I.R.). La Farge's country and western song "Ballad of Ira Hayes"—#3 on the pop chart for Johnny Cash—was a tribute to the Navajo who helped raise the Stars and Stripes over Iwo Jima in World War II. The song is a testament to the fact that pop music needn't be pabulum to be popular. Patrick Sky, the folk musician, was also a Field Representative for F.A.I.R., as was Buffy Sainte-Marie (Dunson, 94). Johnny Cash also recorded an entire album of La Farge's songs devoted to the plight of Native Americans entitled *Bitter Tears* in 1964. Peter La Farge's folk sound was quite distinct for its incorporation of traditional drumming. Unfortunately, his promis-ing career was cut short with his untimely death in 1965.
2. This article was originally published in 1999 before the Native American hard rock band Indigenous (whose sound is remarkably similar to Stevie Ray Vaughn) became popular on certain radio stations that year. Nonetheless, the basic premise put forward here remains viable: since Indigenous became popular as an alternative rock band, without the widest air play, while previous Native American artists were able to become a part of mainstream radio; and certainly today in 2005 the consolidation of the radio airwaves has proceeded more-or-less unabated over the past five years. Nonetheless, there are very real cracks in the monoliths in certain regions and there has been a remarkable word-of-mouth and even television boom in interest in Native American music in the past few years with the popularity of the Native American Music Awards, and the new categories for Native American music at the Grammies.
3. (Communication from Weissman to author 1 Jan. 1998.) Unfortunately, Robbie Bee's approach to women is not as enlightened as John Trudell's is. Though in no way abusive to women the way many hardcore "gangsta" rappers are, Bee uses terms of address such as "girl" and "honey," and sings about looking to score. In all fairness, one can't too quickly judge the intentions of an artist whose work is so thoroughly laced with irony, insinuation, and sarcasm. But in "Pow Wow Girls" Bee sings "…the intertribal honeys are just so fine…Got to make one mine"; and in "Party Time" he chants "Boyz from the Rez/Going to turn you out…Lady, tonight I'm going to make you mine"; and in "Cold As Ice" we find the age-old lament, "Girl, why'd you do me wrong?"
4. A dynamic group of hard core hip hoppers has flourished in Tulsa, Oklahoma, around the rapper/actor Litefoot (*Indian in the Cupboard, Mortal Kombat*, and *Adaptation*, among many other films), who has released several of his own rap albums, as well as having produced a compilation of traditional music interspersed with rap by Litefoot himself, Fun-maker, and the indigenous woman Haida, in addition to rap albums by the Red Ryders and Flawless.
5. José Limón has carefully analyzed this phenomenon in his exceptional work *Mexican Ballads and Chicano Poems: History and Influence in Mexican-American Social Poetry*. And while Limón does not ignore the implications of this observation for his theory in relation to women, the actual work of addressing woman's side of corridos has fallen to others, such as María Herrera-Sobek and Jean Franco. Limón has developed a particularly useful framework and process for understanding the corrido musical form of storytelling. Though none of the artists studied here write or perform corridos, Limón's analysis can be utilized because his work is not narrowly outlined and each musician here is a storyteller in her or his respective genre. Limón utilizes a discursive structural analysis of ideological forms to situate the artist, song, and audience in the broader social context and illustrates the distinction between "archetype" and stereotype.

   Limón's greatest strength is his fusion of two quite distinct—some would say diametrically opposed—analytical formulations: Harold Bloom's literary theory of artist and creativity, and Fredric Jameson's "revisionist" Marxist ap-proach to postmodern cultural criticism. The radical "conflict" in ideas represented by Limón's combination produces a tension that provides insights, not only into corridos and into their composers and their times, but also into other storytelling forms such as rap, blues, rock, and reggae. Limon's strategy to use the contemporary but contradictory elements available in Bloom and Jameson results in a framework for analyzing historical corridos that applies across boundaries of distinct cultural forms.

References

Anzaldúa, Gloria. 1987. *Borderlands=La Frontera: The New Mestiza*. San Francisco: Spinsters/Aunt Lute.

Benjamin, Walter. 1968. *Illuminations*. Introduction by Hannah Arendt. Trans. Harry Zohn. New York: Harcourt, Brace & World.

Carvalho, Jim. 1997. "El Corridero: An Interview with Louie Perez of Los Lobos." *Border Beat* Jan.-Feb.: 20–22.

Dunson, Josh. 1965. *Freedom in the Air: Song Movements of the 60's*. New York: International Publishers.

Franco, Jean. 1989. *Plotting Women: Gender and Representation in Mexico*. New York: Columbia University Press.

Gilroy, Paul. 1993. *The Black Atlantic: Modernity and Double Consciousness*. Cambridge, MA: Harvard University Press.

González, Ray. 1997. "The Language of Tribes: An Interview with Joy Harjo." *Bloomsbury Review* 17(6):18–20.

Harjo, Joy. *In Mad Love and War*. 1990. Hanover, NH: Wesleyan University Press/University Press of New England.

———. 1989. *Secrets from the Center of the World*. Tucson: University of Arizona Press.

———. 1983. *She Had Some Horses*. New York: Thunders' Mouth Press.

———. 1994. *The Woman Who Fell from the Sky*. New York: Norton.

Harjo, Joy, and Gloria Bird, ed. 1997. *Reinventing the Enemy's Language: Contemporary Native Women's Writings of North America*. New York: Norton.

Herrera-Sobek, María. 1990. *The Mexican Corrido: A Feminist Analysis*. Bloomington: Indiana University Press.

Kallet, Marilyn. 1996. "In Love and War and Music." *The Spiral of Memory: Joy Harjo Interviews*, edited by Laura Coltelli, 111–23. Ann Arbor: University of Michigan Press.

Kelley, Robin. "People in Me: So What Are You?" *Colorlines* Winter 1999: 5–7.

———. 1994. *Race Rebels: Culture, Politics, and the Black Working Class*. New York: Free Press/Macmillan.

Kermode, Frank. 1988. *History & Value*. Oxford: Clarendon Press.

Limón, José. 1992. *Mexican Ballads, Chicano Poems: History and Influence in Mexican-American Social Poetry*. Los Angeles: University of California Press.

Lipsitz, George. 1994. *Dangerous Crossroads: Popular Music, Postmodernism and the Poetics of Place*. London; New York: Verso.

Owens, Louis. 1992. *Other Destinies: Understanding the American Indian Novel*. Norman: University of Oklahoma Press.

Segel, Joel. 1996. "Interview with John Trudell." *Cultural Democracy* Spring: 4–6.

Smith, Dinitia. 1997. "The Indian in Literature Is Growing Up." *New York Times* 21 Apr.: Sec. B 1–2.

Underhill, Ruth Murray. 1938. *Singing for Power: The Song Magic of the Papago Indians of Southern Arizona*. Berkeley; Los Angeles: University of California Press.

Weisman, Alan. 1986. *La Frontera: The United States' Border with Mexico*. Tucson: University of Arizona Press.

Weissman, Richard. 1979-97. *The Music Business: Career Opportunities and Self-Defense*. New York: Three Rivers Press/Crown/Random House.

Record Company Addresses

Canyon Records, 3131 W. Clarendon Ave., Phoenix, AZ 85017. 800-268-1141. www.canyonrecords.com.

Four Winds Trading Company, P.O. Box 1887, Boulder, CO 80306. 800-456-5444. www.fourwinds-trading.com.

Indian Funk Records, P.O. Box 1694, Clearlake Oaks, CA 95423. 707-998-4750.

Mekko Records, P.O. Box 891, Glenpool, OK 74033. www.joyharjo.com.

Red Vinyl Records, 8086 S. Yale, Suite 146, Tulsa, OK 74136. www.redvinyl.com

Silver Wave Records, P.O. Box 7943, Boulder, CO 80306. 303-443-5617. www.silverwave.com.

SOAR Corp./Warrior, 5200 Constitution NE, Albuquerque, NM 87110. 800-890-SOAR. www.soundofamerica.com.

Third Mesa Music, 6161 E. Ivyglen, Mesa, AZ 85205. 480-830-7991. www.3rdmesa.com.

Discography

Btaka. 1995. *Indian Funk*. Tape. Clearlake Oaks, CA: Indian Funk Records/Black Bear BB101. Includes "Be Brown" and "Drinkin' Your Life Away."

———. 1995. *Indian Roots*. Tape. Clearlake Oaks, CA: Indian Funk Records/Black Bear BB102. Includes "Indian Life."

Casper Lomayesva (aka: Loma-Da-Wa). 1997. *Original Landlord*. Compact disc. Mesa, AZ: Third Mesa Music. Includes "Original Landlord."

———. 2001. *Sounds of Reality*. Compact disc. Mesa, AZ: Third Mesa Music.

Funkdoobiest. 1993. *Which Doobie U B?* Tape. New York: Sony/Epic ET53212.

Harjo, Joy; with Poetic Justice. 1996. *Letter from the End of the Twentieth Century*. Compact disc. Albuquerque, NM: Red Horse/Silver Wave Records SW914. Includes "A Postcolonial Tale," "Creation Story," "Fear Poem," "Mourning Song," "Letter from the End of the Twentieth Century," and "For Anna Mac Pictou Aquash, whose Spirit is present here and in the dappled stars (For we remember the story and must tell it again so we all may live)."

———. 2004. *Native Joy For Real*. Compact disc. Glenpool, OK: Mekko Records.

In the Spirit of Crazy Horse: Songs for Leonard Peltier P.O.W. 1992. Compact disc. Boulder, CO: Four Winds Trading Company. Includes Buffy Sainte-Marie's "Bury My Heart at Wounded Knee."

Jackalope. 1991. *Dances With Rabbits*. Tape. Phoenix, AZ: Canyon Records CR7005.

———. 1988. *Weavings*. Tape. Phoenix, AZ: Canyon Records CR7002.

La Farge, Peter. 1992. On the *Warpath: As Long as the Grass Shall Grow*. Compact disc. Vollersode, Germany: Bear Family Records BCD15626. Includes "Ballad of Ira Hayes."

Litefoot. 1996. *Good Day to Die*. Tape. Tulsa: Red Vinyl Records RVR9607.

———. 1998. *The Life and Times*. Tape. Tulsa: Red Vinyl Records RVR9609.

———. 1999. *Litefoot Presents the Sounds of Indian Country*. Tape. Tulsa: Red Vinyl Records RVR0970.

Mirabal, Robert. 1995. *Land*. Compact disc. New York: Warner Brothers WB9 45992-2.

———. 2003. *Indians Indians*. Compact disc. Boulder, CO: Silver Wave Records SD935.

Nakai, R. Carlos. 1986. *Journeys*. Tape. Phoenix, AZ: Canyon Records CR-613-C.

———. 1988. *Canyon Trilogy*. Tape. Phoenix. AZ: Canyon Records CR-610.

Redbone. *Wovoka*. 1973. Vinyl Record. New York: Epic. Also includes "Come and Get Your Love."

———. 1975. *Come and Get Your Redbone: The Best of Redbone*. Vinyl Record. New York: CBS/Epic KEG33456. Includes "Come and Get Your Love."

Redhouse Family. 1997. *Urban Indian*. Compact disc. Phoenix, AZ. Canyon Records CR-7023.

Red Thunder. 1995. *Makoce Wakan*. Compact disc. Port Washington, NY: Eagle Thunder Records/KOCH 3-7916-2H1.

Robbie Bee & the Boyz from the Rez. 1992. *Rebel Rouzer*. Tape. Albuquerque, NM: Warrior/Soar SOAR-105.

———. 1993. *Reservation of Education*. Compact disc. Albuquerque, NM: Warrior/Soar WAR-604. Includes "Looney Rooney," "Ebony Warrior," "Party Time." "Cold as Ice," and "Pow Wow Girls."

Sainte-Marie, Buffy. 1992. *Coincidence & Likely Stories*. Compact disc. Los Angeles: Capitol/EMI F2-21921. Includes "Bury My Heart (at Wounded Knee)."

———. 1996. *Up Where We Belong*. Compact disc. Los Angeles: Angel/Capitol CAP-35059.

Shenandoah, Joanne. 1994. *Once in a Red Moon*. Compact disc. Phoenix, AZ: Canyon Records CR548. Includes "America."

———. 1996. *Matriarch: Iroquois Women's Songs*. Compact disc. Boulder, CO: Silver Wave SD9I3.

———. 1995. *Life Blood*. Compact disc. Boulder, CO: Silver Wave SD809.

Southern Scratch. 1994. *Em-we:hejed—For All of You*. Compact disc. Phoenix, AZ: Canyon Records CR8097.

Tohono Raiders. 1988. *Chicken Scratch*. Tape. Phoenix, AZ: Canyon Records CR-8081.

Trudell, John. 1983. *Tribal Voice*. Tape. Los Angeles: Tribal Voice.

———. 1988. *AKA Graffiti Man*. Tape. San Francisco: Rykodisc RACS0223.

———. 1994. *Johnny Damas & Me*. Compact disc. San Francisco: Rykodisc RCD10286. Includes "Johnny Damas and Me." "Rant and Roll," and "See the Woman."

———. 2003. *Bone Days*. Compact disc. Los Angeles: Daemon Records.

Walela. *Walela*. 1997. Compact disc. Triloka Records; Mercury/Polygon 314536049-2. Includes "I'll Turn My Radio On," written by Laura Stewart.

WithOut Rezervation. 1994. *Are You Ready for W.O.R.?* Tape Proenix, AZ: Canyon Records CR-7035. Includes "Dead Indian to the Sellouts," "Was He a Fool?." "Skin I'm In," and "Mascot".

XIT. 1993. *Entrance. Compact Disc. Albuquerque, NM: Warrior/Soar-145-CD*.

———. 1995. *Drums Across the Atlantic/XIT LIVE*. Tape. Albuquerque, NM: Warrior/SOAR-103.

21

From "I'm a Lapp" to "I am Saami"
Popular Music and Changing Images of Indigenous Ethnicity in Scandinavia

Richard Jones-Bamman

Introduction

During the 1940s, members of Scandinavia's indigenous population, the Saami (formerly known as Lapps), began an active campaign to confirm their status as an ethnic minority in Norway, Sweden and Finland (Ruong 1969; Svensson 1976; Eidheim 1987). Despite their small numbers (approximately 65,000–80,000 total), over the course of the following decades the Saami made significant strides towards this goal, particularly in the areas of native language instruction in schools (Svonni 1993) and reindeer herding subsidies and regulations (Beach 1981, 1988). While most of this activity logically occurred within governmental agencies and legislative bodies, music played an unexpected role as well, particularly popular recordings created specifically for Saami audiences by Saami artists. In fact, since the late 1950s, Saami singers have routinely turned to popular musical idioms as a means of stimulating discourse within their culture, and occasionally affecting significant change as a result. This development is all the more remarkable when one considers that the Saami have their own unique vocal genre, *joik*, which is traditionally performed by soloists without any instrumental accompaniment. That popular genres should augment or even displace *joik* performances in recent times, at the very least suggests an important shift within the culture, one that seemingly embraces modernity over tradition. But is this the only interpretation?

The quotations in the title of this article are taken from a pair of popular songs released in Sweden (in 1959 and 1991 respectively) by two young Saami musicians, Sven-Gösta Jonsson and Lars Jonas Johansson. Not surprisingly, given the span of more than three decades separating these recordings, there are clear musical differences between the two, with the earlier performance sounding decidedly mild in comparison to the hard rock-tinged production of the later piece. There is also a difference evident in the personae projected by the two singers in their performances, again in keeping with the shifting norms one anticipates within popular music across generations. Sven-Gösta Jonsson comes across as a smooth and competent, if slightly naive, teen idol in the Ricky Nelson mold, while Lars Jonas Johansson exudes self confidence, typically snarling out his lyrics in the fashion befitting a more contemporary rock performer, such as Axl Rose.

The language used for these recordings is worth noting as well, for it, too, is an indication of change, albeit of a different sort. Like many of his contemporaries in the late 1960s, Jonsson had only a passable knowledge of Saami, so he performed and recorded in Swedish (Andersson 1992). Johansson, a generation later, chose to sing exclusively in Saami, reflecting a trend across Saamiland to revitalize the language by encouraging younger people to use Saami whenever possible. Johansson acquired these skills in school, and has used them primarily to compose and perform pop songs.

But the most revealing distinction between the two recordings lies in the message each song conveys, strikingly distilled in the use of the terms "Lapp" and "Saami." These particular words are loaded with meaning for listeners, both within and outside Saami culture. To the Saami, "Lapp" is a pejorative term, having been long ago affixed to this population by outside observers and officials (Fjellström 1985). On the other hand, "Sámi" (or "Saami" in its anglicized version) is the name by which these people have always referred to themselves (Beach 1988). Thus, Jonsson's self-description as a "Lapp" with reindeer was very much in keeping with stereotypical outside conceptions of this indigenous culture in the 1950s and 1960s. The majority of Swedes saw the Lapps as exotic yet complacent nomads, whose lives rarely intersected with their own. In contrast to this, Johansson's choice of "Saami" was intentionally confrontational. Here, the protagonist steadfastly declares himself a member of an ethnic minority, and challenges anyone to dispute these claims, or dare to call him a "Lapp." This, too, was in keeping with prevailing perceptions of Saami culture in the 1980s and 1990s, by Swedes and Saami alike.

While the differences in musical and performance styles between the two artists can easily be attributed to the predictable evolution of popular musical genres, this shift in language and the replacement of a negative stereotype with a more positive self-image suggests a more profound series of developments. Yet, these recordings merely serve to mark this phenomenon, without offering any explication of the circumstances that initiated and encouraged these particular changes in Saami culture. At the very least, it needs to be shown that Jonsson's and Johansson's songs are actually part of such a process, rather than musical anomalies, conveniently chosen for their obviously contrastive positions. Therefore, any analysis of these recordings should not simply focus on the specific milieu within which each artist found inspiration, but should also take into account the intervening years between the two singers, seeking to illuminate some of the forces which enabled the changes reflected in these songs. Another incentive for adopting a diachronic approach in this task is the overview this provides of other Saami artists, for the line stretching between Jonsson and Johansson is populated with numerous other Saami musicians, several of whose recordings are compelling documents of change during this time period (1959–1991).

Taken collectively, these commercial releases offer a unique perspective that is not afforded by focusing on live performance. Saamiland is vast and sparsely populated, making the possibility of musical tours difficult at best. Live shows certainly do occur, but the primary connection between most performers and their audiences in this environment remains one that is necessarily mediated. Under these circumstances, recordings of Saami music have played a significant role in how the Saami conceive of themselves collectively, and how they would prefer to be perceived by others. As a result, over the last thirty years quite a few recordings have become iconic within Saami culture, marking a particularly noteworthy event or time period. Others have served as pedagogical tools, providing models of performance for would-be musicians; and some have functioned as musical portraits of Saamiland and its inhabitants, potentially reaching audiences far outside the region.

An equally important consideration here is that popular music has figured so prominently in these processes, for many performers (like Jonsson and Johansson) have chosen a pop genre as a vehicle rather than turning to the musical tradition of their ancestors, joik. Far from representing another example of the hegemony of Western musical resources (Slobin 1992), the decision by these artists to adopt and adapt popular musical genres is predicated in the belief this course of action is the most effective way to provoke and control change. From the late 1960s on, Saami musicians have been consciously manipulating recording and broadcast media as a means of both initiating and promoting concerns which affect their communities, and a great deal of this effort has taken place within popular musical idioms. Some of this activity has attracted the attention of the Scandinavian recording industry, but the overwhelming majority of the resulting LPs, tapes and CDs have been produced and/or released by Saami-owned companies, whose distribution networks are more dependent on local Saami organizations and handcraft businesses, rather than on music shops and department stores. These are essentially "homegrown" products for a local market, with very few of them crossing the ethnic boundary until recently. The broadcast media, particularly Saami Radio in Norway and Sweden, have also played a significant role in disseminating this music, largely relying on these same recordings as a resource for their music programming. Whereas Saami musical activity was once limited primarily to traditional contexts of performance, this increased activity in the areas of production and dissemination, has expanded the profile of "Saami" music considerably. It now embraces both traditional and popular genres simultaneously.

These activities have not been without controversy among Saami critics, however, so the voices of these individuals also must be heard in this discussion. Almost from the beginning, there have been those arguing these efforts to merge popular genres with Saami musical ideas necessarily result in something of dubious value to Saami culture. The primary objection lies in the challenge this cultural commodification presents to traditional conceptions of performance. Yet, far from detracting from the value of these recordings, the dialectic raised between these opposing forces has helped create a forum in which significant issues can be and are wrestled with, under the guise of musical performance. In effect, criticism has often stimulated new ideas from musicians, whose recordings in turn predictably generate another round of critical responses, thereby impacting on the trajectory taken by contemporary Saami music.

While the path from "Lapp" to "Saami" has obviously not been a strictly musical phenomenon, music has played a crucial role in this process, as I shall demonstrate through the musicians and their works highlighted below. Although the choices for inclusion are necessarily subjective, I tempered this tendency by soliciting suggestions from Saami musicians, record producers, journalists and avid audience members, during several periods of intensive fieldwork in Sweden and Norway. As an outside researcher, I constantly turn to these sources, not only to keep me aware of emic perspectives, but also to direct my attention toward issues and concerns that quite frankly would have escaped me entirely. Without the informants' willing participation, much of what follows would perforce be quite different.

Sven-Gösta, the "Rocking Saami"

At first listen, Sven-Gösta Jonsson's *Vid Foten Av Fjället* (*At the Foot of the Mountains*) seemingly demonstrates the singer's tacit acceptance of the prevailing stereotypes of a good "Lapp" in the early 1960s. He has his reindeer, he seems more at home in the woods than indoors, and he admits to being able to *joik* (although he does not actually do so on the recording).

The musical vehicle for these lyrics contrasts sharply with this image, however, being totally devoid of any element that might be construed as "Saami" (or "Lapp"). The record combines a familiar U.S. melody (*Red River Valley*), with instrumentation and production values which borrow generously from both mid-1950s British skiffle (acoustic and electric guitars, simple drum set, string bass) and Bobby Darin-style vocalizing. In other words, when compared with other European pop recordings of the era, there is nothing remarkable about this particular effort from a strictly musical perspective. For performances and publicity photographs, Jonsson continued this cultural ambiguity by adopting a public persona that was equal parts U.S. rocker (a pompadour hairstyle) and Saami reindeer herder (deliberately wrapping himself in *gákti*, the traditional woolen costuming associated with the Saami). The resulting image further underscored the impression Jonsson was a man caught between two cultures, straddling the line that divides "Lapp" from Swede, and the past from modernity.

It is this complex juxtaposition, however, which provided the recording with its particular appeal, and which made it potentially open to different interpretations, depending upon one's ethnic background. To those outside Saami culture, Jonsson's Lapp, conforming to widely held beliefs about this minority population, was at once both an exotic and a comedic mediator, sharing a laugh about the "primitive" ways of his people, while simultaneously becoming the butt of the joke. As a result, when Jonsson's period of popularity waned, both the artist and his songs quickly faded from public memory, his records having been consigned to the "novelty" category (Smith and Wiwatt 1990).

Yet, the suggestion Jonsson unwittingly parroted negative opinions about the Saami, perhaps even functioning like a quasi "Uncle Tom," ignores the positive impact this singer had on Saami audiences. In interviews with Saami who were teenagers (or older) when this recording was released, the unanimous response to Jonsson in general, and this song specifically, has been favourable. When pressed for an explanation, these same individuals have spoken frankly about the paucity of positive public images of Saami culture, and an overarching assumption that Saami youth could do little to counteract this situation in the early 1960s. Here, in the guise of the "Rocking Saami," however, was evidence a representative of their generation could stand up proudly and discuss his ethnicity openly, even if the presentation required adhering to existing "Lapp" stereotypes to some degree. While his choice of language, Swedish, could be interpreted as a denial of ethnicity, it was in fact a reflection of a sad reality: in the 1960s most Swedish Saami could not speak their language sufficiently well to have created or to have understood a simple pop song.

More importantly, several of those interviewed suggested that Jonsson used the opportunity afforded by this particular record to comment on issues which only a Saami audience could interpret, through his choice of specific images and metaphors (Stoor 1992b; Andersson 1992). These include references to ritual offering sites ("heathen stones" toward which the song's narrator professes to joik), and possibly even an underground spirit (a "Lapp girl" who mysteriously disappears). Such topics were typically not discussed openly, for they fueled impressions that the Saami still harbored (or secretly acted upon) pre-Christian beliefs. In this light, Jonsson's otherwise mundane recording spoke directly to a controversy that had existed inside and outside Saami communities for over a century, one which moreover accounted for the reasons why neither Jonsson nor any other Saami artist in the early 1960s was prepared to *joik* within the public context that a commercial recording necessarily created.

At the center of this maelstrom of opinions lay the indisputable fact that joik had once been an integral element in the ritual practices of the Saami *noaidi* (plural: *noaidit*), or shaman. Specific joiks, combined with drumming, served as the means by which the *noaidi* entered a trance state, traversed the spirit world, and eventually was brought back to the realm of human existence (Edström 1978; Bäckman and Hultkrantz 1978). These activities were noted by some of the earliest visitors to Saamiland, rarely in a positive light, and ultimately contributed to a power struggle between the *noaidit* and their Christian missionary counterparts. The Christians eventually prevailed, with the *noaidi* effectively disappearing entirely from Saami culture as a ritual specialist. But the condemnation of these practices extended beyond the ritual context as well. To the clergy and their growing parishes, all joiking was understood to be inherently "heathen," if not downright evil, and those who continued to sing in this fashion were subjected to harsh public criticism and potential ostracism from Saami communities (Rydving 1993). While this did not lead to a complete extinction of the genre, joiking was most often relegated to solitary or at least guarded performances, in which those within earshot could be counted on to ignore the infraction. More open displays of joik were generally discouraged, and unfortunately were most often the result of inebriation, which simply fueled objections toward the genre (Edström 1978).

Against this historical backdrop, then, Jonsson's admissions carried considerably more weight, particularly since they reached audiences all over Sweden via the mass media: Here was a young Saami man, dressed in *gákti* and snapping his fingers to a prominent backbeat, singing about his intimate knowledge of the beliefs of his forebears, and boasting of his own prowess in enacting these same beliefs. Even if the actual sound of joiking was entirely missing from the recording, Jonsson's prominent mention of the genre as an element of being a "Lapp," and his refusal to be ashamed by this pronouncement marked a substantial challenge to the perception of joik and its position within Saami culture. While these subtleties may have been lost on the overwhelming majority of Swedes who heard this song over the radio or purchased Jonsson's record, the reactions of my Saami acquaintances suggest that the "Rocking Saami" had opened a figurative door that had long been closed by shame and guilt. In so doing, he precipitated a move toward public joik performance, which was shortly realized in another landmark recording, one also taking advantage of a popular musical idiom.

Nils-Aslak Valkeapää: "Joik from Finnish Lapland" and the Emergence of "Modern Joik"

Saami singer/artist/actor/author Nils-Aslak Valkeapää's 1968 release of a vinyl single, *Johtin Luohtti*, and his subsequent follow up with an EP, *Joikuja/Jojk Från Finska Lapland* (*Joik from Finnish Lapland*), on a Finnish literary label (Otava; OT-LP 50; 1969), ushered in a new era of Saami music which was to have profound influence on all of the recording activities that followed. Whereas Sven-Gösta Jonsson sang about joiking, Valkeapää joiked openly, thereby creating the first commercial recordings of the genre (Jones-Bamman 1993). But the singer's efforts were groundbreaking in musical terms as well. Rather than performing his joiks in the traditional, unaccompanied manner, Valkeapää chose to combine joiking with simple instrumental arrangements, provided in this instance by a lightly plucked acoustic guitar and a string bass. The singer also mixed in field recordings he made in the midst of reindeer herding activities. Barking dogs, the dull bell of the lead animal, shouts from the herders, and the ubiquitous wind were all are heard on these recordings, usually at a sound level far below that of the vocalist or the instrumentalists.

According to Valkeapää, the creation of this particular recording was carefully calculated to bring the whole subject of joik into public discourse, a position that it had not occupied previously except with negative connotations (Valkeapää 1992). Having grown up in a reindeer herding family in Finnish Saamiland, Valkeapää was intimately familiar with the most traditional aspects of this culture, including joiking. But he was also aware of the self-imposed restrictions on joik performance that prevailed, particularly in his immediate surroundings, where the local Laestadians (an evangelical Lutheran sect common among Saami populations) frowned on all such activities (Outakoski 1991). Despite this prohibition, he learned to joik as a youngster, becoming quite competent by adulthood.

In his early twenties, Valkeapää elected to enter a teacher-training program rather than follow the family livelihood, and it was during this period of living away from Saami culture that the whole issue of joik became more focused for him. Like many young Saami, Valkeapää was aware of political developments in Norway, Sweden and Finland that were gaining momentum in the mid-1960s, contributing to what would later be characterized as an 'ethnic mobilization' (Svensson 1976). At the core of this highly charged movement were questions over the rights of Saami reindeer herders and government policies toward these individuals; a second area of concern was the right to language instruction for Saami-speaking children and their families.

Valkeapää, while remaining basically apolitical in most respects, waded into the midst of these controversies with an abiding belief that joik was a fundamental aspect of Saami culture, and therefore deserved to be revitalized and to rid itself of the guilt and shame cloaking its performance for over a century. Recognizing the difficulty of this task, however, he also reasoned a new performance context was required, one removing joik from its "natural" context (i.e., unaccompanied, and most often spontaneous singing), and thereby momentarily suspending performers and audience members alike from the objections typically heaped upon the genre. If this campaign were successful, he felt that joik would eventually overcome all obstacles, including those which hindered the conveyance of joik in more traditional performance contexts.

The inspiration for his first recordings came from contemporary popular models, particularly the urban folk stylings of U.S. artists such as Bob Dylan and Peter, Paul and Mary, whose recordings were regularly heard over the radio throughout Saamiland and the rest of Scandinavia. Valkeapää felt that this music, with its reliance on acoustic instrumentation, was more suited to his needs than rock or other pop forms, particularly since he was concerned about the accompaniment overpowering the vocals. The environmental sounds that Valkeapää later added counterbalanced the U.S. "folk" instrumentation, and brought the performances more firmly into Saami territory. Within this curious mix of elements, Valkeapää felt that joik had its best opportunity effectively to become a new form of popular music for Saami audiences, albeit one which was already familiar in its structure and overall sound.

Underlying these decisions, therefore, was a genuine concern that the joiks remain recognizable, and not be transformed into a form wholly out of character with the genre. Joik texts, for example, often consist of vocables, or vocables mixed with fragments of language, and Valkeapää's new recordings of the genre were no different. What lyrics were discernible, however, were always in Saami. On this issue, Valkeapää never wavered: this was to be Saami music for Saami audiences, and singing in any other language was not an option for consideration, even if a sizeable portion of that audience could not really understand what was sung. Even among those who spoke Saami, there would be those who could not comprehend his particular dialect. Nor would he modify the joiks musically in any way to ensure that his singing meshed with the instrumentalists. Joikers often raise the pitch incrementally over a series of repetitions, particularly as they run out of breath, and also tend to sing in very long phrases, again determined entirely by breath control rather than a predictable musical structure. When a joik is performed traditionally without any accompaniment, such factors have no impact whatsoever, as the singer is in complete control of when and how a joik starts and/or ends. Once instruments are added, however, these same characteristics potentially become a problem. In the case of Valkeapää's first recordings, this issue was only partially resolved. Occasionally the accompanists simply modulated up a semitone, while at other times the pitch discrepancy between vocalist and instrumentalists was palpable. Phrasing, on the other hand, was more carefully worked out, with Valkeapää consistently structuring his joik interpretations to emulate Western song models more closely; that is, he consciously manipulated his joiks to fit within the conventions of popular song phrasing.

The resulting recordings, if judged purely as musical events, are not particularly remarkable; the singing is somewhat hesitant, and the pitch disjunctures between the voice and accompanying instruments are quite notable at times. But the response which this record generated, and the esteem in which it is still held have little competition in Saamiland. When his 1968 single was first played over Saami Radio, the station was deluged with requests to play the piece again and again; eventually it became the theme for the daily program which was beamed out over Saamiland (Gaski 1992). Sales of the EP so thoroughly overwhelmed the small company, which released the record, that the business never completely caught up with its backlog and nearly foundered as a result. A surprising number of individuals and families even bought a copy of the recording without actually owning any means of listening to it (H. Valkeapää 1995); this small EP had become tangible evidence for many that joik, and by extension Saami culture, was viable and capable of moving forward.

But Valkeapää's efforts were not universally accepted among the Saami, and the artist was well aware that this was bound to be the case. To that end, he took action to defend his work on the EP, even before it was released, by creating a short manifesto for the accompanying liner notes. Valkeapää surmised criticism would potentially come from two camps: those who objected to joik in any context on religious grounds, and those who would take issue with the addition of musical instruments to a genre traditionally performed without any accompaniment. In his brief self-defense, Valkeapää (1969, 3) referred to the latter critics as "cultural romanticists" and lashed out at them, both for their attempts to control the development of a living traditional genre, and their objections to his creation of a new performance context. From his perspective, the joiks on the recording had not been rendered meaningless through the recording process, nor had they suffered any damage as the result of the new arrangements he created. To these critics, Valkeapää stated bluntly, "All of the joiks on this record would be recognizable, if performed in a traditional manner" (1969, 3). Furthermore, he reminded his listeners that joik performance was a dynamic tradition that had always encouraged change and improvisation. Yet, he also acknowledged that a recorded performance constrained the degree of improvisation by virtue of the need to conform to the recording process: "When one performs in public, one is forced to restrict the inclination to improvise. The performance context has changed and the text has crystallized" (Valkeapää 1969, 4). Finally, in response to the critics who labeled his initial efforts "modern," Valkeapää asserted, "I have previously been opposed to the label 'modern' joik... however, since I do not want to stand accused of sinful or false joiking, I will accept 'modem joik' as a fine term" (1969, 3).

Once *Jojk Från Finska Lapland* was released, Valkeapää never looked back, nor did he succumb to requests from his myriad fans that he simply continue in the same musical vein. Subsequent recording projects found the singer exploring myriad possibilities, from light pop songs without any joiking to long, highly improvisatory joiks melded with sympathetic jazz and New Age accompaniments. While some of these efforts have at times confounded his Saami audience, he remains the single most important figure in both the development of contemporary joik performance contexts, and the eventual revitalization of the genre in its most traditional form.

The "Joik Renaissance"

While Valkeapää's *Joik Från Finska Lapland* certainly proved to be influential in its own right, perhaps the greater measure of its importance is the sheer amount of recording activity generated in its wake. As Valkeapää explored several different musical directions, a number of younger artists adopted the performance model he presented in this first recording and began tentatively fusing simple joiking with everything from country music to Ramones-flavored rock. Not all of these were particularly inspired (or inspiring), but collectively they constitute a remarkable body of recordings representing a new Saami musical phenomenon eventually termed the "joik renaissance." During the 1970s and early 1980s alone, nearly forty albums and cassettes of Saami music were commercially released, most of which featured joik on at least some of the tracks. The majority fell squarely into the realm of popular music, but there were also attempts to fuse joik with Western classical music (Jones-Bamman 1993).

This activity also marked the emergence of a small Saami music industry, with all aspects of record production (from studio work to publishing and distribution), gradually being taken up by individuals and collectives intent on making Saami music for Saami audiences. Among these new businesses, Jar'galæd'dji, and Davvi Girji, based in Tana and Karasjok, Norway respectively, were the first to function successfully within the Saami market in the late 1970s. They were followed in the 1980s by IDUT, a record company in Tysfjord, Norway, and DAT, a Saami music and book publishing firm with offices in Norway and Sweden. Funding for all of this largely came from government grants, which were often attained with the help of an official Saami music consultant appointed by the Norwegians to expedite the process (Prost 1992; Boine and Utsi 2000).

Although none of these recordings generated the same degree of response that Valkeapää's first EP had, all of the performers enjoyed some degree of notoriety within Saamiland for having produced a record at a time when such an occurrence was still considered an accomplishment for any aspiring pop musician, regardless of ethnicity or nationality. The Saami press tended to treat most of the new releases with positive reviews, almost as though genuine criticism would be counterproductive to the larger issue of emergent Saami pride. Pal Doj, editor during the late 1970s and early 1980s of the Swedish national Saami magazine, *Samefolket*, best expressed this attitude in a short feature article on two new recordings, one by a well-established group (Dædnugádde Nuorat) and the other by a raucous group of very young musicians from Kautokeino, Norway (Jávrras Ivnniiguin): "On the whole, both records can be recommended, even if done so without the greatest enthusiasm. Still, there are not very many Saami records released, so all the new ones that are produced are welcome" (Doj 1980, 5).

In truth, however, very few of these recordings recouped their initial expenses and, by the end of the decade, the most active Saami record label, Jar'galæd'dji, was on tenuous financial ground, while the more cautious Davvi Girji remained only marginally interested in record production. In part, this could be credited to the admittedly small market for this music, but this development also reflected a degree of anxiety over the intense commercialization of Saami music.

These concerns were eventually addressed in an article, *Om joik og kommunikasjon* (*Joik and Communication*), written by Saami professor and historian, Nils Jernsletten in 1977. Jernsletten, an outspoken activist for Saami civil rights, drew a clear distinction between traditional joik and what he somewhat derisively termed "joik songs" (Jernsletten 1977, 119). His argument was grounded in what he viewed as one of the fundamental functions of joik in Saami culture, its power to communicate. Joik is essentially a descriptive medium, with each song representing an accurate portrayal of a person, an animal, an event or an object in the environment. This description is accomplished through a combination of melodic structure, rhythm and to a lesser extent, text, creating a musical gestalt that the singer conveys to his/her audience (Edström 1978). However, the interpretation of a joik, according to Jernsletten (and corroborated by several singers whom he cites), is only accomplished when singer and audience have been raised in the same "joik milieu"; that is, a village or extended family in which joiking is integrated into daily activities. Within this environment, children and adults alike develop the skills and the intimacy both to create musical descriptions and to understand them (Jernsletten 1977, 110). This naturally leads to the development of joik dialects and idioms that are quite esoteric. From this perspective, the conveyance of joik via any medium, be it a radio broadcast or a recording is problematic, for it diminishes the possibility of the song actually being understood. Nor is the situation any better when a person joiks from a stage, as was increasingly occurring by the end of the 1970s. In each of these instances, Jernsletten argued, the communicative quality of joik was severely compromised.

Jernsletten, however, was not condemning the so-called "modern joik" and its new performance contexts, but was instead concerned that this newer manifestation not be mistaken for the traditional genre, for the latter was firmly embedded in Saami culture and therefore worth protecting from unnecessary change. As if in anticipation of this criticism, several of the "modern" joik artists had in fact taken steps in this direction themselves, demonstrating their abilities to joik without instrumental accompaniment, and to create new joiks which met the aesthetic criteria of their respective communities. Singer/actor Ingor Ántte Áilu Gaup is perhaps the best example of this phenomenon, having released both a rousing rock recording and a traditional joik recording (sans accompaniment) simultaneously in 1978. In interviews later, he explained that his primary concern had always been to create joiks that his family members and the people in his village found acceptable (Gaup 1992). While Gaup and some of his contemporaries wrestled with this dichotomy, others within the industry produced recordings of more traditionally oriented material, performed by older singers whose joik skills had in many cases lain dormant until the heady atmosphere of the "joik renaissance" also sparked a flame of interest among this group.

Partially in response to the criticisms of Jernsletten and several of his colleagues, and also as a result of diminishing enthusiasm among Saami audiences, the interest in the musical experimentation of the 1970s began to wane quickly as the decade ended. But there was to be one final recording of the era which was destined to eclipse everything preceding its release in terms of sales and size of audience, a joik that was eventually heard all over Europe.

A Joik is More Powerful Than Weapons: *Sámiid Ædnan*

While Saami musicians wrestled with the appropriateness of different musical idioms and performance contexts, the end of the 1970s was also marked by a growing concern among Saami populations and environmentalists alike, over the proposed construction of a new hydroelectric project
on the Alta River in the northernmost region of Norway, squarely in Saami territory. This action
was to involve damming up the river, thereby flooding thousands of hectares of prime reindeer
grazing pasturage, and displacing at least one Saami community, Máze, that was situated along the
flood path. Those Saami living in the area were justifiably disturbed by this development, seeing
it as one more example added to a centuries-long list of abuses at the hands of their Scandinavian
neighbors. Environmentalists, while certainly aware of the impact on the Saami in the region, were
more concerned with the damage to flora and fauna, and with the fundamental issue of whether
or not another hydroelectric project of this magnitude was justifiable under any circumstances.
A number of political action groups were hastily organized, reflecting these intertwined ideologies, with the result that several protests were staged in and around the proposed site in 1979. As
anticipated, these actions drew considerable attention from the authorities, and from the local and
national press. With the arrival of news crews and television cameras, all of Norway (and interested
parties in Sweden and Finland) were soon well aware of the increasingly tense situation unfolding
in northern Saamiland.

In the midst of this activity, a dissatisfied cohort of younger protestors split off from the main
Saami political organization (People's Action Group or PAG), forming their own assemblage (Saami
Action Group or SAG) with the express intention of significantly raising the level of confrontation
with Norwegian officials (Paine 1985). On 8 October 1979, the members of SAG set up a traditional
Saami *lavvo* (a conical tent, similar in shape and function to a Plains Indian dwelling), on a small
plot of ground directly across the street from the Norwegian Parliament building in Oslo. With
this act, the protestors effectively transformed the space into a symbolic Saamiland. They added
to this transformation by joiking vociferously for passers-by, as they awaited some reaction from
the august body situated in the edifice facing them.

Very quickly, this activity brought both the police and the press, and before long the streets
surrounding the area were clogged with curiosity seekers and various authorities. For their part,
the Saami protestors remained calm, declaring that they intended to stage a hunger strike until
their case was heard by the appropriate government officials. In the meantime, they continued to
joik periodically, and went about the business of preparing for their ordeal, appointing an official
spokesperson and making themselves as comfortable as possible in the confines of a tent erected
in the midst of a large urban area.

Rather than irritating Oslo's citizenry, as one might expect, this dramatic action actually aroused
a great deal of sympathy for the protestors, and served to stimulate a much-needed national dialogue
about the country's indigenous population and their rights. Throughout the protest, Norwegians
continued to stop by the tent to offer their support; for many this amounted to their first real experience with Saami culture. More significantly, a surprising number of observers stepped forward
to declare openly their own Saami heritage, something that many had not done before out of fear
or shame (Paine 1985, 196).

In response to a week of intense scrutiny by Norwegians and an ever-increasing European audience, the government agreed to a moratorium on the Alta dam project until the appropriate council
could be convened to reconsider the entire proposal. This time, however, the officials agreed to
take into account some of the issues raised by the Saami protestors; not a final resolution, by any
means, but one which both sides felt represented a start toward a more meaningful dialogue. Shortly
thereafter, the members of SAG dismantled the tent and returned home, having accomplished
considerably more than they had anticipated. For a brief period, at least, the Saami had undeniably

become both visible and *audible* to an unprecedented extent, and they had used this opportunity to promote an overtly political agenda before an attentive, national audience.

Before the memory of this unusual activity could fade from public consciousness, an enterprising Norwegian pop singer, Sverre Kjeldsberg, waded into the fray with a new recording that eventually moved the conflict surrounding the Alta project into a much broader arena of public discourse. Kjeldsberg was well known to Norwegian music fans for his previous work with the popular group, The Pussycats, a situation that provided him with handy access to both the recording industry and a proven fan base (Graff 1992). But the new record he released in late 1979 was quite unlike anything he had undertaken before. Working with lyricist, R. Olsen, and arranger, E. Monn-Iversen, Kjeldsberg fashioned a musical commentary on the Alta protest focusing specifically on the Saami "occupation" of Oslo. Moreover, it painted the members of SAG in a particularly heroic light, effectively casting the Saami group as brave David figures actively confronting the Norwegian government's Goliath. Rather than giving the song a Norwegian title, Kjeldsberg underscored his sympathetic stance on this issue by calling the recording *Sámiid Ædnan*, a Saami phrase meaning "Saamiland" or "Saami Homeland." Yet, the record's strongest link with the Saami cause, both musically and symbolically, was the inclusion of Mattis Hætta, a young Saami musician from Máze (the affected community in the Alta region), who added a prominent joik performance to the project.

The resulting recording is an interesting attempt both to explain the significance of the protest, and to place this action within a context in which the Saami potentially come off as morally and ethically superior. The Norwegian text opens with a metaphorical representation of the activities, encapsulated in "two small words: *Sámiid Ædnan* —the Saami world," that "came like a puff of wind from the north," and gradually gathered strength until this initially benign force had become a "storm" to be reckoned with. The lyrics then recount the activities in front of the Parliament building, where "joiking was heard day and night." Kjeldsberg's performance begins *sotto voce*, and gradually builds in intensity, until he is fairly shouting at the conclusion of the opening section. Monn-Iversen's arrangement frames this part of the recording with a long, gradual crescendo, coupled with a layered approach to orchestration: by the third verse, the accompaniment has swelled to big band proportions, matching the rather surprising fervor in Kjeldsberg's voice.

All of this comes to an abrupt stop, only to be set in motion again by the entrance of Mattis Hætta, who begins joiking rather cautiously (mirroring Kjeldsberg's performance), and slowly gains confidence with each iteration. For this project, Hætta chose a traditional joik from his home district that made exclusive use of the vocables "lo" and "la" in lieu of any actual Saami text. Whether by design or simply by coincidence, this joik's triadic structure and fairly narrow ambitus made it an ideal choice for a chorus, and ensured the success of the recording. In fact, the song's title (*Sámiid Ædnan*) was nearly forgotten when audiences began referring to the record as "Låla" (pronounced "Lola") because of Hætta's joik.

Eventually, the band returns, nearly overpowering the joiking with its bombastic 'oom-pah' effects, and Kjeldsberg chimes in with the final observation that "A joik is more powerful than weapons…because it has neither a beginning nor an end." Underneath all of this, Hætta can be heard repeating his simple joik, providing the only real Saami "voice" within this complex arrangement that clearly sought to reconstruct some of the sentiments surrounding the Oslo protest, and to use this connection to create interest in the recording.

Apparently this strategy worked, for *Sámiid Ædnan* was not only a huge commercial success in Norway, but was ultimately chosen to be the nation's entry in the 1980 Eurovision Song Contest, an annual popular music event which attracts a television audience of millions. The song was eventually placed last in the contest that year, but its impact in terms of creating interest in the Saami (albeit with the fleeting quality that awaits most pop music hits) is incalculable. Within a few months, people all over Europe were listening to Mattis Hætta joik, and frequently singing along to the "Lo-la" hook. Thanks to a popular music recording, a highly mediated interpretation of Saami culture had made its way into the mainstream of European consciousness.

The success of *Sámiid Ædnan* was not gained without controversy, however, particularly within some Saami circles. While there were predictable outcries about the appropriateness of joiking in such a public manner or its use in such an obviously commercial venture, one of the more thought-provoking arguments against the song focused on the musical and structural arrangement of the recording (Gaski 1992). At issue was a concern over the manner in which the protest activities that inspired the song had been more or less appropriated for interpretation by Kjeldsberg et al. In the space of a typical three-minute pop song, the listener is presented with an obviously abbreviated version of the activities in Oslo and their peaceful but ambiguous resolution, all from a perspective that seemingly favors the Saami side of the story. But the narrator/guide for this presentation is Norwegian, and as such necessarily represents the role of "outsider." This is reinforced by the choice of language (Norwegian rather than Saami) and the manner in which the joik performance is framed and presented; that is, deep "inside" the soundscape of the recording, surrounded by more "outside" forces (e.g., an orchestra). The conclusion of the record, an ascending orchestral passage reaching a final *fortissimo* chord, is even more bothersome in this light, as it would appear to end the inside/outside discourse on a decidedly outside note. There is no doubt as to which "voice" has the last word.

To a number of individuals concerned with the direction of contemporary joik practices, the success of *Sámiid Ædnan* and its eventual achievements outside Saamiland, represented a predictable outcome of the more troubling aspects of the so-called joik renaissance (Gaski 1991; Stoor 1992a). By becoming simply an element of a pop song, and in this instance a pop song created by a non-Saami artist, joik seemed to be in danger of losing its significance within Saami culture, just as historian Nils Jernsletten had warned a few years earlier. A hastily assembled follow-up LP by Kjeldsberg and Hætta (appropriately entitled *Låla!*) did nothing to assuage this concern that the relationship between Saami joik and popular music had apparently developed in ways that even the most "modern" Saami musicians found uncomfortable. These anxieties coincided with the closing of the Saami record company, Jar'galæd'dji, a development which impacted not only the quality, but the quantity of recordings that would be made in the immediate future. Consequently, the 1980s proved to be an era of considerably more circumspection in terms of recording and live performance, as artists and their followers alike took a greater interest in *how* Saami culture was being presented to an audience that now potentially included both "inside" and "outside" listeners.

"I am Saami": Speaking Up For One's Own

When Lars Jonas Johansson growled out "I am Saami" with his band Almetjh Tjöönghkeme, on their 1991 CD, *Vaajesh* (Jojkbox 001), he was actually making a statement that could be interpreted on several different levels. First, he was declaring his ethnicity, and doing so without any hint of the shame that had often tainted the lives of his forebears. For Johansson, this was a particularly important moment of self-realization, because like many in his region, one of his parents (his mother) is Swedish. While there was never any question of his ethnic orientation, it was still important for Johansson to make this public statement, and to do so in the language of his father's people (Johansson 1992a). By electing to sing in Saami, however, Johansson and his band mates consciously delimited the audience for their music, effectively excluding anyone who did not speak the language. This decision was in keeping with their desire to create recordings for an exclusive Saami audience, just as Nils-Aslak Valkeapää had done 20 years earlier. In further support of this, the members of Almetjh Tjöönghkeme decided not to translate their song lyrics, feeling that to do so would undermine their efforts to encourage young listeners to learn and use Saami.

Yet, the issue of language brings Johansson's declamation to another level of interpretation. Johansson and the rest of his group speak South Saami, a dialect that has become particularly moribund over the last century due in large part to assimilationist policies of the past, and the constant interaction between southern Saami populations and their Swedish and Norwegian neighbors. This process has gradually been reversed, but there are currently very few contexts encouraging the active use of this language, particularly when compared with similar situations among North Saami speakers (Svonni 1993). By his own admission, Johansson's skills are rough and his grammar limited, but he has made a commitment to using this language and to encourage others to follow his example. Therefore, when Johansson sings out "I am Saami" in his own dialect, to a knowledgeable audience (i.e., Saami speakers), he is actually saying, "I am <u>South</u> Saami."

Johansson is quite a competent joik singer, as is evidenced both in his live performances and on his recordings. The particular song from which this lyric is taken, however (*Goh Almetjh Lea* [*Just Like Other People*]), is one of a few on the CD that do not include any joiking. The reason for this takes one deeper into the motivations of this particular artist and his desire to be identified distinctly as South Saami. Just as language was adversely affected by generations of ethnic interactions and institutionalized prejudice, joiking was similarly impacted and has all but disappeared from the southern region of Saamiland. In many instances this has not been simply a matter of the practice becoming secretive (as was true further north), but actually has brought about the near extinction of the genre. Under these circumstances, for Johansson to learn to joik has meant that he has had to rely on the only models that were available. Lacking any living traditors in his immediate environment, he turned instead to recordings, which were invariably produced by North Saami artists. Consequently, Johansson's joiking has been heavily influenced by a style which is not a reflection of his own heritage, something he readily admits, but also sees as a matter of some concern. When it came time to record *Goh Almetjh Lea*, Johansson was suddenly faced with a paradox: to add a joik to the song would certainly reinforce his stance as a proud Saami man, but its obvious North Saami sound would undermine his intent to be recognized as South Saami. In the end, he chose to let the song stand without the inclusion of any joik. The language alone is symbolic enough that no listener can miss the surface content ("I am Saami"), while those with more esoteric skills can appreciate the fact that he has remained within a South Saami context in this performance, by not joiking in his North Saami-influenced style.

The final layer in this carefully packaged presentation is the musical arrangement, which Johansson describes as "hard rock." The backdrop for *Goh Almetjh Lea* features electric guitars, electric bass, several layers of electronic keyboards, and a full drum kit, all played with the requisite volume and distortion that typifies heavy metal and other hard-edged rock genres. This is not the only style of music played by Almetjh Tjöönghkeme, yet it was chosen for this particular song by Johansson (who wrote the melody and lyrics), largely because he suspected that younger Saami listeners would be more inclined to identify with this genre, and thus pay more attention to his message. As he explained, "[W]e figured, if we were going to go further and get the youth interested in this, then we must use something which they'll jump on, something they'll grab onto. It doesn't do, just to be concerned with 'culture'; that becomes too heavy. If you are going to turn around the youth, then you have to use a little of their language [i.e., slang] and the musical style they want to listen to ... and blues, that's always popular ... and rock, that's popular, too—that's easy to listen to, that hits home today with the youth, really well" (Johansson 1992b).

If this all seems a bit contrived, it is important to understand that Johansson's motivation for forming the band in the first place was embedded in his own experience as a youngster. While he was able to learn the rudiments of his language in school, he could not help but compare his own situation with that of other Saami youth whom he met through participation in Sámi Nuorra, a Swedish national Saami youth organization. Within this context, Johansson often felt disenfranchised, and eventually turned to his musical interests in an attempt to raise his self-esteem. He was already a competent guitarist and had a flare for performance, but his inability to joik was a decided impediment, by his own reckoning. Turning to recordings for inspiration (particularly those of Nils-Aslak Valkeapää), Johansson began the difficult task of teaching himself to joik, and gradually added these newly acquired skills to his musical performances. Thanks to a talent search in 1998 by a local South Saami organization (in Östersund, Sweden), Johansson was included on an LP, *Aarjede Laavloeh* (Samien LP001), joiking and playing acoustic guitar.

During this recording project, Johansson met several other South Saami musicians, with the result that Almetjh Tjöönghkeme was organized as a vehicle for creating pop music with a decidedly South Saami orientation. From the beginning, the band's explicit goal was to reach other youth who, like the band members themselves, felt cut off from the mainstream of Saami culture, by virtue of their geographical location in the southernmost reaches of Saamiland. Their strategy was simple: compose and perform decent pop songs in their own dialect. They would also trust the attraction of a familiar musical idiom would draw in their target audience and simultaneously open them up to the prospect of learning more about their own language and culture.

Johansson (1992a) was by far the least comfortable with South Saami language, but this only solidified his commitment to ensure that other young people became involved in the struggle to revitalize the entire region: "My goal is to awaken the Saami youth, and above all the South Saami…and moreover to do this with joik and to teach them to listen to Saami music; because I believe that the way to learn a language is to enjoy it and to be interested in it. If you can come in the 'back way' by playing a good song that everyone goes crazy over, and if you sing that song well, they'll want to pay attention to the words, and via that route they become involved with the lyrics. In the end, they might have to approach someone else who can understand it, and this nearly forces them to become a part of it—that's a means of awakening an interest in Saami language" (Johansson 1992b).

Over the few years that the band existed, they pursued this mission with mixed success. They were able to generate a good deal of interest in their music, both through CD and cassette sales, some airplay on Saami radio broadcasts, and occasional live performances. During one of their more memorable concerts in 1992, I watched a small theatre full of young Saami rise to their feet on several occasions, joiking boisterously along with Lars Jonas when he tore into the chorus of one his songs that fuses joik and rock quite effectively. Had it not been for the preponderance of Saami clothing and language that evening, it would have been easy to mistake the event for a typical rock concert without any particular political agenda. But throughout the show, Johansson continually returned to his theme, one which played very well to this audience: I am Saami, I am *South* Saami.

Eventually musical differences (not to mention the difficulty of living very far from one another) led to the dissolution of the group. Nevertheless, in Almetjh Tjöönghkeme's short tenure, Johansson and his Saami band mates demonstrated that the inherently rebellious quality of hard rock could be effectively marshaled to further their particular cause: securing recognition for a minority within a minority, by using music as a means of confirming their identities. To draw an audience into this discursive field, however, required that the musicians continually strike a balance between music which was familiar (rock) and the Saami music they hoped to create. When this was accomplished effectively, as in the recording of *Goh Almetjh Lea*, the band amply demonstrated Saami music could really rock without compromising its essential ties to Saami culture.

Taking Saami Pop to the World Stage

In the period of time that has passed since Lars Jonas Johansson growled out "I am Saami," Saami music and Saami musicians have become considerably more audible, both in Scandinavia and abroad. As in previous decades, much of this contact with audiences has been the result of commercially released recordings. However, a growing interest in so-called global pop (Taylor 1997) has also made it possible for Saami artists to perform live in festivals and concerts all over the world, frequently sharing the stage with other 'indigenous' and 'traditional' musicians and various pop stars.

Perhaps the individual who has been most successful in taking Saami music outside its figurative and literal borders is Mari Boine, a singer/bandleader whose recordings have been widely distributed abroad by both the Realworld and Antilles labels. Like those who ventured into the popular music sphere before her, Boine records exclusively in Saami, but she differs markedly in the manner in which she uses her songs to portray her culture. Whereas Nils-Aslak Valkeapää and those who followed him created music which tended to strengthen the ethnic boundary separating Saami and non-Saami audiences, Boine's recordings and performances demonstrate the permeability of that boundary (Barth 1969). Rather than relying on an exclusive group of Saami musicians, Boine has deliberately surrounded herself with players of markedly different ethnic backgrounds. This syncretic approach most often produces a sound field in which the Saami element (Boine's language, her topics and her joiking) is only one of several obvious "ethnic" elements purposefully mixed together. In effect, Boine creates music which celebrates her ethnicity in relation to other heritages (represented by her band mates), in a much more obvious manner than that of her predecessors. Thus, instead of drawing a musical line around her songs and declaring them exclusively "Saami," Boine's recordings frequently convey a message of inclusivity, placing Saami culture within a global environment that emphasizes parity. To be sure, the Saami element is privileged in these performances, but it is not done so to the exclusion of others.

However, Boine, like those who entered this process before her, has not been without her critics. Some argue that her free adoption of musical ideas from around the globe, and her frequent attempts to combine these elements into a coherent package, actually contribute to a general exotification of "ethnic" music, that threatens to draw Saami music into a generic "indigenous" category. The overarching concern is that Saami music may lose its identity as a unique cultural expression in a marketplace that is increasingly guilty of lumping together such disparate groups as Australia's Yothu Yindi (with some Aboriginal members) and Canada's Kashtin (Innu), simply because the musicians involved share backgrounds as indigenous peoples (Jones-Bamman 1993; Taylor 1997). Others more pointedly dismiss Boine's joiking as too mannered or even as opportunistic, alluding to the fact that Boine taught herself to joik as an adult, after she had begun making recordings. While this calls to mind similar concerns over "authenticity" dismissed by Valkeapää in the 1960s as evidence of a "museum culture" attitude (Valkeapää 1969, 3–4), it certainly points up the extent to which music and particularly joik remain topics of great concern to Saami (Skaltje, 2000).

Within this dynamic milieu, at least one Saami music company (DAT) is actively pursuing a wider market for its artists, but is also proceeding cautiously to ensure that what they release meets the artistic needs of the musicians, while representing Saami culture in a manner that preserves its unique qualities (Boine and Utsi, 2000). The company, originally established as a collective in the early 1980s, was among the first to encourage joik singers to record without accompaniment, thereby adopting a decidedly different trajectory than the musical excesses of many of the Saami recordings produced during the 1970s. Over time, however, DAT's releases have gradually branched out from this fairly conservative base to include artists who freely mix joik and songs in Saami with various idioms from outside the culture, ranging from pop styles and jazz to flamenco. Their catalogue, thus, now presents a continuum of Saami music, rather than promoting a definitive style or benchmark by which others are measured. There is ample evidence within this body of work that joik remains the most significant mode of musical expression, but the variety of approaches to the genre also suggest that both this music and the people who produce it are far from finished exploring new performance contexts and new musical identities.

Coda

When Sven-Gösta Jonsson first introduced Saami culture to a popular audience with his song, *Vid Foten Av Fjället*, he opened the door to a new mode of dialogue based in music. At the center of this lay the question of Saami identity, which like the "Lapp" in Jonsson's song, straddled two realities, one that was encumbered with stereotypes and negative preconceptions rooted in fear and distrust, and the other, a modernity that offered release from this past, but potentially at the cost of self esteem and cultural identification. Within a few years, however, advocates for Saami rights would explore another alternative that drew strength from the past, while employing modern political and economic mechanisms as a means of creating a more positive ethnic identity for all Saami populations (Svensson 1976; Eidheim 1987).

In the midst of these developments, once again popular music came to the fore, this time as a catalyst for change. Nils-Aslak Valkeapää's seemingly simple combination of joik and folk-inspired accompaniment broke through the layers of shame and secrecy which had enshrouded the genre by providing a new performance context, one that avoided comparison with the past by introducing instrumentation, yet was clearly embedded in the past by Valkeapää's own admission: these were the same old, familiar joiks, merely being put to new use.

And yet the revolution that Valkeapää inspired with his first recordings was not limited to music, for his actions grew out of a conviction that a modern Saami identity would never be complete until his people had fully reconciled themselves with their past, and were thus prepared to move toward a future which entailed greater self determination. While Valkeapää's efforts engendered a good deal of criticism, it is important to remember that the artist lashed out most vehemently at those whom he felt sought to deny the dynamic quality of Saami culture, by placing too much emphasis on the past (Valkeapää 1969, 3–4; see also Valkeapää 1983). In creating a new context for joik, Valkeapää was not only freeing the genre from long-held negative preconceptions, but was moving it forward. This new/old joik was thus a trope for change which Valkeapää and his supporters wished to introduce across the culture.

Following quickly along the path that Valkeapää charted, the artists who participated in the "joik renaissance" experimented with Saami music to such a degree that even the most stalwart supporters of this movement found it difficult not to be troubled on occasion. When Saami historian Nils Jernsletten dismissed much of this activity as "joik songs," he was not particularly attacking the musicians involved, but merely reminding the Saami public that the products of this process should not be confused with traditional conceptions of joik, for only the latter was capable of conveying meaning at an interpersonal level (Jernsletten 1977, 119). No popular genre, created for a mass audience, could function in this manner, according to Jernsletten and his supporters. As if in acknowledgement of this predicament, several Saami singers released recordings of solo, unaccompanied joik performances, thereby stimulating the development of a parallel market for more traditional commercial approaches to the genre. These were no less troubling to the most conservative critics, but certainly demonstrated that the complete revitalization of joik that Valkeapää envisioned had been realized.

Such concerns were further exacerbated by the release of *Sámiid Ædnan* and its subsequent elevation to the top of the Norwegian popular music chart in 1979. After a few weeks of continual airplay, thousands of Norwegians were joiking along to the catchy chorus, leaving many Saami uncomfortable with the results, and leading to unprecedented legal disputes over Saami intellectual property (Gaski 1991). While the success of *Sámiid Ædnan* proved to be an anomaly, the recording effectively put an end to most of the experimentation that characterized the 1970s, and led to an era in which Saami musicians were considerably more circumspect and cognizant of their responsibilities to a public that increasingly included non-Saami listeners. This caution was evident throughout the 1980s, with the preponderance of recordings falling more into the realm of traditional, unaccompanied performances. The only other development of note was a slight increase in the number of artists singing in Saami, without including any joik at all. Even Nils-Aslak Valkeapää was surprisingly silent during this period, devoting himself instead to writing, photography and painting projects.

The emergence of the Saami rock band Almetjh Tjöönghkeme in 1990 was not an attempt to reverse this trend, but a calculated move to promote their particular cause. Here again, a popular music genre (Johansson's self-described "hard rock") was brought into service, this time as a vehicle for attracting a crowd of Saami youth whom the band had targeted as disenfranchised. Once drawn into the familiar sphere of this music, the band hoped to stimulate ethnic pride among their listeners and encourage them to participate in their culture to a greater degree by learning and using their specific dialect. While this was obviously idealistic, at the very least it provided a much-needed boost to South Saami populations, who were delighted to hear their language used, even in the context of a heavy metal song. The long-term effects of this band, and particularly the efforts of singer Lars Jonas Johansson, are even more significant. Thanks in large part to the group's performances and recordings, several older Saami singers have shared their repertoire and techniques with Johansson, thereby ensuring that this aspect of their culture is no longer endangered.

Most recently, popular music has largely been used by Saami artists as a means of reaching beyond both cultural and geographical boundaries. Musicians such as Mari Boine have taken Saami music and Saami concerns to a world stage, where pop music is the lingua franca. Her distinctive approach not only fuses Saami musical ideas with pop genres, as her predecessors had done, but does so in an atmosphere populated by several other discrete musical identities. Nor is Boine alone in these efforts. Ingor Ántte Áilu Gaup, a well-established singer from Norway has experimented for several years with joik and Afro-pop in his performances with Bolon X, a Stockholm-based ensemble of West African and Swedish musicians. He has also recorded with saxophone artist, Jan Garbarek on the latter's *I Took Up The Runes* CD (ECM 1419), which features an instrumental interpretation of one of Mari Boine's songs, as well.

While it is doubtful that anyone listening to Sven-Gösta Jonsson singing about his "Lapp" lifestyle in the late 1950s could have envisioned these developments, from that point forward, popular music has served Saami artists well as a vehicle for both commenting on current issues, and provoking change in areas that had either reached an impasse or were simply uncharted. Along the way, many of the resulting recordings stimulated discussion within Saami communities, which in turn led to change that was even more far reaching. Thus, as people within this culture now seek to negotiate an identity as an indigenous population within the new European Union, it can be presumed with some certainty that popular music genres will continue to play a role in this process (Gaski 1997). The results, no doubt, will please some and disturb others, but will ultimately keep the internal cultural dialogue open and productive, if past examples are any indications of the future.

References

Anderson, L. 1991. Interview, 7 and 8 November.
———. 1992. Interview, 13 March.
———. 1995. Interview, 12 May.
Bäckman, Louise. and Åke. Hultkrantz, eds. 1978. *Studies in Lapp Shamanism*. Stockholm: Almqvist & Wiksell.
Barth, Frederik., ed. 1969. *Ethnic Groups and Boundaries*. Oslo: Universitetsforlaget.
Beach, Hugh. 1981. *Reindeer-herd Management in Transition*. Stockholm: Almqvist & Wiksell.
———. 1988. *The Saami of Lapland*. London: Minority Rights Group.
Boine, P. L., and K. Utsi. 2000. Interview, 23 June.
Doj, Pal. 1980. "Samiska 'svenskstopp' i tva nya skivor." *Samefolkets Egen Tidning* 61 (1): 5.
Edström, Karl-Olof. 1978. *Den Samiska Musikkulturen*. Göteborg: Skrifter fran musikvetenskapliga institutionen 1.
Eidheim, Harald. 1987. *Aspects of the Lappish Minority Situation*. Oslo Occasional Papers in Social Anthropology, No. 14.
Fjellström, Phebe. 1985. *Samernas Samhälle*. Stockholm: P. A. Norstedt.
Gaski, Harald. 1991. Og ønskeplate er: En joik med Kjell Karlsens orkester. In *Joikens frie lyder nar lengre enn mange ord*, edited by O. Graff, 97–108. (Tromsø, *Tromura, Kulturhistorie nr. 21*).
———. 1992. Interview, 5 and 6 May.
———, ed. 1997. *Sami Culture in a New Era*. Karasjok: Davvi Girji OS.
Gaup, Ingor, Ántte Áilu. 1992. Interview, 4 May.
Graff, O. 1992. Interview, 7 and 8 May.
Jernsletten, Nils. 1977. Om joik og kommunikasjon. *By og Bygd. Norsk Folkemuseums Arbok* 26: 109–122.

Johansson, L. J. 1992a. Interview, 20 March.

———. 1992b. Interview, 12 March.

Jones-Bamman, Richard. 1993. 'As long as we continue to joik, we'll remember who we are' Negotiating identity and the performance of culture: the Saami joik. Seattle: University of Washington.

Outakoski, Nila. 1991. Lars Levi Laestadiuksen Saarnojen Maahiskuva. Oulu: Oulun historiseauran julkaisuja.

Paine, Robert. 1985. "Ethnodrama and the 'Fourth World': the Saami Action Group in Norway, 1979–1981." In Indigenous Peoples and the Nation State: Fourth World Politics in Canada, Australia and Norway, edited by N. Dyck, 190–235. St John's: Memorial University of Newfoundland.

Prost, E. 1992. Interview, 9 May.

Ruong, Israel. 1969. Samerna I Historien och Nutiden. Stockholm: Bonnier Fakta AB.

Rydving, Håkan. 1993. The End of Drum-Time. Uppsala: Acta Universitatis Upsaliensis, Historica Religionum 12.

Skaltje, M. 2000. Interview, 22 June.

Slobin, Mark. 1992. "Micromusics of the West: A Comparative Approach." Ethnomusicology 36 (1): 1–88.

Smith, Steve. and Leif Wivatt. 1990. Rock dag för dag. Boras: Diagram.

Stoor, K. 1992a. Interview, 8 April.

———. 1992b. Interview, 20 November.

Svensson, Tom. 1976. Ethnicity and Mobilization in Saami Politics. Stockholm: University of Stockholm, Department of Social Anthropology.

Svonni, Mikael. 1993. Samiska Skolbarnens Samiska. Stockholm: Almqvist & Wiksell.

Taylor, Timothy. 1997. Global Pop. New York: Routledge.

Valkeapää, H. 1995. Interview, 23 February.

Valkeapää, Nils-Aslak. 1969. Joikuja/jojk Fran Finska Lapland (accompanying notes to the recording) (Otava OY, OT-LP 50).

———. 1983. Greetings from Lappland. London: Zed Press.

———. 1992. Interview, 8 July.

Part IX

Social and Political Action

22

Cajun Music, Cultural Revival
Theorizing Political Action in Popular Music

Mark Mattern

Cajun music is music of the primarily white, francophone people living in southwest Louisiana.[1] Cajun music is distinct from zydeco music played by black Creoles living in southwest Louisiana. Although Cajun and zydeco music share many common elements, especially common French and African roots, they are distinct and should not be confused. The term "Cajun" is an Anglicized rendition of "Cadien," which is a shortened version of "Acadien," the French word for Acadian. Cajuns came to Louisiana after being expelled from the Acadian region of Nova Scotia for refusing to abandon their French culture, forswear Catholicism, and swear allegiance to the British crown. After years of dispersion and separation, during which time they faced francophobia and anti-Catholicism in their temporary homes in England and British Atlantic seaboard colonies, they were finally reunited after 1765 in Louisiana.

In Louisiana, due in part to hostility from Anglo politicians, most Cajuns were downwardly mobile, and eventually endured an ethnic stigma which portrayed them as "white trash." During the twentieth century, Cajuns were nearly swallowed up in mainstream Anglo culture as several factors combined to break their isolation and exert pressure toward their assimilation and Americanization. These factors included two world wars, which drew thousands of Cajuns into the armed services; nationalistic pressures wrought in part by the wars; the development of the oil industry, which lured many Cajuns out of traditional livelihoods of farming and fishing; radio and television, which introduced new ways of life into traditional Cajun culture; and explicit pressure from the Louisiana state legislature to abandon their French culture in favor of Anglo culture.[2] By the mid-twentieth century, these various factors of ethnic stigma, economic marginalization, and assimilation pressures drove Cajun culture to the brink of extinction.

Beginning in the 1960s, Cajun musicians initiated a cultural revival that would reverse years of assimilationist pressures, partly erase the ethnic stigma attached to Cajun identity, and contribute to economic vitality through tourism. In the late 1960s, when the Cajun Balfa Brothers began playing at folk festivals, most people had not heard of Cajuns or their music. By 1984, when Beausoleil first appeared on the *Prairie Home Companion* radio program, pockets of Cajun aficionados had appeared in cities far from the bayous of Louisiana. By the late 1980s, most people in the United States and Western Europe had directly experienced some form of Cajun culture, and many were on familiar terms with it. Threatened with extinction as recently as forty years ago, Cajun culture is now thriving. Cajun music has been one of the primary forces behind this cultural resurgence, giving Cajuns a focus for movements to recover pride in Cajun culture, to maintain the distinctiveness of Cajun culture while partially assimilating, and to undo years of social and political hostility against Cajuns in Louisiana.

In this article, I interpret Cajun music in terms of three distinct forms of political action. My primary goal is to widen the discussion of political action in popular music to include forms of political action that have received little attention from researchers of the politics of popular music. One of the characteristics of the literature linking popular music and politics is a tendency to emphasize one kind of political action, which I will call confrontational. This confrontational form of political action is marked by the language and practices of opposition, resistance, and struggle. While this literature offers many insights into the politics of popular music, a narrow emphasis on opposition, resistance, and struggle tends to obscure other forms of political action that are actually occurring in popular music. These other forms may at times represent better strategic choices for political actors, and may be inconsistent with confrontational political action.

In the first section of this article, I will discuss three main kinds of political action and briefly illustrate them with examples drawn from popular music. In addition to the confrontational practices of opposition, resistance, and struggle, I develop two other forms of political action that I call deliberative and pragmatic.[3] In a deliberative form of political action, people use popular music to debate their mutual identity and commitments, and negotiate relationships with others. In a pragmatic form of political action, people use popular music to organize for collaborative problem-solving. Each of these forms is distinct from the resistant and oppositional practices characteristic of confrontational forms of political action. I argue that deliberative and pragmatic forms of political action should be viewed as complementing, rather than replacing, oppositional and resistant forms of political action. Finally, I apply the three kinds of political action to Cajun music, and argue that Cajuns benefit from diverse political strategies.

Three Kinds of Political Action in Popular Music

Confrontational political action is typically cast in the language and practices of resistance, opposition, and struggle. Its major characteristics include heightened militancy, perception of incompatible interests, perception of zero-sum power relations and of zero-sum outcomes, and perception of relatively clear distinctions between the forces of right and wrong. One example of music that is usually cast in confrontational terms is protest music, in which musicians decry the injustices and oppression endured by certain individuals and groups and extol the virtues of favored alternatives. Typically, the intent of protest musicians is to oppose the exploitation and oppression exercised by dominant elites and members of dominant groups. Protest musicians typically couch their music in terms that draw sharp distinctions between the forces of right and wrong as they perceive them. They attempt to advance the cause of members of a favored group, who are typically portrayed in zero-sum opposition to members of one or more other groups, by promoting sympathy and support.[4]

Other examples of music cast in confrontational terms can be found in the work of researchers who rely, explicitly or implicitly, on a Gramscian-Marxist framework for interpretation of cultural politics. The work of Antonio Gramsci, an Italian Marxist writing in prison during the 1930s, has been widely used by researchers of cultural politics since its translation into English in 1971. In attempting to make sense of the apparent quiescence of the working class in Italy and internationally, an anomaly in Marxist theory, Gramsci turned to culture as an explanatory variable. He argued that dominant elites maintained control in part through ideological manipulation and control insinuated throughout culture. In part because of the penetration of bourgeois domination—in the form of beliefs and ideologies of everyday life—into culture, workers believe in the legitimacy of the system that oppresses them. Under circumstances of bourgeois political, economic, and ideological domination—or "hegemony"—Gramsci advocated a "war of position" in venues of everyday life including, potentially, popular music, to challenge dominant elites. Many scholars have subsequently used this framework to interpret cultural politics. Within this framework, popular music represents the legitimate expression of members of the subdominant group who resist and oppose oppression by members of the dominant group. It is viewed as a mouthpiece of "the people" and, as such, a communicative arena where group identity and allegiances are defined and cemented, and one of the sites where resistance and opposition occurs.[5]

A confrontational form of political action has a potentially positive role to play in a democratic politics as a way of enlisting support for the political agenda of a particular group, for publicizing a political issue, for drawing citizens into active participation in public life, and for galvanizing action on specific issues. While this confrontational form of political action can make a significant contribution to democratic politics, it is important to note that it is only one possibility among others. Several cautionary notes are in order regarding its potential overemphasis. First, it is important not to limit the strategic political options of popular musicians and others. Sometimes a strictly oppositional and resistant stance can produce beneficial outcomes. Opposition and resistance may be satisfying existentially and may appear to be the only reasonable options for political action in, for example, a context of extreme repression. However, an oppositional stance may also be unnecessarily fractious and counterproductive in alienating potential allies. In these cases, a more conciliatory approach might be more politically fruitful. An oppositional stance may also be doomed to failure when, for example, the choice is posed in either-or terms of winning outright over more powerful rivals. Political actors, especially those in subdominant positions, benefit from the availability of strategies of compromise, adaptation, accommodation, and negotiation of new, potentially democratic, relationships between dominant and subdominant groups.

Second, framing politics as a zero-sum struggle between two opposing forces may motivate the forced erasure of intragroup differences and struggles. In the interests of group solidarity and cohesiveness, viewed as strategically important in a zero-sum struggle with another group, internal differences of political belief and commitment may be viewed not as legitimate expressions of diversity, but simply as mistakes, the result of failure on the part of certain members to realize or acknowledge their true interests. In such a situation, dissident group members may be silenced by a majority or powerful minority. From the point of view of a researcher working within this confrontational framework, it may be tempting to interpret the role of these dissidents in overly simple terms of co-optation—the dissidents have been co-opted by the dominant group—or to drop them from the picture entirely.

Third, framing politics as a zero-sum struggle between two opposing groups may overlook the fluidity between groups. It sets up political relations in black and white terms that deny the presence of border zones between different groups.[6] These border zones represent social spaces between groups of overlapping identity and interest. These spaces may drop out of sight in an analysis couched exclusively in oppositional and resistant terms since they are gray spaces of overlapping, mixed, and dynamic identity and interest that cannot easily be cast in the black and white terms of right against wrong. Worse, they may be uncritically portrayed as the spaces occupied by people who are being co-opted or assimilated by the dominant group, or who are traitors to the cause. Although these charges may sometimes be true, at other times they are not.[7]

The presence of intragroup differences and disagreements, and of border zones between different groups, suggests that we sometimes adopt an interpretive and practical framework of negotiation, rather than an either-or struggle between opposing forces. This framework would emphasize some of the intragroup disagreements and differences over the appropriate stance to members of other groups, and also take better account of the fluidity between different groups. Popular music would be viewed in these cases as a site and a medium for disagreement and debate over both intragroup and intergroup identity and commitments. This takes shape in a *deliberative form of political action*, which occurs when members of a group use musical practices to debate their identity and commitments, or when members of different groups negotiate mutual relations. Although members of a group typically stand on at least some common ground, they likely also retain multiple differences of identity, interest, and commitment that sometimes emerge as disagreements and conflicts. Unless these are simply squelched, members must engage in the communicative interactions needed to adjust for differences, to negotiate potential compromises, to accommodate each other, and to find or create common ground for action on shared interests. For some people, music provides a communicative arena in which this debate and discussion can occur. Since music is both a reflection and a determinant of the identity and commitments of a group, debate and disagreement over group identity and commitments may appear in the world of music as well as in other communicative arenas.

It may be tempting to push this argument further and conclude that all music represents an ongoing deliberative form of political action. This conclusion would be mistaken. Unreflective, habitual reinforcement of individual and group identity and commitment, whether or not through musical practices, is not necessarily political. To deny this is to deny any meaningful distinction between social and political, private and public realms. While all social life is *potentially* political, it is not inherently so. Social life becomes political through disagreement, debate, and conflict, when unreflective, habitual reinforcement of identity and commitments is challenged.

Deliberation is a political process and a form of political action in its own right, as well as a necessary preliminary step in forging agreement on common interests and goals for action in other political arenas to address them. In other words, politics does not only occur *after* the formation of a group in various forms of political action where members of the group assert themselves collectively in various public arenas. The discovery, creation, and recreation of group characteristics is itself potentially a political process and a form of political action marked by disagreement and debate. It is potentially a form of public life in its own right. This form of political action is also applicable to relations between two or more different groups. Music potentially serves as a communicative arena in which members of different groups discuss and negotiate the terms of their mutual relations.

For example, different rap musicians express different, sometimes contradictory, messages and visions in their music. They express different beliefs, attitudes, and commitments, which both reflect existing African-American communities and, at the same time, offer competing visions of what African-American communities ought to be like. Both implicitly and explicitly, rap musicians debate these competing visions through their music as they respond to each other and to their audiences. Since music both reflects and partly determines identity, this debate presumably has at least some determining impact on the beliefs, attitudes, and commitments of members of different African-American communities. Taken together, such debates partly form the character and shape of the communities.

In her application of the concept of dialogism to female rap music, Tricia Rose (146–48, 182) approaches this interpretation. She argues that black women rappers are engaged in an "ongoing dialogue" with each other, with members of their audience, with black male rappers, with black men and women in general, and with dominant American cultural forms. Rose's dialogism resembles deliberation, but is different in that deliberation entails political disagreement and debate while dialogism may simply involve "multidirectional communication." Also, Rose places her dialogism within a larger framework of resistance and opposition, themes which dominate throughout her book. I want to ensure that deliberation stands alone as a distinctive, legitimate form of political action in its own right.

Both of the forms of political action that I have thus far considered—confrontational and deliberative—begin from a presumption of divergent interests. By contrast, the possibility of *pragmatic political action* begins from the premise of shared political interests. Pragmatic political action occurs when individuals and groups use music to promote awareness of shared interests and to organize collaborative efforts to address them. Pragmatic political action may involve efforts by members of a single group to identify and address shared concerns collaboratively, or it may involve attempts to tie together the concerns of different groups in order to build a collaborative effort spanning different groups. This form of political action is characterized by cooperative and collaborative efforts to engage in mutually beneficial problem-solving. It involves power sharing and the building of collaborative working relationships with other individuals and groups. This does not necessarily require mutual admiration or emotional bonding, but it does require mutual respect, meaning the acknowledgement of the validity of others' claims and a willingness to work constructively with others. Pragmatic problem-solving means that people share a common stake in solving a problem, that they identify that common stake, and that they discover or create the common bases for acting upon it. Examples of pragmatic political action in the world of music include megaconcerts such as *LiveAid* and *FarmAid*, which were produced to organize collaborative efforts to solve the problems of hunger and the destruction of the family farm respectively. Another example is Rock the Vote, a voter registration effort which recognizes that we have a mutual stake in increasing voter turnout, regardless of the voters' actual choices at the polls.

These three forms of political action, which potentially occur wherever music is produced and consumed, should not be viewed as mutually exclusive of each other. In practice, it is possible and likely that they will overlap. In other words, the same musical practice might reveal characteristics of more than one of the forms of political action. For example, a concert designed to organize collaborative efforts to solve world hunger might include musicians whose message is couched in highly oppositional, confrontational terms. Also, the different forms may complement each other. For example, deliberation over identity and commitments, in order to define common goals or strategies, may be a necessary prelude to both pragmatic and confrontational forms of political action.

Cajun Music and Political Action

Some might argue that the Cajun case can easily be explained entirely in terms of confrontational politics. This approach would portray Cajuns in terms of resistance and opposition to the oppression that they have experienced at the hands of British colonial administrators in Nova Scotia, to class oppression, and to dominant Anglo politicians in Louisiana. Cajuns would also be portrayed as resisting and opposing the dominant Anglo culture, and assimilation into it. This interpretation has many merits. Cajuns *have* experienced considerable oppression. They *do* face multiple assimilationist pressures. Many *are* economically marginal. In short, this characterization of the politics of Cajun music enables at least some analytical grip. However, there are good reasons to avoid casting an analysis entirely in terms of a confrontational form of political action. First, most Cajuns do not understand themselves in these confrontational terms and second, there are plentiful examples of pragmatic and deliberative uses of music for political action which supersede confrontation in importance among Cajuns.

Only in rare cases does the language of opposition and resistance surface in Cajun music or other communicative arenas, including speech, in Southwest Louisiana. Zachary Richard's "Réveille," which appeared during the early years of the Cajun revival, is one of those rare instances. This song, with its reference to the spilling of family blood, family destruction, and "goddamn British," reveals a more militant political orientation than the vast majority of Cajun lyrics, which emphasize themes of love and everyday mundane life. Another political statement slightly tinged with the sympathies characteristic of opposition and resistance appeared on the first longplay recording (Swallow Records 1977) of Beausoleil, a band named after Joseph Broussard *dit* Beausoleil, an Acadian who led Acadian resistance to the British and later led one of the expeditions to Louisiana. An inscription on the recording jacket expressed the band members' determination to connect their musical efforts to "the injustice of the British exile," and to use their music to resist the "eminent degeneration of Acadian culture." Most of the original lyrics composed during the revival and subsequently have stayed well away from these oppositional and resistant messages. More typical of the original lyrics during the period of cultural revival were some of Bruce Daigrepont's compositions, including "Two-step de Marksville," describing the founding of his family's hometown, and his "Disco and Fais Do-Do," in which he rues his loss of cultural and ethnic roots and affirms his rediscovery of the beauty and value of his culture. In other communicative arenas aside from musical lyrics, one occasionally finds language and practices characteristic of a confrontational form of political action. For example, musicians and cultural activists Marc and Anne Savoy both take militant stances with respect to preserving Cajun cultural heritage. According to Marc Savoy, "We've got to make war on these things that are undermining our wonderful Cajun culture" (Simoneaux 5B). Their Savoy Music Center is nicknamed "The Bunker," and a sign inside the store once stated that "I don't go to work; I go to war!" As with song lyrics, however, these militant, confrontational sentiments are relatively rare among most Cajuns.

Although most Cajuns do not typically view themselves in oppositional or resistant terms, this does not by itself disqualify an interpretation that emphasizes these elements. Analysts need not accept at face value the self-understandings of their subjects of investigation, which might be distorted or partial. However, such self-understandings should at least give pause to the researcher who wishes to explain the Cajun case in confrontational terms.

Perhaps the most serious objection to couching the Cajun case entirely in terms of opposition and resistance is that such an interpretation distracts attention from the more prominent forms of political action which actually appear among Cajuns, and which are at least partially inconsistent with a confrontational interpretation. While explicit examples of opposition and resistance are relatively rare, the prominence of both pragmatic and deliberative forms of political action is striking. Many examples of the collaborative problem-solving characteristic of a pragmatic politics can be identified. These typically involve collaboration among musicians, cultural boosters, civic groups and leaders, and various levels of government. Many also involve collaboration between Cajuns and Anglos. Each is based on the recognition of a set of problems to be solved—most notably cultural survival, ethnic stigma, and economic marginalization—through collaborative efforts among various individuals and groups. Some of the specific steps taken by Cajun musicians and others to address mutual problems and concerns include the organization of music concerts, festivals, workshops, and contests; the establishment of collaborative relationships with government agencies and units of government; and the development of educational and apprenticeship programs. Some of these efforts are described below.

During the mid-1960s, Cajun musicians such as Dewey Balfa and other cultural activists, in conjunction with the Louisiana Folk Foundation (formed in 1965 with help from the Newport Folk Festival Foundation), began sponsoring traditional music contests with cash prizes at local festivals such as the Abbeville Dairy Festival, the Opelousas Yambilee, and the Crowley Rice Festival. Additional money was committed to recording Cajun musicians. These steps encouraged musicians to dust off their instruments and begin playing publicly again. In 1974, these musicians and activists organized the First Tribute to Cajun Music,[8] later to become the popular *Festival de Musique Acadien*, which remains an annual event in Lafayette that routinely draws more than 40,000 music fans. In organizing this First Tribute, Dewey Balfa, Barry Ancelet, and other musicians and activists secured the support of the influential Louisiana politician James Domengeaux and the Louisiana Council for the Development of French in Louisiana (CODOFIL).

Apprentice programs were established to encourage younger Cajuns to embrace their culture and to reknit some of the frayed cultural connections between older and younger Cajuns.[9] Fiddle, accordion, ballad, and other musical workshops were established at local festivals. Dewey Balfa won a "Folk Artists in the Schools" grant in 1977 from the National Endowment for the Arts, the Southern Folk Revival Project, and the Acadiana Arts Council in order to present discussions and demonstrations about Cajun music in classrooms in Southwest Louisiana. Led by activists such as Dewey Balfa, Barry Ancelet, and Michael Doucet, Cajun music continued to increase in visibility and popularity at local, national, and international levels. The process of diffusion of Cajun music was facilitated by increased touring of Cajun musicians. As Cajun music acquired a national and international audience, Cajun musicians and groups began to receive regular invitations to play at preeminent American cultural venues such as Carnegie Hall in New York, at presidential inaugurals, and at other prestigious events locally, nationally, and internationally. In 1982, Dewey Balfa became one of the first recipients of the National Heritage Fellowships, sponsored by the National Endowment for the Arts (NEA) Folk Arts Program. The revival solidified its national prominence with Beausoleil's 1984 appearance on American Public Radio's *Prairie Home Companion*. Two years later, the 1986 Grammy nominations in the folk and ethnic category were swept by Louisiana musicians including Beausoleil and Dewey Balfa.[10] This national and international acclaim brought local fame to the musicians, making them "cultural heroes" (Ancelet, "Dewey" 83). This proved to be of great importance in rekindling interest in Cajun music and culture in younger generations, and in encouraging younger people to begin playing Cajun music.

Another prominent illustration of the collaborative attempts to promote cultural vitality is the *Rendez-vous des Cajuns*, a Grand Ole Opry-like program established in the late 1980s by local activists, the city of Eunice, and the Jean Lafitte National Historical Park and Preserve of the U.S. Department of the Interior. The Rendez-vous, broadcast live over several radio stations in Southwest Louisiana, is frequently hailed as a Cajun version of Garrison Keillor's *Prairie Home Companion*. The *Rendez-vous* provides both entertainment and education. Other types of governmental support for Cajun music and culture include occasional sponsorship of Cajun recordings, funding for heritage centers and theme parks which showcase Cajun and black Creole music, and various policies and resolutions designed to promote Cajun tourism. Cajun music and culture are also supported by civic organizations such as the Lafayette Chamber of Commerce, which sponsors or cosponsors events such as the *Festival de Musique Acadienne* and Downtown Alive![11] and local industry, which helps fund and promote cultural projects such as the Lafayette heritage theme parks. The motivation of these governmental, civic, and industrial organizations is economic as well as cultural, as they seek ways to increase both economic and cultural vitality.

Each of these examples illustrates a pragmatic attempt to forge collaborative relationships, many of them between Cajuns and dominant Anglo cultural, political, and economic institutions. The examples provide evidence, much of it inconsistent with a strictly confrontational analysis, of a flexible, pragmatic orientation among Cajuns and a willingness to work with, rather than against, Anglo individuals and institutions. Most Cajuns shun confrontational struggles with non-Cajuns, preferring instead to develop collaborative and accommodating relationships, characterized by power-sharing and cooperation, that yield mutual gain.

A deliberative form of political action can also be identified that, like a pragmatic politics, at least partly undermines a generalized confrontational analysis. Cajun culture, like other relatively marginalized cultures, faces multiple assimilationist pressures. Some Cajuns fear that change within Cajun culture represents assimilation at work. They seek to preserve elements of a traditional Cajun culture, and object to the introduction of certain new elements. They believe, first of all, that a traditional, authentic Cajun culture can be identified and, secondly, that it should be maintained more or less as it is. Implicit in this view is the fear that cultural change means assimilation or even cultural death. On the other hand, some argue that Cajun culture has long survived by adapting to and accommodating its social and cultural environment, and by incorporating new elements which increase its resiliency and vitality. For them, change is not simply a reality, it is a necessity for survival. This disagreement is debated implicitly and explicitly through musical practices.

Among the preservationists are prominent musicians such as Marc Savoy, Anne Savoy, and "Nonc" Jules Guidry and organizations such as *L'Association de Musique Cadien Francaise de Louisiane*, or Cajun French Music Association (CFMA). These individuals and groups deny the validity of significant cultural change, believing that "we have to make sure that when the next generation comes along, we can give [Cajun culture] to them as it was when we got it" (Marc Savoy, qtd in Simoneaux 5B). The CFMA, which by 1993 boasted eight chapters in Southwest Louisiana and East Texas, and approximately 2,000 member families, sponsors Cajun musical events such as dances, festivals, and contests; organizes local dance troupes and dance contests; provides for French language and dance lessons; and sponsors a variety of social events such as potlucks, family nights, and bus trips. It promotes a basically preservationist and traditionalist agenda by, for example, considering only traditional musicians who sing in French and include a fiddle for their *Le Cajun* awards, and allowing members of its performing dance troupes to perform only dances deemed traditional.[12]

On the side of cultural change and adaptation are musicians and others who believe that change *is* the very tradition of Cajun music. According to them, Cajun music "is very much an ongoing process. It's constantly changing, being reinvented and redefined by people who play it, in response to people who listen and dance to it. It's a process rather than a product. The change is a sign of its life" (Barry Ancelet, qtd. in Simoneaux 5B). This argument is correct in that Cajuns have long created their culture by adapting to and absorbing other cultural influences, and this is nowhere more evident than in the world of Cajun music. Historically, Cajun musicians have borrowed, adapted, and absorbed many different cultural influences. Cajun music is a "gumbo" assembled from elements as disparate as French folk music, American Indian chants, West Indies work songs, New Orleans jazz, Texas swing, bluegrass, country and western, Spanish guitar music, Anglo folk songs, '50s rock and roll, field hollers, and pop music.[13] Of course, the controversial question is how far can this assembling of diverse experiences and sounds go and still produce music which can be called Cajun? Preservationists decry the ongoing experimentation in Cajun music as straying too far from authentic Cajun sounds. Implicit in their stance is the presumption that a traditional, authentic Cajun music and, by extension, culture can be successfully identified in the first place. However, even the music of Cajun musicians viewed as traditional, for example Marc Savoy and Dewey Balfa, marks an assemblage of many different influences drawn from different sources in an ongoing historical trajectory. If this is true, the difficulty of identifying a traditional, authentic sound looms larger than preservationists appear willing to admit. Yet, of course not just any sound can be labeled Cajun.

Cajuns clearly do not agree on how much innovation is appropriate nor, by extension, what *is* Cajun music and Cajun culture. Their music gives them a forum for arguing among themselves over these questions. Music provides people of southwest Louisiana with a communicative forum through which these questions of cultural survival and adaptation can be posed and alternative answers explored. Cajun music both goads debate in other arenas about issues of cultural preservation and change and represents a communicative forum in its own right through which Cajuns implicitly and explicitly consider these issues. Of course, music is only one social and communicative forum among others, but for Cajuns it is a prominent one. The Cajun music revival, which was frequently discussed and debated in southwest Louisiana in many arenas ranging from newspapers to informal dinner table conversations, encouraged in many Cajuns an awareness of issues of cultural preservation and change.

Like the pragmatic forms of political action identified earlier, the presence of this deliberative form of political action should discourage simplistic and generalized portrayals of Cajuns as resisting Anglo domination and exploitation. Although it makes at least some sense to portray the preservationists in confrontational terms as resisting and opposing change and cultural assimilation, we should be wary of generalizing this interpretation. Most Cajuns, preservationists included, live comfortably in both francophone and Anglo worlds. More profoundly, contemporary Cajun identity includes a significant Anglo component, as Cajuns selectively adopt some of the beliefs and practices that characterize Anglo culture and identity. It thus makes little sense to argue that Cajuns are opposing or resisting Anglo culture, since this would imply that they are at least partly at war with themselves. Also, a strictly confrontational strategy implies a clear demarcation between Cajuns and others. As the above analysis should indicate, no such clear distinction can be identified. Instead, the line between Cajuns and others is blurred, and boundaries between Cajun and non-Cajun are porous. This considerably muddies the waters of a confrontational analysis, since it makes clear identification of right and wrong more difficult, and undermines the sensibility of an analysis that emphasizes a zero-sum struggle between two opposing forces.

Finally, Cajun survival into the future requires diverse political strategies. While confrontational strategies may prove beneficial in some ways and at some times, Cajuns also benefit from other political strategies. The benefits accruing to Cajuns from pursuing collaborative strategies have been noted above, and are substantial. Cajuns seek collaboration with Anglos and others because they benefit from collaboration in monetary and political terms. A confrontational strategy would potentially result in the loss of these benefits. Having an arena for deliberation nurtures a critical awareness among Cajuns of important issues that affect them, and stimulates debate and public life in general. These collaborative strategies, and other strategies of accommodation, adaptation, and compromise are precisely the ingredients of cultural resilience. As Ancelet says, "Cajuns are constantly adapting their culture to survive in the modern world. Such change, however, is not necessarily a sign of decay, as was first thought; it may even be a sign of vitality" (Ancelet, "Introduction," *Cajun Country* xviii). For Cajuns, much of their adaptability and resilience is tied to musical practices which allow them to explore new options for adaptation without disappearing as Cajuns.

How much accommodation, adaptation, and change can Cajun culture experience and still remain distinctively and recognizably Cajun? The question is inaptly posed as a mutually exclusive choice between preservation and change. The better question is *how much* change is appropriate in order to keep a culture vital and resilient without tearing the culture from its historical moorings? The answer to this question is unclear. What is clear, however, is that Cajuns are still around to debate this issue in part because of their music and the different forms of political action that their music enables.

Notes

1. This article is adapted from two chapters of Mattern, *Acting in Concert: Music, Community and Political Action.* Some of the information contained in this article is taken from interviews conducted in 1993 with Barry Ancelet, Pete Bergeron, Joe Bodi, Carl Brasseaux, Earline Broussard, Glenn Conrad, Wayne Parent, and Pat Rickels. I would like to thank these individuals for their assistance.
2. For example, in 1916 the Louisiana state legislature mandated that only English could be used in state schools. See Brasseaux (*Founding; Scattered;* and *Acadian*) for a history of Cajun people. See Ancelet (*Makers; Cajun;* and "Introduction") for a history of Cajun music.
3. These three forms of political action through music are more extensively developed in Mattern. They are partially adapted from Harry Boyte, who uses the categories of deliberative, pragmatic, and insurgent (or protest). I call the third category confrontational rather than insurgent or protest in order to better cluster together a genre of political action which includes struggle, opposition, and resistance as well as protest.
4. See John Greenway, Jerome Rodnitzky, and Jeffery Mondak on protest music.
5. See Gramsci's *Selections from the Prison Notebooks.* See Tim Patterson and Manuel Pena for explicit applications of Gramsci to popular music—country-and-western and Texas-Mexican *conjunto* music, respectively. See also George Lewis for an interpretation of Hawaiian popular music which is less explicitly indebted to Gramsci but couched in similar terms. For other examples of literature, much of it indebted to Gramsci, which emphasizes the resistant and oppositional nature of musical practices, see Horace Campbell, Dick Hebdige, and Patrick Hylton on calypso and reggae music; Charles Keil on African TIV music; Peter Manuel on Andalusian gypsy music; Ray Pratt on several forms of popular music; Tricia Rose on rap music; and Kilza Setti on Brazilian Caicara music.
6. See Renato Rosaldo for a discussion of border zones. See also Gloria Anzaldua's *Borderlands.*
7. See Patterson and Pena for two examples of analyses which rely heavily on a "co-optation" thesis. In their analyses, early country-and-western and *tejano* musicians, respectively, were co-opted by external forces such as the recording industry and the dominant Anglo culture. See Lewis for an analysis which treats nonresistant Hawaiian popular musicians as traitors for participating in the tourist industry.
8. Despite its somewhat misleading title, this First Tribute included black Creole musicians as well as Cajun musicians. It occurred on March 26, 1974, at Blackham Coliseum in Lafayette. The 8,000 seats inside were full, and 4,000 more people listened outside in a torrential rain.

9. For example, Nathan Abshire took on several accordion apprentices, while Michael Doucet apprenticed himself to several of the most prominent Cajun fiddlers still alive. Marc Savoy, at 32 years of age, was the youngest musician featured at the First Tribute. By 1978, the Tribute to Cajun Music, which had become an annual event, included eight (out of the total twenty-two) groups whose musicians were entirely under the age of thirty, while two of the groups were composed entirely of musicians under the age of twenty.

10. The other nominees were black Creoles including Clifton Chenier, Stanley "Buckwheat Zydeco" Dural, and Rockin' Sidney (Sidney Simien). Rockin' Sidney ultimately won with his "Don't Mess with My Toot-Toot."

11. Downtown Alive! occurs in downtown Lafayette each Friday after working hours in an attempt to maintain the vitality of downtown Lafayette by encouraging people to stay downtown and patronize the downtown bars, clubs, and restaurants. For this weekly event, an intersection is blocked off for live music and dancing. Downtown Alive! is sometimes complemented by Kids Alive! with performers such as the Children's Cajun Band.

12. In one controversial decision, CFMA banned the use of the popular Cajun jitterbug by its dance performers on the grounds that it is not traditional. CFMA is correct in that the Cajun jitterbug is a relative newcomer to Cajun culture. It was invented within the last thirty years by non-Cajun folkdancers from New Orleans who regularly drove to Mulate's Restaurant in Breaux Bridge near Lafayette to dine and dance to Cajun music. The dance caught on among Cajuns as well as non-Cajuns, and now it is called the Cajun jitterbug. CFMA's position on this is vulnerable to criticism since, if one examines the history of Cajun dance, it becomes apparent that dance forms have been regularly, if not frequently, transformed, added, and dropped and that any attempt to define a "traditional" Cajun dance form requires a dubious assertion of preeminence for a particular time period. As recently as the late nineteenth century, Cajuns danced quadrilles, minuets, waltzes, polkas, and mazurkas. Of these, only the waltz survived into contemporary use. The Cajun two-step was added later, probably imported from Texas during the Texas swing era in the early twentieth century.

13. This diversity of musical influences appears in the work of individual Cajun musicians such as fiddler Dewey Balfa, contemporary innovator Wayne Toups, Beausoleil's Michael Doucet, and Zachary Richard, each of whom cites a variety of influences coming together in his work. Balfa cites Bob Wills of Texas Playboys fame as one of his primary influences (see Ancelet, "Dewey" 79). The music of Wayne Toups is described as "a sound infused with good, healthy doses of traditional Cajun a la Iry Lejeune, overlaid with upbeat jazz rhythms, country and a touch of rock" (Booth 42). The style of Beausoleil's Michael Doucet has been described as a blend of "vast historic knowledge with aggressive eclecticism and brilliant technique. Doucet has played rock, and he understands avante-garde jazz. Such wild influences are amply evident in his daring rhythmic/harmonic forays" (Sandmel). Zachary Richard says of his music that it is "a holy trinity mix of Cajun, Zydeco, and New Orleans rhythm and blues cooked in a rock-n-roll pot" (Simon A-13).

References

Ancelet, Barry Jean. 1989. *Cajun Music: Its Origins and Development*. Lafayette, LA: Center for Louisiana Studies, University of Southwestern Louisiana.

———. 1981. "Dewey Balfa: Cajun Music Ambassador." *Louisiana Life*, 83.

———. 1991. "Introduction." *Cajun Country*, edited by Barry Ancelet, Jay Edwards, and Glen Pitre, xiii–xxiv. Jackson: University Press of Mississippi.

———. 1992. "Introduction." *Cajun Music and Zydeco*. Ed. Philip Gould. Baton Rouge: Louisiana State University, ix–xxi.

———. 1984. *The Makers of Cajun Music*. Austin: U of Texas P.

Anzaldua, Gloria. 1987. *Borderlands*. San Francisco: Spinsters/Aunt Lute.

Booth, Karen. 1985. "An Affair of the Heart." *The Times of Acadiana* 12 Dec., 42.

Boyte, Harry. 1991. "The Pragmatic Ends of Popular Politics." *Habermas and the Public Sphere*, edited by Craig Calhoun, 340–55. Boston: MIT Press.

Brasseaux, Carl. 1992. *Acadian to Cajun: Transformation of a People, 1803–1877*. Jackson: University Press of Mississippi.

———. 1987. *The Founding of New Acadia: The Beginning of Acadian Life in Louisiana 1765–1803*. Baton Rouge: Louisiana State University.

———. 1991. *Scattered to the Wind: Dispersal and Wanderings of the Acadians, 1755–1809*. Lafayette, LA: Center for Louisiana Studies, University of Southwestern Louisiana.

Campbell, Horace. 1987. *Rasta and Resistance*. Trenton, NJ: Africa World.

Gramsci, Antonio. 1971. *Selections from the Prison Notebooks*. Ed. Quintin Hoare and Geoffrey Nowell Smith. New York: International Publishers.

Greenway, John. 1977. *American Folksongs of Protest*. New York: Octagon.

Hebdige, Dick. 1987. *Cut-n-Mix: Culture, Identity, and Caribbean Music*. London: Methuen.

Hylton, Patrick. 1975. "The Politics of Caribbean Music." *The Black Scholar*: 23–29.

Keil, Charles. 1979. *TIV Song: The Sociology of Art in a Classless Society*. Chicago: University of Chicago.

Lewis, George. 1991. "Storm Blowing from Paradise: Social Protest and Oppositional Ideology in Popular Hawaiian Music." *Popular Music* 10(1):53–67.

Manuel, Peter. 1989. "Andalusian, Gypsy, and Class Identity in the Contemporary Flamenco Complex." *Ethnomusicology* 33(1):47–65.

Mattern, Mark. 1998. *Acting in Concert: Music, Community and Political Action*. New Brunswick: Rutgers University.

Mondak, Jeffery. 1988. "Protest Music As Political Persuasion." *Popular Music and Society* 12(3):25–38.

Patterson, Tim. 1975. "Notes on the Historical Application of Marxist Cultural Theory." *Science and Society* 34:257–91.

Peña, Manuel. 1985. *The Texas-Mexican Conjunto: History of a Working Class Music*. Austin: University of Texas.

Pratt, Ray. 1990. *Rhythm and Resistance: Explorations in the Political Uses of Popular Music*. New York: Praeger.

Rodnitzky, Jerome. 1976. *Minstrels of the Dawn: The Folk-Protest Singer as a Cultural Hero.* Chicago: Nelson-Hall.

Rosaldo, Renato. 1988. "Ideology, Place, and People without Culture." *Cultural Anthropology* 3(1):77–87.

Rose, Tricia. 1994. *Black Noise: Rap Music and Black Culture in Contemporary America.* Hanover, NH: Wesleyan University.

Sandmel, Ben. 1984. Jacket notes. Michael Doucet with Beausoleil. Parlez-nous a Boire. Berkeley: Arhoolie 5034.

Setti, Kilza. 1988. "Notes on Caicara Musical Production: Music as the Focus of Cultural Resistance among the Fisherman of the Coastal Region of Sao Paulo." *The World of Music: Bulletin of the International Music Council* 30(2):3–21.

Simon, Dixie. 1993. "Zachary Richard Comes Home to Scott." *Advertiser* 14 Feb.:A-13.

Simoneaux, Angela. 1992. "Growth, Not Change, Is Seen as Key to Preserving Traditional Cajun Music." *Sunday Advocate* 22 Mar.:5B.

Discography

Beausoleil. 1977. *The Spirit of Cajun Music.* Swallow, 6031.

Daigrepont, Bruce. 1981. *Stir Up the Roux.* Rounder, 6016.

Michael Doucet with Beausoleil. 1984. Arhoolie, 5025.

Richard, Zachary. 1974. *Mardi Gras.* RZ, 1005.

23

Nitmiluk
Place, Politics and Empowerment in Australian Aboriginal Popular Music

Chris Gibson and Peter Dunbar-Hall

Introduction

The word "Nitmiluk" signifies, in physical space, a series of spectacular gorges and chasms which stretch for 12 kilometers down the Katherine River in Australia's Northern Territory, approximately 30 kilometers north of the present town of Katherine (see Figures 23.1 and 23.2).[1] As a symbolic feature in the natural landscape, Nitmiluk also reflects divergent histories of conquest, colonialism, and more recently, indigenous rights struggles. For the Jawoyn people who are traditional owners of Nitmiluk, it continues to form a nexus of cultural and spiritual practices, and has become central to political strategies towards self-determination and economic independence from Australian governments. The traditional country of the Jawoyn surrounds the series of sites known collectively as Nitmiluk, and covers a vast expanse of what is now known as the Top End of the Northern Territory. More recently, as the Jawoyn develop models of community management for their lands, the sites delineated by tribal boundaries have become known collectively as the Jawoyn *nation*.

In this article, we provide a reading of Nitmiluk, as a physical site central to the process of an indigenous (re)construction of post-colonial space. This involves situating Nitmiluk as the point of intersection of several threads of cultural and political discourse. First, we outline the project to re-claim and re-inscribe Aboriginal spatial identities after colonial experiences of appropriation and contempt, as read through the expressions of indigenous musical recordings, in particular the text of an Aboriginal rock song, "Nitmiluk," by the group Blekbala Mujik. Second, we examine the reflection of this cultural discourse in the current activities of the Jawoyn's representative organization, which has sought to assert its own presence in the Katherine region of the Northern Territory, and achieve a resolution to the competing claims of indigenous and non-indigenous jurisdictions. In this sense, we hope to point to the importance of popular musical expression as mediator of political and geographical conflict, and as an accessible tool of education, communication and identity construction.

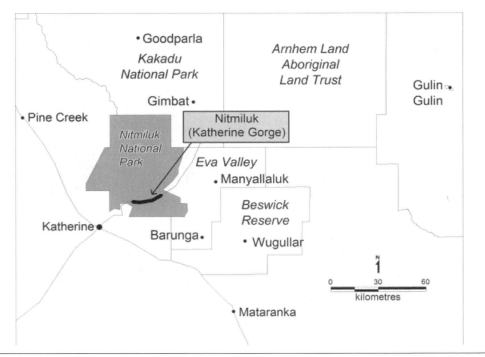

Figure 23.1 Map of Jawoyn traditional lands.

Nitmiluk and Colonialism

Nitmiluk was, and continues to be, a central component of Jawoyn tradition and "law"—a sovereignty delineated over land through complex and holistic systems of responsibility and social organization for at least an estimated 50,000 years prior to European invasion in 1788.[2] In Jawoyn mythology, creation beings including the Bolong (Rainbow Serpent) and Barraya (Kookaburra) have continuously occupied the gorges that make up Nitmiluk, inscribing the country with physical features, social responsibilities, and cultural meaning since the period known as Burr (roughly translated as "the Dreaming").[3] The Jawoyn naming of the gorge (and many other sites throughout the area) is attributed to a particular Burr-figure, Nabilil, who "camped at the entrance to the Katherine Gorge where he heard the song of the cicada (*Nitmi* in Jawoyn language) and called this place Nitmiluk" (Jawoyn Association 1993a, 5). Traditional songs and dances that communicate these stories continue to be practiced as part of Jawoyn oral culture—as exercises in naming and owning. More recently, this same musical practice of naming and owning a site in a song has re-surfaced in Aboriginal rock music. Blekbala Mujik's "Nitmiluk" can be interpreted in this way.

The spectacular geomorphological features of Nitmiluk did not escape the colonizing gaze of non-indigenous settlers and authorities during the twentieth century. The expansion of pastoralism, and the explosion of mining activities that followed the discovery of gold at Pine Creek during the construction of the Overland Telegraph Line in 1872, had tragic consequences for Aboriginal groups throughout the Northern Territory, including the Jawoyn. Jawoyn indigenous sovereignty over traditional territory was disregarded in the often violent process of asserting European sovereignty over land. Jawoyn people no longer had free access and mobility over their country, pastoral stock polluted water sources, and traditional lands became populated by strangers. Jawoyn people were, by the turn of the century, "experiencing the violence and culture shock of colonization" (Jawoyn Association 1993a, 9).

Figure 23.2 Photograph of Nitmiluk.

Colonial histories documented by non-indigenous writers even as recently as the 1980s reflect the denial of the Jawoyn and other local indigenous voices, consequently mapping physical sites for the purpose of legitimizing English rule. According to Forrest (1985:6), in his glaringly one-sided trajectory of pastoral expansion in the Katherine region, "the survey, construction, and operation of the telegraph line *brought people to* the Territory. Alfred Giles, pioneer of Springvale, *was one of the first*" (emphasis added). The conspicuous absence of local indigenous peoples from these narratives, and from the maps that served to legitimate colonial rule at the time, stems from the naming practices of frontier settlers and planners. Sites such as Nitmiluk, and Wurliwurliyn-jang (now covered by the Katherine Town Council chambers) were overwritten with European names—some gentile, others regimented: Wurliwurliyn-jang became contained within the town known as "the Katherine" or "Kathrhyne,"[4] with its militaristic parallel streets ("First Street," "Second Street," "Third Street," and so on), whilst Nitmiluk became "Katherine Gorge" (see Figure 23.3).

The early colonial experience at and around Nitmiluk demonstrates the centrality of naming and mapping practices in acts of dispossession, in perpetuating the "terra nullius" philosophy which underwrote British sovereignty over Australia; rendering landscapes "empty" of competing indigenous meaning (cf. Jacobs 1993; Ferrier 1990; Harley 1988; Huggan 1989).

More recently, Nitmiluk has been central to attempts by indigenous people to re-claim these colonized spaces within wider Australian arenas (both cultural and legal). This includes the part it has played in explicitly geopolitical strategies to re-claim land tenure within Australian land rights mechanisms (the Jawoyn [Katherine Area] Land Claim), formal projects to build indigenous employment and training opportunities (through the Jawoyn Association), and its figurative/symbolic role within more qualitative cultural expressions of local artists and performers, notably musicians such as Blekbala Mujik.

In this context, popular music, alongside other media such as art, dance, and literature, forms a site of expression and empowerment. These expressions are related to debates that currently dominate conventional political arenas, and which intersect with wider Australian institutions, polities, and audiences in complex ways. Perhaps more effectively than formal political avenues, indigenous musicians are able to promote mainstream engagement with themes of indigeneity as

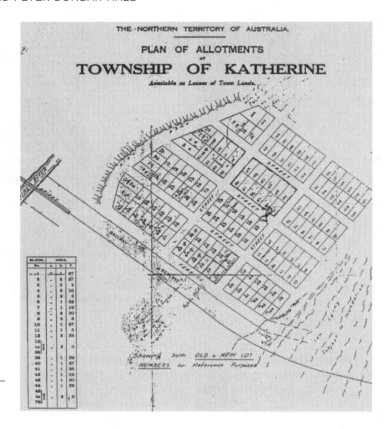

Figure 23.3 Colonial map of Katherine.

part of holistic cross-cultural strategies. As Blekbala Mujik's principal singer/songwriter Apaak Jupurrula argues:

> Music is perhaps one of the few positive ways to communicate a message to the wider community. Take, for example, politicians. They address an issue but people will only listen if they share those particular political views. Music has universal appeal. Even if you have your critics, people will still give you a hearing (quoted in McCabe, 1996).

The sites of expression constructed through music (and their fields of interpreted meaning) remain fluid, sensitive to shifts in government policy (such as the current federal government's turn towards limiting, rather than extending, recognition of indigenous rights) and the wider atmosphere of Australian race relations. In this sense, music also provides a sphere in which wider issues of social and political change can be understood. Indeed, music not only reflects political and cultural shifts, but is bound up in the processes through which these shifts occur and in the ways in which communities perceive and construct place (Feld and Basso 1996; Leyshon et al. 1995; Kong 1995; Lipsitz 1994). Indigenous organizations such as the Jawoyn Association continue to provide challenges to the geography of the nation-state with demands for new, fluid spaces of co-existence, such as on National Park land and pastoral lease-holdings. As this occurs, indigenous popular musicians (and other artists) are becoming increasingly important mediators in the surrounding national "mediascape," writing and singing about "Aboriginal methods for melding the disparate worlds of Aboriginal and non-Aboriginal Australians" (Neuenfeldt 1993:1; cf. Appadurai 1990; see Langton 1993 and Michaels 1994 for an examination of indigenous interventions in the production of television and video footage about and by indigenous communities).

The socio-political concerns of these song writers and performers are articulated in ways which symbolically reclaim space; inscribe markers of indigeneity upon a popular cultural landscape; and delineate empowerment strategies. In the same way, the cultural expressions of Aboriginal identity and place within Blekbala Mujik's songs are reflected materially in the strategies and practices of the Jawoyn Association. Indeed, the song "Nitmiluk" was first performed in public on September 10, 1989, at the hand-back ceremony of the site to its traditional owners, as a commemoration of the Jawoyn's successful land rights claim. By examining "Nitmiluk" as a musical text, we can begin to understand ways in which an indigenous rock group has transferred traditional Aboriginal ways of expressing history and geography (that is, orally, through song) into a contemporary music genre. In this way, Blekbala Mujik has mobilized diverse strategies to signify, re-map, and gain influence over, traditional country.

Blekbala Mujik's "Nitmiluk"

Blekbala Mujik, from the Jawoyn communities of Gulin Gulin and Barunga in the Northern Territory, is one of a number of Aboriginal rock groups to achieve success in the last decade, a period of marked increase in the recognition accorded to Aboriginal performers, artists, and writers. The reasons for this increase in recognition are numerous and varied, among them government and media policies, the availability of recorded, film and print materials by and about Aborigines, the influence of post-colonial ideologies, and the activities of media organizations which specialize in the recording and distribution of indigenous music. Chief among these is the Central Australian Aboriginal Media Association (CAAMA) based in Alice Springs (NT), the company responsible for Blekbala Mujik's recordings. Thus, institutional structures have been central to the growing success of indigenous musicians in Australia (for detail on industry structures in this context, see Lawe-Davies, 1993; Gibson, 1998).

In a similar manner to that employed by other Aboriginal rock groups, Blekbala Mujik combine elements of traditional and contemporary musical styles, incorporate multilingualism in the texts of their songs, and consciously use traditional music to raise awareness about Aboriginal cultures. As Apaak Jupurrula states: "We enjoy different feels, different genres. . . . What I do as a songwriter is base new works around what we already have in the way of traditional music. I tend to build around that and we come up with new ideas" (quoted in Smith, 1996, n.p.). He also discusses proactive uses of music to communicate aspects of his traditional background: ". . . we want to provide some kind of information to the audience that we are strong within our cultural beliefs, that we still maintain our traditional ideology and understanding of a world view, and we would like to share that with the public" (ibid.).

More generally, Aboriginal rock music is diffuse and difficult to discuss as an entity. Like any music it is multifaceted and reflects the diversity of the cultures in which it originates. Despite this, some writers identify trends in its aesthetic stance. Chief among these, and in line with interpretations of indigenous rock music from countries such as America, Canada, and New Zealand (see Broughton et al. 1994; Cohen 1996), is the use of music for protest (for example, Breen 1994). In particular, Aboriginal rock bands have been associated with the land rights movement that has accelerated since the 1970s. This can be heard in music by groups such as Coloured Stone, No Fixed Address, Mixed Relations, and Sunrize Band. Such a view, however, ignores more prevalent uses of music by Aboriginal rock musicians, among them: for educating the broader listening public about Aboriginal cultures, agendas and demands (Yunupingu 1990); acting as an expression of localized Aboriginalities (Stubington and Dunbar-Hall 1994); recording and reviving Aboriginal languages under threat of extinction (National Board of Employment, Education and Training 1996); in public awareness campaigns in Aboriginal communities, especially on matters such as AIDS, alcohol abuse and petrol sniffing (Dunbar-Hall 1996); and in public celebrations of events in Aboriginal life. Ostensibly it is as the last of these that "Nitmiluk" can be understood. This is made explicit in a CAAMA press release about the song's creators: "Nitmiluk...is the traditional place name for Katherine Gorge National Park, handed back to the Jawoyn people in September 1989...the band were asked by the owners to write some music for the hand-back" (CAAMA n.d., 2).

The writing of the song involved a particular set of cultural practices in the buildup to the hand-back of Nitmiluk to traditional owners. Accompanied by senior Jawoyn elders, members of the group camped in the area for two weeks, learning about the role of Nitmiluk in local law/lore and surviving on bush tucker foods. At a crucial point in this process, the song emerged, in ways resonant of the creative processes apparent in music considered "traditional" (Ellis 1985). As explained by Apaak Jupurrula: "We slept on that earth and it protected us. Our lifestyle revolved around that place and old people came telling us of its importance. One night we were strumming around the camp fire and the song and words came from the wind into our collective mind" (CAAMA, n.d, 2). As this quote suggests, there is more to the song than commemoration of the hand-back of land to its owners, as a study of the musical and textual profiles of this song reveals. In the reading presented here, the song is interpreted through references to land and identity, and linked to this, agendas of Jawoyn cultural revival and self-determination.

Recognition for Blekbala Mujik (Kriol for "blackfella music") has come from a number of sources. These include the 1996 *Deadly Sounds* Album of the Year (at an award ceremony dedicated to indigenous performers), nomination for an Australian Record Industry Association (ARIA) award, extensive touring within Australia and internationally, and the use of their song "Walking Together" as the signature tune of the Australian Council for Aboriginal Reconciliation. To date, this group has issued five albums: *Nitmiluk!* (1990), *Midnait Mujik* (1990), *Come-n-Dance* (1993), the self-titled *Blekbala Mujik* (1995), and *Walking Together* (1995). These releases have received wide critical acclaim in a popular music climate that up until recently ignored Aboriginal performers. Their music is variously described as "an exuberant concoction" (Eliezer 1996); "catchy, airplay friendly Aboriginal pop;" "decidedly deadly Arnhem grooves" (Jordan 1995:90); while the group has "musical sophistication, diversity and innovation which pushes them beyond the usual recipes of Aboriginal reggae, Aboriginal country and Aboriginal rock" (Elder 1995).

As a repertoire, the songs on these albums address topics pertinent both to aspects of Australian pan-Aboriginality (for example, Aboriginal identity in general) and to local communities of the Jawoyn speaking area (for example, songs about local events). In its music and text, "Nitmiluk" reflects this ability to signify on different levels of Aboriginality, exhibiting characteristics common to the music of numerous Aboriginal rock groups across Australia, as well as some specific to Jawoyn culture. It is through the second of these contexts, music that can be analyzed as Jawoyn, that the role of a rock song as an expression of current agendas and activities of cultural revival can be understood.

As an example of Aboriginal rock music in the widest sense, "Nitmiluk" employs the integration of two types of music in an overall three-part structure: an opening traditional section of west Arnhem Land song with didjeridu and clapsticks accompaniment gives way to a rock section, performed with electrified guitars and drumkit. This rock section is followed by the return of the opening traditional section. The traditional sections of "Nitmiluk" can be identified as "White Cockatoo" by the appearance of that song as the track immediately preceding "Nitmiluk" on the album *Nitmiluk!* The readily identifiable musical differences between traditional and rock sections of the song are further delineated by the use of different languages for each: the traditional sections are sung in a local Aboriginal language, the rock section in English. Such multilingualism, a facet of Aboriginal life, is not uncommon in Aboriginal song and can be observed in the music of numerous Aboriginal rock groups.

This diachronic use of two styles of music, a feature of music by Aboriginal rock groups such as Yothu Yindi (see Stubington and Dunbar-Hall 1994) occurs alongside a synchronic use when the descending melody of the framing traditional sections is heard as the basis of the melody of the rock section (Musical Examples 23.1 and 23.2).

Music Example 23.1 Melody of traditional sections.

In the be-gin - ning _ There was no-thing on this land ____

Music Example 23.2 Opening melody of rock section.

Music Example 23.3 Country style guitar lick, rock section, "Nitmiluk," by Peter Miller. Used by kind permission of PolyGram Music Publishing Australia Pty. Ltd.

In common with a large proportion of Aboriginal rock music (see Breen 1989, 1994; Castles 1992), especially that from central and northern Australia, "Nitmiluk" relies heavily on a country and western feel, especially in its use of a repeated guitar lick (Musical Example 23.3).

The use of country music sounds has been recognized by various writers as one of the stylistic mainstays of contemporary Aboriginal popular music (Breen 1989,1994; Castles 1992; Mudrooroo 1997). Numerous reasons are given for this, among them familiarity with the style from its appearance on the play-lists of rural radio stations, and thus exposure of it to Aboriginal listeners, or the fact that in their lyrics country songs reflect the lifestyle of workers on the land. Mudrooroo (1997, 111) explains this link between Aboriginal country working conditions and country music in his explanation of the popularity of the style:

> country and western (hillbilly) songs in time replaced most indigenous secular song structures. This was because the subject matter reflected the new Indigenous lifestyle: horses and cattle, drinking, gambling, the outsider as hero, a nomadic existence, country-orientation, wronged love, fighting and fucking—the whole gamut of an itinerant life.

More relevant to the present discussion is the possibility that the topics of country songs, which often express emotions about family and land, appeal to Aboriginal cultural sensibilities and thus the style, through a form of semiotic linkage, has been subsumed into Aboriginal musical life as an expression of relationships to land. Certainly it is not difficult to find country style songs by Aboriginal musicians which in their lyrics express closeness to, love of, and responsibility for land.

A further characteristic of "Nitmiluk" found in much Aboriginal rock music is the inclusion in its inner rock section of didjeridu and clapsticks as members of the rock group lineup. Both instruments seem aligned with the instruments of the drumkit, and thus integrate into the rhythmic profile of the song through a number of one-bar repeated patterns that constitute the basis of the song's accompaniment (Musical Example 23.4).

In Aboriginal rock music, the instrument didjeridu[5] is used throughout Australia and has assumed an identity as a marker of musical Aboriginality (see Neuenfeldt 1997). This nation-wide, pan-Aboriginal use of the instrument is relatively recent and is in contrast to the instrument's traditional origins in northern Australia, above a latitude drawn across the continent from Broome in

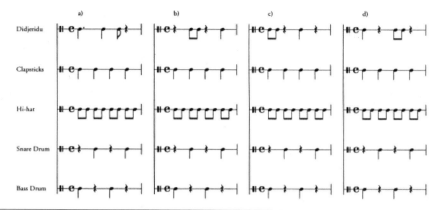

Music Example 23.4 Clapsticks, didjeridu and drumkit rhythms: rock section, "Nitmiluk."

West Australia to Ingham in Queensland (A. Moyle 1971; Stubington 1979). Concomitant with this geographic diffusion of the instrument has been a widening of its musical uses as it transfers from traditional to rock contexts (Dunbar-Hall 1997a). In its various uses of the didjeridu "Nitmiluk" demonstrates ways that the instrument moves between these different musical settings.

Two didjeridu playing styles can be identified in "Nitmiluk." In the opening and closing traditional sections, the didjeridu provides a rhythmic drone. This playing style has been identified by researchers as that found in west Arnhem Land traditional music (one that only employs the instrument's fundamental pitch). This is in contrast to that heard in the traditional music of east Arnhem Land, where in addition to the instrument's fundamental, hooted upper partials and unpitched "spats" are used, and conforms to musicological expectations of west Arnhem Land music (A. Moyle 1971; Stubington 1979). In the rock sections of "Nitmiluk," it is unpitched "spats" that are used in rhythmic interplay with the drumkit. Through this "Nitmiluk" demonstrates that despite Blekbala Mujik's west Arnhem Land origins, the distinction between west and east Arnhem Land traditional playing styles does not adhere in contemporary uses of the instrument. In this analysis, uses of the didjeridu in "Nitmiluk" refer both to localized Jawoyn musical culture and to contemporary, national Aboriginal cultures.

These four aspects of "Nitmiluk" (presence and integration of traditional and rock styles; multilingualism; influence of country and western style; and use of clapsticks and didjeridu as rock instruments), also found in songs by numerous Aboriginal rock groups across Australia, may be responsible for giving the song an Aboriginal "feel"—a pan-Aboriginality that assists in creating relevance for listeners from other Aboriginal cultures, and increasingly, wider non-indigenous audiences. A fifth aspect of the song, its topic, is also one used by many Aboriginal rock groups, but it is here that more specific references to Jawoyn culture are made in "Nitmiluk."

Aboriginal Rock Songs: Tradition and Indigenous Maps

The song topics used by Blekbala Mujik tend to favor issues of importance to Aboriginal communities: conditions of Aboriginal life ("Blackman's School"), invitations to understand and enjoy Aboriginal cultures ("Come-n-dance with Blekbala Mujik," "Walking Together"), the problems of alcohol abuse ("Drangkinbala"), references to Dreamtime personalities ("Dreamtime Dancer"), local events ("Barunga Festival"), the disastrous effects of British nuclear testing on Aboriginal lands ("Ngukliya Fiya"), and the celebration of place ("Kakadu," "Nitmiluk," "Uluru"). The presence on albums by Blekbala Mujik of this last category of songs, those about a place, adheres to a practice found throughout the repertoires of Aboriginal rock groups. Examples of songs about places significant to Aboriginal communities can be heard on recordings by groups such as Amunda, Kulumindini Band, Mixed Relations, North Tanami Band, Sunrize Band, Warumpi Desert Band, Warumpi Band, Wedgetail Eagle Band and Yartulu Yartulu Band (see Dunbar-Hall 1997b; Gibson 1998). Although based around a place, such songs can have different purposes. Some celebrate sites, others express longing or nostalgia for a lost site, describe a tract of land, call for the restitution of land to Aboriginal people, or, as in this case, commemorate the return of land to its owners.

The use of named places and the concept of place in Aboriginal rock songs can be seen as a contemporary expression of Aboriginal relationships to land, one of the defining factors of Aboriginal identity. This contemporary song topic mirrors one found in traditional music, and descriptions of the role of song in the expression of land ownership, and therefore of group and individual identity, appear regularly in the literature on Aboriginal traditional cultures. R. Moyle (1986, 4) for example, in his discussion of Aghar-ringa song from central Australia, notes that "[t]he linking of songs to land is a feature of central Australian society in general... Agharringa men consider the bond between certain of their own ceremonies and Agharringa Country to be such that ownership of the former is a *sine qua non* for ownership of the latter."

References to the role of song as a repository of knowledge about land and land ownership also appear in descriptions of judicial activity in relation to Aboriginal land claims. Davis and Prescott (1992, 73), in their research into action by the Jawoyn to re-possess an area to the north of Nitmiluk, list song ownership as one form of evidence used to establish continuing relationship to land:

in support of their claim to traditional ownership of land in the South Alligator Valley the Jawoyn described events which took place in the creative epoch whereby ancestral beings identified with the Jawoyn traveled across the landscape and performed activities which have become synonymous with particular localities.... It is common within Aboriginal tradition to define the limits of territory through the spatial properties of events which are described by reference to location names in song cycles. These song cycles are often sung in the course of ceremonies to accompany dances which re-enact the events performed by the ancestral beings...

It would not be implausible to suggest that this aesthetic of Aboriginal traditional song, and the practices listed by Davis and Prescott, continue in contemporary musical expression, and can be seen at work in "Nitmiluk."

In constructions of Aboriginal identity, land is widely cited as part of a complex of related concepts. These concepts link a location with ancestral (often called "Dreamtime") beings who created it and/or performed activities there, with language/s spoken there, with the people and events of the past, and those who live there today or have rights to ownership. The centrality of land to Aboriginal cultures in general is explained by Toyne and Vachon (1987, 4–5) in reference to the Pitjantjatjara in the following way:

For Pitjantjatjara men and women, their land is the central and inseparable part of their being.... When [they] talk about themselves relating to the land, they express these relationships in a single concept known as *ngura*. Ngura can be a single camp or a community, the places where people make a living and renew their existence in dance and song... [ngura] is a focus of day-to-day living and philosophical ideas and speculation. And it is a key to understanding the people, their culture and their rights to land.

A relationship commonly exists between the concepts within this identity construction so that reference to one connotes reference/s to the others. Naming a site is metonymically naming related sites and the beings associated with them; beyond that is a connotation of naming the group associated with and responsible for the site. The recitation of the names of beings and place names in song in the language/s associated with a site is a significant role of Aboriginal song: as Davis and Prescott (1992, 2) point out: "place names are usually recited or sung...and the language in which they are publicly uttered confirms the identity of the group that holds primary rights in the territory." They return to this point later: "The social group is affiliated with a particular language because the language is identified with a defined tract of country to which the group is also affiliated" (Davis and Prescott 1992, 71). In these ways the physical world is combined with the spiritual world, and the past with the present, to illustrate group and individual identity in a symbiotic relationship. The overlapping of these simultaneous levels of reference and their potential composite meaning/s are difficult to unravel, and attempts by non-Aboriginal writers to represent them can only ever be preliminary. An analysis of the ideas presented in "Nitmiluk" can demonstrate how elements of place, history, language, and ownership are linked in a musical statement about a site, this statement itself acting as a signifier of identity and the implications of that identity in current policies of Jawoyn cultural revival. It should also be borne in mind that *singing about a place* is also *singing a place*. That is, by performing a song about a place, the events of the past, through which that place came into being, are re-created in the present; through the performance of an Aboriginal rock song about a place, that place is in a state of continual (re)creation. Here, "Nitmiluk" connotes the coming into existence of Nitmiluk, at the same time as it references the gorge's more recent past of dispossession and reclamation. In this way, the song not only writes a Jawoyn *Burr* ("Dreaming") history, but makes references to colonial attitudes and activities in relation to Jawoyn land. Levels of past and present on which the song relies, can be read into the song, not only through these textual references, but also in the song's use of distinct musical styles, while the dependence of the present and the past on each other can be heard in the ways that musical styles interact with each other throughout the song.

The text of the rock section of "Nitmiluk" is:

Verse 1
In the beginning
There was nothing on this land
An echo came from the past
Gandayala breathed the fire of life   [Dreamtime figure]
Whistling sounds were heard
Bolong made the waters flow   [Dreamtime figure]
In the distance land formations stirred
It turned into life

Chorus
Nitmiluk! Nitmiluk!
You're the father of the land
Break the chains and help to set me free
Nitmiluk! Nitmiluk!
You're there for one and all for one
We honor you—we depart in harmony

Verse 2
Mungana's taken you   [Ab. Eng. = white man]
There was nothin' we could do
A fight took place in court
It seemed that we had won
The *bunggul's* been revived   [trad. song and dance]
People praise your mighty name
A jury gave the answer
You're free for everyone

Chorus
Nitmiluk! Nitmiluk! ...

Verse 3
Forgive the white man
They're our brothers and our sisters
Let's join hands together
Share one earth forever
Teach the young our culture
Be happy and be peaceful
This land's for you
This land's for me
Take pride, it is yours, it is ours

Chorus
Nitmiluk! Nitmiluk! ...

The three verses present a story-line that can be summarized as: creation of Nitmiluk; dispossession; land rights claim/court action; return of land and cultural revival; hopes for the future. The specific events/factors of this story-line are the elements which combine to create the nexus of associations through which land ownership and identity are expressed. These elements and their locations within "Nitmiluk" are tabulated in Table 23.1.

Through this analysis, ways that "Nitmiluk" acts as a statement of local identity can be demonstrated. However, the generalized themes of local Aboriginal identity and attachments to land which pervade Blekbala Mujik's "Nitmiluk," also signify another field of indigenous politics—more specifically Jawoyn strategies to "rebuild the Jawoyn Nation," formulated by traditional owners and their own representative non-government organization, the Jawoyn Association (Jawoyn Association 1994). These have been enacted through land use agreements and negotiated sovereignties based on the recognition of Jawoyn native title rights over traditional lands. In this sense, the song contributes to the inscription of Nitmiluk as a physical space of profound importance, mythologizing its position at the cutting-edge of contemporary indigenous struggles.

"Sharing Our Country": The Jawoyn Land Claim for Nitmiluk

The geopolitical significance of the song "Nitmiluk" must be appreciated in the context of indigenous land rights struggles in Australia that accelerated during the 1970s with the growth of pan-Aboriginal political consciousness and the drive for formal recognition of indigenous rights to self-determination. Under land rights legislation passed by the Commonwealth Government in respect to the Northern Territory,[6] Jawoyn traditional owners submitted, on 31 March 1978, the

Table 23.1 Thematic Elements of "Nitmiluk"

Element	Example	Location in song
Aboriginal language	White Cockatoo	traditional sections
Location	Nitmiluk	chorus
Dreamtime beings	Gandayala	v1
	Bolong	v1
Past	Creation and history of site	v1
	Dispossession	v2
	Land claim	v3
Present	Return of land (1989)/ownership	end v2
	Position of land in reconciliation	v3

Katherine Area Land Claim over a wide stretch of their homelands, including Nitmiluk. Despite the stated intentions of traditional owners not to exclude non-Jawoyn people's access to Nitmiluk in the event of a successful land hand-back, the Katherine Area Land Claim was met with fierce opposition from the local non-indigenous population (Jawoyn Association 1993a). The amplification of intense racism, fears of separatism and exclusion in the non-Aboriginal community, particularly in the township of Katherine itself, was no doubt exacerbated by the lengthy process of deliberation on the claim (initial hearings were not held with the Aboriginal Land Commissioner until 1983–84. See also Lea 1989).

During this time opposition to the land claim was being articulated through both "formal" and "intimidatory" means. The incumbent Northern Territory Government actively opposed the claim, supporting the funding of oppositional challenges in the court of the Aboriginal Land Commissioner, whilst the then speaker of the Northern Territory Legislative Assembly led a street rally against land rights (Northern Territory Parliamentary Record, 16 May, 1989, 6056; Jawoyn Association 1993b). Concurrently, the Katherine Town Council attempted to halt the claims process by re-voking the formalizing cartographic strategies of the colonial enterprise discussed earlier. In response to the claim for Nitmiluk, the size of the town's official boundaries were expanded to increase its official area from 33 square kilometers to nearly 4,700 square kilometers, thereby incorporating Nitmiluk into its own territorial domain, and potentially nullifying indigenous land rights.[7] Once again, the map was employed as a device to legitimize (and concurrently exclude others from) territorial power—to know land in colonial terms, to "conquer" and thus incorporate place into a non-indigenous domain. This act of twentieth-century colonialism was later rejected by the Aboriginal Land Commissioner in his final report on the Jawoyn (Katherine Area) Land Claim, as an unnecessary expansion of the town's boundaries, given all projections of growth and urban planning in the foreseeable future (Kearney 1987, 51).

Many local non-Aboriginal residents developed their own racist strategies, including the formation of anti-land rights lobby groups such as "Rights for Whites," and the adornment of suburban front gardens along the local highway to Nitmiluk with mocking "sacred sites" signs (Crough 1993). Whilst opposition to the Jawoyn land claim was generally not violent, at one stage during the claim process shots were fired by an opponent of the Jawoyn claim over the head of a senior elder implicated in the hearings (Jawoyn Association 1993b). A survey of local residents in 1983, conducted by the Katherine Town Council, captures the extent of the sensitivity surrounding the Katherine Area Land Claim at the time. Over 60 percent of local respondents voiced opposition to the potential for Jawoyn ownership of Nitmiluk, citing arguments such as "Aboriginal's [sic] claims not necessary—they have enough land already;" "country—especially National Park, is for everybody—land shouldn't belong to one section of the community;" and "whites had to pay for land—so should Aborigines" (Katherine Town Council 1983, 36–38). Consequently, the geopolitical conflict surrounding the site of Nitmiluk was emblematic of wider political struggles and debates concerning the rights of indigenous peoples in the Australian polity.

The actual hearings for the Jawoyn land claim were also drawn out. The final Land Commissioner's report, recommending the return of Nitmiluk to traditional owners, was not released until 1988. In addition to bearing the brunt of hysteria from sectors of the local non-Aboriginal community throughout the period of the hearings, less than half of the original area claimed (approximately 5,000 square kilometers), was recommended by the Land Commissioner for hand-back to Jawoyn owners (Jawoyn Association 1994). However, the 2,032 square kilometers to be handed back did include Nitmiluk and surrounding areas, allowing the Jawoyn, through their representative non-government organization the Jawoyn Association Aboriginal Corporation (hereafter referred to as "The Jawoyn Association"), to negotiate with the Northern Territory's Conservation Commission the terms of a lease-back arrangement and management plan for their traditional country (see Figure 23.1). This would become a financial and symbolic platform for the development of the Jawoyn's formal strategies for self-determination and economic independence, captured in the use of the phrase "Rebuilding the Jawoyn Nation."

Given this set of circumstances, the performance of the song "Nitmiluk" by Blekbala Mujik at the hand-back ceremony on September 10,1989, signifies much more than a general affirmation of Aboriginal cultural identity and connections to place (which a text-based analysis suggests in the first instance). The themes of sharing country, reconciliation and pride in land in the song react to a tangible set of local circumstances, challenging the mis-informed narratives of exclusion and economic ruin which dominated opposition to the Jawoyn land claim throughout the hearings process. The song declares the Jawoyn's intention to rejoice in the return of traditional lands, whilst retaining access for both Aboriginal and non-Aboriginal populations to the National Park for recreational purposes. Whilst many of the song's themes can be seen as expressions of pan-Aboriginality, they occupy another layer of meaning for Jawoyn people, given the background of racism and division which preceded the Jawoyn's land rights victory. As Blekbala Mujik sings "This land's for you/This land's for me/Take pride, it is yours, it is ours," they are simultaneously answering local critics of Aboriginal land rights who appeal to narratives of separatism, and pointing to further directions which Jawoyn empowerment and regional development strategies could take. The performance of the song at the hand-back ceremony for Nitmiluk, on September 10, 1989, under the banner "Mamgun Mungguy-wun lerr-nyarrang Nitmiluk" ("Sharing Our Country"), occurred at a significant moment in indigenous struggles, and at a turning point in local geopolitical relations between the Jawoyn and non-Aboriginal residents of the Katherine region.

Nitmiluk and the Process of "Rebuilding the Jawoyn Nation"

Since the hand-back of Nitmiluk, the Jawoyn Association has signed the Nitmiluk Tours joint venture with local tourist operators to manage boat tours, camping grounds, and kiosks within the park, providing further community income and securing control over potential employment opportunities for the Jawoyn (Pritchard and Gibson 1996). Nitmiluk has therefore been (and continues to be) a central part of the Jawoyn's strategies for empowerment and autonomy from government welfare funding.

The most recent developments in Jawoyn politics are the formation of strategies to "Rebuild the Jawoyn Nation," which also capitalize on the tangible gains secured through the hand-back and management of Nitmiluk National Park, and capture again the themes of "sharing our country" which pervade Blekbala Mujik's recordings. By the use of the term "Jawoyn nation," the Association aims to crystallize the broad spectrum of its political claims and assertions of indigenous rights. The Jawoyn Association has employed the term "nation" in a multivalent sense, to represent a whole people, a language, and areas of traditional country (Gibson 1995), and in ways to suggest the rights of the Jawoyn to govern over traditional lands, to "care for country" in a region in which they are greatly outnumbered by both the non-Aboriginal population and by the diversity of other more recently-arrived Aboriginal groups who have been dispossessed from their country further afield. As such, it represents the attempt of the Jawoyn to assert their distinct status as indigenous guardians over much of the region. The term "Jawoyn nation" does not, however, represent Jawoyn claims for a "separate nationhood" in a western political sense. The Jawoyn, in line with principles to "share our country," are suggesting a concept of sovereignty which recognizes their indigenous rights to negotiation and decision-making, without implying a parallel monolithic and monopolistic sense of land ownership as that entrenched in Western, capitalist forms of land tenure (Jawoyn Association 1994; Patton 1995). Thus, the Jawoyn are able to assert geopolitical strategies for autonomy which avert the implication of long-term secession from the Australian nation-state and the narratives of separatism espoused by local opponents of land rights.

Among the Jawoyn Association's recent activities as part of this locally specific "rebuilding the Jawoyn nation" project, was the formation of the 1993 Mt. Todd Agreement, between traditional owners, Australian national and Territory governments, and mining company Zapopan NL, in which the Jawoyn were granted title to vast tracts of land previously owned by governments, in exchange for secure tenure for the mine's operations in Jawoyn traditional land near Werenbun. Mechanisms such as the Mt. Todd Agreement have since been incorporated into local indigenous strategies in ways which reflect the "multiple sovereignty" approach of the "rebuilding the Jawoyn Nation" project, attempting to ensure indigenous title and influence over land, yet concurrently accommodating non-indigenous interests in land. These approaches have become more influential since the 1992 "Mabo" decision, and recent legal victories such as the High Court's December 1996 decision in favor of Wik and Thayorre, traditional owners in Cape York, Queensland, who were able to prove the co-existence of indigenous title to land with current non-indigenous pastoral leases. The "multiple sovereignty" approach developed by the Jawoyn, whilst not commensurate with the political desires of all Aboriginal associations (for example, the Aboriginal Provisional Government), is being considered as a way of securing indigenous interests in land, without fulfilling the hysterical fears of separatism which have prompted some conservative politicians to suggest the total extinguishment of some native title rights (see Gibson 1999; and Meyers, ed. 1997 for examples of the growth of negotiated agreements in Australia).

These new concepts of multiple sovereignty and discourses of indigenous nationhood are suggested throughout Aboriginal popular music recordings, and specifically in Blekbala Mujik's "Nitmiluk." The phrase "Sharing our Country," expressed in the song "Nitmiluk" and emblazoned across the stage at the hand-back ceremony, refers simultaneously to the generalized approaches to reconciliation which could apply across Australia and appeal to both Aboriginal and non-Aboriginal audiences, and captures the expression of highly local, specific, and material narratives of nationhood. Regev (1997) argues with regard to popular music that the "nation" is itself a field of meaning, a contested term, a concept which provides the basis for debates about cultural difference, uniqueness and attachments to territory:

> Local culture becomes, in this regard, a field in which different versions of the "nation" struggle to gain recognition, legitimacy, dominance—or separation. Each position in the field formulates a version of the nation's history, invents traditions and produces specific artworks that express its different identity. But the idea of "the nation" dominates and underlies the existence of the field—it is its doxa. (Regev 1997, 128)

Discourses of indigenous nationhood are extended by the Jawoyn Association in their community development strategies through the use of symbols of Aboriginality on the covers of reports, letterheads, and policy documents; and these motifs also appear on cassette covers released by Blekbala Mujik. The official letterheads and reports of the Jawoyn Association feature a depiction of the Bolong of Nitmiluk and Nitmi (cicadas), the same images used as the cassette cover for Blekbala Mujik's *Nitmiluk* (see Figure 23.4). The symbols themselves represent the continued role of tradition—the Bolong and Nitmi—in contemporary land naming and owning practices—denoting specific sites and sounds. This particular design was created by a Jawoyn artist who has since passed away, but the image remains in the public domain as an emblem of the Jawoyn Association's activities (Jawoyn Association 1994a). In this case the use of particular cultural icons to denote national identity by indigenous groups whose rights are not uniformly recognized by colonial nation-states sustains links to the use of Pan-African imagery since the 1970s in many black American and Caribbean music traditions. The use of the symbols of the Ethiopian flag— the Lion and red, green, and gold colors—in the music and culture of reggae and Rastafarian Jamaica provides a precedent to the connections between Blekbala Mujik and the Jawoyn Association's use of the Bolong, and Nitmi image, and brown, black, and gold motifs (cf. Campbell 1985).[8] Whereas the colors and iconography of reggae's pan-Africanism denote resistance to a Babylonian, capitalist/slavery history, the Bolong on the cover of *Rebuilding the Jawoyn Nation and Nitmiluk!* can be read as reacting in similar ways to dispossession and alienation under Australian colonial rule. These symbols of nationhood, a type of localized "flag," assert regional formations of identity that contextualize indigenous empowerment strategies in a sub-national political landscape where

Figure 23.4 Jawoyn Association Emblem.

Aboriginal sovereignty has no current legal recognition. With *Nitmiluk* this sense of nation within nation is voiced through music.

Moreover, the construction of Jawoyn nationhood and the narratives of survival and celebration in the song "Nitmiluk" represent significant attempts to generate new post-colonial space—the Jawoyn Association's political strategies (such as the Mt. Todd Agreement and the co-management of Nitmiluk National Park), and the song by Blekbala Mujik signify fluid, negotiated approaches to land tenure in areas where separatist agendas are both unrealistic and unwelcome. Themes that resonate throughout these formal political and popular cultural texts involve going beyond the strict individualistic undercurrents of Western land ownership, about re-inscribing space with indigenous meaning, but not resorting to a non-indigenous discourse of inclusion and exclusion. The song "Nitmiluk," alongside other activities such as the Barunga Sports and Cultural Festival held annually on Jawoyn land, is part of this process of re-inscribing Aboriginality on the landscape of the Katherine region. The physical space of Nitmiluk therefore occupies the focal point of various meanings: through music, in formal political strategies of indigenous nationhood, and as a contrast to non-Aboriginal cartographic representations of "reality." With Blekbala Mujik's "Nitmiluk," then, to sing the song is in a sense to re-sing the place.

Some Concluding Comments

In this article, we explore links between popular music and Aboriginal cultural and political strategies, in particular the negotiation of colonial histories and cartographies, and the development of a new geopolitical discourse in a regional context. The work of Blekbala Mujik, like that of many other indigenous performers, has a strong emphasis on place-specific songs, on revisionist accounts of community events, and on the celebration and vitality of Aboriginality in contemporary circumstances. We have considered one particular song by Blekbala Mujik, "Nitmiluk," as an example of the general relationship between music and place. However, specific musical characteristics of the song allow us to read "Nitmiluk" through levels of meaning derived from Aboriginal cultural representations. In this case, the use of the didjeridu, traces of country music style, and the multilingual text of the song could be shown to have significance to local Aboriginal listeners, and could be read in geographically-specific ways. Whereas other Aboriginal rock groups (such as Yothu

Yindi and Warumpi Band) use names which are site-specific, and thereby express geographical and cultural origins, the use of the name Blekbala Mujik could be read as Aboriginal in the broadest sense ("blackfella music"). While this song tells the story of one particular site and its associated political contexts, at the same time it can be read as symbolic of wider Aboriginal agendas. These agendas affirm traditional attachments to territory, and the validity of these claims in current circumstances. Yet, these assertions are articulated in ways which suggest the accommodation of these claims within the Australian nation-state. The solution to tensions between the local and the national is one of reconciliation ("This land's for you/This land's for me/Take pride it is yours, it is ours"), a topic common to Blekbala Mujik's wider repertoire. As Apaak Jupurrula explains:

> The underlying feature . . . is about being one, of Australia's people being one, being together in various aspects of what we do, particularly having to live in this part of the world as a collective group, I guess. The concept is actually reconciliation. It's not only a concept that's been emphasized within the political world, but people are beginning to think of it as a very important issue socially as well. (quoted in Smith 1996)

Blekbala Mujik's "Nitmiluk," with its synchronic use of traditional and rock forms, delineates the persistence of indigenous attachments to land; meanwhile the naming of sites within the song offers a significant means of negotiating power and re-presenting place. Taken as a whole, these musical expressions can be read as new cartographies of attachments to land—a series of post-colonial maps.

On another level, while many of the themes of Aboriginal rock songs are written for and received by pan-Aboriginal audiences, they often remain rooted in the specific empowering practices and political circumstances of local communities (cf. Grossberg 1984). Beneath a more general reading of Blekbala Mujik's "Nitmiluk," the song operates as a response to the racial narratives of separatism and exclusion that dominated non-indigenous opinion and opposition to the Jawoyn (Katherine Area) Land Claim throughout the 1980s. The song achieves this through constructing new possibilities for cross-cultural understanding, evading separatist scenarios with appeals for more process-based, fluid regimes of co-existence. Thus, this Aboriginal rock song actively engages with various threads of geopolitical meaning, delineating general strategies for self-determination and cultural pride, at the same time reclaiming local spaces of "multiple sovereignty." Music, rather than simply "reflecting" happenings in the wider world, is *constitutive* of local political relations. As a physical site, Nitmiluk therefore remains both a symbolic marker of indigenous land rights struggles and a source of musical inspiration. Through policy, text, and in song, this landscape of gorges and chasms, of the Bolong and Nabilil, continues to be contested and renegotiated.

Notes

1. This article is based on papers read by the authors at the 1997 conference of the Association for the Study of Australian Literature: *Land and Identity*, University of New England, Armidale, NSW (see Dunbar-Hall 1997c and Gibson 1997). The authors would also like to thank the following people for their advice and input during the conduct of this research: Apaak Jupurrula, Richard Micaelef, John Connell, and Robert Lee.
2. The "Northern Territory of Australia" was annexed in 1863 from the colony of South Australia.
3. The Burr figures and stories alluded to here are documented in a publication of the Jawoyn Association (Jawoyn Association 1993a) which is not restricted to any particular audience. They make up part of the publicly available information about Jawoyn culture approved by Jawoyn people.
4. "Katherine" was named in 1862 by the explorer John McDouall Stuart after the daughter of his patron, James Chambers.
5. Although Aboriginal languages have their own names for this instrument, the term "didjeridu" is now used almost universally.
6. The Commonwealth retains power to legislate for land tenure in Territories of Australia, but not for the States (e.g., Victoria, Western Australia) due to the constitutional entrenchment of the States' primary sovereign rights. Consequently, the Aboriginal Land Rights Act (Northern Territory) of 1976 only covered lands in the Northern Territory.
7. Under the Aboriginal Land Rights Act (Northern Territory) of 1976, only vacant Crown land not expressly put aside by governments for future use can be claimed by traditional owners.

8. The music of Jamaican reggae and attendant Rastafarian imagery (on T-shirts, flags, cassette covers, etc.) is also prevalent throughout indigenous communities in the Top End of the Northern Territory, providing a material basis for the parallels drawn between Blekbala Mujik and pan-African iconography.

References

Appadurai, Arjun. 1990. "Disjuncture and difference in the global cultural economy." *Public Culture* 2(2):1–24.

Breen, Marcus 1994. "I have a Dreamtime: Aboriginal music and black rights in Australia." In *World Music: The Rough Guide*, edited by S. Broughton, et al. 655–662. London: Rough Guides.

———, ed. 1989. *Our Place, Our Music*. Canberra: Aboriginal Studies Press.

Broughton, Simon, et al., eds. 1994. *World Music: The Rough Guide*. London: Rough Guides.

Campbell, Horace. 1985. *Rasta and Resistance: From Marcus Garvey to Walter Rodney*. London: Hansib.

Castles, John. 1992. "*Tjungaringanyi*: Aboriginal rock." In *From Pop to Punk to Postmodernism: Popular Music and Australian Culture from the 1960s to 1990s*, edited by Philip Hayward, 25–39. North Sydney: Allen and Unwin.

Central Australian Aboriginal Media Association, n.d. *Blekbala Mujik*. Press release.

Cohen, Hart, ed. 1996. "Music/Image/Text—A Special Issue on Indigenous Media." *Australian Canadian Studies* 14(1–2).

Crough, Greg. 1993. *Visible and Invisible: Aboriginal People in the Economy of Northern Australia*. Darwin: North Australia Research Unit and the Nugget Coombs Forum for Indigenous Studies.

Davis, Stephen and John Prescott. 1992. *Aboriginal Frontiers and Boundaries in Australia*. Melbourne: Melbourne University Press.

Dunbar-Hall, Peter. 1996. "Rock Songs as Messages: Issues of Health and Lifestyle in Central Australian Aboriginal Communities." *Popular Music and Society* 22(2):43–68.

———. 1997a. "Continuation, Dissemination and Innovation." In *The Didjeridu: From Arnhem Land to Internet*, edited by K. Neuenfeldt, 69–87. Sydney: John Libbey and Perfect Beat Publications.

———. 1997b. "Site As Song—Song As Site: Constructions of Meaning in an Aboriginal Rock Song." *Perfect Beat* 3(3):55–74.

———. 1997c. "Nitmiluk: An Aboriginal Rock Song about a Place." Paper presented at the Association for the Study of Australian Literature conference "Land and Identity," University of New England, Armidale, NSW, Australia, September 29.

Elder, Bruce. 1995. "Sophistication from the Heartland." *Sydney Morning Herald*, review obtained as promotional material for Blekbala Mujik by CAAMA.

Eliezer, C. 1996. "Blekbala Mujik—Blekbala Mujik." *The Herald Sun*, 19 May, unpaginated.

Ellis, Catherine. 1985. *Aboriginal Music: Education for Living*. St Lucia: University of Queensland Press.

Feld, Steven and Keith H. Basso, eds. 1996. *Senses of Place*, Santa Fe, NM: School of American Research Press.

Ferrier, Elizabeth. 1990. "Mapping Power: Cartography and Contemporary Cultural Theory." *Antithesis* 4(1):35–49.

Forrest, Peter. 1985. *Springvale's Story and the Early Years at the Katherine*. Darwin: Murranji Press.

Gibson, Chris. 1995. "Aboriginal Self-determination in the Jawoyn Nation." Hons. diss., Department of Geography, University of Sydney.

———. 1997. "Nitmiluk: Song Sites and Strategies for Empowerment." Paper presented at the Association for the Study of Australian Literature conference "Land and Identity," University of New England, Armidale, NSW, Australia, September 29.

———. 1998. "We Sing Our Home, We Dance Our land': Indigenous Self-determination and Contemporary Geopolitics in Australian Popular Music." *Environment and Planning D: Society and Space* 16:163–184.

———. 1999. "Rebuilding the Jawoyn Nation: the Geopolitics of Regional Agreements and Indigenous Self-determination in the Katherine Region, NT." *Australian Aboriginal Studies* 1, 10-25.

Grossberg, Lawrence. 1984. "Another Boring Day in Paradise: Rock and Roll and the Empowerment of Everyday life." *Popular Music* 4:225–258.

Harley, J.B. 1988. "Maps, Knowledge, and Power." In *The Iconography of Landscape*, edited by D. Cosgrove and S. Daniels, 277–312. Cambridge: Cambridge University Press.

Huggan, Graham. 1989. "Decolonizing the Map: Post-colonialism, Post-structuralism, and the Cartographic Connection." *Ariel* 20(4). Reprinted in *The Post-colonial Studies Reader*, edited by B. Ashcroft, et al., 407–411. London and New York: Routledge.

Jacobs, Jane M. 1993. "'Shake 'Im This Country': the Mapping of the Aboriginal Sacred in Australia—the Case of Coronation Hill." In *Constructions of Race, Place, and Nation*, edited by P. Jackson and J. Penrose, 100–118. London: UCL Press.

Jawoyn Association. 1993a. *Jawoyn People, Land and Life*. Katherine: Jawoyn Association Training Section.

———. 1993b. "Mabo: Putting the Big Stick to One Side?" Paper presented to the 1993 Aboriginal Culture and Heritage Conference "People Place Law," Sydney, 8–11 September.

———. 1994. *Rebuilding the Jawoyn Nation: Approaching Economic Independence*. Darwin: Green Ant Publishing.

Jordan, S. 1995. "Blekbala Mujik." *Rolling Stone* May 1995:90.

Katherine Town Council. 1983. *The Katherine*. Series of social surveys, volume 2. Brisbane: Victor G Feros Town Planning Consultants.

Kearney, William J. 1987. *Jawoyn (Katherine Area) Land Claim*. Report by the Aboriginal Land Commissioner to the Minister for Aboriginal Affairs and to the Administrator of the Northern Territory.

Kong, Lily. 1995. "Popular Music in Geographical Analyses." *Progress in Human Geography* 19(2):183–98.

Langton, Marcia. 1993. "*Well, I Heard It on the Radio and I Saw It on the Television.. *": An Essay for the Australian Film Commission on the Politics and Aesthetics of Filmmaking by and about Aboriginal People and Things. Sydney: Australian Film Commission.

Lawe-Davies, Chris. 1993. "Aboriginal Rock Music: Space and Place." In *Rock and Popular Music: Politics, Policies, Institutions*, edited by T. Bennett, et al., 249–265. London: Routledge.

Lea, John. 1989. "South of the Berrimah Line: Government and the Aboriginal Community in Katherine and Tennant Creek after World War Two." In *Small Towns in Northern Australia*, edited by P. Loveday and A. Webb, 189–204. Darwin: North Australia Research Unit, Australian National University.

Leyshon, Andrew, et al. 1995. "The Place of Music." *Transactions of the Institute of British Geographers* 20:423–433.

Lipsitz, George. 1994. *Dangerous Crossroads: Popular Music, Postmodernism and the Poetics of Place*. London: Verso.

McCabe, K. 1996. "In Tune with the Times." *The Daily Telegraph* 26 January.

Meyers, Gary D., ed. 1997. *Implementing the Native Title Act—The Next Step: Facilitating Negotiated Agreements*. Perth: National Native Title Tribunal.

Michaels, Eric. 1994. *Bad Aboriginal Art: Tradition, Media, and Technological Horizons*. Sydney: Allen and Unwin.

Moyle, Alice. 1971. *Songs of the Northern Territory*. Canberra: Aboriginal Studies Press.

Moyle, Richard. 1986. *Alyawarra Music: Songs and Society in Central Australia*. Canberra: Australian Institute of Aboriginal Studies.

Mudrooroo. 1997. *The Indigenous Literature of Australia: Milli Milli Wangka*. Melbourne: Hyland House.

National Board of Employment, Education, and Training. 1996. *The Land Still Speaks: Review of Aboriginal and Torres Strait Islander Language Maintenance and Development Needs and Activities*. Canberra.

Neuenfeldt, Karl. 1993. "Yothu Yindi and Ganma: The Cultural Transposition of Aboriginal Agenda Through Metaphor and Music." *Journal of Australian Studies* 38(1):1–11.

———, ed. 1997. *The Didjeridu: From Arnhem Land to Internet*. Sydney: John Libbey Publications and Perfect Beat.

Odgen, Pearl. 1989. *Katherine's Earlier Days*. Northern Territory Library Service Occasional Papers No. 9. Darwin: Northern Territory Library Service.

Patton, Paul. 1995. "Post-structuralism and the Mabo Debate: Difference, Society, and Justice." In *Justice and Identity—Antipodean Practices*, edited by M. Wilson and A. Yeatman, 153–171. Wellington: Allen and Unwin.

Pritchard, Bill and Chris Gibson. 1996. *The Black Economy: Regional Development Strategies in the Northern Territory*. North Australia Research Unit Report Series No. 1. Darwin: Australian National University and the Northern Land Council.

Regev, Motti. 1997. "Rock Aesthetics and Musics of the World." *Theory, Culture and Society* 14(3):125–142.

Smith, M. 1996. "Blekbala Songlines." *Drum Media* January, unpaginated.

Stubington, Jill. 1979. "North Australian Aboriginal Music." In *Australian Aboriginal Music*, edited by J. Isaacs, 7–19. Sydney: Aboriginal Artists Agency.

——— and Peter Dunbar-Hall. 1994. "Yothu Yindi's 'Treaty': *Ganma* in Music." *Popular Music* 13(3):243–259.

Toyne, Phillip and Daniel Vachon. 1987. *Growing Up the Country: The Pitjantjatjara Struggle for Their Land*. Penguin: Melbourne.

Yunupingu, Mandawuy. 1990. "Yothu Yindi Band." In *Aboriginal Voices: Contemporary Aboriginal Artists, Writers and Performers*, edited by L. Thompson, 100–103. Sydney: Simon and Schuster.

Discography

Blekbala Mujik, 1990 *Nitmiluk!* CAAMA Music, Cassette.
Blekbala Mujik, 1990 *Midnait Mujik*. CAAMA Music, Cassette.
Blekbala Mujik, 1993 *Come-n-Dance*. CAAMA Music, Compact Disc.
Blekbala Mujik, 1995 *Blekbala Mujik*. CAAMA Music, Compact Disc.
Blekbala Mujik, 1995 *Walking Together*. CAAMA Music, Compact Disc.

24

Culture, Conservation, and Community Reconstruction
Explorations in Advocacy Ethnomusicology and Participatory Action Research in Northern KwaZulu Natal

Angela Impey

Applied or advocacy ethnomusicology has yet to be developed as a formal sub-field in South Africa, yet researchers of music have the advantage of being at the forefront of a social reconstruction impetus that provides opportunities for relevant social engagement, the remodelling of research foci, the expansion of multidisciplinary applications, and the utilisation of participatory methodologies that have yet to be explored in research on performance.[1] This paper is presented in the form of a report of my recent explorations into the operational interface between ethnomusicology, environmental conservation and sustainable development in the Dukuduku Forests of northern KwaZulu Natal. In so far as the study is situated in a community that resides within an environmentally protected area, it extends the notion that culture is as much a part of the treasure of the landscape as are its faunal, floral and marine resources. The premise herein, is that songs, dances and ritual processes present rich repositories of local knowledge about the environment, and are particularly relevant signifiers of local meaning systems in a context where these systems may no longer be learned through apprenticeships or oral tradition, due to geographic displacement and rapid socio-economic transformation. Broadly therefore, the project strives to examine the interdependencies between symbolic practices and natural resource use, and to explore ways in which deep-rooted cultural wisdoms may be recast to contribute towards a more effective organizing paradigm for the sustainable custodianship of the environment, and herein empower the communities to participate more equitably in the development of the region.

The people of the Dukuduku Forests of the Greater St. Lucia Wetlands Park Authority[2] are amongst the poorest in northern KwaZulu Natal. They are also amongst the most controversial. Having been evicted from the eastern shores of the St. Lucia estuary in the 1950s, when the white Nationalist Government proclaimed the area a National Forest, they returned in the late 1980s to claim legitimate ownership of the land, where they now subsist by way of slash-and-burn subsistence agriculture, fishing, craft production and tourism. Not all residents can claim ancestral connection with Dukuduku however. Some attempted to escape violence from other areas of the province;[3] some sought land, employment or other lifestyle opportunities; a small number are immigrants from Mozambique.

Official title lodged with the KwaZulu Natal Land Claims Commission in 1991 by the Dukuduku community attracted extensive media attention as one of the first successful land settlements by a displaced black community in South Africa. Perhaps as highly publicised, however, has been the battle waged by the *Save the St. Lucia Campaign* (an umbrella of more than 200 environmental organisations) that sought to protect the wetland dunes from titanium mining, prevent the rapid deforestation of the indigenous coastal forests, and to encourage greater exploitation of nature-tourism in the area.

Lake St. Lucia is the largest estuary in Africa; it is the oldest proclaimed National Park in southern Africa, and it is the first area in South Africa to be registered a UNESCO World Heritage Site.[4] As a result of its massive tourism potential, it has become necessary for the Ezemvelo KwaZulu Natal Wildlife services to consider a more comprehensive, sustainable approach towards conservation that is concerned not only with the preservation of its plant and animal resources, but significantly with the people, culture and local knowledge. Consequently, decentralised decision-making, recognition of community rights, and the incorporation of local communities into joint management schemes are currently being investigated in an attempt to decrease conflict over resource management, as a means towards ensuring biodiversity, and as a way to boost revenue potential to local peoples. This integrationist approach represents a dramatic departure from the old South African "fortress" approach to conservation, wherein rural communities who fell within areas demarcated for National Parks or Forests would be forcibly removed, with no consideration given to the value of local knowledge in environmental decision-making, and less still to the ways in which locality and natural resources play a fundamental role in the social, cultural and spiritual identities of local communities. However, while material resources may be in place within the new dispensation, and the commercial benefits calculated, the community stakeholders and cultural assets have yet to be identified, thus ensuring that policy development will build on community strengths and participation.

For the 15,000+ residents of Dukuduku's main settlement, Khula Village,[5] the notion of "community" is defined by a spatial boundary and by common economic interests in the resources of the area. Although mostly Zulu-speaking, people represent diverse regional cultural differences, and retain a high level of mobility. In addition, Khula Village is an unusual combination of urban and rural. While having the physical profile of a peri-urban township, it is positioned deep within a national park; and while it functions with an urban infrastructure, it remains politically represented by hereditary traditional leadership.

For the newly settled residents of Khula Village, the construction of locality (i.e., the claim on territory, the recreation of sense of place and the development of social bonds) is likewise being fashioned by conflicting forces. While the concerns of the residents themselves are with the development of a community infrastructure, job creation, and poverty alleviation, development visions for the region are being significantly shaped by its recent accession to World Heritage status, which defines human action in terms of the preservation imperatives of the natural landscape.[6]

Making further impact on this disjuncture is the overwhelming development thrust arising out of eco- and cultural tourism, which feature as the major foci for income-generation in the Greater St. Lucia Wetland Park Authority. As has been demonstrated elsewhere, cultural tourism has the tendency to reduce identity to a singular, generic "Other".[7] Tourism initiatives in KwaZulu Natal capitalise on the global imagination of the Zulu as the quintessential African Warrior Nation, an image that is framed in an idealised, historic moment, and that perpetuates their representation as authentic, potent, and uncontaminated.[8] In as much as cultural tourism feeds on mediated images of the "noble savage", so eco-tourism trades on the recurrent tropes of the African landscape based on images of an endless, pristine wilderness teaming with wildlife, and into which are inserted "natural" but soon to vanish cultures (Bruner and Kirshenblatt-Gimblett 1994).

The contrast between the internal processes of community building (which arise out of the challenges of modernisation), and the externally defined environmental, economic and development visions for the region (which focus on an idealised past and on cultural uniformity), provided the thematic disjuncture which this project aims to address. Since the Dukuduku people are extremely poor, their survival appears to depend on their conforming to the visions and requisites defined by external agencies. However, they are well positioned to develop agency through self-representation, which builds upon environmental value and cultural significance.

Linking Ethnomusicology to Community Development and Environmental Action

My involvement with the Dukuduku community was initiated in 2000 by a request from the Dukuduku Development and Tourism Association to undertake a musical survey of the region and to assist in the conceptualisation and production of a musical display towards a more encompassing cultural tourism initiative.[9] Since the village is located in an indigenous forest system that falls within a World Heritage Site, the livelihood potentials for the community are restricted by the preservationist parameters of the UNESCO Convention. Commercially profitable ventures such as fishing, the collection of mussels, the harvesting of reeds for the construction of wedding or sleeping mats, the collection of medicinal plants, and the use of indigenous wood for the crafting of tourist art are strictly proscribed. The economic value attached to these products on the open market has resulted in massive over-harvesting in the past, and many of these species are now listed as endangered. Khula Village is, however, situated on the key access route to the tourist town of St. Lucia, and the community is well positioned to capitalise on the increasing numbers of local and international visitors to the estuary. With additional exposure gained by its accession to World Heritage status, the development vision of the community has progressively begun to focus on eco- and cultural tourism as their primary route to poverty alleviation.

While I welcomed the opportunity to participate in a community-driven initiative, I was apprehensive about the long-term value of tourism in Dukuduku. Eco- and cultural tourism is vigorously embraced in South Africa as an ideal economic base for underdeveloped communities, but I feared that these ventures could run the risk of corroding the already tenuous social fabric of this community. From an economic standpoint, I was concerned that tourism would inevitably benefit some (the gate-keepers, those with resources, men) and exclude others (the poor, women, the aged). The construction of a cultural spectacle based on a fabricated, historicised cultural image would not assist in the establishment of a community identity, which in reality is based on diversity and difference. Nor would such an exercise assist people in negotiating the complex dialectic between "traditional" and "modern," which feature as concurrent facets of their contemporary lives and identities. Perhaps of greatest concern, however, was that in spite of its privileged geographic location, Khula Village is situated at the epicentre of the HIV/AIDS pandemic in South Africa. Additionally, due to the rising levels of poverty and unemployment in the region, crime has escalated, and is often directed at the affluent outsider. These massive social problems alone attest to the fragility of tourism as a growth industry for poor communities.

However, given that there are so few economic alternatives for the communities in the region, and that nature conservation bodies, NGOs and the corporate sector were resolute in their decision to develop partnerships with communities around tourism and tourism-related activities, I was not in the position to voice my somewhat academic reservations. Rather, while conducting the musical survey, I began to reflect upon ways in which the process of cultural documentation could function to benefit more than simply the tourist gaze. Since the community had shared a ten-year history only, it was clear that people were as yet unfamiliar with one another's histories and cultural practices. Through the application of participatory research methodologies, the process of documentation could begin to stimulate dialogue and exchange between Khula residents, and could provide a platform for people to address issues of identity, meaning and community building. The development of a narrative for eco- and cultural tourist consumption would therefore be linked with an initiative that sought to actively recover the communities' histories, identities and traditional knowledge systems, and operate as a process upon which other kinds of community interventions could be explored.

In January 2001, I established a community cultural and environmental documentation initiative at the Silethukukhanya High School in Khula Village. The aim of the documentation project is to train young researchers to build a community archive of indigenous knowledge and cultural heritage. Through the documentation of songs, dances and ritual processes, the project aims to stimulate public discussion concerning "traditional meaning" (as claimed and understood by Dukuduku residents), identity and self-representation. Further, it aims to encourage dialogue regarding the interface between music/ritual processes on one hand, and land, natural resource use and notions of locality on the other. And finally, it aims to explore methods by which the memorisation of this knowledge can be reconciled with contemporary conditions and economic opportunities.

The school was identified as an appropriate institution to house the project as it operates as a cultural nucleus of the village. Through young, volunteer student researchers, the project could network into the wider community by way of families, friends and neighbours. Information collected would have direct educational value and would contribute materials towards the development of the school's Cultural Studies Focus,[10] which necessarily draws on local knowledge and practices. And further, the project would provide skills training to researchers and would herein open a range of post-school vocational possibilities, otherwise unattainable to the average Khula school-leaver. Lastly, the culture-environment focus of the project would complement other initiatives at the school, namely the restoration of a segment of indigenous forest within the school premises and an indigenous plant nursery.

For the advocacy ethnomusicologist, positioning oneself at the interface between music, environmentalism[11] and community development poses a number of theoretical and methodological challenges. It presents the opportunity for new multidisciplinary intersections that is at once exciting, but also demands that one gains knowledge of new discourses and disciplinary trajectories, all of which have their own ideological agendas and professional priorities. The challenge of placing one's footprint across academic/professional sectors may be equalled by the challenge of repositioning oneself within one's own disciplinary territory. Historically, there has always been something of an uncomfortable relationship between theoretical and applied fields in the human sciences, the subtext being that academia is superior to the theoretically unsophisticated and ethically problematic wanderings of applied work. To some extent this schism remains, despite recent reconsideration that applied anthropology (and by extension, ethnomusicology) be viewed as an integrated theoretical and practical field. Within this frame, the action-orientated undertakings of applied anthropology do not detract from the unity of general anthropology, but rather enrich it through a mutually beneficial relationship (Johannsen 1992, 73).

In developing an applied methodology in Dukuduku, I have attempted to draw on theoretical insights offered in the intersections between ethnomusicology, performance studies, oral history, environmental anthropology, social geography and development studies. In linking these particular disciplines, I was encouraged by Brosius's assertion that "while there may have been a proliferation of research around contemporary environmentalism with particular regard to how environments are constructed, represented, claimed and contested, there is an urgency in the broader field of environmental anthropology to better understand ways in which particular topologies—constructions of actual and metaphorical space—are discursively produced and reproduced" (1999, 281). The underlying concern herein is in how people transform landscapes into places of human action, and how nature is imbued with meaning by, and for social praxis and identity. As Lovell suggests: "Nature—be it in the form of landscape, architecture or any other form of habitat—may be understood differently if considered against the background of human experience. Of course nature is also instrumental in shaping social relational discourses, and it is obvious that it is also part of social praxis. But nature is mutually reflexive in its own rapport to human beings. It serves to shape a human consciousness about emplacement, about the workings of the human body, and provides a reflection against which human imagery of the self, at individual and social levels, can be mapped and experienced" (1998, 9).

The symbolic embodiment of nature and its role as mediator of identity is not new to ethnomusicology or performance studies. Jackson (1989) argues that nature extends beyond cultural categories and ontological classifications. He claims that humans enter into a more complex dialectical relationship with landscape where nature itself becomes inscribed onto bodies, and provides both the foundation and the outcome of contextual interactions. In this regard, Jackson suggests that knowledge through artistic expression (such as dance) may be a particularly revealing way to understand natural agency. The performative aspects of ritual activities are considered essential in anchoring belonging, and in endorsing it through social practice.

Seeger (1987), in his analysis of the musical life of the Suya of Upper Xingu in Brazil, provided insight into the interconnectedness between nature, music, dance, speech and other forms of communication in the construction of sense of place or locale. His work extends the notion that it is through music and dance that fundamental aspects of Suya social organisation are recognised, social time is ritually articulated, and an entire cosmological system is grasped (Stokes 1994, 2). Similarly, Roseman focused on how the Temiar of the Malaysian rainforest inscribe in their songs, crucial forms of knowledge of the landscape in a manner that serves to "map and mediate their relationships with the land and each other" (Roseman 1998, 111). Feld (1982) analysed how the expressive modalities of weeping, poetics and song account for how the Kaluli of Papua New Guinea construct their world. He argues that nature (as manifest in forest, waterfalls, rivers, birds, insects, day and night, and annual seasonal changes) provides a visual-auditory-sensate metaphor of self, place and time, and herein become a "reflection" or mirror for Kaluli social relationships (Feld 1984, 395). Finally, contemporary identity amongst Aboriginal Australians is profoundly invested in land, which is assigned exceptional spiritual and cultural importance. Contemporary economic and political empowerment is associated with access to sacred sites and significant landmarks, which are laid claim to through songlines and dream narratives (Magowan 1994).

Land, locality and belonging play themselves out in the South African annals as a painful and unresolved lament. Unlike the research undertaken by Seeger, Roseman, and Feld, who focus on the musical constructions of place by societies which remain profoundly rooted in their cultural landscapes, the people of Dukuduku have been expelled from ancestral place, successively relocated to regions that were geographically, culturally and politically unfamiliar, and pressured into urban labour migration by rural poverty. Here, locality cannot be solely predicated upon collective identity and a sense of cohesion or cultural commensality, as Lovell might suggest (Lovell 1998, 4). Rather, locality in Dukuduku would have to be mobilised as a more complex and dynamic concept of *recreation of place,* a process that would link political displacement, cultural and spiritual memory, economic well-being and global gaze.

During the first interviews conducted by the student researchers with their elders, it became evident that the legacy of successive displacement and rapid modernisation has rendered most residents unable, or unwilling, to readily articulate their value of sense of place:

(Researcher) How did you feel when you left your ancestors and the land you were used to?

(Baba Dube) We felt deep pain. It is heart breaking to have to leave your place and head for an unknown destination.

(Researcher) Do you get the chance to go and speak to your ancestors?

(Baba Dube) You find that where your ancestors were, there are now only plantations and sugar cane. What could we do? We were defeated. As we are residing here, we were defeated. We are here because we respect the law and don't want to be beaten like those who remain in the forests.[12] (Interviewed by student researcher. Professor Nthombela, Khula Village, April 2001)

However, in describing their cultural practices, many interviewees revealed that the essence of their identity remained invested in the ongoing dependence— functional, cultural and spiritual—on land and natural resources. For the Zulu people in general, music, dance and ritual processes are dynamic loci where landscape most vividly articulates with notions of identity and sense of place. Like the Australian Aboriginals, they relate to land through a form of "songlines" (manifest as *izibongo* personal-praises or *amahubo* ceremonial songs that link ancestors with families, clans, the nation) in which rivers, mountains, forests, and birds are typically recalled to situate one in the geographic, genealogical and political present. Despite the pervasive influences of Westernisation in Dukuduku, rituals continue to depend upon reeds, animal sacrifices, bones, skins, medicinal plants, water and sacred sites as signifying materials through which humanness, identity and value are enacted.

This tree—imphahla[13]—in our culture is used when men are going to an important ceremony. They crush the leaves early in the morning before talking to anyone. Then they bathe in the liquid extract in the middle of the cattle kraal.[14] Culturally, this is the medicine of chiefs and *izangoma* (healers). If you have this tree in your yard, you cannot cut it down because it has been blessed by the ancestors. When a person is possessed with ancestral spirits, and the spirit is weak, the leaves and roots of this tree are crushed in a bowl. You have to use a stick from the same tree to stir the liquid. When you drink it, you will vomit, and this way, your spirits will regain their power. (Gogo Mathonsi interviewed by student researcher, Zama Simelane, Khula Village, October 2001)

Fostering a process of dialogue through the research of Indigenous Knowledge Systems (IKS) appeared to me to be both methodologically challenging and politically apposite.[15] In South Africa, the recovery, protection and mainstreaming of indigenous knowledge has been placed at the forefront of post-1994 development policies, as implemented by the Ministry of Arts, Culture, Science and Technology, and by research bodies such as the Human Sciences Research Council and the National Research Foundation.[16] The recovery of IKS is motivated by an attempt to open new moral and cognitive spaces within which constructive dialogue and engagement for sustainable development can begin, and essential to which, is consideration of how knowledge can be recovered and re-appropriated in real time to advance the survival and growth of local communities (Odoro-Hoppers 1998, 3). IKS in South Africa focuses predominantly on biodiversity and the role of indigenous communities in the protection and utilisation of natural resources.[17] IKS, as manifest in music, dance and ritual processes, seeks the recovery of meaning systems as its principle reference.

Participatory Research and Action

Since the Dukuduku cultural and environmental documentation project is motivated by a commitment to sustainable development, the methodological processes draw fundamentally on the participation of the Dukuduku people, for whom project incentives, processes and outcomes must be meaningful. I have drawn on the Participatory Research and Action model (PRA) as formally promulgated by British sociologist, Robert Chambers (1997), and most commonly applied in health, agriculture and environmental development sectors. Realising the shortcomings of development policies and methods of implementation of the 1950s and 1960s, which sought solutions to universal health access, employment, education and environmental protection through western models of modernisation, Chambers began to explore new development methodologies drawing on bottom-up problem identification and solutions for action.[18] In his words, PRA seeks

> actively to involve people in generating knowledge about their own condition and how it can be changed, to stimulate social and economic change based on the awakening of the common people, and to empower the oppressed. The techniques used in PRA include collective research through meetings and socio-dramas, critical recovery of history, valuing and applying folk culture, and the production and diffusion of new knowledge through written, oral and visual forms. (Chambers 1997, 108)

Chambers' "new professionalism" challenged the hypothesis-driven, extractive approach to data gathering by introducing a model that is flexible, and that places the needs, priorities and capacities of the people first. PRA seeks sustainability by encouraging the people to lead; to determine the agenda, to gather and analyse information and, based on capacities and infrastructure, to construct their own community action plan. The role of the professional herein is to listen and learn, and to function as a research partner, a facilitator or a catalyst to change. Essential to PRA is monitoring and evaluation, which is applied in order to enhance people's awareness of the wealth and value of local knowledge and practices, and to empower their actions.

In addition to PRA, the project has been informed by "appreciative inquiry" or an "assets-based approach." This methodology avoids focusing on problem identification, but emphasises cultural strengths, potential and value. Through recognition of what people have, rather than what they lack, the approach seeks to overcome perceptions of deprivation and powerlessness, and encourages self-representation. In the Dukuduku project "appreciative enquiry" is considered particularly significant in building confidence and hope, and herein challenging the hegemonic trajectory of apartheid, which used culture to systematically undermine and demoralise black South Africans.

Once the school headmaster had agreed upon the project concept and a coordinator was elected from amongst the teachers, it was the responsibility of the coordinator to select a group of senior school students to create a core group of ten researchers. Students joined voluntarily and on the basis of their interests in culture and conservation. The group comprised five female, and five male students between the ages of 16 and 18 years. In addition, we solicited the assistance of three unemployed school leavers as our interview transcribers and translators. A third element of the group comprised six elders who, having taken special interest in the documentation process as interviewees during the early phases of the project, were invited to formally join the process as project advisers and evaluators. Finally, in order to ensure sustainability of the project, we established a mentorship program at the end of the year, wherein members of the original group selected, trained and guided an additional ten young researchers.

When launching initial discussions about the project, and in order to ensure cooperation from school faculty and community members, we solicited participation by the community leader, a number of the community elders, the school headmaster and interested teachers. With the guidance of this group, we identified a strategy for documentation, aiming first to train young researchers to interview the elders of the community, whose memories of cultural practices and natural resource utilisation provided a precious, and endangered, source of information. Significantly, we were directed to focus on the *izangoma* (healers) who operate as the essential custodians of information about the environment, linking people to landscape through their knowledge of medicinal plants, their spiritual connectedness and ritual action. It was also suggested by the group of elders that we focus on information regarding rituals of attachment—birthing ceremonies, marriages, funerals and ancestral rites—that continue to provide cultural anchorage to the Dukuduku people in spite of their long history of displacement and social change. Significantly, these rituals depend on the continued use of natural resources to symbolically link people to one another, to their ancestors and to the material world. They are also the sites where songs and dances comment most powerfully upon social and historical identity and sense of geographic place.

In keeping with the techniques of PRA, and as a way to begin to ascertain perceptions of social and environmental place, our first exercise focused on the conceptual mapping of Khula Village and the surrounding forest settlements. Each member of the research team drew a map of his/her homestead and surrounding area, identifying relevant markers (shops, churches and significant natural features such as forest areas, lakes, burial grounds) and the homes of cultural spokespeople whom he/she wished to interview. We then amalgamated all of the drawings to create a composite map, marking the homes of each student researcher and preparing to progressively mark the homesteads of all community members who participated in the documentation process. In the process of creating the composite map, the students had to explain why he/she chose to include certain features; an exercise that stimulated animated discussions that revealed conceptualisations of the area as an historical, social, political, cultural and environmental domain. This exercise represented our first step towards rethinking locality and belonging.

In discussing the aims and objectives of the documentary project, we designed a loose list of questions that would operate as a directional framework in the interview process. In so doing, we applied two exercises: pie charts were used to clarify and prioritize the research agenda,[19] and a matrix provided diagrammatical representation of the interrelatedness of significant musical/ritual practices and natural resources.[20] The matrix is a good example of how the application of a simple visual exercise may stimulate an unexpected level of discussion. In this instance, the exercise facilitated comprehension of the significance of the culture/nature interface, and student researchers were thereby made aware that the survival of those cultural practices that are recognised by the people to constitute the essence of their identity is dependent upon the continued stewardship of certain natural resources. In the words of one student, "Without these rituals, we cannot call ourselves Zulu."

Most researchers chose to conduct their first interviews with grandparents or elderly relatives with whom they felt comfortable. Once each had completed two or three general interviews, they decided to focus on cultural processes that were of particular interest to them, all of which are marked by a specific repertory of songs and dances: female rites of passage (e.g., *ngcekeza* first-menstruation ceremony; *umemulo* coming-of-age ceremony) and the ritual use of natural resources in cleansing, medicating and providing ancestral protection to young women; marriage ceremonies (which are complex, highly ritualised ceremonies and involve a protracted series of symbolic exchanges between families that draw significantly on images of land, ancestors and natural resources); the life-passages of boys, focusing on the passing on of indigenous ecological knowledge related to farming, hunting, and fishing; musical instruments and music making (for example gourd and mouth-bows, whistles, ocarinas and drums, all of which are made from natural resources specific to the region, but are severely endangered); and death, funeral ceremonies and ancestral worship:

> Though their physical graves are left behind, we have to collect the souls of our ancestors to our new home. When a new home is completed, you collect them by taking a branch of a tree called *umlahlankosi*.[21] If it is a female ancestor, you have to collect her with a branch called *umGanu*.[22] You go to their graves and you tell them: "Now my ancestors, I have come to collect you from this abandoned home to a new place." When you collect them using a car, this is what happens. You will go with a few older members of your family and at the graves you will tell each of your ancestors that you are there to collect them to a new home. From there you tell them that they must get into the car and go. Inside the car you don't talk to anyone. If the car stops in town, and it happens that your relative comes and talks to you, you just keep your mouth shut. He will see you carrying *umcansi* (a small reed mat) and

the branches of this tree, and he will understand. (Baba Thethwayo, interviewed by student researcher, Mduduzi Mcambi, Khula Village, April 2001)

All interviews conducted by the student researchers are recorded on audiotape and are transcribed and translated from isiZulu into English. Students have been taught to record songs and instrumental performances on a high-quality DAT recorder with external microphones. Central to the documentation and evaluation process is the use of video to record both the interviews and cultural events that take place in the community. Video materials are essential in soliciting feedback through community screenings, and for increasing the network of participants. Video operates as an extremely powerful medium in giving voice to the elderly in particular.

The project does not only envisage community empowerment as a byproduct of cultural dialogue and exchange, but also facilitates skills development and capacity building through the operational methods of cultural documentation. Through a joint venture established between the University of Natal, the Living Lakes Partnership Program,[23] and the Wildlands Trust, a local conservation NGO, we have built a dedicated computer laboratory at the school which houses twenty-six reconditioned computers, and a small audio-visual unit.[24] To ensure maximum use of documented information, all interviews are stored electronically, and all video material is copied and made available for public viewing in the audiovisual unit. One of the outcomes of the project being developed by the participants is a project Web site, the aim of which is to stimulate dialogue between the people of Dukuduku and indigenous forest peoples globally.

People and agency call for the translation of data into the basis for action. Through a series of PRA workshops with student researchers, elders, members of the Ezemvelo KZN Wildlife services and members of the public, we have begun to explore ways in which the memorisation of indigenous knowledge can empower the community through improved educational resources, by networking with municipal resources and infrastructure, by feeding into existing income-generating ventures such as eco- and cultural tourism and establishing new ideas for income-generation, and by increasing local input into decision-making. As I had anticipated, since undertaking the initial musical survey, two cultural tourism ventures have been established in Khula Village, both of which are run as independent businesses by individuals who have privileged status in the community. Nevertheless, the documentation project has been able to add value to both enterprises. One company has built a traditional Zulu homestead and has constructed a narrative about Zulu life in Dukuduku based on stories, songs and themes developed by the student researchers. The representation of Zulu culture is not one of historicised uniformity, but rather follows the theme of memory, mobility and cultural dynamism. So too does it feature the notion that Zulu cultural identity is strongly located in land, nature and senses of place. The second enterprise follows the form of a "village safari" that takes place in an open vehicle. The tour addresses the historical experiences and contemporary conditions of the Dukuduku residents. One of the stops en route is the school computer laboratory, now a source of pride to the community, and an emblem of progress and opportunity. Here, tourists are presented with an explanation of the student documentation initiative, and recognition is given to the value of cultural emplacement through the collection of songs and oral narratives. Included in this presentation is recognition of the value of electronic media in building skills and in providing a global mouthpiece through which aims and experiences of the documentation initiative may be shared. With no intervention on the part of the project participants, the tour leader has chosen to include the project as a tourist attraction.

In advocating participatory research, so too am I mindful of the restrictions of this approach. While we may have the advantage of being in close proximity to communities in South Africa where such interventions are possible, processes can be frustratingly slow, time-consuming and often difficult to sustain. Chambers' analogy of "handing over the stick" herein deeply challenges the inclination of the researcher to shape research priorities and, for the sake of expediency, steer the processes.

However, processes chosen by others provide opportunities for cultural analysis on several levels. In attempting to do so, I have become appreciably aware of the complementarity of praxis-orientated and theoretical ethnography. Participatory methodologies generate vast amounts of information through discussion, negotiation and memorisation. Memories of the past become an index of contemporary senses of place, and processes of emplacement become shaped by the way narratives of the past are recreated in the present. The "scripting" of this information, in the Fabian (1990) sense, may provide insight into the making, refashioning and performance of identity and meaning. Music, dance and ritual processes are herein particularly potent indicators of the way people build relationships and recreate a sense of place.

Through the application of a documentation-reflection-action process, the Dukuduku project aims to set in motion a conscious repositioning of self and locale. Promoting dialogue through the recovery of cultural and environmental heritage may be an empowering process and may stimulate new forms of cultural production that challenge hegemonic relations and contest the reductionist global gaze, as is typically promoted through eco- and cultural tourism. Further, it is hoped that through active reflection of sense of place, the project may encourage stewardship of the environment, and assist in raising the volume of local voice to promote the well-being of an otherwise marginalised, fragmented people.

Notes

1. I would like to thank Louise Meintjes for her commentary on an earlier draft of this paper.
2. The St. Lucia Wetlands Park is approximately a quarter of a million hectares in size, and is located on the northeastern coast of KwaZulu Natal. Its boundaries extend from Mapelane and the St. Lucia estuary in the south, to Kosi Bay on the Mozambican border in the north. The Park comprises a variety of habitats, including grassland savannah, coastal dune forests, wetlands, beaches and mangroves, and is sanctuary to an exceptionally wide variety of animal, bird, marine and plant species. The Dukuduku forests are located in the southern region of the Park, some 250 km north of the city of Durban.
3. In the run up to, and following the first democratic elections in 1994, there was an escalation of violence in KwaZulu Natal between supporters of the African National Congress and the Zulu nationalist Inkatha Freedom Party.
4. According to the "Convention Concerning the Protection of the World Cultural and Natural Heritage" adopted by UNESCO in 1974, a World Heritage Site relates to an area in which the natural and cultural assets are considered of outstanding universal conservation and aesthetic value. Once granted this status, UNESCO helps to protect and manage the site, and encourages participation of local communities in the preservation of its cultural landscapes. See: www.unesco.org.
5. The Dukuduku forests historically have been known as a place of refuge. Despite its volatile past, Khula Village has become associated with hope, regeneration and opportunity, and hence the choice of the name "Khula," which means "we are small but growing".
6. While the UNESCO convention draws attention to the importance of cultural diversity with in areas assigned World Heritage status, little work is being undertaken to document indigenous cultures in South African World Heritage sites, particularly in relation to their value in environmental decision-making. See Griggs, 1994. www.cwis.org/fwdp/artrack.html
7. See Urry 1990; Smith 1989; and MacCannell 1989, amongst others.
8. For further discussion on cultural tourism in KwaZulu Natal, see Hamilton 1998.
9. The Dukuduku Development and Tourism Association, more recently named the Simunye Association, is a community-based organisation comprising community leaders, elders and environmental NGOs.
10. Cultural Studies falls within the Arts and Culture Learning Area, which is one of eight categories of learning within Outcomes Based Education (OBE). OBE was recently introduced into the South African high school system by the National Ministry of Education as a more flexible, open learning system, basic to which is the privileging of the needs, experiences and capacities of the learners in the attainment of knowledge and formal certification. Within it, Arts and Culture are defined as an integral part of life, embracing the spiritual, material, intellectual and emotional aspects of human society. Culture embodies not only expression through the arts, but also modes of life, behaviour patterns, heritage, knowledge and belief systems.
11. Brosius's (1999) definition of environmentalism is that referring to the broad field of discursive constructions of nature and human agency.
12. Some of the Dukuduku people have not settled in Khula Village, but remain in the indigenous forests where they are treated as illegal squatters.
13. *Brachylaena discolor*
14. The cattle kraal is a sacred space in the Zulu homestead; it is where family ancestors are addressed, oxen are ceremonially slaughtered, and family *amahubo* ceremonial songs are performed. The kraal is strictly designated as a male space.

15. Indigenous Knowledge Systems (IKS) refers to a combination of knowledge systems encompassing technology, social, economic, philosophical, legal and governance. The term refers to the body of knowledge that exists outside of formal education systems but that have enabled communities to survive.

16. Although fairly contentious in South Africa, the designation "indigenous" is broadly applied to people of African decent.

17. This position was ratified by the 1992 UN Convention on Environment and Development.

18. This paradigm shift owes much to the work and inspiration of Brazilian educationalist and political activist, Paulo Freire (1972), who maintained that the poor and exploited should not be judged according to externally imposed systems and standards, but can and should be enabled to analyse their own reality. The Freirian model, referred to as Participatory Learning and Action (PLA), has been associated with adult education movements in Latin America, and has been influential in the shaping of pro-poor initiatives in developing countries throughout the world.

19. Using the image of a pie that can be divided into different size slices, the pie chart operates as a simple diagram that is used by groups to negotiate the relative importance of issues.

20. The matrix is a simple table used to assess one set of items/issues against another.

21. *Ziziphus mucronata* (buffalo thorn)

22. *Sclerocarya birrea* (marula)

23. Living Lakes Partnership is a worldwide project that promotes sustainable development of lake areas in the world. See: www.livinglakes.org.

24. The building of a computer laboratory and the acquisition of so many computers enabled the school to lobby the Ministry of Education for a dedicated Computer Studies position. Computer classes are available to all school students and computer literacy workshops are conducted over the vacation periods for members of the community.

References

Brosius. J. Peter. 1999. "Analyses and Interventions. Anthropological Engagements with Environmentalism." *Current Anthropology* 40(3): 277–309.

Bruner, E. and B. Kirshenblatt-Gimblett. 1994. "Masaai on the Lawn: Tourist Realism in East Africa." *Cultural Anthropology* 9(2): 435–70.

Chambers, Robert. 1997. *Whose Reality Counts? Putting the First Last.* Intermediate Technological Publications.

De Negri, B., E. Thomas, A. Llinigumugabo, I. Muvandi, and G. Lewis. 1998. "Empowering Communities. Participatory Techniques for Community-based Programme Development". In *Trainer's Manual (participant's handbook), Volume (1)*2. Nairobi: The Center for African Family Studies (CAFS), in collaboration with the Johns Hopkins University Center for Communication Programs and the Academy for Education Development.

Fabian, Johannes. 1990. *Power and Performance. Ethnographic Explorations through Proverbial Wisdom and Theatre in Shaba, Zaire.* Madison: University of Wisconsin Press.

Feld, Steven. 1982. *Sound and Sentiment: Birds, Weeping, Poetics and Song in Kaluli Expression.* Philadelphia: University of Pennsylvania Press.

———. 1984. "Sound Structures as Social Structure." *Ethnomusicology* 2: 383–409.

Freire, P. 1972. *Pedagogy of the Oppressed.* London: Penguin Books.

Griggs, R.1994. The Cultural Dimensions of Environmental Decision-making. Center for World Indigenous Studies: www.cwis.org/fwdp/artrack.html

Hamilton, Carolyn. 1998. *Terrific Majesty. The Powers of Skaka Zulu and the Limits of Historical Invention.* Cape Town and Johannesburg: David Philip Publishers.

Jackson, Michael. 1989. *Path Towards a Clearing: Radical Empiricism and Ethnographic Inquiry.* Bloomington, Indiana University Press.

Johannsen, Agneta. 1992. "Applied Anthropology and Post-modernist Ethnography." *Human Organisation* 51(1): 71–81.

Lovell, Nadia, ed. 1998. *Locality and Belonging.* London and New York: Routledge Press.

MacCannel, D.1989. *The Tourist: A New Theory of the Leisure Class.* New York: Schoken Books.

Magowan, Fiona. 1994. "'The Land is Our *Marr* (essence), It Stays Forever': The Yothu-Yindi Relationship in Australian Aboriginal Traditional and Popular Music." In *Ethnicity, Identity and Music. The Musical Construction of Place,* ed. Martin Stokes, 135–55. Oxford; New York: Berg Publishers.

Odora-Hoppers, Catherine. 1998. "Indigenous Knowledge and the Integration of Knowledge Systems: Toward a Conceptual and Methodological Framework." A discussion document prepared for the Human Sciences Research Council (South Africa).

Roseman, Marina. 1998. "Singers of the Landscape: Song, History, and Property Rights in the Malaysian Rain Forest." *American Anthropologist.* 100(1): 106–21.

Seeger, Anthony. 1987. *Why Suya Sing: A Musical Anthropology of an Amazonian People.* Cambridge Studies in Ethnomusicology: Cambridge University Press.

Smith, V.L., ed. 1989. *Hosts and Guests. The Anthropology of Tourism.* Philadelphia: University of Pennsylvania Press.

Stokes, Martin, ed. 1994. *Ethnicity, Identity and Music. The Musical Construction of Place.* Oxford; Providence: Berg.

Urry, J. 1990. *The Tourist Gaze: Leisure and Travel in Contemporary Societies.* London, Newbury Park: Sage Publications.

Glossary

The following glossary provides brief definitions of some of the terms that are used in ethnomusicological literature today yet are seldom defined in glossaries or dictionaries for music students. Drawn from diverse fields, including musicology, anthropology, sociology, geography, and cultural studies, many of these terms are frequently discussed and vocabularies are often modified during dialogues that take place in academic forums and in the ethnographic and theoretical literature. Further discussions about the way these terms are used by ethnomusicologists, including refinement of their meanings, will hopefully take place in the classroom and beyond. To explore the concepts in greater depth see the articles in the collection as well as sources cited in the bibliography for the volume. In addition, you may want to consult dictionaries, encyclopedias, or handbooks that provide in-depth treatment of terminology, placing concepts in historical and social contexts within specific disciplines. See a brief list of glossaries and dictionaries at the end of this section.

A

acculturation   A process by which a culture adapts and is transformed due to the adoption of cultural traits from another society.

advocacy ethnomusicology   A division of applied studies in ethnomusicology. Advocacy-based researchers in ethnomusicology and anthropology facilitate community-based action using knowledge and experience drawn from their fieldwork and specialized understanding and interest in a region or culture.

agency   The ability of individuals to operate independently of the constraints of social structure.

assimilation   Absorption or integration of an individual or minority group into another society or group resulting in loss of independent traits in favor of the dominant society. While this term is sometimes used interchangeably with acculturation, assimilation more often refers to absorption due to forced immigration.

authenticity   The quality of being authentic; the concept is connected to ideas about legitimacy or validity of practices or ideas and is often criticized for its grounding in nostalgia and its adoption by commercial enterprises.

B

borders   Political or geographic spaces in which people interact. They are not neutral lines of separation, but symbols of power that enforce inclusion or exclusion. *See also*: **boundaries, frontiers**

boundaries   Perimeters that define a community or nation. Boundary sites may contain events and meanings that are inaccessible to some communities. *See also*: **borders, frontiers**

C

civil rights   The fundamental rights of every citizen to freedom of expression, movement, and ideas.

class   A group of people who are unified by their socio-economic similarity. The differences between class groups create differences in material prosperity and power expressed in social values, beliefs and customs.

codes   Set of culturally recognized signs or rules which guide how meaningful action is interpreted.

collective action   Relatively spontaneous action carried out by an assembly of people in response to conditions or circumstances that are perceived as problematic. Their actions are often in opposition to existing social norms.

colonialism   System of occupation, exploitation and control of political and economic systems of a territory or country by another.

commodification   Transformation of noncommodities into products that can be bought or sold. Artifacts, actions, objects, and ideas are evaluated in terms of economic exchange and the competition and/or power that accompanies it.

cultural imperialism   Aggressive promotion and advancement of one culture over another, believing its values are superior to others. Imperialist groups use the benefit of their economic and/or political influence to modify or replace other cultures.

cultural tourism   A term used widely by the travel industry to describe travel and activities related to heritage, the arts, local heritage, leisure, and natural resources of a particular area.

culture   The ideas, beliefs, and practices of individuals and groups of people; a social group of social system that shares these ideas, beliefs and practices. Recently this term has been identified with the boundaries around regions (identified as nations) and social groups that the economically and politically powerful have created.

culture industry   Social, political, and economic structures that contribute to the production of beliefs and practices and shape it through standardization and commodification.

D

diaspora   People who live outside of their homelands due to voluntary or forced migration. They consistently maintain connections to their place of origin while in new localities.

diffusion   Movement of cultural ideas or traits from one society to another, the original meanings may change as they spread.

discourse   Language as well as nonverbal signifying systems in use that contribute to the construction of social knowledge and conventions.

E

emic   Insider's perspective on cultural practice including self-description (reflexivity) and conforming to community values and practices. *See also: **etic***

enculturation   The process of learning and incorporating cultural knowledge, practices, and values.

essentialism   Belief that traits that include gender and race are innate rather than socially constructed.

ethnic group   A group of people whose members share awareness of a common cultural identity.

ethnicity   Mutual identities among social groups who share common cultural, historical, racial, religious, or linguistic practices, norms, and belief systems.

ethnocentrism   Judging or interpreting a social group by one's own standards.

ethnography   Systematic description of a way of life based on first-hand observation of people in particular social settings.

ethnoscape   Landscapes that are comprised of diverse and ever-changing populations who reconstruct and reconfigure their histories and everyday lives in response to new media forms and places.

etic   Outsider's perspective on cultural practices. *See also:* **emic**

exoticism   Adopting behaviors or evoking places or social situations that are different from local practice

F

feminism   A social theory and political movement concerned with political, economic, and social equality, including freedom of choice, for both women and men.

fieldwork   Collecting empirical data typically by participating in and/or observing a social activity.

frontier   Marginal sites where real or imagined interaction, adaptation, conflict and blending take place. *See also*: **borders, boundaries**

G

gender   Culturally constructed identity, typically designated as female or male, that carries a complex of assumptions about behaviors, practices, values, and roles.

globalism   Policy or attitude that places world-wide interests before those of national or regional concerns.

globalization   Increased connectivity and interdependence among social groups, economically, politically, and culturally, resulting in an increase in global cultural exchange and, some argue, a simultaneous reduction in global cultural and political differences.

glocalization   Indicates emerging forms of social power in which citizens create products or provide services for use in the global marketplace that are customized for use locally.

H

habitus   Habitual practices and assumptions of a particular social environment that are internalized and expressed in bodily actions and behaviors. This generative process challenges and recreates culturally constructed meanings and values.

hegemony   The ability of a dominant class to exercise social and cultural power over economic, social and cultural events and expressions.

human rights   Fundamental moral rights for life with dignity that people are entitled to regardless of their race, ethnicity, language, gender, sexuality, nationality, or abilities. These rights are often codified and enforced through binding agreements and treaties.

hybridity   Creation of dynamically mixed cultures, sometimes identified as syncretic, but beyond cultural blending, it is also connected to self-empowerment and defiance of authority.

I

identity   The distinctive characteristics of an individual or group which are constructed, negotiated and defended in different contexts, on individual, community, national and international levels.

ideology   Unified set of ideas, beliefs and symbols used to interpret one's place in the world.

imagined community   Communities—often nations—in which social bonds are imagined rather than experienced, collective experience is reinforced through technological developments that have become the means of representing them.

indigenous peoples   Original inhabitants of a geographic area.

intellectual property (IP)   Legal ownership of an idea or creative work, protected in some cultures with copyright, patents, and trademarks.

intellectual property rights (IPR)   Rights for individuals and groups to control their core beliefs and principles.

invented traditions   Practices or processes used by nations and other social groups which seek to instill values, norms that imply an (imagined) continuity with the past.

M

mass media   Information produced by a few for consumption by many people. Also, forms of communication (newspapers, magazines, radio, television, film, Internet, etc.) and institutions that create and distribute information to reach mass audiences.

mediascape   Setting or environment for the transmission of messages and people, reflecting the global production and dissemination of information via the media.

mediation   In popular music studies, how media forms (including radio, television, video, etc.) represent music to the listener/viewer.

modernity   Literally the condition of being modern, refers to the idea that through processes of social and cultural change, the present is different from the past.

multiculturalism   Promotion of the coexistence of a number of different cultural groups in a common space with support for the maintenance of distinctive cultural identities.

music industry   A range of institutions and associated markets including record companies, retail organizations, magazines, newspapers and journals, musical instrument/equipment makers, sound recording and reproduction technology, advertisers, and agencies for royalties and rights.

N

nation   A community of people who recognize each other as sharing a common identity, with a focus on a real or imagined homeland.

nation-state   A sovereign state with government, boundaries, and symbolic markers such as a flag, anthem, as well as a popular self-image.

nationalism   Ideologies that support the construction of a nation based on cultural, linguistic, geographic, historical, and/or racial claims.

neocolonialism   The continued economic and political control by countries that conquered and dominated much of the world between the sixteenth and twentieth centuries.

O

orientalism   Term adopted to refer to European and Euro-American fascination with, and cultural appropriation of, Asian cultures. The stereotyping of ideas in academic writing, literary and artistic expression is said to embody and maintain a colonialist and imperialist attitude.

P

pluralism   A condition in which political power is dispersed among diverse ethnic, racial, religious, or social groups.

postcolonialism   Applied widely to events and agendas that reference the European colonial system (especially during the nineteenth and twentieth centuries) and its ongoing impact on the development of identities.

postmodernism   Often refers to the practice of rejecting or abandoning broad schematic perspectives in favor of fragmented, discontinuous and ephemeral views.

R

race   A mode of classifying human beings that distinguishes them based on inherited biological or physical characteristics. It is now widely believed that racial categories are socially constructed and contribute to political and economic inequality among social groups.

racism   Belief in the superiority of certain racial groups that leads to prejudice towards people of other races. The attitudes and behaviors expressed in popular cultural practices have reinforced and challenged racist discourse.

reflexivity   Process of examining, questioning, monitoring and reflecting on one's own experience. In ethnomusicology it is used especially to refer to positioning of the fieldworker in relation to those she/he is working with, to maintain a mutuality in social interaction.

repatriate   To restore or return material goods or ideas to individuals, groups, or nations that represent the original owners. These include human remains, sacred objects, recordings, songs, place names, and other artifacts.

S

schizophonia   Separation of a sound from its source. Refers especially to the impact on everyday sound environments of electroacoustical representations of original sounds.

sexuality   The expression of sexual identity, though sexual activity, or the projection of identity. Sexuality is shaped by beliefs, values, attitudes, behaviors, physical appearance as well as socialization.

social movement   Collective attempt to bring about or to resist social change that typically operates outside of institutional and political structures, especially issues that the political or institutional processes have failed to address.

soundscape   The acoustic environment, used to refer to characteristic sounds of a place.

subculture   A social group organized around age, ethnicity, race, class, gender, or sexuality that exhibits values, beliefs, attitudes, and/or lifestyles that distinguish it from—and place it outside—the existing mainstream society.

syncretism   The fusion of two or more culture traits to create a new composite practice.

T

technoculture   Communities and forms of cultural practice that negotiate and are often transformed by technology.

traditional knowledge (TK)   Constantly evolving creations, innovations and cultural expressions that are passed from generation to generation.

transculturation   A process in which individuals and groups move to a new society and selectively adopt elements of the culture, involves both agency and loss of cultural traits.

transnationalism   The migration of members of a particular ethnic group from their homes to another country, who continue to maintain close contact with traditions they left behind.

Sources

Barfield, Thomas. 1997. *The Dictionary of Anthropology*. Oxford, UK; Malden, MA: Blackwell.

Barker, Chris. 2004. *The Sage Dictionary of Cultural Studies*. London; Thousand Oaks, CA: Sage Publications.

Barnard, Alan, and Jonathan Spencer. 1998. *Encyclopedia of Social and Cultural Anthropology*. London; New York: Routledge.

Brooker, Peter. 2003. *A Glossary of Cultural Theory*. London Edward Arnold.

Calhoun, Craig. 2002. *Dictionary of the Social Sciences*. Oxford; New York: Oxford University Press.

Drislane, Robert, and Gary Parkinson. "Online Dictionary of the Social Sciences" Athabasca University and ICAAP. Available: http://bitbucket.icaap.org/.

Edgar, Andrew, and Peter R. Sedgwick. 2002. *Key Concepts in Cultural Theory*. Rev. ed. Routledge Key Guides. London: New York.

Hartley, John et al. 2002. *Communication, Cultural and Media Studies: The Key Concepts*, 3rd ed. Routledge Key Guides. London: Routledge.

Horner, Bruce, and Thomas Swiss. 1999. *Key Terms in Popular Music and Culture*. Malden, MA; London: Blackwell.

Johnson, Allan G. 2000. *Blackwell Dictionary of Sociology: A Users Guide to Sociological Language*, 2nd ed. Oxford, UK; Malden, MA: Blackwell.

Kennedy, Michael. 1995. *The Oxford Dictionary of Music*. Oxford: Oxford University Press.

Payne, Michael, ed. 1996. *A Dictionary of Cultural and Critical Theory*. Oxford, UK; Cambridge MA: Blackwell.

Randel, Don Michael. 2003. *The Harvard Dictionary of Music*, 4th ed. Cambridge, MA: Belknap Press of Harvard University Press.

Sadie, Stanley, and John Tyrrell. 2001. *The New Grove Dictionary of Music and Musicians*, 2nd edition. London: Grovemusic. Available: www.grovemusic.com.

Shuker, Roy. 2002. *Popular Music: The Key Concepts*, Routledge Key Guides. London: Routledge.

Winthrop, Robert H. 1991. *Dictionary of Concepts in Cultural Anthropology*. New York: Greenwood.

Research Resources

This list of research resources includes books and articles, audio and video recordings, and Web sites that together are providing a foundation for contemporary research and classroom study about music and the discipline of ethnomusicology. They have been selected, from among many possible sources, for their connections to the subjects in this collection. The ultimate goal of this list is to provide resources for new research that has been inspired by the studies presented by the twenty-four authors in this collection.

Books and Articles

The books and articles listed here include some of the most widely cited sources in contemporary ethnomusicological research. The reader is reminded that they are just a few among many excellent ethnographic, analytical and theoretical studies that can play a significant role in exploring a topic of interest. The bibliographies and notes found in the listed books and articles should be used to find other related sources for more in-depth information on a subject of particular interest. For a comprehensive, annotated list of recently published books see *Ethnomusicology: A Guide to Research*, published in 2004.[1] In addition, students, teachers, performers, and others seeking information on contemporary issues in ethnomusicology are encouraged to use online databases that provide access to the most current information on books and articles as well as other media.

Allen Ray, and Lois Wilken, eds. 1998. *Island Sounds in the Global City: Caribbean Popular Music and Identity in New York*. New York: New York Folklore Society.

Anderson, Benedict. 1991. *Imagined Communities: Reflections on the Origins and Spread of Nationalism*. Rev. ed. London: Verso.

Aparicio, Frances R. 1998. *Listening to Salsa: Gender, Popular Music, and Puerto Rican Cultures*. Hanover, NH: Wesleyan University Press.

Aparicio, Frances R., and Cándida F. Jáquez, eds. 2003. *Musical Migrations: Transnationalism and Cultural Hybridity in Latin/o America*. New York: Palgrave Macmillan.

Appadurai, Arjun. 1996. *Modernity at Large: Cultural Dimensions of Globalization*. Minneapolis: University of Minnesota Press.

———, ed. 1988. *The Social Life of Things: Commodities in Cultural Perspective*. Cambridge: Cambridge University Press.

Askew, Kelly. 2002. *Performing the Nation: Swahili Music and Cultural Politics in Tanzania*. Chicago: University of Chicago Press.

Attali, Jacques. 1985. *Noise: The Political Economy of Music*. Minneapolis: University of Minnesota Press.

Austerlitz, Paul. 1997. *Merengue: Dominican Music and Dominican Identity*. Philadelphia: Temple University Press.

Averill, Gage. 1997. *A Day for the Hunter, a Day for the Prey: Popular Music and Power in Haiti*. Chicago: University of Chicago Press.

Bakhtin, Mikhail. 1981. *The Dialogic Imagination*. Austin: University of Texas.

Baranovitch, Nimrod. 2003. *China's New Voices: Popular Music, Ethnicity, Gender, and Politics, 1978–1997*. Berkeley: University of California Press.

Barz, Gregory F., and Timothy J. Cooley, eds. 1997. *Shadows in the Field: New Persepctives for Fieldwork in Ethnomusicology*. New York: Oxford University Press.

Bayton, Mavis. 1997. *Frock Rock: Women Performing Popular Music*. Oxford: Oxford University Press.

Béhague, Gerard, ed. 1984. *Performance Practice: Ethnomusicological Perspectives*. Westport, CT: Greenwood.

———, ed. 1994. *Music and Black Ethnicity: The Caribbean and South America*. New Brunswick: Transaction Publishers.

Bennett, Andy, and Kevin Dawe, eds. 2001. *Guitar Cultures*. Oxford; New York: Berg.

Bergeron, Katherine, and Philip V. Bohlman, eds. 1992. *Disciplining Music: Musicology and Its Canons*. Chicago; London: University of Chicago Press.

Berliner, Paul F. 1993. *The Soul of Mbira: Music and Traditions of the Shona of Zimbabwe*. Chicago: University of Chicago Press.

———. 1994. *Thinking in Jazz: The Infinite Art of Improvisation*. Chicago: University of Chicago Press.

Blacking, John. 1973. *How Musical Is Man?* Seattle: University of Washington Press.

Blum, Stephen, Philip V. Bohlman, and Daniel M. Neuman. 1991. *Ethnomusicology and Modern Music History*. Chicago: University of Chicago Press.

Bohlman, Philip V. 1988. *The Study of Folk Music in the Modern World*. Bloomington: Indiana University Press.

———. 2003. *A Very Short Introduction to World Music*. Oxford: Oxford University Press.

Bohlman, Philip V., and Michael B. Bakan, eds. 2004. *The Music of European Nationalism: Cultural Identity and Modern History*. Santa Barbara: ABC CLIO.

Born, Georgina, and David Hesmondhalgh, eds. 2000. Western Music and Its Others: Difference, Representation, and Appropriation in Music. Berkeley, CA: University of California.

Bourdieu, Pierre. 1984. *Distinction: A Social Critique of the Judgement of Taste*. Cambridge: Harvard University Press.

———. 1977. *Outline of a Theory of Practice*. Translated by Richard Nice. Cambridge: Cambridge University Press.

Brackett, David. 1995. *Interpreting Popular Music*. Cambridge: Cambridge University Press.

Broughton Simon, et al., eds. 1999. *World Music: The Rough Guide* 2nd ed. Vol. 1, *Africa, Europe, and the Middle East*, Vol. 2, *Latin and North America, Caribbean, India, Asia and Pacific*. London: The Rough Guides.

Browner, Tara. 2002. *Heartbeat of the People*: Music and Dance of the Northern Pow-Wow. Urbana: University of Illinois Press.

Buchanan Donna A. 1998. "Bulgaria's Magical Mystère Tour: Postmodernism, World Music Marketing, and Political Change in Eastern Europe." *Ethnomusicology* 41(1):131–58.

———. 1995. "Metaphors of Power, Metaphors of Truth: the Politics of Music Professionalism in Bulgarian Folk Orchestras." *Ethnomusicology* 39(3):381–416.

Burnett, Robert. 1996. *The Global Jukebox: The International Music Industry*. London: Routledge.

Butler, Judith. 1993. *Bodies That Matter: On the Discursive Limits of "Sex."* New York: Routledge.

———. 1990. *Gender Trouble: Feminism and the Subversion of Identity*. New York: Routledge.

Byerly, Ingrid. 1998. "The Music Indaba: Music and Mirror, Mediator, and Prophet in the South African Transition from Apartheid to Democracy." *Ethnomusicology* 42(1): 1–44.

Chun, Allen, Ned Rossiter, and Brian Shoesmith, eds. 2004. *Refashioning Pop Music in Asia*. London; New York: RoutledgeCurzon.

Clark, Walter Aaron, ed. 2002. *From Tejano to Tango: Latin American Popular Music*. New York: Routledge.

Clayton, Martin, Trevor Herbert, and Richard Middleton, eds. 2003. *The Cultural Study of Music: A Critical Introduction*. New York: Routledge.

Clifford, James. 1988. *The Predicament of Culture: Twentieth Century Ethnography, Literature, and Art*. Cambridge: Harvard University Press.

———. 1997. *Routes: Travel and Translation in the Late Twentieth Century*. Cambridge: Cambridge University Press.

Clifford, James and George E. Marcus, eds. 1986. *Writing Culture: The Poetics and Politics of Ethnography*. Berkeley: University of California.

Cohen, Dalia, and Ruth Katz. 2004. *Palestinian Arab Music: A Maqam Tradition in Practice*. Chicago: University of Chicago Press.

Cohen, Sara. 1991. *Rock Culture in Liverpool: Popular Music in the Making*. New York: Oxford University Press.

Connell, John, and Chris Gibson. 2003. *Sound Tracks: Popular Music, Identity and Place*. London; New York: Routledge

Crafts, Susan D., Daniel Cavicchi, and Charles Keil. 1993. *My Music*. Hanover, NH: Wesleyan University Press.

Dawe, Kevin, ed. 2004. *Island Musics*. Oxford; New York: Berg.

DeNora, Tia. 2000. *Music in Everyday Life*. Cambridge: Cambridge University Press.

Erlmann, Veit. 1999. *Music, Modernity, and the Global Imagination*. New York: Oxford University Press.

———, ed. 2004. *Hearing Cultures: Essays on Sound, Listening and Modernity*. Oxford; Berg.

Eyerman, Ron, and Andrew Jamison. 1998. *Music and Social Movements: Mobilizing Traditions in the Twentieth Century*. Cambridge: Cambridge University Press.

Feld, Steven. 1982. *Sound and Sentiment: Birds, Weeping, Poetics, and Song in Kaluli Expression*. Philadelphia: University of Pennsylvania.

———. 1984. "Sound Structure as Social Structure." *Ethnomusicology* 28: 383–409.

Feld, Steven, and Keith H. Basso, eds. 1996. *Senses of Place*. Santa Fe, NM: School of American Research.

Feld, Steven, and Donald Brenneis. 2004. "Doing Anthropology in Sound." *American Ethnologist* 31(4): 461–74.

Finnegan, Ruth. 1989. *The Hidden Musicians: Music-Making in an English Town*. Cambridge: Cambridge University Press.

Floyd, Samuel A., Jr. 1995. *The Power of Black Music: Interpreting Its History from Africa to the United States*. New York: Oxford University Press.

Forman, Murray. 2002. *The 'Hood Comes First: Race, Space, and Place in Rap and Hip Hop*. Middletown, CT: Wesleyan University Press.

Foucault, Michel. 1972. *The Archaeology of Knowledge*. Translated by A.M. Sheridan Smith. New York: Pantheon.

Friedson, Steven. 1996. *Dancing Prophets: Musical Experience in Tumbuka Healing*. Chicago: University of Chicago Press.

Frith, Simon. 1996. *Performing Rites: On the Value of Popular Music*. Cambridge: Harvard University Press.

———, ed. 2004. *Popular Music: Critical Concepts in Media and Cultural Studies*. 4 vols. New York: Routledge Press.

Frith, Simon and Andrew Goodwin, eds. 1990. *On Record: Rock, Pop, and the Written Word*. New York: Pantheon.

Frith, Simon, Will Straw, and John Street, eds. 2001. *The Cambridge Companion to Pop and Rock*. New York: Cambridge University Press.

Garofalo, Reebee, ed. 1992. *Rockin' the Boat: Mass Music and Mass Movements*. Boston: South End Press.

———. 1993. "Whose World, What Beat: The Transnational Music Industry, Identity, and Cultural Imperialism." *World of Music* 35(2):16–32.

Geertz, Clifford. 1973. *The Interpretation of Cultures: Selected Essays*. New York: Basic Books.

Gibson, Chris, and John Connell. 2005. *Music and Tourism: On the Road Again*. Toronto: University of Toronto Press.

Giddens, Anthony. 1979. *Central Problems in Social Theory: Action, Structure and Contradiction in Social Analysis*. Berkeley: University of California Press.

———.1991. *Modernity and Self-identity: Self and Society in the Late Modern Age*. Stanford: Stanford University Press.

Goertzen, Chris. 1997. *Fiddling for Norway: Revival and Identity*. Chicago: University of Chicago Press.

Gouk, Penelope, ed. 2000. *Musical Healing in Cultural Contexts*. Aldershot: Ashgate.

Guilbault, Jocelyne, et al. 1993. *Zouk: World Music in the West Indies*. Chicago: University of Chicago Press.

Hall, Stuart. 1981. "Notes on Deconstructing 'the Popular'." In *People's History and Socialist Theory*, edited by Raphael Samuel, 227–40. London: Routledge and Kegan Paul.

———. 1997. "Old and New Identities, Old and New Ethnicities." In *Culture, Globalization, and the World System: Contemporary Conditions for the Presentation of Identity*, edited by Anthony D. King, 41–68. Minneapolis: University of Minnesota Press.

Hayward, Philip, ed. 1999. *Widening the Horizon: Exoticism in Post-War Popular Music*. Sydney: John Libbey.

———, ed. 1998. *Sound Alliances: Indigenous Peoples, Cultural Politics, and Popular Music in the Pacific*. London: Cassell.

Hebdige, Dick. 1987. *Cut 'n' Mix*. New York: Comedia.

———. 1979. *Subculture: The Meaning of Style*. London: Routledge.

Herndon, Marcia, and Suzanne Ziegler, eds. 1990. *Music, Gender, and Culture*. Intercultural Music Studies, 1. Wilhelmshaven, West Germany: Florian Noetzel Verlag.

Hesmondhalgh, David, and Keith Negus, eds. 2002. *Popular Music Studies*. London: Oxford University Press.

Hobsbawm, Eric and Terence Ranger, eds. 1983. *The Invention of Tradition*. Cambridge: Cambridge University Press.

Inda, Jonathan Xavier, and Renato Rosaldo, eds. 2002. *The Anthropology of Globalization: A Reader*. Malden, MA: Blackwell.

James, Deborah. 1999. *Songs of the Women Migrants: Performance and Identity in South Africa*. Edinburgh: Edinburgh Press for the International African Institute.

Jarviluoma, Helmi. 2000. "From Manchuria to the Tradition Village: On the Construction of Place via Pelimanni Music." *Popular Music* 19:1: 101–24.

Jones, Steve, ed. 2002. *Pop Music and the Press*. Philadelphia: Temple University Press.

Kaeppler, Adrienne, and Olive Lewin. 1988. *Come mek me hol' yu han': The Impact of Tourism on Traditional Music*. Kingston: Jamaica Memory Bank.

Kartomi, Margaret, and Stephen Blum, eds. 1994. *Music Cultures in Contact: Convergences and Collisions*. Basel: Gordon and Breach.

Keil, Charles. 1991. *Urban Blues*. Chicago: University of Chicago Press.

Keil, Charles, and Steven Feld, eds. 1994. *Music Grooves: Essays and Dialogues*. Chicago: University of Chicago Press.

Keyes, Cheryl L. 2002. Rap Music and Street Consciousness. Urbana: University of Illinois.

King, Richard, and Timothy J. Craig, eds. 2002. *Global Goes Local: Popular Culture in Asia*. Vancouver: University of British Columbia Press.

Kirshenblatt-Gimblett, Barbara. 1998. *Destination Culture: Tourism, Museums, and Heritage*. Berkeley: University of California Press.

———. 1995. "Theorizing Heritage." *Ethnomusicology* 39(3): 367–79.

Kisliuk, Michelle. 1998. *Seize the Dance: BaAka Musical Life and the Ethnography of Performance*. New York; Oxford: Oxford University Press.

Koskoff, Ellen, ed. 1987. *Women and Music in Cross-Cultural Perspective*. New York: Greenwood .

Krims, Adam. 2000. *Rap Music and the Poetics of Identity*. Cambridge; New York: Cambridge University Press.

Kruse, Holly. 2003. *Site and Sound: Understanding Independent Music Scenes*. New York: Peter Lang.

Levin, Theodore. 1996. *The Hundred Thousand Fools of God: Musical Travels in Central Asia (and Queens, New York)*. Bloomington: Indiana University Press.

Leyshon, Andrew, David Matless, and George Revill, eds. 1998. *The Place of Music*. New York: Guilford.

Lipsitz, George. 1994. *Dangerous Crossroads: Popular Music, Postmodernism and the Poetics of Place*. London: Verso.

Lysloff, René T. A., and Leslie C. Gay, eds. 2003. *Music and Technoculture*. Music/culture. Middletown, CT: Wesleyan University Press.

Magrini, Tullia, ed. 2003. *Music and Gender: Perspectives from the Mediterranean*. Chicago: University of Chicago Press.

Manuel, Peter. 1993. *Cassette Culture: Popular Music and Technology in North India*. Chicago: University of Chicago Press.

———. 1988. *Popular Musics of the Non-Western World: An Introductory Survey*. New York: Oxford University Press.

Marcus, George E. 1998. *Ethnography Through Thick and Thin*. Princeton: Princeton University Press.

Mattern, Mark.1998. *Acting in Concert: Music, Community, and Poltical Action*. New Brunswick; London: Rutgers University Press.

McCann, Anthony. 2001. "All That is Not Given is Lost: Irish Traditional Music, Copyright, and Common Property." *Ethnomusicology* 45(1): 89–106.

McClary, Susan. 1990. *Feminine Endings: Music Gender and Sexuality*. Minneapolis: University of Minnesota Press.

Meintjes Louise. 1990. "Paul Simon's Graceland, South Africa, and the Mediation of Musical Meaning." *Ethnomusicology* 34(1):37–73

———. 2003. *Sound of Africa! Making Music Zulu in a South African Studio*. Durham, NC: Duke University Press.

Mendoza, Zoila S. 2000. *Shaping Society through Dance: Mestizo Ritual Performance in the Peruvian Andes*. Chicago: University of Chicago Press.

Merriam, Alan P. 1964. *The Anthropology of Music*. Evanston, IL: Northwestern University Press.

Mitchell, Timothy. 1996. *Popular Music and Local Identity: Rock, Pop and Rap in Europe and Oceania*. London: Leicester University Press.

———, ed. 2001. *Global Noise: Rap and Hip-Hop Outside the USA*. Middletown, CT: Wesleyan University Press.

Moisala, Pirkko and Beverly Diamond, eds. 2000. *Music and Gender*. Urbana: University of Illinois Press.

Monson, Ingrid. 1999. "Riffs, Repetition, and Theories of Globalization." *Ethnomusicology* 43(1): 31–65.

———. 1996. *Saying Something: Jazz Improvisation and Interaction*. Chicago: University of Chicago Press.

———, ed. 2000. *The African Diaspora: A Musical Perspective*. New York: Garland.

Nattiez, Jean-Jacques. 1990. *Music and Discourse: Toward a Semiology of Music*. Princeton: Princeton University Press.

Negus, Keith. 1999. *Music Genres and Corporate Cultures*. London: Routledge.

———. 1996. *Popular Music in Theory: An Introduction*. Hanover; London: Wesleyan University Press.

———. 1992. *Producing Pop. Culture and Conflict in the Popular Music Industry*. London: Arnold; New York: Routledge, Chapman, and Hall.

Nercessian, Andy. 2002. *Postmodernism and Globalization in Ethnomusicology: An Epistomological Problem*. Lanham, MD; London: Scarecrow.

Nettl, Bruno. 1983 *The Study of Ethnomusicology: Twenty-nine Issues and Concepts*. Urbana: University of Illinois Press.

Nettl, Bruno and Philip V. Bohlman, eds. 1991. *Comparative Musicology and Anthropology of Music: Essays on the History of Ethnomusicology*. Chicago: University of Chicago Press.

Nettl, Bruno, with Melinda Russell, ed. 1998. *In the Course of Performance: Studies in the World of Musical Improvisation*. Chicago: University of Chicago Press.

Neuenfeldt, Karl, ed. 1997. *The Didjeridu: from Arnhem Land to Internet*. Sydney: J. Libbey/Perfect Beat Publications.

Oliver, Paul, ed. 1990. *Black Music in Britain: Essays on the Afro-Asian Contribution to Popular Music*. Milton Keynes; Philadelphia: Open University Press.

Pacini Hernandez, Deborah. 1995. *Bachata, a Social History of a Dominican Popular Music*. Philadelphia: Temple University Press.

Pacini Hernandez, Deborah, et al., eds. 2004. *Rockin' Las Américas: The Global Politics of Rock in Latin/o America*. Pittsburgh: University of Pittsburgh Press.

Porter, James and Timothy Rice, eds. 1998–2002. *The Garland Encyclopedia of World Music*. 10 vols. New York: Garland.

Post, Jennifer C. 2004. *Ethnomusicology: A Research Guide*. New York: Routledge.

Pratt, Ray. 1990. *Rhythm and Resistance: Explorations in the Political Use of Popular Music*. New York: Praeger.

Qureshi, Regula Burckhardt. 1995. *Sufi Music of India and Pakistan: Sound, Context, and Meaning in Qawwali*. Chicago: University of Chicago Press.

Qureshi, Regula Burckhardt, ed. 2002. *Music and Marx: Ideas, Practice, Politics*. New York: Routledge.

Radano, Ronald M. and Philip V. Bohlman, eds. 2000. *Music and the Racial Imagination*. Chicago: University of Chicago Press.

Ramnarine, Tina K. 2003. *Ilmatar's Inspirations: Nationalism, Globalization, and the Changing Soundscapes of Finnish Folk Music*. Chicago: University of Chicago Press.

Randall, Annie J. 2004. *Music, Power and Politics*. London: Routledge.

Rees, Helen. 2000. *Echoes of History: Naxi Music in Modern China*. Oxford: Oxford University Press.

Reyes, Adelaida. 1999. *Songs of the Caged, Songs of the Free: Music and the Vietnamese Refugee Experience*. Philadelphia: Temple University Press.

Rice, Timothy. 1994. *May it Fill Your Soul: Experiencing Bulgarian Music*. Chicago: University of Chicago Press.

Román-Velázquez, Patria. 1999. *The Making of Latin London: Salsa Music, Place and Identity*. Aldershot: Ashgate.

Rose, Tricia. 1994. *Black Noise: Rap Music and Black Culture in Contemporary America*. Hanover, NH: Wesleyan University Press.

Roseman, Marina. 1991. *Healing Sounds from the Malaysian Rainforest: Temiar Music and Medicine*. Los Angeles: University of California; Sydney: Oceania Publications.

Ross, Andrew, and Tricia Rose, eds. 1994. *Microphone Fiends: Youth Music & Youth Culture*. New York: Routledge.

Ross, Andrew. 1992. "New Age Technoculture." *Cultural Studies*, edited by Laurence Grossberg, Cary Nelson, and Paula Treichler, 531–55. New York: Routledge.

———. 1991. *Strange Weather: Culture, Science, and Technology in the Age of Limits*. New York: Verso.

Sadie, Stanley, and John Tyrrell. 2001. *The New Grove Dictionary of Music and Musicians*. 2nd edition. London: Grovemusic. Available: *Grovemusic Online*.

Sanjek, Roger, ed. 1990. *Fieldnotes: The Makings of Anthropology*. Ithaca: Cornell University Press.

Sarkissian, Margaret. 2000. *D'Albuquerque's Children: Performing Tradition in Malaysia's Portuguese Settlement*. Chicago: University of Chicago Press.

Schade Poulsen, Marc. 1999. *Men and Popular Music in Algeria: The Social Significance of Raï*. Austin: University of Texas Press.

Schafer, R. Murray. 1977. *The Tuning of the World*. New York: Knopf.

Scruggs, T. M. 1999. "'Let's Enjoy as Nicaraguans': The Use of Music in the Construction of a Nicaraguan National Consciousness. " *Ethnomusicology* 43(2): 297–321.

———. 1998. "Nicaraguan State Cultural Initiative and 'The Unseen Made Manifest." *Yearbook for Traditional Music* 30: 53–73.

Seeger, Anthony. 1987. *Why Suyá Sing: A Musical Anthropology of a Amazonian People*. Cambridge: Cambridge University Press.

Simonett, Helena. 2001. *Banda: Mexican Musical Life across Borders*. Middletown, CT: Wesleyan University Press.

Slobin, Mark. 1993. *Subcultural Sounds: Micromusics of the West*. Hanover, NH: Wesleyan University Press.

Slobin, Mark, ed. 1996. *Retuning Culture: Music Changes in Central and Eastern Europe*. Durham, NC: Duke University Press.

Small, Christopher. 1987. *Music of the Common Tongue: Survival and Celebration in Afro-American Music*. New York: Riverrun.

———. 1998. *Musicking: The Meanings of Performing and Listening*. Hanover, NH: Wesleyan University Press.

Smith, Susan J. 1997. "Beyond Geography's Visible Worlds: A Cultural Politics of Music." *Progress in Human Geography* 21: 502–29.

Solís, Ted. 2004. *Performing Ethnomusicology: Teaching and Representation in World Music Ensembles*. Berkeley; Los Angeles; London: University of California Press.

Sterne, Jonathan. 2003. *The Audible Past: Cultural Origins of Sound Reproduction*. Durham, NC: Duke University Press.

Stokes, Martin. 1992. *The Arabesk Debate: Music and Musicians in Modern Turkey*. Oxford: Clarendon; New York: Oxford University Press.

———. 2004. "Music and the Global Order" *Annual Review of Anthropology* 33: 47–72.

———, ed. 1994. *Ethnicity, Identity and Music: The Musical Construction of Place*. Oxford: Berg.

Stokes, Martin, and Philip V. Bohlman, eds. 2003. *Celtic Modern: Music at the Global Fringe*. Lanham, MD: Scarecrow.

Sugarman, Jane C. 1999. "Imagining the Homeland: Poetry, Songs, and the Discourses of Albanian Nationalism." *Ethnomusicology* 43(3): 419–458.

Swiss, Thomas, John Sloop, and Andrew Herman, eds. 1998. *Mapping the Beat: Popular Music and Contemporary Theory*. Malden, MA: Blackwell Publishers.

Taylor, Timothy D. 1997. *Global Pop: World Music, World Markets*. New York: Routledge.

———. 2001. *Strange Sounds: Music, Technology, and Culture*. New York: Routledge.

Théberge, Paul. 1997. *Any Sound You Can Imagine: Making Music/Consuming Technology*. Hanover; London: Wesleyan University Press.

Thornton, Sarah. 1996. *Club Cultures: Music, Media and Subcultural Capital*. Hanover, NH: Wesleyan University Press.

Turino, Thomas. 1996. *Moving Away From Silence: Music of the Peruvian Altiplano and the Experience of Urban Migration*. Chicago: University of Chicago Press.

———. 2000. *Nationalists, Cosmopolitans, and Popular Music in Zimbabwe*. Chicago: University of Chicago Press.

Veal, Michael E. 2000. *Fela: The Life & Times of an African Musical Icon*. Philadelphia, PA: Temple University Press.

Wade, Peter. 2000. *Music, Race, and Nation*. Chicago: University of Chicago Press.

Waksman, Steve. 1999. *Instruments of Desire: The Electric Guitar and the Shaping of Musical Experience*. Cambridge: Harvard University Press.

Wallis, Roger, and Krister Malm. 1984. *Big Sounds from Small Peoples: The Music Industry in Small Countries*. New York: Pendragon.

Walser, Robert. 1993. Running with the Devil: Power, Gender, and Madness in Heavy Metal Music. Hanover, NH: Wesleyan University Press.

Washabaugh, William, ed. 1998. *The Passion of Music and Dance: Body, Gender and Sexuality*. Oxford: Berg.

Waterman, Christopher. 1990. *Jùjú: A Social History and Ethnography of an African Popular Music*. Chicago: University of Chicago Press.

Waxer, Lise. 2002. *The City of Musical Memory: Salsa, Record Grooves, and Popular Culture in Cali, Colombia*. Middletown, CT: Wesleyan University Press.

Whiteley, Sheila. 2000. *Women and Popular Music: Sexuality, Identity, and Subjectivity*. London: Routledge.

Whiteley, Sheila, Andy Bennett, and Stan Hawkins, eds. 2004. *Music, Space and Place: Popular Music and Cultural Identity*. Aldershot, Hants, England; Burlington, VT: Ashgate.

Wong, Deborah. 2004. *Speak it Louder: Asian Americans Making Music*. London; New York: Routledge.

Young, Richard, ed. 2002. *Music, Popular Culture, Identities*. Critical Studies, 19. Amsterdam New York: Rodopi.

Zipp, Bruce, and Pratima V. Rao, ed. 1997. *Borrowed Power: Essays on Cultural Appropriation*. New Brunswick: Rutgers University Press.

Audio Recordings

The Recording Industry Association of America (RIAA) has noted a decline in the production and sale of audio CDs in their year-end statistics during the last few years. It is widely understood that this is due to the popularity of other media sources, especially online digital download recordings such as mp3s. Nevertheless, RIAA statistics show that 745.9 million audio CD units were shipped in the United States (worth over $11 billion) in 2003[2] and the International Recording Media Association (IRMA) indicates that there were over five billion audio CD units replicated worldwide in 2004.[3] Considering unique titles (the latest statistics are from RIAA in 2002) there were 33,443 unique titles produced in the United States and 90,000 around the world (including re-releases).[4] Since ethnomusicologists are concerned with all forms of musical expression, a discography that identifies the hundreds of thousands of titles currently in circulation is clearly impractical. The following selected list of recordings from the inventories of recording labels frequently found in college and university libraries includes both studio recordings by music producers as well as field recordings by ethnomusicologists. Detailed notes on music, musicians, and instruments accompany many of these recordings. The list should be used as a key to the wider range of titles available on these and other recording labels. You will find additional citations to recordings in online databases for library collections, recording companies and other commercial establishments. For more comprehensive selected lists subdivided geographically see the "Current Discography" published three times each year for the Society for Ethnomusicology (http://www.ethnomusicology.org/) and the list of audio recordings from 1994–2004 published in *Ethnomusicology: A Guide to Research*. The list should be used as a key to the wider range of titles available on these and other recording labels. You will find additional citations to recordings in online databases for library collections, recording companies and other commercial establishments. For more comprehensive selected lists subdivided geographically see the "Current Discography" published three times each year for the Society for Ethnomusicology (www.ethnomusicology.org) and the list of audio recordings from 1994–2004 published in *Ethnomusicology: A Guide to Research*.[5]

ARC Music (W. Sussex, UK, http://www.arcmusic.co.uk/)
> *Bhangra: Original Punjabi Pop.* 2003. ARC Music EUCD 1795. Compact disc. Punjabi pop music of India. Performed by Jasbir Jassi; Ashok Masti; Jaspinder Narula; Ashoo Punjabi; Rajinder Raina; Preet Brar; and Simran & Tripat.
> *Crossing Borders.* 2001. ARC Music EUCD 1660. Compact disc. Global jazz-fusion. Performed by Trilok Gurtu, Re-Orient, Atzilut, Nour-Eddine, Ravi, Hossam Ramzy, Jason Carter, Oliver Shanti, Sirocco, Hariprasad Chaurasia, Larry Coryell, and others.
> *Festival Mondial des Cultures Drummondville.* ARC Music EUCD 1579. Compact disc. Recordings made in 1997, 1998 and 1999 at the annual Festival Mondial des Cultures in Canada. Groups presented from Israel, Spanish Asturias, Albania, Slovakia, Lithuania, Ukraine, Turkey, Yakutia, India, China, Korea, Japan, the Philippines, Mexico, Colombia, Peru and Chile.
> *Music of the Silk Road.* 2004. ARC Music EUCD 1845. Compact disc. Traditional music from Armenia, Azerbaijan, Iran, Afghanistan, Turkmenistan, Uzbekistan, Kyrgyzstan, Mongolia, China, and Turkey. Various performers.

Auvidis (Gentilly, France, http//www.auvidis.com.)
> *Bali: Balinese Music of Lombok = Musique balinaise de Lombok.* 1997. Auvidis/Unesco D 8272. Compact disc. Recorded by David Harnish, 1983–1989. Music of the minority Hindu Balinese population of Lombok. Includes music for large gamelan, small ensembles, solo instrument, and vocal ensemble.
> *Musiques traditionnelles d'Ukraine = Traditional Music from Ukraine.* 1998, 1993. Auvidis Ethnic B 6871 (Silex: 225211, 225216). Two compact discs. Recorded in 1992 and 1993 by Hubert Boone and Olèna Chevtchouk. Various performers.
> *Trinidad: Music from the North Indian Tradition = Musique de la tradition d'Inde du Nord.* 1999. Auvidis/Unesco D8278. Compact disc. Recorded 1991–1994 in Trinidad and Tobago. Various performers.

Buda Musique (Paris, France, http://www.budamusique.com/)
> *Inde: Kobiyals, Fakirs & Bauls = Oral Traditions of Bengal.* 2001. Buda Records 1977782. Compact disc. Recorded by Gautam Nag at the Boral Baul Festival, Calcutta in 1999. Various performers.
> *Kolyma, chants de nature et d'animaux = Songs of Nature and Animals.* 1995. Buda Records 92566-2. Compact disc. Sibérie: 3. Performed by people of four villages in the Kolyma: Kolymskoe, Cerskij, Andrjuskino and Nelemnoe. Cukc even Jukaghir: Kolyma Cukc, Even & Jukaghir

Canyon Records (Phoenix, Ariz., http://www.canyonrecords.com/)
> *Blackfoot Confederacy: Setting the Record Straight.* 2004. Canyon Records CR-6372. Compact disc. Songs of the Blackfoot Confederacy sung by members of the Blackfeet, Kainai, Piikani and Siksika Nations.
> *Veteran's Honor Songs.* 2003, 1993. Canyon Records CR-6214. Compact disc. Includes songs honoring service in World War I and II, Vietnam, and Desert Storm. Performed by the Black Lodge Singers.

Narada World (Milwaukee, Wisc., http://www.narada.com/)
> *Border: La Linea.* 2001. Narada World 72438-10265-2-6. Compact disc. Emigration and immigration songs from Mexico. Lyrics in Spanish, English and Mayan. Principal performer: Lila Downs, with supporting musicians.
> *Playing for Change.* 2004. Narada. Compact disc. Celebrates the freedom and the lives of street musicians in Los Angeles, New Orleans, and New York. Various performers.
> *SOS Planet Earth.* 2004. Narada World 72435-82103-2-3. Compact disc. A benefit CD, the funds earned from its sale will go to several named foundations. Performers: Johnny Clegg; Toure Kunda; Sergent Garcia; Seba; Youssou N'Dour; Peter Gabriel; Rokia Treare; Wazimbo & Orchestra Marrabenta Star de Moçambique; I Muvrini; Sting; Bebel Gilberto; Zuco 103; Sacred System; David Hewitt; Chris Hinze; Dalai Lama.

Naxos World (Hong Kong, http://www.naxos.com/)
> *Bhangra Beatz.* 2000. Naxos World 76012-2. Compact disc. Popular music of Pakistan, India and the diaspora. Compiled from material originally issued by Kiss Records in 1993, 1996–1997 and 1999. Performers: Anakhi; Jassi Premi; Balbir Bittu; Jazzy B; Balwinder Safri; Sukshinder Shinda; K.B. & the Gang; Soni; The Sahotas; Bhinda Jatt.
> *Electric Highlife: Sessions from the Bokoor Studios.* 2002. Naxos World 76030-2. Compact disc. Highlife songs of Ghana. Sung in Akan, Ewe, Ga, Nzima, and English. Various performers.
> *Russian Songwriter: A Collection from Boris Grebenshikov.* 2002. Naxos World 76039-2. Compact disc. Political singer songwriter Boris Grebenshikov, vocal and guitar with other supporting musicians.

Nimbus (Monmouthshire UK, http://www.wyastone.co.uk/)
> *Buddhist Music of Tianjin. Naxi Music from Lijiang.* 2000. Nimbus NI 7064/5. Two compact discs. Performers: Tianjin Buddhist Music Ensemble and Dayan Ancient Music Association.
> *Ca Trù, the Music of North Vietnam.* 2001. Nimbus NI 5626. Compact disc. Recorded by Robin Broadbank. Performers: The Hanoi Ca Trù Thai Ha Ensemble.
> *Dance Music from Brazil: Choros and Forró.* 2000. Nimbus NI 1741. Four compact discs. Recorded 1992-1995 in Salvador, Pernambuco, and Recife. Performing groups: Os Ingênuos and Oficina de Cordas.

Ocora Records (Paris, France, http://www.radiofrance.fr/divers/boutique/cd/)
  Colombie: Palenque de San Basilio = Palenue of San Basilio. 2004. Ocora C 560187. Compact disc. Songs from Palenque of San Basilio, the first settlement of emancipated Blacks in the new world. Various performers.
  Honduras: Chants des Caribs Noirs = Songs of the Black Caribs. 2002. Ocora C 560162. Compact disc. Recorded in Cristales, Guadalupe, and Plaplaya, Honduras. Performers: Wabaruagun Ensemble.
Pan Records (Leiden, The Netherlands, distributed by Arhoolie, http://www.arhoolie.com/catalog/pan.shtml/)
  Baishibai: Songs of the Minority Nationalities of Yunnan. 1995. Pan 2038CD. Compact disc. Field recordings made in Yunnan province between 1982 and February 1994, by Zhang Xingrong. Various performers.
  Rabi: The New Home of the Exiled Banabans from Ocean Island. 2000. Pan Records PAN 2095. Compact disc. Music of the people of Rabi (in Fiji) who originated from the Micronesian island of Banaba (Ocean Island), now part of the Republic of Kiribati.
  Tuvalu: A Polynesian Atoll Society. 1994. Pan Records PAN 2055. Compact disc. Field recordings by Ad and Lucia Linkels in 1990. Includes diverse traditional and contemporary forms. Various performers.
  Women's Love and Life: Female Folklore from Azerbaijan. 1996. Pan Records. PAN 2028CD. Compact disc. Azerbaijani field recordings made by Taira Kerimova, 1979–1990. Various performers.
Piranha (Berlin, Germany, http://www.piranha.de/)
  Ashkelon: Moroccan Mawal. 1998. Piranha CD-PIR 1260. Compact disc. Moroccan and Judeo-Moroccan mawal and traditional songs in popular style, with ensemble of both traditional and modern instruments. Performer: Emil Zrihan, vocal; with supporting instrumentalists.
  Ballads at the End of Time. 2003. Piranha CD-PIR 1787. Compact disc. Serbian popular music played by the LaDaABa Orchest led by saxophonist Boris Kovac.
Putumayo (New York, NY, http://www.putumayo.com/)
  Asian Groove. 2002. Putumayo World Music PUT 202-2. Compact disc. Performers include: Bally Jagpal; Karmix; Mo' Horizons; A.S. Kang; Badar Ali Kahn; Mungal with Nitin Sawhney; Yulduz Usmanova; Deepak Ram; Susheeta Raman; Bally Sagoo; Kam Dhillon.
  Greece: A Musical Odyssey. 2004. Putumayo World Music PUT 225-2. Compact disc. Contemporary Greek music performed by Apenanti, Melina Aslanidou, Kostas Mantzios, Anastasia Moutsatsou,George Dalaras, Elly Paspala, Children of the Revolution, Melina Kana, Pantelis Thalassinos, Theodosia Stiga, Sofia Papazoglou, Gerasimos Andreatos, Glykeria, and Kostas Makedonas.
  World Reggae. 2004. Putumayo World Music PUT 221-2. Compact disc. Performers from Ivory Coast, Cape Verde, Nigeria Cameroon, Algeria/France, Brazil, India, New Caledonia, French Guiana. Performers include Kana; Apache Indian; Intik; Majek Fashek; Maria de Barros; Gnawa Diffusion; Alê Muniz; Más y Más; Chris Combette; Alpha Blondy; Bernaud Uedre; and Kaïssa.
Rounder (Cambridge, Mass., http://www.rounder.com/)
  The Hidden Gate: Jewish Music Around the World. 2003. Rounder 1161-5084-2/11661-5085-2/1161 615 083-2. Two compact discs. Hebrew, Yiddish, Ladino and Judeo-Arabic music. Performers include Chava Alberstein; Ofra Haza; Savina Yannatou; Yasmin Levy; The Klezmatics; The Klezmer Conservatory Band, and others.
  Radio Freedom: Voice of the African National Congress and the People's Army Umkhonto we Sizwe. 1996, 1985. Rounder CD 4019. Compact disc. Music and political commentary recorded from broadcasts of Radio Freedom, the underground station of the ANC and the Umkhonto we Sizwe. Recorded in 1985 in Lusaka, Zambia and Addis Ababa, Ethiopia.
  The World of Gnawa. 2001. Rounder 82161-5080-2. Two compact discs. Recorded from 1990–1995, Casablanca and Marrakesh, Morocco. Gnawa musicians of Morocco. Various performers.
Rykodisc (Salem, Mass., http://www.rykodisc.com/)
  Utom: Summoning The Spirit: Music In The T'boli Heartland. 1997. Rykodisc RCD 10402. Compact disc. Field recordings by Manolete Mora. Music of the T'boli people of the Philippine island of Mindanao; "utom" refers to a T'boli form of composition in which the sounds of the natural world are incorporated into the music.
  Voices of the Rainforest. 1991. Rykodisc RCD 10173. Compact disc. Recorded by Steven Feld. Sounds of the rainforest and music of the Bosavi people of Papua New Guinea.
  The Yoruba/Dahomean Collection: Orishas Across the Ocean. 1998. Rykodisc RCD 10405. Compact disc. Field recordings by Melville Herskovits, Josefina Tarafa, Juan Liscano, and Laura Boulton. Ritual songs and drumming from religions of the Yoruba/ Dahomean diaspora: Haitian vodou, Brazilian candomble, Cuban anteria, and Trinidadian shango.
Shanachie (Newton, NJ, http://www.shanachie.com/)
  Ghazal: Moon Rise Over the Silk Road. 1999. Shanachie 66024. Compact disc. Improvisations by Persian and Indian musicians. Performers: Kayhan Kalhor, kamancheh; Shujaat Hussain Khan, sitar and vocals; Swapan Chaudhuri, tabla.
  If I'd Been Born An Eagle. 1997. Shanachie Records 64080. Compact disc. Vocal and instrumental music of of Tuva. Performers: Huun Huur Tu
Sharp Wood Productions (SWP) (Utrecht, The Netherlands, http://www.swp-records.com/)
  Batonga Across the Waters. 1996. Sharp Wood Productions SWP 005. Compact disc. Traditional Tonga music from Zambia and Zimbabwe. Recorded by Michael Baird, Nov.-Dec. 1996 and by Bert Estl, April 1997. Various performers.
  Origins of Guitar Music: Southern Congo and Northern Zambia '50, '51, '52, '57. '58. 2000, Sharp Wood Productions SWP 015. Compact disc. International Library of African Music. Songs with guitar and various other instruments from northern Zambia, Congo, Malawi, and Zimbabwe.

Zambia Roadside: Music From Southern Province. 2003. Sharp Wood Productions SWP 019. Compact disc. International Library of African Music. Music of the Tonga people from Southern Province, Zambia. Recorded by Michael Baird in 1996 and 2002.

Zambush. Vol. 1: Zambian Hits from the 80s. 2004. Sharp Wood Productions SWP 027. Compact disc. International Library of African Music. Documents a period in Zambian music history when bands were transforming traditional sounds from rural regions into urban, electric pop.

Smithsonian (Washington, DC, http://www.folkways/si.edu/)

Abayudaya: Music from the Jewish People of Uganda. 2003. Smithsonian Folkways Recordings. SFW CD 40504. Compact disc. Lullabies, political songs, children's songs, religious rituals, hymns, and celebratory music. Sung in Luganda, Lusoga, Lunyole, English, and Hebrew. Various artists.

Badenya: Manden Jaliya in New York City. 2002. Smithsonian Folkways SFW CD 40494. Compact disc. Recorded 2000-2001. Vocal and instrumental performances on bala, kora, n'goni, tambin, djembe, dundun, guitar, and bass. Performers: Abdoulaye Diabate; Abou Sylla; Keba Bobo Cissoko; Adjaratou 'Tapani' Sissoko; Mahamadou Saliou Suso; Bah Bailo; Famoro Dioubate.

Bamboo on the Mountains: Kmhmu Highlanders from Southeast Asia and the U.S. 1999. Smithsonian Folkways SFW 40456. Compact disc. Folk music of Kmhmu people from Laos and Vietnam and those living in the U.S.

Bosavi: Rainforest Music from Papua New Guinea. 2001. Smithsonian Folkways SFW CD 40487. Three compact discs. One booklet (80 pp.) by Steven Feld. Guitar bands of the 1990s, sounds and songs of everyday life, ritual, and ceremony of the Bosavi of Papua New Guinea. Various performers.

Raíces Latinas: Smithsonian Folkways Latino Roots Collection. 2002. Smithsonian Folkways SFW CD 40470. Compact disc. Latino roots music from the Caribbean to the Andes and from Brazil to the American Southwest. Various performers.

Safarini: In Transit, Music of African Immigrants. 2000. Smithsonian Folkways SFW 40457. Compact disc. Popular music by African immigrants to the U.S. Pacific Northwest. Various performers.

Tuva, Among the Spirits: Sound, Music, and Nature in Sakha and Tuva. 1999. Smithsonian Folkways SFW 40452. Compact disc. Recorded 1995–1998 by Joel Gordon and Ted Levin. Folk music and nature sounds from Sakha and Tuva performed by Huun-Huur-Tu and other performers.

Sterns (Sterns/Earthworks and Sterns Africa, http://www.sternsmusic.com/)

In Griot Time: String Music from Mali. 2000. Stern's Africa STCD 1089. Compact disc. Recorded 1992-1998 by Banning Eyre. Djelimady Tounkara; Super Rail Band; Yayi Kanouté; Adama Tounkara; Kandia Kouyaté; Lobi Traoré; Sibiri Samaké; Oumou Sangaré; Sali Sidibé; Salif Keita; Toumani Diabaté; Habib Koite; Ali Farka Touré; Basekou Kouyaté and Dirck Westervelt.

Kwaito: South African Hip-hop. 2000. Sterns/Earthworks STEW42CD. Compact disc. Rap and popular music from South Africa. Sung primarily in English, Zulu, and Sesotho. Brenda Fassie; Arthur; Bongo Maffin; Aba Shante; M'du; Boom Shaka; Jimmy B; Spokes "H".

Topic Records (London, UK, http://www.topicrecords.co.uk/)

Before the Revolution: A 1909 Recording Expedition in the Caucasus and Central Asia by the Gramophone Company. 2002. Topic Records TSCD921. Compact disc. From the International Music Collection of the British Library Sound Archive. Field recordings made in Central Asia in 1909. Vocal works sung in Armenian, Azeri, Bukharan, Chechen, Ingush, Kabadian, Kazakh, Kumyk, Kyrgyz, Persian, Pushto, Sart, and Old Turkic.

Music in the World of Islam. 1994, 1976. Topic Records TSCD 901/902/903. Three compact discs. Vol. 1. Human voice & lutes; Vol. 2. Strings, flutes & trumpets; Vol. 3. Reeds & bagpipes; drums & rhythms. Recorded 1960–1975, principally in the field, by Jean Jenkins and Poul Rovsing Olsen.

Zanzibar: Music of Celebration. 2000. Topic Records TSCD 917. Compact disc. From the International Music Collection of the British Library National Sound Archive. Field recordings by Janet Topp Fargion. Music from Tanzania. Various performers.

Traditional Crossroads (New York, NY, http://www.traditionalcrossroads.com/)

Afghanistan Untouched. 2003. Traditional Crossroads 80702-4319-2. Two compact discs. Recorded in 1968 by Mark Slobin. Tajik and Uzbek music; Hazara music; Pashtun music; Herati music; Kazakh music; Turkmen music.

Music of the Sultans, Sufis, and Seraglio. 2000. Traditional Crossroads CD 4301-4304. Four compact discs. Music of the Ottoman Empire in Turkey. Performed by the group Lalezar on kanun, kemençe; ney, tanbur, percussion, and vocals.

Women of Istanbul. 1998. Traditional Crossroads CD 4280. Compact disc. Cabaret songs popular in Istanbul from 1920 to mid 1940s. Recorded 1929–1953. Various performers.

Trikont (Munich, Germany, http://www.trikont.com/)

Africa Raps. 2001. Trikont US-294. Compact disc. Rap music of Senegal, Gambia, and Mali. Various performers.

Suburban Bucharest: Mahala Sounds from Romania. 2004. Trikont US-0323. Compact disc. Recorded ca. 1936–2004. Historical and contemporary music that documents musical influences from Serbia, Turkey and the Middle East. Various performers.

Stranded in the U.S.A.: Early Songs of Emigration. 2004. Trikont-US0326. Compact disc. Compiled by Christoph Wagner from an archive of 78s recorded between 1922 and 1959. Songs represent a social history of immgration among various ethnic groups.

VDE-GALLO (Lausanne, Switzerland, http://www.vdegallo.ch/)

Afrique du Sud: Le Chant des Femmes Xhosa. cp1996. VDE-Gallo CD-879. Compact disc. Folk songs of the Xhosa of South Africa. Performers: Ngqoko Women's Ensemble with accompanying local instrumentalists.

Bosnie: Chants Soufis de Sarajevo. 1998. VDE CD-927. Compact disc. Sufi music from Bosnia and Hercegovina. Performer: Nesidu-l-Huda.

World Music Network (London, UK, http://www.worldmusic.net/)
> *The Rough Guide to African Rap.* 2004. World Music Network RGNET 1126CD. Compact disc. Includes rap music from Gambia, Mali, and Senegal. Artists include Prophets Of Da City; Manu Dibango; Positive Black Soul; X Plastaz; Mabulu, and others.
> *The Rough Guide to Brazilian Hip-Hop.* 2004. World Music Network RGNET 1141CD. Compact disc. Artists include Somos Nós A Justiça; Elza Soares; Black Gero; Stereo Maracanã; MC Partideiro; Instituto & Sabotage, and others.
> *The Rough Guide to Cajun Dance.* 2004. World Music Network RGNET 1139. Compact disc. Cajun music. Artists include: Steve Riley & The Mamou Playboys; Beausoleil; Zachary Richard; Magnolia Sisters; Balfa Toujours; Dewey Balfa, Marc Savoy & D.L. Menard, The Balfa Brothers, and others.
> *The Rough Guide to Tex-Mex.* 1999. World Music Network RGNET 1037. Compact disc. Artists include: Flaco Jiménez, Los Pinkys, Jimmy Sturr, Los Dos Gilbertos, Lydia Mendoza, Tony De La Rosa and Conjunto Bernal

World Village (Burbank, Calif., http://www.worldvillagemusic.com/)
> *Drop the Debt.* 2003. World Village 479008. Compact disc. Supporting the Jubilee Debt Campaign to end world debt. Performers include: Cesaria Evora, El Hadj N'Diaye, Sally Nyolo, Oliver Mtukudzi, and others.
> *Festival in the Desert.* 2003. World Village 468020. Compact disc. Recorded live in 2003. Performers: Takamba Super Onze; Afel Bocoum; Tartit; Robert Plant & Justin Adams; Sedoum Ehl Aïda; Lo'Jo + Django; Oumou Sangaré; Ali Farka Touré; Tinariwen; Adama Yalomba; Tidawt; Ludovico Einaudi & Ballake Sissoko; Kel Tin Lokiene; Kwal + Foy-Foy; Tindé; Aïcha Bint Chighaly; Igbayen; Baba Salah; Blackfire; Django.
> *Tinariwen: Amassakoul.* 2004. World Village 468026.Compact disc. Malian Touareg group whose songs are rooted in political events that have affected the Touareg people during the second half of the twentieth century.
> *Warsaw Village Band.* 2003. World Village 468028. Compact disc. Polish songs and dances that combine traditional shepherd's songs, punk rock, and electronic remixes on vocal, fiddle, cello, jew's harp, krzaqattack, baraban drum, and frame drum. Performers: Katazyna Szurman; Maja Klecz; Sylwia Swiatkowska; Wojciech Krzak; Piotr Glinski; and Maciej Szajkowsi.

Video Recordings

There are hundreds of valuable videos and films available for use in ethnomusicological research and study, I include here a briefly annotated list of commercially available sources that present issues of particular interest to readers of this volume. Many will generate lively discussion both inside and outside of the classroom. Some of the topics explored through music and dance in the following sources include issues connected to race and racism, gender and sexuality, national identities, politics of resistance, indigenous rights, censorship, technology and the music industry, the impact of media on local communities, transnationalism, the diaspora, and borderlands. All listed titles are in English or have English subtitles and all titles listed are available in either VHS and/or DVD format. A continuing source for information on videos, audio recordings, and other media is the Society for Ethnomusicology Web site (www.ethnomusicology.org) for film/videography lists compiled by ethnomusicologists three times each year. See also the videography in *Ethnomusicology: A Research Guide.*[6]

Amandla! A Revolution in Four Part Harmony. 2002. Directed by Lee Hirsch. Distributed by HBO/Cinemax. Video. 108 mins. Details how protest songs were used in the struggle to end apartheid in South Africa.
Amrit beeja = The Eternal Seed. 1996. Produced by Meera Dewan. Women Make Movies. Video. 43 mins. Combines music, poetry and humor as rural women protest agribusiness, preferring their traditional methods of farming.
Arab Diaries 2: Youth. 2000. Produced by Ali Bilail, Samia Chala, and Muriel Aboulrouss. Distributed by First Run/Icarus. Video. 26 mins. Part of a five-part series, *Youth* examines the difficulties faced by young women in Lebanon, Egypt, and Algeria. The Algerian segment features two female rap musicians whose lyrics express political dissent. In various languages with English subtitles.
Beating the Drum. 1998. Directed by Fiona Cochrane. Distributed by the Australian Film Institute. Video. 51 mins. Musicians, scholars, promoters, and audience members discuss controversies over concepts of "world music," cultural appropriation, and ownership.
Beats of the Heart. 2000–2003. Shanachie Home Video. Directed by Jeremy Marre. Fourteen videos, ca. 60 min. each. Originally published between 1979 and 1988, this series of documentaries examines different music scenes—often politically charged—from around the world. See the following titles listed in this compilation: *Chase the Devil: Religious Music of the Appalachians*; *Konkombe: Nigerian Music*; *No. 17 Cotton Mill Shanghai Blues*; *Rhythm of Resistance: Black South African Music*; *There'll Always Be Stars in the Sky: The Indian Film Music Phenomenon*; *Romany Trail*; *Roots, Rock, Reggae: Inside the Jamaican Music Scene*; *Salsa: Latin Pop Music in the Cities*; *Shotguns and Accordions: Music of the Marijuana Growing Regions of Columbia*; *The Spirit of Samba: Black Music of Brazil*; *Sukiyaki and Chips: The Japanese Sounds of Music*; *Tex-Mex: The Music of the Texas-Mexican Borderlands*; *Two Faces of Thailand: A Musical Portrait*.
Bhangra Jig. 2001. Directed by Pratibha Parmar. Distributed by Women Make Movies. Video. 4 min. Short video about how young Asian people in Scotland celebrate desire and self-pride through dance and music.
The Bhangra Wrap. 1995. Directed by Nandini Sikand. Through the Looking Glass Productions; Distributed by NAATA/Crosscurrent Media. Video. 20 mins. Documents popular music of Punjabi youth in Canada and the United States that fuses folk bhangra of India and Pakistan with techno, reggae, and rap.
Breaking the Silence: Afghan Music. 2002. Directed by Simon Broughton. Distributed by the Danish Film Institute. Video. 60 mins. Documents the return of music to Kabul after the fall of the Taliban. Filmed just weeks after the Taliban left,

it describes the conditions of music in Afghanistan during the last twenty years

Buena Vista Social Club. 1999. Directed by Wim Wenders. Artisan Entertainment. Video. 105 mins. Documentary on the group of Cuban musicians recorded by Ry Cooder in 1996, includes interviews with musicians and concert footage.

Chase the Devil: Religious Music of the Appalachians. 1990, 1982. Directed by Jeremy Marre. Distributed by Shanachie. Video. 60 mins. Beats of the Heart series. Footage from Virginia, Tennessee, and Kentucky, with performances by Dee and Delta Hicks, Nimrod Workman, Virgil Anderson, and the Roan Mountain Hilltoppers.

Chutney in Yuh Soca: A Multicultural Mix. 1993. Directed by Karen Martinez. Filmakers Library. Video. 36 mins. Three short films: *Chutney in Yuh Soca* on East Indian and African populations of Trinidad and Tobago; *The Gospel Truth* on a black family in Great Britain; and *Songs For Our Daughters* on West Indian women in Britain.

The Coolbaroo Club. 1996. Directed by Steve Kinnane, Lauren Marsh, Roger Scholes. Coolbaroo Club Productions in association with Annamax Media; Distributed by Ronin Films. Video. 55 mins. The story of an Aboriginal-run dance club in Perth in the 1950s and its role as a political organization in a hostile environment.

Cruisin' J-Town. 1995, 1975. Directed by Duane Kubo. Video. 30 mins. Distributed by NAATA. Japanese American musicians discuss their ethnic identity and their assimilation into mainstream American society. Features performances by jazz fusion artists including Dan Kuramoto and the band Hiroshima.

Dancing in the Moonlight. 1988. Directed by Trevor Graham. Distributed by the Australian Film Institute. Video. 52 mins. The Fifth Festival of Pacific Arts in Townsville, Australia in 1988 with interviews with musicians and others who discuss the impact of colonialism, the preservation of linguistic and musical practices, and media access for indigenous groups.

The Darker Side of Black. 1994. Producer, Lina Gopaul. Filmakers Library. Video. 59 min. Explores issues such as machismo, misogyny, and homophobia in black popular music in Jamaica, London, and the U.S. in rap, hip hop, and dance-hall. Features interviews with Cornel West, Tricia Rose and others.

Desi Remix Chicago Style. 1996. Third World Newsreel. Directed by Balvinder Dhenjan and Manjeet Mudan. Video. 46 mins. On the efforts of three Punjabi bands in Chicago and London to use their music as a bridge between the competing cultural influences of India and America.

The Devil's Dream. 1991. Directed by Mary Ellen Davis. Cinema Guild. Video. 68 mins. Social and political conditions in Guatemala with excerpts from "The Legion of the 24 Devils" folk dance-drama.

Do Re Me. 2001. Directed by Peng Yang. The Documentary Department of Xinjiang TV Station. Video. 30 mins. Depicts a music shop in Kashgar, Xinjiang province, where craftsmen make instruments and teach tourists to play them. English subtitles.

Down to the Crux. 2000. Directed by Michael Lucio Sternbach. Video. 45 mins. Explores connections between avant-garde jazz and the civil rights movement in the 1960s. Features music of John Coltrane, Archie Shepp, Albert Ayler, and others.

Dream Weavers = Hinabing Panaginip. 1999. Directed by Fruto Corre. Bookmark. Video. 45 mins. Documents the T'boli of Lake Sebu in the Philippines. Shows how this indigenous group has kept their artistic traditions alive in spite of incursions from the lowlands.

Exploring the World of Music. 1988. Produced and directed by Martin D. Toub. Annenberg/CPB Project. Twelve 30 min. videos. See especially: Vol. 1: *Sound, Music and the Environment*; Vol. 2: *The Transformative Power of Music*; Vol. 3: *Music and Memory*; Vol. 4: *Transmission, Learning Music*. Vol. 11: *Composers and Improvisors*. Vol 12: *Music and Technology*.

Family across the Sea. 1990. Directed by Tim Carrier. South Carolina ETV. Video. 58 mins. A delegation of Gullah people travels from the United States to Sierra Leone to trace their heritage though a ballad of South Carolina and Sierra Leone.

The Flute Player. 2003. Directed by Jocelyn Glatzer. Distributed by the National Asian American Telecommunications Association. Video. 53 mins. Documents musician and activist Arn Chorn Pond's return to Cambodia after living in the United States for twenty years.

Following One's Way. 2000. Directed by Diego Fernando Hernandez. First Run/Icarus Films. 26 min. Documents the struggle of a Colombian singer to balance family responsibilities and meet the expectations of the music industry.

Free to Sing? The Music of Suman Chatterjee. 2003. Directed by Sudipto Chatterjee. Distributed by Epic Actors' Workshop & Choir. Video. 57 mins. Documents a political singer from Calcutta, with interviews, song sequences and scenes from Calcutta. Narrated by Pete Seeger.

From Angkor to America: The Cambodian Dance and Music Project of Van Nuys, California, 1984–1990. 1991. Directed by Amy Catlin. Apsara Media for Intercultural Education. Video. 37 mins. A Cambodian refugee family revives classical dance and music traditions while in the United States.

Genghis Blues. 1999. Directed by Roko Belic. Distributed by Roxie Releasing. Video. 88 mins. Follows bluesman Paul Pena, who has taught himself throat-singing, on a visit to Tuva.

Gimme Somethin' to Dance To!: What Is Bhangra? 1995. Directed by Tejaswini Ganti. New York University Program in Culture and Media. Video. 18 mins. Documents the rising popularity of bhangra music, originally from the Punjab and popularized in England, then North America.

Glattalp. 1987. Directed by Hugo Zemp. Jüüzil of the Muotatal. Centre National de la Recherche Scientifique. Video. 30 min. In rural Switzerland, people reconstruct the Jüüzli in the Alpine landscape. The scenes embody local and national identities and recall an idealized image of the past. In German with English subtitles.

Googoosh: Iran's Daughter. 2001. Directed by Farhad Zamani. Distributed by Atash Productions. Video. 155 mins. Reflects on the career of Googoosh in the context of the Iranian revolution. Conceived before the singer resumed public performances, this production includes footage of films in which Googoosh starred and interviews with songwriters and lyricists. In Persian, Farsi and English, with English subtitles.

Graceland. 1998. Directed by Jeremy Marre. Rhino Home Video. 75 mins. Paul Simon recounts the story of his 1986 album Graceland. Includes interviews with engineer Roy Halle, and musicians Joseph Shabalala, Ray Phiri, Bakithi Kumalo, Linda Ronstadt and Philip Glass.

Haiti Dreams of Democracy. 1988, 1987. Directed by Jonathan Demme and Joe Minell. Distributed by Cinema Guild. 52 min. Music and theater as vehicles for the expression of political views in post-Duvalier Haiti.

Her Mother before Her: Winnebago Women's Stories of Their Mothers & Grandmothers. 1992. Jocelyn Riley Productions. Video. 22 mins. Six Winnebago women talk about their mothers and grandmothers. Includes Winnebago songs.

Hip Hop: The New World Order. 2002. Directed by Muhammida el Muhajir. Video. 50 mins. Distributed by DVD Music. Explores impact of hip hop on global youth and popular culture.

Hmong Musicians in America: Interactions with Three Generations of Hmong Americans 1978-1996. 1997. Directed by Amy Catlin and Nazir Jairazbhoy. APSARA Media for Intercultural Education. Video. 57 mins. Recounts the social and musical history of the Hmong from China to Laos to America.

I'm British But—. 1989. Directed by Gurinder Chadha. Umbi Films; National Asian American Telecommunications Association. Video. 30 min. Uses bhangra and bangla music and the testimonies of young British Asians to uncover a defiant popular culture.

In the Light of Reverence. 2001. Directed by Christopher McLeod. Distributed by Bullfrog Films. Video. 73 min. A series of three films exploring tensions between indigenous peoples in the U.S. and New age believers, tourists, and commercial developers: *Devil's tower* (Wyoming); *Hopi land* (Northern Arizona); *Mt. Shasta* (California).

Inca Music, Journeys and Rituals. 2002. Directed by Anja Dalhoff. Distributed by Filmakers Library. Video. 52 mins. Documents two Peruvian musicians on a trip into the rainforest where they visit local communities that retain indigenous traditions to varying degrees and respond to globalization in contrasting ways.

The Internationale. 2000. Directed by Peter Miller. Distributed by First Run/Icarus Films, New York, NY. Video. 57 mins. How the Internationale has affected social activists from the Spanish Civil War through Tiananmen Square.

Know Your Enemy. 1990. Directed by Art Jones. Distributed by Third World Newsreel. Video. 27 mins. A critique of mass media bias against rap music and culture with interviews and performance footage, including archival material from the Black Power Movement.

Konkombe: Nigerian Music. 2000, 1988. Directed by Jeremy Marre. Video. 60 mins. Beats of the Heart series. A kaleidoscope of Nigerian pop music. Includes performances, interviews, and recording sessions with Sunny Ade, Fela Anikulapo-Kuti, I.K. Dairo, Sonny Okusun, Lijadu Sisters, and others.

Ladies First: Women in Music Videos. 1996. Produced by Robin Roberts. University Press of Mississippi. Video. 25 min. 1 book (218 p.). Includes excerpts from five music videos discussed in the accompanying publication: Homecoming Queen's Got a Gun (Julie Brown); Hey, Baby (Maggie Estep); Heterosexual Man (The Odds); Independence Day (Martina McBride); Ladies' First (Queen Latifah).

The Language You Cry In: The Story of a Mende Song. 1999. Directed by Alvaro Toepke and Angel Serrano. Distributed by California Newsreel. Video. 53 mins. Traces cultural and musical connections between 18th-century Mende of Sierra Leone and the Gullah people of present-day Georgia.

A Little for My Heart and a Little for My God: A Muslim Women's Orchestra. 1993. Directed by Brita Landoff. Filmaker's Library. Video. 60 mins. Portrait of Algerian *meddahatts*, female musicians who customarily entertain gatherings of women, including weddings, engagements, and circumcisions.

Material Witness: Race, Identity and the Politics of Gangsta Rap. Video. 1995. Directed by Sut Jhally. The Media Education Foundation. 42 min. Michael Dyson talks essentialism and identity within the context of race, and discusses hip hop culture and the conflicts around gangsta rap.

Mecate: A New Song. 1984. Directed by Felix Zurita de Higes. First Run/Icarus Films. 50 min. Documentary on the Peasants Movement for Artistic and Dramatic Expression (MECATE) in Nicaragua that shows how music, theater and poetry are used to improve their lives. In Spanish with English subtitles.

Media Assassin. 1989. Directed by Art Jones. Distributed by Third World Newsreel. Video. 17 mins. Politically charged analysis of hip-hop, black culture and racism in America.

Money for Nothing: Behind the Bu$ine$$ of Pop Mu$ic. 2002. Produced by Kembrew McLeod. Media Education Foundation. Video. 78 min. Examines the centralization of radio station ownership, the integration of popular music into the advertising and commercial aspects of the consumer market, and discusses independent bands and record labels.

Musicians in Exile. 1990. Directed by Jacques Holender. Distributed by Rhapsody Films. Video. 75 mins. A performance documentary that features Hugh Masekela, Julian Bahula, Jonas Gwanga, Duddu Pukwana, Quilapayun, and Paquito D'Rivera in New York City, Paris and London.

The New Klezmorim: Voices Inside the Revival of New Yiddish Music. 2000. Directed by David Kaufman. Ergo Media. Video. 69 min. Explores the Klezmer revival through performances and interviews with performers and students.

No More Disguises. 1989. Directed by Tom Sigel and Boryana Varbanov. First Run/Icarus Films. Video. 6 min. A music video focusing on the faces of China interspersed with images of the Tiananmen Square Incident of 1989.

No. 17 Cotton Mill Shanghai Blues. 2003, 1994, 1984. Directed by Jeremy Marre. Distributed by Shanachie. Video. 60 mins. Beats of the Heart series. Shot in Shanghai, Beijing, and the Islamic region of Xinjiang, documents musicians working in and around the Cultural Revolution.

Nobody Knows My Name. 2000. Directed by Rachel Raimist. Distributed by Women Make Movies. Video. 58 mins. Shows facets of hip hop through the lives of women performers in Los Angeles. Includes commentary on turntablists, hip hop artists and their families, and working with major record labels.

Our Nation: A Korean Punk Rock Community. 2001. Directed by Timothy Tangherlini and Stephen Epstein. Distributed by Filmakers Library. Video. 39 min. Documents the punk scene in rapidly changing Korea and provides a socio-historical overview of the youth subculture including the impact of the emerging consumer capitalism and the social impact of globalization on Korean culture.

Peshavar Rubab. Silent Voices. 2001. Directed by Daniel Ridicki. Distributed by Factum, Zagreb, Croatia. Video. 26 mins. Afghan rubab players who were refugees in Peshawar during the time of Taliban. In Farsi with English subtitles.

Plena, canto y trabajo = Plena is Work, Plena is Song. 1989. Directed by Pedro A. Rivera and Susan Zeig. Distributed by the Cinema Guild. Video. 29 mins. Cultural and political history of the Puerto Rican *plena*. In Spanish with English subtitles.

The Popovich Brothers of South Chicago. 1994. Video. 60 min. A musical portrait of the South Chicago's Serbian-American community, as reflected by the Popovich Brothers, a tamburitza orchestra that provided a constant source of traditional Serbian music over fifty years.

Radical Harmonies. 2002. Directed by Dee Mosbacher. Distributed by Woman Vision. Video. 90 mins. Documents the women's movement in music with interviews and performance footage.

Rap, Race & Equality. 1994. Directed by Stephen and Grant Elliott. Filmakers Library. Video. 52 mins. Early rap artists, including Ice T, Chuck D, KRS One, Queen Latifah and Ice Cube, speak about racism, economic and social inequality and race relations.

Resistencia: Hip Hop in Colombia. 2002. Directed by Tom Feiling. Distributed by Faction Films. Video. 51 mins. Documents street culture and the impact of rap in Colombia. Looks at the current political and economic crisis in Colombia through the eyes of activist-artists. In Spanish with English subtitles.

Rhythm of Resistance: Black South African Music. Directed by Jeremy Marre. Distributed by Shanachie. Video. 60 mins. Beats of the Heart series. Traces the connections and relations between rural and urban practices and features Ladysmith Black Mambazo, Juluka, Philip Tabane & Malombo, the Mahotella Queens, and Abafana.

Righteous Babes. 1998. Directed by Pratibha Parmar. Distributed by Women Make Movies. Video. 50 min. Profiles women in rock to show the impact of feminism on popular culture and Third Wave activists.

River of Sand. 1998. Directed by Robert Lang. Filmwest Associates. Video. 49 min. Political singer songwriter Bruce Cockburn accompanies filmmaker Robert Lang to Mali to study the effect of desertification on people's lives and to explore Malian music. Performances by Toumani Diabate and Ali Farka Toure.

The Romany Trail. 2002, 1992, 1981. Directed by Jeremy Marre. Distributed by Shanachie. Beats of the Heart series. Two videos. 120 mins. Vol. 1: Gypsy music into Africa; Vol. 2: Gypsy music into Europe.

Roots, Rock, Reggae: Inside the Jamaican Music Scene. 2000, 1988, 1977. Directed by Jeremy Marre. Distributed by Shanachie. Video. 60 mins. Beats of the Heart series. Shot in Kingston in 1977, includes rehearsal and concert footage of performances by Toots and the Maytals, Jimmy Cliff, the Heptones and Ras Michael.

Sabemos Mirar. 1991. Directed by Dolly Pussi. First Run Icarus Films. Video. 25 mins. Examines rock music as an outlet for Argentinean youth to express their feelings of powerlessness, focusing on the band Bersuit Bergaravat. Includes a performance by Mercedes Sosa at a protest in Buenos Aires. In Spanish with English subtitles.

Sacred Sounds: Music of the World, Songs of the Soul. 2000. Directed by Carmine Cervi. Distributed by Films for the Humanities & Sciences. Video. 58 mins. Filmed at the 1999 Festival of World Sacred Music in Fez, Morocco. Features performances from Christian, Islamic, and Jewish traditions.

Salsa: Latin Pop Music in the Cities. 2000, 1988, 1979. Directed by Jeremy Marre. Distributed by Shanachie. Video. 60 mins. Beats of the Heart series. Documents Latin dance music from New York to the Caribbean. Includes performances, interviews and recording sessions with Celia Cruz, Tito Puente, Ruben Blades, Charlie Palmieri and Ray Barretto.

Shotguns and Accordions: Music of the Marijuana Growing Regions of Colombia. 2001, 1983. Directed by Jeremy Marre. Distributed by Shanachie. Video. 60 mins. Beats of the Heart series. Explores x*vallenato* music in the Valledupar region of Colombia.

Singing our Stories. 1998. Directed by Annie Frasier Henry. Full Regalia Productions, Omni Film Productions. Distributed by the National Film Board of Canada. Video. 49 mins. Singing by Native American women from several parts of the U.S. and Canada.

Singing to Remember. 1991. Directed by Tony Heriza. Asian American Arts Centre. Video. 16 mins. A portrait of Ng Sheung Chi, master singer of Chinese storytelling songs who emigrated to the United States in 1991.

Son de la tierra. Song of the Earth: Traditional Music from the Highlands of Chiapas. 2002. Directed by Jorge. Distributed by the Chiapas Media Project. Video. 17 mins. Tzotzil elders discuss the importance of traditional music and the effects of Western dress and viewpoints on this music. Filmed and produced by indigenous videographers. In Tzotzil with English subtitles.

Song Journey. 1994. Directed by Arlene Bowman. Distributed by Women Make Movies. Video. 57 min. Documents movement among First Nations female musicians rebelling against the monopoly of the men's drum circle.

SongoLoLo: Voices of Change. 1993, 1990. Directed by Marianne Kaplan. Cinema Guild. Video. 54 min. Examines the role of black resistance to apartheid in South Africa through a look at two of the nation's leading cultural activists and popular performers, poet Mzwakhe Mbuli and writer/performer Gcina Mhlophe.

Songs of the Adventurers. 1987. Directed by Gei Zantzinger. Constant Spring Productions. Video. 47 mins. Documents performances of difela, poetic songs of Sotho migrant workers who traveled from their homes in Lesotho to work in the mines in South Africa.

Songs of the Badius. 1986. Directed by Gei Zantzinger. Constant Spring Productions. Video. 35 mins. Documents dance music of the Kriolu people of Santiago Island in Cape Verde.

South of the Border. 1983. Directed by David Bradbury. Ronin Films. Video. 60 min. Surveys protest music in Mexico, El Salvador, Guatemala, and Nicaragua where popular music contributes to a tradition of social commentary and political protest.

The Spirit of Samba: Black Music of Brazil. 2000, 1990, 1982. Directed by Jeremy Marre. Distributed by Shanachie. Video. 60 mins. Beats of the Heart series. A musical tour of Brazil from the ghettos of Rio to the African-rooted Bahia region. Includes conversations with and performances by Gilberto Gil, Milton Nascimento, and Chico Barque.

The Spirit Travels: Immigrant Music in America. 1991. Directed by Howard Weiss. Cinema Guild. Video. 55 mins. A survey of the musical contributions of different immigrant groups to the American culture, featuring performances of Irish, Greek, African- American, Jewish, Central Asian, Chinese and Puerto Rican musics.

The Split Horn: The Life of a Hmong Shaman in America. 2001. Directed by Tabbart Siegel. Distributed by Filmakers Library. Video. 58 mins. Shows the life and culture of Paja Thao, a Hmong shaman, who emigrated to Appleton, Wisconsin with his family.

Stopping the Music: Music Censorship in South Africa. 2002. Directed by Douglas Mitchell. Distributed by the Danish Film Institute. Video. 54 mins. Explores the relationship between a protest singer and the former security branch policeman who was assigned during the apartheid era to stop his music.

Straight Up Rappin'. 1993. Directed by Tana Ross and Freke Vuijst. Green Room Productions, distributed by Filmakers Library. Video. 29 mins. Documentary about rap, providing social commentary on street life in urban America.

Strange Fruit. 2002. Directed by Joel Katz. Distributed by California Newsreel. Video. 57 mins. Traces the history of the song made famous in Billie Holiday's performance. Delves into the songwriter's background as a union activist; includes reflections by folksingers, civil rights activists, and modern-day jazz performers.

Sukiyaki and Chips: The Japanese Sounds of Music. 2003. Directed by Jeremy Marre. Distributed by Shanachie. Beats of the Heart series. Video. 60 mins. A look at contemporary Japanese music that combines foreign-influenced music with traditional music of the past.

Susumu: A Tone Poem in Three Movements. 1990. Directed by Gei Zantzinger. Constant Spring Productions. Video. 30 mins. Jazz composer Sumi Tonooka's tone poem dedicated to three generations of Japanese-Americans affected by WWII internment.

Swing in Beijing. 2000, 1999. Directed by Shui Bo Wang. Distributed by First Run/Icarus. Video. 73 mins. Surveys the avant-garde performing arts in Beijing, exploring artist responses to censorship, modernization, and Western recognition.

Tabaran. 1992. Directed by Mark Worth. Distributed by the Australian Film Institute. Video. 52 mins. Documentary of the Australian band, Not Drowning, Waving, their work with Papua New Guinean musicians (1988-1991) and music and video industries in Papua New Guinea and the emergence of string bands.

Tales from Arab Detroit. 1995. Directed by Joan Mandell. Olive Branch Productions. Video. 45 min. Music in an immigrant community in Detroit, Michigan revealed through the performances of Bani Hilal an epic story-teller from Egypt.

Tan-Singing of Trinidad and Guyana: Indo-Caribbean "Local-Classical Music." 2000. Directed by Peter Manuel. Distributed by Peter Manuel, Leonia, NJ. Video. 51 mins. Documents the musical life of South Asians in Trinidad, Guyana, and the Caribbean diaspora of New York City.

Tex-Mex: The Music of the Texas-Mexican Borderlands. 2001, 1990, 1982. Directed by Jeremy Marre. Distributed by Shanachie. Video. 60 mins. Beats of the Heart series. Explores the Texas-Mexico border region and the music that combines corrida, norteña, and other forms to both entertain and provide social commentary. Includes performances by Lydia Mendoza, Flaco Jimenez, Little Joe Hernandez and others.

There'll Always Be Stars in the Sky: The Indian Film Music Phenomenon. 2003, 1983. Directed by Jeremy Marre. Distributed by Shanachie. Beats of the Heart series. Video. 60 mins. Explores India's film music industry and the musical forms associated with it. Includes a behind-the-scenes examination of soundtrack creation that uses large ensembles and powerful "playback" singers.

Told in Heaven to Become Stories on Earth: A Study of Change in Randai Theatre of the Minangkabau in West Sumatra. 2000. Directed by Wim van Zanten and Bart Barenregt. Distributed by the Institute of Cultural and Social Studies, University of Leiden. Video. 48 mins. Depicts the reactions of present-day Minangkabau to film clips of Randai theater from the 1920s and 1930s.

Umm Kulthum: A Voice like Egypt. 1996. Directed by Michal Goldman. Filmakers Collaborative. Video. 68 mins. Documentary about the Egyptian singer Umm Kulthum, 1898–1975, who became a powerful symbol of the aspirations of her country.

The Underground Orchestra. 1998. Directed by Heddy Honigmann. Distributed by First Run/Icarus Films, New York. Video. 108 mins. Profiles street musicians in Paris who have fled political repression.

Viento e Terra - Vent de terre. 1996. Directed by Antonietta De Lillo. Metafilm Production. Video. 40 min. Documents a community near Naples, Italy transformed by the changing economic landscape during the 1960s. Features music of industrial laborers that provided opportunities for residents to express and confront their social and political problems.

We Have No War-songs: Gypsies: The Professional Amateurs of Life. 1995. Directed by Izzy Abrahami. Filmakers Library. Video. 53 mins. Explores Gypsy heritage and identity through their religion, music, and dance practices.

We Jive Like This. 1991. Directed by Deborah May. Filmakers Library. Video. 52 mins. Street music, dance, poetry, and theatre of youth in South Africa which provides an outlet for self-expression to heal the effects of apartheid.

Wisconsin Powwow; Naamikaaged: Dancer for the People. 1996. Produced by Thomas Vennum. Smithsonian / Folkways Recordings. Two videos. 67 mins. Documents the powwow held by Ojibwe people in northern Wisconsin. Naamikaaged follows a young Ojibwe, Richard LaFernier, as prepares for and performs at the powwow.

Web Sites

The Web sources listed below have been selected from among hundreds of sites that are potentially useful for educational and scholarly research and exploration of issues connected to contemporary performance in music. The list provides examples of how the Web and the organizational structures linked to media, preserve, document, present, support and discuss musical practices. The selection is organized into the following broad topical areas: *archival sources* made available on the Web through digitization, *cultural advocacy* organizations and sites that respond to perceived needs of the changing social, political, and environmental landscape; *marketing music events*, especially international events for the general public, including festival and tourism organizers; *media advocacy* sites working to regulate and to respond to the needs of users, *media programming* sites constructed by media organizations for educational purposes; *virtual exhibits* of ethnographic and other archived information. All sites were current in March 2005.

Archival Sources

Africa Focus Image and Audio Collection. http://digital.library.wisc.edu/1711.dl/AfricaFocus/. An online collection maintained by the University of Wisconsin-Madison Libraries with digitized images and sounds from Africa available for personal or educational use. In 2000 there were over 3000 slides, 500 photographs, and 50 hours of sound from 45 different countries.

Africa Online Digital Library (AODL). http://africandl.org/. A project of Michigan State University in collaboration with institutions in Africa, AODL provides multimedia materials for both scholarly research and public use.

The Archive of the Indigenous Languages of Latin America (AILLA). http://www.ailla.utexas.org/. A digital archive of recordings and texts in and about the indigenous languages of Latin America, contains recordings of narratives, ceremonies, oratory, conversations, and songs.

British Library National Sound Archive (in development). http://www.bl.uk/collections/sound-archive/nsa.html/. Collections are organized into seven main subject areas: classical music; drama and literature; jazz; oral history; popular music; wildlife sound; world and traditional music. The archive expects to have collections digitized and available to the public by 2006.

DART: Digital Anthropological Resources for Teaching (in development). http://www.columbia.edu/dlc/dart/. A collaborative project between Columbia University and the London School of Economics that will provide customized access to digital resources for teaching undergraduate anthropology.

Digital South Asia Library. http://dsal.uchicago.edu/. A project of the Center for Research Libraries that provides digital materials for reference and research on South Asia. Includes historical and contemporary visual and textual materials from collections in the United States, South Asia, Europe, and Australia.

EVIA (in development). http://www.indiana.edu/~eviada/. A joint effort of Indiana University and the University of Michigan to establish a digital archive of ethnomusicological video for use by scholars and instructors. Currently in the planning phase, the project is focused on providing online access to musical performances recorded on video in the last two decades.

Folkstreams.net. http://www.folkstreams.net/. A collection of online documentary films about American folk or roots culture. Includes background information on the history and significance of the traditions and the films.

Global Jukebox (in development). http://www.alan-lomax.com/style_globaljukebox.html/. A codified audio-visual archive of that maps, samples, classifies and correlates the song, dance and speaking traditions of the world within their broadest cultural contexts. It currently contains 6,000 coded songs and 1,500 coded dances from 400 world cultures.

Save Our Sounds Project (in development). http://www.saveoursounds.org/. A joint project between the Smithsonian Institution and the Library of Congress to restore and preserve original recordings, make digital and archival copies, and make recordings accessible online and on CD.

Scran. http://www.scran.ac.uk/. A UK-based learning image service with over 300,000 images, movies, and sounds from museums, galleries, archives and the media that are available for educational use.

Smithsonian Global Sound. http://www.smithsonianglobalsound.org/. A network of institutions working to preserve and distribute music from archives worldwide. The Web site offers audio downloads, streaming media, and educational resources from the Smithsonian Folkways collection, the International Library of African Music (ILAM) in South Africa, and the Archive Research Centre for Ethnomusicology (ARCE) in India, among others.

The Virtual Gramophone: Canadian Historical Sound Recordings. http://www.collectionscanada.ca/gramophone/index-e.html/. A multimedia Web site devoted to early recorded sound in Canada with a database of images and digital audio recordings as well as biographies of musicians and histories of music and recorded sound in Canada. Focus is on 78–rpm and cylinder recordings and images.

Cultural Advocacy

Aboriginal Canada Portal. http://www.aboriginalcanada.gc.ca/. A portal to Canadian aboriginal online resources, contacts, information, and government programs and services in all areas, including language, heritage and culture.

The Acoustic Ecology Institute. http://www.acousticecology.org/edu/index.html/. A project of the Art and Science Laboratory in Santa Fe that provides access to news, academic research, public policy advocates, and articles and essays about sound and listening.

Beyond the Commons. http://www.beyondthecommons.com/. A collection of sites and materials (essays, syllabi, bibliographies, Web links, discussion) connected to concepts of "enclosure" and by extension to issues of intellectual property.

Center for Political Song. http://polsong.gcal.ac.uk/index.html/. Based at Glasgow Caledonian University, the Center seeks to promote an awareness of all forms of political song. Their online site links users to news, research discussion, song lyrics and audio links, a local collection catalog, and a list of other related sites.

Cultural Heritage Initiative for Community Outreach (CHICO). http://www.si.umich.edu/chico/. A portal for projects, including cultural exhibits from around the world, based at the School of Information, University of Michigan. Topics range from flamenco to powwow traditions, salsa to gamelan. Sites serve as a teaching aid for students and general audience.

Cultural Protocol. http://www.abc.net.au/message/proper/. full text document from the Australian Broadcasting Corporation (ABC) constructed to help media professionals understand the importance of respecting Indigenous Protocols. Includes information on production, recognition, copyright, contacting communities, ethical issues, and a list of resources.

Cultural Survival. http://www.cs.org/. A site that promotes the rights, voices and visions, of indigenous peoples with information on conflict and migration; culture; health; indigenous enterprise; law & self determination; natural resources. Includes articles, news briefs, documents, and links.

Ethnomusicology as Advocacy. http://www.dolsenmusic.com/advocacy/. An internet information project by Dale Olsen, Florida State University, that introduces "cultures in peril, transition, or near extinction" in a case study format. Includes text, audio, and photographic information.

Freemuse: The World Forum on Music and Censorship. http://www.freemuse.org/. An independent international organization advocating freedom of expression for musicians and composers worldwide established in 1998 at the World Conference on Music and Censorship. Their objectives include documenting, informing and supporting musicians and organizations regarding human rights violations. Includes articles, interviews, reports, speeches on human rights, censorship, artist opinions.

The Hemispheric Institute of Performance and Politics. http://hemi.nyu.edu/. A consortium of institutions, artists, and scholars dedicated to exploring the relationship between performance and social and political life in the Americas. They are currently developing an archive of video for Web delivery and sponsor a Web *cuaderno* site for multi-media projects.

    Web Cuadernos. http://hemi.nyu.edu/eng/cuaderno.shtml/. Sites housed at the Hemispheric Institute with online multi-media materials that focus on performance and politics in the Americas. Selected current programs include: The Death of the Inca Atahualpa; Performance and Censorship in Colonial Mexico; Mapuche Campaign for Self-Representation; Repasos: Art and Life in Chile Under Pinochet; Political Performance.

Indigenous Portal (ATSIC). http://www.indigenous.gov.au/ip.dll/. Maintained by the Aboriginal and Torres Strait Islander Commission (ATSIC), the portal provides online access to indigenous services and information, including educational materials.

World Intellectual Property Organization (WIPO). http://www.wipo.int/. An international organization dedicated to promoting the use and protection intellectual property.

    WIPO: About Intellectual Property. http://www.wipo.int/about-ip/en/index.html/. Provides documents and discussion about Industrial Property, Copyright and Related Rights, Emerging Issues in IP, Intellectual Property in Everyday Life, and Women and Intellectual Property.

World Forum for Acoustic Ecology. http://interact.uoregon.edu/MediaLit/WFAE/home/. Founded in 1993, this association is concerned with the study of the social, cultural and ecological aspects of the sonic environment.

Marketing Music Events

European Forum of Worldwide Music Festivals (EFWMF). http://www.efwmf.org/index.php/. A network of festivals established in 1991 with a membership that shares a transnational approach to presenting "world, ethnic, traditional, folk and roots music."

Folk Alliance. http://www.folkalliance.net/. The North American Folk Music and Dance Alliance identifies itself as a service association for the music and dance industry with a goal to increase public access to music and dance events.

IMZ: The International Music + Media Center. http://www.imz.at/. A global non-profit association of leading producers of cultural programs focusing on classical, contemporary and world music, jazz and dance.

International Festival and Events Association (IFEA). http://www.ifea.com/. A professional association for festival and event leaders worldwide.

MASA: Market for African Performing Arts. http://masa.francophonie.org/english/index.htm/. Established in 1993 by the Agence Intergouvernementale de la Francophone to support African performing arts and to incorporate them into international mainstream.

WOMAD. http://womad.org/. WOMAD (World of Music, Arts and Dance) sponsors music festivals, performance events, recordings, and educational projects from around the world. The Web site includes festival information, news, forums, and online audio/video recordings from performances.

WOMEX. http://www.womex.com/. An online site for *World Music Expo*, a series of conference, showcase and trade events that have occurred annually in Europe since 1994. The events and the Web site (virtual WOMEX) are concerned with "world, roots, folk, ethnic, traditional and local music of all kinds."

Media Advocacy

Central Australian Aboriginal Media Association (CAAMA). http://www.caama.com.au/. Established in 1980 and owned by the Aboriginal people of Central Australia, CAAMA interest is in promoting indigenous culture, language, dance, and music and educating the wider community about diverse practices.

Electronic Frontier Foundation (EFF). http://www.eff.org/. A nonprofit group of lawyers, technologists, and other volunteers working to protect digital rights.

Future of Music Coalition (FMC). http://www.futureofmusic.org/. A collaborative effort involving members of the music, technology, public policy and intellectual property law communities to educate the media, policymakers, and the public about music and technology issues.

Indigenous Media Arts Group (IMAG). http://www.imag-nation.com/. A Vancouver-based aboriginal organization that is comprised of local media makers. They sponsor an annual film and video festival, training and other media related events, with a goal to disseminate aboriginal production.

International Recorded Media Association (IRMA). http://www.recordingmedia.org/. A worldwide trade group that includes raw material providers, manufacturers, replicators, duplicators, packagers, copyright holders, and other related industries.

Independent Media Center (IMC). http://www.indymedia.org/en/index.shtml/. A collective of independent media organizations journalists that offer "grassroots, non-corporate coverage" of events.

Recording Industry Association of America (RIAA). http://www.riaa.com/. A trade group of major record labels that represents the U.S. recording industry with a mission to "foster a business and legal climate that supports and promotes our members' creative and financial vitality." The organization has been actively involved in copyright and other file sharing cases.

Media Programming

ABC Online: Message Stick (Australian Broadcasting Corporation). http://www.abc.net.au/message/. Message Stick is a portal to Indigenous Australian information on the Web. Provides links to indigenous sites and reference information for use in business, media and education.

> Message Stick: Indigenous Radio (ABC). http://www.abc.net.au/message/radio/. Includes a series of programs that focus on indigenous art and culture.

ABC Online: Music Deli (Australian Broadcasting Corporation). http://www.abc.net.au/rn/music/deli/. Presents a wide range of musical styles including live recordings from musical festivals in Australia.

BBC Music Features (British Broadcasting Corporation). http://www.bbc.co.uk/music/features/. Features present in-depth coverage of selected topics, highlighting popular artists and genres.

> Echoes of Africa. http://www.bbc.co.uk/music/features/africa/. Links to music in eight broad geographic regions through audio clips and photographs with some contextual data.

> Rekjyavik Underground. http://www.bbc.co.uk/music/features/iceland/. The contemporary music scene in Rekjyavik organized by musical group and genre.

> Reggae. http://www.bbc.co.uk/music/features/reggae/. Music, fashion and dance through the musical styles that have contributed to the genre.

BBC World Service: Rhythms of a Continent: Africa. http://www.bbc.co.uk/worldservice/africa/features/rhythms/index.shtml/. Audio links to programs look at the role of music in selected regions of Africa today, including South Africa, Malawi, Tanzania and Kenya, Ivory Coast, and Zimbabwe.

BBC Radio 3. http://www.bbc.co.uk/radio3/. Broadcasts a wide range of musical genres and styles via DAB, Cable, Satellite, Internet streaming, Internet Radio Player, FM Radio and Freeview. Some of the programs and developed Web sites to support them include:

> Guide to World Music. http://www.bbc.co.uk/radio3/worldmusic/index.shtml/. A portal for world music BBC programs and information on festivals, awards, and other events.

> Africa on Your Street. http://www.bbc.co.uk/radio3/africaonyourstreet/index.shtml/. Explores the African music scene in the UK with audio clips, news, and performance schedules.

> World on Your Street. http://www.bbc.co.uk/radio3/world/onyourstreet/index.shtml/. Creates a musical map of the UK through sound. Includes performances by professional musicians as well as music that occurs in everyday life.

NPR (National Public Radio). http://www.npr.org/. Among the music programs offered by this U.S.-based source of noncommercial news, talk and entertainment programming include:

> All Songs Considered. http://www.npr.org/programs/asc/. A multimedia online music program that provides online audio and contextual data for recordings. A wide range of styles and genres are presented.

> World Music. http://www.npr.org/templates/topics/topic.php?topicId=1044/. Web site with programs on musics from around the world. Includes audio and written information.

Virtual Exhibits

Canadian Museum of Civilization. http://www.civilization.ca/cmc/cmce.asp/. Hosts a virtual museum with numerous folklore- and ethnomusicology- related exhibits.

> Opus: The Making of Musical Instruments in Canada (*Canadian Museum of Civilization*). http://www.civilization.ca/arts/opus/opuse.html/. Based on an exhibit mounted between 1992 and 1995, the site provides the full text of the exhibit catalogue by Carmelle Bégin (150 pages, with illustrations). The site also includes audio and video clips of instruments and interviews with makers.

Ethnomusicology Musical Instrument Collection (University of Washington). http://content.lib.washington.edu/ethnomusicweb/index.html/. An online collection of about 250 instruments from around the world housed at the University of Washington. Includes photographs and descriptive information.

Experience Music Project. http://www.emplive.com/. Explores and celebrates musical diversity through online exhibits, interviews, and audio links to music and musicians representing a wide range of popular music forms.

Library of Congress American Memory Collections. http://lcweb2.loc.gov/ammem/. Selected collections and online topical exhibits from the Archive of Folk Culture, the Library of Congress and other collection are housed at this site. Collection materials presented here include photographs, manuscripts, and audio- and video-recordings.

California Gold: Northern California Folk Music From the Thirties. http://lcweb2.loc.gov/ammem/afccchtml/cowhome.html/. Drawn from the WPA California Folk Music Project Collection.

Fiddle Tunes of the Old Frontier: The Henry Reed Collection. http://lcweb2.loc.gov/ammem/hrhtml/hrhome.html/. Fiddle tunes performed by Henry Reed of Glen Lyn, Virginia.

Hispano Music and Culture of the Northern Rio Grande: The Juan B. Rael Collection, from Northern New Mexico and Southern Colorado. http://lcweb2.loc.gov/ammem/rghtml/rghome.html/.

"Now What a Time": Blues, Gospel, and the Fort Valley Music Festivals, 1938–1943. http://lcweb2.loc.gov/ammem/ftvhtml/ftvhome.html/.

Omaha Indian Music. http://lcweb2.loc.gov/ammem/omhhtml/omhhome.html/. Recordings made between 1895 and 1897.

Southern Mosaic: The John and Ruby Lomax 1939 Southern States Recording Trip. http://lcweb2.loc.gov/ammem/lohtml/lohome.html/.

Voices from the Dust Bowl: The Charles L. Todd and Robert Sonkin Migrant Worker Collection, 1940–1941. http://lcweb2.loc.gov/ammem/afctshtml/tshome.html/.

Music in the Afghan North, 1967–1972. http://www.wesleyan.edu/its/acs/modules/slobin/html/index.html/. Presents fieldwork and publication materials from Mark Slobin's research in Afghanistan in the 1960s and 1970s. Includes introductions to ideas and topics, excerpts and full text of his 1976 study, *Music in the Culture of Northern Afghanistan.* Includes photos, audio and video clips to accompany the written text.

National Public Radio: Honky Tonks, Hymns, and the Blues. http://www.honkytonks.org/. This public radio series provides background information on various southern musical traditions through photos, text, and sound. Radio segments are available online as well as guides, bibliographic information and Web links.

Public Broadcasting Service (PBS): Online exhibits. http://www.pbs.org/.

River of Song (PBS). http://www.pbs.org/riverofsong/. Based on a Smithsonian Institution series for public television and radio that explores the richness and vitality of music along the course of the Mississippi River.

Accordion Dreams (PBS). http://www.pbs.org/accordiondreams/main/index.html/. A companion Web site for a film produced for PBS by Hector Galán in 2000, explores the Mexican American *conjunto* tradition.

American Roots Music (PBS). http://www.pbs.org/americanrootsmusic/. A companion site for a multi-part series on blues, gospel, country bluegrass, Cajun, zydeco, Tejano, and Native American musics

Smithsonian Center for Folklife and Cultural Heritage: Online Exhibitions. http://www.folklife.si.edu/explore/online_exhibitions.html/. Online exhibits include audio, video, photographs, and written information.

The Silk Road: Connecting Cultures, Creating Trust (2002). http://www.silkroadproject.org/smithsonian/. Produced in partnership with the *Silk Road Project.*

Mali: From Timbuktu to Washington (2003). http://www.folklife.si.edu/resources/Festival2003/mali.htm/.

Creativity & Resistance: Maroon Culture in the Americas (1999). http://www.folklife.si.edu/resources/maroon/start.htm/.

Borders/Fronteras (1996). http://www.folklife.si.edu/frontera/start.htm/.

Virtual Museum of Canada (VMC). http://www.virtualmuseum.ca/. A product of the Canadian Heritage Information Network and the museum community to produce ongoing virtual exhibits on Canadian heritage with audio, video, and photographic data along with descriptive information.

The Astonishing World of Musical Instruments (Virtual Museum of Canada). http://www.virtualmuseum.ca/Exhibitions/Musique/. Documents a collection of about 550 instruments housed at the Laboratoire de recherché sur les musiques du monde (LRMM).

Staying in Tune: Traditions and Musical Instruments of the Francophonie (Virtual Museum of Canada). http://www.virtualmuseum.ca/Exhibitions/Instruments/Anglais/accueil_en.html/.

Musical instruments from French-speaking countries coordinated by the Canadian Heritage Information Network (CHIN) and the Department of Canadian Heritage, Quebec Region. Includes photos and sound samples from collections in North America, Europe, and Africa.

Through the Eyes of the Cree: The Art of Allan Sapp (Virtual Museum of Canada). http://www.virtualmuseum.ca/Exhibitions/allensapp/index.html/.

Biographical, historical, visual and audio documents on artist and musician Allan Sapp.

Wesleyan Virtual Instrument Museum. http://learningobjects.wesleyan.edu/vim/. A project of the Wesleyan University Music Department and the Learning Objects Development team. Provides links to several hundred instrument using photo, video, and audio files. Organized by genre, ensemble, material, and geographic region.

Notes

1. Jennifer C. Post, *Ethnomusicology: A Guide to Research* (New York: Routledge, 2004).
2. The Recording Industry Association of America: 2003 Yearend Statistics. Available: http://www.riaa.com/news/newsletter/pdf/2003yearEnd.pdf
3. When CD ROM, CD Video, DVD, DVD ROM and DVD Audio are added to this the number is 17 billion. International Recording Media Association. IRMA Statistics: CD & DVD Replication Worldwide 2002-2004. Available: http://www.recordingmedia.org/news/stat-replication_worldwide.html.

4. Lyman, Peter, and Hal R. Varian. 2003. "How Much Information 2003?" School of Information Management and Systems, University of California, Berkeley. Available: http://www.sims.berkeley.edu/research/projects/how-much-info-2003/optical.htm.
5. Jennifer C. Post, *Ethnomusicology : A Guide to Research* (New York : Routledge, 2004).
6. Ibid.

Index

A

Abeles, Harold, 214
Aboriginal music (Australia), 9, 11, 168, 364, 383–398, 405, 406
Aboriginal music (Malaysia), 147–157
Aboriginal rock (Australia), 9, 11, 383–398
Abu Lughod, Janet, 156–157
Acadian, 371–381
Accordion, 289, 376, 380
Acculturation, 283, 284
Acoustic as "authentic", 343
Acoustic community, 203
Acoustic ecology, 9
Acoustic environments, 9, 192
Acoustic materials, 192, 196
Acoustical reality, 192
Acoustical sound, 171
Acoustical space, 34–39, 45–48, 195, 199–206, 323,
Adhan, (azan) (Islamic call to prayer), 21, 199–206
Ading Kerah, 150–152
Advocacy ethnomusicology, 401–410
Advocacy, 10, 365, 401–410
Aesthetics
  authenticity of, 191–192, 195
  boundaries, 62, 64
  bodily, 94
  commodity, 138–139, 144
  contemporary, 387–388, 391
  indigenous, 284
  local, 358
  national, 230, 237
  performance in West Africa, 164, 179
  production, 35, 38, 41
  recordings that reflect, 210
  technology, 206
  world music, 17–18, 22–23, 25–26, 29–30
Afghanistan, 109–111, 117–121, 122, 123, 125, 126
Africa, 6, 7, 17, 98, 100, 109–110, 127, 143, 161–179, 194, 276–277, 283–284, 298, 305, 333, 345, 366, 401–410, 100, 396; *see also* Individual countries
African diaspora, 17, 261–262, 268–269; *see also* pan-Africanism
Africa Djolé, 169
Africa, North, 110, 122

African Americans, 23, 47, 97–108
African-Caribbeans, 277, 283–284, 289
Agency, 93, 157, 251, 403, 405, 409
Ahmed, Leila, 115
Ahyoung, Selwyn E., 276
AIDS, *see* HIV/AIDS
Aleksandrov, Alexander, 246, 250–256
Almetjh Tjöönghkeme (musical group), 361–363, 366
Amateur musicians, 92, 116, 126, 162, 166, 169, 232
Ambient music, 193, 195, 196
American Indian Movement (A.I.M.), 338
Amplification, 76, 199–206, 210–212, 215, 343,
Amunda (musical group), 391
Ancelet, Barry, 376–379
Anderson, Benedict, 226, 245
Andes, 312–315, 324
Anthems, *see* National anthems
Anthropologists, 2, 3, 10, 17, 58, 68, 73, 93, 94, 148, 311
Anthropology, 17, 404; *see also* Ethnography; Ethnomusicology
Antilles an identity, 140–143
Apartheid (South Africa), 100, 407
Appadurai, Arjun, 27, 29, 203, 204, 271
Appalachians, 71–72
Applied anthropology, 10, 404,
Applied ethnomusicology, 10, 401–410
Appropriation, 3, 24, 91, 139, 142, 171, 193, 262, 383; *see also* Sampling
Arabia, 114
Arabian peninsula, 109, 114, 122
Architectronics, 33–49
Architecture, music, 33–39
Argentina, 111
Aristide, Jean–Bertrand, 261, 269, 270
Armstrong, Robert Plant, 324
Arom, Simha, 194
Asaf'ev, Boris, 255
Asian Americans, 87–94
Askew, Kelly, 8
Assimilation, 138, 229, 231, 232, 269, 298, 332, 340, 343, 361, 371–372, 373, 375, 377, 378
Attali, Jacques, 48
Audiences, 1, 3, 10
  Aboriginal (Australian), 385, 387, 390, 396, 398

African American, 97–102, 104
Asian American performance, 87, 91
  behaviors, 17–30, 246
  Cajun music, 377
  diasporic, 263, 266, 268–269, 272, 275–277, 283–285,
    289–290
  festival, 73, 76, 77
  Malaysian, 147
  and musical meaning, 255
  Native American, 331, 333–334, 339, 342, 346
  performer and audience relationships, 34, 40, 164, 169,
    192, 210–213, 215, 217, 302–304
  Saami of Scandinavia, 351–365
  rap, 374
  tourist, 55–64
Australia, 11, 168, 289, 333, 364, 383–398, 406
Australian Broadcasting Corporation (ABC), 2
Australian Record Industry Association (ARIA), 388
Authenticity, 7, 10, 17–18, 22–30, 43, 58, 67–68, 72–74,
    76–77, 91, 94, 179, 191–197, 209, 212, 232, 276, 284,
    290, 298–299, 343, 364, 377–378, 402–403
Authoritarianism, 244, 255,
Averill, Gage, 8
Azerbaijan, 110

B
Babylon, 112, 113, 396
Baily, John, 111, 117, 121
Bakan, Michael, 8, 57, 60
Balfa Brothers (musical group), 371
Balfa, Dewey, 376–378
Bali, 5–6, 55–66
Balkans, 110, 123
Ballet Africains (Paris), 183
Ballet National du Mali, 164–165, 178
Baltics, the, 251
Bamako (Mali), 7, 161–179, 183
Bamba, Sorry, 168
Basso, Keith, 9
Baumann, Max Peter, 138
Bayton, Mavis, 214–215
BBC (British Broadcasting Corporation), 2
Beach Boys, 45
Beausoleil (musical group), 371, 375, 377
Beck, Ulrich, 49
Becker, Howard S., 302
Beckerman, Michael, 68
Bee, Robbie, 339
Bee, Tom, 339
Beethoven, Ludwig van, 42
Belarus, 251
Belonenko, Alexander, 249
Bender, Barbara, 323
Bendix, Regina, 72, 74
Benjamin, Walter 203, 345
Bennett, Stith, 212
Berlin, 169, 276
Bhangra, 289
Bihar, 278–279
Billboard, 40, 46
Black Americans, *see* African Americans
Blekbala Mujik, 11, 383–398
Blues, 102, 215, 269, 289, 331, 333, 338, 344, 346, 362
Bobo, Jacqueline, 97–98
Boden, Dierdre, 203
Body, the, 6, 9, 24, 87–94, 101–102, 148, 151, 212,
    216–217, 295–307, 405
Bohlman, Philip V., 8

Boine, Mari, 364, 366
Bolivia, 9, 311–327
Bolon X (musical group), 366
Boogie Boys, the (musical group), 101
Borders and frontiers: 6, 8, 94, 139, 203, 341, 344–346,
    364, 373–374
Boundaries 6–7, 9, 10, 47, 156, 203, 289
  cultural, 192, 197, 366
  ethnic, 268–269, 335, 343, 345, 353, 364, 379
  and frontiers, 55–64
  national, 8, 228, 237s
Bourdieu, Pierre, 42
Boyd, Malcolm, 244–245
Brezhnev, Leonid, 248
British-Asians, 287–289
Brosius, J. Peter, 404
Brown, James, 143
Bruner, Edward 73–74
Btaka (Btaka Brown), 334, 341, 343
Buddhism, 22, 87, 94
Bulgaria, 70
Buonaventura, Wendy, 122
Burkina Faso, 161, 169, 170
Byrne, David, 27, 193, 305

C
CAAMA, *see* Central Australian Aboriginal Media
    Association
Cajuns, 371–381
Calendric ritual, 77
Calonarang, 58, 60–64
Calypso, 275–277, 283–284, 286–287, 289–290, 333,
    336
Canada, 36, 92, 285, 286, 289, 364, 387
Capitalism, 5, 33, 48, 138, 168, 323
Caribbean, 6, 7, 8, 138–144, 261–272, 275–291, 295, 345,
    396
Carnival
  Bolivia, 312–322
  Caribbean, 268, 271
  Trinidad, 276, 283, 284, 286, 289, 291
Cash, Johnny, 331
Casper (Casper Lomayesva), 332, 334, 345–347
Cassettes and cassette players, 60, 167, 190
Caucasus, 110, 251; *see also* Individual countries
Celebrations
  carnival (Indian Caribbean), 283
  carnival (Andes), 312–22
  local drum and dance (West Africa), 161–170,
    176–179, 183
  national day (China), 233–236
  New Year (Afghan), 119
  public (Australia), 387
  religious (Bali), 62–63
  solstice (Górale), 77
  sports (Haiti), 267
  wedding (Indian-Caribbean), 275, 276, 279, 280–282,
    290
  wedding (Iran), 117
  wedding (Middle East), 122
Censorship, 120
Central America, 344
Central Asia, 110, 127, 251; *see also* Individual countries
Central Australian Aboriginal Media Association
    (CAAMA), 387–388
Ceremonial dances, 59, 62
Ceremonial repertoires, 62
Ceremonies, 17, 59, 61–63

Chambers, Robert, 406–407, 409
Chatterjee, Partha, 226
Chayantaka (in Bolivia), 311–324
Chicago, 156–157
Chicano rock, 344
China, 8, 225–238
Chinese Communist Party (CCP), 218–229
Chinese, the, 202, 203,
Choreography, 56, 79, 87, 94, 164
Chow, Rey, 204–205
Christianity, 22, 46, 109, 115, 122, 124
   missionaries, 229, 354
Chutney, 6, 8, 275–291
Chutney soca, 276, 284, 286, 291
Cirlot, J. E., 111
Clapsticks (Australia), 388–390
Class
   consumer, 36–37, 42, 46–47
   Haitian immigrants, 262, 265–267
   musicians, 29
   social, 6, 8, 139, 143, 296, 304
   struggle (Cajuns), 375
   struggle (in China), 227–228, 229
   women's status, 110, 123, 127
Classical music, 214
   Afghani, 118
   Chinese, 231
   European, 20, 42–43, 190, 244, 298, 357
   North Indian, 284
   Syrian, 26
Coding, 23, 68, 69, 76, 77, 93, 99, 115, 124, 138, 272,
   296
Collins, Patricia Hill, 99
Colombia, 295, 299, 301–302, 305, 307
Colonialism, 142, 191
   in America, 335, 341–343
   in Antilles, 140
   in Australia, 383–387, 392, 394, 396, 397–398
   in Egypt, 27
   in India and the Caribbean, 276–278
   in Malaysia 148, 150
   in Nova Scotia, 375
   in Singapore 200
   in West Africa, 162, 164, 169, 183
Coloured Stone (musical group), 387
Commercialization, 168, 179, 214, 358
Commodification, 4–5, 17, 18, 24, 29, 30, 58, 59, 141,
   179, 189, 194, 353
Commodores (musical group) 269
Communism, 69–72, 247–49, 251, 253, 256–257
Conakry (Guinea), 161, 162, 166, 170, 178, 183
Congas, 166, 173, 300
Connell, John, 4
Constance, Zero Obi, 276
Consumption, 4–5, 7, 17–30, 35–37, 43–44, 46, 56, 58,
   60, 194, 230, 271, 404
Cooley, Timothy J., 6
Coolidge, Rita, 331, 334
Cosgrove, Dennis, 323
Coulibaly, Soungalo, 169
Country music, 331, 357, 389, 397
Cowley, John, 276
Creole
   language, 140, 142, 267, 268
   music and musicians, 283, 371, 377
Csordas, Thomas, 157
Cuba, 295
Cudjoe, Selwyn R., 278

Cui Jian, 232–233
Cultural imperialism, 7, 190, 193
Cultural industries, 27, 205,
Cultural loss, 24
Cultural politics, 72, 179
Cultural revival, 5, 11, 29, 61, 321–379, 388, 392, 393
Cultural Revolution (in China, c. 1964–1974),
   229–230
Cultural tourism 5–6, 55–64, 403–403, 409–410
Cyberpunk, 189, 196
Cyborg, 213, 215, 216
Czechoslovakian State Orchestra, 38

D
D.P. Express (Haitian band), 263, 267
Da Brat, 98, 103
Dahl, Linda, 214
Dalal, Muhammad Qadri, 18, 20, 24
Dances and dancing, 4, 5–6, 8, 9, 11, 18, 20, 21, 28
   Aboriginal Australian, 384, 385, 391
   Bali, 55–64
   Cajun, 378
   Chayantaka in Bolivia, 317, 324
   Górali in Poland, 68–81
   Haitian, 266–268
   Indian Caribbean, 276, 279, 281–284, 289–290
   Latin, 295, 296, 298, 302–306
   Middle East, 110, 113–114, 117–123, 127–128
   Native American, 333–334, 339
   South Africa, 401, 404, 405–408, 410
   Temiar in Malaysia, 147, 149
   West Africa, 161–164, 166–170
Dangdut (Javanese genre) 195
   disco dangdut, 195
Daughtry, J. Martin, 8
Davis, Angela Y., 98, 100
Davis, Stephen, 391–92
De Zoete, Beryl, 59
Deep Forest (musical group), 193–195
Deng Xiaoping, 230
Derrida, Jacques, 27
Dery, Mark, 217
DeVale, Sue Carole, 110
Dewind, Josh, 262
DeWitt, Mark, 5
Diamond, Beverley, 6
Diaspora, 8, 17, 93, 140, 275–290, 335–336, 345
   African, 17, 261–262, 268–269
   Haitian, 261–272
   Polish, 69
   South Asian, 275–290
Didjeridu, 168, 169, 388–390, 397,
Digital technologies, 193, 195
Displacement, 149, 156, 205, 261, 333, 335–336, 344–346,
   359, 401, 402, 405, 408
Djembe, see Jembe
Doj, Pal, 257–58
Doubleday, Veronica, 6, 122
Doucet, Michael, 377
Dramé, Adama, 169
Dreaming, the, 384, 392
Dreamtime, 390, 391, 392, 393
Duan Baolin, 231
Dunbar-Hall, Peter, 5, 9, 11
Dupuy, Alex, 262
During, Jean, 124
Duvalier, François, 262, 264, 265, 267, 269, 270
Dylan, Bob, 192, 331, 334, 356

E

Eastern Europe, 251; *see also* Individual countries
Economic issues, 2–5, 8, 11, 49, 71, 137–144, 156–157, 189, 191, 197
  Aboriginal Australia, 383, 394, 395
  African American, 99–100, 124–125
  Bali, 60
  Cajun, 371, 373, 376, 377
  Górale in Poland, 68, 81
  Haitian, 262–265
  Indian-Caribbean, 278, 287
  Latin Americans in London, 300–302, 307
  Malaysia, 200
  Middle East, 128
  Native American, 332, 333, 335, 346
  Saami in Scandinavia, 365
  South Africa, 401, 492–405, 407
  Temiar in Malaysia, 154
  West Africa, 166, 169, 179
Ecuador, 324
Education, 9–10, 128, 212, 228, 231–232, 234, 280, 296, 302, 333, 339, 376, 377, 383, 404, 407, 409,
Educational institutions, 165–166
Edwards, J. Michele, 114
Egypt, 27, 109, 110, 112, 114, 122, 123, 127
Eiseman, Fred, 60
Electronic media, 189–192, 197, 203–205, 209–217, 235, 236, 283, 301, 304, 343, 362
Embodiment, 6, 9, 295–307, 312, 314, 320–324
Emplacement, 9, 156, 312, 323, 324, 405, 409, 410
Empowerment, 91–92, 94, 97–106, 156, 197, 215, 401, 405,
Endo, Kenny, 90
England, 27, 42, 100, 299–300, 371
Ensemble al-Kindi, 17–30
Environmental issues, 3, 5, 9, 11
  acoustics, 192–193, 196, 199–206, 323–324
  in commercial spaces, 33–49
  conservation, 401–410
  impact of changes, 149–150, 262, 359
  use of sounds, 356
Erlmann, Veit, 6–7, 17, 27, 28, 139, 142
Ethnicity/ethnicities, 4–6, 9–10, 48, 73, 137–139, 142, 192, 226, 244
  Aboriginal Australian, 168
  Arab, 24, 25, 27, 29
  Asian American, 87, 89, 94
  Cajun, 371, 376–377
  Chayantaka in Bolivia, 312
  in China, 232–235
  Górale in Poland, 67–68, 72, 77, 81
  Haitian, 261, 266, 267–269
  Indian–Caribbean, 277, 278–279, 283–284, 287–288, 291
  in Latin America, 295–307
  Native American, 343, 346
  of New York rock musicians, 210
  Saami in Scandinavia, 351–366
  in Singapore, 200–204, 206
  in West Africa, 162–163
Ethnochoreologists, 73
Ethnographers, 68–69, 71–72, 73, 76, 80, 276
Ethnographic legitimacy, 191–192
Ethnography, 17, 68–69, 72–81, 93, 109, 211
Ethnomusicologists, 1–11, 17, 34, 38–39, 72–73, 148, 190–192, 196–197, 255, 257, 404
Ethnomusicology, 1–11, 35–36, 48–49, 55, 189–197, 206, 211, 217, 311, 401–410

Ethnopsychology, 149, 157
Europe, 2, 6–8, 19–20, 26–27, 29, 42–43, 72–73, 78, 80–81, 109, 117, 123, 125, 127, 156, 162, 166–169, 173, 178, 189, 232, 244–225, 251, 261–262, 284, 298, 300, 337, 340, 345, 353, 358–360, 371, 384–385; *see also* Individual countries
"Evil that Men Do, The" (Queen Latifah), 99–100
Exorcism, 110, 120, 127
Exoticism, 26, 43, 56, 59, 64, 169, 191, 194, 195, 352, 354
Eyerman, Ron, 10

F

Fabian, Johannes, 410
Farmer, Henry George, 113–116
"Fear Poem", (Joy Harjo), 337
Feld, Steven, 9, 18, 20, 23, 29, 48, 142–143, 196, 211, 323, 405
Female rap artists, 97–106
Feminism, 6, 93, 97, 99–100, 104–105, 109, 125, 215
Ferguson, James, 209
Fernandez, James, 233
Festivals, folklore, 6
  drum and dance (West Africa), 162–164, 168, 170, 178
  folk, 371, 376–378
  Górale, 67–81
  international, 265, 268, 363
  local
    Australia, 390, 397
    Haiti, 271
  national (China), 234–235
  regional (Andes), 324
  religious (Trinidad), 279
  sacred music, 21–22, 27–30
  temple (Bali), 62
  women (Middle East), 112, 116, 124
Fez Festival of World Sacred Music, 22, 27–29
Finland, 8, 10, 351, 355, 359
Firqat al-Turath (Heritage Ensemble), 21
Folk music, 331
Folk festival, 6, 67–81
Folkloric music and musicians, 22, 161–162, 165, 167, 170, 271
Folklorists, 2, 3, 72, 73, 101, 321
"For Anna Mae Pictou Aqash" (Joy Harjo), 337
Forrest, Peter, 385
Foucault, Michel, 311
Foxy Brown, 98, 101, 103, 104
Frame drum, 6, 109–128
France, 7, 17, 43–44, 140–143, 169, 295
Francophone culture, 168–169, 371–379
Friedland, Roger, 203
Friedson, Steven, 245
Frith, Simon, 192, 304
Frontiers, 55–59, 343–347
Funk, 143, 268–269

G

Gabriel, Peter, 27
Gajraj, Terry, 285–286, 289
Gamelan, 58–63, 192, 195
Garbarek, Jan, 366
Garofalo, Reebee, 10
Gaup, Ingo Ántte Áilu, 366
Gay, Leslie C., 6, 7–8
Geertz, Clifford, 226–27
Gender, 4, 6, 9, 40, 42, 45, 46, 87–94, 109–128, 139, 210, 214, 233, 234, 276, 295–297, 303–307, 312, 333, 338–339; *see also* Feminism; Women; Masculinity

Geography, 4, 8, 9, 55, 63
Geopolitics, 8, 335, 385, 393–398
Germany, 169, 295, 333
Gibson, Chris, 9, 11
Gilroy, Paul, 261, 298, 345
Glassie, Herbert, 277
Glinka, Mikhail, 243, 249–50, 252
Global imagination, 17, 27–28, 402
Global market, 25, 26, 137, 139, 179,
Global/local relationship, 137–44
Globalization, 4, 6–8. 10, 17, 23, 29–30, 137–144,
   156–157, 169–170. 178–179, 193, 197, 271, 297
Gold, Gerald, 262
Górale (in Poland), 67–81
"Górale, Górale," 77
Gramsci, Antonio, 372–373
Greek Empire, 113–114
Greene, Alex, 34,
Griot, *see* Jeli
Gu Jiegang, 231
Guilbault, Jocelyne, 6, 8, 276
Guinea, 161, 164, 168–171, 173, 175, 179
Guitar, 25, 39, 104, 143, 168, 183, 190, 209–222, 282, 289,
   336–337, 338, 353, 355, 362, 363, 378, 388–389
   electric guitar, 209–222, 253, 262
   bass guitar, 214–216, 297–298
Gupta, Akhil, 209
Guyana, 275, 285–286
"Guyana Bobo" (Terry Gajraj), 286
"Guyana kay dulahin" (Anand Yankaran), 285
Gypsies, *see* Roma

H
Haetta, Mattis, 360–361
Haiti, 8, 261–272, 333
Hall, Stuart, 45, 297
Hanna, Judith Lynne, 121
Hannerz, Ulf, 276
Haraway, Donna, 194, 215
Hard rock, 334, 338–339, 351, 362–363, 366
Harjo, Joy, 334–38, 342–343, 345, 347
Harmonica, 289
Hart, Mickey, 193
Hassan, Shéhérezade Qassim, 112, 122, 124
Healing ceremonies, 124, 147–148, 156–157, 245
Heather B, 98
Hebdige, Dick, 193
Heidegger, Martin, 27, 245
Heimarck, Brita, 60
Herat (Afghanistan), 119, 121
Herder, Johann Gottfried, 73
Herndon, Marcia, 6
Hinduism
   in Bali, 58, 60, 62–64
   in Trinidad, 280, 284, 289,
Hip hop, 98–99, 101–105, 196, 214, 339, 340–342,
   347
Hirabayashi, Roy, 90
HIV/AIDS, 102, 270, 387, 403
Hobart, Angela, 59
Hobsbawm, Eric, 226
Holland, *see* Netherlands, the
Homeland, 8, 17, 229, 235, 261–263, 266–67, 268, 271,
   277–278, 285, 287, 290, 345, 360, 394
Homophobia, 104–105
hooks, bell, 90, 91, 101
Hopkins, Simon, 141–142
Hu Yaobang, 230

Human rights, 4, 253
Hungary, 79
Husayn al-'Azami, 25
Hybridity, 8, 10, 23, 29, 333, 343–344, 346

I
I Wayan Limbak 59
I Wayan Lotring, 59–60
Iberia, 110
Ibo Combo, 264
Ice Cube, 102, 340
Iconicity, 18, 23, 26, 200, 352
Identities/identity
   Antillean, 140–143
   Chayantaka in Bolivia, 311–324
   Ethnic, 4, 9–10, 77, 279, 296, 297, 365
   Górale in Poland, 67–81
   Jawoyn in Australia, 383–398
   Latin Americans in London, 295–307
   National, 4, 8, 9, 37, 164, 233, 243–257, 344, 396
   Saami in Scandinavia, 351–366
Identity construction, 311, 383, 391
Identity politics, 11, 91, 94, 204, 333, 344–346, 383–398
Imagined community, 203–205, 245, 247, 271, 311
Impey, Angela, 6, 11
Improvisation, 19, 20, 79, 114, 122, 301–302, 303–305,
   357
India, 100, 118, 123, 127, 195, 201, 202, 256, 275–291,
   305
"Indian Animal" (Sundar Popo), 285
"Indian Life" (Btaka), 341
Indian subcontinent, 110, 118, 123, 127, 195, 201, 202,
   256, 275–291; *see also* Individual countries
"Indian Soca" (Drupatee Ramgoonai), 286
Indian-Caribbean music, 275–91
Indigenous Knowledge Systems (IKS), 404, 406, 409
Indigenous knowledge, 404, 406, 409
Indigenous land rights, 385, 387, 393–395, 398
Indigenous peoples
   Australia, 383–398
   Bolivia, 311–324
   Scandinavia, 351–366
   South Africa, 401–410
   United States, 331–347
Indigenous rights, 383, 386, 393–395
Indonesia, 55–63, 192, 195, 245
Intellectual property, 4, 365
Intelligent Black Women Coalition (I.B.W.C.), 100
International Council for Traditional Music (ICTM), 5,
   10, 72
International Festival of Mountain Folklore (Podhale,
   Poland), 67–81
"Internationale", 237, 246–247
Internet, 3, 11, 27–28, 139, 166, 244
Iran, 110, 118, 123, 124, 126
Iraq, 24, 25, 110, 111, 112, 115, 122, 124, 125, 127
Ireland, 295
Isis, 98, 100
Islam, 5, 22, 25, 109–112, 114, 115–117, 122, 123, 124,
   126, 127, 199–206
Islamic call to prayer, 7, 9, 21, 102, 199–206
Islamic chant, 21,
Islamic community, 199–206
Islamic Council of Singapore, 206
Islamic cultural contexts, 6, 162, 163, 192, 195
Islamic music, 5, 25
Israelites, 110, 112, 113, 114,
Ivory Coast, 161, 169, 170

J

Jackson, Michael, 405
Jakarta (Java), 57
Jamison, Andrew, 10
Japan and the Japanese, 89, 92, 93, 148, 150–152, 229, 231, 234, 295, 304
Japanese Americans, 87–94
Japanese language, 70, 87
Java, 57, 60, 192, 195
Jawoyn Association, 384–387, 393–397
Jawoyn people (of Australia), 383–398
Jazz, 38, 39, 40, 213, 269, 301, 331, 333, 334, 336–339, 357, 364, 378
    Latin jazz, 301, 303
Jazz fusion, 333, 334, 336–339
Jeli (griot), 161, 163–165, 174, 178
Jembe, 7, 161–179
Jenbe, *see* Jembe
Jenkins, Jean, 111, 112
Jensen, Gordon, 58
Jernsletten, Nils, 358, 361, 365
Jewish women, 125
Jews, 113
Johansson, Lars Jonas, 351–352, 361–363, 366
Johnson, Mark, 211
Joik, 351–66
Jones-Bamman, Richard, 10, 11
Jonsson, Sven Gösta, 351–355, 364–366
Journey (musical group), 39
Judaism, 22, 109, 115, 121, 122, 124
Judd, Ellen, 229
Juste, Farah, 261, 269–270

K

Kaeppler, Adrienne, 5
Kaluli (of Papua New Guinea), 9, 196, 211, 323, 405
Karasov, Deborah, 36
Kashtin (musical group), 364
Kassav (musical group), 140–143
Kecak, 58–60, 63–64
Keil, Charles, 34, 217,
Keita, Fodeba, 183
Keita, Mamady, 166
Kelley, Robin, 333
Keyboards, 195, 214–215, 217, 282, 337, 362; *see also* Piano
Keyes, Cheryl L., 6
Khrushchev, Nikita, 248
Kijima Taiko (Japan), 92
Kinley, David H. III, 262
Kinship, 9, 150, 152, 277, 279, 285–86, 290, 297, 312
Kirshenblatt-Gimblett, Barbara, 73–74, 77
Kjeldsberg, Sverre, 360–61
Kleczynski, Jan, 69, 80
Kolberg, Oskar, 69
Kondo, Dorinne, 91, 94
Konpa, 264, 268–269
Kora, 169, 183
Korean and Koreans, 92, 150–151
Korean Americans, 91
Koskoff, Ellen, 6, 110, 128, 130 n40,
Kreasi baru (new creation), 59–64
Kulumindini Band (musical group), 391
Kurai, Shuichi Thomas (Rev. Tom), 89, 92, 93
Kurdistan, 127
Kurds, 118, 124, 126, 127
Kuti, Fela Anikulapo, 143
KwaZulu Natal, South Africa, 6, 7, 401–410

L

La Farge, Peter, 331, 334, 342
"Ladies First" (Queen Latifah), 100
Laguerre, Michel S., 266
Lakoff, George, 211, 216
Lanser, Susan, 99
Lapp, *See* Saami
Latin America, 276, 295–307
Lauryn Hill, 103, 105, 342
Lawless, Elaine, 101
Lee, Benjamin, 236
Lee, Ton Soon, 7, 9
Les Diables Bleu, 265
Lesbianism, 104–05
Life-cycle events
    Górale in Poland, 77,
    Middle East, 112, 115, 117–123, 125–128
    West Africa, 162
    Singapore, 200, 202
    Indian Caribbean, 275, 276, 280–282, 290
    South Africa, 407–408
Lil' Kim, 98, 103, 104
Lipsitz, George, 333, 344
Litefoot, 334, 347
London Symphony Orchestra, 43
London, 42, 295–307
"Looney Rooney" (Robbie Bee), 339
Lorde, Audre, 101, 104
Los Angeles Matsuri Taiko (LAMT), 92
Los Angeles, 10, 91–92, 156–157, 344–345, 346
Los Lobos (musical group), 344
Louisiana, 11, 371–379
Love, Monie, 97, 100
Lovell, Nadia, 404–405
Lowe, Lisa, 94
Lukács, Georg, 48
Lysloff, René T. A., 7, 11

M

MacRae, Grame, 58–59
Madonna, 39
Magrini, Tullia, 6
Mahabharata, 279
Malawi, 245
Malaysia, 7, 8, 9, 147–57, 200, 202, 405
Male(s), 97, 101–105, 109–111, 115–117, 119–121, 123–128, 210, 214, 215, 283, 290, 296–297, 303, 306–307, 341–342, 374; *see also* Masculinity
Mali, 161, 164, 169, 170, 173
Malinowski, Bronislaw, 68
Malm, Krister, 138
Mandela, Winnie, 100
Manuel, Peter, 35, 256, 275, 276, 283, 287, 288, 291
"Marajhin" (Mighty Sparrow), 286
Martin, Judith A., 36
Martinez, Karen, 276
Marx, Karl, 246
Marxism, 246–247, 372–373
"Mascot" (WithOut Rezervation), 340
Masculinity, 88–89, 92, 126, 214, 306,
Mass media, 2, 7, 35, 49, 142, 189–190, 193, 197, 205, 231, 244, 331, 351
Master Musicians of Jajouka, 28
Mathkor (pre-wedding celebrations), 276, 280–82, 290
Mattern, Mark, 10, 11
Mawlawiyya (Whirling Dervish), 5, 18, 21, 24–26, 28, 29
MC Lyte, 97–98, 103, 342

McCann, Anthony, 5
McClary, Susan, 296
McPhee, Colin, 59
Mead, Margaret, 58
Means, Russell, 339
Mediation, 5, 27, 28, 34, 48–49, 105, 166, 203–205
Mediterranean, 6, 109, 114, 125
Meintjes, Louise, 143
Melanesia, 127
Memory, 9, 74, 111, 113, 121, 256, 290, 323, 405, 409; *see also* Nostalgia
Merriam, Alan P., 55
Mershon, Katherine, 59
Mesopotomia, 109, 112, 114, 121
Mevlevi, 18, 20, 24–25, 111, 124
Mexico, 341, 343–344
Meyer, Leonard, 23
Meyers, Carol, 114
Meyers, Suzanne, 114
Mia X, 103
Miami, 261, 265, 271
Miao Ye, 232
Middle East, 6, 20, 22, 25, 109–128, 157; *see also* Individual countries
Middleton, Richard, 191
Mighty Sparrow, 286
Mikhalkov, Sergei, 246, 248–250, 254–256
Miller, Bill, 334
Mini djaz, 264–269
Miniature paintings, Persian, 117–118
Mirabal, Robert, 334
Misogyny, 105, 115, 340
Missionaries, Christian, 229, 354
    Hindu, 284
Missy Elliot, 102, 103
Mitchell, Timothy, 18, 27
Mittler, Barbara, 228, 233
Mixed Relations (musical group), 387, 391
Modernity, 28–30, 156, 333, 351, 353, 365
Modernization, 72, 152, 189, 195, 206, 403, 405, 407
Moisala, Pirkko, 6
Moldova, 251
Monk, Meredith, 29
Montague, Jeremy, 114
Morgan, Joan, 104
Morris, R. Conway, 110
Moudallal, Sabri, 21, 25
Moyle, Richard, 391
Mozart, Wolfgang Amadeus, 42, 43
"Mozart in Mirrorshades" (Sterling and Shiner), 189–197
Multiculturalism, 74
Music industry, 1–4, 7, 33, 48, 137–144, 333, 341, 346
    Haitian, 271
    Saami in Scandanavia, 357
    transnational, 18, 22, 25, 27–29
Music, as architecture, 33–49
    and commercial space, 33–49
Musical instruments, 6, 9, 109–128, 161–179, 212, 216–217, 297–300, 324, 356, 408; *see also* Individual instrument names
MUZAK, 5, 34, 38, 40–41, 47,
Myers, Helen, 191–192, 276, 283–284, 291
Myoman Pendit, 57

N
Nabajoth, Eric, 142
Naipaul, V. S., 290
Nakai, Carlos, 334

National anthems, 77, 228, 237, 243–260
Nationalism, 8–9, 36, 225–237, 244–225, 247, 249, 262, 271
Native Americans, 10–11, 331–347, 378
Ndegé Ocello, Me'Shell, 104
Nefertiti, 98, 100
Nelson, Havelock, 97
Netherlands, the, 142, 295
Nettl, Bruno, 36, 55, 109,
New Age, 193–95, 251, 334, 357
New York City, 7–8, 18–20, 22, 28, 29, 91, 92, 171, 209–218, 262, 295, 305
New York, 156–157, 346
New Zealand, 387
Ney (reed flute), 111, 117
Nie Er, 231, 234
Niranjana, Tejaswini, 292
Nirvana (musical group), 39
"Nitmiluk", 383–398
No Fixed Address (musical group), 387
Noise, 44, 48, 201–203, 209, 213
Nordberg, Devin, 46
Norteña, 344
North Africa, 17, 110, 122
North Tanami Band (musical group), 391
Northern Territory, Australia, 383–398
Norway, 10, 295, 351, 353, 355, 357–360, 366
Nostalgia, 40, 45, 190, 196, 256, 257, 262–63, 266, 268, 271, 391

O
Odaiko, 88
Odalan (Balinese festival), 61–62
Oja, Carol, 60
Olsen, Dale, 11
Omosupe, Ekua, 104
Ong, Aihwa, 93
Opera
    Chinese, 202–203, 231, 237
    Russian, 249
Oppression, 92–93, 140, 205, 227–229, 267, 342, 372–375, 407
Orientalism, 25–27, 91, 122, 191, 194, 244
Oslo, 359–361
Oswald, John, 193
Otherness, 1, 3, 5, 23–24, 59, 60, 64, 149–150, 156–157, 191–193
Oud, *see* 'Ud
Owen, Louis, 342

P
Pakistan, 123
Pan-Aboriginality, 168, 388–390, 393, 395, 398
Pan-Africanism, 100, 396
Papua New Guinea, 9, 17, 127, 196, 323, 405
Pareles, Jon, 1, 3
Paris, France, 27, 43, 140, 141, 162, 166, 169, 265
Parks, Rosa, 100
Participatory research, 404, 406–410
Patriarchy, 103–104, 115, 338, 341, 346
Patronage, 29, 43, 64, 190, 264, 266, 268, 269, 271
Pebblee Poo, 101
Pelisero, Tom, 38
Pendit, Nyoman, 57
People's Liberation Army (China), 230, 234
Peoples Republic of China (PRC), *See* China
Performance practice, 9, 117, 152, 269
Persian culture, 109, 111, 115, 117, 118, 119, 124

Phillips, Carl, 277
"Phoulourie" (Sundar Popo), 287
Piano, 39, 117, 214, 298, 300
Picard, Michael, 57
Picken, Laurence, 110, 123
Pitjantjatjara people (Australia), 391
Pluralism, 205, 268
Podhale (Poland), 67–81
Poetic Justice (musical group), 334–338
Polak, Ranier, 7
Poland, 67–83
Political action, 10–11, 359, 371–379
Political science, 4, 228
Political scientists, 3, 10, 142, 247
Politics and music, 227–228, 230; see also Cultural
    politics; Identity politics; Politics of representation;
    Politics of popular music; Politics of the body
Politics of popular music, 137, 371–379
Politics of representation, 189–197
Politics of the body, 307
Polka, 79, 331, 334
Popo, Sundar, 275, 283, 285, 287
Popular culture, 189–190, 199, 290, 331, 335, 339
Popular music, 1–2, 4, 8, 10, 11, 40, 189–190, 192–193,
    196, 209–210, 304, 306–307, 311, 332; see also
    Individual genres
  Afghanistan, 118
  Australian Aboriginal, 383–398
  Cajun, 371–379
  China, 232–233, 236–237
  Gender, 105
  Haitian, 261–262, 268, 272
  Indonesia, 195
  Malaysia, 200
  Native America, 332–333, 344
  Saami in Scandinavia, 351–366
  South Asian, 284
  West Africa, 163
Porter, James, 245
Porter, Susan, 214
Postcolonialism, 11, 17, 142, 148, 194, 197, 383, 387,
    397
Postman, Neil, 197
Postmodernism, 44, 138, 139, 142, 189, 190, 257, 344,
    346,
Prescott, John, 391–392
Princesa, 105
Private sphere, 285
Professional musicians, 92, 116–117, 119–126, 161–163,
    166, 168, 170, 172–179, 232, 301, 302
Property rights, 4
Protest music, 337, 372, 387
Public Enemy, 100
Public sphere, 285, 335
Puerto Rico, 295, 302, 305
Punjab, 279, 289
Punk, 210, 215, 338
Purdah, 115, 128
Putin, Vladimir, 243, 249–250, 252–255, 257

Q
Quechua language, 312–321, 324
Queen Kenya, 98
Queen Latifah, 97–100, 103, 105, 342
Queen Mother Rage, 98, 100
Queen Pen, 104–105
Qureshi, Regula, 42

R
R&B, See Rhythm and blues
Race, 6, 8, 9, 10, 41, 46, 47, 87–89, 104–105, 143, 225,
    265, 283, 287, 300, 304, 386
Racism, 78, 90, 91, 104, 262, 298, 335, 339–340, 346, 394,
    394, 395
Radano, Ronald, 47
Radio Afghanistan, 121
Radner, Joan, 99
Raï, 17, 139, 142, 143, 333
Ramayana, 58, 59, 279
Ramgoonai, Drupatee, 285–286
Ramnarine, Tina K., 6, 8
"Rant & Roll" (John Trudell), 338
Rao, Apurna, 120
Rap, 97–108, 214, 331, 333, 340–342; see also Hip hop
Rara, 271
Real Roxanne, 98
Recording industry
  French, 143
  Haitian, 271
  international, 3
  Scandinavian, 353, 360
  transnational, 139
Red Thunder, 334
Redbone, 331, 334
Reddy, Michael, 211
Redhouse Family, 333
Regev, Motti, 396
Reggae, 196, 269, 331, 333
Regionalism, 69–71, 75, 77, 232, 234–235, 237, 395–397
Reinhard, Ursula, 125
Religious geography, 63
Religious practices, 58–64, 111–128, 149, 152, 192,
    199–206, 279–280, 283–284, 356
Repertoires, 18, 19, 21, 24, 25, 28, 29, 30
  Aboriginal Australia, 388, 390, 398
  Bali, 59, 61, 62
  Górale in Poland, 68–69, 80
  Middle East, 119
  Saami in Scandinavia, 366
  West Africa, 163–164, 166–169
Representation, 7, 8, 11, 18, 20–30, 56, 58, 59, 67–68, 72,
    74, 76, 78, 89–91, 97, 105, 189–197, 225–237, 397,
    402–404, 407–409
Resistance, 10, 44, 47, 92, 105, 190, 229, 233, 234,
    372–376, 396
Rhythm and blues (R&B), 215, 269, 336
Ribeiro, Indra, 276
Rice, Timothy, 11
Rich, Adrienne, 335
Richard, Zachary, 375
Rihtman, Cvjetko, 110
Rising Sun (film), 87–94
Rituals, 6, 11, 29, 111, 212–213, 245–246
  Afghanistan, 126
  Ancient Middle East, 112–114
  Bali, 60, 62–63
  Chayantaka in Bolivia, 312
  China, 228–229
  and Gender, 125–126
  Górale in Poland, 67–81
  Haitian, 265–268, 271
  Macedonia, 127
  in Persian culture, 111, 117
  Saami in Scandinavia, 354
  South Africa, 401, 404–410

Sufi, 20–23, 116, 117–118, 121, 124, 127
Syria, 21, 289
Trinidad, 279–283
Robertson, Robbie, 331
Rock, 6, 7, 9, 11, 40, 43, 137, 189–190, 194, 195, 197, 331, 333, 209–218, 297–298, 305, 331, 333–334, 336–339, 344–346, 378; *see also* Hard rock
 Aboriginal Australian, 383–398
 Chicano, 344–345
 Chinese, 232, 237
 Saami in Scandinavia, 351, 353–358, 362–363, 366
Roma, 123, 126, 127
Roman Empire, 113–14
Román Velázquez, Patria, 6, 9
Rose, Tricia, 105, 214, 374
Roseman, Marina, 7, 8, 9, 405
Ross, Andrew, 190, 216
Rouget, Gilbert, 113
Roy Choudhury, M. L., 115–116
Rumi, Jalal al-Din, 18, 24, 111
Russia, 8, 68, 243–260
"Russia, Our Holy Power", 250, 255–257
Ryden, Kent, 321, 324

S
Saami Action Group (SAG), 359
Saami Radio, 353, 356, 363
Saami, 10, 11, 351–366
Sacramento Taiko Dan, 92
Sainte-Marie, Buffy, 331, 334, 342
Sakata, Hiromi Lorraine, 119
Salsa, 6, 9, 268, 269, 295–307
Salt-N-Pepa, 98, 101, 102, 105, 342
Sámi, *See* Saami
Sampling, 195–96, 214
San Francisco Taiko Dojo, 87–89, 92
San Francisco, 87–89, 92, 340
San Jose Taiko, 90, 92
Sanghyang (trance dance), 59
Sarmini, 'Umar, 25
Saxophone, 39, 299, 335–337, 366
Scandinavia, 10, 344, 351–366
Schafer, R. Murray, 9, 193, 203, 204, 206, 323
Schechter, John M., 324
Schiller, Nina Glick, 262, 266–267
Schizophonia, 156, 192–194, 206
Schubert, Franz, 42
"See the Woman" (John Trudell), 338
Seeger, Anthony, 49, 405
Seger, Bob, 45
Semai (of Malaysia), 151, 152
Senegal, 161, 170, 173
Sense of place, 9, 10, 321, 323, 324, 333, 402, 405–406, 410
Sequence (musical group), 98, 101
Sexuality, 6, 9, 101–03, 105, 111–112, 115, 119, 121–124, 128, 216, 295–297, 306–307, 332
Shah, Sonia, 93
Shakkur, Sheikh Hamza, 18, 22, 25
Shakuhachi, 88
Shamanism, 127, 150, 157, 354
Shanghai, 233
Shannon, Jonathan H., 5
Shanté, Roxanne, 97–98, 103, 354
Sha-Rock, 98, 101
Sharp, Cecil, 71
Shenandoah, Joanne, 334
Shields, Rob, 37

Shiloah, Amnon, 110, 127
Shleu-Shleu, 264–265
Simon, Paul, 27, 193
Singapore Muslim Action Front, 202
Singapore Muslim Assembly, 202
Singapore, 7, 199–206
Sister Souljah, 98, 100
Skah Shah (Haitian band), 263–265
Slobin, Mark, 6, 118, 262, 276, 289
Slovakia, 67, 79
Smitherman, Geneva, 103
Soca, 269, 275, 288–289; *see also* Chutney soca
Social action, 10, 11, 234
Social activists, 138, 194,
Society for Ethnomusicology (SEM), 10
Sociologists, 3, 10, 99, 406
Sociology, 4, 55, 228
Soh Daiko (New York), 92
Solomon, Tom, 9
"Song of the Canned Sardine Spirit", 153–156
Soukous, 139, 142, 143, 269
Soul, 143
Sound recording(s), 35, 191, 193; *see also* Cassettes; Recording industry
Sound signature 213,
Soundmark, 200
Soundscape 37, 152, 191, 193, 196
 Islamic, 201–202, 236, 323, 337, 361
South Africa, 401–10
South America, *See* Latin America
South America, 127, 295, 344; *see also* Individual countries
"Souvenir d'Haïti," 262–263
Soviet Union, 243–249, 256
Space, public, 37, 47, 119, 203; *see also* Public sphere
Spain, 127, 295
Spanish language, 295, 300–307, 313–414
Spies, Walter, 59
Spirit medium, 147–149
Spirit songs and practices
Spiritual geography, 25
Stalin, Joseph, 243–244, 246–251, 254–256
Sterne, Jonathan, 5, 6, 8
Sting, 27
Stoeltje, Beverly, 235
Stokes, Martin, 5, 9–10, 289, 311
Sub-Saharan Africa, 109, 127
Sufism, 18–30, 111, 113, 116–118, 121, 124–127
Sumer, 112, 113, 114, 121
Sunrize Band (musical group), 387, 391
Suppan, Wolfgang, 72
Surinam, 275
Suryani, Ketut, 58
Sustainable development, 11, 401, 406
Sweden, 10, 351, 353, 355
Swedish language, 352
Switzerland, 169, 295
Synthesizer, 88, 190, 195, 196, 214, 301, 303
Syria, 5, 17–30
Szymanowski, Karol, 68

T
Tabou Combo, 264–265, 268–269
Tagg, Philip, 298
Taiko Center of the Pacific, 90
Taiko, 87–94
Talking Heads, 143

Tanaka, Seiichi, 88, 90–91
Tarab, 18–21, 24–25
Tatra Mountains (Poland)
Taylor, Timothy, 23
Techno, 191, 193, 195–96, 339
Technoculture, 7, 11, 190–191, 193, 197
Temiar (of Malaysia), 7, 8, 9, 147–157, 405
Tenzer, Michael, 60
Tex Mex, 344
Théberge, Paul, 191
3M Corporation 34, 38
Tilley, Christopher, 323
Ti-Manno (musician), 263, 267
TLC, 102, 105, 342
Toner, P. G., 3
Touhy, Sue, 8
Touma, Habib Hassan, 110, 113, 124
Tourism, 1, 3
    Bali, 55–64
    Cajun in Louisiana, 371, 377
    Podhale, Poland, 67–81
    South Africa, 402–404, 409–410
Tourists, 3, 5–6, 36
    Bali, 55–64
    China, 228
    Podhale, Poland, 67–81
    Southwestern United States, 331, 333, 343
    South Africa, 403–404, 409
Toyne, Philip, 391
Transnationalism, 5, 8–9, 17–18, 23, 28–30, 87, 93–94,
    138–139, 261–272, 268, 269–272, 345
Trinidad, 8, 275–290
Trudell, John, 334, 338–339, 342, 347
Trumpet, 298, 300, 301, 305
Tuan, Yi-Fu, 323
Tubman, Harriet, 100
Turino, Thomas, 8, 256
Turkey, 20, 24, 77, 109, 110, 113, 122, 123, 125
Tusler, Mark, 92

U
Ubud (Bali), 5–6, 55–64
Ubud Tourist Information Office, 57–58
'Ud (Oud), 18, 25, 116, 117
Ukraine, 251
Ullestad, Neal, 10, 11
"Unbreakable Union", 246–257
UNESCO, 194, 402, 403
United Kingdom, 100, 141, 276–277, 287–289, 295,
    301
United States, 331–347
Uttar Pradesh, 278–279

V
Vachon, Daniel, 391
Valkeapää, Nilk-Aslak, 355–357, 361–365
Venezuela, 295
Vertovec, Steven, 281
Video, 2, 7, 44–45, 98, 100, 102, 103, 234, 271, 304, 386,
    409
Villafañe, Eldin, 306
Violin, 76, 79, 117, 214
Vodou, 267, 279, 271

W
Waila, 334, 344
Walela, 334
Walker, Lisa M., 104

Walker, Madame C. J., 100
Wallis, Roger, 138
Walser, Robert, 211
Warumpi Band (musical group), 391
Warumpi Desert Band (musical group), 391
"Was He a Fool?" (WithOut Rezervation), 341
Weddings, 77, 115, 119–123, 125, 126–127, 162, 202,
    275–76, 280–82, 285, 289
Wedgetail Eagle Band (musical group), 391
Weeks, Jeffrey, 296
Weiss, Julien, 18, 20, 22, 24–27, 29
Whirling Dervishes of Damascus, The, 25
Whisnant, David, 71–72
White Top Festival (Virginia), 71, 73
Wilcken, Lois, 271
Wild, Stephen, A., 3
Williams, Raymond, 296
Williams-Forte, Elizabeth, 112
WithOut Rezervation (W.O.R), 334, 340–343, 345
Women
    Aboriginal Australia, 391
    African American, 97–106, 374
    China, 229–234, 236
    Indian-Caribbean, 276–277, 280–285, 290
    Indonesia, 61–63, 192
    Latin Americans in London, 304–307
    Middle East, 109–128
    Native America, 337–338, 341–342, 345
    in New York rock music, 209, 214–217
    North American in taiko, 88, 92–94
    Singapore, 205
    South Africa, 408
    Syria, 26
    Temiar in Malaysia, 147, 149, 156
West Africa, 163, 168
Wong, Deborah, 6, 11
Workshops, music, 138, 139, 166, 169, 279, 376
World beat, 17, 23, 27, 29, 139
World music industry, 18, 22, 25, 29
World Music Institute (New York, N.Y.), 20, 22, 23
World music, 1–3, 5, 7, 17–18, 20, 22–30, 109, 137–144,
    168, 193, 195, 197, 276, 277, 290
Wu Yuqing, 228

X
XIT (musical group), 339

Y
Yamada, Mitsuye, 92
Yamamoto, Traise, 89
Yankaran, Anand, 285
Yartulu Yartulu Band (musical group), 391
Yayasan Bina Wisata (Tourist Management Foundation)
    (Bali), 57, 61
Yeltsin, Boris, 249, 251, 252
Yoon, Paul, 87, 91
Yothu Yindi (musical group) 364, 388, 397
Youla, Fodé, 169
Yo-Yo, 98, 100, 102

Z
Zaire, 193
Zanetti, Vincent, 170, 179
Zbójnik, Franciszek Swider, 69
Zemp, Hugo, 194
Ziegler, Suzanne, 6, 122–123
Zimbabwe, 8, 256
Zydeco, 371